NOT MY HEART TO BREAK

W WINTERS

NOTE: This is a work of fiction.

Names, characters, places, and incidents are a product of the author's imagination.

Any resemblance to real life is purely coincidental. All characters in this story are 18 or older.

willowwinterswrites.com

LONGING TO HOLD

There's a moment when I forget he's not mine. This small spell of time, when I let my thoughts carry me away.

He holds me. He kisses me. He makes all of this better.

That moment when I'm his and everything is all right, is gone in an instant. It's quick and fleeting, moving so fast that it slips through my grasp. If I could catch it, I'd hold on to it forever.

I always thought this thing between us would only ever be just that. A passing moment, a pleasant dream that helped lull me to sleep at night.

If I'd known what was to come, maybe I would have thought twice. I couldn't have prepared for this.

Longing to Hold is a short prelude to the *Hard to Love* series.

CHAPTER 1

Laura

OUR EYES MET FOR A FRACTION OF A SECOND. IF THAT. IT WAS IN passing.

Him on one end of the cafeteria, and I at the other.

The clatter of trays hitting the tables in our high school cafeteria and the even louder chatter and laughter of everyone else faded into the background. The sounds weren't worthy of white noise. It all disappeared.

Despite being across the room I felt him then, his hands on me; I knew they'd be rough and possessive. His lips hit mine, hot and full of hunger, as if he'd been deprived of my touch. I could feel the hard cinder blocks scraping my back as he pushed me against the wall. I could hear the soft moans and heavy breathing I'd give to him the second his lips left mine and he stared deeply into my eyes.

Peering down at my tray, I can only hope my cheeks aren't as red as they are hot. It's hard to swallow, but I do. The perfectly red apple with no bruises or nicks holds absolutely no desire for me to eat any longer, but I bite into it again, not tasting a damn thing while I keep my head down.

I could look up to see if he noticed, but Seth King's table is full of other students, his crew as I've dubbed them, and mine is empty. One look and someone would see me staring at him; there's no one else here at my table to hide me or my sordid thoughts.

So I keep my head down and avoid the curious gazes of anyone watching. Just like I've been doing for weeks now. Ever since my dad died.

My throat's tight. It gets like that whenever I think of my father, and I nearly choke on the small piece of fruit in my mouth. Apple juice goes down the wrong way and I pretend that's why my eyes sting.

I'm dealing poorly with the loss and everything that happened just before it. I'm certain that's why everyone avoids me now.

It didn't used to be like this. I was never one of the popular girls, but I wasn't a pariah either. That must be it. I've become an emotional wreck, so now everyone keeps their distance. It seems fitting enough.

It's been weeks and only Cami talks to me since the car crash. Everyone else lets me be. I don't blame them. The simplest of questions or even a friendly wave—it's all met with a delayed response because my mind was elsewhere, or worse. I've cried out of nowhere more times than I can count. So now they leave me alone. I'm grateful, because it's embarrassing and I hate it. I hate how weak mourning has made me.

Everyone lets me be… everyone except for Seth King.

That has to be why I'm thinking of him like I am. Of all the thoughts of what he'd do to me.

He doesn't talk to me, not really. He doesn't do anything but walk me home. I didn't ask him to and at first I didn't want him there. I don't need an audience for my grieving and no one owes me anything, whether he knew my father or not. I told him just that, but it didn't deter him and to be honest, a piece of me was grateful that someone was there with me.

When the school bell rings and all my textbooks are swept up and safely zippered into my backpack, I know he'll be there. Waiting for me as if he's supposed to be there. He doesn't even know me; not like that.

He doesn't tell me he'll be there, but I know when I walk out the double doors at the back of the gym, feeling the cool autumn air sweep my hair behind my neck, Seth will be standing at the edge of the parked cars. Which is directly in my path to walk home.

Seth's friends have been there as well lately, surrounding him when I get out.

I know the crowd of his friends, although I had no idea they even knew my name until recently. Everyone knows about them. They have a certain reputation.

They're the boys who are trouble. I know Derrick and all the things people say he does. Seth is their ringleader. That's a good way to put it.

Before I've even taken a step out of the building, I can hear Seth's voice. Most times, he glances through the people around him and sees me before anyone else does.

They usually disperse before I get there, but sometimes they're still talking. Especially Derrick; he doesn't seem to get the hint like the others do.

I'm not the kind of girl to allow a man to tell me to do anything. Certainly not Seth. I listened though. Not a piece of me wanted to be alone on the way home. All the evidence of how low my life had gotten was waiting for me. So I let him. He stands right at the entrance to the field, where anyone heading for the north side of town can walk right through a gap in the fence . Students like me.

I go to him; he walks me home. It's as simple as that.

But last week, his crew was talking and I didn't want to be a part of it. I didn't need Seth to walk me home and I definitely didn't need to wait around for him. I thought, I'm strong enough and I've had enough of Seth acting like my babysitter or whatever he thinks this is. I'm not one of them and I don't need to be a burden.

I walked around Derrick and Seth, not wanting to interrupt their conversation and not wanting to anticipate that he was waiting for me. Even though he'd been doing it every day I wanted to make it clear that I didn't assume it was going to last forever and, more importantly, that I didn't need him to. I didn't need his sympathy or whatever it was that convinced him he should be watching over me like he did.

After all, I barely know him. I know *of* him. It's different. His crew is older and they're all seniors. I'm only a sophomore.

Their fathers run the gang—*if that's what it's called?*—that my father was a part of.

I'm just the lonely girl Seth has to babysit, I think. Maybe his father told him to do it as a favor to my now dead father; I don't know. I don't care either.

So last week when I saw that their conversation wasn't coming to an end, I decided that if he's busy, I'll go about my business, refusing to be the inconvenience I knew I was.

Seth didn't like it, though. He didn't like me walking around them. He didn't like that I didn't wait.

I know that he didn't because of the way he yelled out my name. His voice was deep and full of irritation. The little hairs at the back of my neck stood up and it wasn't because of the chill that accompanies the end of October.

I couldn't even look over my shoulder at him. Instead I stood there for only a moment, frozen, watching the tall grass between the posts of the white fence waving in the breeze. And then my right foot moved, followed by my left. I kept my head down and continued forward.

He wasn't the boss of me and he still hadn't given me a reason as to why he was doing all of this. I still don't know for certain.

So I kept walking. None of them owe me anything. Regardless if they were close to my father or not. If they want to help because my dad worked with them, they can send money or something, I'm sure my grandma could use the help with the bills.

At least that's what I was thinking when I ignored him yelling after me.

Until his strong arm came from behind, wrapping around my lower belly. His forearm was solid against my hip and my back hit his chest.

"Wait for me, Babygirl," he whispered although his tone was rough and demanding. *Babygirl.* The name is probably inconsequential to him. I bet he calls a lot of girls that three-syllable nickname. It hit me hard though, like it meant more. It's like a memory you can't place. When it feels so familiar and comforting, but you don't know why. That's what his harshly spoken whisper, almost a reprimand, did to me. The girl I used to be wouldn't have tolerated it before. But that girl is long gone, and she took my will with her.

Seth's breath was warm on my neck. It traveled lower even through the cold. His hand slipped under my cardigan and lingered on my hip as his thumb brushed the exposed skin there. The layering tank top I had on beneath my sweater had ridden up when he moved to hold me.

It was maybe a third of minute, all of twenty achingly long seconds of him standing next to me, his heat enveloping me. I swear he runs hotter than everyone else.

I nodded, not trusting myself to speak and it's then that I noticed the other guys, most certainly Derrick, must be right behind me. I *felt* their presence. They followed too and they were close enough for me to hear although they whispered. The few students who walked around us stared. Great, I thought, now I've made a scene.

I heard Derrick's voice. That's what made me turn around to face all of them, something about having a good night, but he said my name with it. *Have a good night, Laura.* That's all it was. Derrick's first words to me were casual and seemingly innocuous.

I was going to say, *you too* like a normal person, even if it was weird that he'd speak to me. He never had before. But when I turned, Seth was there, too close, and with a look in his eyes I didn't care for. Concern, disappointment, maybe something else as well when his gaze met mine.

It's been thirty-four days since the first time he walked me home. I count because I'm waiting for it to end.

Only twenty-two of those thirty-four days he actually walked me home. Twenty-two days of him by my side every step of the way after school. The weekends I've been alone to obsess over the change in events.

And seven days since that day I can't shake, when I disappointed him. When he called me *Babygirl*. It was last Thursday. And here I am, still wondering about it, replaying it and debating on where I should stand today if they're talking again. I won't walk off, because I don't want him to look at me like that again.

It's a foolish reason, but I know it to be true.

So all of this, this sexual tension between us, I know I've made it up in my mind. It's embarrassing and I hate it. If there was anything at all between us, he would have made that clear. He doesn't even speak to me apart from occasional niceties when we walk the fifteen minutes to my grandma's townhouse. Nothing. And if I know anything at all about Seth, it's that if he wanted me in any way, he would have been damn clear about that.

I'm just a girl who lost her father, and Seth is a boy who feels the need to make sure I'm okay because he knew my father. I'm sure that's all this is. But my mind wants it to be more.

Setting my apple down on the full tray of food I probably won't be able to stomach, I make a mistake and I look over at them. At the table of boys who are trouble at best, and dangerous at worst.

I just miss making eye contact with Seth's right-hand man, literally sitting to his right. Derrick's good looking; I get a glimpse of him first before cowardly averting my eyes and looking back down at my tray. He has the same dark brown hair as Seth but his is longer, swept to the side. He actually styles his hair. Seth's is shorter, but still long at the top. Long enough to barely grip maybe, but not much longer than that. Short enough not to have to style.

I've been doing that recently, I think with a touch of humor as I tap the plastic fork on the tray. I've been comparing every man I see to Seth. I always come to the same conclusion: they can't hold a candle to Seth.

It's his eyes though and his dominating aura around him that draw me to Seth. The piercing blue gaze, the broad shoulders and that strong jawline. Everything about him radiates power and sex appeal.

One more glance, just one, and I drink him in. Even though

Seth's not overly muscular, he's toned and has enough of a defined outline of muscle that anyone who sees him knows he works out, or rather, that he could hurt them easily enough. It's what keeps his jaw sharp, I think. It's a clean line, severe like his gaze can be.

Apart from that, he's charming and classically handsome. When he smiles, *God when he smiles*, his pale blue eyes brighten, shining with humor, and his cheeks soften in a way that makes him more than approachable.

He doesn't smile much, though. Not recently.

I peek up, trying to disguise my curiosity as just coincidence that I'm looking his way again to see if he's smiling now.

My breath is stolen when our eyes lock and my heart does a weird thud; maybe it's pretending to be dead, just like I am. To no longer exist since he caught me in the act of daring to look his way.

Fuck, I'm shit at this. I've never been a good liar and I don't hide a damn thing well. I can't look away though, not when he's still staring back at me. I'm caught, literally and figuratively, stuck right where I am, feeling my skin tingle and my cheeks burn.

My heart's caught too.

It only beats again when he nods to the right, his head tilted, almost imperceptibly, motioning with it to come to him.

I can see myself doing it, walking over to him. I'd have to leave my tray behind though, because there isn't a place for me. There isn't room at his table. What would I do? Stand there like an imbecile waiting for his next demand? I'm foolish enough as it is.

What if when I got there, he hadn't called me over? What if all of it is all in my head?

I wonder if he knows what I'm thinking just by looking at me. I think he does because the corners of his mouth slip down as my lips part. As if I'd spoken the excuse. As if he could hear it from all the way over there.

"Hey," I hear a familiar voice say and the word comes with the clank of a tray hitting the cheap table. It jostles as Cami sits, her blond hair bouncing with tight curls as she tells me, "Sorry I'm late, fucking algebra." Picking up her apple she asks me, "You doing all right? You look a little flushed."

Emotions swarm up my chest and my cheeks heat even more. "Fine," I answer her without looking in her eyes and refusing to look Seth's way again. "I'm fine."

I hate lying, but I'd rather do that than admit how irrefutably *not fine* I really am.

CHAPTER 2

Seth

DERRICK SHUTS THE DOOR TO HIS LOCKER AND IT BANGS LOUDER than it should. I don't care; I keep the back of my head resting on the cool metal of the steel lockers and stare down the hall at room 4W with my hands in my pockets. I've never had a class in that room, but Laura has two of them every day in 4W.

"You really that pissed over her not coming to sit with you?" Derrick sounds exasperated and I turn back to him, not bothering to move even though the warning bell rings. The halls are mostly vacant, so I have plenty of time to get to the other wing of the school.

"She doesn't listen," I say, biting out the complaint lowly, although there's not much emotion in my comment. Laura Roth has a bad habit of doing what she wants, when she wants. And the bottom line is that she doesn't want me. Which is for the best, but I'll be damned if I don't want her.

"She's mourning," he reminds me and I give him a glare that would shut anyone else up.

"You don't have to remind me." I don't hide the anger in my tone as I make my way past him and down the corridor. I have nearly every class with Derrick. Thank fuck. I don't know how I'd get through the day without him there. I'm not a scholar, I'm not booksmart. With the life I lead, none of the curriculum taught within these walls means a damn thing.

"Get to class, you two," Miss Talbot calls out to a couple kissing in a corner. She's a nice enough lady, married and with kids of her own in college. Even her reprimand to those students sounds motherly. Her voice carries over to us along with her gaze and the moment she sees us, her lips slam shut. She visibly pales and looks to her right, clapping and telling someone else, apparently his name is Steven, that he can't be late again. She doesn't say shit to me or Derrick. No one does anymore.

Teachers like her are simply counting the days until we're gone and they don't have to deal with us. I don't blame her. I don't blame any of them. I get it now, more than ever. Quite frankly, I've been counting down the days for years.

"I'm just saying," Derrick speaks beneath his breath, "she's not trying to be a problem, she's just out of it." My gaze narrows as I take in my friend. We're nearly the same height, but I'm still just a hair taller than him.

"Who said she was being a problem?"

"Cut it the fuck out. You know what I mean." The last student in front of us shuts her locker and practically runs off with two thick textbooks in her arms. Derrick gives her a tight smile that she returns with a blush and a quickened pace to get by us. "You're getting all pissed off because she didn't come over to sit at the table, but why would she? She makes it obvious she'd rather be alone." He continues, and soon the two of us are standing outside of our classroom sooner than I'd like. The door is still open and Derrick places his shoe against it deliberately, keeping it open. "You're letting her get to you. … that's a problem whether you want to admit it or not."

I catch our English teacher's gaze as Mr. Chasting stares back at me before looking to his notebook and greeting the class. Not bothering to say a word to the two of us. He knows we'll come in, sit down, and deal with this last year just like he deals with us. Quietly, causing as few problems as possible and simply sliding by until we can walk across the stage at graduation and everyone can be done with this charade.

My response to him is firm. "She's not a problem and it's not a problem."

"You're right," he says, agreeing with me, catching me off guard. "You're the one with the problem. She's just a sweet girl you can't seem to leave alone."

"You know why."

"I do and I think it's fucked. My advice?" he offers although I don't want it. "Let it be," he hisses and I look over his shoulder to see a girl watching us from inside the class. I think her name is Sandra or maybe Susan. She's quick to avert her eyes and pretend like she wasn't trying to listen.

I barely react to Derrick's comments. I've heard it all before. I know how he feels and I don't give a shit. I can't stay away from her. I'm just walking her home. That's it. I owe her that at least.

"You've made your opinion known," I remind him, turning around to lean my back against the wall outside of the classroom. Seems like I need anything and everything to hold me up lately. It's fucking draining, dealing with all the shit that's gone down.

Derrick sighs audibly, as if I'm the worst thing he has to deal with. God knows that's not the case. Letting the door go, he stands beside me. The door shuts softly with a click and it's quiet for a moment before a resounding bell rings through the hall.

Now we're late. No one cares, though.

"I'm just saying," he continues, "she lost someone and maybe you should just leave her alone."

"Everyone lost someone." The words are lost in the vacant hall. "Including me," I add and turn to look Derrick in the eyes. Slipping his hands into his pockets, he nods solemnly. "I haven't forgotten," he answers.

"It's all different now, and if I want to deal with it this way, I need you to back me up." I feel tense and unsure, knowing everything has changed and I need Derrick here. I won't survive without him.

"I back you on everything, but you're supposed to trust me, and you know that means I won't be shy telling you when I think something's fucked."

A thin smirk graces my lips but it comes with a humorless huff of a laugh that sounds sick to my ears. "Everything's fucked." The past weekend was the hardest and the only bright light I had was knowing that come Monday, I'd have Laura to look out for again. Even if for only a moment.

I can hear him swallow thickly, and it's quiet for a minute.

"People mourn differently, yeah?" I ask him although it's rhetorical. They're his own words given back to him. Words he gave me when we stood over the ashes this past weekend.

His sneaker kicks against the cheap linoleum floors and I feel like a prick. "Sorry, I'm just being a dick now," I tell him and close my eyes, pushing down the pain of the brutal truth we've been hiding.

"No, you're right." He brushes it off but his voice is tight. "I like the way I handle it better."

"We should get to class," I speak when neither of us says anything for a long moment. His words stop me from moving more than an inch though.

"We're all dealing differently and when the news breaks, I know it'll be easier in some ways." I hate that he's talking about it at all. We made a pact not to say anything. A cold prick travels over my skin, starting at the back of my neck and working its way down slowly. My hands form into fists and I press the right one against the wall, letting my knuckles turn white.

The story is that our dads took off and we didn't want to file a report. We don't need the police getting involved. Death is a part of this life. So is getting even.

I don't look at him when I speak. "It will get easier," I answer him, feeling my throat get so tight the words almost don't make it out. "This is what we signed up for. We knew what we were doing." I don't know who I'm trying to convince anymore.

"I know. And I'm here with you. Your right-hand man. I just feel like…" he trails off and scratches his jaw, staring down at his feet instead of meeting my gaze.

"Out with it," I say, biting out the words.

"Everyone lost someone and we're all dealing with it differently. But I don't get why you won't leave her alone."

"I'm just protecting her." The answer slips out easily enough. It's what I've told everyone.

Derrick scoffs. "Don't bullshit me."

"Fine," I answer him, subconsciously nodding as I tell him, "You're right. I want her and it's fucked. But I'm just being there for her, I'm not pushing anything."

He shakes his head slowly, his eyes pinned to mine. "You're waiting. You know it's going to happen. She wants you, you want her. It's going to happen and you're making sure it does."

"It will be her call if it does," I answer him, at peace with that decision.

"You can never have her. A lot of shit went down and more is coming. You really want to drag her into it?"

"She's already a part of it and you know it."

"Don't do this to her. You want to feel better, and I get it. But this? This is wrong." His conclusion is spoken hard and clear.

"Are you going to stop me?"

"No." His tone drops, as does his gaze. "I'll still be here. I won't stand in your way."

"Good. Drop it."

On some level I should feel relief that he's going to drop it, but I don't.

I don't think I can stop myself. And he's right; I don't deserve her after what I've done. But I can't help myself.

CHAPTER 3

Laura

My shoulder's sore. I carried all my books around today rather than going to my locker and the damn strap has been digging into my shoulder. It hurts more than I try to show.

Secretly, as I make my way through the thinned crowd to the open double-doored exit, I hope Seth asks if he can carry my bag for me. I'm not a damsel in distress, but my pride is kind enough to acknowledge that it hurts. He always asks, and with my luck, I think: *today will be the day he doesn't ask and I'll have to ask him.*

I swallow the thought the moment the chilly November air hits me. Everyone scatters in front of me, but I stay where I am, my feet planted on the asphalt just outside the doors.

"Oh, sorry," I mumble when someone behind me brushes past and I realize I've been blocking the doorway.

A nervous heat ricochets through my body from my tiptoes all the way up to my ears, which turn red hot. I imagine they're about as red as my nose must be when I shiver and a cold gust of wind smacks me right across the face.

Unwilling to stand here any longer, growing colder by the second, I force myself forward toward the field.

My heart drops with each passing second. I have no right to be upset. This raw tightness in my throat can get the hell out of here. And it can take my insecure thoughts with it. One step. He's not mine. Therefore, there is no loss. Another step. I knew this wouldn't last.

Another step and I whirl around at the sound of my name.

Seth's face is flushed as he jogs to catch up to me. Tall and handsome, and literally running after me. *Blip*. My heart does a thing that feels like a mix between a sink and a flip.

"Couldn't wait for me?" he asks although it's obviously rhetorical, stopping just in front of me. He's so close that his heat is immediate and with another gust of wind, I'm hit with his heady masculine scent.

"Sorry." My apology makes him noticeably flinch. With a tight smile, I shift my weight and adjust the strap of my bag.

"Let me get it." Seth doesn't ask, he tells me, and he reaches for my bag before I even have a chance to hand it over.

"Thank you." Relief is immediate.

"No problem." All sorts of emotions threaten to show themselves and instead, I bury them down. I shouldn't be this happy that he's here. We're still nothing. I'm just getting used to it. I look forward to it, even. I don't know what I'll do when he stops, but I don't want to think about that either.

"Are you still stalking me?" I manage to ask, even as the gratitude fills me.

"Of course," he answers with a cocky, asymmetric grin. "Technically," he adds and starts walking, his stride long enough to quickly put distance between us. He turns around to walk backward just as we get to the open gap in the fence. I'm faintly aware of the eyes on us, but I ignore them all. "Since I'm in front, you're the one who's stalking me," he teases with that handsome smile and my God, I laugh. It's genuine and loud enough for him to hear it.

"You wish," I tell him with a smile and feel the heat in my cheeks when he slows down so I can catch up. He made me jog a little to do it; maybe he wanted to make this chase even.

It will never be even though, I'm certain of that.

It's been thirty-four days and it's then I decided I needed to write the little moments down. As the days blend together, the tension between us changes into something warmer, something closer. It's easier and lighter.

Day 1: He told me he'd walk me home and that day I held his hand.

Day 24: He called me Babygirl. The first time he held me, even if it was only to stop me from leaving without him.

Day 36: He started meeting me outside my classroom and immediately takes my backpack without prompting when he sees me.

Day 45: It's too cold to walk, so Seth insists on driving me home. That's the day the news broke about his father. I hugged him and refused to let go for the longest time. And he let me, holding me back in return.

Day 46: My hand brushed against his more than once in the car and I swear I couldn't breathe because of it.

Day 50: I thought he was going to kiss me over the console. But he didn't.

Fifty days with Seth King so close. Fifty days of subtle touches and longing glances. It's not in my head. I know it's not. I just want him to kiss me. I'll be the one who loses in the end of whatever game he's playing. Because I'm already falling. I'm tired of fighting, though. I don't know how I can stop myself.

CHAPTER 4

Seth

"YOU'RE A BAD INFLUENCE," LAURA COMMENTS AS SHE PICKS AT the hole in her jeans. There's a broad, beautiful smile on her face though and a tempting tease in her tone. I fucking love it.

"Yeah," I answer her, grabbing another beer. "I know." The football game is on in the main room of The Club, so I invited her back here, to the back room.

Weekdays are no longer enough. I need her on the weekends too. Derrick warned me against mixing business with my personal life, but I can't tell the difference between the two anyway.

There's a pool table in front of us, and then there's only this amber brown leather sofa. Just those two pieces of furniture in the dimly lit back room, and just the two of us. Whenever I meet her gaze, the strong girl I know Laura to be is suddenly shy. Shy looks damn good on her. It only makes her look that much more fuckable.

"I don't really drink." The chilled beer in her hand moves to the other. Her thumb drags up the side of it, leaving a trail in the condensation against the cold glass.

"You have to at least try it," I say and brush my shoulder against hers, inching closer. Then I shrug as I add, "Or not," and take a swig of my own. Resting my elbows on my knees, I lean forward and tell her, looking over my shoulder, "You're right, I'm a bad influence. I'll drink it. I just didn't want to be rude and not offer you one." I want to ease her nerves, but I know part of the reason she's nervous is because she's waiting for me to make a move. She's getting bolder with every passing day. It'll happen soon; I know it. I'm fucking dying for it.

"'Kay," she answers me, and then takes a swig of her own. Her nose scrunches, but she swallows. Watching her lick her lips afterward makes my cock harden. I have to rip my gaze away and I focus on the cracked door as a roar of cheers drifts back to us.

"Someone did something good," she says quietly and I can hear her take another drink.

"Did you want to watch the game?" I question her, almost praying she says yes just so we're not alone back here. Everything is her call. But damn she's pushing me to give in with that innocent and tempting look in her eyes.

"As much as I like it out there, no, I want to play," she says and gestures to the pool table. Right. I drop my head, remembering that's why we're back here. It's not so I can fuck her on this sofa like I want to do. With Laura, the days feel like they're passing slower and slower until that moment she lets me walk her home. That short amount of time is a blur, leaving me wanting and waiting in agony until I can see her again. She's addictive. Her soft glances and gentle touches are my drug. *I want more.*

More than that, *she wants more.*

"What are we betting?"

"What do you want?" she asks me in return, the question deliberately seductive, and I have to swallow tightly, taking a long drink of my beer. I nearly finish the damn thing.

"How about if you win, you can pick where we go next Sunday," I offer her, knowing it's a win for me too.

"I like it here. I told you I was curious what it was like."

"I still can't believe you've never been here," I say before finishing the beer and stand, grabbing the rack to get the game started before all the blood in my head moves to my dick and I forget about the pool game again.

Laura follows my lead and says, "I don't see how you can't believe that… as I'm not twenty-one so I shouldn't be in a bar and this isn't exactly *my crew*."

"Crew," I repeat and lean back, grabbing the cue and lining it up. "You don't need to be in the *crew*," I emphasize the word, mocking the way she said it, "to hang out in here. Didn't you want a job? We need a new waitress and you don't have to be twenty-one for that."

She's quiet for a moment, not answering and I would give anything to know what she's thinking. Everyone knows The Club is our hangout and she's right, not everyone is welcome. It's only a bar, but it's where all the cash is funneled and laundered so all the dirty shit we do comes out clean in the books.

She finally relaxes her shoulders, letting the bottle sit on her knee to tell me, "I really love the atmosphere though. And the people… it's nice to be around here, I guess that's how I can put it."

"Well, I'm glad you came."

Just as I'm pulling back the pool cue, Laura calls out, "Uh, no. Ladies first." She pulls at the stick from behind me, and playfully nudges my shoulder. She teases, "And to think, I thought you were a gentleman."

I loosen my grip on the cue and when she has it fully in her grasp, I raise my hands, letting my gaze roam down her body. From the tight cream sweater to the faded pair of jeans with a hole in the knee, she looks utterly desirable. The cut on her sweater is lower than most of them. At school she's always hidden behind baggy sweatshirts. It doesn't escape my notice that she decided to wear a sexed-up version for today's venture. A not-date with yours truly.

"Whatever gave you the idea that I'm a gentleman… I take it back. You should know I'm practically a savage." My joke is rewarded with a sweet laugh and a complementary blush coloring her cheeks.

Laura rests the pool cue against the table so she can take another sip of beer before telling me, "I may have picked up on the savage part."

"You like the beer?" I ask her and she shrugs.

"So far I don't hate it."

I wait, taking my time for my next comment until she's lined up and pulled back.

"I heard you liked something else today," I start and watch her ass sway, her hips rocking as she teases the cue, letting the slim wood thread through her fingers as if she's a pro with it. I've got a full hard-on just from watching her, and I might be a bastard, because I'm not ashamed of it in the least.

"What's that?" she asks, squinting just so and ready to strike.

"Heard you told your girl Cami that you like my ass," I confess just as she pushes her weight forward, barely hitting the cue ball and bumping into the table as well. With her mouth hung open, although it comes with a smile she can't contain. A vibrant rose hue colors her chest all the way up to her cheeks. The balls smack against one another and only three break away, not giving her a damn thing.

"Speechless?" I question when she doesn't say anything, the butt of the pool stick hitting the floor as she holds it against her body.

My lips are on my beer, but my eyes stay on her as I drink.

"You're not a savage," she finally responds with more confidence than anything else, "you're an ass." She says it all with the most beautiful smile. I belt out a laugh, holding my hand out for the cue. She's resistant, pursing her lips, but gives in, passing me the stick.

Our fingers brush one another when she does. Electricity strikes me, coursing through my arm and then down my body. It's hot and the heat lingers long after she's sulked back to sofa, sitting on the armrest with her arms crossed against her chest. I want to feel that all the time. The way she makes me feel with such a simple touch.

"I don't remember saying a damn thing about your ass by the way," she says and shrugs. I make my hit quick, lining up an easy pocket shot. *Crack*. I move to the other side of the table, lining up another that should break up the rest of the balls. It's a more difficult setup, requiring a little more strength.

"Is that memory of yours selective?" I ask her and immediately pocket another ball. With the stick in my right hand, I round the table, daring to look back at her.

She's seething but the embarrassment, or anger, whatever's got her panties in a bunch, is mixed with desire that's been coming to the surface more and more with every passing day.

It's quiet until I pull back.

"You do have a nice ass," she mutters, and I look over my shoulder to see her shrug, bringing her beer to her lips, her eyes focused on the ass in question.

"Glad I can give you a good view," I offer and just miss the next pocket.

Laura's giddiness is accompanied by a squeal of "my turn" and her quickly coming up behind me while her left arm brushes against my back and her fingers dance over mine. Every touch is deliberate, seductive, and I am drowning in all of it. I don't let go of the stick at once. When she tugs it, her eyes meet mine and the air sparks between us, getting hotter and lighter.

"My turn," she whispers, and I let go, not saying a word. I back up to the other end of the sofa, memorizing every curve of her body. She calls the side pocket and with a soft touch, the ball rolls lazily into the pocket. I have to wait until her back is to me to adjust myself. I'm uncomfortably hard, my cock pressing against the zipper of my jeans.

"We didn't come up with a bet," she reminds me when she misses her next. We trade places with little conversation, but the heat between us is there, and when she hands me the pool cue, she hesitates, forcing me to look into her eyes and see the smoldering heat that stirs in them.

"Right," I nod when she hits the cue ball, misses, and makes her way back to the other end of the sofa, handing me the pool stick. I'm still standing where I was, watching her. Instead of going back to the table, I make my way to her, planting the stick down right in front of her, both of my hands around it as I ask her, "What is it that you want, Babygirl?"

Her beautiful blue eyes drop to my lips in a heartbeat. I know it's one heartbeat because my own pounds in my chest with lust and need.

"I can have anything?" she questions in a breathy whisper, slowly raising her gaze back to mine.

I lean in closer until my lips are only inches away from hers. "Anything you want." The tension sizzles between us.

Her chestnut hair falls in front of her, draping around her shoulders and I reach forward to tuck a lock behind her ear. I don't get the chance to though, because Laura's small hands reach up, grabbing on to mine. There's desperation in her touch, want and need swirling in a deadly concoction in her eyes.

"Seth," she says, trying to speak my name easily, but lust mingles with the single syllable. She closes her eyes, breathing in deeply, letting her chest rise and fall.

All I have to do is lean forward. That's it.

But the door whips open and Derrick's voice booms in, startling Laura.

She gasps and backs away, leaning deep into the sofa as I glare at Derrick.

"Oh shit, sorry," Derrick says and looks between the two of us. "I didn't mean to…"

"It's fine," I answer but my tone denotes that it's anything but fine. Clearing my throat, I ask him, "What is it?

"We need you. Some," he pauses and glances at Laura who looks down and away, like she's not listening as he continues, "information just came in."

I know exactly what he's referring to and it can't wait. Fucking figures.

"I have to go," I tell Laura rather than answering Derrick. "I'll drive you back."

"You don't have to," she answers sweetly, not at all bothered that our non-date ended as quickly as it began.

"It's not about what I have to do. Do you want me to?" I regret asking her that the moment the question slips out. Derrick's still here watching and I'm on edge waiting for her answer.

"Yes… please. I want you to."

Derrick butts in, responding to both of us. "We have to go that way anyway." He speaks to Laura this time. "So even if you said no, I'm sure Seth would have insisted." He's friendly toward her but I can see the warning when he looks back at me, the politeness when he looks at her. He still hasn't changed his mind.

I haven't changed my mind either.

"I hate your fucking guts," I mutter to Derrick and he only chuckles in response. Like all of this is some joke to him. The evening sky is already black, not a star in sight and with no streetlights in Laura's neighborhood, the only lights are from the windows lining the rows of townhouses.

"No you don't," he finally says, pulling out a cigarette and lighting it. "I was surprised you brought her to The Club. Didn't even know she was back there with you."

Nervousness pricks down my neck. I know exactly why he wouldn't think I'd bring her there.

"She wanted to do something this weekend. I offered to take her."

"Of all the places?" he questions, but doesn't say anything else as I put the car into drive and make a right, driving back to the highway.

"You kiss her yet? Or was that your first and I completely cock-blocked you?"

"The latter," I answer, tightening my grip on the wheel. My palms heat talking about this with him. He'd given up all the warnings for weeks now.

"So no kiss?" he asks like it's unbelievable.

"No kiss," I answer him, not bothering to hide my resentment toward him for interrupting us. I'm not just taking it slow. I'm letting her lead. Which is taking a longer time than I'd hoped. It's fucking torture but that's what I get.

"If that's not a sign, I don't know what is."

"What are you talking about?" *What sign?*

"That I just happen to walk back there and stop it. You're in too deep with her. And you know it."

"This again?" Anger forces my muscles to coil. "I told you, it's none of your business."

"It is my business, because you're my friend. My best friend. I'd give my life for you," he stresses in a pained statement.

"I'd do the same for you and you know that," I say and pause, making sure he accepts that as fact, "but she's not up for discussion."

"Could you even love her? Knowing that she doesn't know."

She'll never know. I've already decided that. She will never know the truth. It'll kill her. I won't allow that to happen. An intense wave of protectiveness jolts through me, leaving a cold sweat to cover every inch of my skin. Having to slow down at the stop sign, I look Derrick in the eyes and say, "There were only five of us in that room. They're all dead now except for you and me. She will never know."

"They could have told someone else. You don't know."

My head shakes in anger, denying what he's saying. No one else knows. They can't.

"I'm just saying, are you sure you want to go after her and not end this? It's not too late to walk away. She'll be all right, man. I'm telling you. She'll be fine if you walked away."

"I'm not walking away, Derrick. It'll be best for us if you never bring that shit up again."

He starts to apologize, but I cut him off, easing into traffic and aiming to end this conversation, "I made up my mind on how this is going to happen. If anything gets in my way, or threatens to get between me and Laura, there will be hell to pay. I want her, and I'm going to have her."

I know if she were to find out the truth, she'd hate me. I'll do everything I can to keep it a secret.

"She's going to fall for me," I speak out loud, wanting Derrick to know it, to accept it and get the hell over his reservations.

"Are you going to be able to give her that back?" he asks in a calm, even voice riddled with true concern. "Can you really fall for her, knowing what you did?"

If I were a better man, I'd keep her away because I don't know the answer to Derrick's question. I wouldn't dream every night for her to kiss me. He has it right. It's selfish of me to want her to be with me.

I'm not a better man. She makes me feel like one, though. That's why I can't stop.

I don't answer his question, and he doesn't bring it up again.

All I need is for Laura to kiss me. One kiss, and then I won't hold back a damn thing anymore.

HARD TO LOVE

She was too good for this world. I was too much of a bastard to push her away.

I grew up in this life, and now I run these streets. Blood and violence taint everything I touch.

Everything but her. She was my constant through it all.

Just a touch would singe and soothe.

Just a look would tempt and torment.

She became my escape and my addiction.

I only survived because she was by my side.

I should've known better than to indulge.

I should've known better than to let her fall for me.

It was only a matter of time before the danger bled into what we had.

I was Laura's downfall. Problem was, she was mine too.

PROLOGUE

Seth

On the west coast and several years before meeting the Cross brothers.

This hour of night, the floor-to-ceiling windows reveal nothing but black outside. Pitch black. Inside, though, the lights shine brightly and keep everyone in this place invigorated. The bass of the music thrums in my veins just as it lightly vibrates the hardwood floors beneath my polished oxfords.

Wrapping my hand around the steel rail that runs along the second-floor loft, with my office behind me, I watch the bright blue lights fade to nearly black in time with the beat. Bodies sway, drinks are poured, and life moves on.

My bar is the hottest spot in all of Tremont. The women, the money, all the shit that goes down in the back rooms—it's all mine. Everyone wants in those black glass double doors. Thank fuck for that. It took nearly a year to get my name back, to get the money, both dirty and clean, flowing easily without someone wanting me dead along the way.

A year of recovering from the damage that was done.

A year without her.

A year cleaning up the mess and taking care of shit that nearly broke me. Between all the fights and all the drugs, none of it compares to what happened last year. Two days until the date.

A gruff exhale leaves me as I force away the memories and focus on what's in front of me. The perfect location, the perfect setup. The perfect fucking life I've been building.

The name of the bar mirrors every inch of what's inside. *Allure.* It's designed to lure in customers and to keep the drinks flowing, the hips moving, and the money streaming in. The bar is seductive with polished black marble waterfall counters that gleam, their shine visible from all the way up here. The deep cobalt velvet sofas on opposite sides of the seating area are just as enticing as the women who perch themselves there with crystal glasses containing pink cocktails in their manicured hands as they let out peals of feminine laughter. Black crystal chandeliers drip from the ceilings.

Club Allure is about escaping from reality via luxury and illusions of grandeur.

The basement though… and the back rooms… those are the real moneymakers, all of it under the table, and how I earned the fear and respect that comes with my name.

It's also what led to enemies. You haven't made it in this world until someone tries to take what's yours. Until someone wants to challenge you. Until someone wants you dead.

I learned that hard lesson a year ago. And the ones who came for me? Their deaths didn't go unnoticed by anyone else who thought they could take from me.

An eerie prick travels down my spine as my mind wanders to places in the past. Back to when I was a different man. Things change when the ones you love the most leave you. Just as I think about everything that happened before this, just as the memories invade the present, I swear I hear her voice.

It's only a memory. *She's only a memory.* I remind myself like I've done so many silent nights, only to have my gaze drawn to the sound again.

The crowd doesn't part for her; she blends into it, which is what she always wanted.

I see her though, and everyone else blurs as I focus on her alone.

My grip tightens on the rail and everything pauses around me. My blood runs scorching hot. Her dark brunette hair cascades down to her lower back. In distressed dark denim shorts and a silk cream tank top that hangs low on her back, she makes her way straight to the bar. I watch as the corners of her lips turn up at recognizing the two men behind the bar. They've been my crew since the first day… she was there too.

She was always there, always a part of us.

Connor sees her first, dropping the empty glass he's holding on the counter to reach across the bar. When he calls out, "Babygirl," Roman looks up from the set of four shots he's pouring and grins at her.

It's too loud on this floor to make out everything they're saying. It's all smiles and hugs, though. Warm, friendly greetings. It steals any heat I had and leaves a chill to settle over my shoulders, slowly wrapping its way around me as the time ticks away.

The two of them barely let her get a word in as they talk, but she laughs—fuck, I can hear that sweet mirth all the way up here. Just like I can see the rosy flush in her cheeks when she agrees to take a shot with them. Just like I can see the dip in her throat that I used to lick when she throws back the shot of clear liquid.

It's been a year, but I swear I remember the way she tastes.

It takes a minute before she asks them something. She rocks on her heels as she waits for an answer and both of the guys look around the first floor.

It's when they point to Derrick that the hate creeps in. That chill on my skin turns to ice and I decide I'm sick of waiting.

She asked for Derrick. Not me.

My eyes are trained on her as I make my way down the stairs. My jaw is set as it is, and I can't change that fact for the world right now. Past the masses dancing on the floor, I make my way easily to where Derrick's seated in a leather wingback chair on the far edge of the wall where security is located.

A woman turns around, tall and slim, when I brush past her. I barely notice anything about her except the short red dress that clings to her curves. She smiles when she sees it's me, her eyes hopeful but she quickly lowers her gaze and backs away.

Maybe it's the hate in my glare that told her I'm not in the mood for these games tonight.

I'm barely contained, hardly capable of a single rational thought as that last moment I had with Laura runs through my mind. The past and the present swirl in front of me, hitting me harder and more forcefully than the strongest cocktail I could drown myself in.

Laura plants a kiss on Derrick's cheek… It's short lived and her smile is sorrowful.

The anger that carved itself into a glower relents and dims. Even a year isn't enough time. There will never be enough time passed to make it better.

Regret is my enemy. Guilt its friend.

I'm standing there like a lion stalking his prey when Laura turns around, not looking where she's going, brushing stray strands of hair from her face as she bumps right into me.

"Sorry," she quickly breathes, and then she looks at me. Her blue eyes have flecks of gold in them, and like a concoction of emotion they swirl as she stares at me. Her lips are slightly parted, and they stay like that. Open and waiting with disbelief.

"Laura." I say her name and feel the thrill of doing just that simmer in my blood.

"Seth," she whispers. Her shoulders drop slightly and then she covers herself, as if instantly cold.

"I um, I had something to give Derrick," she tells me, but her eyes don't stay on me. They stray, unable to keep my gaze. I watch the cords in her neck tighten as she swallows; I can't help but notice how her hands keep nervously playing with the hem of her shirt.

"You afraid to see me, Babygirl?" I ask her lowly and that gets her attention. Those beautiful blues find mine and for a moment, I feel everything all over again.

The undeniable lust, the tormented love, and finally, the loss. It all echoes in her doe eyes.

"Should I be?" she asks me, her cadence caressing. Her teeth sink into her bottom lip as she holds her breath waiting for my response. That lip I used to nibble as she moaned my name. Lips that used to kiss me and only me.

"You should leave." I push out the words, feeling a wash of cold run over my flesh. It comes back in waves, but the loss takes so much with it.

She swallows thickly with a nod and turns to leave without another word. Her thick hips sway and my gaze stays pinned to her until she disappears behind the double doors. She doesn't look back.

She never did.

"You fucked up." Derrick's deep voice carries over the beat of the music. His eyes stay glued to the television that displays over eight feet of the white and blue bars of an equalizer, changing with the rhythm.

It mocks me. The fact that everything in this place keeps moving, mocks me.

He takes a swig from his beer bottle, not bothering to look at me.

I have to close my eyes and breathe. Without her here, all that's left is anger.

I already know I fucked up. I take in a steadying breath as my teeth grind together.

The music keeps going. The women keep laughing.

My muscles twitch, consumed with a feeling of restlessness, the need to move, to do something.

"We both fucked up." Derrick's remark makes me open my eyes. Slowly and with a loathing for all of this, for everything I've built since she's been gone.

"Boss," Connor calls out, sliding a tumbler of whiskey over to me. I stare down at the glass, remembering everything. Watching it play out like a movie across the surface of the amber liquor.

Rowan calls out, "Boss," at the same time as someone else, but all I can picture is the night she left. The memory goes backward in time until I'm with her that morning, kissing her lips, feeling the dip of her waist. The voices around me lower in volume until I hear "Seth" instead.

There's never a minute. Never a quiet moment.

If there was, none of that shit would have happened.

I hear her tell me she loves me. I can practically feel her lips against the shell of my ear and the warmth that traveled down my shoulder that morning.

I didn't know I'd never feel that warmth again. I didn't know. But I should have.

It was all my fault.

With the single bellow of a roar torn from deep in my chest, I throw the glass in my hand recklessly at the flat-screen TV. The glass shatters, falling like rain, crashing into the liquor bottles lining the bar.

Connor and Rowan have to duck and cover their heads as I seethe, drawing in a breath and then another. I'd feel more remorse if she hadn't spoken to them, laughed with them. I'd feel guilty if she hadn't given her smiles to them so easily, when she didn't have a damn thing to give me.

I'm a bastard; I've always been a bastard.

"Get out," I say and my command ricochets in the large open space. Stunned faces stare back at me, the bar silent save for the occasional tinkling of glass shards. No one moves and that's their mistake too.

"Get the fuck out. We're closed." The low threat isn't hidden and a sea of women in short dresses suddenly start moving. No one looks at me for more than a split second as the patrons grab their shit and head for the door.

My crew stays where they are, their eyes on me. All but Derrick. He doesn't look at me. He takes a swig and stares at the broken TV as if it's still a visual for the nonexistent music. Even as Connor and Roman ask me if I'm all right, I watch him staring blankly at the broken glass.

"If you want to help me," I begin as I finally look Roman in the eyes to answer him, feeling the rage subside but something else still lingers as I continue, "clean up this fucking mess."

The two men who are some of my best friends look at me with sympathy. I see it staring back at me in their eyes and it makes me grit my teeth. With the sound of my blood rushing through my ears, I grip the collar of Connor's shirt and bring the steadily spoken, low threat to his attention as I say, "Don't ever let her in here again."

CHAPTER 1

Thirteen months prior

Seth

My cock is stiff in the matter of a half second watching Laura do a feline stretch on my bed. The mattress protests with a groan until she settles down cross-legged and lays the book she's been studying in her lap. It looks heavy and uncomfortable, but I know she'll read it until she's tired, taking notes on that bright green pad of paper. She'll be tired enough that she stays, though. That's all I want.

"Why are you staring?" she asks and then taps the pen in her hand on the edge of the book. Once, twice, before looking up at me with a cocked brow. I was going to answer, but then she slips the end of the pen between her teeth.

She laughs at my groan and then reprimands me. "You're impossible."

"Maybe I just like seeing you on my bed," I offer her.

Even with her tough-girl act, she smiles. "You're cute."

The way she sways slightly, reveling in the small statement does something to me. It took years to get to this point. Years of me fighting and struggling to feel stable.

Years of her by my side, carrying me along the way when I was too fucked in the head to see straight.

She glances down at her book and then back up at me. "Are you just going to keep watching me read?" Her tone is playful, a little taunting. It makes me that much harder.

I have to get out of here in thirty, meet the guys and tell them what's going down. I have time to enjoy her though.

I'll always make time for that.

"Lie down and spread your legs for me." I give her the command and wait for her reaction.

She bites down on her bottom lip, trying to contain her smile. Closing the hardback, she places it on the bedside table, scooting her glass to the side with the spine of the heavy anatomy textbook. "You like it, don't you?" she asks as she shimmies her way down the bed.

"Like what?" I ask her, feeling my cock twitch and not wasting another second to remove these jeans. I kick off the denim and pull my t-shirt over my head, noting how Laura's gaze drops down my chest, then to my boxer briefs the moment the shirt isn't in her way anymore.

I don't know if she does it on purpose or not, but the way she rocks her crossed legs from side to side on the bed, like she's impatient for me… fuck, I'm too hard.

"You like the dom thing?" she asks in a whisper and a blush sweeps up from her chest to her cheeks.

She asked me to try it out a few months ago. I tell her what to do. She listens.

"Fuck yeah I do."

I stare at her as I shove my briefs down. I love how she swallows when she sees my dick and her breathing gets deeper when I stroke myself.

"You already wet?" I ask her, a little cockier than I should be. With a little nod she hums an "uh-huh" in that seductive drawl she gets when I'm playing with her.

It takes a moment. It always does. Rocking in and out of her slowly, waiting for her to adjust, my skin is fire against hers as I rake my teeth up her slender neck. I can feel my warm breath in my face, followed by hers as I lazily kiss her. Taking my time, feeling her body writhe under mine. Her kiss is tender and sweet. Her nails dig into my shoulders, sending a slight pain that urges me to go in deeper. Once, twice, then her breath hitches, her doe eyes widen, and my name is a strangled moan in the air between us.

"There it is," I groan in her ear as she pushes her head back into the mattress. With each of my forearms pinned against her shoulders, I don't give her an inch of movement. When I pick up my pace, slamming myself deeper inside of her, she has nowhere to go.

"Take it, Babygirl," I grit between my teeth as I fuck her harder, faster, mercilessly. Feeling her warmth wrap around my cock, she's already screaming her pleasure in the crook of my neck.

I pound into her, feeling her climax and reeling in the way her cunt pulses around my cock. She's a damn good lover, urging me on and taking everything I have to give her.

With the steady pounding of the headboard against the wall, I pick up my pace, feeling my own release coming.

Not yet. I want her to cum again. I want to feel it all at least one more time.

I slow down, repressing my urge, going against everything I want.

And then I do it all over again.

My heart's racing and my blood ringing with adrenaline as I pick up my head to breathe when it's all over. She whimpers when I pull myself out of her, that sound I can't get enough of. Every sound she makes is like that. It's everything.

With her hair a messy halo and her eyes half lidded but still full of lust, she looks well fucked. She should always look just like this.

Checking the clock, I only have five minutes, but Laura will give me shit if I don't hold her for a minute. Her thighs shake when I clean her up.

My exhale is easy as I get back into bed, listening to it creak as Laura sidles up next to me.

It's quiet for a moment. I kiss her hair. She told me once it's what made her fall in love with me. When she was falling asleep, I kissed her hair. As if love is that easy.

"You going to get another this year?" she asks me as her fingertips run down the length of one of the bands across my right bicep. I have a sleeve of tattoos running from my wrist up to my shoulder, but around my bicep are three thin bands with untouched flesh between them. One for each year I won't ever forget. The first year, my mother died and the second, my father was murdered. The third year, I got revenge.

"Another band?" I question her, feeling a crease settle between my brow just as she nestles into me with a soft sigh. Her eyes never leave the tattoo.

"Yeah?" she asks.

It's been two years since my last tattoo. Because that's how long we've been together. Maybe she doesn't realize it's been that long. I sure as hell do though. I didn't get one last year. And I'm not planning on getting another.

It was all before this. These past two years have felt like… like after. There's no other way to describe it. She's here; I have my crew. There are no more demons left to fight. It's all just something I think of simply as after. "I think I might get something different," I answer her.

"You're running out of room," she humorously replies and looks up at me. Her pale blue eyes glimmer with affection. "Between the gears from your bike there might be a little space to put something."

A huff of a laugh leaves me and I settle back on the headboard, although the alarm clock tells me I'm already running late.

"Maybe I'll get something for you," I suggest and watch how she pulls back slightly to get a better look at my face. Her disbelief makes me smirk.

I grin as I whisper at the shell of her ear, "Don't be too scared."

"Not scared," she says, and pushes me away playfully as she answers. She still doesn't know if I'm serious or not and I like it that way.

Stretching my arms over my head, I roll out my shoulders and get out of bed. Grabbing my clothes, I get ready for tonight.

She looks surprised that I'm getting dressed. Shit, I didn't tell her.

Sometimes she leaves when I'm gone, but damn do I want her to be here when I get back tonight.

Zipping up my pants and buttoning them, I explain, "I have to go meet up with the boys. You staying here to study?"

"Yeah, I really have to. If I do well, the advisor said I could apply to the nursing program and have a good shot."

"You will. You'll ace that shit."

She offers me a small smile but doesn't say anything. It's not like either of us were good at school. There was too much shit going on. Too much real shit that took up everything we had.

I get her insecurity, I understand it. But she's with me. No more of that. "You'll ace it, and then you'll move in with me," I tell her, as if saying it makes it an absolute.

Laura's eyes are silently warning me not to bring this up and she bites the inside of her cheek. I don't push her; I don't have time to fight about this again.

Instead I pull my shirt down over my chest, lean over the bed, and give her a kiss. And then another with my hand spearing through her hair.

"You go to school. Be a fine-ass nurse. I can take care of us. Your schooling and all that."

My words are meant to reassure her, but the bright light that's always a constant in her eyes dims, as does her smile. She fights to keep it in place.

"I know you don't know how this is going to work. But I've got you. I've got us."

She's quiet and that doubt is still there. She wants a certain life—a quiet, honest living with white picket fences—a different one from this, but her place is with me. She knows it, I know it, everyone does. "I'll make sure you get everything you want. I promise," I tell her, and my voice is resolute.

"I love you," is all she responds. That, and a kiss that deepens then turns into more.

I'm going to be so fucking late.

CHAPTER 2

Laura

EVERY TIME I SEE THIS HOUSE, IT HURTS. THE JINGLE OF THE KEYS AND the sound of a car driving down the road behind me are all that I have to comfort me as I walk through the front door.

When I was a kid, I loved the slate floors of my grandma's house. I remember thinking the coffered ceilings were the kind of thing castles had. I remember rocking on the front porch swing and the thoughts I had of stealing Mr. Timms's roses from next door. His front yard was always prettier than Grandma's overgrown shrubs. She worked at the diner until the week she died. She didn't have time to smell the roses, let alone tend to them in her small front yard.

Whenever I'd pluck a few roses, Mr. Timms always knew it was me and Grandma would make me go over and apologize once he told her. Stubborn old man liked his garden.

That was then. Seen through the eyes of a child. I know better now. It's a run-down house on a busy street in an old city. To add salt to the wound, the roses next door are grown over with weeds even though Mr. Timms still lives there. This street was destined for failure. I didn't know it back then, and I'm sure Grandma didn't see it when she bought the place after her husband of two years ran off with someone else and never looked back, abandoning her and her only son.

The train, the highways, the steel mill behind the development. It's all undesirable. My grandmother watched the neighborhood change as she aged. She hated what this town became when the steel mill went out of business decades ago and half the people here didn't have a job anymore.

I still remember the roses though. And I'll never take down that porch swing.

Shutting the door behind me, I take in what's left of her home. Half the furniture is gone since holding the last estate sale. I kept Grandma's chair though. I had it refurbished for her when the chemo stole her energy. I don't want to sit in the chair. I don't want to move it either.

I just want it to stay in the corner by the lamp where she read the newspaper and gossiped on the phone to Esme, another waitress from the diner.

Breathing out a tired sigh, I push off from the door and stare down at the bills in my hand. Grandma had plenty of them. And they keep coming.

I should sell this place, pay off the debts, and move in with Seth. At least that's what he says. But that's a little too much like moving on from the only person who was a constant in my life and putting all my faith in a man. A man who won't even tell me he loves me. Even if I love him, he scares me. All of this scares me.

The sound of the door creaking open startles me and I reward the newcomer with wide eyes and taking the Lord's name in vain.

It's only Cami.

"Shit," she says and cringes when she sees my hand over my chest. "Didn't mean to freak you out." She ducks her head a little with a grin as she shuts the door and says beneath her breath, "My bad."

"You could have knocked," I tell her and toss the stack of envelopes onto the side table at the entrance. It's butted up against the stairs that lead to the second floor. The hard maple side table has been there for years. When I was a kid, I thought about jumping off the balcony on the second floor and landing on the table. A neighborhood friend was chasing me when we were playing tag. I was a reckless and stupid girl. Hell, I'm still lacking in that department.

"Since when do I knock?" Cami walks right past me down the narrow hall and I follow her then stop when she gets to the kitchen. Leaning against the threshold and crossing my arms, I watch her open the fridge and take out a can of cola.

"You kinda look like hell," Cami comments with a wrinkled nose and then adds, "and you need to go grocery shopping."

"And to think… you're the bright light in my world," I say to mock my closest friend and her constant peppy tone.

She laughs as she cracks open the can, drinking soda at 9:00 in the morning. Her long blonde hair is a mess; it's obvious she hasn't brushed it yet, and she's still in her pajamas.

"You're looking rough yourself."

"Long night," she says cryptically and takes another sip, but she can't disguise the devilish smile she's hiding.

Her grin is infectious, and I join her at the small oak table in the kitchen.

"Shut up," I say then gasp as my eyes go wide. "Derrick?" I question her, feeling all those ooey gooey and excited emotions racing inside of me.

"Mm-hmm." She can't even speak as she nods her head. Beaming, her full lips are upturned as her cheeks turn red.

"Did you guys…?"

She shakes her head quickly and shoves the can of soda a few inches in front of her, looking at it and then me. "Not yet. I just don't want it to be a one-time thing, you know?" She talks quickly when she's nervous. Not even taking a breath, she continues. "He came over and we watched a movie. It was awful." She looks past me and shakes her head. "Like truly awful. I don't know why I let him pick." She breathes in for the first time, deep and easing the tension through her shoulders as she adds, "But it doesn't matter, because he pulled me in all close." She gets up and goes around the table. "Like this, you know," she tells me as she wraps her arm around my shoulders and makes me laugh.

"And then..." I draw out the last word, waiting for her to tell me the good stuff.

She shrugs, strutting back to her seat and taking a drink while she makes me wait.

"You're insufferable."

"And you love me."

I pull my lips into a grimace for half a second but then add, "I do love you."

"I love you too... and I loved it when he kissed me." She can't contain her giddiness as she practically dances in her seat. "Not even just once, but five times."

"Any makeout sessions?" I question and she nods as she replies, "Yup." The *P* pops as she says it. "Twice."

"So the yearlong crush is finally becoming something," I say then smile as I get up and search for coffee. I listen to Cami regale me with the details of last night, putting the grounds in the top and pushing the button to start the coffee maker.

"Slow and steady," Cami says, then downs the last of her soda and gets up to grab another one. "Not like you two," she adds.

The coffee machine hisses, and I couldn't agree more.

"Different strokes and all that," I half-heartedly reply. We did go too fast. It's hard to come back from all of that. We were both tumbling downhill, and there's no going slow when your life is free-falling. Better to fall fast together than apart.

"Any update on that matter?" she asks.

"Well since you're making out with his best friend..." I trail off and exhale heavily while I stir sugar into my coffee and the spoon clinks against the ceramic mug. "...you should know," I conclude before looking her in the eye.

Sitting back in her seat at the table, she asks me, "Seriously. You going to be okay?" Both of her hands are wrapped around the Coke can as she leans forward.

"You're so intense sometimes." I try to shake it off like Seth does, but Cami sees through me.

"Have you told him?" she asks.

I run my nail along one of the gouges in the wooden table as she talks. This table's been through a lot, but it's another thing I'll never get rid of. Grandma said it belonged to her mom. So, really, it's the only heirloom I've got. I've sat here and celebrated; cried and mourned. I sat here as I studied… even if I didn't do so well in school. The first kiss I ever had was in the kitchen threshold and shortly after that, Seth took me on this table.

Yeah, I'm never getting rid of this table.

"It's okay if you didn't."

I confess, "He knows."

"And?"

"And he was all… you know, as good as he could be about it." It hurts. Everything hurts, so I drink my coffee like it'll wash all these bad feelings down.

"It's a lot to go through at once."

"His solution is for me to move in with him, and he'll just take care of everything," I say as I toss my hand in the air and then stare down at my coffee through glossy eyes.

I won't tell her how he still didn't say it. He still didn't say that he loves me. It's so stupid, but with everything going on, it means so much to me that Cami's the only one in my life who will say it. She may be the only one to ever tell me those words again.

"Don't cry." Cami's voice is consoling. "You're going through a lot," she repeats.

"I'm not crying," I tell her a little too sternly and calm myself down, shaking out my hands. "I'm fine."

"You're not fine. And that's okay." Ever positive and nurturing. I love her, but she doesn't get it. We may both be in our early twenties, but she hasn't gone through an ounce of what I've seen in the last three years. Let alone my childhood.

"What am I going to do?" I ask her, not knowing myself.

"You think too much," she tells me after a long moment of silence.

"You don't think enough."

"That's not the first time you've said that," she jokes, and I let a puff of laughter leave me.

"First things first. You're going to study while I go through the bills. We have more than enough to pay the minimum on all of them..." She pauses as she hesitates but adds what I already know she's going to say, "I still think you should tell Seth. He would pay them off."

"And I'd be in debt to him and he'd have more of a reason for me to sell it all and give it all away."

She stares at me for a moment, not saying what's on her mind. Straightening in her seat, she drinks the rest of her second can of soda, making me even more jealous of how skinny she is. "You study, we pay the bills, and then we meet up with our men who are oh so bad for us and have a damn good time." She ends with a smile and the one I give her back is genuine.

"Yeah," I answer her, taking a sip of the much-needed coffee. "You're right. That's a good plan."

She gets up to toss her can in the recycling bin, but she stops where she is and turns to me with a serious expression. "I'm happy you told him."

I swallow the bitter coffee, not knowing what to say. Happy and that moment don't belong together.

CHAPTER 3

Seth

"WHAT'S UP WITH THIS GIRLY SHIT?" DERRICK'S VOICE BELLOWS from behind me. He's not even through the front doors of this place and he's already being a prick.

I give it a moment, letting my eyes settle on his pale pink button-up paired with dark jeans. "You talking about that shirt you're wearing?"

It looks ridiculous. Derrick is jacked. He works out constantly and he was already built to be a big man.

He grunts a laugh and says, "The girl I'm seeing likes it. Fuck off." My chuckle is deep and short lived.

"Must really like this one," I comment. I've never known him to settle down or even remember the names of the different chicks he's with every week. Not until now. Times are changing, though. For all of us.

Standing in the middle of all this construction, of what will soon be my club, change is all I can think about.

"Girlfriend material?" I ask him.

"Something like that," he says, keeping his answer cryptic. Landing a hand on my shoulder, Derrick gives me a squeeze and adds, "Finally coming together, brother."

"That it is."

He squeezes again, commenting that the couch in the corner is too fucking girly for our club, as if he has any taste at all, and heads past me to the bar. It's not stocked yet, but the guys keep a stash on hand in the fridge. Drills are going, the TVs are being mounted, and the furniture is set in place now that the floors are down. The crew we hired is fast and on point.

Laura picked out the furniture, well most of it, including the sofa Derrick's not a fan of. It'll all come together. She shares my vision, and the guys will get on board.

Cracking open a bottle and tossing the cap into the bin with a clink, Derrick's voice echoes as he asks, "Where are the fights going to be?"

Selling guns is how we got this far, old business that was set in stone when we took over, but the fighting and betting? That's a steady flow of cash I didn't know was possible. A bar to push the dirty money through is the cherry on top.

"It's called underground for a reason," I answer him and steal his beer before he takes his first swig.

"Fucker," he comments when I tell him thanks.

"Grab yours and follow me," I tell him just as Connor comes in. He's got his sleeve rolled up and I can see the shamrock tat on the inside of his forearm. He's Irish through and through. He even gave me shit about having Mexican beer in the bar. *What Irish pub carries Dos Equis?* Ours does, because it's damn good beer.

I've got five guys in my crew. We started this shit together; we'll always be together. Growing up in this town, we saw how things were run. It took one too many blows but now it's ours. Simple as that. Connor's got a scar on the left side of his jaw to prove it. He's the shortest of us, the leanest too, but he's the one I'd pick in a knife fight. Ten out of ten times. The Irish in him, that crazy bastard side, gives him the edge he needs.

Together, the five of us own this town. And this bar is going to be the crowning jewel of our empire.

Connor takes a look around and I watch him, waiting for his reaction. He moves the pack of beer in his right hand to his left and then back again.

"What do you think?" I ask.

"Legit cash flow in the bar, fight club downstairs. It's perfect."

"You like that girly-ass sofa? A fucking sofa in a bar?" Derrick says and regards Connor, who looks in his eyes and then at his shirt.

"What the hell are you wearing?" Connor asks.

"Screw both of you," Derrick says and shoves his beer into Connor's chest then starts unbuttoning his shirt. He tosses it on the back of a sleek steel barstool, its seat lined with cobalt velvet.

Wearing just his white t-shirt on top, he leaves the button-up where it is and snags back his beer.

"Don't feel peer pressured now," I quip and make my way to the back left of the large open space, past the bathrooms that are being renovated and I head down a narrow hall. The sound of construction dims until it's nonexistent as we hustle down the steel stairs. It's nothing but luxury on the first floor, or at least it will be, but down here, it's raw and primitive.

With a flick of the switch, the lights come on; thin rails of white light form stripes along the ceiling. They go from wall to wall so nothing will be missed. Spotlights will be installed next. Everything's on schedule.

"Ring in the center. Stage at the back for security to watch over everything. We'll be here at the head, calling the shots." I can see it all play out. It's only cement floors and drywall with spackle at the moment, but I can already hear the bell going off, the cheering, the crunch of bone.

"Vale Tudo," Connor says as he makes his way around the back of the basement. It's nearly a two-hundred-foot square.

"What the hell does that mean?" Derrick asks; he has to speak up as Connor's halfway down the room and Derrick's coming up beside me. He's my right-hand man. My best friend. I wouldn't be here without him. He wouldn't be here either. And we both know it.

"Anything goes… It's Portuguese fighting."

My answer comes without a second thought, "Oh, fuck that."

"Eye gouging and nut kicking… No, sir," Derrick comments.

Connor laughs and bellows from the back of the room, "Pussies."

"Seriously, though," Derrick says and holds up his beer as if he's toasting, "it's going to be killer." Derrick looks around even though I hadn't broken eye contact with him and I take him in. It's been a long damn time since he's been like this. Carefree and relaxed.

"Things are finally looking up," he comments as he looks around the room and Connor makes his way to us.

"You need a beer," he tells me, taking out a beer for me and then cracking one open for himself. It fizzes and he curses as he sucks the head from the top of the beer to keep it from spilling.

Derrick laughs at him and I take a moment to open mine carefully so I don't suffer the same fate.

"This is it, boys. We have the legit business from the bar, but this gets us in deeper, so we know what's going on and we have the cash to stay in the thick of it."

"That it is," Derrick says and then asks me, "Speaking of the thick of it. You hear from Wright?"

"That's why I wanted you two here, away from the construction crew upstairs."

"Figured as much," Connor comments.

My shoulders feel tighter as I lift the beer to my mouth but stop short of taking a sip. "He said Mathews is storing everything at the docks."

"All of it's there?" Derrick asks just beneath his breath.

"All but the cash. That he keeps in a safe in his house."

"We don't need to go for the cash, right?" Connor clarifies.

"Right. Just his drugs. He's growing too quickly, taking up too much territory and getting too close for comfort."

"Time for him to take a hit," Derrick says.

"And then another," I add.

"Where in the docks?" Connor questions.

"Roman staked it out last night. He knows right where it is. He said two men stayed there all night. A pair of dogs too."

"Fuck, not dogs," Derrick groans and grimaces. He got his leg torn up pretty good by a dog a few years back.

"It'll be taken care of. Don't worry," I reassure him. "In and out. We grab the haul and go."

"You think he'll know it was us?"

"Nah, we're throwing it out. We don't need his shit supply. It's laced up and cut so much it's hardly worth a dime. He's going to be looking for someone selling."

"Good," Connor says.

"When are we going?"

I look at Derrick to answer his question. "Tonight. Let the girls come here and we'll have Roman keep an eye on them. We'll go out and take care of it. Come back when we're done and no one will be the wiser."

All three of us grew up in this life. All three of our fathers died going against the men who took over. Men who didn't belong here and didn't give a damn about the people who live here. It was only a matter of time before we took this place back.

Revenge was sweet, but cleaning out this place the last two years has been hard as hell. People like Mathews need to stay back and this is how that happens. They inch closer, we steal their shit, wreck their warehouses, kill their men. We make it unprofitable and violent. We do whatever we have to in order to never go back to what used to be.

"No one owns Tremont but us," Derrick declares.

"Damn right," I tell him and clink my beer with his.

Connor lifts his beer and Derrick and I follow suit as he starts our toast. "Here's to the money, the dirty and the clean."

Derrick goes next. "Here's to the women, the ones who please us and the ones who make us scream."

I finish it out. "And here's to chaos, may we make that bitch our queen."

CHAPTER 4

Laura

"THREE HUNDRED IS LEFT OVER," CAMI TELLS ME AND POINTS TO the spreadsheet on her computer. Her chipped pink nails are a sign of the stress I know she's feeling right now. She put it all together, accounting for every cent of the money coming and going.

With my shoulders relaxed, I play off every bit of anxiousness that's been pulling me down, hoping to give her a little lift up. She doesn't need to carry my burdens. Damn do I love her for doing it though.

"So that's three hundred for the next two weeks to live off of after all the bills. That seems good, right?"

"After gas and food… that's tight, but it's workable," she confirms.

"And you're sure they're okay with just fifty a month?" I ask her again and then I want to kick my ass for second-guessing her and bringing in "bad mojo," as she'd call it.

"The hospitals?" she questions. Nodding, she makes her voice seem more chipper than it has been. "Yeah, they'll settle for what you can afford. Fifty a month for these bills is… appropriate. Insurance doesn't cover it. Eight bills total, so four hundred a month to cover someone else's medical bills. That's what you can afford… Barely."

"At least the new bar is coming." I'm trying to be optimistic as I sit back at the kitchen table. I stare through the threshold to the large bay window at the front of the living room. It needs new trim and the whole house could use a fresh coat of paint. Everywhere I look I see dollar signs and evidence that times are changing.

"Right. When the new bar comes, you'll make more money bartending. For now, you have the Clubhouse… and… and Seth… if you ask him."

I move my gaze back to Cami. "I don't want to ask him."

"He's—"

"Not yet," I say to cut her off. "I just… just give me time to figure everything out," I plead with her to understand. I don't want to be indebted to Seth more than I already am. Even if I love him, I still need a sense of independence. Especially now.

I have nothing but this little piece of independence. As small and shitty as it is, it's mine still. If it's gone, all I am is Seth's girl. If I don't pass this test, I'll never be anything but his girl. His burden too.

I don't ever want to be anyone's burden. Not like my father was. I will always love him and I hate to think ill of the dead, but it is what it is. He was a burden to my grandma. Hell, he was a burden to me. I won't be that. I won't allow it.

"I get it," Cami says. Breathing in, she taps her empty can on the table at the same time as I see a bright red shirt on my porch.

"What the fuck?" I can feel confusion line my face and then recognition when what's happening dawns. My heart races. "Who the hell is that?" I whisper the question and Cami turns to look out of the window too.

I see the guy's profile; I don't recognize him or his shaggy hair. And then I see my bike. In his hands.

"He's stealing my bike!" I jump out of my chair so fast it falls onto the floor, clattering as I rush past Cami and make my way to the door.

Bat, bat, bat. It's a mental reminder I scream in my head with every step. It isn't the first time in this neighborhood I've needed an edge on my side.

I keep a baseball bat between two umbrellas in the entry stand. Hating the feel of it in my hands, but damn grateful to have it, I snatch it and then unlock the door. Feeling a wave of disgust and anger rush through me, I watch the guy walk out into the middle of the street, both of his hands on MY bike and surrounded by a man on each side of him.

"Hey!" I scream out in the street, hearing my front door slam open and then shut behind me. "Hey fuckers!" I yell louder, my footsteps pounding down the uneven stone steps as I hustle my ass toward them in the middle of the street. The bat is in my hand, swaying heavily, but my grip is white knuckled on it.

It doesn't escape me that if it was just one of them, he could get on the bike and take off, but as it is, all three guys turn around and face me.

One of the assholes has a broad and gorgeous smile on his baby face. Freshly shaven or incapable of growing hair on his chin, I don't know. And I don't care. The asshole is smiling at me. That's when I notice his eyes are red. So are the guy's next to him. With blond hair down to his shoulders, the second guy looks like he doesn't give a shit about anything. He's just here for the ride.

The one holding the bike looks me up and down like, "What are you going to do about it?" with the same bloodshot eyes.

They're young. Young and dumb. I may be around their age, but age is a number, while youth is inexperience. The shit we've gone through—Seth, me, the crew—it's enough to age someone decades. We've been through more than some people go through their entire lives. These guys in front of me? I can see in their eyes that they haven't experienced the turmoil life is.

Three assholes out for a walk, high as fucking kites and taking what they want along the way as a joke.

My life isn't a joke. They don't get to take from me. No one gets to take from me.

The adrenaline causes the blood to course too fast through my veins. I can barely breathe, barely keep from shaking I'm so furious.

"Laura!" Cami's yelling my name from the porch, but I don't turn around. I'm not taking my eyes off these bastards.

"That's my bike." I grit out the words, my chest heaving.

"Looks like it's his now," the first guy says, and the others laugh. They laugh at me. "Possession is nine-tenths of the law," one of the others says. Even glancing down at the bat in my hand, the bat that sways slightly and brushes against my leg, they continue to laugh.

Taking one deep inhale full of rage and disbelief, I whip the bat above my head and crash it down onto the bike. I don't think twice. I just do it.

It's all the hurt and bitterness inside. I let it out. There are times to contain and times to explode. I'm hoping this is one of the latter, because I do it again. Screaming incoherently all the while.

I land the bat down with tired, aching muscles that somehow find explosive energy in the single act. The wooden bat is raised and swung.

Crashing down upon the bike my dad taught me to ride on before he died.

Smack! The wood hits the asphalt and the shock from the impact travels up my arms.

I used to ride it to his grave after the car accident. The memory brings a prick to the back of my eyes. Maybe this is what I get for thinking ill of him. Instant karma. The universe decided I wasn't allowed to have the bike anymore.

I lift the bat again, hearing the men back away. Calling me crazy. With both hands on the bat, I swing with everything I have, hitting the gears, smashing the handlebars again and again.

All I can hear is my frantic breathing and Cami telling me to calm down, saying that I'm all right.

With hot tears streaming down my face, I look up to see the three men looking more awake, more sober than they were when they stole from me.

"Now it's no one's fucking bike," I spit at them, tossing the busted bat at their feet then moving to walk away.

"Get out of here!" Cami screams at them. Her hand on my shoulder is soothing in some ways. I don't think I can speak right now.

"Are you deaf?" Cami urges them on when they hesitate, staring at me like I'm a sight to behold. Sometimes when you take from people, you take more than just a dumb bike.

They don't care. Or at least they didn't.

I wonder if they'll laugh and grab something off of another person's porch again.

The tears keep coming, but I don't brush them away; I won't give them that satisfaction of watching me clean myself up. I'm fine like this. I'm just fine.

I watch them leave, picking up their pace as they get closer to the street corner. Occasionally, they turn around to see if I'm still here. And I am. Standing right where I was when they left and waiting for them to disappear.

I don't even realize Cami's cleaning up my bike until I hear the clink of the broken gears against the metal trash can she dragged into the middle of the street. I'm grateful that this time of day isn't busy. Because heaven forbid a car come down this road now and beep at me or tell me to get out of the way. I can still feel the thrum of anger.

It's a good thing I put that baseball bat down. I don't like it. I just want it to go away. I don't like this side of me.

"I lost it," I say then finally swallow the sharp pains in my throat and wipe under my eyes. Falling to my knees I help pick up the mess, the tiny bits of metal and the bent wheel, the splinters of wood. All the small pieces go in the trash can.

There are also some pieces under my knees. They dug into my skin. I guess with the adrenaline, I didn't even feel it.

"Those guys were assholes," is all Cami says. But she knows, just like I know, that I lost it.

"And to think, I thought my anger issues were dealt with," I joke and that makes her laugh although the sound is choked.

She hugs me tight, both of us still on our knees in the middle of the street. "You okay?" she whispers.

Although I nod and pull away, hurrying to clean up, I'm not okay. I haven't been okay for a while now.

I feel hot and my head is light when I finally stand up and drag the bent, broken bike to the curb. Sniffling, I wipe the rest of the tears from my heated face.

I barely look over my shoulder when I hear a car pull up. "Fuck," I murmur and roll my eyes when I see who it is.

"What the hell is going on?" I can hear Seth freaking out before his door even shuts. The slam seems like an overreaction as it echoes down the street.

My heart's all sort of wonky. Hurting and flipping and full of distress. *So much for not being a burden.*

"What the hell happened? You okay?" He's staring between the bike and me. My legs that aren't scratched, my elbows that aren't bruised. He's trying to figure it out, I know he is, but right now I can't speak. How the hell did my bike get so damaged when I'm seemingly fine, although I'm sure it's obvious I've been crying?

"Babygirl," he says and his voice is consoling as he cups my chin and then brushes away the remaining tears.

"I'm fine," I tell him and then I have to clear my throat. My voice is so raw. "I didn't fall. I…"

"She took a bat to it," Cami finishes for me. She takes a seat on the stone steps to the porch, brushing her hands off on her pajamas. "Some guys tried to steal it and your girl lost it."

"What guys?" Seth's voice turns stone cold.

"Three assholes. Never seen them before." Cami does all the talking, even though she pauses to look at me. I can't look her in the eyes as my gaze drops.

"You fuck them up?" Seth asks. His voice is even, low but even. He just wants to know; he's not judging me. God, do I love this man. I shake my head in his hand and then move from his grasp. I don't deserve him.

Taking a deep inhale, I calm myself.

"I just lost it," I explain to him.

"So you wrecked your bike?"

"Better the bike than them, right?" I try to make it sound like a joke. He doesn't think it's funny though. There goes my gaze, back to the weeds in the cracks of the sidewalk.

"I mean, you should have seen it," Cami butts in before Seth can reply. I feel embarrassed, guilty, remorseful. My stomach churns and I feel sick. "I can guarantee you they think she's crazy."

"You should have called me—"

I cut Seth off. "They aren't going to steal from me again." Finally looking him in the eyes, I tell him, "They aren't coming back here and taking things off porches again."

In my periphery, I can see Cami nodding, although her expression is solemn.

"I handled it," I say with finality.

Seth shifts his weight, staring down at me. He feels very much like the judge, jury, and executioner right now. As if that's what I need.

"What would you do if someone stole your pen?" he asks me as Connor's car pulls up behind Seth's. I barely keep from rolling my eyes, knowing Seth must've called or messaged and told him to come. All because I'm a little messed up right now.

"My pen?" I say, trying to remember what the question even was.

"Like next time, say someone steals your pen. What are you going to do?"

I imagine someone at the Club doing that. Not like they took it accidentally after signing their check. But deliberately taking from me… at the Club? No one would be that stupid.

"There won't be a next time," I say and my voice holds an edge to it. Seth closes the distance between us with a few easy steps. Placing a hand on each of my forearms, he squeezes, consoling and relaxing.

Pulling me in closer to him, he gentles his voice. "Just humor me. Say someone steals your pen, what are you going to do?"

"Take it back." He nods at my response but then I add, "And then stab the hand they took it with. I'd keep stabbing that hand with the same pen until there was nothing left of the pen anymore."

Seth's eyes widen comically, but the Cheshire cat smile grows on his face even more. "You're psycho, Babygirl."

"I'm joking. Ish." The "ish" makes Cami laugh. The tension in the air seems to dissipate.

Seth's smirk widens to a grin and I give him a small smile in return.

"Come here," he says and holds me against his chest, wrapping his arms around me. I didn't even realize how cold it was outside today until I feel how warm he is.

"Next time, call me," he whispers into my hair. "Please."

"There won't be a next time," I answer into his chest, breathing in his scent. The essence is fresh but masculine. And if I breathe in deeper, I can smell a hint of the cologne I got him for Christmas. I heard smell is the scent most likely to hold memories. With everything that's happened while I've been at Seth's side, you'd think they'd all be bad. Like the smell of him would bring me nothing but pain. It's the opposite though. I feel safe, I feel cherished. I never want to forget the smell of him. I wish I could bottle it up and put it in an aromatherapy roller ball or something.

"You're adorable but fucking psycho, you know that?"

I pull away at his comment. "What was I supposed to do? Let them steal my bike?"

Any worry he had when he arrived has turned to a smile. "I would have gotten it back for you and made sure they knew never to do that shit again."

"Well you weren't here, so I did it for you." I stand on my tiptoes for a quick second to offer him a peck. Although the kiss is more for me than him, I think. "You're welcome," I add with a little more sass than I should have right now.

"Mmm." His groan is more than a turn-on and he grabs my ass before I can turn around and leave him like I planned on doing. Pinning me to him, he tells me, "I'm not done with you yet."

The spike of heat and want is immediate. A feeling of calm washes over me. I could stare into his soft blue eyes forever. Well, I can try. But when he leans down for another kiss, I close my own and let him press his lips to mine. He nips the bottom one and when I smile, he takes that as his cue to deepen the kiss. The embrace is heated and brings a singe of desire that overwhelms every other feeling.

"My little hotheaded psycho," he murmurs when he breaks the kiss, his lips still close to mine.

"Stop," I say and jokingly push him away, but both of us are smiling. "I'm not psycho," I tell him and I finally roll my eyes, although of course it's in response to my own statement. I really lost my shit. Over a bike. It's just a bike.

"Yeah, you are. I fucking love it, though."

There's that word. *Love*. He didn't say he loves me. Not quite, but it feels like he did.

"You two need a room?" I hear Connor's question laced with heavy sarcasm before I hear his footsteps stopping just behind Seth.

"If I wind up dead in a gutter, she did it," Seth tells Connor, not answering his question.

"Oh, fuck off," I tell him playfully as Seth laughs at my reaction. He's good at soothing me, teasing me, working me up. He's good at *me*. That's the best way I can put it. Turning to look over my shoulder as I make my way up the steps, I tell Seth as they follow me into the house, "I'm going to leave long before I reach my breaking point with you."

CHAPTER 5

Seth

"YOU WANT TO TALK ABOUT IT?" I ASK HER, WATCHING HER STRIP out of her clothes to get into the shower. She's still in her old room in her grandma's house, even though the master's been cleared out.

I get it, I do. I've stayed plenty of nights here and I know this is her place. It's her safe spot. I get it.

This room is just small. She's got a twin-size bed and barely any room in here with her bulky dresser. She has to have the damn dresser because there are no closets in this old house.

She wrinkles her nose at me, as if I'm pushing her too far. She's the one always asking me to talk, though.

"Is that a no, you don't want to talk?"

"No." The way she eyes me before answering puts a smug look on my face. She's not psycho, she's defensive and scared. After everything that happened these last few years, she should be.

"All right then," I tell her and lean back in her bed, taking up the whole damn thing as I stretch out my shoulders and stare at her ceiling fan. "What'd they look like?" I question her even though she's not going to tell me. She doesn't have to say a word though, because I told Connor to get the descriptions from Cami. I'll figure it out and make sure they don't ever make my girl feel like that again. She doesn't have to know. She just needs to be safe.

"I don't remember," she answers half-heartedly, shrugging her shoulders as she steps into the stream of the shower. With the bathroom door open, I've got a great view from where I'm lying.

I think about talking louder over the running water, of pressing her again on whether or not she's going to sell this place. It's not the right time though. It's never the right time with her.

The house is in a rough part of town, every piece of it. From the staircase that creaks, to the trim that's dented and stained, it's all worn down, but the old home is sentimental. If she wants to keep it, we can. Shit, I'll even fix it up. I want her with me though. In my house that she helped me build, that *she* furnished. I got that damn house for her.

Isn't that what compromise is?

I'm debating about approaching the subject, when I turn over and see her family photo on the dresser. Her dad, her grandma, and her at some park when she was just a kid. I get that this house is all she's got left of them. I swear I do. I just don't like it.

Now's not the time, but I don't know when it will be time though. Shit.

Pinching the bridge of my nose, I listen to the water splashing and talk over it, raising my voice to make sure Laura can hear me.

"You really shouldn't pick fights." I don't tell her it scares me. I don't tell anyone that anything scares me.

"You can stop reprimanding me," she calls out in a singsong voice after opening the sliding glass door to make sure I hear her response. The shower door closes and then opens again for her to add, "And I didn't pick the fight, I finished it."

Her smart-ass mouth brings a warmth to my chest as I chuckle and run a hand down my face. She shouldn't have to finish any fights. That's the problem.

It's my fault for letting her stay here.

Letting her. She hates that word.

Now there's a real fight to pick. Not tonight though. Not with everything going down.

The creak of the faucet precedes the sound of the water stopping, the shower door sliding open and the pitter-patter of her bare feet in the bathroom.

I watch her dry herself off, then wrap her hair up in the towel. All the while, I eye her curves. She takes her time rubbing lotion into her legs and I'm pretty sure she's prolonging touching herself just to tease me.

She dries her hair and lets the towel drop to the floor in a puddle at her feet. With one hand on either side of the threshold, she stands there butt naked, looking utterly fuckable. And then she speaks.

"You don't fuck with crazy."

Grabbing my hard cock through my jeans I tell her, "Speak for yourself."

She gives me a ridiculously gorgeous smile that's infectious and tells me I'm awful before making her way to the bed.

"Come here." I give her the command even though she was already coming to me.

She crawls up my body, slow and deliberate, but keeps her hair to the side since it's still damp.

"You really are impossible," she tells me and she could be saying I'm her Prince Charming with the look she's got in her eyes. I love the way she looks at me. No one's ever looked at me like that before. No one other than her.

"I don't think you've got much room to talk," I respond, wanting to bring up the situation again if for no other reason than to get her fine ass to move in with me and be safe.

"When I said that, I meant no one wants to mess with a crazy person," she explains. "That's what my dad used to tell me. You never know what someone crazy is going to do. They could bite your nose off if you push them, you know? They're crazy. So if you react like that, like you've lost your mind, no one's going to want to mess with you. It's not worth losing your nose over."

I have a hard time keeping a straight face; she's serious as all hell right now. "So you were *acting* like you're crazy? You were in full control the whole damn time?" I question her, letting my tone prove that I think what she's saying is bullshit.

Pursing her lips she thinks for a moment, looking past me. Instead of answering me, she says, "I didn't pick the fight." The humor and confidence are gone.

"I know you didn't," I tell her with sincerity. Spearing my hand through her hair, I bring my lips to hers and kiss her. I nudge my nose against hers and whisper, "You did what you had to do."

"Exactly." Both of her hands wrap around mine when she speaks. And I kiss her again, but she pulls away.

"I have to get ready," is the excuse she gives me. Her ass sways as she walks, tempting me even though she doesn't seem interested.

"You wanna?" I ask her, and when she turns to look at me with a hint of confusion, I thrust my hips in her direction.

She only laughs before telling me no and saying I'm a shitty Romeo.

"What if I kiss you here?" Getting on my knees at the edge of the bed so I can tower over her as she stands at the end of it, I suck her neck. I feel her thighs hit the edge of the bed and hear her moan before I plant a single kiss there and pull back.

"You're hot," she tells me with a moan and smiles. "But I don't want to be late, and you're not getting laid right now. You should come up with something better while I'm getting dressed."

Damn it. I watch her walk away.

"You know all my lines already," I call out to her as she closes the bathroom door, leaving me with blue balls in her too-small bed. Even being shut down I'm smiling, because she's all right and she's happy.

We're all right. Everything is going to be all right.

Not even five seconds pass before the bathroom door opens again. I only raise up my head, to look at her.

She clucks her tongue and puts both hands on the door again. Her small breasts have a bit of weight to them and they sway when she sways.

"Sometimes I do feel crazy," she tells me and I see the hurt there, plain as day in her eyes as they gloss over.

"You're not crazy," I say. I'm quick to sit up but before I can get off the bed, she's already walking to me. I wait there on the edge, the bed bowed in the center from my weight.

She stops before she can walk between my knees. When she's hurt, all I want to do is love her. Lay her down and fuck her until the sad eyes are only in my memory.

Crossing her arms, her breasts are pushed up. She is not helping my situation at all. "Tell me what you need, Babygirl," I speak softly and caress her, placing a hand on each of her elbows. I know what she needs.

She finally decides on her next words. "I love you, and you need to make this up to me."

"Get on the bed," I tell her, standing up so she can take my place.

"That's not—"

"Get your ass on that bed." I'm firmer this time and she can't hide the smile. She gets on the bed on all fours before rolling onto her back and lying down for me.

"Knees bent, legs spread," I tell her, and the grin widens even with her teeth sinking into that bottom lip.

I make my way between her legs; she has to move her heels out further so my shoulders fit between her knees.

I start with a single kiss on the inside of her knee. "Let me show you how much I worship this…" I say then pause to plant another kiss, further up her thigh.

She's already breathing heavy, already wriggling on the bed ever so slightly.

I smack her clit with the back of my hand. Her top half jolts up, her eyes go wide and her mouth drops open. "Keep still," I tell her and push her chest back down. She obeys.

She says she wants a dom; I'll give it to her.

"Like I was saying," I say and plant another kiss on the inside of the opposite knee. "Let me show you how much I worship…" I keep my warm breath close to her skin as I speak and watch the goosebumps slide up her body, following my path of open-mouth kisses.

"... This perfectly sane..." I can't even keep a straight face while I talk, so I smile against her skin. The warmth of her feminine laugh and the way she covers her face fuel me to continue.

Another kiss. "Never unreasonable..." I say and shake my head between her thighs, letting my nose graze just above her clit.

"Completely stable..." I continue then suck on her clit, which cuts off her laughter instantly.

Her legs close tighter around me, and I push them back open, reminding her to be still.

"Beautiful," I add and plant another kiss. "Smart," I say and lick her from her entrance to her hard nub. "Woman," I say then breathe against her clit while her hands find my hair. Pulling on what little she can grab, I don't stop sucking and licking until she's trembling under me.

Then I take her like I have so many times. On this too-small bed, in this broken-down house, filled with so many memories just like this. Lying next to her when it's all over, I think again about how I get it, even if she thinks I don't. I get why she wants to stay.

"You'r not coming in?" Laura questions me when I stop the car at the front of the Clubhouse. I haven't even put it in park yet, but she knows the drill. She turns off the radio and looks at the Club and then back at me. The Club is an old bar Connor's dad used to own. He had bikes and he liked to think of him and his friends as a motorcycle club. Connor inherited it when they were gunned down. This place is everything that represents how we got here. We inherited what was ours to have and the life that comes with it.

"We just have to run and pick something up," I lie.

Laura clucks her tongue after unbuckling her seat belt. Narrowing her beautiful eyes, she tells me, "You picked me up so I wouldn't drive here. So I couldn't leave while you were out doing something stupid."

"Beautiful and smart," I say then tilt my head to the side and give her a charming smile. "How'd I get so lucky?"

"What are you doing, Seth?" she asks and her tone is serious.

"Just something stupid. I'll be quick, I promise. You won't even get your second drink down before I'm back." I give her a quick kiss that she doesn't return, and her expression is the same as it was when I lean back.

She settles into her seat, her clutch in her lap and she looks at me. Really looks at me. "I wish you wouldn't do dumb shit."

I can't return her gaze when I lie to her. I'm staring at my thumb tapping restlessly on the steering wheel instead as I say, "I'm working on it."

I'm getting in deeper. That's the way this works. There isn't an out. One day she'll see that. She just needs time to adjust.

The leather protests as she leans over the console and plants a kiss on my jaw. "Don't get yourself hurt," she tells me and then gets out of the car without sparing me another glance.

I promise her I won't and watch her go. She looks back and gives me the smallest of smiles. I know it's more for me than it is her. Or at least that's how it feels in this moment.

I keep the radio off as I drive away after watching her walk in. Roman was at the door, so he's got her taken care of. The twenty-minute drive is quiet on the way to the warehouse. Nothing but black night and cool spring air blowing from the open windows.

Quiet is good for moments like this. Preparing for the "dumb shit," as she calls it. I go over the plan with every turn I take until I'm parked beside two unmarked vans behind Linel Centers.

"Already got the plates," Derrick tells me when I get out. There's nothing back here in the mountains but woods. Crickets chirp in the distance as I open up the double doors to see the back of the van is empty. It's colder than it was when I left Laura. Seems fitting.

"Other one is empty too," Derrick tells me and then Connor appears, the keys to the other van clattering in his hand. "We're all set, Boss."

"What about the fireworks?" I ask them and Connor tells me those are all set too.

"All right, let's do this." I give the command as I shut the doors, but Derrick grabs my arm. "What about the dogs?"

Half of me wants to mess with him, tease him about being scared of some dogs, but tonight is all business. "Tranqs are in the glove box of my car. Grab 'em."

Derrick pats my shoulder and I can see the instant relief on his face. While he's off getting the tranquilizer guns, I tell Connor to take that van and I'll ride with Derrick.

This isn't the first time we've done this shit. Won't be the last. Roman and Liam are at the Club, but they're on call and they know it. Sometimes in our line of business, the more, the better. But late at night, in the dark with a surprise like this, the fewer, the better. We only need three.

I probably could have done it with just two, but someone needs to be driving and someone else on the walkie while we're moving. So three it is. Besides, I don't know how much shit Mathews has in his stores.

Reaching in my jacket pockets, I hand Connor one of the two walkie-talkies. "Let's do this."

The gravel crunches under my boots as I round the back of the van and I look up to the moon. Not a star is in sight, just vacant dusk and a sliver of light. Every five minutes I swear the night sky is getting darker.

"You drive," I tell Derrick and hear Connor close his door. He starts his van before Derrick can move. The empty van sways as Derrick swings himself into his seat.

"You good? Got your mask?" I speak into the walkie and pull my mask from the glove box. It's a simple ski mask. I'm sure there are cameras, so we're taking every precaution. I don't have to wait long for a response.

"All good, Boss."

The van revs to life and four streams of white brighten the dirt road ahead of us.

With the walkie's talk button pressed down, I speak to both of them, going over the plan one more time.

"As soon as we're lined up at the docking site, Connor will set off the first round of rockets a block down. They're all set, right, Connor?"

"Got 'em in place. And they're the best ones too. They're low and sound like gunshots."

I wait for the click and continue. "There are only two men on-site and they stay out of the storage unit. I bet Mathews is too scared one of his men will steal from him, so he keeps it light. We get their attention with the fireworks. They run toward the noise or to their cars, I don't give a shit where, so long as they're far enough back and going after something that isn't there. We back the truck up, over the fence and right into door of the storage building at the dock. In and out, no talking. Not a damn word unless someone's going to die. Got it?"

"Got it," they both answer without stress, with nothing but seriousness.

"We'll take this shit back here, dump it, change the plates, and head back to the Club like nothing happened."

"It's a plan," Derrick comments as we round the corner, getting us out of here and where we need to go.

It's silent while we drive. Just like the drive down here. All the while, I let the adrenaline flow. It courses through me, urging me to get it done as quick as we can without missing a beat. I glance at Derrick, whose hard expression mirrors what I feel. It's why this crew works; we all need the same, want the same. I focus on the plan and why we need Mathews to back the hell up. This will hurt him and it'll make him think twice about inching closer to Tremont.

Time goes by too fast, but not fast enough just the same.

I can already smell the water. There's a saltiness to the air with the windows down. We have five minutes until we're there. If that.

Five minutes of calm although it feels anything but. My muscles are tense and my throat tight. This spike in my veins is a different kind of high. My second favorite. The only thing that tops this is when I'm under Laura. Or on top of her, for that matter.

This right here, I fucking love the intensity. The need to fight severely, quickly. The desire to protect what's ours… It will never grow old. It's everything. Laura should know that. She just needs time.

When Derrick sees me putting on my gloves, he does the same. One block to go, and the small bait store on the corner comes into view. The fixture is an old shed and shut down for the night. Everything down here is closed. There shouldn't be any witnesses. Other than the two men working for Mathews.

"Masks on," I tell them and put on my own. It's hot with it in place, but a necessity. Just like the gloves. The mask is cheap, but my gloves are thin leather and expensive as shit. I can't have gloves slipping off or hindering my movements when I'm in the heat of it all.

Thump, my heart pounds in my chest, fighting against my rib cage as we come around the corner. There are three white storage sheds made of steel. Each surrounded by chain-link fences ten feet high. They look about twenty feet apart from each other. One has two dogs inside the perimeter, with a doghouse in the far corner. That's it.

There are two men on that property. At least there should be, but I don't see either of them yet.

"Here," I speak into the walkie and watch as Connor's van comes to a stop in the rearview. We're in a good position to keep a lookout and not be seen. Turning off the vans, we wait.

This is the worst part. The waiting. Not being able to move.

We need eyes on the men doing patrols. I wait a minute and then another, feeling the ring in my blood, the need to be fast and not sit and wait. It could be a setup. Wright could be two-timing us. The glance from Derrick tells me he's on edge just like I am.

We can't wait. When you're still, that's when your enemies catch up to you.

"Now." The second I say the word, I catch sight of a man coming around the corner of the dock. Smoke billows from his blunt as he rounds the building from inside the fence.

Crack, crack, crack!

The rockets go off somewhere unseen, but they hit the building farthest away from the one we're after.

The man screams what sounds like a name, dropping his smoke and grabbing the gun at his waist. He races to the gate of the fence furthest from us. His back is to us; he doesn't have a clue we're here.

So far, it's all going according to plan, but anything can go wrong.

Wait, wait. I can barely keep still in my seat, willing both of them to move. To get to their cars, to go toward the distraction. Something. Anything.

My foot taps anxiously on the floorboard of the van as I stare at him and see him wave a guy over. The second guy comes around from the other side.

"Again," I speak into the walkie and just like that, a second round goes off just as the two men move to open the gate. They take cover behind the doghouse, but the German shepherds are there, barking and going crazy. They sound vicious even from here and with a series of curses, one of the men smacks a dog over his head with the back of his gun. The yelp of the wounded animal is swallowed by the pandemonium of bangs and cracks from both the fireworks and the shots fired by men who think they're under attack.

"How many?" one yells over the supposed gunshots.

"I don't know!"

The two men scream while the sounds ricochet throughout the docks.

I can imagine what's running through their minds. They're dead men. It's too many blasts, too many guns, which means too many men for only the two of them.

I'm eerily calm watching it play out. It's only been two minutes, maybe five since we've pulled up. We don't have a lot of time before more of Mathews's men get here.

Everything's quiet, save one shepherd barking, hovering over the other dog and hollering as if he's the one in pain. The men don't look back toward the dogs or toward us, instead they stare down the road, searching for the location of the gunmen coming after them.

"Now!" I can barely hear the one man yell, the one who seems to be leading things. The one who may be high. I expect them to go down the street toward the shots, slowly making their way to gauge the threat. That's what I'd do.

He fires a few shots aimlessly, as does his partner, but they both run to the parking lot. That's when I relax slightly, feeling a smirk pull up my lips into an asymmetric grin. *They're running.*

"Again," I speak into the walkie, and the night fills with smoke as more fireworks go off. The second man is barely in the vehicle when they take off, still shooting behind him. With the squealing of their tires, we turn on the vans, revealing ourselves for the first time.

The fear in the eyes of the man shutting his door is palpable. "Go!" he screams even as their getaway car is in gear.

"Connor, once more and then back it up." I give the command. The rockets go off again and both Derrick and I hold our guns out of the window as Connor turns his van around, firing at the car as they fire recklessly at us. A bullet hits the side of the van. And then another as they drive by. The pings make my chest tighten and my blood turn ice cold each time.

With my jaw clenched tight, we keep firing as the car disappears. My gun empties first, and it only takes half a second to reload. Connor's van has already flattened the chain-link fence as he slams the van into the building, the roof of it crumbling down onto the hood. When he drives forward, it falls to the ground, but more of it collapses when he reverses again, slamming into the building and opening it wide up.

The lone German shepherd lets out a territorial bark from back in the corner of the place. Poor thing won't move away from the other. Derrick's already got the tranq and he pulls back to load it the second he steps out of the van.

"Leave them," I call out before Derrick can lift the gun. I shouldn't have said shit. But my voice was deep and I tried to disguise it.

He looks at me, standing beside the van and then back at the dogs. One's lying helpless; I don't know if he's dead or unconscious. The other isn't leaving his side.

I can see Derrick swallow, tense and uncertain before shoving the tranquilizer gun into the waist of his jeans at his back.

If he were to shoot, it'd be evidence left behind. The less we leave, the better.

Connor's already opened the back of his van and Derrick does the same to ours as I pull back the bent steel door and make my way over the rubble to see what's inside.

It's dark in the building, but the brake lights from the van give me everything we need. In the ten-by-ten-foot space, there are eight crates and nothing else.

Setup. I think the word as I walk around them. I don't trust Wright, but so far, he told the truth. He was paid off with cash, plenty of it.

It takes a moment to pry the top off of one with my pocketknife. They're a light wood and look like something fishermen would use. Or at least that's what I imagine they're going for. I've never touched a fishing pole in my life.

Without hesitation, I crack open the one in front of me, knowing the clock is ticking away and Mathews's crew will be here soon.

Under a bed of straw is at least a dozen bricks of snow.

I heave the crate into Derrick's chest as he makes his way to me, feeling the anger consume me. It's so close. He's five miles from my turf. Setting up storage here is unacceptable.

As we haul the crates into the vans, all I can think is how I wish I'd brought gasoline, so I could light this place on fire when we're done.

Next time.

It takes only minutes with the three of us. Less than ten minutes in all to load, to get back in and take off. I keep looking in the rearview, but no one's there. When we get back to Linel Centers, we switch the plates on the vans, then park them inside to hide the one with the bullet in it. Roman will take care of that on Monday.

Moving the bricks out from the crates, we dump every last one of them down the drain. The plastic wrap cuts easily with a knife. The white powder, hundreds of thousands of dollars of it, disappears in a swirl down a filthy drain.

The large room is silent as we do it. At least at first. I've learned from each hit we do, that it takes time to cool down. It takes time to let it all turn still again.

No one says a word until we're opening up the last crate.

"First round's on me, gentlemen," Connor speaks up, breaking the silence, and takes out a flask from his car. Derrick chuckles, helping me with the last of it and takes a swig when Connor offers it. I follow suit.

Another five and we're done. It's over.

"Damn good night," Derrick comments and I nod in agreement.

Looking at the clock on the wall, an hour has passed; I broke my promise to Laura. She's definitely on her second drink by now. Fuck, I hope she didn't wait for me.

CHAPTER 6

Laura

PICKING UP THE TWENTY OFF THE POLISHED WOODEN COUNTER, I TURN on my heels to face the register. My sneakers slip easily on the worn linoleum floor as I tick my blunt nails against the metal buttons until I hear the *ping* and the cash register opens.

How much shit could he have possibly gotten into in just an hour and a half last night? Every time I know he's out there, doing something—something that could get him killed—I watch the clock like it's going to have answers for me.

Like last night. I glance at the clock that never has anything for me but how long he's been gone. I stared at it for an hour and a half, making small talk in between and drinking with Roman while he watched the clock on his phone like he was waiting for something too.

I was sitting there feeling every tick of the clock squeeze my heart harder and harder when Seth sat down next to me on the leather bench in the back of the Clubhouse, put his arm over my shoulder and kissed my jaw. He was happy and relaxed, like there's not a worry in the world.

Before I could even speak, he was making me want to thank him. *"I know I'm late, but I grabbed you the vodka you like,"* he said.

It's Grey Goose Citron and the bar was out of it. So yeah, I wanted to *thank* him.

Touching me, kissing me, giving me gifts and acting like he got stuck in traffic on the way down here.

One shot and thirty minutes later, I was laughing along with everyone else. Feeling the ease of being among friends. Even if half of them knew what Seth was doing last night and I still don't.

"Thanks for the beer," Mickey says from the far end of the bar. "Keep the change." The wrinkles around his eyes deepen when he gives me a wave and heads for the door. He's a regular. Well, a regular during the day. At night things are different; busier, louder, more… intense. Technically we're closed then and it's just a hangout. The crew—and us—aren't charged. We kick out anyone who isn't one of us due to the "private party." It's always intense, and a good time if I'm being honest, when the crew is here.

The "private parties" are what got me through so much shit.

During the day, it's just a slow old Irish bar. Lunchtime always picks up though, right about now.

"Thanks, Mick," I call out to my regular before he can make it through the exit. The front door is old wood, dark brown except for a little black on the outside of it. Where the fire from next door caught it a few years back. The bar is in need of updating, but Seth and the guys say they like to see the memories. I get that. I like to see the memories too.

"Good luck on the test," Mick calls back to me and I flash him a smile. His bill was only twelve bucks, so I scoop eight bucks from the register and slip the cash in the back of my anatomy book that's open next to the register. I keep my finger wedged in the pages I'm reading though. I can't lose my place.

With the pen in my hand, tapping it against the notebook, I take tabs on the three remaining guests. Two are women, whispering over large pours of red wine in the back corner at a high top table. The picture frames above their heads are of the old times. Black-and-white prints from when Connor's family first came here from Ireland. Those are my favorite pictures in the bar.

The women's glasses are still relatively full, although twenty minutes ago, they were sucking the wine down like I'd given them water. The look on the brunette's face combined with a few whispers I heard tells me she most likely dumped someone, or got dumped.

Either way, they're good for another chapter of notes.

The other patron is another regular, staring up at the TV above the leather bench I sat on practically all last night. An old soccer game is on. Or a new one. I don't know and I don't care; sports aren't my thing. I assume it's an old one though, judging by how Cormac doesn't yell, "Oh, come on!" every five to ten minutes.

So, back to studying I go.

I only get two lines written in my notebook when I hear the front door open. "Welcome to the Club," I say and greet the new guest with a smile. It's automatic but it drops nearly instantly. Just like the lump that sinks down my throat before it gets stuck.

"Officer Jackson, what can I do for you?" I keep my voice upbeat and barely catch sight of Cormac taking another swig of his beer while looking over his shoulder at the cop in full uniform who just walked in. The old man eyes him, but then turns back to the television.

The officer's slick boots don't seem right in here. They look brand new with the way they're shining. Putting down the pen, I watch as he walks to the bar.

I like Jackson just fine. I always have. But I don't like him coming around because he's not one of us, and that badge on his chest could lead to problems I can't have.

I instantly wish I hadn't told Roman it was fine to take off for lunch. He hangs out here, just in case. That's what the guys tell me when I say I can manage being on shift alone when it's so slow. Just in case.

I'm pretty sure this is a *just in case* moment.

With both forearms on the bar, holding his sunglasses in one hand and releasing a deep exhale, Officer Jackson hesitates. He still hasn't said a word. I wait on pins and needles while he drags the barstool closer to him and takes a seat. He's got to be close to thirty now. He's nice enough looking, average height although he does have a good build on him. Young for a cop, but damn did this job age him.

He's come in here before, usually to escort the drunken barflies out. A few of the older women in town don't know their limits. A couple of those few have tempers. Jackson is always the one who comes. Seth said he likes Jackson well enough. I doubt he'd like him if he knew he was here right now though.

"Everything all right?" I ask him. "Looks like you've been working out."

He huffs a quick laugh and then thanks me.

"You want a beer?" I ask him. The corners of my mouth even lift a little, thinking he's just on his lunch break. But again, the smile drops when he shakes his head. Any hope I had of this drop-in being about grabbing a bite to eat or a drink vanishes.

"You have any idea where Seth King is? I believe he's your boyfriend?"

"He *is* my boyfriend, you've got that right," I say and nod then take a step back to put down the pen in my hand. He knows damn well Seth's my boyfriend, but he asks me every time like maybe that status has changed. My back is to him as I bend down, open the small fridge and grab a cold bottle of IPA. "I think Seth said he had some errands to run today." I talk loud enough so Jackson can hear me, pop the top of the beer and turn back around to face him. "He should be here tonight, though. You need him for something?"

Taking my eyes off Jackson, I slide the beer down to Cormac who thanks me, pushing his mostly empty bottle forward.

"You're on top of it here, aren't you?" Jackson asks me.

"I can keep count of four, five... Hell, on a good day, six," I joke with him.

He laughs and leans back although his hands stay on the bar top. "You don't have any idea where he is?" he asks again, and I feel a vise grip my heart. This vise is special though; it's made of cast iron and feels like it's been sitting in the freezer the way it gives me chills and makes everything inside of me sink.

"Sorry, I don't," I answer Jackson. I'm saved by another customer walking in. I recognize her as someone who's been coming around more often lately. What the hell is her name... Cindy, maybe? She usually comes in later in the day and eyes up the guys when they first get here. She always leaves before it gets dark. Part of me thinks she wants to play with fire and she just doesn't have the balls to stay and do exactly that.

"We only have a few things available on the lunch menu," I tell her as she sidles up to a spot right between Cormac and the officer. There are two seats between her and either of the guys. "Short-staffed at the moment," I explain and pass her the paper lunch menu for the day. "We've basically got anything that can be deep-fried, but not the usual burgers."

She nods and gives a polite smile. The kind that doesn't show any teeth. She glances at the officer too. Even with her menu lifted as if she's reading it.

"Sorry about that," I tell Officer Jackson and wait for anyone other than me to do any sort of talking.

"You're a good girl, Laura." Jackson catches me off guard with the way he says it.

Swallowing thickly, I nervously peek at Cormac, who's staring at us just like the nosy woman at the bar.

"Thank you?" I try to keep my voice even, but it shows my anxiousness.

Officer Jackson gets off his stool and talks while rapping his sunglasses on the bar. "The guys they're dealing with aren't going to let them get away with it. Get out while you can."

"I don't know—"

"I'm sure you don't," he says, cutting me off and then he tells me to have a good day before walking out.

Cormac sucking his teeth is the only thing that rips my eyes away from the closed front door.

I don't know how long I stand there staring. Hearing his last words on repeat in my head.

"He's got one thing right," Cormac tells me as I focus on stopping my hands from shaking. My back's to everyone as I pretend to be writing something down in my little notebook.

"What's that?" I manage to ask Cormac, turning to face him and leaning the small of my back against the counter.

"You are a good girl," he tells me even though he's already watching the television again.

I don't know what to say to him, so I don't respond.

"You know what you want?" I ask the woman who's still holding a menu with only five things listed on it. Cindy, or whatever the hell her name is, is frowning for the first time since she walked in.

"Not yet," she answers, and I have to try hard not to roll my eyes.

I know why Cormac thinks I'm a "good girl." It's the same reason the crew trusts me. That night is just as vivid right now as it was back then. I imagine it is for everyone who was there. That night changed everything.

I remember every detail of it as I stand with my arms across my chest, looking back at the door, and replaying that night three years ago, over in my head.

Good girl.

Cormac was there, plus everyone in Seth's crew now was there and then some. It wasn't his crew then though. And the event didn't take place here; it was a different bar. This place was empty. Connor's father had died a few weeks before. A lot of people I knew died back then. Men my father used to hang around.

It all happened at a place called Hammers. Stupid name for a bar, but it'd been around for as long as the town's existed. A little more than three years ago I was sitting at a table at that bar. I had just turned sixteen. I knew I shouldn't have been there, but when my father had to run an errand for the boss, I was supposed to wait for him at that table. My grandma rented out the spare bedroom in the house and with the new tenants upstairs, Dad didn't like me to be alone there. He was reckless with himself but a protective father. In many ways he was a shit dad, but I always knew he loved me and this was a way to show me that. Even if it was fucked up and I didn't want to be there.

I'd have a car soon. It's all I kept thinking. I hated Hammers. I hated it because if I was there, it meant my dad was out doing something he shouldn't be. For men who scared me.

The guys in the bar always told me what a good girl I was, and some of them, like Cormac, I even liked.

It didn't mean I wanted to be there though. Just the thought of that place makes my skin crawl.

Hammers was owned by the boss, Michael Vito. I knew all about him and his family. He took over when his dad died and he stirred things up. At least that's what my dad told me when I asked why so many people were getting killed. The first memories I have are of my family and friends, who used to be fine with the Vitos, acting like they were scared. Michael wanted to be feared, whereas his father was respected.

They all worked for him. I didn't want to be anywhere near that table or in that bar. But my dad told me to stay seated while he was gone, just like he had so many times before.

Vito walked in while I was sitting at my spot. It got quiet; it always did when he walked in. Another thing I hated. I had my seat and I was to keep my butt planted right where it was and do my schoolwork. My father told me that every time he left. For years, that's what I was supposed to do. I knew Grandma would be done at the diner soon, so if he didn't get back soon, she'd find out he dropped me off at the bar again. She'd come and get me. She didn't like this place at all. She never did though.

Thinking about Dad and Grandma makes my throat tighten.

My father didn't make the best choices in life, but he left me there because it was supposed to be safe. Everyone knew me, and everyone knew I was the daughter of a man who worked for the Vitos.

Even Michael Vito knew who I was. When he spotted me sitting there, he knew. My textbooks were open as I read Lord knows what and pretended I didn't feel his eyes on me. I pretended the bar didn't get quiet again.

I remember the sound of his heavy boots. Unlike his father, Michael carried a lot of weight to him. I remember his voice. How it was harsh when he gripped my shoulder too hard to not mean for it to hurt.

He told me to go to the back room.

The back room is where I was never supposed to go. I knew very well what happened to women who went to the back room. I could hear it. Everyone could.

Seth was there along with all of his friends. He scared the hell out of me at school. They all did. I wasn't a dork, I wasn't a cool kid, and I wasn't an athlete. I wasn't a kid who sold or did drugs either, like they were. I was just a girl who was stuck there. I knew who Seth was though, and when I looked at him, I wanted to see that it was okay and that I should listen.

Because I wanted to be a good girl. I didn't want to cause problems. Especially not for my dad who excelled at making plenty of problems for himself all on his own.

I should be a good girl and do what I was told. That's what my father said all the time. And I may have had a mouth on me, but I really did try to be good.

When I looked at Seth though, after being told to go to the back room, his expression was anything other than one of a boy who thought it would be okay if I listened. Instead his face was darkened with fear and then anger, so much anger.

"No," I blurted out without thinking. I wasn't thinking of anything other than the sounds of the girls who went into that back room. They liked it. At least I think they liked it.

But other people went into that back room too one night and they screamed. Their faces were in the paper the next morning, printed in stark black and white. Just like the pictures of the crime scene where their bodies were found.

I didn't know which option Michael meant for me, but I didn't want either of them.

"Are you telling me no?" His breath reeked of cigarettes. I'll never forget it.

"My dad told me to stay—" Before I could finish, the back of his hand whipped across my face. My neck snapped to one side and I barely stayed standing upright. I was only able to keep my footing because of the table behind me and the fact that my palms landed hard on it.

Vito yelled something in Italian, but I have no idea what it was; no one from around here is Italian. I never did understand how and why the Vitos used to run this town.

When I straightened myself to look up at him, he sneered in my face for me to get in the back room and get undressed. I don't think the others heard him, but looking at their faces, they had an idea.

"No."

He didn't slap me; he closed his fist and punched me. The burn in my nose comes back as if he's just done it, but he's gone. Long gone.

"If someone's going to show everyone else their true colors to hurt you—let them." My grandma said that once. She said sometimes people need to see. They have to look at it and swallow that harsh pill. That's all I was thinking as I lay there on the dirty floor with the taste of blood in my mouth and what I thought was a broken nose and jaw. Sometimes you have to take a hit from your enemy for them to be seen as what they are.

I did. I took the hit. And when I landed facedown and dizzy with Vito's boot pressed against my back, I didn't think the hit would do what it did.

I lay there with the coppery taste of blood in my mouth, all the while zoning in and out of semi-consciousness. My vision hazy, I thought it was the beginning of the end. I couldn't fight back; I knew I couldn't. The best chance I had at surviving was simply being unconscious. Still, I tried to get back up, with the fear and the desperation clinging to me. Simply because I would've rather been dead or unconscious than willingly go into whatever that bitch fate had planned for me.

The one thing I'll never know is why I didn't cry. Inside, it's all I was doing. Outside, I was willing my muscles to push me up. I wanted him to hit me again. However many times it took.

What happened next didn't last long; it felt like hours, but it was twenty minutes of brawn and bullets. I lay there crying, knowing I was going to die. I got sick once when I heard the gunshots and the yells.

I watched with horror when he was dragged to the back room. He was barely conscious, but they waited until he was with it enough in order to tell him his reign had ended. It wasn't just a brawl. It was a massacre that ended with Vito being shot in the back of the head, execution style.

The men in the bar weren't going to stand by and watch while Vito took advantage of the daughter of someone who worked for him. They weren't going to let him stomp his boot into my back while I helplessly lay on the dirty ground, flat on my stomach, which is what he was going to do after the first punch was thrown.

Even through the haze of my injuries, I saw everything from the worn wooden floors that held a stale stench of beer. I watched while a man punched Cormac in the face for shoving another man in a suit. I watched him nearly be beaten to death. It was the suits mostly, them against everyone else.

Same with Seth; he was almost strangled to death. The only reason he lived is because Derrick shot the man choking him in the back of the head. They were so close to me, the blood sprayed onto my face and neck.

Everyone lost someone that night, but it felt like we won something else.

I have to close my eyes so I don't cry at the memory.

I was still shaking, tasting vomit and blood when Seth picked me up. Half his face wasn't even recognizable; he'd been bludgeoned so badly. He walked me home and the other guys came by in twos and threes. They stayed with me until my dad got there, crying and apologizing like it was all his fault.

I begged them not to tell my grandma, but she found out. Everyone in Tremont knew what happened. They knew why things had to change.

And I was the good girl, the one who stood up against Michael Vito. Even if I didn't fight back. Even if I didn't want to be there.

Seth's father is the one who took the lead after everything went down, and he was killed along with the men who followed him within two weeks. Sometimes I wonder if his dad was still here and the crew I know today didn't make it their mission to ensure revenge, if we'd still be here. He promised me once, when he first kissed me, that he'd take me far away from this place. That was two years ago, and here I stand, in a different bar in Tremont. Different bar, different fears.

My phone pings at the same time the woman at the bar tells me she's ready. It takes a few minutes to do the rounds and I call back an order of fries to the cook, an old lady named Holly who only agreed to work here if she could stay in the back. She's a recovering alcoholic, but jobs in Tremont aren't growing on trees, as she explained.

I don't think anyone can tell I'm emotional. Not Holly and not Cormac. I just look pissed, maybe? Grandma used to joke that I inherited her resting bitch face. I don't know. I don't ask and I don't wait for anyone in here to say a word to me.

When I get back to my phone, I see Cami's response from me asking her to come to the appointment tomorrow with me. That's what the ping was.

What's it for? she asked me and then two minutes later when I didn't respond, she added, *Is everything all right?*

Yeah, I text back, *just that heart thing*. When I was at the doctor's two weeks ago, they said I had arrhythmia. I had a moment in the office. The stress was just getting to me, but they want me to "get it checked." Cami knows all about it. Seth too. I looked it up in detail when I got home. It's fine. It'll be fine.

What time? she asks.

3:45

I'm so sorry babe, I can't go. I have work until six but I'll keep my phone on me and I'll come by tomorrow night?

Sounds good, I text back, feeling a different kind of pain on top of the previous one that won't let go. I should have figured she'd be working on a weekday. I just wanted someone to go with me.

Cami was freaked out at first. She texts me now what she told me back then. *Don't mess with shit that deals with the heart.*

I want to tell her about Jackson; I want her to tell me anything at all to get my mind off of things.

Instead, I text her back, *Don't I know it*, and I join Cormac in watching the game.

CHAPTER 7

Seth

"THE MEET'S ALL SET UP." I'VE JUST ABOUT FINISHED THE RUNDOWN with the guys at the far left side of what will be our bar. The brown paper is laid out on the floors and the furniture is covered in cloth. The painters are coming back tomorrow since I had to kick them out early for this meet. Club Allure is coming together, piece by piece. "We've got a fight next weekend, so let's get the ring moved downstairs."

"The place isn't finished," Connor interrupts me. He's leaning against the primed walls next to Cade, who's in charge of the books, and Liam. Liam is Connor's brother and looks just like him. Especially now that they're both wearing dark jeans and dark t-shirts. Cade's the odd one in a crisp white shirt and black khakis. The rest of these guys couldn't give two shits about appearing professional. Cade comes from a different background though. He's all about numbers and left a top accounting firm to come work for me.

In another life, I'd wear suits every damn day. We don't do that here though. The men before us who wore suits destroyed any desire I had to put on tailored clothing.

"Doesn't matter," Cade speaks up, turning his head to face Connor and leaning forward so he can see him. He's the one who came to me with the idea of a fight club.

"You think anyone betting on the fights downstairs gives a shit what this floor looks like?" Derrick asks Connor, his question dripping with sarcasm.

The three of those men side by side look like they could be their own Irish crew. If things were the way they were two years ago, they'd probably be dead. The Irish didn't last too long when Michael Vito took over. The three of them are as Irish as they come. Cade comes equipped with a hint of an accent too; he's first generation. With tats trailing up his right arm, it's easy to tell him apart from Liam. He's taller than Liam too, with lighter, longer hair on the top of his head. Liam looks more clean-cut. His short hair's always neatly trimmed, as is his facial hair. Even though Cade left the business world, you'd think Liam was the one who was trying to be white collar based on how they look.

"You two," I say as I gesture on both sides of Connor to the other two Irish men. "You get the say since this gig is your baby. Have it here, in the basement? Or keep it where we have been?"

"Here," Cade says, his accent peeking out. Liam agrees with his friend. The two of them are tight, another reason they'd have been knocked off years ago. I remember telling Connor that it was on him if Cade and Liam couldn't be trusted. I have a hard time trusting people. These two are the only two guys out of the five in my crew I've brought on in the two years we've been running this shit. I don't like new blood, Connor, Derrick, Roman and I have been through everything together. We don't need anyone else. Cade and Liam can be trusted though and it's better to keep them close. So it's just my five guys and me.

That's enough for now.

"Good. I'm ready for things to start changing and the first—"

"Yo," Derrick says, cutting me off and leans his head to my right. The dark black glass for the front double doors was just installed and Laura's admiring it from where she's at the other side of the bar, still holding one door open.

"I knocked," she bellows when I call out her name to get her attention. She looks cute in a tight pair of jeans and a cropped top that shows off her stomach. Just the sight of her makes my cock twitch. My first instinct is to smile, thinking she's come to surprise me, but then I see her expression.

"Come on down," Derrick calls out to her.

"Give me a minute," I tell the guys, not liking the look on her face. It's the one she gets when she's scared but she's trying not to be. I know it well. I take a few slow steps toward her as she takes the shortest path across so she doesn't have to walk the entire distance of the place.

"It's really coming together," she says sweetly, greeting me with a quick peck and then saying hi to the guys.

"Yeah, it is. We need a few more permits," I tell her and wait. She's got both hands shoved in her pockets when she asks if there's a room we can talk in.

I don't like it. The way her shoulders are hunched in and how quietly she's talking.

"Everything all right?" I ask her as I place my hand on the small of her back and bring her around to one of the back rooms. Her doctor appointment is tomorrow. It's the first thing I think of with how she's acting. She said it wasn't a big deal. She said her heart skips sometimes and I took credit for it. Looking at her now, I feel like a jackass for making light of it. Her exact word was "harmless." She said it was harmless and the procedure was routine for diagnosis.

She better not have lied to me. Maybe I should go with her.

"Let's just talk," she answers and I pick up my pace.

The small corner room, opposite from where the guys are and what will be used for storage of unopened liquor, isn't furnished and the floors are covered with brown paper. Other than that, there's only blue painter's tape on the trim.

Laura lets out a deep exhale before I've even shut the door.

"What did you do?" she asks and her question comes out frantic. She sounds scared and it instantly makes my muscles coil, ready to beat the shit out of whoever's gotten her so worked up. But then what she says hits me.

What did I do? Relief is the first thing I feel, but then it's quickly followed by confusion.

"Whoa, hold up, what's wrong?" I ask her, taking her elbow so I can pull her in, but she pushes me away, backing up to the other side of the small room. Nervous pricks run up my arm.

"I don't like this. I don't like any of this."

With her arms crossed, she faces me from the other side of the room. I stay where I am, waiting and crossing my arms just the same.

"What did you do?" She repeats her question.

Speaking clearer this time, I ask, "What happened?"

She's stubborn. Babygirl is a stubborn broad, but she also knows I'm not going to lie to her. Which means I'm also not telling her a damn thing. It's a rule we have in the crew; it keeps the people we love out of harm's way. She doesn't need to know.

Uncrossing my arms and slipping my thumbs into my back pockets, I take a single step forward and raise my brow. *Waiting.*

A look of despair mars her face when she uncrosses her arms and confesses, "Jackson came to the bar."

A spike of rage goes through me. Just one, a blip.

"What did he say?" I ask calmly, evenly, although my voice is lower now. We have an arrangement, and for Jackson to go behind my back and tell Laura something that's got her worked up… I'm going to have to have a word with that prick.

"He said the guys you're dealing with aren't going to let you get away with it," she says. Her voice cracks and it fucking shatters me.

Another spike of rage hits me, but this one simmers. "That seems cryptic," I tell her, keeping a poker face even though I'm already second-guessing if Jackson is talking about Mathews or if he's referring to something else. What does he know that I don't know?

Nothing.

The answer in my head is arrogant, but I can't see how he knows something I don't.

"What did you do?" Her tone pleads with me as she closes the distance between us.

The tough-girl bit falls pretty quick with her. "Please," she begs.

The second her hands reach my arms, I bring her in, holding her tight. It's what she needs, and she's quick to hold me back.

"Please, Seth," she whispers this time.

My chin rests on the top of her head as her grip on me tightens. "You're worried," I tell her, rocking her small body and staring at the blank back wall, picturing everything that happened and at what point someone would have known it was us. Jackson can't know. No one knows. He's confused or he's trying to start shit. I'll set him straight either way.

"How could I not be worried?" Laura responds with despondency.

"Jackson's bluffing, saying anything he can to get to you," I lie to her. Or maybe it's the truth. If it was though, I don't think I'd feel the way I do. Ice cold and like something bad is going to happen.

I move to hold her tighter, hating the way everything's feeling hot and numb all at once, but she breaks away, her hands on my chest as she shakes her head.

"It's not a bluff; he was worried about me." She raises her voice as she speaks but it's the emotions getting to her.

"There's no reason for you to worry," I tell her, trying to calm her down by grabbing her hands, one in each of my own.

I kiss her knuckles before telling her that I'm sorry Jackson freaked her out and that he's just a jackass.

She's not in the mood for my jokes though, if her ripping her hands away from me and pacing is any indication.

"You need to calm down," I tell her as I square my shoulders.

She asks with wide eyes, full of both hope and desperation, "Why don't you just get out of all that?" When I don't answer, she adds, "You have this bar." Like that's some sort of justification.

The bar only works because we'll do the deals here, host fights in the basement, and launder money through the alcohol sales. I struggle for a reason to give her. One day she'll realize it all. She's too smart not to piece it together. She's just messed up in the head right now and unable to see it. It's not this bar or that life. They're one and the same.

She doesn't budge right now though. "Please, give it up."

"What am I going to do?" I ask, feeling a deep crease settle in the middle of my forehead as my lips form a straight line. "Men in the life don't leave the life."

"You don't have to keep this up," she begs me, and I hate it. Every few months she does this. She can't just accept it?

"You knew who I was. There was never a question." I have to contain my frustration so I don't raise my voice.

"I thought things would change!" she yells, and I know the guys can hear. "When things got better, I thought you'd stop!"

"The guys are here." I bring up that fact to try to get her to keep her voice down. "Don't do this now." Even though it's a command, I know I'm asking her. Shit, I'd beg her not to do it in front of them.

"When are we going to do it, Seth?" she says and her voice cracks when she questions me. Her teeth sink into her bottom lip to keep it steady and the moment she wraps her arms around herself, I wrap mine around her shoulders. My chest touches her crossed arms and then her chest when she finally relaxes.

The anxiousness I feel seeing her broken down like this dims when she presses her chest against mine from her collar to her hips, and wraps her arms around me. Rubbing soothing motions up and down her back, I try to console her the best I can. Kisses in her hair, telling her it's going to be all right. I don't know what else I can do.

She knows I can't leave the guys; I can't leave the life. What the hell would I do? I don't know anything else.

That's the next step in this conversation. And then she tells me I can be anything. She believes it, too. My throat's tight when I kiss her hair again, and I breathe in deep, inhaling the smell of her shampoo. It's some floral scent.

"I love you," she whispers into my chest. I don't know if she meant for me to hear it or not, she spoke it so softly, so I don't answer. I just kiss her hair again and try to ignore that feeling in my gut that everything is all wrong.

"I hate this shit," I speak without thinking. I don't even know why I said it.

Laura takes a step back, no longer holding me and I have to straighten my expression, making sure she doesn't see anything but confidence.

"Hate what?" she asks, nearly breathlessly. Her eyes are larger, darker, swirling with a concoction of emotion that I can't quite place.

"I hate fighting," I tell her honestly. "I hate you not being happy."

"I am happy," she's quick to tell me, ignoring all of the shit that just happened so she can give me what I want. She comes to that realization at the same time that I do, and she swallows tightly. A moment passes in silence, and then another. Reaching her hands up to my collar, she stares at the stubble on my jaw as she composes herself. "I'm just scared, Seth."

"Don't be," I say, putting every ounce of reassurance I can into my tone. "I'm right here; you have nothing to be scared about."

"You're not always here, though."

I bite down hard on the tip of my tongue to keep from telling her I would be if she'd move in with me. Round and round we go. In a fucking circle.

I hate when she does this shit. Sucking in a breath, I watch her staring up at me. Wide eyed, waiting for a response and not realizing how much it pisses me off.

She's always done this, though.

Even when I first started walking her home from school. She still had the bruises and cut lip from Vito. I was busted up pretty good for a while too. It was only surface damage. That shit heals just fine. My pops took over along with his crew. If they were the first generation, we're the second for this organization. His reign didn't last long though. The Vitos weren't going to go down in a single night. Pops knew that; we all did. So someone had to keep an eye on Laura. I volunteered.

"You don't have to babysit me," I remember her telling me as I followed her down the dirt path along the field. She walked to school by herself usually, but we were engaged in an all-out war with whoever was left in Vito's crew. No one was allowed to be alone. I stayed behind and kept my distance. Apparently it wasn't far enough for her.

"You don't have to babysit me."

"I kinda do," I called out since she was maybe six, ten feet ahead of me. It was turning to autumn and I remember how the breeze went by as she turned to face me. She may be small and meek and not wanting any of this shit, but there was so much fight in her. Still is.

She faced me, the cornfield to her back, her cheek bruised. Her bookbag fell to the crook of her arm so she could open it and pull out a sweater.

"My dad ask you to?" she asked without looking at me. She was putting all of her energy into pulling on that thin blue sweater like it was going to help her with how cold the air had just gotten. It was way too thin, but I didn't have anything for her. Shit, I was only wearing a t-shirt.

"No," I answered her and licked my bottom lip. The cut there was still pretty bad and I ran the tip of my tongue over it, remembering the weekend before. She had balls. It was more than that though that made me volunteer to watch her. She looked to me. When the moment came and she was scared, she looked at me for help. That bruise on her face? I did that to her. I might as well have. As far as I'm concerned, I'm the one who put that mark on her face. A bar full of men and it took two blows before any of us stood up to Vito. Two punches to this girl's face. Even me. Even knowing what I knew.

I never should have sat idly by. Not when it came to her, and not when it came to all the other guys I grew up with, who Vito had knocked off one by one.

My throat got tight and I had to clear it, shoving my hands in my jean pockets and kicking the dirt as I waited for her to get moving.

"Your pops didn't ask me to, no."

"Then why?" she bit out and when I looked up, she was finally looking me in the eyes. Could she see? All the guilt I felt? I wanted to make it up to her, but I couldn't say that. When she looked at me, I should have stepped up. I shouldn't have let her be the one to say no to Vito, even if I'd never said a word to her before. She shouldn't have been the one to stand up to that man.

I couldn't speak so I just shrugged. "If you want me to go, just tell me." I implied I'd leave, but I was a lying bastard back then.

"I'd never do that," she barely whispered and pushed the words out quick, like they were toxic and crazy. Like the thought of telling me to leave would be the worst sin she'd ever make.

A moment passed, and there were so many things I wanted to say, so many things I needed to tell her, but I couldn't say any of them. So I grabbed her arm, and directed her to walk. My hand slowly moved from her elbow, down to her wrist. I didn't take her hand in mine; she did that. It took ten minutes of walking for her to do it. But she's the one who did that and I've never felt anything better.

It took her almost a year of going through turmoil together before she caved and finally let me kiss her. Two years have passed since then, and sometimes I still feel like I did the moment she slipped her hand into mine and let me walk her home.

Laura's soft voice brings me back to the present. "Seth, I just—"

"You're scared," I say to cut her off when her plea breaks up the memory.

"Shouldn't I be?" she says, stressing the words like they're some ultimate truth.

"Come here." I give her the command with both of my arms outstretched but she shakes her head. "Hey," I say, hardening my voice and that gets her attention. "Didn't we agree I should boss you around? Or do I need to get out whips and chains?" I joke with her about that BDSM shit. It does what it should and cracks a smile on her face.

"That's only for the bedroom," she tells me and rolls her eyes, but her soft smile is still there. I motion for her to come to me and she does. Resting her head on my shoulder even though she's focused on twirling the ends of her hair around her fingers.

"You're scared," I tell her again. She's quiet but I know she's listening because her motions stop. "Steven Jackson knows some things, but not everything. Maybe he is scared for you, maybe he thinks something happened. I don't know, but I can tell you," I pause to wrap my hand around the nape of her neck and wait for her to look at me before continuing, "he doesn't know shit."

I don't know if it's a lie or the truth, but her gaze already softens with relief. Her pouty lips drop open slightly, but I keep talking before she can say anything.

"He doesn't know what he's talking about because we don't tell him everything. Only little things he needs to know to keep him off our back." Her eyes search mine and I don't know what she'll find after that half-truth leaves me.

"If something was wrong, or if you were in danger, you know I'd hide you away." I run my hand through her hair as I add, "I'd probably lock you up in that safe at the house." I grin at the ridiculousness and she lets out a broken laugh and then sniffles.

I let a minute pass, just rocking her, allowing her the moment she needs to realize Jackson isn't the be-all and end-all. I am.

"I'm sorry he got you all worked up and upset," I tell her and kiss the crown of her head.

"I'm sorry I let him," she says. Her apology is quiet, and I hate it. Before I've even straightened my spine to stand upright, she's coming at me, kissing me and wrapping her hands around my shoulders to keep me lowered for her.

Her lips are hot, and her tongue is greedy. Everything inside of me simmers. "Greedy girl," I groan against her lips when she finally pulls away.

My right hand has already drifted to her ass, keeping her hip pressed against my thigh. My left is roaming, feeling curves I know so well and wanting to sear her skin, branding it with my touch to make sure she still belongs to me.

"Seth," she murmurs. The combination of tearstained cheeks and lust in her eyes makes me hard as stone for her. "I love you," she tells me. "I hope the guys didn't hear," she adds before she takes another breath. She's quick to do that. To deny me the opportunity to say it back. She's afraid I won't. I get it. I don't mind it either. She likes to protect herself however she can.

"I'm sure they did," I answer her and then reach behind me to the doorknob, making sure it's locked. The click is in time with the thump in my chest. "They aren't going to hear you yell at me anymore though," I tell her and unbutton my pants.

Laura's thighs clench as she stands there, in a ten-by-ten-foot room with me and nowhere to hide. Desire dances in her eyes.

"We can't," she hisses, accompanied by the zip of my pants being undone.

"If they can hear you yell at me, they can hear me fucking you, so you better be quiet."

My sweet innocent girl gasps and it thrills me. I love that I can still surprise her. "Don't let them hear you," I command her as I take a step forward, kicking off my jeans and sliding down my drawers as I go. She takes a step back until her shoulders hit the wall, as if she can escape me. As if she'd want to. "I want them to hear all the banging from me fucking your brains out against this wall. Not you moaning my name. Just this." Splaying my hand on the drywall above her head, I slap my hand hard once against the wall. I lean my lips to the shell of her ear and say, "You need to be quiet. Do you hear me?"

My cock is already leaking precum at the thought of being inside of her and everything being right again. Her small hand reaches out between us and she rubs the moisture over the head of my dick, making me groan. Dropping my lips to the crook of her neck, I kiss and suck and nibble while she strokes me until I've had enough.

It takes everything I have to step back and tell her to strip down. I want her ass completely naked. Both of us. Our clothes are nothing but puddles of fabric on the floor. Before I lift her up, I run my fingers between her slick folds, teasing her, rubbing her sweet nub and testing her ability to be quiet. Her nails dig into my shoulder as she bites down on her lip. Her head slams against the wall as she rocks herself on my hand. She's breathing too heavily, making too much noise.

I don't give a shit though. It wouldn't be the first time my crew caught us going at it. They know to get the hell away and leave us alone.

With a hand on each of her ass cheeks, I lift her up and she wraps her legs around my waist. "Bite my shoulder," I demand, and she does it instantly. It's a good thing she doesn't hesitate, because I slam into her out of pure unadulterated need. My thrusts are primal and the harder she bites me, the harder I fuck her. My body is covered in a cold sweat and hers is hot to the touch on every inch. I take her like we both need, and I have no regrets about that.

No fucking regrets. Not anymore.

CHAPTER 8

Laura

I can't even cross my legs; I'm so sore. Seth has some sort of magic over me. I don't know what it is. The moment I'm in his vicinity, I'm a puppet for him. Whatever he commands, I do. Whatever he tells me, I believe. My body bends to his and I love it.

It does terrify a small piece of me, though. That little voice is quiet right now, sated by what happened in the back room last night.

And then again when Seth met me at his place and took me to bed.

That second time reminded me of our first time. I keep comparing the two and I find nothing identical. Back then when I first gave into Seth years ago, the temptation to touch him, the urge to let him do whatever he wanted to me—I had never experienced it with anyone else. I knew nothing, except that I wanted him to finally touch me, to have me like I'd been fantasizing about. It would have happened sooner if my dad hadn't died shortly after Seth started hovering over me. He was my protector for nearly a year before I kissed him.

I remember being up on my tiptoes, my hand pressed against his chest and I kissed him as though I had done it a thousand times before. And I had in my mind. Every time he opened the door for me. Every time his fingers brushed against mine when we walked. Every time he laughed at the bar and with the rough cadence his hand landed on my thigh and stayed there. In the very forefront of my mind I leaned into him and kissed him, thousands of times or more. So that day, after having a drink and feeling the buzz of both intoxication and lust, I planted my lips directly onto his.

I never imagined the groan of satisfaction. That deep, masculine sound was unexpected and a pleasant surprise that travelled down to my belly, and then further. His rough hands gripped my hips and he lifted me up, keeping his lips on mine, never breaking the heated embrace.

Last night was slow and leisurely; that first night was a rush of primitive need. He couldn't take my clothes off fast enough, until my bare back was on the table and my ass was hanging off. I'd have been mortified if he hadn't dipped his head to my breasts and sucked, nipped and ravished every inch of my flesh. How could I be embarrassed by my body when he worshipped it the first glance he got?

I was naked while he was still clothed. Again, it's a difference. Last night was slow, relaxing, and he stripped first, then he took his time peeling my clothes off.

"I'll go slow," he whispered at the crook of my neck when he had finally made it to that moment. The moment when I was no longer a virgin. I remember how hot I felt. How suffocating those prolonged seconds were between knowing it was going to happen, and it finally happening.

"I don't want you to go slow," I told him, my mind clear and my desire evident. "I want you."

In one swift stroke he took me, hard and unabashed. He watched me as my eyes widened; he never stopped watching between heated kisses.

"I'll make sure you love it," he promised as he pounded into me with reckless abandon and I don't know for certain if the promise was for me or for him.

My thighs tighten and I can still feel him. That night I knew I could never go back. I wasn't sure if he could go back to pretending the attraction wasn't there. He made damn sure I knew the next day when he took me into the bar and kissed me in front of everyone. There was never any "going back" with Seth.

When my phone buzzes in my hand, I instinctively jump from my seat in the waiting room and then hiss at the slight pain that throbs between my legs. It's a good ache, but it's embarrassing as fuck when the receptionist eyes me from behind the glass divider. Like I'm some kind of nuisance. I don't want to be here anymore than she wants me here.

I want to be a nurse; I don't want to be a patient. I hate being a patient. Mostly because of insurance.

I've already got my clipboard of paperwork filled out. Now I just wait in this room, sitting in one of the chairs that look like they're from the '80s while a cooking show plays in the upper right corner on a tiny little TV.

I check the text I received, thinking it might be from Seth, but it's not. *Tell me something good.*

Cami's text makes me smile.

No news yet, I'm waiting to be seen. YOU tell me something good. I'm eager for her to distract me. I want to know all about what she and Derrick did last night. I feel like I'm in on the details because she told me, but Derrick didn't tell Seth. I know because last night Seth told me he thinks that Derrick's seeing someone seriously.

You have to tell me what they say. As I read the text Cami sent back, a little disappointed that it's not full of juicy details, an elderly woman in an oversized t-shirt comes into the waiting room from the doctor's side and then leaves through the front doors. I glance at the woman at the front desk, wondering if this means it's my turn, but nope, nothing yet.

Tap, tap, tap, my shoe is at war with the wooden leg of my chair.

Cami texts me again and I nearly shriek in the room. The gasp is certainly audible and when I look at the receptionist, she's looking at me disapprovingly. Fucking hell. This isn't the library.

Giving her a tight smile, I return to my phone and read the text again.

Derrick and I slept together last night.

I've known Cami for half a decade. She's slept with three men in her life before last night. Derrick is the fourth. All three were young love… for Cami. The guys told her they loved her, fucked her, and moved on. Derrick won't do that. I know he won't. He wouldn't have touched her if he didn't want more from her. He knows she means a lot to me. He told Cami that's why he didn't make a move sooner. He was afraid of getting into trouble with "the boss," meaning Seth.

So this is the end of 'let's take it slow'? I ask her.

I have to wait a few minutes to get a response, and in the meantime, I text her about half a dozen times: *How was it? How big is he? Where did it happen?*

It's practically an interview when she finally texts back.

He told the guys last night he was into me. He said he claimed me, like the guys used to do at the Clubhouse, you know? His dad and them.

She rambles in her messages, sending them in chunks. And all the while my heart does a little flip for her. But also for me. Seth was fucking with me. Maybe he wanted to see if I knew. Dammit, I'm more disappointed than I should be that I'm not in on a secret Seth doesn't know of.

He said if I'm with him, we're exclusive. That he'll be out late some nights, but it's for work. He said I can't ask questions and I have to trust him. He told me that it's hard for some girls to trust like that and he asked me if I could.

And you said yes? Right? I text back with my questions even though I already know she did. Cami knows everything I've been through with Seth. Late nights after we've had fights are the worst. It's easy to think he's just avoiding me, that he's off somewhere trying to get me—and our fight—off of his mind.

Those nights, I called Cami.

She'd come over or stay with me on the phone, easing my worries. Somewhere deep down, I knew Seth wasn't going to leave me, but it didn't make the thoughts in my head stop. We've had three big fights, all about the stupid shit he does and how we can get out of it. All three times, I watched that clock. All three times, he eventually came home, then sat next to me like he belonged there. Even if I wasn't talking to him when he left. All three times, I kissed him hard, loving that he made the choice to come back to me.

He's a man who doesn't leave. All of the guys in the crew are the same. Derrick will be to Cami what Seth is to me; I know it.

She didn't grow up in the life, but she gets it. Her dad was a truck driver and not around a lot. Maybe that's why it's easier for her? I don't know. But she stays calm in the storm. Derrick's lucky to have that.

My phone pings.

I told him to shut up and kiss me. He wasn't telling me anything I didn't already know.

This time I do squeal and I don't bother to look up at the receptionist. She can deal with it.

"Laura Roth?" a doctor calls out into the room, looking at a clipboard and lifting the papers before looking up to see me. The doctor looks young at first, but then I see the age around her eyes and mouth. She's done up with dangling earrings, her brunette hair piled high in a bun, and a black dress under the professional white coat.

I wave. Like an idiot. I'll blame it on being caught off guard by Cami's last text.

"Come on back." Her voice is calming yet chipper as she holds open the door and leads the way to whatever room we're going to. "I'm Dr. June. It's nice to meet you." She's polite and confident. I find myself making up stories about her on the way through the hall.

I wonder if she has a date after work. Or maybe it was a lunch date. She's even wearing heels and that seems like a bold choice. I've already picked out the white sneakers I want to wear when I'm a nurse.

"Have a seat," Dr. June says as she directs me to a blue examination table with vinyl upholstery that seems cheap but is probably easy to clean. It's covered by a sheet of white paper that crinkles when I sit down.

"So I see here you were at your gynecologist and she identified what she believes to be a potential arrhythmia?"

I nod my head, remembering that day and a certain feeling in particular. I'm experiencing it again right now, this draining of everything inside of me right to the pit of my stomach.

"Can you tell me when you first experienced these symptoms?"

I move my gaze from her to the stark sink and the clear canisters filled with odd-shaped swabs. "I um—" I stop speaking to clear my throat. "I wouldn't have known if I hadn't been there, so I don't really know."

"The chart indicates you grabbed your chest and seemed to struggle to breathe." I can hear the paper fall as Dr. June drops the clipboard to her lap. "Is that a normal occurrence?"

"I'd just found out." It hurts all over again. "I went in because I was bleeding, and I'd just found out that I miscarried. I didn't even know I was two months along." My eyes prick with tears, but I keep them back. "I didn't know I was pregnant. … So, no, it's not a normal occurrence. I was just reacting to the situation."

"I can understand that," Dr. June says and nods, trying to ease the thick tension. I hate this room. I hate being the one sitting on this table.

She asks me the same questions the gynecologist did. If I've felt fatigued, light-headed, or experienced any rapid heartbeat and shortness of breath in the last six months. All of them are a yes, but it's because of Seth and the shit he puts me through, so I lie, which I know I shouldn't do, and tell her no.

"I've already answered these for the other doctor, my gynecologist," I say and cut her off from asking more questions, feeling like this is all déjà vu.

"I know, but for the tests we have to conduct, we have to do this at our facilities." Paperwork. Legalities.

"I understand."

"So today, I'm going to listen to your heart and do a checkup of sorts. We're also going to do an echocardiogram to take a look at what's going on physically. It's an ultrasound …" Her voice drones on as she lists what she has planned for me and her reasoning for the tests. I've already read up on it, so I'm ready. Her stethoscope is cold as she listens to my heartbeat, occasionally pausing to tell me to breathe in deep.

All the while, I think about moments like this that I may face as a nurse. With me on the other side of things. If there's ever a woman talking about her miscarriage and on the brink of tears, I promise myself not to keep a smile plastered on my face and tell her that I understand.

You can never understand what anyone else's pain is like. She doesn't know Seth told me he wanted kids. And that I told him I didn't; there was too much going on.

I was already pregnant when I told him that. I put that out there into the universe, not knowing I was already carrying the baby Seth wanted. I practically asked fate to take that baby away from me. From us.

I'll never forgive myself for speaking those words out loud. For even thinking them. I wish I could take it back. I would if I could. You're never ready for a baby.

"You may want to ask someone to go with you." Dr. June's suggestion brings me back to the present.

"For the stress test?" I clarify, shifting and making the paper crinkle under me. I was barely listening to her telling me I'll have to come back in next week.

"Yes. It's just a treadmill and I don't think you'll have any problems, but it may be comforting to have someone with you."

I'm grateful the stethoscope is nowhere near me, suddenly worried that she can hear just how battered my heart feels. I don't want to lie to her even more than I already have, so I don't tell her I asked the only two people I have to come today and neither of them could.

CHAPTER 9

Seth

FROM THE PARKING LOT OF THE OLD GAS STATION, YOU COULD THROW A stone and hit a car on the highway. It's that damn close. It's loud too as the three of us huddle for this meet.

Behind me is the old worn-out sign, bleached by the sun but you can still read *Gas and Convenience Store*. Under it is my crew. Roman, Connor and Liam are talking about something. I don't know what. I can't hear shit with the highway here.

Derrick looks with me, and then tells me, "Should be simple." Maybe he thinks he needs to ease my concerns, so I nod. "Yeah," I respond.

I can't shake this feeling in my gut though. Ever since Laura came home from the doctor's two nights ago, something feels off. Not just with her, but with work too.

It's like someone's watching me. A gust of wind passes, and I the feeling comes over me again. I don't like it.

Leroy holds out his hand for a shake before saying a word. His crew's behind him like mine is, at a distance and leaning against a black sedan. His grip is strong and he looks me in the eyes as he says, "I'm looking forward to doing more business with you fellas."

I can see in my periphery that Derrick's lips kick up in an asymmetrical grin at "fellas."

Leroy's from down south and he needs shipments coming in. We can provide that. We have in the past, but these should be steady, or so he claims. Shipments come into the dock, we collect, we deliver. Like Derrick said, *should be simple*.

"You know our take," I tell him and then my gaze is pulled past Leroy when one of his crew reaches behind him. My hand burns with the need to go for my gun when I see the quick motion, but the guy is just reaching for a smoke. With the cigarette in his mouth, he takes out a lighter from his back pocket and passes it to the guy next to him. "Fifteen percent," I tell Leroy, keeping my expression easy, even though adrenaline is scorching through me.

I know you need trust in these relationships. At least trust that they need the partnership and can't afford to fuck you over. I have that with Leroy. I have for a year now although this proposition is new. I just can't shake this feeling though.

Not everyone is an enemy. But damn does it feel like they are sometimes.

Leroy shifts his focus to Derrick, who's silent. The gravel under his feet crunches noisily while we wait. "What if I increase the load, can your boys handle that?" he asks me, and I nod.

"We got it covered."

Another second passes. "If I increase the product per shipment, seems like it should be dropped to ten percent, doesn't it?"

"How's that?" Derrick pipes up. I roll out my right shoulder, watching Leroy's men talking. A freight truck rushes by on the highway above them and two of them turn to look. It's not a high-tension situation, but negotiations at the last minute aren't welcome.

"More product, more money, but you're still only doing one run," he explains to Derrick.

"We agreed on fifteen," I tell him.

Leroy puts both of his hands up, a move that makes the men behind him still, their eyes focused solely on us now. *Thump, thump* my heart pounds and the back of my neck pricks. His hands are lowered as quickly as they went up, and his men settle. They're watching closely now though.

"I got a call yesterday. I may have more product than I thought. Terms for me have changed," Leroy says then sniffs and thumbs the tip of his nose. "Like I said, it's more product, more money, still one shipment. Ten percent of this load is more than fifteen percent of the previous."

"How much more?" I ask him.

"Forty."

Forty thousand.

I still hesitate and he adds, "How long have we been working together? Two years now? I don't want to work with anyone else. You're my guy."

Another truck goes by as I take in what he's saying. I don't like changing arrangements.

"We've got the cash in the car," he says. As he moves to call over one of the guys, I see a familiar car pull up to the gas station. It's an old, light blue Mustang. The paint is worn out, but I think Jackson likes it that way.

"We got company," I murmur and nod my head for Leroy to see.

"He's not one of yours?" Leroy's brow arches.

"We have him contained, but he doesn't get a paycheck," I explain.

"No exchange then?" he questions. I eye Jackson, parked at a pump and sitting there, not even bothering to get gas. Fucker.

"No, we still exchange. We have a deal at twelve percent because it's more work for us, more heat too if anything happens." I hold out my hand for Leroy.

It takes a few seconds, but he agrees and his handshake is just as firm as it was when he first pulled up. "It's always nice doing business with you."

Turning to Derrick, I tell him to get the details and the cash—all twelve percent of it. "I'll take care of this."

"Until next time," Leroy says, giving me a nod as I walk off. Dust kicks up from the parking lot as I walk the twenty feet or so over to Jackson.

The highway's louder at the front of the store than on the side where the parking lot is. A car beeps on the bypass above, quick and short, but in multiple successions and it aggravates me just as much as the sight of Jackson does right now.

I could fucking snarl, remembering how he got into Laura's head.

It takes everything in me not to grab him by his throat and slam him up against his car. The only reason I don't do it is because of the deal going on behind me. If Leroy thinks I'm in over my head with the cops, he could back out. Shit, I would if it were me, but we need this cash. We need everything we have right now. The twelve percent from Leroy with a higher take? That's good for us. I probably would have taken the ten given it's still one run. A steady cash flow is what we need while we get the bar up and running.

With my jaw clenched, I stare down at Jackson. My shoulders are tense and I breathe in the dusty air just to keep from screaming at this asshole.

"Come to tell me you're worried for me?" I raise my voice as I speak so he can hear, not changing the expression on my face.

"Worried for you?" Jackson keeps his door open, standing with it between him and me and that makes me uneasy. I want his hands where I can see them. Which is ironic, given who he is.

"Get out and shut the door," I demand and he cocks his head, staring at me like this is a showdown.

"You want to have this conversation while I'm thinking you're hiding a gun between the two of us?" I question him and that gets him moving. The door shuts as another round of cars rushes behind us, below us. We're surrounded by activity.

Jackson's my height and my build. Ever since we were kids, we were built the same. At least physically. Mentally, we were always opposites.

Before he's finished taking the two steps it takes to get close enough to talk, I tell him, "Don't ever go to Laura again." The threat in my voice is clear as day. I don't do subtleties when it comes to her.

Jackson isn't fazed. It should piss me off, but instead I find myself questioning things.

"She deserved a heads-up and so do you, which is why I'm here."

"You leave her to me," I tell him again, gritting the words out between my teeth.

"A moment of weakness," he says and then glances at the pavement before looking me in the eyes. "I apologize."

My muscles twitch; my back feels like it's tighter than a coiled rope ready to split and unravel.

"Wright is a snitch," Jackson says, changing the subject. My mind is still on Laura, still on the stress he caused her. Hearing Wright's name though, the source of our intel and a lower-level mule for Mathews, catches my attention.

"If he snitched to us, you don't think he told Mathews?" Jackson questions me.

"Told you what?"

"You stole half a mil in product—at cost." He emphasizes cost and it takes a lot for me to stay calm in this moment. I have to keep my voice low and even, show no emotion. Leroy's men are watching.

With that in mind, I look over my shoulder. Derrick's at the corner of the store where I can see him. The car's parked in the back. I imagine he's having Roman do the bitch work of moving the cash from one car to the other. As long as Derrick's in view, I know everything's going as planned.

Other than what Jackson just told me. *Wright's a snitch.*

"It wasn't us and I don't know what you're talking about."

Jackson shakes his head and sucks his teeth. "Don't do that to me. Not with all the shit I've covered up for you. Don't fucking do that to me." I don't expect the anger, or the hurt. That's what it is in the way he looks at me with his nostrils flared. He's hurt.

"We've known about them coming down here. We grabbed Wright. We had him spilling everything. Then you go and fuck with them?" Contempt laces his last line.

Clenching my fist and cracking my knuckles with my thumb, I take a moment. Letting this information sink in as I watch Leroy and Derrick shake hands before our respective crews part ways. Mine stays where they are, waiting for me while Leroy and his men take off in two vehicles, one after the other. Jackson and I both watch in silence.

"These guys like Mathews don't just get angry; they make examples of the people who steal from them."

"And you were going to stop him?" I question him. I remember when we were just kids. This is a small town and I knew all the neighborhood kids. We'd play cops and robbers back then. He was always the cop and I was always the robber. The "bang" of our toy guns didn't come with the same kick back it comes with now.

"We were getting the intel we needed to get the feds involved."

"Are they?" I ask him.

"Are they what?"

"Involved?"

His gaze drops and I already have my answer. No. Mathews must not be big enough. Either that or Wright didn't give them good enough intel.

"What do you want from me?" I ask Jackson, wanting this conversation to be over so I can figure out how we're going to handle this.

"Come in—get protection. Especially for Laura. It doesn't have to be like this."

Protection? I scoff at the very idea that Jackson would be bringing this shit up. "You remember what it was like. It *does* have to be like this."

"This is too much. They're too big. The collateral—"

"Is my problem," I say, cutting him off. "I can handle this."

His expression falls when I raise my voice. I can feel the words still ringing in my throat long after they're spoken.

Opening his car door, he tells me grimly, "Then, at least I warned you. You know where I am if you change your mind."

CHAPTER 10

Laura

I hear Seth before he says a word to me. The door isn't shut quietly; it's practically slammed. Gripping the edge of my nightgown, for a moment I wonder if it's him or someone else since it was shut so hard. But then I hear the jingle of the keys as they hit the bowl we keep in the kitchen. It's an old ceramic bowl my grandma gave me. At least he didn't throw the keys in there hard. I'd have to kick his ass if he ever broke it.

I must have dozed off; the clock on the nightstand tells me it's nearly nine. When I check my phone, still hearing Seth slamming what sounds like the fridge door, I see a handful of messages Cami sent. Shit, we were supposed to go out. She gathered, in the series of texts I'm reading, that I forgot or that I was busy.

Writing her a quick reply, I tell her I'm sorry. I never miss our dates. Ever. I feel like complete shit that I fell asleep.

I answer the two questions she asked me as well. They're questions about birth control. I promise in the next message I'll make it up to her.

She's quick to tell me it's okay. She's already replaced our date with one with Derrick.

I would feel relief, but Seth's still out there.

There's a little nagging piece inside of me. Digging and clawing, making me feel that something really is wrong. It heats my skin; it sickens my stomach. It tells me to worry. This is what he does when I'm not looking. He bangs shit around and lets out his stress that way.

As I'm walking in the hallway, not trying to be quiet, but quiet nonetheless, I hear the slam of his fist on the counter. My heart jolts in my chest, seizing for a moment until I peek out from the threshold and see my towering man hunched over, both forearms resting on the counter, his head laying between them. His broad shoulders stretch the white t-shirt he's wearing tight over his muscular back. Every muscle ripples as he breathes in deep in what looks like an attempt to calm himself.

"Everything okay?" I ask a little quieter than I'd planned, feeling that aching whisper scream inside. My fingers twitch with the need to hold him, to come up behind him and comfort Seth as he's done for me so many times. But I wait.

Some nights are bad and he doesn't like to be touched then. Not when he first gets home. Maybe it's because he wanted to throw shit around like he is now, but he couldn't because I was home.

He lifts his gaze to me and instantly softens. His exhale is short as he stands up straighter, running his hand over the back of his head. "Sorry, Babygirl. I didn't know you were home. Thought Cami and you were going out?"

Seth clears his throat and then opens his arms, urging me to come over to him. I don't waste any time molding myself to the side of his body, feeling his heat. With one arm around my waist, he hugs me back and then lifts the beer on the counter to his lips with his free hand.

"You okay?" I ask once the glass clinks on the counter, noting he takes his time with the swig, probably to get his thoughts in order.

"Fine," he breathes out although stress is prominent in his answer. "How did the studying go?" he asks me, changing the subject. He does that a lot, but I can still see the torment that clings to him. Maybe he thinks he hides it well, but he doesn't.

"So you don't want to talk?" I ask him, hoping maybe all he needs is a push.

All he gives me is a weak smile though. I already knew he wouldn't confide in me. It's just not who he is. Grabbing both of his hands and making him leave the beer on the counter, I tell him to come with me.

His fingers barely grip mine until I give his hand a squeeze.

"You all right?" he asks and a new worry rips through his expression. It's fresh, not tired. And fear, not stress.

I have to laugh a little when I answer him, "I'm better than you are." I'm still walking him to the sofa in the living room when he gives me a huff of a masculine laugh in response. Seth's house is larger than my grandma's. Nicer in a lot of ways simply because it's new and in an up-and-coming part of town. The sofa though, it's my favorite. The entire living room really. Probably because I picked out every piece.

The sofa is a soft cream chenille with a pale blue paisley pattern on the outsides of the armrests and all the way around the back of it. When I picked it out, I was thinking of myself and thought for sure Seth would say no. Instead, he told me to get whatever I wanted to go with it. So I got a thick, plush royal blue rug to go with the sofa, covering the hardwood floors, solely so I could get on my knees like I'm doing now, unbuckling his pants and helping Seth relax.

I can give him this. Freely. He gives me so much and never asks for a damn thing. So this? I can give him this.

He spears his hand through my hair as the sound of the zipper mixes with my faint moan.

"Laura," Seth protests weakly and my response is to grip his jeans in both my hands, ripping his pants down as I stare up into his heated gaze. He's already hardening. I can see his length get stiffer by the second through the thin fabric of his boxer briefs.

"Sit down." I give him the firm command while keeping our eyes locked, and he smirks at me. From this angle, he's even more handsome, which doesn't make any sense. He's just towering over me. Maybe it's the rough stubble, the way he smiles, or the lust in his eyes. But my heart does that little pitter-patter, the beat that's out of rhythm. Maybe it really is all because of him. *He makes my heart skip a beat.*

"Let me do what I want to you," I whisper and inch my fingers up to the waistband of his boxer briefs. His hand is still in my hair, and he scratches his blunt nails against my scalp before wrapping my hair around his wrist. Pulling my head back, I'm forced to look at him, rather than his hardening cock that's barely contained by the thin fabric in front of my face. He doesn't pull hard, not enough to give me any pain, but it's authoritative.

I think for a moment he's going to say something; his gaze is so penetrating and he stares for so long. All the while, my core heats, my heart flutters, and I can barely breathe.

Seth releases me without a word, letting me strip him down, dropping slowly to the sofa, spreading his strong legs wide for me.

His cock is ready, standing tall when I reach out and stroke him. My fingers nearly don't wrap around the entire thing. I run my thumb up one of the thick veins all the way to his head. Spreading a bead of precum over the velvety top of him, I almost lick my lips.

"I like it when you blush like that," he murmurs. Looking up at him, I hold his gaze as I lean forward and let the tip of my tongue slip through his slit while holding him with both hands to keep him where I want him. He hisses and the *S* sinks deep into my heat, forcing me to clench around nothing.

I wrap my mouth around the head of his cock and hum a sweet moan as I taste the saltiness of what little cum is there. Opening my jaw as far as I can, I sink down his length and feel his smooth skin massage my lips as I bob. It's only a tease, only to get a little moisture on his cock. Releasing him with a pop, I look back up at Seth, whose lips are parted as he breathes ever so slowly. His hips thrust in my hand the next time I lean down, teasing his head with a gentle suck.

I could worship his cock like this for hours, but he doesn't let me.

A squeal leaves me when he reaches down, grabbing me by the hips to sit in his lap. "Seth!" I object, but that doesn't stop him from ripping my nightgown over my head. I'm mid-laugh when his open-mouth kiss lands on the dip in my throat. The giddiness in my voice is quick to morph to a strangled moan when he touches me. His hands grip my flesh, and his mouth devours my sensitized skin.

I anticipate him maneuvering me onto my back upon the sofa, with him on top. That's how he likes it most of the time. But he doesn't. Instead he places my back to his chest, still kissing my neck, and spreads my legs so my thighs are resting over his.

"Seth," I moan as his cock presses against my folds. The head slips against my clit and I writhe against him, my breath hitching.

He's not merciful as he pushes himself inside of me with a single stroke. My back arches, and my front feels cold without him here. Seth keeps my neck at his lips by gripping my throat with his hand. I'm staring at the ceiling, wide eyed, feeling the sweet stretch that lingers with pain when his other hand meets my throbbing clit.

He's relentless as he strums my swollen nub and pistons his hips up to fuck me just like this. My screams of pleasure are as ruthless as his touch. He doesn't stop until my throat is sore, my limbs are trembling and I've orgasmed more times than I can keep count.

CHAPTER 11

Seth

There are two platform stages in the basement of Club Allure. The one in the center, a sixteen-by-twenty-foot rectangle, has bright lights shining down on it. They're highlighting two men as they circle each other. The drop is only two feet if one of the hulking men falls off. It's the platform of a professional boxing ring, minus the ropes. It looks like Jameson might fall off the edge. The blood from the cut above his eye is dripping down his face and he can barely keep up with protecting his body with his fists, let alone keep the blood from blinding him.

If he falls, he's still fair game. Just harder for everyone else to see the ass beating he'll take. Judging by the cheers and the frown on Cade's face, this match isn't an upset. There are four more after it though, and regardless of how this match turns out, these men will keep betting. For the thrill, for the entertainment. For the addiction of being a part of something so primitive. All of which is good for us. We haven't had a fight yet that didn't line our pockets. This is the first one down here; the first of many.

In front of where Derrick and Liam are standing on top of the second stage, the one against the back wall, I approach Fletcher. Derrick and Liam are watching it all go down while Cade takes the bets. At least sixty bodies form a swarm around the ring, filling the room with their cheers and yells. It's all white noise. The real money is made away from the lights, in the shadows of the room while surrounded by the chaos.

With men like Fletcher. He runs things up north of here. He has for years and when shit got rough the first year of taking Tremont back from Vito's men who wanted it just as much as we did, Fletcher took our side.

Back then, he said he was rooting for the underdogs. I wonder if he bet on Jameson tonight.

"King," Fletcher greets me and I grip his hand firmly, keeping my gaze on anything but his pocket square. He always wears a suit I can't stand.

Ostentatious is one way to describe the pale blue suit that's wrapped around his body in a slim fit. With the yellow patterned handkerchief tucked in his pocket, garish is the word I'd use for this one. Fletcher is flashy, from his heavy gold watch to the diamond stud in his ear. His look comes outfitted with a lit cigar. Money talks, but the wealth he has, he decides to make scream. I may not prefer his attire, but he's just the man I want to do business with tonight.

"Good to see you, Fletcher."

"Your bar is coming together nicely," he says, starting with small talk. Upstairs isn't finished, and it won't be for another few weeks or more. I want it perfect when we open the doors to the public. Down here is just fine. No furniture, nothing that can be stained with the blood that will most certainly be spilled. These heathens would be fine with cardboard boxes.

"Thanks. I heard you're building one uptown?" I question him and he shrugs.

"Not like this," he says.

"Wasn't asking because I'm worried about competition," I say to reassure the worried look on his face.

He huffs from his nose before straightening the gaudy handkerchief. "I just want you to hear it from me. I'd never step on your toes."

"Likewise," I say with a nod and move on to business. "The next shipment has been moved up a week. Leroy has extra product, and he's happy for me to hand it on over to you."

"You want me to cut out Mathews?" Fletcher questions, a glint in his eye. He's had to deal with Mathews because there was no one else. It's what led to that fucker getting closer to Tremont. This is one more blow to Mathews while giving me favor with both Leroy and Fletcher. It's a win on all sides and both of them know it.

If I need an ally against Mathews, Fletcher is my man.

"Who's that?" I ask with a smirk and he lets out a bellow of a laugh. Fletcher sells what Mathews sells. All the heavy shit. Pushing Mathews back by destroying his stash only helps Fletcher keep his territory. *Stick with the devil you know*, comes to mind when I think about the last conversation Fletcher and I had.

"Know what I love about you?" he asks me, wrapping an arm around my shoulders. "You treat your friends well."

I give him a tight smile and nod. "I take it you're happy to not have to rely on the man cutting into your turf?"

"This last week has been less bloody," he tells me with a seriousness that chills my spine. "I want to keep it that way."

"It's been coming to that. A war on the streets."

Fletcher nods and says, "That's what happens when a new dealer moves in."

"I heard he's moving out," I'm quick to comment as Fletcher lights up a cigarette. He takes a long puff and exhales as the men surrounding the stage to our right, let out the kind of roar that comes with disbelief. Looks like Jameson's coming back. That's what happens with the Irish. You can't count them out until they've hit the ground.

"He can sell his shit elsewhere," Fletcher says, practically spitting the words out. "It was a mistake to ever buy from him… This Leroy… he's all right?"

"Been with him for a while, he's better than all right."

"What have you been buying, though?" Fletcher questions me and I don't like it. "That soft shit isn't the same type of deal."

I level him with a hard stare. "You don't have to worry about Leroy."

He's slow to nod, then drags on his cigar before saying, "Tremont has some good shit. The pot, the coke, the E.... but when are you going to expand, Young Buck?"

Young Buck. I hate the nickname he has for me even more than the suit I'm currently forced to look at.

"We're stable, controlled, that's how I like it," I tell him and then I put my arms up, gesturing to the room and the stairs as I add, "Money's flowing. That's what counts."

"You're growing into what was already here—there's so much more to be done," he says, giving me the hard sell.

I made a deal with Jackson years back. Back when I was selling for Vito and he knew and he was in the academy. I'd keep things as they were. The cocaine, the pot, there's a demand for it from certain people in this town and the surrounding areas. I fill it, but keep it contained to just that.

Meth and heroin aren't an option. We both agree on that. It's how Jackson's mom died. I think it's the only reason the two of us work. He needs me keeping that shit out and I need him to keep the cops off our back.

Uptown, Fletcher makes a pretty penny from that shit. As does Mathews. As does Leroy.

They can sell, split and fight each other for it.

"Not interested at the moment," I answer Fletcher as I have for the past two years.

He lets out a low whistle, and I watch him watch Jameson land an uppercut against his opponent's jaw. The blood splatter only fuels the audience to scream for more. Even if it is an upset.

My eye catches sight of my men. Derrick and Liam are still surveying the room from the platform stage. Roman's in another corner, making another deal. Cade's got a grin from ear to ear as he's taking more bets.

"I like the system I've got going," I tell Fletcher, but I didn't need to give him that. He doesn't need or deserve an explanation. I wish I could pluck the statement from the air when he looks back at me. I'm taller than him, but it still feels like he's looking down at me.

"You're still learning," he says as he squares his shoulders and faces me. "There's more money to be made. You haven't even scratched the surface, my friend."

He puts his hand on my shoulder and I keep my expression firm. A moment passes, and anger swells inside of me. I won't repeat myself, and I won't humor him with more of this conversation.

"Are you good for the drop next week?" I ask bluntly and he drops his hand from my shoulder.

"Always open for your business," he tells me, and I offer him a tight smile, leaving him where he is and telling him to enjoy the show. He still urges me to "think about it" and I reassure him that if I'm in the market, I'll turn to him first.

The part that irritates me the most is that there's too much truth to Fletcher. The real money is in the harder shit. I'm the youngest leader of any crime organization for thousands of miles. And I do have a lot to learn. I picked up the pieces after a year of grappling for power. I took the deals I knew were already in place because we needed the money and the connections. Someone was going to take them, and I literally killed for it to be us.

Men like him, they aren't my friends. They don't need explanations. They'd get rid of me if they thought they could get away with it. I'm more than aware of that little fact.

"You look pissed," Derrick comments as I step up onto the stage to stand next to him.

The collar of my shirt feels tighter as I swallow down the rage. "What'd he say?" Derrick asks, referring to Fletcher.

"Everything's fine and set," I answer him and add, "Just pissed at myself."

"What happened?"

"I'm too fucking friendly," I tell him and the grin I give him makes him shake his head.

"Just your friendly neighborhood thug," he comments with humorous sarcasm.

"Something like that," I say and cross my arms, watching the fight and trying to hear the punches over the cheers.

"Did you decide what we're going to do about the potential problem?" I can feel Derrick's eyes on me, waiting for an answer to his question. I watch blood drip down Jameson's arm. I watch his jaw clench tighter as he lands blow after blow, the veins in his neck bulging.

Swallowing, I answer Derrick without looking at him. "There's no sign Mathews knows for sure."

"Right," he comments.

"All we can do is be ready if they come for us." Finally, turning to him I add, "And we can tie up the loose end."

"Loose end?" he questions but his gaze lights with the answer before I have to say it. "Wright."

"Wright," he repeats, although this time he breathes out long and heavy as he does.

"The sooner the better," I tell him.

"How do you want it done?" he asks, and I tell him I don't care.

A minute passes and the ref calls the fight, lifting Jameson's fist into the air. The man looks like he's barely standing on his own, like he needs that hand to be lifted just so he can stay upright. But he won.

"I thought you said Wright was with the cops?" Derrick's brow is lined with confusion. We don't fuck with the cops and they don't fuck with us.

"He is," I answer Derrick and lift a shoulder nonchalantly. "I'm tired of being friendly." I say the joke in a deadpan manner. "Kill Wright. From here on out we don't trust anyone to stay quiet."

Derrick huffs a laugh, although it's tight. "No more Mr. Nice Guy."

CHAPTER 12

Laura

THERE ARE NO STREETLIGHTS ON MY GRANDMA'S STREET. THEY'RE something the city never put in. So when I park, I don't turn off the car yet. I want that bit of illumination from my headlights as I take out my phone and peek at what Cami texted back.

I grin when I see her message about how she still hurts. But it's a good kind of hurt. I know the feeling. *Is every time like this*? she wrote in the last text.

Only the good ones, I reply before tossing the phone back into my purse. Taking a quick look around, I turn off the car and palm my keys. I've never liked the dark. But I especially don't like it here anymore.

I catch sight of a black sedan idling a few cars up. It would be hard to miss it. It's a sleek car and looks expensive; it looks like it doesn't belong here. The red brake lights come on and the car pulls away a little too fast, making their tires squeal. It's odd they'd drive away so quickly and because of that, I try to read the license plate, but all I get are the first two numbers. One and seven. I try not to care that I didn't see the rest of the plate. It's a habit I have, but this is just a random car.

It sends this weird vibe through me, though. Seeing that car take off… I can't shake it even though it's just a car. I don't know most of the people on this street anymore.

It's nothing, I tell myself and think about Cami's text again. But the odd feeling, that little stir of anxiousness, sits like a rock in the pit of my stomach.

All the good feelings from taking the practice entrance exam this morning seem to drain from me as I take the stone stairs up to the porch. I practically aced the test. I can't believe it. I didn't actually think I'd do well enough to even consider putting in my application anywhere. I never did well in school, so why would I? A hint of a smile tries to pull my lips up, but then I hear the gentle creak of the rusty porch swing. It lingers in the quiet air like the memories do. *Grandma would have been so proud.*

This place will always have memories around every corner and in every crevice, even if it's lifeless. Lacking everything it held when I was a kid. The dark and the quiet are reminders of everything that's gone. Everything that will never come back.

My eyes are on the ground while I walk, which is why I'm so shocked when I reach up to put the key in the door, only to find it already open.

The wooden frame is splintered. Confusion hits me first. I haven't even put the key in yet.

Thump.

The lock is still turned; I can see the hunk of metal as the door brushes open with the slight touch of my hand. Gasping, I try to stay calm, but I don't see how I can as the reality registers.

Thump.

The shoe print on the door is black against the white door. Someone kicked in the door.

"Fuck," I say and the curse leaves my lips in a whisper.

I'm half a step back, feeling the racing need to run take over when I smell smoke.

And then I see the bright red and orange flames beyond the cracked frame.

It's on fire. My grandma's house is on fire. No! God, no!

"Help!" I scream, gripping the keys so hard in my hand it feels like they've broken my skin.

My hands are shaking as I fumble in my purse. My keys drop harshly onto the concrete porch. Then something else, maybe my sunglasses; I don't know and I don't care.

I just need my phone.

I'm still shaking when I finally find it. Struggling with both hands to grip it and dial 9-1-1, I drop my purse and stand there on weak legs as I stare straight ahead, watching the bright red expand alongside billowing white and gray smoke. The hallway is clear, telling me it's the kitchen. The kitchen is on fire. The flames are high, almost to the ceiling. It's too far gone. *No, no, please tell me this is a nightmare.*

The operator is cool, calm and professional. Whatever he sounds like, I'm the opposite. Tears prick my eyes and my voice cracks as I tell him the address and that my house is on fire. Tell isn't the right word; maybe scream or cry would be better to describe it. My mind is a whirlwind, my lungs fail me and so does any form of common sense. He's asking me questions, asking if I'm safe and away from the fire.

He's going to tell me to step back. To get far away and keep my distance until help comes.

His voice comes through clear from the other end and I'm right.

I've never been one to just step back. Even with my blurred vision, I can see the fire is raging. But what if whoever broke in is still in there? What if I could find this bastard?

The phone drops in a swift motion, landing at my feet. A door slams open to my right, Mr. Timms's house, as I take a step into Grandma's.

"There's smoke from the back of your house!" Mr. Timms yells at me. I barely even hear him, although I recognize his ever-harsh tone. I sure as shit don't respond as I push open the door, feeling the wave of heat surround me instantly. I have to cover my mouth and nose with the crook of my arm.

The vise around my heart tightens as I walk quickly to the living room on the left. My coughing is involuntary as I pull open the coffee table drawer and take out a gun. The metal shines with the flick of flames as I get closer to the kitchen.

There's no chance whoever started this fire is still here. It's a raging storm of heat and flames at the back of the house. There's so much smoke; how long has it been going?

The sirens swarm from outside, but there's so much damage. Too much.

I can't even get to the bathroom, or the kitchen sink. My sobs are impossible to contain as I watch the destruction overwhelm this old house where I grew up.

A sound that resonates like the crack of a whip forces me to scream. Mr. Timms yells something from outside. He's closer now, yelling at me or the fire trucks. He sounds frantic but all I can hear is the sound of my home being burned to the ground as I watch.

I hear a crack, a snap and then a loud bang as the fire seems to grow along the wall like a vine. The pictures slam to the floor, leaving the shattered glass to skitter across the hardwood. I scream, covering my mouth as I stare in disbelief. A younger version of myself seated in my father's lap is slowly charred, lit aflame, and engulfed.

"The pictures," I say as my hands shake and I make a move to gather the ones closest to me and farthest away from the kitchen. Slipping the gun in the waistband at the back of my jeans, I feel the cold metal graze against my skin. With both hands up in the air, the smoke violates my lungs.

The first cough makes me heave in air, but the air is thick with soot and I collapse to the floor. I'm light-headed, taking in quick short pants, but I can breathe at least.

"Laura!" Seth's voice cuts through it all, like a bright light on the darkest of nights.

My neck cranes back to see him in the doorway. "Laura!" he screams louder as he runs into the house, his arm covering his face.

"Seth!" I scream as loud as I can and crawl to him, keeping my body low on the ground.

He breathes my name so softly when his eyes reach mine, I don't know how I heard it. Maybe it was the ghost of a memory filling in that actuality.

His movements are effortless as his arm wraps around my waist. I can hear my plea for the pictures at the back of my throat. I even reach for them, but Seth is strong, and the moment is hopeless. I'm so lightheaded more than anything. It makes me weak.

I don't have a single picture of my father. I don't have any pictures of my grandmother.

They're all in this house.

The vision blurs in front of me as my skin feels cold and my head light. Outside is brighter than it's been this late. Everyone's porch light is on and everyone's watching. When my ass hits the hood of Seth's car, parked recklessly in Mr. Timms's front yard, I see how large the flames have gotten, how the house is completely engulfed. Maybe whoever did it had just been here.

I could have saved it all, if only I'd been here earlier.

Seth's hands are on me and he's talking, he's shaking me, but I can't stop crying. I can't stop this trembling.

I've never felt like it was all gone until this moment. It may have been empty, but it was still here. It held so much of me. Now what do I have?

My breathing is ragged as Seth pulls me into his hard chest. I feel him stroking my hair as I try to calm myself. Drying my eyes on his shirt, I watch as the hoses are pulled. I can smell the singe of burned wood as the flames rage against the downpour of water.

The firefighters are barking out orders nonstop. So much is going on that I can't focus; people talking, people looking at me, crowds gathered to watch my childhood home burning to nothing.

"Shhh," Seth soothes me. I close my eyes and listen to his heartbeat. I hear him shush me over everything else.

A paramedic is at our side too soon. I don't want to go; I don't want to leave, but Seth makes me.

I have to grab his wrist, holding it too tightly. "Someone broke in," I tell him, feeling my dry lips crack as I do. I stare into his dark eyes. They widen, a sense of recognition taking over. Carefully slipping my gun to him, hiding it under his jacket, I tell him before the medic returns to take me away, "Someone did this on purpose. Someone burned it all down." It's only when I'm in the ambulance with an oxygen mask over my face that I remember the black sedan. One and seven. I want to text Seth, but I don't have anything. Not my purse. Not my phone.

I refuse to forget. Someone might have seen whoever it was. Whoever it was may have taken everything from me. Whoever it was, is a dead man.

CHAPTER 13

Seth

MY SKIN IS ICE COLD BUT EVERYTHING INSIDE OF ME IS ON FIRE. A raging fire hotter and more violent than the one at my back. I can feel the heat, smell the burned wood, and it means nothing. The chaos has everyone's full attention, but it means nothing to me.

Someone did this.

They tried to hurt her. They tried to send a message.

Mathews is the only one I can think of. But why go after Laura?

The heavy doors to the ambulance close one at a time and the sound of them shutting, removing her from my vision snaps my gaze to the EMT.

"You can't ride with her, but she'll be the top priority in the emergency room. We already called it in."

You must be family. That's what the guy said to me when they ripped her away.

There are only two things keeping me from chasing down the ambulance and staying on its tail as they take her to the hospital.

The first is that Charlie said she's okay and that she'll be all right. It's just smoke inhalation they're concerned about. More importantly, he said he'll stay by her side until I'm there. I've known Charlie for years; he works with us on and off the clock. No one's getting near her room and Roman is already on his way to the hospital.

The second is that Jackson is in plain view when the ambulance leaves.

Dressed in his finest blues, his badge is on clear display and it reflects the light from behind us. It's waning as the water subdues the fire. I'll deal with Jackson first, and then I'm not leaving her side.

"Mr. King," he calls out and I huff in irritation. His footsteps are even and grow louder as he makes his way to me.

"Since when am I Mr. King to you?" I ask him when he stops in front of me, although my voice is lifeless, not hiding a damn thing I'm feeling.

The agony is something I didn't expect. It fucking hurts. The anger is better. Seeing her on a gurney in the back of an ambulance tears me up inside.

"I did this to her," I tell him, knowing exactly what I'm doing. I don't have many friends outside of my crew, but I need Jackson. I need all the help I can get.

Surprise colors his expression before he responds. He clears his throat and glances to his left and then right. "It was arson," he tells me as if I didn't know. A fire this large, this fast, there had to be an accelerant. Even if Laura hadn't told me, it doesn't take a genius to know.

"I figured as much," I tell him, looking coldly into his eyes at the thought of someone breaking into Laura's house.

"There were explosives too, Seth."

His lowered voice and this knowledge make my blood go cold. "They didn't go off. Duds I guess, but if they had, it would have blown up most of the block."

Leaning forward he asks, "You know who did it?"

I shake my head, trying to swallow the overwhelming feelings that make it hard to stand up right now as I say, "But I have suspects."

He tried to kill her. He tried to kill Laura. I can barely breathe.

Jackson's eyes read, *I told you so*, but he's a friend not to say it out loud and grind the heel of his shoe deeper into the pain and regret.

"I can't believe he'd go after a woman." *My woman.* "Fucking coward," I spit.

Breathing out, Jackson watches the fire behind me for a moment before telling me, "It's a good thing you got in there and dragged her out."

"Yeah," I answer him in a breath and turn to watch the blaze, but I can't do it. It almost took her away from me.

All I keep thinking as my muscles tighten to the point where I'm trembling is, *Mathews is a dead man. All of his men are dead. Anything he's ever touched, is dead.*

Rage is an adulteress. She comes at my weakest times, like now. Seeing the fire play on the metal of the police car, I imagine what I'll do to Mathews. It had to be him. He'll die a slow death. The rat, Wright? He can die slow too. Everyone who had a part. They will all suffer.

"Was she here when it happened?" Jackson asks with a careful tone, like what he's asking might make me snap. I shake my head no, remembering the little bits I've heard from Mr. Timms giving his statement as I held Laura.

"She came home and saw the fire, and ran in."

Jackson blows out a grunt. "Of course she did." His comment forces the faintest of laughs from me. *She's safe. She'll be all right. She's safe.* Just then I get a text from Roman. He's at the hospital now and ensuring Laura gets a private room.

Good. *Stay with her*, I tell him but he already knows.

"What are you going to do?" Jackson's question resonates with me. It's what I've done that's led to this.

"What do you think?" My answer is spoken darkly. He holds my gaze, taking it in with the seriousness it deserves. "If you have any insight to offer, now's the time," I prod when he doesn't respond.

"If I did, I'd tell you. Are you sure it's Mathews?" he asks me and a list of names runs through my mind, the many faces I've seen who hold nothing but contempt for me.

"No," I answer truthfully.

Jackson seems to consider something, but he only says, "If I hear anything, you'll be the first to know."

"I appreciate it."

He nods solemnly and stares past me. The night sky is darker than it was moments ago, and the streets are emptying out. Mr. Timms is seated on his porch, staring between the wreckage and me. My hard gaze doesn't deter him. The old man knows how this life works.

He knows this happened to her because of me. Everyone knows that.

"She's going to have to file a report," Jackson tells me and I nod in agreement.

"I'll tell her," I say although he looks anything but reassured.

"Do you have a statement to give?"

"No. I have to get to the hospital. To make sure she's okay," I tell him when I hear the sound of tires coming up behind us a little too fast. Both of our hands reach for guns, both of us on edge. Derrick's car screeches to a halt and Jackson and I both visibly relax when we see him get out and slam his door. It feels like war all over again, because that's what this is. An act of war.

"You do that." Jackson's already walking off, heading over to the fire truck when I call after him, "Thanks."

We may be on opposite sides of some things, but there's a loyalty between us that hasn't faded. Not yet. I imagine one day it will. All that will be left are the ashes of what used to be.

It seems like there's a lot of that going around.

"Yo." Derrick is at my side and out of breath before Jackson's even across the street. It's so dark now, I know he won't be able to see how bad it is. Not until morning.

"Is she okay?"

"We have to go to the hospital," I tell him and make my way to my car. My throat's tight and my jaw clenched as we walk past the last few onlookers.

"We see her, get her home, and then we have business to attend to." Feeling his eyes on me, I turn to look at him. A chill sweeps across my back, blowing the cold down my spine as I lower my voice. "We're killing Wright tonight, but first we need information. We need to know what he's been telling people and if this is Mathews's doing."

"Fuck." Derrick's response is accompanied by a mix between a groan and a snarl. With both hands running over his buzzed head he turns to look at Laura's old house. I watch it sink in. The disbelief, the outrage and then the guilt.

He swallows hard and looks down at the asphalt before looking back at me.

"We get her safe and then we settle this."

"Wright will be easy. If this is because of Mathews…" I trail off and shake my head, knowing that's a fight I'll need heavy backup for.

"We have Fletcher," he reminds me as I open my car door. "And cash to buy men who don't have a dog in this fight."

Looking between him and the rest of the scattered crowd, I wonder how easy it's going to be to get to Mathews. To get revenge and ensure it doesn't happen again.

"I know we have men and the arms to do it," I finally respond and meet his gaze. "I just want it for myself. I want to kill this prick myself."

CHAPTER 14

Laura

Seventeen. I keep thinking about the number and checking every plate that drives by the Club as I sit here in the front corner booth. I swear the worn amber leather smells like smoke. Everything smells like smoke still. Even after I washed up and put on clothes that had been tucked in drawers at Seth's house for a year now.

All I smell is smoke.

Another car rides by and it's not black, it's a dark red SUV, but I still check its plate. I've been doing this all day. I don't need to find its owner though, not if what Derrick said in the hospital is true. Still, I watch, I check. I'm on guard and trapped here in this booth.

Seth doesn't want me to leave the Club; I think he's having Roman keep an eye on me.

I'll be better when they find that car. I remember that feeling I had. Why didn't I listen to it? Gut instincts happen for a reason. That air of danger was meant to warn me. I know it deep down. And yet, I couldn't even remember more than two numbers. It's okay though, if what Derrick said is right.

Cami's voice jostles me from my thoughts about last night. "Hey, you good?"

"Yeah," I answer her as quickly as I can. I have to clear my throat and take a drink of the Sprite she set down in front of me.

"Ugh," I groan and nearly spit it out, not expecting the strong taste of vodka. With the back of my hand over my mouth, I barely keep it down.

"I thought you liked vodka?"

"You spiked it?"

"You need a drink," she says, emphasizing the word *need* before sitting down next to me. The seat groans and I watch another car go by. It's black this time, but another SUV and not a sedan. Still, my heart starts to race, pounding against my rib cage. I want them to find whoever it was so I can stop worrying that he'll come back. That's what it comes down to. I fucking hate this feeling that claws at me.

"I know you're shaken up," Cami says, trying to soothe me. She has no idea. I have no intention of telling her that it wasn't an accident. She doesn't need that worry in her life. But I wish I had my friend to confide in.

As she consoles me, telling me the insurance company will pay out and how she's certain some things will be able to be recovered from the house, I wonder if this is what Seth feels like when I try to talk to him after a hard day. Her hand lands on my knee under the table and she looks at me with wide, innocent eyes. "It's going to be okay," she tells me like she means it. Like she knows for sure it will.

I've heard it so many times. *It's going to be okay*. It never is.

"I hope so," I answer her weakly.

She pats my knee, giving me a sweet smile.

"You *know* it will," she says with a raised brow, and a look on her face that says, *we're choosing to be positive.*

In this moment, I almost want to tell her the truth just so I can see that look fall.

I want to tell her how I told Seth about the black sedan and how Derrick knew right away who it belonged to, or at least he thinks he does. I want to tell her all this shit happened because of the men we love. Dumb for dick. It's a saying Cami has when certain women come into this bar. We are dumb for dick.

That would take that smile right off Cami's face and wake her up about who she's dating.

All the snide thoughts ping-pong around my head and I know they're only there because I bit my tongue when Seth leaned down to kiss me before he left. I didn't have the words to give him last night. I felt it all bottled up, but nothing would come. This morning though, I'm full of plenty of words. They aren't meant for Cami though.

"Right," I tell her, forcing a smile to my face. "I know everything will be okay," I lie to her.

She grabs the edge of the open textbook on the table, dragging it to face her so she can read it.

"I'm not sure you're going to get much enjoyment from *Physiological Integrity* by—" I say as I grab the book so I can lift it up and peek at the spine of the textbook.

"I don't even know how to pronounce the first word," Cami says, cutting me off and then she laughs. It's contagious so I end up laughing too, for the first time today. She glances at the papers in front of me.

"Applications," I say, answering her unspoken question. "I got a really good score on that practice test I took so I'm applying. I'm really going to do it. I think I have a good shot at getting into a lot of good schools."

"Oh." Just like that, her happiness vanishes. "Where are you going?" she asks and her hands find her lap. She picks at her thumbnail—a nervous habit she's had for as long as I've known her.

"Not far," I reassure her.

"Right," she says and nods her head with her eyes closed and that simper reappears. "Seth wouldn't want you to go very far." With her worries eased, I add another to mine.

The school I want to attend, one I thought I'd never be able to get into, is across the country. *Maybe I could just leave for a little while.* The voice in my head is small and hesitant. *Just a little while, just to get some distance.*

"Hey." Cami's voice brings me back to the moment. "It's going to be all right," she says, encouraging me.

"I know," I answer her and snag my pen as if I'm going to fill out these applications. I've been staring at them all day and I can't bring myself to do it. I lie to her again, but it feels easier this time because I picture Seth telling me the same, like he has so many times, "It'll be all right."

I've never thought of myself as strong. Never.

I grew up surrounded by men with guns. Men who made threats and made jokes about women who looked like me. Jokes about how easy women were. My father would tell me that all men were pigs but him.

He was a pig too, though.

I suppose it didn't bother me that I wasn't a strong woman until tonight. Until I'm here sitting cross-legged on the floor of Seth's living room, sunk into the deep blue rug I picked out for him, staring at cardboard boxes filled with my few remaining possessions that weren't destroyed by the fire or the water damage.

"We can get the smell out," Seth tells me from the kitchen. I listen to him open the fridge and get a beer. It's followed by the sound of a drink being poured and I figure that one's for me.

The words I've been thinking all day are stuck somewhere deep down my throat. Like I've swallowed them, even though inside I'm begging for them to come up. He needs to hear exactly what I'm thinking.

He needs to know.

I have to stare at the large black imprint on the cardboard box to say it. It comes out all wonky, like it's scratched its way up. "I want you to get out of the business."

"What?" I hear him reply from the kitchen and close my eyes. I feel lighter already having gotten that off my chest. Even if I know exactly how he'll respond.

"You need to get out." My voice is louder this time, stronger, and for a moment I question if I was really so weak. Until I see him.

Seth makes me weak.

"Get out?" he questions but it doesn't sound like it. His expression is emotionless at best, and disapproval riddles his gaze.

He hands me the drink he made. Smells like Sprite, and I imagine there's vodka swirling in it alongside the ice cubes. He knows it's my favorite, which makes this conversation hurt all the more.

I can't say it again, not while he's looking at me like that. It feels like my chest is hollowed out. Like my own damn heart abandoned me. My throat's dry when I try to explain, but still nothing comes. Yeah, I was never a strong woman.

"You want me to get out of the life," he says, repeating my words back to me with no emotion behind them and then stares straight ahead, still standing while I'm seated. His gaze is on the blank TV screen that's hanging on the wall when he takes a drink of his beer. "It's not like that, Babygirl."

"Then what is it like?" I ask him, listening to the ice clink against the glass and taking a heavy gulp and then another. There isn't enough alcohol on the West Coast to save me from this moment.

Seth's quiet and so I lift my gaze to his. "Because I don't like the way it feels anymore. I don't think—"

"You knew," he says, cutting me off, and his tone is accusatory. It's what he always goes to. I knew he was in the life when I started seeing him. I did. I admit that. Times were different then. It was kill or be killed. There was no in-between. I fell in love; how could I not? I'm not the strong one. I was never the strong one.

The bottom of his beer clinks down hard on the coffee table. The cords in his neck tighten as he swallows and looks down at me. He opens his mouth, but he doesn't have any more words for me.

It hurts so fucking much. "I love you," are the only words I can whisper. That's what it always comes down to for me.

And so it's a stalemate, but I can't face a stalemate anymore. I'll take the hit. I'm terrified, but I'm trying to be strong.

Dropping down to his knees, he cups my jaw in his hand. I don't even realize my bottom lip is trembling until his thumb is there, running over it, caressing me and gentling the pain that keeps me from looking into his eyes.

"I'm sorry," I whisper and he whispers back, "Don't be. There's nothing to be sorry about."

He doesn't get it. He doesn't understand and I can't say it.

It's this life or me.

I can't say it because it's wrong. I can't. I can't do it.

The first kiss is gentle, caressing. I'm eager for it, but when he deepens it, I pull back, covering my hunger for him with my hand over my mouth. Bracing myself on my left hand, I lean backward and dare to meet his gaze.

A raw desire, coupled with a primitive agony, stares back at me. I swear I must have known this man in another life. He was made for me and I for him, but I don't want this life.

"I can't live like this." I don't know how I manage to speak, each word dangling there between us like easily broken threads. "I want you to get out of it," I repeat. "I need you to."

Seth takes a moment, watching me, considering my words before standing up and turning his back to me.

He's silent as he heads to the kitchen and I continue watching him from where I am. I watch him finish the beer and then grab his keys from the blue bowl.

"Don't go," I say. The next words rush out of me. "I need you." How selfish I feel in this moment is almost unbearable. Especially when he turns to look at me again.

He raises the hand holding the keys in the air, to point at me. "And I need you," he says like it's a confession that will bury him.

"Don't leave, Seth. Please, we can talk this out."

A smile akin to a sick joke graces his face but it quickly disappears. "There isn't much talking that can change our situation, Babygirl."

Hopelessness is all I can hear in his tone. He can't be the hopeless one. I cover my face with both hands, feeling an onslaught of emotions. Tears prick but I don't let them come.

Be strong, Babygirl. I hear Seth's voice in my head. Even at my lowest moments, the memory of him is there. It will kill me to lose him. It will kill me to stay.

My shoulders are shaking as I rock myself. I've never felt like this. This misery that feels so much worse than mourning. It's worse because I have control over it. I can make it stop. I can just say the right words. I can pretend it's okay. I can stay here with him and pretend I don't feel this ominous sense of dread. That I'm not constantly scared for not just me but him too.

The keys slam down on the counter and within a split second, Seth's strong chest is pressed to my back. His arms are around me. He rocks me until I've stopped. It's easy to calm down when he's here. His smell, his voice. The way he loves me even if he doesn't say it.

I have nothing without him. I have absolutely nothing. I cling to him.

"It's okay," he tells me and even with all the misery I want to believe him.

"I have nothing left," I finally speak.

"I need you to leave because I'm terrified," I confess to him. "Bad things happen here. I don't have control over any of it." My words make him pull back, breaking his hold on me.

He doesn't say anything for a long time. I grab the cocktail he made me and practically chug it. It does nothing. There is no relief from this whatsoever.

"You need time—"

"No," I say, shaking my head and cutting him off before he's finished.

"You need time for me to show you it's okay. You need time because it's been a rough few years."

"It can get rougher," I speak without thinking. It's the truth though, and the look in his eyes tells me he knows. He's all too aware. I rest my cheek on the sofa, thinking maybe I've been like Cami all the time we've been together, and I've just now crossed to the other side.

I'm not strong enough for this side of things. I wish I were, but I'm nothing compared to him. He should know that. It's easy to see.

"Hey, come here," he says and his voice is gentle. He's always soft with me. This strong man with rough edges and a past that would frighten most… his tone caresses me. I can't help it. I'm drawn to him like a moth to a flame.

I crawl over to him, settling down in his lap. He's so tall and his shoulders are so much wider than me that it feels perfect here. He's warm, and when I lay my cheek against his shoulder, peeking up at him and wondering why he picked me, he kisses me. Stopping my questioning, stopping the pain. It's all replaced by an immediate spike of heat. An immediate desire.

Does he feel it too? How it soothes every inch of me. How that lust turns to wildfire in my blood and nothing stands a chance in its path. With his fingers at my chin, he keeps me still while he breaks the kiss. When I open my eyes, feeling the forgotten beads of moisture in my lashes, he's there, staring at me. His light blue eyes shine with devotion. It's real. I know it's real.

His cadence is rough when he says, "Let me make you feel better."

"We have to talk about this," I tell him as if it's a demand, but I'm begging him. "I lost everything."

"I'm sorry," he says, rushing the words out. "I will make it up to you, but you can't leave and neither can I." The resolution in his tone forces me to bury my face in the crook of his neck. I know I won't be okay either way.

His whisper, his touch, and the air around us are all I have to stay whole. "Let me make you feel better."

CHAPTER 15

Seth

W*hat about the chair in the living room?* I text Derrick and wait. All I can hear is the sound my foot was making earlier. The tapping on the leg of the steel chair as I stared at Wright's body.

Four hours of digging for information with Connor's blade, and he swore he didn't tell Mathews. He screamed it, he begged for us to believe him. But I didn't. Hours later, at home in the kitchen, my foot's motionless but the anxiousness is still there.

The black sedan doesn't belong to one of Mathews's men, it belongs to one of Fletcher's.

I don't want to believe it. More than that, I still don't believe Wright, not even his dying words.

I don't know. It's in rough shape. It takes me a moment to remember what Derrick's talking about. Right, the wreckage from the fire.

Try to save it, I text back and inhale as deeply as I can. I can't even salvage a fucking chair, let alone this fucked-up situation.

If Wright didn't tell Mathews, and it was Fletcher…

Are you ready?

Ready to find out if Fletcher double-crossed me. *Yeah,* I message him, *I'm ready*.

How is she? he messages before I've even set my phone down. The whole crew knows; they all know someone wanted Laura dead.

We assumed it was Mathews, but thinking it might be Fletcher… fuck, that means we have no one to back us up. Leroy won't go after Fletcher. We can't trust Mathews.

Derrick's the only one who knows we're not okay. I lean forward on the counter, my forearm brushing the beer, which is now warm and still full. I can't move from this spot. I can't do it.

She was trying to leave me last night. She's never done that before.

I could see it in her eyes that I'm losing her, so I lie to him, *I can keep her; she's just going through shit right now.*

To my right, I picture her there, sitting on the rug and looking up at me with goodbye in her eyes and I lose it. Tears pricking at the back of my eyes, I slam my fist down on the counter.

She loves you.

Derrick's message means so little. She does love me, and I thought I could keep her forever because of it. But love isn't that easy. It's not that strong either.

I lay with her in bed until she fell asleep, and then I took out all that pain and rage on Wright. He didn't feel enough of it though. Even with his dying breath, he didn't feel loss like I was feeling.

Maybe Fletcher's henchman will feel it. Luke Hartley. The owner of the black Audi with license plate number 175632. The fucker who took off. Something tells me I'm not going to believe him either. It'll be more than four hours though. It's going to take more than four hours to make him feel this pain that's inside of me right now.

Leroy's guy said 220.

Derrick's text forces me to move to the bedroom. Every step is careful and quiet and I don't look to my right as I pass the living room. I swear the ghost of last night is there, watching me.

Two hundred and twenty thousand for him to send up four men in case we need them to go after Fletcher. The code to the safe is our anniversary date. It's three days and one year after the shit at Hammers went down. It took me that long to get her to love me enough to give in.

I only get the first two numbers punched in before I rest my forehead on the safe, feeling the cool metal against my hot skin.

Derrick texts something else, probably asking if he should tell Leroy's guy it's a go or not. I have to enter in the rest of the code and check the tally inside. There's a pad of paper I use to track it all.

It'll be close and it'll slow down business, but we can manage.

I text him confirming it's a go, and that I'm on my way before slamming the safe door shut and getting out of this house as fast as I can.

When I start the car, I sit there for a moment, staring at the damn house I had built in the middle of nowhere to protect us. She would have been safe here. If she'd listened to me. I need to remember to tell her that. I can convince her.

If she'd listened and moved in with me by now, she'd have been safe. I should have made her move in. I should have told her she needed to let go sooner.

Fuck, it's my fault. It's all my fault.

A series of pings comes through on my phone, and I have to calm myself down, shaking off this regret, this feeling like I'm losing her to read what Derrick's telling me.

They've got Luke, but more importantly, Fletcher's warehouse was broken into, their stash stolen.

Mathews? I question him. Mathews went after Fletcher? Mathews thinks Fletcher is the one who screwed him over.

Derrick's reply back sends a chill down my spine.

I don't know, but Fletcher thinks it was us.

CHAPTER 16

Laura

Dr. June's been off during the procedures. I've been here for at least two hours, subjected to stress tests and being poked and prodded.

No black dress and heels today for the doctor. She's wearing the sneakers I'd wear as a nurse, which I find ironic.

"Everything okay?" I ask her as she looks at my chart. She entered the room at least a minute ago and didn't even say anything to me. She's just looking at the results of all the tests.

"Fine," she says then gives me a tight smile and returns to the clipboard.

I don't really feel fine. There's nothing that's fine. The way she's been makes me think something is very, very wrong.

In most cases, medication is all that's required to manage arrhythmia. But then there are the more severe cases.

I channel my inner Cami, wishing she were here. We're going to be positive, I tell myself. Dr. June just got dumped is all. Yeah, that makes me feel better. *When did I get this bitter?*

"You didn't bring anyone?"

I stare back at Dr. June when she sighs heavily and lowers the clipboard to the metal cart to her right.

"Forgot to ask," I lie to her. She doesn't need to know that Cami stood me up. That little tidbit makes me feel a little more lonely. I've realized I don't like being lonely.

"I'm going to prescribe you a medication," Dr. June tells me before pulling out a pad of paper from the back of the clipboard. I watch as she scribbles out a prescription. "You can have it filled at any pharmacy. Make sure you take it daily," she drones on, like she's reading from a script.

I interrupt her telling me about possible side effects to ask, "So everything's fine?"

"Well, you have an irregular heartbeat, but it's treatable with a calcium blocker. Your heart itself is in good condition, which is a great sign. The arrhythmia is virtually harmless, but this medicine will do the trick to keep it beating normally."

"Medicine to keep your heart beating normally," I echo and I can't help it when my eyes water.

"Yeah." The doctor finally shows some emotion as she says, "We should all have access to it, shouldn't we?" Her sad joke mirrors the look of despair I've been feeling from her for the past two hours.

"That's a joke." She quickly corrects herself and gathers the clipboard as she stands. As if I didn't get it.

"I know," I tell her solemnly. I'm such a weirdo, I want to stand up and hug this woman. A woman I know nothing about. A woman I've been inwardly bitter toward. Am I really that lonely?

"This is for you." Handing me the script, she tells me how I can exit the office once I've changed out of my patient gown. She's back to her robotic self with a fake smile as her parting gift.

I accept it and tell her I hope she has a great day. Everyone says that, but I do mean it. I hope she can at least feel that I mean it.

When she's gone, I sit back on the crinkled paper and stare at the prescription before getting dressed. Pills to keep my heart going. I'm going to really need these.

Checking my phone, I see Cami hasn't answered. It's so not like her. She told me she'd come. Regardless, I let her know that I'm all right. I haven't told her about last night yet. Maybe she already knows, maybe Seth told Derrick and Derrick told her.

My face crumples as I lean forward, as does the fucking paper under my ass. It mocks me, and oddly enough, I'm fine with it.

I deserve to be mocked. How did I really think this was going to end?

I text Cami again, telling her I really need her and that I have to tell her something. All the while I get dressed, I watch my phone, waiting for the buzz or for it light up. Anything.

But I get nothing.

Even as I'm driving, I expect her to say something. I convince myself her phone is broken and when I do that, I feel slightly better. Nothing compared to the relief I feel when I see her car in Seth's driveway.

Oh thank God, I think and breathe out in relief. She's been waiting for me to get back. I knew it, I knew her phone was just broken or something.

I haven't parked a car this fast in a long damn time. Gathering my purse, I climb out and prepare to tell her everything. She needs wine for this and I need vodka.

Maybe we should go out first and get enough booze to last us through this.

Even as I'm coming up to the door, I think I already know what she's going to tell me and it calms the deepest part of me.

You love him. I can hear her voice over the sound of the keys. She locked the door. Of course she did, she's in there all alone. I have to fiddle with the lock to get the door open, and through the clang of metal, I hear her tell me that I love him and that love will find a way.

She's told me before. *So long as you choose love, it will all work out.*

Breathing out at the door, rocking the key out of the lock, I let her unspoken words sink in. She's right. I just need her to remind me. And I need Seth because I love him.

It will all be okay.

I center myself for the first time since the fire two nights ago. I have to laugh a little as I push open the door and speak loud enough for her to hear me in the living room. "I didn't even need the pep talk; you've given me so many, I can hear your voice in my head."

My smile fades when I don't see her in the living room. She's not in her usual spot. We each have a spot.

I turn on the light in the hallway, and even though the light's off in the bathroom, I still check for her there. "Cami?" I call out, and she doesn't answer.

That gut feeling, that instinct of danger I felt two nights ago? It's back. It's chilling. "Cami?" I call out louder as I head for my bedroom door.

Why would she be in there? *Maybe she had to sleep. She's only sleeping*, I lie to myself. I know it's a lie. I'm so aware of it before I hear the creak of the bedroom door opening.

Sobs hit me hard and fast as I fall to the floor on my knees.

"Cami," I whisper her name and reach toward her. "No, Cami."

She's so cold. She's so cold.

Years ago

Everyone in this cafeteria is somehow both staring at me and not looking at me at all. Everyone except Seth and his friends. They're two tables over, sitting at the one closest to the doors, and when I look up they don't mind that my eyes catch theirs every once in a while, but everyone else immediately looks away.

They all know what happened two weeks ago and what happened this past weekend. Shit, the bruise on my cheek is still there although it's an ugly green and I can't stop crying every ten minutes. Just as I'm reaching up to touch the bruise, as if I'll be able to tell if the makeup is still covering it or not, Cami sits next to me.

Our table is empty except for the two of us, so when her tray hits the table and she climbs into the cheap benches our high school bought, the whole thing jostles.

I imagine I'm looking at her just like everyone else is looking at me. Slack-jawed. None of my so-called friends sit by me anymore. She did though.

"I'm sorry I wasn't here after the accident," she tells me as she cracks open a soda. "Are you doing okay?"

I'm still staring at her when she turns in her seat, tucking her right foot under her and then squares her shoulders. "I feel like a shit friend; I just found out on the way down here."

I don't say anything. She's talking about my dad and the accident. I don't want to cry. Not when everyone has such a good view of the spectacle I am.

"You want to get out of here? You want to yell? You want to cry?"

"No," I finally answer her and stare down at my tray. There's only an apple and a cold slice of pizza. I don't want to eat. Everything has changed and nothing's all right.

"What can I do?" Cami asks me and it's the first time anyone's asked me that. Seth tells me what to do, he has for over two weeks now and I appreciate it some moments, but I need time to myself, time to process.

Other than him and his crew, no one else asks me anything. They don't talk to me. It's like they're suddenly afraid of me.

Cami reaches her arms around me. It takes me a moment to realize she's hugging me. That's the moment I realize how big her boobs are and the thought actually makes me laugh a little on the inside.

"What the hell is wrong with me?"

I don't realize I've said it out loud until Cami shakes her head, her long blonde hair swishing around her shoulders. "Not a damn thing," she tells me and spears her fork through a grape. She eats them all like that, with a fork.

It's quiet for a moment, but Cami keeps trying to make small talk, keeps hinting at asking whether I need something or if I'm all right. She asks me if she should just shut up and I tell her no.

"Whatever you do, please don't stop talking. I need to talk about something."

"Anything?" she asks and her gaze drifts to the crew of guys we were both once afraid of.

"Almost anything," I correct her and a hint of a smile graces her lips. Again, this sad laugh comes over me, but this time the sound is heard.

"You're going to be okay," she tells me. "I love you."

It's the first time she's told me that. Everything about her makes me think I've found my friend soul mate.

"I'm happy you're here," I tell her with sincerity and then smile and say "I love you" back.

I have a moment to sniffle and get a grip while she takes a large bite of her pizza.

"You ever wish you could just pick up and leave?" I ask her. It's all I've been thinking about for the last three days. I can't though. Grandma needs me now more than ever.

Cami eyes one of Seth's friends, I think his name is Derrick. Then she licks a bit of sauce from her lip and tells me yeah, she has. "Everyone wishes they could leave and start over sometimes."

There's so much comfort in what she says. "Where would you go?" she asks and then takes a bite. She covers her mouth, still chewing when she tells me enthusiastically, "I know where I'd go."

"Where?" I question her and she finishes her bite and washes it down with her drink before telling me with the widest smile, "I'd love to go to Paris."

"The city of love," I breathe out and pick up my apple. As I'm taking a bite, she tells me how her uncle went and brought back a pop-up picture book for her when she was a kid. "It's my favorite; I still have it. Paris Up, Up and Away.*"*

"When you go—"

"I'm taking you with me," she declares, cutting me off then continues eating, like I should have known better. I should have known we'd go together.

"I'd love to go to Paris," I tell her weakly before the tears fall again and this time I don't know why. I was doing so good.

Cami holds me tight and when she sees someone staring, she tells them to fuck off.

We never went to Paris. She has to go to Paris.

"Cami, you have to wake up. Cami, wake up."

CHAPTER 17

Seth

"THE CAR WAS PARKED OUT FRONT," DERRICK EXPLAINS AS I DRAG the metal chair across the concrete floor. The basement of Club Allure has seen more blood in the last two nights than I ever intended. We make do with what we have though.

"It was him. He's saying something different though," Connor informs me as I sit across from Mr. Hartley.

I let my head loll to the right as I take in the knots at his wrist. "He's been fighting it, looks like." The coarse rope has left dark pink marks around his wrist. There's a hint of blood on the loose threads too.

"Had to tie his chest to the chair too. Wrists and ankles weren't doing it," Connor tells me, his gaze steady on our unwelcome guest. The rope is wrapped twice across his chest. "He kept falling over."

"Is that what caused the gash on his head? Or did you two start the party without me?"

Roman's out front, keeping an eye out. The four of us, Derrick, Connor, this Luke fuck, and myself, are the only people within four miles of Linel Centers.

"Seth," Derrick says then scoots his chair forward and I glance at him but I have to do a double take. The way his forehead is creased, his lips pressed in a firm line and his eyes reflecting doubt… I don't like it. I don't like it at all.

Connor steps forward, ripping the rag out of Luke's mouth. Luke's body heaves forward as he sucks in air in between coughs.

I share a look with Derrick then one with Connor, both of them chilling me to the bone. Derrick nods his head at the man in the chair, whose gaze is focused on the floor. "Listen," he mouths to me. My muscles ache to let out the rage. It takes everything I have just to stay in my seat.

"You'll never get away with it," Luke says, threatening us the moment he's able to speak. His cadence is rough and from the split lip and gash in his head, I can guarantee he's hurting.

"The threats always come first," I tell Luke, speaking lowly, but I sit back in my chair, listening to the ranting man.

I crack my knuckles one by one, waiting.

Luke's head raises slowly and his brown eyes find mine, the hate firmly in place. "First the warehouse, then me? Fletcher will never let you get away with it."

"We didn't hit the warehouse."

"I didn't hurt Laura," Luke spits out immediately after my admission. He said her name. I can't sit here and listen to this man say her name and get away with it. The steel chair I'm sitting on is practically nothing, flying backward as I lunge forward. The skin on my knuckles stretches tight and nearly splits as I land a blow on Luke's jaw, screaming at him, "You don't get to say her name."

His chair falls backward, the steel clanging against the cement as I tower over him, heaving in air.

Connor's behind me in a split second, his hands on my biceps, pulling me back. He doesn't have to pull hard; I wasn't going to beat the shit out of him.

"He can't say her name," I explain to Connor, who looks up at me bewildered. It takes a hard look from me before he corrects himself.

Groaning on the ground, Luke spits up blood, and then looks me in the eyes as he says, "I would never go after a woman. Fletcher…"

He has to pause and spit and when he does, I can already see the bruise forming from his lower jaw up to his high cheekbone. "Fletcher wouldn't go after the women. He'd never do that, and you fucking know it."

He's out of breath by the time he adds *bastards* to the end of his statement. Derrick eyes me all the while he hauls Luke and his chair back upright to a sitting position.

I lower myself in front of Luke, crouching so he's at eye level. "Then why was your car there?"

I expect him to deny it. To call my girl a liar, which will earn him a matching bruise on the other side of his pretty boy face. He doesn't though.

"It was stolen," he tells me. For a moment, doubt sets in. Everything that was hot, turns cold. I don't let a damn thing show on my expression though.

"When we found him, he was in the car," Derrick tells me quickly.

"Fletcher would kill me if I fucked with you. He said we needed you and then this shit happened."

Grabbing the back of his chair, I pull Luke closer to me, listening to the metal scrape against the floor as I do. My face is inches from his when I ask him, "Who stole your car?"

A faint smile wobbles on his lips and the bastard starts to cry. "You won't believe me."

"Who stole your car?" I scream the question in his face, feeling the rage tear its way up my throat.

Luke lets out a sick laugh and looks away to tell me, "I don't know."

Cursing, I step back, shoving Luke's chair when I do although he doesn't topple over. I believe him. And that's a big fucking problem.

Doubt and insecurity crawl their way up my spine.

"You better think of something," Connor tells the henchman. "I don't think my boss is too happy about the current situation."

"I thought it was a stupid fucking kid who'd figured out it was mine and got wise."

"Care to elaborate?" Derrick asks. I keep my back to Luke all the while, listening, trying to piece everything together.

"Someone stole it while I was collecting dues. I was pissed."

"You file a police report?" Connor asks with a smirk on his face. He's fucking with him. Men like us don't call the cops. Luke sneers at him.

"Boss," Derrick interrupts me when my phone starts vibrating against the metal. It's still sitting on the steel chair. Turning from where I stand, I wait for him to tell me who it is. "Fletcher."

I shake my head no, and Derrick drops the phone. The vibrations get louder.

"How did you get it back?" I question Luke.

"I didn't. Whoever it was, parked it on Fifth and Rodney. I figured they learned it was my car and what I'd do to them. They didn't touch it. Not a scratch."

Luke's expression looks hopeful although his eyes are a well of despair.

"Call him back, put him on speaker." I give the command to Derrick. "If you want to live, you'll be quiet until I tell you to speak."

"Do you believe me? You have to believe me."

"I don't trust anyone anymore," I answer him. That bit of hope he has falls. I see it, I recognize it. "I mean what I say. Don't speak until I call for you."

"Don't have to call his boss," Derrick says. The second he lifts the phone, it's vibrating again. I watch him tap the screen and then nod.

"Fletcher." I answer the call on speaker and Fletcher's voice is quiet on the other end, but it still fills the large empty room.

"King." It's quiet as I listen to my heart pound. "It seems there are some misunderstandings."

"Is that what we're calling it?" I ask Fletcher and I can hear him huff into his phone. Short and humorless.

"I don't believe it was you," Fletcher tells me and my gaze lifts to Derrick's. I can see Luke in my periphery, looking between the three of us. He's tense, and I'm sure he's aware that his life depends on this call.

"We took your man," I say, speaking clearly. I need him to know, to show him my cards.

"Because you believed it was me," he surmises.

"I believed it was him," I answer honestly.

"Because she told you—"

"She stays out of it," I say, cutting him off. For the first time, anger slips into the conversation and I stare at Luke, who's eager to scream out, but he's silent. "She stays out of it," I repeat. Calmer, with more control.

The air is tense and hot. It suffocates me.

"She stays out of it," Fletcher agrees. "Someone is playing us, King, and I don't like it. I don't care for the fact that you played into their hand."

"It has to be Mathews," I speak and close my eyes, trusting my gut. Gut instincts get you everywhere in this life.

"He stole my stash the way you stole his. He stole my right-hand man's car to set me up. He played us, pitting us against one another.

"He's done it before," Fletcher continues. "It's how he's able to grow as fast as he does. Everyone who doesn't deal with him finds themselves at war with someone else."

He's waiting on a response from me, but all I can think is how much I've fucked up. How bad this shit has gotten. Everything is fucked.

"Did you kill him?" Fletcher asks when I don't say a damn word. I tilt my head toward Luke, giving him the permission he's been dying for.

"I'm here, Boss," Luke tells him. His eyes dart between all of us as if he expects us to kill him as he's speaking to Fletcher. I stand still, not knowing what will happen next.

It's a cardinal sin to break trust in this way of life. It's paper thin to begin with and I shot a cannon through it.

"What would you have done?" I ask, knowing where I stand. He thought it was us. His first instinct when his warehouse was robbed, was that it was us. I'm not the only one who made that judgment, but I'm the one who acted first.

All I can hear is the heavy breathing to my left from Luke, whose wild eyes tell me he thinks he's done for. Fletcher takes his time answering.

"I can't answer that," he finally speaks and his answer pisses me off.

Stepping closer to the phone, and feeling the anger write itself on my face, I question him, "And why is that?"

Derrick watches me closely. I can feel his eyes boring into me, but he doesn't say a damn word.

"Because I don't love anyone," he answers. "I have no wife; I have no kids. You love Laura."

I can hear Derrick swallow, and then his hand is on my shoulder. We fucked up. We never should have touched Luke.

"I can make you a promise right now that before I question your men, if that time were to ever arise, I'll speak to you first."

"That's all I can do."

"It would be wise to let her go. You're good at what you do, but not when it comes to her."

"Untie him," I tell Connor in a murmur and instead of engaging Fletcher and his romantic advice, I move the conversation to what matters. "Mathews needs to pay for this."

"We need more men," he says and Fletcher's voice is easier now, closer to the way it was just the other night.

"We have them; I have the money. I've got the cash to give to the crews down south."

"I want to be clear that I am loyal to you, King. But if you do something this stupid again, I will kill you."

"I hear your threat loud and clear." I did what I had to do. I did what any man would have done. If he tries to kill me, I'll happily kill him first. There is no love lost between Fletcher and me. I will use him, and he will use me. That's all this is. We trust that the other is needed, and when that need no longer exists, one of us will kill the other. I can already see it playing out before my eyes.

"It's a promise, not a threat."

"Boss," Luke speaks up as the rage rings in my blood. "His address." Luke pushes out the words as if they'll stop a bomb from going off.

"Fuck," Fletcher hisses into the phone. "Mathews had his car."

My stomach churns and I don't know why.

"And?" I question.

"I had to check you out. You can't be pissed." His preface to this confession sits uneasily in the pit of my gut. "We're still cool and that's how we're going to stay," he states firmly.

"What did you do?" I ask and the contempt is clear in my voice.

"If someone from Mathews's crew was in my car, he could have your home address."

The room tilts and spins. "Laura," I breathe.

I end the call instantly, texting her not to go home, but she's already messaged me. She said I have to come home. That was an hour ago.

CHAPTER 18

Laura

IT WAS SUPPOSED TO BE ME. IT SHOULD HAVE BEEN ME.

The thoughts don't stop as I rock on the floor, staring at Cami. With a trembling bottom lip, I try to say her name again, but my throat is raw.

At first I thought I should run, in case whoever had been here was waiting for me. I can't leave Cami though. I can't leave her. Not like this.

I want to touch her, but instead I shove my hands into my lap. Her skin is already cold. She's been dead for hours now. I bet she came to drive me. She liked to do that, surprise me with coffee that's probably sitting in her car this very second.

She came to be a friend, and it got her killed. I got her killed. I'll never be able to forgive myself.

The carpet is harsh on my legs as I crawl backward, trying to keep myself from returning to her side. Every few minutes I think it's not real. She's not actually dead. I'm wrong, I'm seeing things, this is all a bad joke.

And then I touch her, I cry out her name. I shook her once and the clots on her throat gave way, letting a small trickle run down to her shoulders and onto my hand.

Her blood. Cami's blood.

She's really dead.

My hands are shaking. Even when I grip them together as tight as I can, feeling the blood rushing inside of them, they don't stop shaking.

I should have been the one who was here. It should be me who was tied up. The gouges around her wrists are so deep. Like they used wire to do it.

I can't stop staring at her. Every inch of her. Every bit of evidence showing what they did to her.

And I know damn well it was supposed to be me.

The taste of salt from my tears is overwhelming, as is the heat on my face. Everything is hot and I can barely breathe; I'm suffocating, waiting in the bedroom for Seth to answer me.

My eyes flick from the black screen back to Cami as I turn it on and wait, but there's no response.

Heaving in a breath, I have to use the cold wall to stand upright, but my legs are too shaky. That's when the tears start again. Heavy, hard sobs.

She's dead.

This life costs more than I'm willing to give.

My inhale is shaky until I hear a bump outside. I freeze, even with dizzy vision, I go stone-still. I've been here long enough for whoever did this to her to come get me if they wanted. Maybe they wanted to see my heart shatter before they killed me too.

Silence, followed by more silence. It was something crashing against the house. I know I heard it.

Thump. Again I hear the sound and this time it's accompanied by the muted howl of the night wind. It's just the trash can hitting the back of the house.

It's just the trash can hitting the back of the house. I tell myself again, hoping it will calm me down but it doesn't. The wind screams and the plastic can bangs against the back of the house again.

With my eyes closed, I breathe in and out. It's okay. I'm okay.

"Please answer me, Seth." I whisper the words, only to open my eyes and see no response and Cami's dead body on the floor.

Her skin is so pale.

It takes everything in me to lean down. Even as bile rises in the back of my throat, I carry through with it, hot tears streaming down my cheeks. It's easier to close her eyes than I thought it would be. Her thick lashes feel wet beneath my fingers and I don't know if it's from my clammy hands or tears that had gathered there.

I don't say goodbye to her, but I know it's the last time I'll see her when I lift my hand and her eyes are closed.

My steps are hurried and loud as I make my way to the bathroom, turning the faucet up as hot as it'll go and viciously rubbing my hands clean.

It's too loud. The water is so loud I can't hear anything that could be going on around me, so I'm quick to shut it off even though I don't feel clean enough.

My back hits the bathroom wall as I stand there, staring at myself in the mirror. Disheveled hair, wild eyes, and hot pink cheeks. It's obvious I've been crying. It's obvious I'm lost.

It's obvious I can't stay here.

I have nowhere else to go, though. Nowhere around here is safe. I'm not safe. Jackson was right. I have to save myself.

Time slows as the next thoughts come to me. The clicks of the ever-present clock seeming to tick longer with pauses between each one, punctuating each moment of clarity.

The money is in the safe. A safe that couldn't be opened by Cami because she didn't know the code. That's why they tied her up. They wanted the code; they wanted the money.

Tick.

The money they killed her trying to get.

Tock.

The money meant for a better life according to Seth, and it cost my best friend her last breath.

Tick.

Money Seth will use for guns, drugs, gambling.

Tock.

Money I need to get the hell out of here.

Tick.

It's over just like that.

Maybe five seconds have passed. But it feels like an eternity. It feels like the weight of the world. It feels like the end.

I'm still shaking when I hear the rapid beeps as I enter the code into the keypad. The click of the lock unlatching and the ease with which the heavy metal door opens only brings a new pain.

If only I had told Cami the code.

If I could go back in time and tell it to her, let it slide that the code was our anniversary date, I would have even though she never would have asked. Maybe she would have been in less pain. Maybe it would have been faster if she could have just told them the code.

With cloudy vision, I try to shut down the visuals of what happened to her hours ago.

I don't know how much money is here. I've never asked and I don't count now.

There are stacks and stacks of cash neatly arranged into bundles that are easy to grab by the fistful. I have to back away for a moment, questioning myself but the question is gone as quickly as it came.

I can't wait for next time.

I can't keep going like this.

There's a backpack, one I'd planned to take to nursing school if I ever got into one, in the far corner of the closet. I know it's there and the memory of it forces me to move quickly on these insecure legs. I unzip it on my way back to the safe, and dump its contents, unused notebooks and packs of pens, onto the safe floor.

I take a stack of cash and then another.

I have my car, money, and enough fear to push me far away from here.

Seth's face is there every time I close my eyes. The hurt, the disappointment. Picturing his sad eyes makes me waver, but only enough that I pause. I don't stop packing.

I've begged him. I've told him I can't stay.

Another stack and the backpack is full. It's six large stacks in total and a little more than a quarter of what was in here.

I have trouble zipping it up. The little metal zipper slips from my fingers and then snags on the bills the next time I try.

I'm a hell of a mess. Scared and damaged. In raw pain from losing Cami, but also from knowing how I'm leaving Seth right now.

I won't wait for him anymore. With that thought, I shut the safe door, leaning my back against it as I heave in oxygen, praying for it to calm me down enough to drive away. I'm faster packing a bag, grabbing everything I can without bothering to remove the hangers. I shove it all in, eager to get the hell out of here.

A small voice whispers to wait. It begs me to check my phone again, to give Seth one more chance.

Oh, how my body bends to that will. I wish he would have texted. I wish he would have been waiting for me right then and there. To stop me from going alone. I want him to come with me.

I need him to. Or in this last moment of weakness, to force me to stay. I wish he were here now to shove me in the safe, like he said he would. Because I don't want to leave. Even now, I'm so aware I don't want to leave.

But Seth isn't here. He didn't text me back. And he isn't going to leave this life. He'll never leave it.

This life is who he is. I know that it is.

My swallow is harsh and ragged, like broken glass slicing its way down when I get to the front door.

My hands are so cold now, they're numb. My entire body is by this point.

I stare at the red door, envisioning Seth walking through it. I wait for one beat of my heart and then it's followed by another fucked-up beat that skips all over. But he doesn't come.

I would have been dead for hours and hours, and then what? What would he do "next time?"

The bookbag drops to the tile floor with a thud as I walk around the counter, pull out the junk drawer in the kitchen and grab a small pad of paper and a pen.

I have to scribble the pen for a moment to get the ink flowing, so I move to the second sheet. Letting the tears flow, I take out another clean sheet to write down my last words to him.

He'll never forgive me. I already know that.

I don't think I'll ever forgive myself either.

The clean sheet is stained by a fallen tear before the tip of the pen can mar the perfectly white paper with a slash of black.

I'll always love you.

I write that line first but the others aren't good enough. *Please forgive me.* I think that thought every other line, but I never write it. *I had to.* I don't have to, I'm choosing to and I know it. He knows it too.

The only truth I can bear to give him is that I'll always love him.

Then I write my final thought.

Even if you hate me, I'll always love you.

There can't be any blood in my hands or face; they're cold and numb. I know that much from the pricks that travel along my icy flesh. It's all drained from me. I don't know how long I stand there, wishing for better words that don't come.

Wishing it wasn't over, but knowing that it is.

It's over.

I'm leaving him.

The resolution gives me enough strength to move, but I still linger at the door, gripping the edge of it as I whisper, "I'm sorry, babe," to Cami. "I love you."

I think about her as I wipe my face and drive away in the dark night. The headlights shine ahead of me, two yellow streaks in a sea of nothing.

It's my fault. I knew who Seth was, I just never thought that there wouldn't be a way for our lives to fit together. It was always so perfect, so easy. He was my everything.

Occasionally I glance at the backpack in the passenger seat, the money I stole from him. When I get to a motel hours and hours away with sleep dragging me down, I finally check my phone for the first time since I left.

There's nothing from him. Nothing after the texts I sent him to come home and that I wasn't okay. He saw them though. He saw but he didn't answer.

Derrick messaged me, though. Reading his text sends me into another sobbing frenzy on the scratchy sheets of the motel.

Tonight is the first night of many where I simply cry myself to sleep, hating who I am and how little I'm worth. And it's the first night in years that Seth doesn't message me back. He never messages me back.

CHAPTER 19

Seth

FUCK.

"No, no, no." With my hands running down my face I keep praying to whatever God would even bother to listen to me to make Cami wake up. To make this entire night go away. Erase it from fate's plans. None of this should have happened.

"Please, God," I beg, but no one's listening to me.

Derrick hasn't moved. Not an inch. His body is over Cami's, his forearm resting above her head. His face is near her stomach, and his shoulders heave every so often. I've never seen the man cry in our entire existence, but he cries for her.

"We're too late," I tell him again, with a dry throat and hope he hears me this time. My fist slams against the wall when he tells me "no" like this isn't real. The pain of my knuckles bashing against the wall isn't enough. The pain is miniscule compared to everything else. So I do it again and again, letting the anguish wash over me. The drywall cracks and crumbles so easily.

I don't even realize I'm screaming until Derrick yells at me to shut the fuck up.

Picking up his head, he stares at me, both of us breathless, wounded and guilty.

"This is because of me," he tells me with red eyes. The pain is etched in every feature of his expression. "She's dead because I couldn't—"

"She's dead because Mathews wanted to hurt us. They wanted to steal from us. They wanted to kill her."

"It's on me," he emphasizes, lowering himself until his forehead rests on her stomach. "She died because of me."

"We'll get them back. We'll make them pay."

Time passes in silence.

"Where's Laura?" he asks cautiously. He didn't see the note when we came in. It's the first thing I saw. The blood, the trail of it to the safe. The emptied backpack.

"She took off," I answer him and I swear the confession strangles me. Each word tries to choke me, hating the very thought of it.

"Where she'd run to?" he asks and the lack of contempt, the lack of sympathy… he doesn't get it.

"She didn't run from them; she took off for good," I explain. It hurts more than I thought it would to say it out loud. "She left me."

With bewildered eyes he shakes his head and that's when I turn away from him, leaving him where he is over Cami and walking away. I have to wipe my face with my forearm as I head back to the kitchen and to the front of the house.

I feel restless, anxious, tormented and angry. It turns to pacing, thinking about how to get revenge against Mathews for hurting Laura, for trying to steal from me, for scaring the one girl I've ever loved away from me.

I can picture Laura finding Cami; that breaks me down to nothing. I am nothing when I imagine that scene. I know how she would have reacted. But I can't see her emptying the backpack and shoving the money inside. I can't see her packing up her things. I can't picture her leaving me.

Never did I think she'd leave me. I can't imagine it, even though it's already done.

The ghosts in the living room call to me. She wanted me to leave. I did this. I did all of this.

Another vicious scream tears from my throat as I swipe my arm down the counter. My body's hot, my head feels light and I do it again. The bang and clatter of the broken glasses and pans hitting the tiled floor urge me on.

I destroy everything, everything I touch, why should this place be any different?

It takes me a long moment to realize she took the cash and what the consequence of that is. I needed that cash. We needed every fucking cent of it.

"Fuck!" I scream out the word, but it doesn't make anything better.

This is what it feels like to be at rock bottom.

It takes a long time for me to actually cry. To let it all out and feel the deep-seated pain in the very pit of my stomach. For me to accept that Cami is dead and Laura is long gone.

Getting revenge for Cami is the sole focus of our crew.

That's the only thing that keeps Derrick moving. The guys are silent. Everyone is. No one asks where Laura is either. They know she left; they don't know about the money though.

If I told them, they'd want to go after her. So instead I have to be smarter, harsher, more violent to get the message across.

She screwed me. Laura screwed me over when she left. She left me at my worst, and made everything harder. I have to tell myself she couldn't have known, but that only helps for so long.

It takes hours of standing in a scalding hot shower to try to wash it all away, the pain of what I've caused, the agony of what I lost. It doesn't leave me though. There's no cleansing these sins.

When I fall into bed, I take her note with me. It crinkles when I grip it, no matter how much I try to let up on my grasp. I can't help it; I hold it with everything I've got.

I have her note, and the messages she sent.

The dim light from the phone is the only light in the room, and I stare at it for hours. Reading the texts about her doctor's appointment, then about Cami. I reread the lines she sent, wanting me to come home. Needing me.

Instead I was out, making a hard life even harder. Getting us into deeper shit.

All the while she was dealing with a dead girl whose blood is on my hands.

There's a mix of regret and hate.

As the weeks move on, I get colder, harder. The realization of what I've chosen fuels me to do unspeakable things. Mathews never stood a chance. Neither did Fletcher.

Laura doesn't text me again other than to tell me she's sorry and I don't respond to that message. She doesn't come back to Tremont or anywhere within a five-hundred-mile radius. Well only once, and it wasn't for me. A year had passed and she came back for a single day, hoping not to run into me even though she stepped into my territory, into my bar. I knew it when she saw me there, bumping into me by accident, that she wanted to leave without running into me.

That hurt stays long after she's gone. I thought I wasn't capable of feeling like that anymore, until she showed up.

Derrick keeps tabs on her. He has since she left.

The regret fades. The hate takes over.

I loved her more than she loved me, because I never would have left her.

Every day that passes, I start hating her more.

She said she loved me and she left.

She stole from me and she left.

She never looked back; she just left.

She should have known one day I'd come back for her. I'm going to make her feel the same regret I feel.

Eight years later

I wonder if Laura knows it's me, for about half a fucking second. The way she averts her eyes and refuses to look at me gives me the answer

I'm looking for. The East Coast has been good to me. I wouldn't have chosen it for myself, but it's where Laura ended up.

It's pitch black and the stores in the shopping center are closing down. I've been parked here for a good three hours now, just watching. It's what I'm paid to do and what I need to do tonight.

I'm supposed to watch Jase Cross's girl. I've been working with the Cross brothers ever since I left Tremont in Derrick's hands. There was no one left to kill there, no challenges to face. So I followed Laura, keeping my distance and getting comfortable.

Fate's a prick.

She's with the girl I'm supposed to be keeping an eye on. I suppose it makes sense. My life's a sick joke.

Fuck, just looking at her dredges up everything. Every splinter of emotion I thought I'd long buried. The sick concoction of it all slips into the crevices of my bones as my eyes wander over the curves of her collarbone.

Then lower, to the dip at her waist.

It's hot and cold. Anger then lust. Fuck, I can't keep still in this piece of tin knowing she's right there. So damn close, I could go get her if only I wanted to. Some moments I do, but I don't know that I'm ready yet and I need her to come to me. A piece of me *needs* her to be the one to come to me.

Her eyes catch mine once, then twice. She turns stiff in the car across the vacant parking lot.

I bet she thinks I'm here for her. She thinks this is about her, and maybe it was when I first moved here. Now though, I have plenty to keep myself occupied here before I attend to her.

If she thinks what's between us is over, she's wrong.

If she thinks I'm going to let her get away with it, she's out of her fucking mind.

The wine bottle is nearly empty in her hands as she sits in the driver's seat. I've been watching her and Bethany, Jase's girl, drink at the bar, go into a shop, drink at another bar, and go into another shop all damn night. They're both on the verge of fucked up when Bethany knocks on my window, wanting a ride.

The slow smirk is hard to hide when I roll down my window. She thinks she can trust me. She hasn't learned that in this life, you can't trust anyone. Not even the ones you love.

Bethany's a sweet girl but oblivious. It's nearly sick how much I revel in her unsuspecting question to simply take them home.

Bethany gets in easily enough, feeling safe and secure because she knows her boyfriend is my boss. She knows I won't do a damn thing to hurt her.

She has no idea what I want to do to Laura, though. She isn't aware that I know her. I know Laura more than I know anyone.

The click of Laura's car door echoes in the empty lot as does the staccato of her heels as she makes her way to my car. I remember those blue eyes spearing into mine when she peeks at me through her thick lashes.

She gets in without a word, but the air burns hot. Her friend is clueless. Utterly unaware.

I can't hear a damn word Bethany's saying of the confession that spills from her and I wonder if Laura can hear it. If she has the patience for it, the mental capacity to think of anything other than what I'm going to do to her once Bethany gets her ass out of this car.

The few miles it takes to drop off Bethany are far too long. Every second is drawn out by the deep breaths Laura takes.

My grip tightens on the wheel, thinning the tight skin on my knuckles and turning it white. The click of the turn signal distracts me from whatever Bethany's saying, but not from the sweet cadence of Laura's response.

Her voice is a memory that thickens the tension between us.

It takes fifteen minutes until Bethany's out of the car, closing the door and asking me sweetly to take Laura home.

I've been in this town for years now. I've come close to seeing the girl who stole my heart and left me with nothing, face to face, more times than I can count. I've been patient though. *Good things come to those who wait.*

It's not until Bethany closes the front door, that Laura speaks to me.

"Seth." Laura speaks my name like a sin. She has to clear her throat after she says my name, the nerves eating away at her and showing easily enough.

The leather groans in the back of my car as she adjusts in her seat.

I'm already down the pebbled path of the driveway, minutes from the highway and debating on which way I should go. Left to her place, or right, to mine.

"Seth, please," she begs me although I don't know what for.

I'm silent, remembering all the times she begged me before when she was under me, writhing and loving me.

I love you. How many times did she tell me that just minutes after moaning my name like she used to do?

I can hear her swallow and in the rearview mirror, I watch as her chest rises and falls heavier with each passing second that I don't acknowledge her.

"Seth, would you say something please, you're scaring me."

Scaring her? If she knew what I became when she left me, she'd be fucking terrified.

My gaze moves to the mirror, watching her nervously bite down on her lower lip. Those plump lips I used to bite myself.

Licking my own, I let out a deep sigh and sit back into my seat, easing the tense muscles and letting more time pass simply to torture her.

She leans forward, refusing to just wait like a good girl. Her hand grips the top of my seat, her fingers brushing my shoulder. The short touch is gentle, seemingly innocuous, but it lights up every nerve ending in me.

"Seth, please, just talk to me." As she speaks, her voice cracks and her eyes turn glossy.

I can feel how her heart breaks only inches from mine. Her pain is like a hit of ecstasy after years of being clean. I want more of it; I crave it like an addict.

"What do you want me to say, Babygirl?" I question her and wait at the red light, right at the fork that decides where we're going.

I can hear the hitch in her breath, I can feel the heat that revs up inside of her. Was it *Babygirl* that did it? Or simply having me answer her after nearly a decade of silence?

Inhaling deeply, I get a heavy dose of her sweet scent. Fuck, it's just like I remember. Everything about her is exactly what I remember. I didn't make it up in my mind. She's intoxicating.

"Anything," she breathes as the red light turns green and I make my decision, knowing exactly what I'm going to do to her tonight, how I'm going to make her pay for leaving me and fucking me over. "Just tell me anything."

Locking my gaze with hers I ask her, keeping my voice low to try to hide the anger, "How did you really think this was going to end?"

DESPERATE TO TOUCH

I ran from him, even though my heart knew better.

Love was one thing, but survival another.

He chose a life of crime and I never wanted any of it; I only wanted him. I left when the danger bled into my life, taking more than I was willing to sacrifice.

I should have known he'd come for me. Men like him always get what they want.

The temptation in his eyes, the heat of his touch… it's all still there, but his gaze is harsher now and his grasp unrelenting.

He's not the boy I fell in love with, although pieces of what we once had are still there. *I can feel it.*

I know what he wants from me, and I know it comes with a steep price. I'll pay it though, if for no other reason than to touch him again. Just once more.

I'll close my eyes and forget about the risks that come with this life and with him. I only hope he doesn't do the same.

Desperate to Touch is book 2 in a series.
Hard to Love must be read first.

"Monsters are real, and ghosts are real too.

They live inside us, and sometimes,

they win."

—Stephen King

PROLOGUE

Laura

The first year Seth moved to the East Coast, years ago

THE JOURNAL IN MY HAND IS THICK AND THE EDGE OF ITS PAGES ARE WORN. As though she didn't just write in its pages daily, but instead read and reread the scribbled confessions of the past three years constantly. The spine itself is cracked and it divides the journal in two.

Guilt riddles its way into my thoughts. I shouldn't be reading a patient's journal, not when she only gave it to me because I told her I'd fix it for her. She trusted me because I'm her nurse. I'm supposed to help Delilah and take care of her.

The poor woman who lives on pills during the day and is haunted by nightmares when the sun sets gave me all her secrets. I know I shouldn't take it, but the second half of the journal starts with the description of a barn Marcus took her to.

Marcus. Just seeing his name chills me down to my bones. I don't even realize that I've stopped moving, breathing, that I've simply halted in the middle of the narrow hall until a sweet new resident asks me if I'm okay. I think her name is Bethany.

"Fine," I tell her and force a smile, although the scribbled name, Marcus, lingers in my mind. The whispered hiss, Marcus, repeats itself faster and faster as I make my way to the office to read what she wrote about him. The

Rockford Center deals with mental health, so naturally, drugs and violence are a conversation starter. Many of my patients talk about Marcus. Marcus and the Cross brothers. Recently, Seth King is a name that's going around too. I have to close my eyes, swallowing thickly as I shut the door to the dark office, leaning my back against it and simply trying to breathe.

Seth King, the man I loved on the other side of the country. The man I ran away from. He gave me time, but I knew he'd come for me. It's been a week since I first heard he was here, only miles from me, and I've been praying. I begged God to give me a sign, to tell me what to do. Opening my eyes, I stare down at the notebook. My salvation.

I photocopied every page of Delilah's journal, hiding in the small back office of the Rockford Center. I can still remember how anxious I was and how heat smothered every inch of my skin. Knowing I could be fired instantly, I still had to do it. I'd only just started working at the center, my first job as a nurse. I had to do whatever it took to survive. I suppose I'd been saying that a lot back then.

That journal was my leverage for when Seth inevitably came for me. Filled with multiple entries all about Marcus, the boogeyman, the Grim Reaper. A faceless villain who made deals in back alleys, running the streets around these parts, battling for power along with the Cross brothers. Unlike Carter Cross and his brothers, no one knows who Marcus is. They've never seen his face, but his signature power plays and ruthless reputation are notorious.

I thought that if Seth came for me demanding the money I stole, I'd give him the copies. I thought maybe it would be of value to him because I knew he came to work with the Irish mob who ruled this part of the East Coast, a.k.a. the Cross brothers. And they'd give anything to uncover any details on their faceless nemesis, Marcus, and his secrets.

They were all in the worn journal. This woman Delilah, my patient, had seen him. Felt him. She *loved* Marcus. She had a single journal when she was first admitted. It described details of where they met and what he wanted with her. It was leverage. Several years have passed; my patient's collection has grown as she's come in and out of the Rockford Center, when her mental state is too harmful to be away from the help we give her. She has a journal for every year, five years now, and I never stopped photocopying them. I could give Seth information on Marcus, in hopes that he wouldn't hold our past against me.

I kept waiting and waiting for Seth to come for me. Didn't he know he'd have to be the one to make the first move? I wouldn't even be able to look him in the eyes or say his name out loud.

Seth King.

Years came and went yet he never approached me. It wasn't relief I felt, it was like a prolonged mourning. Maybe he wanted me to feel his presence, to know I couldn't have him. I remember the first night that thought came to me, and how hard I sobbed against my pillow at the thought. I'd take my punishment; I deserved it.

Fate is a cruel sorceress, but this time I love her. Because last night, I saw him. I spoke to him. He called me *Babygirl* and even through the fear, I want him to say it again.

CHAPTER 1

Seth

SHE STILL DOESN'T KNOW HOW BADLY SHE FUCKED ME OVER.

I try to keep that in mind as I wait for Laura. Waiting for her is all I've done since she said good night two weeks ago. Each hour has felt like an eternity. She whispered it when she opened the back door of my car, sliding out with tears running down her cheeks. She never cried in the open; she hated the tears. "Useless" is what she used to mutter when she was on the verge of tears.

Back then I always held her while she let it all out. That night, fourteen days ago, I merely watched as she stayed as silent as she could, wiping the tears from her cheek. Maybe that's why she whispered "good night"—she didn't trust herself to speak too loud or else I'd realize she was crying.

I already knew though. She should know better than to think she can hide from me.

If she thinks I don't know how much it hurts, she's dead wrong.

The tick of the clock in Jase's office doesn't stop. It reminds me that I'm getting closer to seeing her again. She's to meet me, to come prepared to pay for the damages. She doesn't know though, just how much she fucked me over.

"Anything else on Walsh?" Jase questions his brother, Declan, as I sit in the corner chair, a dark leather wingback. I listen to the two of them go over the details Declan's been able to gather on the crooked cop hell-bent on revenge against the man known as Marcus. Only half my attention is on them. Until Declan says something about pitting the two of them against one another.

For a moment, I'm torn from my obsessive thoughts of seeing Laura tonight. The thoughts have been coming and going throughout the day. In the dark of night, alone in my bed with nothing but the memories of her, not a damn thing could get through to me. Certainly not sleep.

"Seth, what do you think?" Jase asks me, rolling up the sleeves of his crisp white dress shirt. Watching him lean back against his chair, the tailored suit jacket draped behind him, I'm reminded that I have shit to do other than deal with the woman who broke what semblance of a heart I had.

"I think being between the two of them is a piss-poor place to be," I say, speaking up so Declan can hear me from where he is on the other side of the expansive office. His head is down as he types on the keys of his sleek laptop. It's state of the art and expensive as fuck with all the software loaded onto it. He's constantly searching for more information on Cody Walsh, the cop and former FBI agent who came to this town wreaking havoc.

"It would be easier if Walsh wasn't blackmailing us to help him find Marcus."

"It's not like we can give him Marcus anyway. He'll learn that it's not that easy," I comment but the foresight of what will happen along the way, and more importantly, after, breeds a disdain for the scheming cop. Months of surveillance on Marcus's men have given us nothing but a list of men who work for the man. Nothing about him in particular. We don't have a damn thing to give Walsh.

"Then how does him blackmailing us play out?" Jase's unspoken concerns are read easily with the worry in his expression. If we can't help Officer Walsh find Marcus, he could turn in the evidence he has on Jase and me. Then we're fucked.

"We need to get something on Walsh. We can't trust that he doesn't have backups of the tapes. We could bury ourselves helping him and in the end, he'd turn us in anyway."

"I agree with Declan," I say as I nod solemnly. My voice is even and calm. The threat of going away for murder is there… but all I can focus on is Laura, and making her sweet ass pay for leaving me.

"Even if Walsh does turn in the evidence, we have ways to get around a conviction," Jase says and his menacing glare moves to the lit fireplace on the right side of the room. "As soon as we're able, I want him dead."

I used to feel chills at the thought of murder. They would climb up my spine, sending a freezing cold deeper into my blood as they crept their way up. Not anymore, though. It's been quite some time since I've felt any remorse or apprehension at the depravity I engage in.

"It must be done," I agree.

"When the time comes, we burn his house down, raid his office and get any evidence you can find."

"His car too," Declan adds. "He has PO Boxes in the upper east. Those need to be ransacked as well. All three of them."

"What the hell is he doing with those?" A crease settles deep between my brow.

"Maybe that's where he stores his evidence?" Jase questions, and a hopeful glint resurrects itself in his dark gaze. "Former FBI agents have their quirks and habits. We need to learn every single one of this prick's."

I only nod. There's no telling why Walsh does what he does. He seems to work alone, but the more we learn, the more is amiss. The evidence in his possession could put us away for murder. I'm not willing to allow that. Not when I just got Laura back.

No fucking way is some crooked cop getting in the way of my plans. I wish I had my crew here. For the first time in years, I feel like I truly need them. Maybe it's because Laura's back. Or maybe it's because the danger has a tighter grip around my throat. They're on the other side of the country, though. I haven't spoken to them in a long damn time.

I offer my suggestion and say, "We can put some men on the post office. See how often he goes to the PO Boxes, if ever."

"Agreed," Declan chimes in. "We need to watch him day and night. I can't find shit on him from the last three years and before that he was an agent so I don't trust it."

The ticking of the clock sounds with the crackling of wood and hiss of the fire as the three of us consider our reality. We're dealing with two pricks who have information on us, yet we're lacking when it comes to knowledge about them.

"All of our resources are going toward watching the army of a ghost," Jase says, referring to Marcus's men, "and to a fucking cop who could bring us down."

"We'll take care of it," I comment evenly and reassuringly, joining Jase to stare at the fire. Instead of seeing a cocked trigger, or the match that would cause an explosion, I see blue eyes in the flames. Parted lips. I swear I can hear Laura's moan.

"You all right, Seth?" The question doesn't come from Jase or from Declan. The office door creaks open as Carter steps in, his footsteps heavy as he enters.

"Fine," I answer Carter Cross, the oldest brother and rightful leader of this crew. His ruthlessness and reputation precede him.

He murmurs low and then takes in each of his brothers. "I think we should reconsider Marcus."

"Fuck Marcus." Jase's voice is harsh as he speaks. Marcus is the one who gave the cop the leverage. The bastard set us up. Walsh isn't the only one who wants to take Marcus down.

Carter merely smirks, the only hint of humor that's graced this office for months. He's taller than his brothers. Broader shoulders too with an air about him that's deadly. Jase could charm anyone; he's handsome and well spoken. Declan's quiet and smiles easily enough. Carter's harder, brutal. Even his jawline is harsh. Recently though, since he's found Aria, a different side of him is showing.

"Any unspoken truce we had with Marcus is gone," Jase continues, his anger getting the best of him. "He fucked with us on a personal level. He stole our supply, he captured—"

"All in the past. The enemy of our enemy is our friend."

"Which one, brother?" Jase's gaze narrows. His animosity for the two men shows without even the thinnest veil to hide behind. "You'd choose Marcus over Walsh? When Marcus is the one who set us up! He gave us over to Walsh when we did nothing to him. He's a traitor. I won't rethink a damn thing."

"Your emotions are getting the best of you." Carter's lack of emotion, his logical thinking combined with unforgiving lethal force, is what made the Cross brothers what they are. If nothing else, I admire it.

My gaze moves slowly between the two brothers, as does Declan's. I understand Jase's anger and his fear.

"What would you have us do?" Jase questions. Their dark gazes meet, and neither softens. Carter's hand falls in the pocket of his crisp black suit as he seems to debate an answer.

"Surveillance will take time. Do we have it?" he asks.

"Yes," Declan speaks up, cracking the tension but not breaking it. In gray slacks and a white Henley, Declan's attire makes him stand out from his brothers. He always does though. But it's his quiet, watchful nature that allows him to blend in with crowds. He doesn't have the same intensity about him that Jase and Carter do. At least not in public. I've seen him though. I've seen the real him and it's nothing like the man on the other side of the office.

Carter nods, running his thumb over his freshly shaven chin, the stubble already starting to show. He's a beast of a man, dressed up in a tailored suit.

"My only thought, and something I hope you would consider… if we get rid of Walsh, who will get rid of Marcus?" Carter questions and for a moment, Jase's head tilts as he considers his brother.

I'm nodding my head in short, nearly undetectable movements when Carter looks at me. I've found companionship with Jase, and friendship with Declan. Carter though has never allowed a step toward anything other than a working relationship. He's guarded, and until recently, I'd hardly spoken to him in the years I've worked for the Cross brothers. He'd be in the room, he'd speak. But not to me. Never to anyone other than his brothers. Guarded is a word that doesn't do him justice.

The trust simply isn't there. I respect that. I understand it more than he knows.

"You certain there's nothing you'd like to tell me?" Carter questions. "To tell *us*?"

A prickle of unease travels along my skin. Hot and sickening, but I answer calmly and with a no-nonsense tone. "Not a damn thing. If there's something you'd like to ask, I'll do as I've always done. I'll tell you whatever you want to know."

Declan and Jase are quiet as Carter squares his shoulders and contemplates a moment. "Something's going on with you," Carter finally speaks.

My palms are clammy as I clench and unclench my fists. "If you're doubting—"

"You are in this family. I don't doubt your loyalty or your ability… yet." Although Carter's tone is harsh, there's a softness I haven't seen from him before. *You are in this family.*

I am in no family. I haven't been for quite some time.

"Like I said, there's something going on with you." As Carter repeats the accusation, Jase leans back against his desk. The skin on his knuckles turns white as he grips the edge of it.

"Old ghosts," Carter surmises. "For weeks now."

Ever since I saw Laura with Bethany, Jase's girlfriend. I only nod, swallowing thickly.

"If something's going on—"

"It's personal," I reassure him and keep my tone even but without any room for discussion. "It won't get in the way of anything."

"If I've noticed the change, Seth… those ghosts are already in the way."

CHAPTER 2

Laura

I'M TRYING TO REMEMBER EVERYTHING SETH SAID TWO WEEKS AGO, BUT all I can hear is *Babygirl*. All I can feel is the prick at the back of my eyes. *He asked me how I thought it would end*… that's right. That aching feeling in my chest returns and I swallow, dry and harsh as I sit in my car. My seatbelt's off and the constant pinging from the dash is driving me crazy until I pull the keys out of the ignition.

I begged for his forgiveness while all he did was stare at me through the rearview mirror. I tried to explain, but his gaze remained brutal and unforgiving. I put my hand on his shoulder once, and that was the only time he really looked at me. First my hand, and then into my eyes.

He wrote down an address, this address. In the note, he told me to come in two weeks—which has felt like forever. And he gave me a time… five minutes from now.

Don't make me come for you.

I read the line noting how quickly my heart beats, then the pause and the sudden shortness of breath. A wave of overwhelming emotions crashed down around me. The thought of him coming for me will always make me feel conflicted. I want to run from him, but I also want him to capture me, to force me to stay. Because I'm selfish, just like my heart is when it ticks and skips like it's running and it's out of breath.

I stopped taking my medication for arrhythmia when I got settled here. My hand instinctively hovers over my chest as the *thump, thump, thump* goes off beat. With my eyes closed, I breathe in deep and tell it to calm down.

I haven't needed a pill in years. Seth King fucks up my heart. No one can tell me otherwise. It's all his fault.

Ping.

Jolting from the buzz on my lap, as I sit in the car outside of the address Seth gave me, I silently scold myself. *Calm the fuck down.*

The heat from the vents hits my face and I'm quick to flick the button off. It's cold for an autumn night, colder than it's been since March if I remember right, and the wind is unforgiving too.

With the blush of the sunset on the horizon, I'm close to a moment I knew would come one day. For better or for worse. I'm safe in my car… safe for now.

It took me twenty-five minutes to drive here. All in silence. That's all it took. It felt like forever, but forever is over far too quickly now that I'm sitting here staring at the massive house. It's all old light gray stone with dark blue roofing… the slabs all the way up there look like stone too. It's hard to tell this late at night though. There are two stories with a wraparound porch. There isn't a piece of furniture at all outside though. The old Victorian has been cared for. It's obviously been meticulously maintained, which must take effort given that it's out here, surrounded by miles and miles of woods.

Taking my gaze away from the gorgeous house, I read the text and then I have to read it again.

You want to go out soon?

My brow furrows, a deep line settling in my forehead.

My first thought is: *what is Cami doing on the East Coast?* After all, who else would be texting me?

A vise tightens around my dry throat. *Cami's dead.* Fuck, my head is so messed up.

It's been like this since I saw Seth days ago. Since he called me Babygirl. The past has a way of creeping in. All the things once forgotten come back. With the pain lingering in my chest, oh how I wish Cami were here. I wish it were her who sent that text.

It's been a long time since I've had moments like I've been having, where I've forgotten about everything that happened when I left. I don't hold the guilt or any of the fear. In those moments, my mind plays tricks on me to convince me Cami's still alive, still happy. I've only left her on the other side of the country for school and work. It's a nice thought for a moment, but then my eyes prick with hot tears and the memory of the night I left comes flooding back in a rush.

I'll never forget that imagery. I'll never forget how cold her skin was. Or the feel of her lashes against my fingers when I closed her eyes. I hold my fingers now, willing the sensations to go away.

My body's heavy as I fall against the driver seat. Breathe in, breathe out. Just keep breathing.

Ping. Bethany texts again. She's not Cami. She'll never be Cami.

A new friend to replace me, Cami's voice whispers in my head and my throat tightens as I read the text Bethany sent: *I miss you. I really do.*

I don't even have time to think about what happened between Bethany and me. I haven't seen her since she left my apartment, pissed off at me. I did what I had to do. It was a few days after I'd seen Seth. I did what I thought was right.

I'll tell her everything. She'll understand. Some friendships come and go but some, like the one I have with Bethany, are meant to be forever friendships. I want so badly to make it up to Bethany and explain. Just like I want to do with Seth.

She'll understand.

Failure and regret are kneading together in the pit of my stomach. I've made so many mistakes. Countless times I've prayed and wished that I could just go back so I could do things differently. If only I could have known…

I miss you too and whenever you want, I'm there. I type out my response and hope she can feel just how much I miss her too.

Tonight? Bethany's answer is immediate and my teeth bite into my bottom lip as I suck in a deep breath.

Dammit. I can't tonight.

Tomorrow then? she asks.

Tomorrow. I respond immediately and then quickly add, *I am all yours tomorrow.*

I don't realize I'm holding my breath until she replies, *Can't wait* and I finally exhale.

I can make things better. I can make them right again. Closing my eyes again, I see Cami's face. *Not everything can be made right.*

With another exhale, I try to shake off the nerves that curl and coil around my insides. Preparing to toss my keys in my bag, the jingle of them is all I can hear other than my wonky heart when I look up and see Seth standing there.

My heart tumbles over itself at the sight of him. I've only seen him in a suit once before. For his father's funeral. Back then, the suit looked like a hand-me-down. He could have afforded whatever suit he wanted, but he chose a loose black one, with a black tie that was never tight around his throat. The knot hung loose and the second the casket was lowered to the ground, he ripped it off, followed by his jacket. It was snowing that day, but he couldn't have cared less. He never did like suits.

It seems that time has changed all that. The expensive cloth is cut perfectly to fit Seth's broad shoulders. The black is pristine, the cufflinks a detail I'd never envisioned on him. He lifts his arm just slightly, glancing down at his wrist and the shine of a silver watch, or maybe platinum, reflects back at me.

His clothes are all wrong, all different from what I know about the boy I fell in love with. But his eyes, they're the same. His stubble and hard jaw, they're what I remember. His cheekbones seem more defined with how trim he keeps his facial hair and the lines around his eyes are faint, but they tell tales of an older man, not one in his twenties. The look he's giving me though, with his lips slightly parted, his tongue peeking out just for a moment to wet his bottom lip... it's reminiscent of before, but just like his clothes, it's worn differently.

Skip, trip, thump. He doesn't stop staring as I take him in. Like he's waiting for something. My heart responds but I don't. I'm as still as can be in my seat, feeling the heat the car has stopped providing even without it being on anymore. It engulfs me as Seth's stare penetrates through everything.

He doesn't stand there for long, his large hands clenched into fists at his sides. They unclench and his right smooths down the black pressed suit pants he's wearing. Irritation grows in his expression, but I'm in no rush to move.

I hate how he looks at me, but I love that he's looking at me at all.

I reach out to the passenger seat without breaking Seth's gaze before he can open the door himself. He's hiding from me. Behind those blue eyes, I see nothing anymore. Maybe a hint of lust and a wall of hate, but not him. I don't see him anymore and it fucking hurts. It's a jagged rip to my heart.

Before I step out, I reach behind me for my purse; inside it is the notebook. Only the first one though. I didn't bring them all.

As I stand toe to toe with him, swinging the thin black strap of my blush satchel over my shoulder and feeling the gust of wind send a chill down my spine, I close the car door without looking back. The thudding click of it shutting is all I can hear. Even the woods that surround us are silent.

It's hard to believe Seth's right in front of me. The wave of heat from his hard body towering over me is addictive. He's so close that his scent fills my lungs and it brings memory after memory as I stand breathless in front of him. I could touch him; I know I could.

He could touch me if he wanted to as well. Neither of us moves though.

"I told you not to make me come for you." His deep voice is a low baritone, a threat not so veiled laying within the syllables.

What was left of the light from the sun is waning and the moon doesn't provide a damn thing tonight. The shadows come quicker than they have any other night. My God, does the darkness make Seth look even more tempting. Fear is ever present, the unknowing and lack of control driving my anxiety to pump my unbalanced heart harder.

I pay it all no mind. Seth is here in front of me.

"Did you hear me?" he asks, although it's not a question. It's more a statement of his discontent.

"I'm sure that's not what you meant in that note, Seth," I finally speak, my voice more even than I dreamed it would be. How it comes out so calm and collected, I have no idea.

Goosebumps line my arms as another gust of wind pushes at my back, gathering my hair and causing it to tumble over my shoulders. I cross my arms as my nipples pebble.

"I'm here," I tell him. As if stating the obvious was needed.

The anger and edge of threat are absent, and the heat in Seth's eyes roars when he glances down my body and then back to my own wandering gaze.

Time passes, too much of it, before I break the silence and break our caught stares to say, "I didn't make you come far, did I?"

CHAPTER 3

Seth

SHE'S HERE. LAURA'S IN MY GRASP. AND SHE'S COMPLETELY UNAFFECTED. I can't fucking take it. It's a black hole that whirls around me. Nothingness, yet I'm falling. Hard and fast.

This gut-wrenching concoction of desire and anger, betrayal and longing… it's too much. I can't focus on any one aspect of this moment. Control feels like a concept I can't grasp as the blood rushing in my ears drowns out everything else.

Closing my eyes, I inhale long and deep. She is the woman I used to love. When I was someone else. Nothing more. I try to convince myself of that truth.

Her words linger, confirming the statement.

I didn't make you come far, did I?

Her comment pisses me off more and more with every step I take toward the house. The anger laces with desire. Her smart mouth has always gotten me hard.

I gently place my splayed hand on her back, to lead her into my house, hiding my eagerness.

Inside. I need to get her inside.

I can barely feel her, but I don't miss how her eyes close at my touch. All it takes is a gentle push and Laura walks fast enough so that I barely have contact with her.

The soft satin of her red dress caresses my fingertips. I know she's cold in the thin material. She chose this dress, tight around her ass and low cut, for a reason. Everything she does is for a reason.

Every step closer to the door, I gather more and more composure. I remember who I am today and not what we had before.

The past needs to stay where it is. Those ghosts are long gone. Carter's assessment follows me, hardens me... it warns me to be careful.

As Laura passes the threshold, I notice her long hair, once naturally dark but now lightened, falling over one shoulder. She peeks over her shoulder but not at me though; instead she looks back to her car. Maybe second-guessing everything, maybe wanting to run. I wonder if she can feel the difference inside of me. I feel it every damn day. I'm highly aware that I'm not the same man she remembers from the past. How could I be? That night changed everything about me.

When she chose to run, so did something inside of me. And it never came back.

The clack of the front door closing is followed by the lock clicking into place. Laura's body shudders at the sound, and I watch closely as her plump lips, colored the same dark red as her dress, part as she sucks in a breath. She may not want to admit I've gotten to her, but I damn well know I have.

She can pretend to be the confident seductress when she looks in the mirror. But I see underneath it all.

The mix of dark woods and grays, all the masculine clean lines of my home is at complete odds with Laura. She stands out, unable to hide in the neutrals of the open floor plan. She aims to move to the sleek ashen davenport sofa in the living room. Even picking up her pace, turning the air between us businesslike, she takes a few steps forward, only for me to catch her elbow and move her forward, toward the office.

Her quick glance and questioning gaze are gone as quickly as they came. I couldn't give two shits where we do this, but she won't decide it.

She decided to run from me. To steal from me. She doesn't get to decide anything else.

Never fucking again. She doesn't have a choice.

I've had countless days to plan what I'd say and do. Years ago, back in California. And years here, knowing she was close enough to see with only minutes of driving. Even as I walk her through the hall and open the carved walnut office door, ushering her inside, the plan is changing.

Some days it's a debt owed and I want her to pay me back, however I choose.

Some moments the hate for her leaving me at my worst is so strong, that I don't want a damn thing to do with her. I want her to know how close I am, and to know I don't care enough to seek her out.

Smelling her sweet scent, and listening to the steady beat of her heels clicking against the wood, part of me wants to charm her, to beg for her forgiveness and offer her the world. I could give her that. Everything is different now. That part comes with something else. It starts as an inkling of sorrow, but it's quick to spread, like oil slicking across the water. It's thin, but covers every inch in blackness. I want to beg her to love me again. I want her to see how wrecked I was. How I feel like nothing without her. I am nothing anymore, but why would she want me? Why the hell would she ever come back?

She makes me weak.

"Your home is lovely," Laura comments politely with her slender back to me as I shut the office door. Both of her hands grip the strap of her purse, giving away the nerves she's hiding. "The inside isn't like the outside… it's so modern and open."

I'm different; I know I am, but so is she. We're nothing like we used to be. I assess her as she appraises my office. Taking in the rows of books, organized by date of publication. I collect the rare ones because I like the way they smell and look, but I haven't read them. I don't intend to either.

Her footsteps are gentler in this room and the angular edges of her dress seem to soften as I watch her move from one end of my small office to the other. Her footsteps are muted although it's hardwood beneath her heels. She's walking more carefully, with more hesitation.

I love that. The façade fades as the seconds pass.

She's still the same girl I know, even if she wants to appear otherwise.

Her hair is curled, meticulously so when she still sat in her car. But the wind has seen to ruffle her blond tresses. I like her even more with her hair slightly messy. She should aim for that next time, a "just recently fucked" look.

I want to ask her why she did it, why she dyed her hair. It's gorgeous on her; she has the tan in her skin to pull it off. I love the memory of her from before more though. She was perfect before.

Her nails are painted a darker shade of red than the short dress that hugs her curves. Even her makeup is flawless. It's obvious this look—this sex kitten appeal, is deliberate.

I would like to pretend she did it for me. But two weeks ago, she looked similar. Perfectly put together and dressed with an edge of a vixen. The thought hits me as she glances up at me: *this is who she is now.*

Is it a lie? Is she still the woman I fell for?

Laura turns the moment my eyes read hers, preventing me from imagining running the tip of my finger along her skin. From the crook of her neck, all the way down her back. I could see myself doing it again and again until she begged me to unzip her dress. "Did you decorate it yourself?" Again, she's polite.

I fucking hate niceties.

"I hired someone," I say and my answer comes out flat as my eyes gauge her expression. Her knuckles are white from her tight grip, but her smile is forced. The longer the seconds draw out, the tighter her grip gets.

Maybe she's realizing what I am. Maybe she's come to the conclusion that she doesn't trust the man I've become. I wouldn't blame her.

I take my time, slipping off my jacket and folding it neatly before placing it over the arm of an amber leather executive chair in the corner of my office. The cufflinks are next to go, sitting them on the end of the antique bookshelf to the left of my desk. I focus on them, avoiding Laura's prying eyes although I can feel them on me. Every step I take circles her as I move closer to where she is until I finally look up at her, feet away, but I feel miles apart with the way she looks at me.

"Are you scared of me?" I ask her and take a step forward. She doesn't move from where she is in front of my desk. "Maybe of what I may tell you?" I take another step forward, blocking the light from the floor lamp in the far corner and causing shadows to darken her face. "Or maybe what I may do to you?"

"If you wanted to hurt me, you would have already," she answers me with such certainty, although it's practically whispered.

She doesn't say anything else; she doesn't give a hint of what's she's thinking or feeling. She doesn't apologize. She doesn't ask me for anything. The tension thickens as she waits for a response from me.

How long would she have lived without me and been perfectly fucking fine? All the while, I've died inside.

"You stole from a criminal," I practically hiss. "So many others would have killed you simply to set an example."

"You didn't tell them," she responds without letting a second pass. I had so much left to say, so much to make her feel the anxiousness I feel. It vanishes when her gaze softens with agony. "You didn't tell them I took the money. Your crew never knew." The sound of her swallowing mixes with the desperation in her voice. My gaze falls to her slender neck and then drifts down to the dip below her throat. She must have difficulty breathing now, because her lips part just to inhale and she leaves them that way. Her chest rises and falls and finally she takes a half step back.

"Derrick?" I ask her and she nods slowly, bringing my attention back to her face. Her expression gives nothing away, even if her posture gives away everything. "What else?"

"What else what?" she questions, again evenly.

"Tell me everything Derrick told you."

"We haven't spoken in a long time," she says then breaks my gaze as the corners of her lips pull downward. Looking behind her, she rests against the edge of the desk, setting her purse beside her. Her hands tremble slightly until she clasps them together, hiding her emotions as she pretends to relax in front of me.

What a lie she's become. Or is it only for me? Sucking in a breath, I rip my gaze away from her and wait for her response. "Tell me."

"The last time I talked to him was a few years ago, when you first moved here."

"So you've known—" I start to say, and it comes out like an accusation.

"That you've been here?" she says as she cuts me off and I only nod. "I knew when you started working with the Cross brothers because of the whispers. I called Derrick and he confirmed it."

"What did he say?" I shouldn't feel this heat in my blood. This apprehension that she may not like what Derrick told her. I'm not here to soothe her or comfort her though. That's not what this is about.

I will never let her in like I did before. Never again. I learned my lesson. She made sure of that.

"He only said you heard about the Cross brothers and how quickly they were taking over… I asked him if you came for me." Her voice hitches for the first time and she has to swallow thickly before continuing. I watch pain flash across her expression and she doesn't try to conceal it. "He said you didn't."

Tap, tap. My pointer finger rests on the desk as I lean my thigh against the side of it opposite from her. *Tap, tap*. I wonder if that hurt her. *Tap, tap*. I watch her face as she waits for me to say something, but I don't.

"I came up with a plan when I heard you were here," she confesses.

"A plan?"

"I had information I thought you'd want." I don't respond to her comment. I merely stare in her doe eyes, watching the way the gentle gold flecks among the blue brighten with emotions in their depths.

"Like a deal? You wanted to make a deal with me?" Anger roils inside of me, overwhelming my focus. *A deal to get me to leave her alone.*

"Yes," she whispers this time and her fear isn't something she can hide, judging by how she inches away from me.

"You thought I came to hurt you?" I question her.

"At first."

I ignore my immediate reaction to hearing her admit that. "I have a deal too. I've thought of a lot of them over the past few years."

"What's your deal?" she asks and lifts her chin slightly, her bright blue eyes boring into mine. Back to business maybe. I'm not sure what's going on in that pretty little head of hers.

"You do everything I say."

Her eyes search mine until she blinks rapidly and looks past me, shaking her head. "That's not a deal."

My words echoing in my head sound more and more inviting. "Yes, it is."

"What do I get in return?" She licks her lips quickly, leaning forward as if she's scrambling to hold on to something before adding, "Deals have two parties."

"You get to live," I offer her in all seriousness. I don't care who she's become. Laura's mine. I will get everything I want from her. I *need* it.

"I'm already living."

"You stole from me. There's a debt owed and a corresponding punishment. I would never let someone else steal from me and live."

"Just kill me then," she says and her voice cracks although she's quick to clear her throat. "Just kill me if that's what you want." Despite her shattered veneer she holds her head high. She accepts my glare and doesn't falter, her eyes brimming with tears.

Before I can respond, she says something else. I don't hear it though as I take a seat; I simply watch as she pulls herself back together. She's damn good at it. *At not needing me.*

I take my time, giving her a moment to breathe. At the head of the desk, I grip the armrests, waiting.

"Did you hear what I said?" Her composure is back, although her breathing is ragged.

"You said you wanted an exchange. You want to change the details of our deal."

Her doe eyes beg me to consider, and they hold a vulnerability that her tense curves fail to deliver. As she takes a step forward, I think she wants to sit in the other wingback chair, but her legs give out. She grips both arms of the chair across from me as her chest rises and falls with a quickened pace. She can't hide the fear of coming back to this life. *Of coming back to me.*

As her bottom lip slips between her teeth, I note that she can't hide the desire either.

"I've wanted this for too long to consider your proposal," I tell her, spreading my legs wider and leaning forward in the wingback chair opposite hers. My elbows rest on my knees as I lean closer to her, only inches away as I whisper, "You know what I want. I want you."

"I can give you something you want more," she speaks clearly, although her last words waver when her gaze drifts to my lips.

Lies. There's nothing I want more.

I would have told her that and meant it with every bone in my body, but then she tells me, "I can give you Marcus."

Laura

What would he do to me?

Even as I reach in my satchel for the notebook, my hand trembles. I can't imagine Seth hurting me. I can't. Even as he looks at me the way he does. That's not what scares me.

I'm scared to go back, back to him and all this shit he comes with. I don't want this life. I've never wanted it.

A voice in the back of my head whispers: *you're afraid to fall in love with him again.* I ache for him. So deeply. Agony shreds me when I see who he's become. I want to cry more than anything. I don't know how I'll survive this. All I have to cling to is a collection of photocopied pages, as if they'll save me from this.

"You're lying," he says and his voice is firm.

"I'm not; I haven't lied. I can give you information on Marcus."

"Yes you have," he bites out quickly and for the first time since I've been in here, I see a flash of sadness in his dark cobalt gaze. I can't respond to him. Not even when he turns away from me, leaning back and tapping his index finger on the desk again. He's so broken. I didn't do this to him. It's not because of me. With the notebook of photocopied pages between my fingers, I lie to myself again: *I didn't do this to him.*

"There's a patient at the Rockford Center. She's been in and out of there for years although she's not a resident currently," I explain as I hand over the notebook. It's a hardcover, black and nondescript, of her first collection of memories. Holding out the bound pages, I can't look in Seth's gaze. I can't and I won't, but he doesn't take it. He doesn't accept it and with every long second that passes, it only hurts more. "She's been with Marcus. She knows about him."

"Many people work for—"

"*Been* with," I interrupt him to emphasize, "she was his lover."

His fingers graze mine as he takes it. A hot and longing need for him is threatening to consume me. With my eyes closed, I try to ignore what the rough feel of his touch does to me. It's like a sparkler, hot and brightly lit, yet quickly extinguished. A part of me yearns to move forward, to light my entire body. I've always been weak for him. My soul in love with his, needing his. I keep my eyes closed even when I hear him turn the pages.

I left this man years ago but in this moment, it feels like I'm leaving him again. Simply because I refuse to give in. It feels like I'm running although I'm merely standing still in front of him.

"She wrote detailed descriptions of every location he took her."

"We have intel on his habits and the locations of his businesses." Seth speaks calmly, as if the information gathered in front of him is nothing new. With my eyes widening, I finally look at him, and then my body jumps when he tosses the heavy notebook down on his desk. The slap ricochets through my body.

"Like I said," he says and my gaze falls to his throat, watching the cords tense as he swallows and adds, "you'll do everything I say."

"There are more," I tell him quickly, ignoring his statement and even I can hear how begging my tone is.

I've fallen for this man once. If I do it again, I'll cross the point of no return. I'm sure of it.

His gaze is hungry as he exhales with disdain. "Give me all of them," he commands.

"I don't have them with me."

"You'll bring them next time then," he says. He's bossing me around and telling me what to do.

"I'll do what I please," I bite out, remembering who I am.

Seth smirks at my response, appearing not at all flustered.

"It will please you," he tells me and his tone is different. His cadence caresses every inch of my skin. Leaning forward, he rests his hand on my knee, and damn does my body respond to him. "I will make sure of that."

"Seth," I breathe his name.

"There are other things that need to be done first. I plan on taking my time."

Seth

Hearing her whisper my name like that…

I want her more than I will ever admit. Just like I'll never admit how dire the situation is with Marcus. I don't have this information, but she'll give it to me.

I burn for her to give me many things before that happens.

Her pain as I punish her. And her pleas for me to take her back.

One thing I'd planned to do since I moved back, one thing that has never deviated is sitting right behind her in the top drawer on the other side of the desk.

She watches me all the while and I wonder what she sees. What she thinks. What she feels. The drawer slides out with a creak and it's the only sound in the office.

For a split second, I wonder if I should do it. If I should give it back to her. Laura needs to feel it though. She needs to know.

With the folded paper in my hand, I take a moment to clear off the left side of my desk, slipping a pile of folders inside the drawer. Now all that's left is my laptop and a few odds and ends. The steel pen container is moved first. I set it on the windowsill behind me; clearing off what remains on the desk will take less than a minute. I want her ass right here, on this desk, once she's done reading what I'm holding.

"This is for you." I hand her the note, not going back on the promise I made to myself, although I know without a question of a doubt, that she'd get up on this desk right now with no hesitation. She needs that note first. I told myself for years that if ever I were to see her again, she needed to have it back. There's dried blood on the edge of one side although it's turned a dark brown now. There are other stains on the once clean paper as well. I can still see right where she'd cried and the paper took in her tears, seeping into the crisp creased folds and warping them. It's harder to see it now though. It blends in with all the other evidence that the paper has existed for far too many years.

I watch her eyes as she unfolds the note. I watch her pupils dilate and note their glossy sheen as she rips her gaze away and looks anywhere but at me.

Her inhale is ragged and sharp.

"This isn't for me."

"It is. It's for you to read. I've read it enough."

The paper crinkles in her hand. The creases are so soft; I didn't think it could crinkle anymore.

She needs to be reminded that she told me she'd love me forever.

She promised me she would. She can read it and know it every day of her life like I have since she left me.

"I want you to read it every day. It's only fair—it's what I did for years."

Her voice is raw when she answers the command with, "At least you had a note," and then tosses it onto the desk. Like she doesn't want it.

I didn't want it either. It would have been so much easier without it. If she'd just left me because she hated me.

"Is this what you want?" she asks as a tear rolls down her cheek, unable to hide it any longer. She angrily wipes it away.

"Partly," I admit out loud and shock myself. Her disgust shows and she grabs her purse this time, as if she'll leave.

"Sit down," I command as her ass lifts from the seat. She stills where she is. Debating maybe. "We aren't finished, Babygirl." I meant for the word to get to her. Not to me. But it settles in my chest, spreading the ache I've been doing my damnedest to suppress.

She's slow to take her seat, but she does.

"Want to know what I missed?" I ask her although at this point, I'm just speaking my mind. No filter; I let it all out. "The way you say my name," I say and close my eyes, focusing for a moment on the motions of my thumb. *Tap, tap*. "I missed it."

Even with my eyes closed, I can feel hers on me. I swear my body knows hers. The vulnerability of it all wanes as I flick through the scenes of what happened when she left.

"I missed the taste of you," I comment lowly and tilt my head when I look back at her. Her skin is a gorgeous blush color and her pale blue eyes are rimmed with a pink that matches her complexion. Desire dances between us. My cock hardens and her thighs tense as her inhale skips.

"I remember thinking one night," I say and point to the desk, "as I read that note, is any pussy that good?" Hardening my voice, I remind her of the anger.

She needs to be punished. She has to be.

Her red-rimmed eyes fill with lust. There's an undeniable heat.

"I want to taste you, Laura," I say and then realize it's not a command. She needs to be told what to do though. And every action reinforced.

Desire outweighs the rage. It outweighs everything. The image of her under me, her thighs parted, enters my mind. It's all I can focus on. With my zipper pressing tight against my erection, I get up from the chair and tell her to strip. I add, "I want you down to nothing."

I think, for a moment, there's no way she'll do it.

"Say please," she retaliates, although it's softly spoken and submissive, laced with a sadness too. A new roar of fire ignites inside of me.

"Please," I say and my voice comes out deeper, from a raw place inside of me as I lean forward, "Get your ass up here."

The hesitation in her expression is clear, but that doesn't stop her from toeing off her heels. She's quick to obey me. The hope that blooms from that knowledge is unwanted.

"I want you here," I say and splay my hand on the space to my left I cleared moments ago. All but the notebook and my laptop, which I move now, keeping my head turned as I go and pretending like I'm not obsessed with the peripheral image of her doing exactly what I tell her to do.

The balls of her feet pad on the floor as she makes her way around to the other side of the desk, climbing on top of it. Her heavy breathing invades my senses and fuels the rapid pump of my heart. She's naked, and I'm fully dressed. I swear if I were to move even a muscle right now, I'd take her, savagely and roughly on top of my desk.

Control. I grasp for it. I cling to it when her gaze searches mine for direction. I won't be reckless with her. That's why I lost her. Recklessness.

"Put your ass here and spread your legs." My voice is even and she listens, bringing the sweet scent of her femininity closer to me. I don't move, watching her crawl closer to position herself with her legs in front of her and her ass only inches from my hand on the desk.

My head falls to the side as she places one heel to the left of my hand. I let my nose brush against her calf, then kiss the inside of her knee.

"Seth." She calls my name as if she's falling and I don't respond. Not for a moment and then another. I'm waiting for that other heel to be placed and her thighs to part for me.

It takes her a long minute to do it, but she does.

She's propped up with her hands bracing her. Her breasts are small but they fall heavy, swaying slightly as she breathes.

Bringing my hand to her heat, I brush my knuckles against her soft flesh and then higher up her body, until my hand is at her stomach. "Down," I command, pressing against the base of her sternum and pushing her to lie on her back.

Her body burns under my touch.

"You shaved," I comment as I move my fingers back down. With both hands, I spread her thighs farther apart and she doesn't protest in the least.

"You shaved, you chose a dress and heels, but you came ready to bargain." I'm barely conscious of my own words as I stare at her pussy. Her clit is swollen and she's already glistening with desire. I run my middle finger between her lips, playing with her, toying with her cunt and watching goosebumps spread along her skin.

"You had to know I'd take you, didn't you?" I ask her. The way I'm seated, I can't see her eyes. I'm glad for that because it means she can't see my expression when she gasps as I push my finger inside of her.

She whispers the words, "I missed you too."

A painful recognition spreads through me, suffocating me, knowing it's true; it hurts to hear her say that even more. I lean down and take a languid lick, ignoring the longing in her response and focusing on how her back arches.

She's hot and sweet. I lap at her, taking my time, from her entrance to her clit. A strangled moan fills the air along with the sound of her nails scratching on the desk. As if she wants to grab hold of something.

Letting a low groan come from my chest, I enjoy her, drawing this out. Her thighs close in on me when she writhes on the desk and it's only then that I pull back.

She won't get off. I won't let her. I want her to miss it. To miss how I would do this to her the way I missed it.

"You don't get to cum. Not until I decide you should."

Standing up quickly, I push the chair back just as it nearly falls. I turn my back to her and when I hear her draw in a sharp breath, I tell her to stay.

"Don't you dare move." My heart pounds against my rib cage; maybe it's desperate to get back to her. A cold sweat lines my skin. "You do what I say and when," I state, reminding her of our arrangement.

"I told you no to that deal," she whispers, the desire still coloring her upper chest, throat and cheeks. She doesn't move though. I watch her to make sure she listens. Her eyes are closed as I slowly pace, ignoring her comment about her telling me no. I grab her throat with my right hand, feeling the pulse of her hot blood as she quickly looks up at me, wide eyed and full of concern.

"I missed that mouth of yours," I comment and then lean down, kissing her harshly. I expect it to be short lived, but when she parts her lips ever so slightly, even with the taste of her still present on my tongue, I deepen it. And she does the same.

There has always been a disconnect with us. Our bodies do one thing; our minds tell us another. With the fever of lust covering every inch of my skin, I pull away from her, although my grip on her throat is unmoving.

"You'll stay with me," I say absently, telling her without thinking and my mind plays tricks on me. It goes back years ago. If only she'd stay with me.

"No," she answers weakly, a raw vulnerability lacing the single word.

"You will and you'll pay off the debt with your cunt." I grasp for any reason at all for her to agree. To remember her guilt.

"Don't be crass," she bites out even as her voice trembles. She seems to come out of it, out of the haze of longing. Wiping the corners of her mouth, she stares back at me, not giving in to my demand. "I won't do it, Seth."

"Crass? Are you too good for that kind of language now?"

Even at my mercy, Laura's strength shines through. I wonder what she looked like when she left me. I wonder if she cried. Derrick swore to me there's no way she left without falling apart. I want to see her fall apart. I want to know what this version of her looks like when she does.

"I'm not yours anymore," Laura tells me calmly, still lying spread on my desk. The taste of her is still present on my tongue.

"You owe me," is all I tell her, firm and deliberate.

"You owe me too," she whispers after a moment and the crack in her guard splinters. Suddenly, she looks all too familiar. I have to let her go. In an instant, the room feels colder. The ghost of her in my living room stares back at me. Cross-legged on the floor with the scent of smoke filtering through my lungs.

"I owe you?" I question with feigned disgust. She's quick to sit up, to cover herself from me. The moment is lost. "What is it I owe you?" I dare her to answer me. To bring up her home, to bring up Cami. Fuck.

If she'd listened to me, if only she'd stayed close—I could have kept her safe. It could have been different. It didn't have to end the way it did.

I'm so close to screaming the words. *It didn't have to end like it did. You should have listened to me.* So close, I can feel them scratching up the back of my throat.

"I wish I'd never fallen in love with you," she admits and scrambles to get off my desk. *Stay still*, I warn myself. *Stay still.* If I move, I'll grab her. She reaches for her clothes, heedlessly throwing them on.

"You will stay with me. You will do everything I tell you to." I give the commands as if all of her objecting will vanish. I still don't trust myself to move. I swear I'll lift her beautiful ass over my shoulder and lock her in a room.

"You wanted to humiliate me? To prove to me you could still have me if you wanted?" she questions with disdain and the thought of what she's implying had not once occurred to me. Not once. I didn't even know until a moment ago that I could have her.

"You have no idea what I want from you!" I don't know why I scream. I don't know why I shake as she zips up her dress and slowly faces me.

"Yes, I do, and I'll tell you right now, Seth, it won't happen. I won't let it."

"I left you alone for years. I won't any longer," I tell her and my words are rushed.

"I'm not a plaything. I'm not yours anymore," she tells me as she grabs her heels from the floor.

"Yes. You are. That is exactly what you are."

She turns from my heated gaze, frantically looking for her purse until she can snatch it, ready to leave me.

"You'll come back tomorrow night. Five o'clock," I say calmly even as a panic stirs in my blood watching her race out of the door.

I don't follow her. I stay perfectly still, not trusting myself to move. It's not until I hear her car start from outside that I brace myself against my desk. It's still warm from where she laid herself bare for me.

The rev of her engine and the peeling out of her tires comes and goes until I'm alone.

She left me again. My eyes catch sight of the note on my desk. She left me again.

With a roar ripped from my throat, I grab the floor lamp and slam it against the bookshelf. Heaving in the darkened room, I can't let go of it.

She left me again, but she'll be back.

I'll have her again.

She'll be back.

CHAPTER 4

Laura

THE BAGS UNDER MY EYES STILL FEEL HEAVY. I PUT ON ENOUGH concealer to hide them though. I'm an expert at that now. I doubt anyone in this coffee shop can tell how much I cried last night.

With the small chatter and the subtle pop music, no one in Baked and Brewed is paying me any mind. I picked a table in the back corner and from here I can see everything in this place. It's cute and quaint, smelling of freshly brewed coffee and cinnamon from something they just baked. The new shop is on the corner of Fourth and Washington. With walnut furniture, all simple and clean, but pops of mint green from the steel signs and chairs, it's certainly eye catching. Every table has a short clear vase with a few sprigs of baby's breath too. It's all sorts of happy and relaxed in this coffee shop. Completely at odds with how I'm feeling.

But this is the place Bethany picked. And so I'm here.

Blowing on the hot cup of caramel coffee, their flavor of the day, I think back to last night. Back to the moment I know I lost myself as I wait for Bethany to walk in the front door.

Is any pussy really that good?

His voice is deep and rough in my memory. I don't know if I've made it up, rethinking about that moment time after time in such a short period, or if he really sounded like that. There was a sense of awe, followed by a sense of loss that coated his words. I was a fiddle for him to play right then and there.

I thought after he took that first lick he'd lift his head and meet my stare to tell me, "No, it isn't that good." Swallowing thickly, I force down a sip of the coffee, not tasting it at all.

The way he treated me… I've never let a man treat me like that before. He's fucked me every way possible, but yesterday I let him touch me, not knowing if he respected me anymore. I'm ashamed I let Seth make me feel the way he did. The vulnerability is something I've never felt sexually with him and I hate it. I am ashamed and humiliated. I've never hated him before last night.

I've heard there's a thin line between love and hate, but damn, I never knew how true those words were.

What's worse is that I know it's the same for him. He has a mix of love and hate for me. I could *feel* it. It's all deserved.

That's why I never should have gotten on his desk. The way I craved him loving me… it's not possible for him to do that anymore. I should know better. That fleeting thought left me the moment his touch registered. I'm not interested in a hate fuck or being played with and treated as less than. If that's what he thinks this will be, I'll refuse, consequences be damned.

Seth's not apologetic; he's only demanding. It terrifies me most because I want to obey him. I want to do whatever he tells me because I am sorry. I hate what I did to him. I hate myself. He makes me hate myself.

Maybe a piece of me thinks he should be treating me like that… like I'm "less than."

"You okay?" Bethany's voice startles me and pulls me back to the present. Back to the hot mug I've got both hands wrapped around and the small ceramic plate of bite-size lemon cake squares.

"Yeah," I answer Bethany, setting the mug down and listening to the bells above the coffee shop door chime as an older man makes his way out. I didn't hear Bethany come in. "I didn't see you come in," I tell her.

As she pulls out the mint green metal stool on the other side of the table, the feet scrape against the floor and she simply stares at me.

There are at least six more patrons in the shop, a pair of maybe sixteen-year-olds—I don't even know if the two girls at the far end should be sipping on those lattes—and a few single adults scattered around the place. One's reading a book, others are scrolling through their phones and one man with white-as-snow hair is reading a newspaper. Bethany's got her back to all of them and her attention is centered on me.

"Sorry I'm late. I got into a little thing at home."

"Does it have to do with your sister?" I ask her in response, keeping my mind focused on the fact that everyone else has something going on in their life too. It's not all about me. It never will be. There's always someone else who needs help. It may seem inconsistent with logic, but that's what gets me through. Bethany nods and I'm quick to tell her, "I'm here for you, you know?" I put my hand over hers on the table and she takes it and squeezes it but then lets go as she sits back.

She seems to look right through me when she tells me, "It looks like you need someone more than me, to be honest." Bethany's blunt. She's always blunt. There's a kindness about the way she says things, but it cuts straight to the heart of the matter. She's a lot wiser than she appears, given how young she looks. She's been through hell and I know all about it. She came out fighting though.

We're silent as a waitress wearing a white apron with a mint green logo for Baked and Brewed stamped square on the front of it, places a cup of tea in front of Bethany.

"Thank you." Bethany smiles and then her dark red lips leave a smudge of lipstick behind on the white mug. That lipstick is what we first bonded over. "Lipstick courage" is what she responded when I complimented the shade. Later that night, she told me the name of it and I ordered a tube without thinking twice. There's a lot to be said about lipstick courage.

She stares at it a moment before tucking her brunette locks behind her ears.

"So, spill it," she requests.

It's been almost two weeks since I've seen Bethany and the last time we spoke in person things didn't go so well. It was my fault and I can still feel the distance between us. I hate it. Rubbing my hand down my face, I come to a certain realization. *Seems like I'm full of hate today.*

"I owe you an apology—"

"Stop it," she says, cutting me off. "You already apologized, for one." She swallows without looking back at me. It looks like she's lost weight since I've seen her. Meeting my gaze, she says, "Second, I know now."

"You know what?" I ask her, my fingers reaching for the ceramic mug.

Even with concealer under her eyes, I can tell she hasn't slept. Or maybe I'm just making it up, and I want to avoid talking about me, and move the conversation to her dilemma.

"That you know Seth," she confesses. She leans forward and says, "You knew him when I dragged you to his car. You could have told me." The last sentence she practically whispers and as she says it, I retract my hands from the table and move them to my lap.

"How do you know?"

"Jase." Bethany's answer is the name of her now-boyfriend. And Seth's employer. It's odd to think of Seth working for someone. He was never the type to take orders from anyone other than his father. He was bred to rule. It's simply who he is.

"What else did he tell you?" I question, my words coming out carefully. I feel a sick prickling along my skin. Bells chime above the café door and the sound steals my attention for only a fraction of a second. It's all too intense. Whenever Seth is involved, it's too intense.

"He told me not to tell you… so shhh, don't tell anyone I told you."

I roll my eyes as I comment, "As if I ever would," and try to take another sip of coffee. Again, I can't taste a thing.

All I can wonder is how much Jase knows. Did Seth tell him something? Did he tell him everything? I haven't told a soul. I can't even speak it out loud.

With a prick at the back of my eyes, I ask Bethany, my voice cracking, "Did he tell you what happened when I left? What made me leave?"

Her thick hair swishes as she sips her tea, never taking her eyes off of me. Maybe she's waiting for me to tell her, but there's not a chance in hell I will. I can't. I can't tell her about Cami.

With the silence separating us and adding an air of dread to our corner of this little café, Bethany tells me, "He only said that you two were together back when you lived in California and then you left." I nod. I fled, I ran, I took off. *Left* seems like such an insignificant word.

She adds when I don't respond, "Jase said it looks like Seth followed you here."

"He didn't." I'm quick to correct her. Derrick told me he didn't. If he had, he would have come for me sooner. "He didn't come here for me."

Why does it hurt so much? Why does my heart twist and turn before going *thud*, *thud*, then pausing in my chest?

"Jase seems to think otherwise. I walked in on him and Carter talking about it."

The furrow of my brow works in time with my curiosity. My interest, and my concern piqued, I lean forward to question, "Why were they talking about it?"

Bethany shrugs, as if it's not a big deal. I don't want my name to be spoken by either of those men. The Cross brothers aren't known for generosity. They're brutal. Especially Carter. That sick prickling heats and makes my entire body burn with anxiety.

"Why did you leave?" she asks me and I'd be grateful for the change of subject away from the Cross brothers, had it been any other subject.

My finger plays at the rim of my mug, gliding along it as I inhale and exhale, forming the words in my mind first. I'm careful and deliberate with my answer when I say, "Things got hard and a bad thing happened to someone close to me." I peek up and Bethany's eyes are assessing. She's the best nurse at the Rockford Center, in my possibly biased opinion. It's one of the reasons I was drawn to her. She's damn good at what she does and she loves people in general. She loves making a difference and helping them. "Don't you dare treat me like one of the patients," I warn her.

Putting her hands up in the air, she protests that she never would. "If you don't want to tell me, that's okay." She resumes her position and cocks a brow at me before adding, "I won't push you."

Her reaction actually makes me huff a humorous laugh. "I've literally heard you tell that to patients."

She joins in my humor, giving me a genuine grin. It lightens the mood slightly, and I'm grateful for it. "I can't talk about it and get worked up. We're in a coffee shop, for fuck's sake. I don't even have mascara with me to touch up." I look her square in the eyes and see my friend again. The bond nearly physical between us, I joke, "I can't walk out of here with black streaks down my face."

She agrees, saying, "This place doesn't have a bathroom either. So no crying…" and then she persists in order to understand, "…but you left, you were emotional. The breakup was mutual?"

"Not really." My gut churns with my response.

"So you left him?" Fuck it hurts to hear her ask that. My heart agrees, stalling and refusing to resume beating until I respond. I nod and give a small *yeah*, ignoring the pain that claws at my gut.

There's no way in hell I'm going to be able to eat those lemon cake squares.

"And then he moved back but he's been here for a while and …" I trail off and when Bethany doesn't say anything, I steel myself to confess the truth to her.

"And the night at the shopping center, our night out was the first time I'd seen him and spoken to him."

I'm surprised by the sorrow that worries Bethany's expression when she says, "And I just let you go with him. I'm sorry." Her voice cracks.

"You trusted him," I say to defend her and make sure that defense is audible. "It had to happen, Bethany. It was bound to. I'm happy you were with me when it did."

Her smile is weak, and the conversation pauses for a moment while she composes herself. "What did he say?" she asks once she's finally got a grip on her regret.

How do I tell her he didn't say a word to me? Again that shame rises at the fact I'd let a man get to me the way he did. More than that, protectiveness spreads through me. I find myself wanting to defend Seth. I don't want her to think of him like that. He wasn't always an asshole she'd hate this very second if she knew what transpired.

He was good.

I did this to him.

With a shuddering breath, I skip over the details of that night, only giving her the bare essentials: *He dropped me off and told me to meet him last night.*

Telling her what happened yesterday proves to be difficult too. I don't know how much of my perception is real. Was he cold to me like I remember? Or was he waiting to see what I'd do, like I was doing with him?

"It looks like more happened than just that, Laura," Bethany prods, when I try to gloss over it.

"The thing is, I'm not okay. Not emotionally. I keep finding myself back in that place I was when I left. It's like I'm grieving all over again."

"So this is about the bad thing that happened to someone close to you? Or leaving Seth?"

"I think both," I admit to her, truly unsure.

"An emotional state isn't linear." She reminds me of something I already know, and her eyes tell me she knows that I know.

"I know, but grief is supposed to be in stages and—"

She cuts me off, her voice pleading with me to understand. "Those stages misrepresent emotions. I just got into this with Aiden." She makes that last comment under her breath, fiddling with her napkin and then popping a lemon square in her mouth. Aiden is our boss at the Rockford Center. We don't always see eye to eye on things. It's good for the patients though. If one method isn't helping them, we have others.

"No, I know, and I agree with you. The stages are a depiction of the mental capacity to deal with shock and stressors that are too much to handle. Denial isn't an emotion, it's a coping mechanism. The stages are a timeline and they move in order and never in reverse because it's about coping, not about emotional ability." I stress the last line with the side of my hand hitting the table. "Yesterday, it felt like I was on a roller coaster, a scary one that I don't want to be on, and it kept moving back without warning, sending me down the same hill I ran from." The emotions, the wretched feeling I'm describing—it all creeps knowingly toward me again.

"It's not the stages of grief you're talking about. It's simply loss."

"It is," I admit quietly and close my eyes. "I'm feeling the loss all over again."

"Loss*es*," she says, stressing the plural, "and memories… they're chaotic, they come and go as they please with no patterns at times. They can be triggered."

"Well him being back in my life…" I start to tell her, grabbing hold of the reason, and therefore a semblance of control. "Seth saying…" I almost tell her *Babygirl*, but I don't want to give Bethany that much. It feels like a violation of what we have. "Seth saying my name…" I look her in the eyes only after I've spoken the last line of deception and continue, "It's bringing back a lot of shit for me."

"That makes sense." She nods in understanding, and it helps. It makes such a difference just to feel understood. "You're wrecked. You look it, too."

"Well thanks, bestie," I joke and it makes us both ease into a short laugh. I have to sniffle, although I haven't cried and when I do, she continues.

"So you are emotional… in a negative way."

"Right."

"Were you afraid of what he'd do?"

"No, I was afraid of how he'd make me feel."

"How did he make you feel?" she asks.

"All sorts of ways."

"But did you get butterflies?" There's a note of optimism in her question.

I peek at her over my coffee, taking a large gulp and praying it gives me energy I desperately need. It's only lukewarm now. "Yeah, I got all sorts of butterflies." Every scene from yesterday washes over me. And even if he was… harder, harsher even, a heat I can't deny betrays my pride. "He…" I can't finish the statement without a blush warming my cheeks.

With wide eyes and an eager grin, Bethany reacts and says, "Oh my God, you're blushing. Since when do you blush?"

A laugh bubbles from my lips and I shake my head. I swear Seth will always give me butterflies. As if in response to that thought, my heart flutters that odd beat and I place my hand over the wild thing, trying to calm it.

"So …" Bethany presses.

"He thinks he can tell me what to do and I'll simply be his." For the second time today, I roll my eyes. It's followed by a smirk though as I add, "But he went down on me yesterday."

If it's possible, her eyes go even wider with this confession.

"He didn't get me off, though." I don't hide my disappointment.

Her response is comical and gets the attention of the older man with thin white hair as she exclaims, "Bastard!"

I smile into my coffee, sipping it. Even though it's not hot, it's delicious. "Yeah, he's a bastard. It's a little more serious than the way I'm saying it," I confess.

"The Cross brothers are always a little more serious."

"He's not a Cross brother."

"He's one of them. And they are more… intense. I understand that."

The air changes between us at the reminder of the occupation of our love interests, if I can even call Seth that anymore, making the lighthearted conversation steer back into the severity it will always claim.

"Sorry you didn't get off," Bethany says, trying to keep it light even though I know she can feel it too.

"Don't worry. I got myself off last night to spite him."

She laughs first and then I join in.

"Were you thinking of him?" she questions and even though I don't laugh anymore, there's still the hint of a smile on my face when I nod. It's a sad smile though.

I thought of who he *used* to be. I don't tell her that.

Bethany chuckles and downs the rest of her tea. I don't laugh anymore. All the memories flicker back to me, ending with Cami and I have to set my mug down. Guilt worms its way up my throat, knowing I haven't told Bethany about Cami.

"You didn't tell me any of this in all the years we've been friends, you know?"

"I didn't tell anyone. I just wanted to forget."

"I get that. Doesn't look like you'll be able to forget now."

"I don't know how I'll get through it," I respond absently, not realizing how true the statement is until it's out there.

"You'll figure it out. You're a smart girl."

"Not when it comes to him." My heart tumbles at the very thought of him. Which reminds me... "I need to swing by the pharmacy and head out," I tell Bethany as I reach down to my satchel on the floor and search for my keys.

"Birth control?" she questions.

"Arrhythmia."

She blinks rapidly, a frown marring her face before picking up her teacup again. "I didn't know. I'm learning a lot about you today."

Worry and panic dance in the pit of my stomach. It's a short little number, but I know why. I'm afraid Bethany won't like me if she learns it all.

"I was diagnosed right before I left California. I didn't get the pills until after I'd moved away. You know how it is, I got busy with school and work. I didn't have any symptoms so I didn't refill my meds over the years. But I can feel it now."

"You shouldn't play around when it comes to heart problems." Bethany's comment sounds like something Cami said once. With a chill stretching lazily down my spine, my gaze catches a woman in the window the second I think of Cami. She's gone before I can see her fully. It was just a profile, but I swear it was Cami. She looked just like her.

"Hey, seriously," Bethany says and reaches out her hand, grabbing my right hand that's gripping the keys so tight I can feel the sharp edges digging into my fingers.

"Get your medicine and take it." She talks to me the way she does with the patients she cares so much about.

If I had any energy left, I'd tell her to knock it off. Instead I answer, "I know. I will."

"Promise?"

"I promise."

"You need to sleep too," she adds as she reaches for her purse and we both stand. It's the first time I get a full view of her getup. She looks like she's going out on a date in that black silk blouse and dark jeans. "You look like you didn't sleep at all."

"I took sweets last night to help." My comment stops her dead in her knee-high, black-leather-booted tracks. "It's just to help me sleep," I add to justify it. "I had a vial in my medicine cabinet from years ago when I first moved here."

"Sweets? Where the hell did you get sweets?" The surprise is just as evident in her voice as the contempt. As if I'm some sort of drug addict. She knows just as well as I do that plenty of our patients know exactly where to get all sorts of drugs. A lot of them self-medicate before they're even diagnosed.

"I had problems sleeping a while back," I explain to her, willing her to calm down. "A patient at the center said it would put me to sleep in an instant."

"You trusted the crazies?" Bethany says and eyes me like I'm a damn lunatic.

"No," I object, "although, eventually yes."

With her eyes closed, she looks like she's praying for mercy and patience. "I couldn't sleep; everyone could tell. Margret mentioned it every day. I tried melatonin, valerian—I even tried NyQuil for fuck's sake, until that wasn't working anymore. I tried everything I could get over the counter."

"You couldn't just go to the doctor's to get something?"

I shrug and say, "I tried everything; sweets were my last option. But it worked. It just lets you sleep."

"You know the men who sell it."

"It helps with addiction… you just sleep through the withdrawal." I try to justify it, but the truth is that the entire reason I resisted taking my patient's advice at first is because the sweets are dealt by the same men who sell everything else on street corners.

"If you say so," she says lowly and crosses her arms.

I'm quick to change the subject and ask, "When do you come back to work?"

"On Monday," she tells me and then counts the days. "Just four more days. I wish this weekend would be over already."

"I just switched my shift for tonight. I have today off, but I'll be working tomorrow and Sunday. I think I'm on for Monday too."

"Good, let's talk then?"

"Of course. I have to tell you what you missed at work too." I scrub at my tired eyes, careful of my mascara. "The world is changing quickly, isn't it?"

"Yeah it is. Go get your prescription."

"Love you," I tell Bethany. Gratitude swarms me knowing I have her as a true friend.

"Love you too," she tells me earnestly, pouting her lip just slightly and pulling me in for a tight hug.

I think about how I truly thought Cami would be the last person to ever say those words to me.

When I left, I knew Seth would never forgive me, because I couldn't even forgive myself. I bought a new place with the cash, I settled down and went to school. I didn't talk to a soul though. I was dying inside until I met Bethany.

Bethany hugs me tighter when I try to let go. She's stealing the method I use. Only two months ago, I did the same to her. I laugh a little, and she tells me again she loves me. It breaks me so I hold her back even tighter.

"Have hope," she whispers when I don't let go, bringing to mind the image of Seth and me together. I finally unwrap my arms from around her and close my eyes, telling her goodbye for now. When I open them, I swear I see that woman outside the window again. The coldness comes back and I swear she looks just like Cami from the back. Goosebumps travel quickly, gracing every inch of my skin.

"Laura?" Bethany's questioning voice rips me away from the woman and when I look again, she's gone.

"You okay?" My friend's tone is full of concern so I force a smile, ignoring the coldness that washes over me. "Yeah, yeah, I'm okay."

"Love you," I whisper when the chill comes back and I feel eyes on me once again, but I don't dare look to my right, toward the window.

"I love you too," Bethany tells me. My words weren't meant just for her though.

CHAPTER 5

Seth

Secrets get you killed in this business, but Laura doesn't have a damn thing to do with them. No one needs to know anything more about her other than what they can discover on their own.

"Who is she?" Jase still isn't letting up. He's asked me twice already today. Irritation swells in my chest as I release a silent exhale and school my expression.

My gaze stays glued to the clock behind the bar and the checklist repeats in my mind. It'll be different today with Laura.

I'll approach the situation with control. She needs it, but I need it more.

Last night I wasn't myself. Tonight, things will be different.

With the tick of another second gone by, I've forgotten all about Jase and his fucking prying.

"You don't trust me?" he questions and an inkling of uneasiness creeps through me. The floor-to-ceiling windows in The Red Room offer little light as I grab my jacket. With rain threatening, the sky is darker than it should be for 3:00 p.m. The bar isn't open yet and I don't plan to be here when it does. When she has a day off, so do I. Simple as that.

I came for the meeting earlier, which is now over. All the men in charge of different operations were called to discuss the new developments overall. A management meeting, so to speak. Although the brothers never tell *all* of us *everything*. Trust and secrets go hand in hand.

The bar is quiet; it's just Jase and me left on this floor.

Slipping on my jacket, I finally face Jase, my back to the front door.

"I don't trust you?" I say, echoing his question back to him. Letting him see the ridiculousness of his statement. I don't trust easily, but I trust Jase. In those meetings, I know all the players and the information that is shared. If any details are omitted, I know why. I'm part of the inner circle and clearly a trusted member of his team. So yes, I trust him.

"It's hard to tell with you keeping secrets." He's pushing me, pressing me for information I've made clear I don't want to give. Worse, he's been digging for it anyhow.

"You know I trust you with my life," I speak under my breath and with an edge of warning, hating that I have to say the words out loud.

"It's not about that."

"What's it about then?"

"Secrets, Seth. It's about the fact that you're hiding something."

"I have this… alert…" I start to tell him and then second-guess myself, but not for long. "When I moved out here, I had a friend set it up. I had to know who was looking into me. So any time someone searches for me, digs into my past… I get an alert." I pause and note how quiet he is. "The searches were constant when I first started working with you. You know how it is. You need to know if someone's looking into you and what for. Fuck, I know Declan has the same or something similar active on every single one of the names associated with your family."

"Declan does?" Jase questions. He knows I'm close with his youngest brother. Closer to him than I am with any of the other Cross brothers. Jase narrows his eyes, like he hasn't caught on yet.

"He has one for Bethany too."

"When did he make one for Bethany?" he asks, truly unaware.

"I asked him to make one for her when you went to her house that first day."

"That first day?"

Instead of answering his question, of telling him how much I had his back when it came to Bethany, I continue. "I made one for Laura too. I did it the second she left me. And I know you already know. I know when *anyone's* looking into her. I know you know who she is." I take a step forward, feeling the expensive suit jacket get tight around my shoulders. Cocking my brow and keeping the air between us as light as I can, I say, "So answer me this, who doesn't trust who?"

Jase's smirk is slow to form but it does, easily enough. The smirk and resistance for him to admit it bring that irritation back to the surface. I struggle to keep hold of my restraint. Maybe he can't feel the rage that's seeping into my remarks. I can though; the heat, the tightness in my chest. My jaw's clenched when I tell him, "I'm aware you already know the answers you're asking for. You've been looking into my background and then hers for weeks, yet you pretend like you don't know who she is?"

His gaze doesn't leave mine. Instead he stares back with a friendly look, although the intensity is at odds with the darkness in his eyes. "Don't get pissed. Since when are you this sensitive?"

"Sensitive?" I dare to bite back in what's nearly a snarl. "She's mine. And she doesn't concern you. I told you that. You don't need to look into her background."

"The fuck I don't." He puts on a façade that this is a relaxed conversation, but the tension grows around us by the half second. "Everything you do concerns me. Concerns all of us. You bring her in, whether you see it like that or not, and she's around us. She has access to the same information we do, how we act, where we are. I know her name, her résumé and credentials. I need to know more. *We* need to know more."

"Like what?" I question. "What do you need to know?"

"What does she want with you? And what do you want with her?" His questions are blunt and I break the hard stare between us to look back at the darkening sky behind us.

I answer him and my voice is low, barely speaking, "I don't know. I have no fucking clue and that's the truth."

"I'm going to need you to be careful with her."

"Why's that?" I say and turn back around to face him. Who the fuck is he to tell me what to do with her? "Is she a threat?" The menacing tone is more than apparent in my question.

"She's Bethany's friend." All emotion is restrained in Jase's voice. His answer is simply matter of fact. It takes me a long moment to realize what he's getting at.

He adds, "I don't need you interfering, messing with Bethany's head or getting to her."

Jase is my boss. He's powerful in ways I gave up any interest of being. So I glare back at him, listening to the thud in my chest and for the first time it feels the same as the first time I was arrested. With nothing else to do but wait, I slammed my fists over and over against the cinder block walls of the cell. *Thud. Thud. Thud.*

Licking my lower lip, I let my response linger on the tip of my tongue. Tasting it, debating it before finally looking Jase in the eyes to say, "She's always been mine and that's the only answer you need."

Taking a step back, I pivot on my back heel and turn my back to him. The soles of my polished oxfords groan as I turn on the waxed floors of the high-end bar. The bar I helped build. Carefully and quietly guiding Jase. I've done more than enough for them. They will not interfere. Or I'll make them regret it.

"At least you can admit that," Jase calls from behind and I pause. "You think it will stay that way?"

His question is met with a rise of anger. "What do you want from me?" I practically sneer the question as I whip around to face him and close the distance in an instant.

"To know what you're going to do. That's what I want, Seth."

"Leave her alone. She's mine and I'll take care of her how I want to."

Jase's clean-shaven jaw flexes at my defiance. With his dark jeans and light gray Henley he doesn't look like the man I know him to be. He's far too charming in his appearance. Far too laid back. Everything he does is intentional. Showing up to a meeting like this today, I knew he'd dispense bad news. It's all in delivery, in appearances. "Maybe I haven't been clear enough," I speak plainly, calmly, so that nothing can be misinterpreted. "I have no intention of sharing information about her. She's mine and she'll remain separate from the business. There are no exceptions."

"We have Marcus and Walsh both breathing down our necks. The batch of sweets that was stolen, our man murdered and even though we framed it like we planned it that way, we still don't know who did it." Jase pauses, his eyes searching my own.

"We've got problems, Seth. We can't find the stolen product. There's too much shit going on and too many unanswered questions. I don't like it." I nod, hearing the sincerity and concern. The bar is silent as the tension wanes. "I don't like you giving me even more questions and not answering them." He slips his hands into his pockets and I take a half step back. "She is an unknown variable. A distraction when you should be focused."

"I still have it for her," I admit to him.

"Have it?"

"Whatever it is that you get with a girl," I say.

Jase only nods, his dark eyes assessing. Wondering if I'm telling the truth. I'm wondering too. I know I'll tell him whatever he wants to hear so he'll back off.

"She's mine. She won't be a problem."

"You can guarantee that there won't be a single problem from this?" he asks although it's evident he already has an answer. Like he can sense the problems that will arise.

"She isn't a problem at all. More than that…" I pause as I decide to give him the intel she gave me yesterday, even though I haven't read it all yet.

"There's a former resident at the center your girl works at—Delilah something—she has drawings of the places Marcus took her." His sharp eyes narrow at me, as if I've been keeping back information. He can fuck off with that.

"I'm going through the notebook but it's old. Laura's got more and she's bringing them today. I'm going through them, with Declan of course."

"Declan knows?" The fact that Declan's in on it has the hair that must've risen on the back of his neck falling back into place.

"Of course," I answer and give him a knowing look. "I talked to him before he left the meeting. He said not to transfer anything digitally. So I'll mark the pages I think may be worth a damn and give them to him."

"I'm curious to see if anything is relevant," Jase says easily, his shoulders relaxing for the first time since he's entered this damn bar.

"I know it's been tense with the shit Walsh and Marcus have been pulling. You don't have to question where my loyalty lies."

"It's not your loyalty I'm worried about."

"What is it then?" I ask him straight up. I need to put this to bed. Jase breathes in deeper, looking more tired than he has in a long damn time.

He shakes his head, which renews a surge of irritation. "There's something I haven't told you." He talks as he runs his hand down his face.

"Is that right?"

"We got a message from Marcus. Mailed with no return address, no postage or prints… It's his handwriting though. Something about Fletcher's right-hand man."

Hearing the name *Fletcher* sends a trail of unease down my spine.

"When?" I ask.

I'm answered with a question of his own. "Who's Fletcher?" He adds, "Yesterday. Just after you left."

"A dead man," I answer him. "Fletcher is long dead and in the ground. Can I see the note?" I ask, letting him know I remember where my place is in this organization. I'll make demands when it comes to Laura, but for business? It's up to them. I don't want to be in charge. I'm not interested anymore.

Reaching into his back pocket, he hands me the folded note:

Which will it be? Fletcher's right-hand man? Or Laura's father?

My stomach sinks and a cold wash of reality hits me hard. He knows. Marcus knows. Every hair stands upright on the back of my neck. Jase takes in every small change in my body language while reading that note. I know he does. The clenched jaw and difficulty staying still. I know he sees it all.

"What does it mean: *Which will it be?*" I ask him, repeating Marcus's question. It's harder and harder to breathe with this fucking tie on.

"I don't know but do you see why I'm concerned now?"

CHAPTER 6

Laura

THE DOOR DOESN'T OPEN SLOWLY, IT'S WRESTED OPEN WITH INTENT and impatience.

The wind wails behind me, blowing past my shoulders and slipping into the sides of Seth's open jacket. It's a dark gray today, slim fit and accompanied with a black leather belt that probably costs more than the most expensive pair of shoes I own. I'm not cheap with my shoes either.

With a shiver tickling my shoulders, I pull the delicate cardigan tighter around me.

"You're early," he says as his tone and posture change, softening. The harsh grip he had on the door slowly slips and that makes my breath catch. That the sight of me could do that to him.

"Who did you think I was?" I ask, realizing his greeting was meant for someone else. "You were expecting someone?"

"No one… but you're never early." He's displaying more than a five o'clock shadow. He must not have shaved this morning. "Come in," he tells me, opening the door and holding it until I pass through, walking past him with each heavy and foreboding step. The roar of the fire in the living room straight ahead isn't the only sound I'm picking up on. There's also the steady thumping in my chest, harder than I've ever heard it.

Maybe it wishes to flutter and skip for the man behind me. The man who places his large hand at my hip, squeezing gently until he presses his hard chest to my back.

Thump, thump. The beat in my chest rages against my rib cage. If only I hadn't taken that pill, I know how wild my heart would be for him. Caged but uncontained.

He lowers his lips to the shell of my ear and I focus my sight on the fire; I barely noticed it yesterday. The flickers of yellow and orange flames slip through black stones in the modern fireplace. There's no wood, no fuel to speak of, but it roars intensely.

I can hear the moment he parts his lips, and my eyes instinctively close.

"Tell me why you're early, Babygirl," he whispers and the gentle tickle of his warm breath travels down my shoulder, both front and back. Eliciting a warning down my spine yet the goosebumps cause my nipples to perk and my core to heat as it travels down my front.

His hand moves to the front of my hip, curving against it.

"I didn't like the waiting," I answer him.

"No dress today?" he asks a little louder this time, less inviting, with less desire and more intrigue.

Instead of responding verbally, I shake my head. The crook of my neck must be more sensitive with his stubble rubbing against it as his thumb slips along the waistband of my favorite pair of blue jeans. I know it's more sensitive because even the shake of my head brings a spark of knowing as the strands of my hair brush along my heated skin.

I have to step out of his hold just to breathe. I take one step in my tan leather booties and look down at myself. Dark skinny jeans and a simple oversized cream cardigan covering a blush tank top. It's a more casual look than yesterday's. "I had a date before you," I comment, subconsciously teasing him.

I can see an alternate life in this instant. One where I'd never left him, one where we're still together and the vision gives me shivers. In my mind, I watch as I place my purse down on the coffee table, taunting him about my coffee date until I confessed it was only Bethany. And he smiles all the while, knowing I was toying with him, knowing he had me all to himself. I can practically hear the laugh I make when he jumps on the sofa in front of us I'd so casually laid on, giggling as he slips between my legs and nips my neck for teasing him.

Another life, a different one.

But I can *feel* it.

"I know you were with Bethany." Seth's response is all business and the moment he steps around me, not touching me, his absence gives me a different kind of coldness.

The one that lingers with this reality.

"You're tracking me?" I question him although it falls flat. Of course he is. He doesn't even bother to answer. "Spies?"

Again, I get no answer. He simply walks to the kitchen, a small one at that for the large, open-concept main floor.

I listen as he pours the drinks, noting how there's no art on the wall except a single piece. It's a black-and-white modern artwork, very sexual with the silhouette of a woman's figure straddling over a chair. It's so close up, and the contrast muted, that at first glance, it's only lines. Abstract art with no meaning. But then I can see what it is clearly, because I remember the day he took that photo of me.

My breath leaves me and I lose my composure the second I recognize it.

"I thought about getting rid of it." Seth's confession comes from the kitchen and rips me away from the memory I long to go back to.

His dark blue eyes pierce through mine, holding me captive as he lifts two glasses off the counter. "Sit," he commands and caught in his trance, I move. I even place my purse right where I had in the fucked-up reality my head had conjured a moment ago. Instead of tossing it playfully, I set it down methodically and sit back against the gray sofa, gripping the edge of it and trying to hold on to my sanity.

"I bought it just before you left. Before that night. It hadn't come in yet, but I got it for you." My nails dig into the sofa, and suddenly the fire raging across from me seems too much. The heat is too overwhelming.

"I don't like you bringing that day up," I'm quick to tell him, feeling the anxiousness roll inside of me.

It's quiet for a long moment. With my eyes closed all I can hear is the fire, followed by the sound of our glasses being set on the slick all-black coffee table and then of Seth drinking from his.

"It stayed covered for… it had to have been three or four years. I'd forgotten about it until I unwrapped it along with everything else that was shipped here."

The sofa dips with his weight as Seth sits on the opposite end of the sofa.

"It stayed on the floor, leaning against the wall with its back showing, for a long time."

I finally peek up at him through my thick lashes and dare to question, "Why? Why not get rid of it?"

"It was a reminder of what I lost. Those memories can give a man a lot of power. And motivation."

I only nod my head before reaching for the glass. It's cold and the beads of condensation are welcome when I grip it.

With my eyes on the painting, hung up to the right of the fireplace, not centered above it, I take a sip of the vodka and soda.

"Do you like it?" Seth asks easily. "I thought about taking it down before you came, but I wanted to know if you remembered."

"My birthday," I say, giving him the information he'd need to know that I recall exactly when the photo was taken. "I remember… I love it."

His exhale is easy as he takes another drink. I watch as he swallows and he only glances at the art piece before looking into my gaze. "I thought you'd like it for the bedroom," he admits and a flash of emotion plays in his eyes. He breathes out like his thought is funny before downing the drink and abruptly standing. "I couldn't throw it out," he says with his back to me as he walks to the kitchen. "I couldn't touch it."

As he makes himself another drink, not bothering with ice and simply adding more whiskey to his tumbler, I hold on to mine. Feeling the diamond pattern carved into the heavy lead crystal.

Even with the cool drink, my throat feels dry and tight.

"A painter hung it while I was out. He thought I meant to hang it. And I couldn't touch it to take it down."

"I'm sorry it bothered you," I speak and my voice cracks before I down my own drink.

He's there, placing his glass on the coffee table and holding his hand out for mine when I finish.

On his walk to the kitchen, he doesn't respond to my comment other than to say, "Everything happens for a reason, doesn't it?" Damn, do I hate that response right now.

He can't hear my faint *yeah* from where I am as he stands in the kitchen. After handing me my glass, this one full to the brim rather than only halfway, Seth takes off his jacket and unbuttons his shirt.

My pulse quickens when he continues to undress himself until he's only in his suit pants. I watch as he takes off his shoes, slipping his socks into them like he used to do. His muscles ripple with power and precision. The fire emphasizes every dip I crave to touch.

He's older, his shoulders broader, his body more muscular and toned. I can't take my eyes from his taut skin and the way his body moves. The warmth from the fire is nothing compared to the heat that kisses every inch of my skin while watching him.

"Getting comfortable?" I ask him. Again, nearly teasing. He looks up at me first, dropping his polished black shoes to the ground next to the fireplace, closest to the hall we walked down last time. With an asymmetric smirk, he comments, "You didn't change, did you?"

"So much of me has changed," I answer him without thinking about what to say. Without forming a list in my head of every aspect of my life that doesn't at all resemble who I used to be.

With my manicured nail tapping along the glass, I speak up, telling him something I decided I had to confess hours ago when I was thinking about how tonight would play out. "I made excuses for you today." My hardened voice and the confidence in it, makes him hesitate before he takes back his seat in nothing but those pants. Everything about him reads powerful and dominant. "I blamed myself for your actions."

With his legs spread, he leans back with his drink, his gaze moving between me and the fire, but landing on me in the end when I don't take my gaze from his.

He sips his drink rather than responding and I tell him, "I won't do that."

"Do what?"

"Blame myself."

"Then don't," he answers easily enough. My bottom lip wavers until I take another unsteady sip and close my eyes.

"What you did yesterday..." I trail off as I remember how I felt on his desk and the wave is an onslaught to my confidence.

The sound of him leaning forward forces my eyes to open wide, the sofa groaning, before I feel him closer to me.

"What did I do that was so wrong that you felt the need to make an excuse?" His question holds a taste of menace.

"You wanted to humiliate me."

"The fuck I did."

Anger rolls off of me in harsh and unforgiving waves. "Yes you did, you acted like I—"

"I wanted you to know how I coped with you leaving; I wanted you to *feel* it." His words are rushed, pushed through gritted teeth. Clearly he's referring to the note. Which is an entirely different matter.

"You had me lay on that desk so you could prove your power over me." I know that's why. I know it is and I can't even breathe as I wait for him to deny it. "To demean me."

He shakes his head. "I wanted to taste you again, that's not humiliating."

"Could any pussy taste that good?" I mock him, feeling that humiliation once again.

"I didn't say it like that," he speaks clearly, sucking on a piece of melted ice between his teeth. He lets it fall back to his empty glass. It pisses me off how he hides the emotion he clearly had a moment ago.

"How is that not humiliating?"

"I wasn't aiming for humiliation," he admits. His gaze unwavering, he fixes me with a calm and dominating stare, not moving. "I was just telling the truth."

Not knowing how to respond, I move to the next item on the list. "Worse, you wanted me to feel bad about the note. You wanted me to feel guilty."

"You are guilty. You're the one who left." Again his answer is matter of fact. *Guilty.* I can't stand it. I can't stand the word. As if all of this is my fault. The control he has makes me lose what little of it I have.

"You're the one who didn't change!"

"You're the one who wanted me to change."

I don't know how I'm able to stand, my legs feel so weak. But I do, as quickly as I can, reaching for my purse to leave.

"Sit down." Seth's authority makes me pause.

"Everything hurts," I admit to him. "I can't be here without hurting. I can't see you without hurting."

When I look down at Seth, through the glaze of tears I hold back, I feel a wave of fear and desire mix. It swirls through my blood and I lose my own thoughts, my concentration. I lose everything to the way he looks at me.

"You're going to do what I say, because you want to… and there's no humiliation in that."

"I never said I wanted to."

"You're here early, Babygirl. You didn't have to say it." *Babygirl.* The desire is immediate and warms everything. He stands and steps forward, taking my purse and tossing it back down onto the table. My breath comes faster, my head feeling lighter.

He whispers, his lips only inches from mine. "Know that I want you, too, because I stare at that painting every day, wishing I could go back to that moment."

Taking his seat again, he repeats, "Sit down." And this time I do.

"You're going to obey me, because it will take that pain and that guilt away."

I close my eyes slowly, careful to hold back any tears and calm myself down. "Not everything. I don't agree to doing whatever you say."

His answer is spoken with confidence. "You will. You're better at it now than you were back then."

"Don't do that," I say and glare at him. Feeling a wash of anxiousness.

"What?"

"Bring up the past." My heart thrashes in my chest, as if it's at war.

"You will do what I say, and I will be mindful of what I tell you to do and how I say it." Seth's proposition eases a burning pain that's quick to ignite every time I think back to what used to be.

As he waits for me to agree or to continue this fight, I consider what he said… the *guilt*.

God it hurts.

"I just want it to stop," I whisper, feeling the pricks at the back of my eyes.

"Want what to stop?"

"The guilt." Admitting it out loud brings a torrent of emotion.

"Strip down," Seth commands me, not responding to the emotion I'm clearly displaying. Not giving it any credence in the least. He doesn't try to comfort me, and damn my desire, I want him to. I want to crawl into his lap, I want to beg for his forgiveness.

"Strip down to nothing," he demands in a calm and controlled voice. His glass clinks as he sets it on the table and then leans back, his large hands clasped as he waits for me to obey.

The discord of what I want, what I need, who I am and what I used to be rips apart who I know myself to be.

The crackle of the fire feels like a whip against my bare shoulder when I slip off the cardigan. It glides slowly down my skin and I feel it settle against my shoes into a puddle of fabric. The blush tank top is harder to take off. Not physically, but emotionally.

I'm so aware of the fear. I feel like nothing when he looks at me. But I want to feel like everything. I have to close my eyes to do it, to pull the tank top over my head and do as he wishes.

"Look at me," he says and it's as though his command physically strikes me. Inhaling and exhaling, controlling my breathing and holding on to the fact that I refuse to leave here without trying, I do it.

I don't know what I'm trying to do though. Even as I kick off my shoes and my jeans are stripped from me by my own hands, I don't know what I want.

As if reading my mind, Seth sits up straighter on the sofa, his erection evident against his suit pants. The fabric is tighter along his length, outlining it and he rubs it once before telling me, "You want to feel better and so do I."

I do.

God, I desperately do.

His eyes darken, the fire flickering within them. "Your bra and then your underwear."

I do as he says. The clasp easily parting and the sound of my bra hitting the floor is louder than it ought to be.

When I step out of my underwear, I'm a half step closer to him, but before I give in and let go, I make him promise me something. "Tell me you don't just want to embarrass me and toy with me."

I can't explain why it means so much to me. But I need to believe it's more than that for him.

"I want to toy with you, yes. But you were never embarrassed before. Humiliating you doesn't get me off." His gaze roams down my body, his lips parted as he exhales. "I want you to listen to me. That's what it boils down to. I just want you to listen to me."

He has to look away, back to his drink that's empty when he tells me the last bit. *He just wants me to listen.* He stalks off, leaving me naked as he goes back to the kitchen, feeling miles away.

He thinks if I'd listened things would be different. The whispered explanation brings a new hurt and new guilt.

"Stop it. Stop thinking. Do what I tell you to." Seth reappears without a glass in hand.

So many years have passed but I still want to please him. I wonder if that will ever change.

"What do you want?" I ask him as calmly as I can. I can still remember the first time I was conscious of that desire. I wanted to please him.

As I watch Seth push the coffee table toward the fireplace, I recall that night.

It was at the old bar, the one my father used to leave me at all the time growing up. And it was just after his funeral. Derrick called me "Babygirl." *Derrick* did. I knew him to be a friend of Seth's. I even liked him. He would look out for me. It was he who welcomed me into the bar to wait for Seth.

I wasn't *Derrick's* Babygirl and my reaction must've told him as much. "Oh," he'd said with a smile. "You want that just for Seth, don't you?" His question wasn't teasing, only knowing. At that moment Seth walked in. Everything was chaotic back then, after Vito was killed. Seth's father was in charge; he hadn't been murdered yet in the war for that territory. Still, Seth was needed and commanded more than anyone else. It was like his father was grooming him.

Seth came in and needed a beer. Looking distracted, he kept heading to the bar but man after man stopped him. They needed him and he gave them the time they wanted. Those days, he still walked me to and from home at night. Just me, not letting anyone come with us. He made time for me. We hadn't even kissed, but he liked to touch me when I was around him. He always held my hand, touched my back; he'd run his finger down the back of my neck absently when Derrick talked to him. He hadn't done a damn thing sexual, but it felt like everything to me that he wanted me near enough to touch. He never made the first move though. Not that quickly after things changed, and not for months later.

I was no one when it came down to it, and he was going to be everything. I could feel it.

I would only be his Babygirl. With that thought in mind, I got a beer for him and put it in his hand as he talked. I wanted to please him, and I had. The way he looked at me, ignoring whoever had been speaking, did something inside of me.

I can feel the same stare now as Seth rounds me years later. He did exactly what I expected him to; he ruled, like the king he was meant to be.

Myself, on the other hand? I wasn't even strong enough to be his Babygirl.

"Did you sleep last night?" Seth's question brings my gaze to his, makes me focus on the present.

"Some," I answer honestly. He doesn't look in my eyes when he stands in front of me, because he's focused on my chest. It's not until his hot touch grips my right breast and my head falls back just slightly that his gaze reaches mine. With his thumb and forefinger, he rolls my nipple and I have to bite down on my bottom lip to keep from moaning out at the sharp pleasure.

"Did you touch yourself?"

"What?" My eyes widen as I betray myself. I know it's obvious. I've never been a good liar.

"You used to. You used to punish me with it too. Taking care of yourself and letting me know you had." He squeezes my left nipple harder than the right, causing me to lean forward until he pulls back. A wave of pleasure rushes through me, stirring in my belly when he releases his hold.

With my lips parted, I breathe in deeply, sucking in a breath when Seth does it again. Both of my nipples, both at once.

"Look at me," he commands and I do. Staring into the depths of his eyes as he rolls my nipples between his deft fingers. "Did it feel like this?"

"No," I answer immediately.

"Did you think of me?" he questions and I hate to admit it, I hate knowing I thought of the good moments with him. All the nights I gave myself completely to him.

I can't answer verbally, so I only nod.

He plucks them both at once and the hot sensation is linked to my clit. I nearly stumble from the pleasure.

"You're a bad submissive." Hearing him say submissive forces a smile to grace my lips. He turns away from me, moving to a chest that sits by the fireplace, just under the painting hung on the wall. Standing there, watching his muscular shoulders, I dare to toy with him. "You're not my dom."

"That's where you're wrong, Babygirl." He stands up as he breathes out, holding a leather paddle in his right hand and slapping it down on the palm of his left. I instantly clench, feeling how hot and wet I am already. His burning gaze heats my own as he tells me, making his way to me, "Your body knows it. One day you'll get it through that thick skull of yours."

My body's tense with the sight of the paddle. Braided strips of black leather are wrapped around the entire length. His gaze is heated when he tells me to bend over and grab the back of the sofa, but not to rest my knees on the cushion.

It's awkward to stand like this, since I'm so short. I listen though, knowing full well he plans to use that paddle on my ass.

Thwack! He doesn't waste any time. The moment both my hands grip the sofa, he spanks me with it. The burning pain ricochets through me, starting at my right ass cheek, and I swear, by the time it returns to my core, it feels like heaven. The pain and pleasure are braided together as tightly as the leather.

Seth takes his time, kicking my clothes out of the way before touching his palm to my heated flesh. He squeezes my sore cheeks and in return, I moan a strangled sound. Leaning my forehead against his sofa, I try to keep still when he smacks my ass with the paddle again.

"Three times," he tells me before quickly bringing the paddle down again. The pain is more intense this time, the strike unexpected and I scream out in brutal agony as my legs buckle and beg me to brace myself on the cushion of the sofa. I don't though; balancing on the balls of my feet, I make sure I stay where I am. My face is contorted until the leather slips through my thighs, brushing against my clit. He rocks it, letting the pleasure build as he wraps my hair around his other wrist and pulls back so I can no longer rest on the back of the sofa. "No more touching yourself or all of your punishments will be as hard as that last one was. Understood?"

With my eyes closed, I agree. "Understood."

He's never been like this before. Never with me. The control, the patience, I know that is his nature, but this is so much… more.

He releases me too quickly, far before I'm ready to let go and fall from the cliff of my release. The pleasure wanes, the pain of my punishment returns and I find myself needy and turning around to see what he's doing.

I turn at the perfect moment, seeing him in all his naked glory as he kicks off his pants, the last remaining garment covering him from me. Every inch of his body reminds me of Adonis. He is sex personified. My inhale is sharp when he turns around, and his gaze is narrowed as he tsks me.

"I didn't say you could turn around," he scolds me, although the lust in his voice and the desire in his gaze are so clear, it feels nothing like a reprimand.

"You didn't say I couldn't," I argue lustily, setting the side of my head back down, taking him in and letting him know just how much I want him. How much I need him.

"Keep your eyes on me then," he speaks calmly as he walks behind me. With one hand stroking himself, I can already see the beads of precum at his velvety head. "How many men did you fuck?" he asks and I blink twice, rapidly.

Hesitating, he urges me to answer with his hand splayed on my lower back. He brings his knuckles up my back to my shoulders and then back down.

"It's been eight years," I tell him as if that's an answer. His erection presses between my folds, thick and hard as he rocks against me. The groan he lets out, *fuck*, I could cum to that sound any night. He bends down when I close my eyes, enjoying the sensation. With his hips pressing against my ass and his cock nudging my clit, the pleasure builds again.

"Open your eyes," he commands, his stubble brushing against my shoulder and I watch as he closes his own and kisses the crook of my neck.

I miss this.

I have dreamed of him doing just this for years.

"How many men did you fuck?" he asks me again, this time in a whisper, his warm breath sending shivers of want down my body.

"Many," I answer him and remember how none of them compared. How at first it was hard trying to find someone who I could hide my past from, but share my present. Then it was simply about trying to find anyone who could fill a portion of the void.

Seth chuckles, deep and rough, his chest vibrating against my back. "You're my little slut now." His comment only makes me hotter for him.

"So tell me, my little whore, how many pricks got to play with what's mine?"

"Not *whore*," I argue, barely able to get out the words as I shake my head against the fabric and practically moan my reply. "Slut." I repeat the word, clenching around nothing again and imagining him inside of me.

"My little slut," he whispers and the feel of his warm breath along my skin brings the pleasure closer to the surface, closer to igniting all of me.

"How many pricks got to play with what's mine?"

I stare back at him, unable to answer as he grips my hair at the back of my neck, still rocking his hips, still playing with me. Still wanting me.

I can't speak as the pleasure builds.

"You're not allowed to cum until I know how many times to deprive you. I need to know how many times."

Defiantly, my back arches as my orgasm rips through me.

Seth stills behind me and I clench against the shaft of his cock. It's a blinding pleasure. I can barely breathe.

"Ever defying me aren't you, Babygirl?" Seth scolds me, taking more of my hair in his fist and pulling back when I look away from him. The tight grip sends a stinging pain along my skin, but it only heightens the pleasure.

"Does thinking about being punished get you off?" he asks.

"Thinking that you cared who I fucked… that gets me off." The admission comes out willingly, easily.

Seth King still wants me. He wants me to be his. That realization comes with one of my own. I want to be his. I've been waiting to be his again.

CHAPTER 7

Seth

IT TAKES EVERY OUNCE OF CONTROL NOT TO CUM WITH HER. HER CHEEKS are flushed, as pink as her ass where the braided marks have left impressions on her skin. She's everything I remember and more.

The memories don't do her justice.

Knowing how easy it was to get her off drives me insane. How much she still wants me, enough to let this strong woman, want to be called my little slut… fuck, I could cum without even entering her.

The fire at my back is nothing compared to the crackling air between us.

"How many?" I question her. Ignoring the screaming rage in my head, demanding she be punished for not listening to me. She wasn't allowed to get off until I'd punished her for each and every one.

"Not enough," she answers, her eyes closing but the moment I pull back on her hair, just slightly, just enough to control her, her baby blues sink into mine and she adds, "I tried to fuck the memories of you out of me."

"Did it work?" With the question lingering between us, my heart slams against my chest, racing to get out of me.

"Not even for a single moment," she whispers, and the pain creeps back into the depths of her gaze. The longing, the need.

I slam into her, my plan, my control, completely gone. I can't restrain the need to have her, to take her and make her mine like she ought to be in this moment.

Deep inside of her, to the hilt, I watch as her neck arches, her head falling back with a wretched scream of pleasure. Her cunt spasms around my length, the warmth and heat stroking a desire that forces my balls to draw up. I could let go just like this. Gripping her hair, feeling her curves, hearing her screams and buried deep inside her as she orgasms from the forceful thrust.

A cold sweat breaks out along my skin, every inch of it covered, trembling with the need to move. I wait, letting her adjust, refusing to give in to the baser need.

A second passes, Laura's body sags and that's my cue to piston my hips. Control and desperation are at war with one another as I fuck her with complete possession. Pulling her hair back, I whisper along the crook of her neck, "You are mine," never pausing the steady pace of my thrusts.

The sound of it, of my hips meeting her ass, mixes with the short moans that slip out of her parted lips every time I sink inside of her.

This. I have missed this dearly. I ravage her and nothing has given me more meaning in my life. Harder, faster; I fuck her more and more ruthlessly until Laura's grip slips, unable to hold on. Letting go of her hair and wrapping my arm around her waist, I shove her to her knees, mine resting just on the outside of hers on the sofa cushion. I don't miss a beat as she thrashes under me, screaming louder and with a frenzy she can't control. Even the sound of her nails scratching against the sofa fuels me.

She screams my name. Mine.

"You're mine," I remind her. Whispering the heated truth. "You're mine."

"Seth," she begs me, but I haven't a clue what for. She could beg for anything now, and I wouldn't stop. I can't. But when I'd finished, I could have promised her the world, just to keep her under me.

"You're mine." The savage words are gritted between my teeth before I rake them down her slender neck. Her lips never close, her screams of pleasures and heavy breathing never pause. Her nails claw down my thigh as she reaches behind her and the hint of pain urges me to fuck her harder and faster.

She's lost in the pleasure, limp and sated, but on the verge of cumming yet again. Her body trembles with the need but her glazed gaze and whispered pleas prove to me she's uncertain if she can take it.

"Take it, Babygirl. You. Are. Mine. Take it." I can't stop. Not yet.

I can't let go. Not until she admits it.

I won't tell her to though. I won't command her to acknowledge what I deserve to hear.

With both of my hands gripping her hips to keep her upright, she takes it all. For over an hour, I refrain, letting her cum time and time again.

I don't let go until Laura screams out, pulsing around me, "I'm yours."

She's limp on the sofa, her thighs pressed together as she turns from side to side. Her skin is a beautiful pink, her hair a messy halo. She's a vision of beauty and nothing less. "Mmm," she moans, biting her bottom lip as she rolls onto her side again, swaying her legs and moving her hands to rest between her thighs.

"Did I break you, Babygirl?" I ask her.

"Hmm," she breathes, her blue eyes searching for mine when she finally looks up. "Seth? You ruined me long ago."

Her body trembles, even as she clings to me when I lean down to pick her up. The evidence of her giving into me surrounds us. From the damp spot where she was just laying, to the clothes strewn around the room.

Her cheek rests on my shoulder as I walk down the hallway, to my bedroom. "You'll stay here tonight." The statement seems to wake her, to make her more sober than she's been for the last hour that I've had her at my mercy. Her grip slips on me, but I hold her just the same.

With a short intake of breath and a hesitancy in her touch, I expect her to protest. She doesn't though. She doesn't do a damn thing when I pull my sheets back, slipping her into the large four post bed and then covering her small body.

"Sleep." I give her the command and her wide doe eyes stare up at me. The look in them is resistant and questioning, but she's quiet.

It's not until I'm leaving the room, until my back is to her and my hand is on the doorknob to close it behind me that she speaks up.

"Seth," she calls out.

"Yes?" I question her, waiting for her defiance so I can shut it down. She will stay here tonight and any other night I want. *She's mine.*

"The other notebooks… I brought the photocopies in a file box." Her voice is clear and I debate whether or not she'll even be able to sleep until she blinks. It's slow, sleep longing to keep her eyes shut. When I don't respond, I simply watch her figure, the moonlight playing with the shadows along her curves under the white comforter. *My gorgeous girl.* Then she adds, "It's in my trunk."

"I'll get them. Go to sleep."

She doesn't agree. She doesn't protest either. She simply watches me as I close the door, making a mental note to reward her in the morning.

CHAPTER 8

Laura

EVEN THOUGH I'M NOT THERE ANYMORE, I CAN'T HELP THINKING: IT'S been a long damn time since I've woken up in someone else's bed. I like to leave in the middle of the night, if I bother staying after a round in the sheets with a man. I only remember staying with one of the guys I'd actually slept with in his bed till morning.

And I never bring them back here. Never. My loft is my safe place.

So as the hot water sprays against my skin, feeling especially brutal against my ass, I think there's only been one other time, one other guy who I've laid in bed next to and slept till morning.

I don't even remember that poor guy's name. It was a decent night, but I only stayed because I'd come off a long shift before the date. It was just fine. Everything about every other guy is always… just fine.

Turning around to wash away the soap that's lathered on my front, I open my mouth and drink some of the hot water. The steam fills the stall and I stare absently at the grayish-blue subway tile. I thought about objecting more than I thought about sleeping when Seth was there, staring at me expectantly. The moment the door closed and I closed my eyes, all I could smell was him. That woodsy, masculine scent that reminds me of home.

Nothing reminds me of home… nothing but Seth.

All I could smell was him; all I could feel were his hands on me, his cock inside of me. *Fuck*, even now as I wash myself, my hands reach lower and I swear I can still feel him pulsing inside of me.

Even with the heat surrounding me, I shiver. Loving the way it feels, loving the memory of it.

The moment I closed my eyes last night and let myself be consumed by the remnants of Seth, I fell deep asleep. It was dreamless, but peaceful. I haven't slept like that in years.

Ding-dong.

The doorbell sounds loudly in my bathroom. The loft is small enough to hear that thing from any corner of my home.

I'm quick to turn off the spray and dry off haphazardly before throwing on a cotton bathrobe. I'm nowhere near presentable, but I can at least peek through the peephole. As I walk, I catch a glimpse of the large clock on the wall in my living room. It's a farmhouse design, galvanized silver and oval with barn wood behind the moving hands. It's not even noon yet. I've been home for nearly two hours since Seth and I parted, him to work, whatever that might be.

It reminds me of what else I was thinking about in the shower.

It's been a long damn time since I've slept in a man's bed. An even longer time since I've woken up to an early morning lazy fuck. With the tingling sensation still ringing along my skin, I open the door for the delivery woman.

With her hair pulled into a tight bun and a ruby red smile, she asks my name and makes me sign before handing me a long rectangular white box.

I'm glad it's a woman, since my robe slips open just slightly as I sign. She can't see anything, but still.

Kicking the door shut behind me, I wonder what's in the box. There's a single ribbon, satin and dark red, in the center of it. It's easy enough to untie. There's no note, no sender information. Only my name. Not even an address.

At the realization, I turn back to look at my front door. Questions are ringing in my head. I'm sure she's long gone, so instead of chasing her, I merely purse my lips and open the box.

Long-stemmed flowers. Their soft floral scent hits my senses just as quickly as the smile on my face and warmth up my chest.

With my bare feet padding on the floor and water still dripping from the tips of my hair, I trace the petals of the blush buttercup ranunculus and the white anemones. It's a full bouquet and given that it's fall, I imagine it wasn't cheap.

Grabbing the step stool so I can reach the top shelf, I take out my expensive vase, not the basic clear ones that are on the bottom shelf.

I cut each stem, remembering when Seth gave me a similar bouquet. It was our first year anniversary. I think it's the first real gift he ever got me. Technically we never gave ourselves a date. But every year, on the date of our first kiss and our first night together, Seth gave me a bouquet, and this one was the first. These flowers and these colors. Much smaller and not quite as fancy as these are, but the same flowers.

I can't believe he remembered. Men never remember details like this.

I leave the vase in the center of my coffee table, and when I'm done cleaning up, I lie down on the sofa, still in my robe, and question everything I thought up until yesterday.

What am I doing? The question nags at me. More importantly, I hear Seth's voice in my head from only weeks ago, asking me how I thought this would end.

CHAPTER 9

Seth

"THE NOTEBOOKS ARE MOSTLY RAMBLINGS. BUT THERE ARE drawings of where Marcus took her." The woman, Delilah, likes to sketch. I wondered how accurate they were until I drove past one of the streets she referred to. She'd drawn a park, specifically Lincoln Park. It was the first place she'd met Marcus according to the notebooks. It's the place that started it all. It was like she'd taken a photograph. It was that detailed and that accurate.

"Drawings?" Jase questions from where he sits behind his desk. Declan's occupying the chair next to mine, on the opposite side of the desk. I answer, although Declan knows just as well as I do.

"Some in New York, where she's from, but she came down here years ago for a case and that's apparently where she met Marcus. She drew the locations."

"Maybe it's something she did back when she was a lawyer?" Jase surmises.

"More like she learned it from a cop," Declan speaks up and steals our attention. "I've been going through Walsh's computer. He's uploaded his old cases and in his files, he drew the sites. Quick sketches."

"Maybe she learned it from him? She was a lawyer, right? Did they work a case together?" This is the first time Declan's telling me this.

"Could be," he says then shrugs and sits back in his seat. The leather groans and with the turn of the clouds, Jase's office darkens. He has to get up to turn on the lights as the day shifts to night behind the large window to the back of him.

"She was with Walsh and Marcus. She has information on both of them. She met Walsh first."

Sitting forward, I nod as I clasp my hands in my lap. My thumb runs along my knuckles as I tell him, "There's a lot in these notebooks that could be useful if the information is still accurate. Like how Walsh used PO Boxes to communicate with informants. He used them to send her letters too. It's a safe place for an information exchange. Or at least he considers it to be since they're purchased and paid for by an LLC that's run through the Cayman Islands."

"Our surveillance shows he's still using them," Declan adds.

"Good, let's see who he's still talking to and if there's something sensitive we can use to our advantage."

It shouldn't surprise me that the information Laura gave us is already paying off.

"Do you think he's still seeing her?" Jase asks and I look to my right, waiting for Declan to speak up. I gave him the latter half and the first one I'd already read, and I took the earlier portion. "Declan has the most recent entries of her diaries."

"It appears she still occasionally has contact with him and she's made it clear she isn't over him. What they went through, it certainly changed her career path and mental state."

"An up-and-coming lawyer, to an in-and-out resident at a mental institution… I'd say so."

"Anything in there about Walsh?" Jase questions.

I thumb through the pile of papers in front of me as I shake my head. "Not anything after the first year of entries. She hasn't written anything about him recently."

"It's possible that she may not know Walsh is looking for her?" Jase says and I can feel the steady tapping of the heel of his foot under the desk. His ass is riding on this just as much as mine is.

"Is he?" Declan asks.

"He mentioned her at the very least. So she's on his mind."

"As far as we know," Declan answers, "he hasn't contacted her."

I add in my thoughts. "It's odd that he hasn't. He's obviously not over what happened years ago and it involves her. She was a key piece in whatever happened in New York that led to him leaving the FBI."

"He has to know where she is. It's only a matter of time before he contacts her." Jase sounds confident and I'm confident he will as well.

"Maybe he's waiting for something," I suggest and that gets Jase's gaze pinned to mine, eager to know what I think after reading the diary entries.

"For what?"

"For Marcus to be out of the way." Declan nods in agreement with me.

It's quiet for a moment, the room still and the only sound the click of the HVAC system and the low hum of air as the heater's engaged.

"We wanted something to barter with. I don't think information on Delilah is enough. If it was, Walsh would be there already."

"We could kidnap her, trade her for it, but I don't see that ending well. And we don't know where she is right now. She's a ghost until she needs help and meds. Should be soon though."

"He'd lie, get her back, then put us away with a copy of the recordings he didn't give us."

"Agreed. We have to play it another way." Jase sits back in his seat, staring past us and at nothing in particular. "If things go wrong, we take her. As an insurance policy. But for now, we play it differently."

"At least we know our next move, steps ahead." Declan is the least tense of the three of us. "I'll have the team keep eyes on her. Just in case."

"Good." Jase still doesn't look at either of us. He's thinking. The wheels spinning, all the possible moves playing out. I can see his thoughts clearly, easily reading him after all the years of getting to know him.

"What are you thinking?" I ask him when the tapping of his foot stops.

"We have two things on Marcus."

I name the two, completing his thought. "A list of men who work for him that we've been following and journals of a woman he seems to have affection for. Although we don't have her location. She goes off the grid, but always goes back to the Rockford Center eventually."

"As well as the knowledge that she's been seeing Marcus," Declan adds and Jase nods, the two sharing a look. "The question is, which do we give to Walsh?"

"If Walsh wants something in exchange for the recordings, I say we don't let on to the woman. Being in between the two of them is a risky move and she's our fail-safe."

Jase's gaze drops and his nod is nearly imperceptible.

I continue, "We don't want to get deeper into it. We just need the evidence he has on us to vanish."

"You think he'll really hand them over?" Declan asks.

"If he trusts us." I explain, "I think trust would be easier to get if we keep the information about the woman and Marcus to us. Keep it business."

"We give him a list of Marcus's men that could lead him to Marcus. In return, he gives us the recordings," Jase says as if he's testing how he feels about the deal.

"It seems like a fair trade to me," I respond and sit back in the seat, attempting to relax but every muscle in me is tight, knowing Marcus knows about Laura.

"I don't trust him," Declan pipes up.

"We don't have a choice but to trust him." Jase answers before I have to.

The sky darkens by the minute behind Jase.

"I'll give him the list," Jase decides. "I'll leave it in his mailbox at the station. We keep the intel on her and eyes on her just in case Walsh wants to fuck us over, but this way he can find Marcus."

Gripping the arms of the chair, I nod, letting go of the tension and uncertainty. It's out of my control. All I can do is hope this is enough for Walsh and that he keeps his end of the deal. And that he finds Marcus. I want him—and everything he knows—out of the picture.

Just as I'm about to stand and leave, Jase asks, "Any other updates?"

I eye him questioningly, feeling my expression show my confusion. "On what front?" I ask him.

He cocks his brow and when I glance down at Declan, he's smirking, pulling the stack of papers in front of him into his lap. He's highlighted a few things, but most of them appear to be drawings. Locations where Marcus may be or go to often.

"Did you ask Laura about her dad?" Jase asks and coldness sweeps along my skin. Any confusion, any ease, vanishing in an instant. Dread is a prickly fucker, crawling along my skin.

"No. No updates."

"We aren't..." Declan clears his throat, his posture shifting and humor leaving at my response. "We're not trying to piss you off."

His explanation doesn't mean shit to me. "I told you—"

"Yes, she's yours," Declan says, interrupting me. "Very possessive male of you." Declan's joke doesn't help. All I can think about is what Laura would do if she knew the truth about her father. *What she'd think...*

"Just asking if everything on that front is all right?"

"Just fine," I answer Jase. Standing, I fasten a single button on my jacket.

"I'd feel better about you seeing her if it didn't turn you into a stone wall."

Jase and Declan look up at me, both waiting. I debate on telling them something, anything. A protectiveness overwhelms me when it comes to Laura. The less anyone knows, the better.

Just like Delilah, Marcus and Walsh. Just the fact that we know anything at all about them, creates a weakness that anyone can exploit. I don't want any more of that for Laura than there already is.

"Bethany asked me how you're doing last night," Jase says and exhales audibly, standing to walk to the bar on the other side of the office. "She's prying and wants information about what you're thinking in regard to her friend."

"You can tell her you don't know anything," I suggest and then hold a hand up to signal no when he offers me whiskey. Declan nods though, so Jase pulls out two glasses and they clink as he shakes his head, his lips forming a thin line.

"I did and she told me to ask."

"You sound pussywhipped."

"I'd like to make her happy, Seth. In case Walsh fucks us and I end up having to go away for a while," Jase admits harshly, his words drenched with the fear of the unknown. He takes a swig of his own drink before handing Declan his and taking a seat once again. All the while I stand and watch the emotions play on his face.

"You really like her? Is that something I could tell her?" he asks with a defeated tone.

For a moment, for some fucked-up reason, I see Derrick sitting there instead of him. I see the man I left behind. The friend who defended Laura. My partner who I couldn't look at anymore because he wanted Laura back just like I did, and he was man enough to admit it. Man enough to keep in contact with her and he had the balls to look me in the eyes and tell me.

It's been years since I've said a word to him. In this moment I want to tell him. I want to tell him I have her back.

"I've missed her and I don't plan on letting her go so easily this time."

Jase nods, again his focus drifting to nothingness behind us before he asks, "Was that so hard?"

He has no idea how much it fucking hurts to say that I missed her out loud to anyone. Telling her is brutal, telling anyone else? Agony.

"We don't know the history. But if you need to talk," Declan offers, leaving the suggestion that they're there for me implied.

A question nags in the back of my head. "Did Bethany tell you anything about me and Laura I should know?"

"Nothing apart from her thinking that Laura still loves you but she's afraid you don't love her back."

His statement hardens me. Love is a word and nothing more to Laura.

You don't leave someone if you love them.

With my jaw clenched I debate on saying just that, but it shows more about me than anything else. Parts of me they don't need to know about. My phone pings and I'm grateful for the distraction until I read the text.

My blood turns to ice and I have to read it again.

"What's wrong?" Declan asks.

"Laura just thanked me for the flowers." I'm not even cognizant that I answered him until he speaks again.

"Then why do you look like—"

I cut off the question and do my damnedest to keep my expression from showing how close to the edge of recklessness I am. "I didn't send her any flowers."

CHAPTER 10

Laura

I felt eyes on me the moment I got out of my car and walked into the doors of the Rockford Center. It's a weird prickling sensation that claws at me from behind.

Even now, as I pick up the tray with the last two cups of pills on it, I swear I can feel someone watching me. It's an eerie feeling. As I slowly turn, just peeking over my shoulder toward the elevators, I truly expect someone to be there.

This late at night, most of the patients are settled into their beds. Visiting hours are over. I tell myself no one is here, but I can't help but feel that I'm wrong. Call it my gut instincts.

I anticipate someone staring at me, but all I find are the simple silver doors, closed and the night hall quiet.

Letting go of a breath I didn't know I was holding, I make my way in my favorite scrubs, a pair of white ones with deep red roses on them, to my last two patients.

They were supposed to get their pills five minutes ago, but the patient I checked on before them refused to take his. It took me a while to convince him the pills are helping, not hurting. Schizophrenia is a bitch.

That patient comes and goes as if this place is a revolving door.

He never keeps up with his medication when he leaves. His symptoms get worse and he finds himself back here. Self-admitted or because his addiction and lack of employment lead him to a judge ordering him a sentence that includes a term here.

It kills.

With the thought settling deep in my gut, and the vision of that man's face in my head, I have to close my eyes just before the 3F on the door greets me. It's a calming breath that leaves me. And then another after a deep inhale.

My eyes slowly open when the prickle at my neck comes back. There's no one but me at the end of the hall. A door to my right, and across it, a door to my left. No one else is here. Aiden is in the back with the paperwork, Mel is on a smoke break. She'll be outside for at least another twenty minutes since her patients are all accounted for and sleeping. She'll do her last round, checking on their breathing, and then switch off, just like I will. We only have forty minutes left until the end of shift at 1:00 a.m.

Maybe I'm just coming down from the high I was on with Seth. The realization is sobering. That's what the odd feeling is. It's the reminder of all that happened and the fact that I was ignoring it.

The tray takes both of my hands to hold, so I have to balance it before turning the doorknob, and using my hips to bump open the door to E.J.'s room.

We weren't given her name, only initials.

Yet another thing that makes me feel uneasy. We've never had a patient whose information was guarded. We only have her medical history. Nothing else. Not a name. Not an address.

Aiden never should have accepted her in here under those conditions. With that thought resonating inside of me, I set the tray down and then look at her.

Really look at her.

Her brunette hair is matted as she lies lifeless on her side on the mattress. Her bed is made neatly, it always is, and she lies on top of it, rather than under the sheets. I know she's cold because of the goosebumps on her skin; hell, even I'm cold in this place at night.

A horrid guilt rolls through me; how could I ever think of turning someone away?

"E.J.," I say as I swallow the previous thoughts and pick up the small paper cup containing three colorful pills. And then a cup of water. I don't sit on her bed like I do with some of the other patients. I keep my distance with her, she's more receptive that way.

I sit in the chair in front of her nightstand. It hasn't moved from the last time I was in here. She doesn't like me to move it though.

It's a rare moment when I see someone in here who truly wants to die. This woman's only thirty-two, and I have no idea why since it's not in her charts and she hasn't spoken to anyone, not that she could now anyway, but she doesn't want to live another day. She has a bandage at her throat from recent surgery. The antifreeze destroyed her esophagus and she nearly died. Death's door was only a minute away from her and not for the first time either. That attempt was made in this facility and that knowledge will never leave me.

She blinks slowly and then her deep brown eyes look up at me. Rolling onto her back, she accepts the pills and then the water, downing them without thinking twice.

When she closes her eyes as I check the bandages, tears fall down her cheeks and land heavily on the bed on either side of her head.

She only sniffs once and then she swallows thickly, gripping the sheets.

"Does it hurt?" I ask her and she shakes her head. Even if she wanted to talk, her voice would be hoarse and difficult to hear. Surgery saved her life and with time, she'll be able to talk again. Not right now though, not while she's in recovery.

I wish whatever was hurting her inside would leave. I wish it would go away. The thoughts in her head that make her desperate to die are something no one should have to deal with. I can hardly look at her without feeling her sorrow. It's palpable. Whatever happened to her, I wouldn't wish it on anyone.

"It looks like you're healing well," I comment even though I know she doesn't care. My blue gloves snap as I take them off, depositing them on the tray with the last set of pills. I never leave anything in here for E.J. I'm sure she'd think of a creative way to die with any items that are left behind.

"If you want anything at all, you know to just hit that button. I'll get you anything." Even to my own ears, I sound desperate at the last sentence. "A radio if you want music." All the rooms have televisions in the upper right corner, but she's never turned hers on.

She only shakes her head, licking the tear that had rolled its way to her lip.

"I hope you sleep well and you have the sweetest dreams," I tell her sincerely. I don't always talk to my patients like this. They're all different.

Her lips part, as if she'd say something, but she's quick to shut them. "Should I get you a pen and paper?" I ask her, but she only shakes her head again, falling back to her side and tucking her hands under her head. I leave her there, staring at the empty chair.

I'm still thinking of her when I enter the last door. Melody's room. Which is why I nearly scream and throw my tray at the sight of a man at the end of her bed.

Thump, thump. My chest hurts from the sudden pounding.

What the hell is he doing here? It takes me more than a second to note his uniform. "Officer," I greet the man as he holds his hands out in defense.

"Nurse Roth," he says and his voice is gruff at first, but his tone and demeanor apologetic. He clears his throat, and it's only then that Melody looks up at me. She's in her young twenties and on antipsychotics. She'll more than likely be on them all her life. When she tilts her head at me as I glance between the two of them, her straight blond hair falls over her shoulder. A lock slips into her loose blouse, so loose I can see straight down and I know she's not wearing a bra. Knowing Melody, that large gray shirt is probably all she's wearing, even with this officer in the room.

It's then that I see the name tag: Walsh. *Holy fuck!*

"Melissa showed me in," the policeman explains, rising from his chair. The legs drag against the floor as he stands, pushing the chair back. With his hand held out, he introduces himself to me. "Officer Walsh."

The cold sweeps along my shoulders and down my back as I take his hand.

"You can call me Laura."

This is the first time we've met, although I know all about him from Delilah's notebook. She drew a picture of him once and I'm shocked to see how much the man in front of me looks like the sketch, but older. Years and years older.

He's good looking to say the least. Although obviously tired. The darkness under his eyes doesn't distract in the least from his pale blue eyes. I may remember pieces of what Delilah wrote about him, but I've heard other things recently. Whispers from patients who talk about Marcus. They say Walsh is a dead man for coming down here when he should have stayed in New York.

"It's nice to meet you, are you visiting?" I ask cautiously and he shakes his head as I thought he would.

"I have questions to ask Miss Trabott."

Setting the tray down on the dresser I explain to him, "I don't know that Melody is in a condition to answer any questions right now. She's not well, on heavy psychotics."

"I understand that," the officer says and eyes me, looking me up and down as if he's sizing me up. It feels like he knows exactly what I'm thinking. I hope regardless of whatever he sees, he gets the impression that I'll kick him out. I have before. Authorities can either take the patients into custody, or they can leave them alone after visiting hours. This place needs to run on a schedule and with strict procedures. Cops don't get free rein just to visit. "Melody asked me to come in. She has information about a murder."

Melody's sweet when she responds, nodding and gathering her skinny legs to sit cross-legged on the bed.

"Officer, I don't know if you're aware—"

"A murder case she's a suspect in… Laura."

All of the blood drains from my face as I stand there, stunned. Melody? Murder?

"It's not just me. He has other suspects," Melody explains and her voice drags from the drugs. She talks slowly, but with purpose and there's always a sweetness behind the words. When she's alone, she rocks and hums to herself.

"Accomplices, you mean?" Officer Walsh questions her. He's kind in the way he looks at her. As if he's not accusing her of murder.

"They were good people. Don't you agree?"

Walsh's demeanor changes. "They were, but a *priest* is dead."

"Officer," I interrupt, the cup of pills in one hand, and a cup of water in the other. "I don't want to… hinder an investigation. But it's important she take these at a certain time and if she's being questioned—"

"I waive my rights; I don't need a doctor or lawyer present." Melody gives me a soft smile, as if thanking me and I ignore her.

"With all due respect, Officer, her doctor would need to approve her mental state before anything she says would be admissible in court."

Walsh searches my gaze; it's quiet. Too quiet. The way he looks at me, like he knows something I don't… I don't like it.

"I can take them," Melody pipes up just as I part my lips to tell him he has to come back during visiting hours. She reaches up for the cups, throwing the pills back and then does the same with her cup of water. She huffs a small humorless laugh as she crumples the little white cup in her hand. "I can't believe the priest was in there," she whispers.

Tossing the small crumpled cup into the larger paper one, she sets both down on the nightstand, staring at it when she speaks. "Why would he go there?"

Officer Walsh leans forward and the movement steals my attention. He looks at me as he asks Melody, "Did you know about the others going there? Maybe just the man who hurt you?"

"I don't know anything," she answers him in a whisper, but she can't look at him.

The rush of blood that met me when I opened the door, slows to a trickle. Melody's quiet. Her gaze is still focused on the cups on the nightstand. Or something else that's there maybe. There's nothing else present except for a clock, but maybe in her mind, something else is staring back at her.

"What happened at the farm?" I ask the officer, remembering something I read a week ago. Six men were killed in a fire at a farm off the highway, just before the state line. They hadn't identified the bodies yet.

"A fire," Officer Walsh answers and I'm quick to look back at Melody. The sweet girl who hums to herself. She came in the day I read that article, which was the day after it happened.

"Five members of a gang from upstate were locked in an old cattle farm two nights ago…" He watches Melody for her reaction before adding, "And a priest."

Her eyes close solemnly and then Melody readjusts, seeking refuge with her blanket as she covers herself up to her waist.

"The five deserved it," she speaks up and then looks back at the officer. "You know that one did, you know what he did to me," she says, pressing Walsh to agree with her. Her body sways first and then the action turns to a gentle rocking. It speeds up with every passing second of silence. "I'm not sad that they're gone."

"Did the priest deserve it?" Walsh asks her and Melody's large eyes gloss over.

"I don't know," she whispers on every rock. "I don't know anything."

"I think that's enough for tonight," I say to break the moment, moving between Walsh and Melody. The officer rises, ready to object, but I don't let him. "I don't know what's right and wrong. I don't know what she did, but she's my patient. She's not well, and she's not in the right mind to talk right now. You can always take her in for questioning."

Gathering the tray, I open the door to Melody's room and wait for Walsh to leave. He tells her to feel better before leaving. She tells him good night and the exchange is odd to me.

I don't know if he's with her or against her. If he wants her to feel like he's her friend, he's certainly accomplished that.

The door closes with a resolute click. Keeping my pace even and doing everything I can to remain professional, I walk straight ahead to the end of the hall then to the left, to the nurses' station.

Slipping the tray on top of the pile, I watch as Officer Walsh signs the check-in sheet. Signing himself out.

"I appreciate you letting her talk," he says absently, not looking at me as he does. The pen hits the paper and he stares at it, looking at all the names, I guess.

His large frame towers over the small desk in front of me and it makes him appear all the more foreboding.

The manner in which he speaks throws me off. *Letting her talk*. As if he's not grateful that he was questioning her, just that she needed to get something off her chest. That's the real reason.

"You can't get reliable information from her," I tell him although I can't look him in the eyes. There are things Delilah wrote and I know they're coloring my perception of this man. "She's not in the right mind."

"She's never in the right mind," he tells me. When he closes his eyes, he runs a hand down his face, letting his need for sleep show. "She could barely focus when she first came to me."

I don't know what to say or what to think. I don't know much about her, only what's on her chart, what she prefers to eat and the songs she must like, because she hums them constantly. I'm not her therapist or her doctor. Only her nurse.

"You've talked to her a lot?" I ask him, probing to see what he knows.

He nods once and then leans against the desk with the palms of his large hands bracing him. "She came to me for help; I tried to… but the evidence." A frustrated sigh leaves him. "I did everything I could but there wasn't enough to charge him with anything and he didn't confess. I thought we were close to getting one, but he didn't give us anything."

"I'm sorry," I say automatically and search for more. "I wish things had turned out better for both of you."

Something I say makes his gaze narrow.

"How do you think she and her friends managed to pull it off?" he asks me and then clarifies. "The five men who hurt them being burned alive in the barn. How did they do it?"

"I—I don't know," I answer him and he gauges my reaction. I add, "Maybe it wasn't them?"

"They're my only suspects. A murder of revenge. That's my working theory. Five young women and men, all of whom have never stepped out of line in their lives. One night, they conspired and committed murder. How did they do it?" he questions me again.

"I can't tell you." I'm certain surprise colors my eyes when he looks at me. I'm not a cop or an investigator. I don't know why people do the things they do. I'm shocked by weekly events here. I could only imagine what transpired that led to the fire that night.

"Someone helped them," he concludes.

"Who would help them? The priest?" I take a guess, still confused and not completely on board with Walsh's working theory.

"I don't think so. I don't understand how Father John plays into all this." I can see the wheels turning in Walsh's head, trying to piece together what happened.

"If it wasn't the priest who helped them… then who?"

"Someone they see as a vigilante. That's my theory."

"A vigilante?" The longer I stand here talking to him, the more and more I feel insane. Or maybe he's the one who's lost it. My mind whirls with all the secrets I know and it makes it more difficult to pretend I don't know what he's getting at. He called Marcus a vigilante. Delilah wrote about it.

"Someone who wanted the men dead for a different reason. Someone who would benefit from the event occurring and make himself look like a hero in the process."

"Who would want them dead?" I play along, pretending I don't know what he's implying.

"You know who."

"I don't understand. I'm afraid you have me at a loss," I lie.

"Marcus. I'm sure you've heard of him. Everyone in this town has," he comments and I feel my cheeks burn. For a moment, I doubt that I've held the secret of taking Delilah's notebooks close enough. I question if he knows. Or is it just that he assumes everyone knows about Marcus? The way he looks at me, though… It feels like he knows I know all about him and all about Marcus.

"A girl is hurt, and not well. This man seeks her out, knowing he can get her to do unspeakable things in order to feel better. In order to feel like she got the justice she should have gotten from the legal system."

I don't want to know about any of this. I'm her caretaker and that's the only reason I intervened. The words are there, ready to be spoken. Instead I find myself thinking and pray I swallow the thought quickly enough that the officer doesn't see it written on my face. *Is that what happened with Delilah?*

I'm drained as I get to my loft and sag against the door. There's not an ounce of me left to keep me upright. My keys jangle as I toss them on the counter.

I'm torn when it comes to Officer Walsh. What I read about him and what I saw tonight are at odds, painting contrasting mind pictures. I don't know what to think about the man, but I can't get what he said out of my head.

I find myself slipping into old habits, inserting myself between the business of powerful men with unjust causes just as easily as I sulk to my living room to gaze at the bouquet.

Some nights I'm numb from work. It's a brutal reality to be submerged in. That's why I told Seth I want to stay at my place after long shifts. He agreed. Nearly everything I suggested, he agreed with this morning. Technically, yesterday morning.

I sag into my sofa and then kick off my sneakers, one by one without untying them. Tonight, this exhaustion isn't from work. It's because I'm questioning my own ability to think straight.

How did I get to this point in my life where I constantly question my sanity and my judgment? When did it get this bad?

A knock at the door sounds, as if answering the question. The large black hands on the clock on the wall read 1:47. I'm hesitant to rise, but almost certain it's Seth.

There's no one else who should be here. For a moment, I question if I should get a knife. I don't have a gun and as the doorknob rattles I curse myself for that.

"Laura," Seth calls out before the door is cracked open and I let out a strangled breath. *Thank fuck.*

"Way to give me a fucking heart attack," I reprimand him although I don't have the energy to speak loud enough for him to hear me.

I'm still inwardly calming myself when Seth comes into view, closing the door behind him.

"I made myself a key," he comments, holding up the shiny silver piece in his hand and then letting it fall, clanging with the other keys on the ring. It takes me a minute to respond. I'm too caught up in how he's dressed. There's no suit today, only faded jeans and a black t-shirt. Simple and yet everything I remember. Running his hand over the back of his head, he ruffles his hair before tossing the keys down on the counter… right next to mine.

The memories come back. Memories of how we used to do just that and it never felt wrong or off or confusing. Not like it does now.

"Of course you made yourself a key… I'd ask how, but…" I leave the thought unfinished and lean back into the sofa, gathering the throw blanket to pull over myself.

"You look good," I tell him offhandedly. Seth looks down at himself and then back at me. I cut him off before he can say a damn word. "I look like hell because that's how I feel."

"Long day?" he asks and stalks into the living room. Stalking is exactly how he goes about it too. Careful steps as he eyes my loft.

"Yeah," I answer him and then watch him. "Like what you see?" I ask and my tone hints at how pissed off I am. It's late, I'm tired, and he's come here unannounced.

"Twentieth floor loft with floor-to-ceiling windows that overlook the park," Seth says and glances outside, but it's so dark that you can't really see a damn thing. He has to pull back the thick curtains and stare for a second and then another until he concludes the same thing.

As he takes a casual seat in the dusty rose velvet chair across from me, I tell him, "Never thought of myself as a city girl but when I moved here... I wanted a change."

I mindlessly pick at the throw blanket, as if there are little fuzzes to be plucked but there aren't.

"Dyed your hair, got your dream job and an upscale place," Seth speaks and looks anywhere but at me.

"Hey, a girl who changes her hair is a girl who's changing her life." Why does it hurt so much to say a simple quote? Is it the unspoken judgment Seth reeks of? Or is it the shame that I did just that: I ran away and changed my life.

"You're still the same girl," Seth comments and leans forward in the small chair. With his elbows on his knees he asks me, "You like it here?"

"Yeah," I answer him honestly. "It's small, but I like it a lot."

He only nods, leaning back in the chair and I have to let out a long yawn. Seth looks so out of place in here. My décor is feminine and chic. His rough edges and masculinity stand out in this room. They'd stand out anywhere though.

He's busy staring at the flowers and that's when I remember he didn't answer my text. "Hey, the number you messaged me with the other day... that's yours, right?" I ask him and he nods once. "I um... thank you for the flowers."

"I got your text," he answers and that hard lump in my chest grows. He stands from the chair and walks past me to the kitchen. I don't bother to look and I'm not surprised when I hear the sound of the fridge opening.

"Make yourself at home." My comment is complete with a full-on eye roll and then I lay my head back, resting my eyes.

"You want a drink, Babygirl?" Seth asks and I tell him no.

"If I have one, I'll pass out," I say.

When he comes back empty-handed I tell him he's welcome to whatever he wants and that I was just joking, but he shakes his head, slipping his hands into his jeans.

"If I'd known you were coming, I'd have gotten you IPA." I hint at the reason I'm a little miffed.

"See," he says as he gives me a weak smile, "same girl."

The way he looks at me melts something inside that hurts. Something that's not meant to burn. "Not all the same," I murmur, pulling my legs into my chest. I've fallen asleep here too many times to count. Work's draining and the long shifts are hard on me some days.

Days like today.

"They remind me of the flowers I got you," he says as he steps slowly toward them and pauses to observe the bouquet.

"They are them." I can practically hear the simper that lingers on my lips in my voice when I tell Seth, "I'd never forget.

"Cami said it was a sign that you'd gotten both my favorite flowers and hers. She used to joke that the buttercups were her favorite and the flowers were really meant for her as a thank you for…" I trail off as I almost tell him how she pushed me to kiss him. Cami urged me to go after what I wanted and to stop thinking. Seth didn't make the moves first. He always let me do it. Times have changed.

"Buttercups?"

"The ranunculus. These ones," I say and I have to lean forward to reach. I don't like the way he looks down at me when I look up at him. He's uncertain; I can see it so clearly.

The realization makes me withdraw, pulling the throw blanket tighter around me before tossing it off altogether. I'm falling into old habits, when I shouldn't. Everything is different now.

"I have to wash my face and get ready for bed," I tell him with a sigh as I stand up. "I had a twelve-hour shift and another tomorrow."

There's only so much a person can take. I aim to walk around him, but he stops me, cupping my elbow in his hand and then pulling me into his chest. *Have I ever given into his warmth as easily as I do now?* Sagging into his chest without hesitation. Closing my eyes and breathing him in. My arms wrap around him and I hold him lightly as he pets my hair and then plants a kiss on my temple.

"I'm tired," I whisper. "And I don't know what we are." Insecurity rises and with the last statement my eyes open. "What are we doing?" I ask him.

With sleep pulling me under, it's hard to remember why I gave myself to him last night.

"We're feeling better," he reminds me.

It's difficult to imagine that this is better. With all the doubt surrounding me.

"Do you forgive me for leaving you?" The moment the question is spoken, I wish I could take it back. Seth's warm embrace turns stiff and it takes a long moment before he answers, "Don't asks questions you don't want the answers to."

A sad smile plays along my lips. It turns sadder when he goes about petting my hair again and the arm he has around my waist holds me closer to him.

Maybe one day. I don't believe the thought enough to speak it.

Peeking up from his hold, I get a good look at the tattoo on his bicep. The thin lines are clean but so close to one another, I can only imagine the ink will bleed together and all it will be is a solid black ring.

"You got more," I comment and run my finger along them.

"More years to remember," he tells me solemnly.

"Didn't you skip a year?" I say but my memory is so foggy.

He only looks down at me questioningly. His eyes are tired and he needs to shave. "Your stubble's turning into a beard."

He doesn't say anything, again he only watches me as I leave his embrace, making my way to the bathroom. It's hot and cold with him and I don't know what to think.

"Is there anyone else?" he finally asks the moment I turn to go to the bathroom and get on with bed, with or without him.

"Anyone else?" The confusion settles into a crease in my forehead.

"Are you seeing anyone else?"

"No." I huff out the response. "I haven't seen anyone in… over a month now."

"Good. When I said you're mine, I meant it." His tone is hard and unforgiving, like I've done something wrong.

"Why do you want me?" I breathe out with exasperation.

"To have you when I want." Seth's answer is bullshit and selfish.

So I hurt him back. "That's the only reason you ever kept me, isn't it?"

"Only reason you ever stayed, isn't it?" My response may have been a slap to the face. His is a bullet to my heart.

With my back to him, I sulk to the bathroom, turning on the faucet to run as hot as it can. With a hand on either side of the sink, I stare at the clear water swirling down the drain, waiting for the steam to come.

Seth isn't quiet when he comes up behind me, and I meet his gaze in the mirror.

"I mean it," Seth says again like it's a warning.

"Mean what?" I say and whip around, pissed off.

"You're mine."

"Seth… I am very much aware of that." It's all I can say. I won't deny it.

"Good." He gives the one-word response before grabbing my thighs and pulling me into his arms. His touch is fire, possessive and full of need.

It shocks me. Even as my back hits the tiled wall of the bathroom and his lips crash against mine. The wind is knocked out of me from the sudden wave of desire.

His fingers dig into my flesh as my legs wrap around his hips. His hard touch softens as he nips my bottom lip and pulls back, breathless.

With his body pressed against me and my hands on his muscular chest, I stare into his eyes wanting to know what the hell has gotten into him.

Before I can speak, he nudges his nose against mine and my eyes close from the tender touch. He kisses me once, short and soft.

Then he kisses me again and this time he deepens it. The water's still running, but I couldn't care less. I moan into his mouth and let him love me the way he knows how.

He nips my bottom lip, my breasts pressing flat against his chest as he leans forward, pinning me where I am.

Instantly, I'm hot and I feel suffocated. I crane my neck, to breathe cooler air, and he takes that as a sign to rake his teeth down my neck. The hint of pain as he drags his teeth and then bites down on my shoulder only ignites pleasure deep down in my belly and then lower.

"Seth," I moan.

"I fucking love it when you say my name," he groans in the crook of my neck before picking me up, one arm keeping me pinned to him.

He turns off the water, turns off the light. He doesn't ask at all if I was done. I hadn't even begun but none of it matters.

With the lights still off in my bedroom, he lays me down, never separating his body from mine and continues his slow, deliberate nips and kisses down my body. He peels my clothes down as he goes. When he gets to my waist, I have to prop myself up to take off my shirt. With my arms above my head, the shirt covering my face for just a moment, Seth unhooks my bra and viciously sucks my nipple. Gasping, I arch my back, and nearly buck him away from me because of the sudden onslaught of pleasure. He's everywhere at once, his hands, his lips, his hard body pinning me down, feeling my curves, worshiping every inch of me.

He only breaks long enough to remove his own shirt and then his pants after he's removed mine.

With both of us naked and panting he braces himself over me, in the perfect position to have me. I can't help but to reach up and kiss him, again and again, on his jaw, his lips, down to his neck. My touch isn't as rough and primal as his, but it's just as needy.

"Touch yourself," Seth says, pulling back when I kiss him again. My lips brush against his, the electricity vibrating through my body. It takes me a moment, my head spinning with desire to realize what he said.

"What?"

"You heard me," he commands, "touch yourself the way you did when you thought about me."

Thump. My heart pounds from the tone of his voice.

Unconsciously my left leg wraps around his thigh, wanting to urge him on, to have him lose control with me.

"I want you," I whisper, practically begging him.

"Touch yourself first, Babygirl." The depths of his eyes reflect only lust and that gives me hope in the uncertainty of what he's doing. "I want you to know the difference," he says, his voice deep and jagged with his own need that he's resisting. "I need you to feel what you can do all by yourself and then feel what I give you."

I crash my lips against his frantically and before he can pull away, my right hand moves to my clit. My nipples are pebbled against his chest and every small movement feels like heaven against them.

A small protest of a moan slips by me when Seth sits up on his knees, watching me in the dark bedroom as I touch myself beneath him. My head falls to the side as I circle my clit, but Seth's quick to put an end to that.

With his hand on my throat, he forces me to look up. "I want to see you," he whispers roughly with his other hand wrapped around his cock and I cum, just like that. I could see him stroking himself as I do the same to myself and the very thought of him losing himself on me was my undoing.

"So easy," he teases me in a murmur, leaning down to kiss me as the waves of my orgasm rock through me, heating my skin, paralyzing my senses in overwhelming pleasure.

Before the pleasure has waned, Seth grips my hips and flips me onto my belly in a swift movement that causes me to yelp in surprise. Lying flat on my belly, he teases my entrance, his thick head probing and playing.

"So easy, so wet. Tell me it's just for me."

With my eyes closed his command envelops me. Of course it's just for him. It's always been him.

"Just for you. It's all just for you." I barely get the words out, still struggling to breathe. In a forceful stroke, Seth enters me, brutally and with a blinding pleasure that has me screaming his name. My nails dig into the sheets and a cold sweat layers every inch of my skin. He waits a moment, his forearm brushing my shoulder until his front is against my back. Simply hovering over me, touching me although his weight doesn't push me down.

"You were made for me," he whispers at the shell of my ear, slipping his hand between my hip and the bed, not stopping until his fingers brush my clit. "This is how you did it?" he questions.

"Yes," I answer quickly and honestly.

He circles my clit and I bury my face into the sheets, moaning low in my throat from the sweet, decadent pull in my core. Bringing me closer to the edge once again. Just as a sheen of heat lifts from my body, as the coiled pleasure threatens to burst, Seth thrusts his hips, never relenting in the attention he pays to my swollen and sensitive nub. And again, and again. Picking up his pace and steadily fucking me deep and raw and possessively.

I have to bite down on the sheets. I try to move away from him; it's all too much. At the same time, I want more, I want him deeper, I want to feel him pulsing inside of me.

"Seth." The only word I can say is his name. Even the friction between my breasts and the sheets is igniting as he ruthlessly fucks me from behind.

He made his point with the first thrust. He made his point without even touching me. I know I can never have what he gives me with anyone else, let alone my own touch. He doesn't stop though, not until my voice is hoarse and raw, my body and lips tingling with a heated sensation that feels like it will last forever.

CHAPTER 11

Seth

PARKED IN THE LOT ACROSS FROM THE ROCKFORD CENTER, THE POLICE station is about a mile down the road and easily monitored. From here, in the driver side of my car with the window rolled down, the cop cars come and go, seemingly insignificant at a distance. I remember a time when I'd get anxious from just the thought of one.

Time changes a lot of things.

An old man in blue jeans and a thin dark gray hoodie mows the circular patch of grass out front of the large cement building directly in front of me.

Other than the small garden of roses on either side of the sidewalk that divides the grass, there's no color at all. The upper half of the three-story building is painted gray. The lower half is the same shade as cement.

Men and women go in and out of the Rockford Center, but the police station is far busier. There's only been a handful of nurses, out on smoke breaks, the mailman and now the gardener taking up residence out here. Even the parking lot is barren. Employees park around back and that leaves only myself and one other parked car with no one occupying it in this lot.

It's an odd choice to plant roses in a place like this.

It reminds me of a book we had to read in school, *I Never Promised You a Rose Garden*. It was about some girl in a place like this. I didn't read it, Laura did though. She cried at the end. I wonder if she likes the roses out front, or if they make her want to cry like the book did.

The smell of freshly cut grass hits me as the breeze drifts into the car. Picking up the paper bag next to me, I realize the sandwich inside it isn't quite hot anymore. It's still warm though.

I must've been sitting out here for longer than I realized. At least the coffee is still hot. I picked up everything from the corner diner by the bar; they have the best coffee in town. It's something sweet, caramel drizzle, or some shit like that, for Laura.

She may have eaten lunch already. I don't know. My phone's been in my hand, the bag on the passenger seat, and all the while, I've just been sitting here, watching, not going in.

The flowers have fucked with my head more than they should. They're just too much like the ones I gave her. It's unsettling. It feels like a sign or something. A signal that what we're doing is wrong. That it's not supposed to be this way.

I always knew I'd see Laura again, talk to her. Sometimes my thoughts would be only of a moment. One moment where we recognized each other and maybe even kissed, but never more than that.

A girl at the bar one night talked about star-crossed lovers and ever since she rattled on about it, I wondered if that's what we were meant to be. Because every time I'm around her, it hurts and I know it hurts her too.

It's like falling down a spiral where nothing else matters; I can't even see anything but her when she's in front of me. But I know I'm falling. Some falls you don't recover from.

Last night, sleep evaded me, the image of the flowers and reckless thoughts haunting me every time I closed my eyes.

My phone pings and I'm grateful to be ripped from my thoughts. The message I get isn't what I want to see though. Cursing under my breath, I don't respond.

Declan's got nothing.

The box the flowers came in was in the trash in her kitchen. I searched for it the second she passed out last night. It didn't have any identifying information. No note, no nothing. Declan can't find a record of any flowers ordered online to be delivered to Laura's address either.

It doesn't sit right with me.

If she wants to believe they came from me though, I'll let her believe it.

It's something more though, something unsettling deep in my bones. It feels like a warning. Like her leaving me is going to happen all over again. I barely survived the last time. She's the same, better even. But me? I'm a fucking shell of the man I was when I was with her.

Declan messages again and I have to respond to his text which reads: *Did he get the list?*

Looking past the center and to the police station, as if I can see Walsh opening the note I dropped in his box outside his office, I text Declan back: *Yeah. I left it at his office.* A list of all six names with the note, *they'll lead you to the man you're looking for.*

Declan sends a series of texts and I read them one by one. Little things he's wondering about from the copies of the diaries he has. He wants me to read them to get an idea of what I think about his conclusions. It's years of scattered thoughts from a tormented woman and right now, that's the last thing I want to do.

"Seth?" Laura says my name like it's a question.

"Shit," I hiss and get over the jolt that pinned me to the back of my seat. My back teeth grind and I have to unclench the paper bag to put it down. "You like scaring the shit out of me, don't you?"

My comment comes as I shake off the unease of being startled without her knowing. Her smile never falters. With her hair pulled high into a bun on the top of her head and a pair of scrubs with a print of coffee cups and hearts, she looks like she doesn't belong here. It's too much sweetness for a place that's made of stone.

"I thought it was you sitting out here." She rocks on her heels before lowering herself to the open window, folding her arms over it and getting closer to me. "I needed some fresh air… didn't expect to see you."

It strikes me for a moment how easy she makes it seem. Like there was no hesitation, no reason she shouldn't come to me.

My gaze darts to her lips as she licks them and the wind rushes, making her shiver.

"I was just thinking of you and brought you some coffee."

"As an apology for keeping me up all night?" she jokes and then hums, "Smells good."

Grabbing the bag and the coffee, I hold them in my lap. "Kiss first."

As the smile grows on her face, so does something warm inside of me. Something that covers the nagging feeling that everything's wrong. It comes with that first step down the spiral staircase. Blindly moving. Just like she does when she lets me hold her chin between my thumb and forefinger and steal a kiss from her. And then another.

There's always another when it comes to her.

CHAPTER 12

Laura

"God I wish Bethany were here."

"Anything I can help you with?" Aiden asks me and it's only then that I realize I spoke the thought out loud.

"Oh, no. No, just… nothing." I force a smile to my face and tap the pen in my hand on the chart. "All good," I tell him when he doesn't look away.

He keeps looking a moment longer, even after I turn my attention back to Melody's sheet.

My coffee's lukewarm now, but it hits the spot as I take a nice long sip and then look at the clock. One more hour until things wind down.

"She'll be here tomorrow." Aiden's comment reminds me that he's still standing by the nurses' station. "I have to say, I missed her."

"This *place* missed her," I say then add, "I'm glad she'll be back to pick up some of these rounds."

Aiden's chuckle isn't forced and it reminds me that he's a nice guy. I haven't been able to think of him the same since E.J. was admitted. It's hard not to think of it as a political decision. The check was big enough, so he let the rules slide for her.

Whoever has her here, with her information hidden, they want her alive and taken care of. I guess that's all that matters.

I watch him leave, waving at Mel who's counting pills that go into each of the little cups behind the half wall with a windowpane for the upper half.

Just as I'm returning the clipboard, I get that nagging prick that someone's watching me on the back of my neck and instead of being quiet about it, I whip around quickly, fear gripping my heart in a cold vise that chills my body.

The back of a black hoodie and dark jeans disappears behind the corner to the hall where my patients are.

I don't like it. Not the look of him or the feeling that resonates in my gut. Grabbing the sign-in sheet for a half second, I don't see a new name. No one signed in recently and I know every name on this list. Every single one. His name isn't here and it damn well should be.

My strides are purposeful as I round the corner.

"Excuse me," I call out, eager to get to the man as he nears the very end of the hall. He stops between the doors that lead to either Melody or E.J.

When he turns around, he tilts his head questioningly and a thin scar on his chin shines from the fluorescent lights above us.

"Do you mind signing in, please?" I ask him cordially, through an innate dread that creeps along every inch of my skin. He's handsome, although rough around the edges. Something about him… my soul doesn't like him.

"Yeah, yeah," the guy says as he smiles at me, and it's a charming smile, with perfect teeth. It makes him look younger too, but it doesn't reach his eyes. He scratches his chin, at the scar, maybe in an attempt to hide it. "This way?" he questions me, urging me to walk with him and I don't want to. The need to check on both the patients beyond those doors rides me harder than anything else in this moment. He was headed to one of them.

It's then that I realize it's quiet, there's no one else here. No patients on their way to the game room or the library. No visitors other than this man in the lone hall and every door down this way is closed.

"Yes. Let me show you," I speak politely, hiding everything I'm feeling and brushing aside my nerves. I feel paranoid. Shaking my head, I breathe out in exasperation.

"Something I said?" the visitor asks. His blondish hair is long enough that it tousles as he walks next to me.

"No, sorry. Just something I was thinking about before I saw you." I direct him to the clipboard, picking up the pen and holding it out to him. He takes it, but not quickly enough. His slender fingers linger. Standing this close to him, I note that he's taller than me. He doesn't carry a lot of weight to him, but he's lean and toned.

The cords in his throat tense when he says, "Thank you."

Shoving my hands into my pockets, I only nod.

"Who are you here for?" I ask him when I see he's only filled out his name. Jacob something. I can't quite read his last name from this angle.

"Just checking on a friend is all," he says softly, with a hint of an accent although I can't place it. Southern, maybe?

I'm stern but still polite, still kind even, when I explain, "You have to write—"

"Laura." I'm cut off by a familiar voice.

Officer Walsh nods a greeting at Jacob, and then apologizes for interrupting. After looking at the silver watch, which looks expensive and doesn't match the read I got on Jacob, the visitor who never said who he was visiting, tells Officer Walsh it's all right and he has to get back to work anyway.

I watch the man go, not listening to a damn word coming from Officer Walsh.

"Do you know him?" I ask the man to my left, a police officer who should have the kind of sense about a person that I've learned to have.

He blinks at me once, his thick lashes covering those pale blue eyes for a moment before his brow raises and he catches sight of the black hoodie just as the elevator doors close.

"Should I?" Officer Walsh asks me.

I debate on telling him the thoughts that are racing through my mind. "Did he do something?" Officer Walsh asks, widening his stance to face me and moving his head lower so he cuts off my view of the elevator doors.

In this moment, Walsh looks trustworthy, *feels* trustworthy. "Tell me now, Laura. I can go get him. Just tell me."

Although it's a command, he speaks so softly, with such empathy, I almost tell him how I don't have a good feeling about that guy.

But he's a cop for fuck's sake and feelings aren't evidence of shit.

I shrug and say, "Just rubbed me the wrong way for some reason."

"Don't take gut instincts for granted," Walsh advises and then he seems to remember he has to sign in. He does, marking Melody down as well. "Maybe it's good I got here when I did."

A chill flows over my shoulders, as if agreeing with him.

"Maybe," I agree. Peeking over my shoulder, I watch Mel separate more cups on a new tray.

"You're here for more questions?" I ask him, changing the subject.

"I thought you would prefer it if I came during visitor hours."

I don't hesitate to tell him, "You thought right." He gives me a tight smile and nods, nearly walking away but then he stops to tell me, "You're protective of them. That's a good thing."

I search his eyes, wrinkled at the edges from his genuine smile and then ask, "Why not bring her in if you think she did it?"

He pauses, looking down at the linoleum floor before slipping his hands into the pockets of his dark blue uniform pants. "She was in a support group before this. She needed to be."

"She needs more than a support group," I urge him. I want to tell him that she's so much better after the therapy sessions. And after a week of regular medication, she's more active, carrying on more conversations than normal. "She's doing well here."

"I'm not suggesting that she's not." He runs his hand over his chin and tells me, "Sometimes… people need justice. And it's hard to define what that is. Five men died that night and in my opinion, they should have been dead long before it for the things they'd done and gotten away with. My job is to protect and serve. It's not so different from yours when you think about it."

"So you don't want to take her in even though you think she did it… because you're okay that she did it."

"I didn't say that," he replies and shakes his head. "I just need to be sure that what I'm doing will help her."

"Do you think she really did it? You still have the theory that Marcus helped her and the others get revenge." Saying Marcus's name to Walsh seems wrong and makes me uneasy but he doesn't react, he doesn't even look away from the sign-in sheet. Not until he speaks again.

"I think she knew and what I found today… I think she knew about the priest being there and I want to know why."

His admission startles me. "There was only one name on the list of confessors before the priest left. Witnesses verify he left the church a quarter after seven. It was Melody's name—she was the last one to see him before he burned to death with the rest of them."

"And still… you aren't going to bring her in?"

"She has motive for one of the murders. We have circumstantial evidence now for the priest. That's all I've got."

I nod, understanding. "If she confesses here though… would it count?"

A sad smile graces his lips. "Count?" He rocks on his heels and looks up at the ceiling before swallowing tightly. "I don't want her," he admits to me in almost a whisper. His pale blue eyes seek mine out, begging me to understand.

"You want Marcus," I surmise.

"That's all I want. If she can give me something on him…"

"What about the others? Her friends from the support group. The ones you think came up with all this? Why don't you ask them?"

"I have. No one mentioned Marcus or admitted to anything. I know Melody's case. I'd spoken to her when she came to me a couple of months ago. I think that's the only reason she's opened up. She's the only one who's given me anything. She's the one with remorse."

I could point out that she's also drugged and not in her right mind, but I bite down on that thought in favor of something else. "Have you brought them in? The others to question them?"

"I don't want to. The thing is, there isn't an ounce of me that thinks they'll do something like this again. I also don't believe they would have done it at all had Marcus not urged them to do it. Given them the solution and laid out the plan."

"Do you know that's what happened for sure?" I ask him. "Sometimes people do things… you don't expect."

"Trust me, I've seen my share. It's my gut feeling. Marcus will never stop. Since I've shown up, the death rate has only increased. He's keeping me busy."

I struggle, knowing more about Officer Walsh and Marcus than he realizes. I feel like a crook and a liar.

"I have questions for Miss Melody." Walsh plasters a thin, short-lived smile on his face.

"Officer," I say and stop him, feeling compelled to say something, "if there's anything I can do to help, please let me know."

A genuine smile replaces the forced one. "I appreciate that."

CHAPTER 13

Seth

WATCHING A CLOCK IS A SHIT WAY TO EAT UP TIME. BUT THEN again, so is staring at a phone screen, wishing you were reading a different message.

I called Derrick about Fletcher a few days ago and asked if there was any talk of him or his crew recently. I killed Fletcher before he could kill me. It's that simple. Along with him, I took out all of his men who had any authority. I let them scatter. His name shouldn't be breathed by anyone of relevance.

Derrick said he'd look into it.

Today he sent me a response. It was detailed and thorough, with the names and addresses of five men who still hang together and were a part of Fletcher's crew.

That's all I've got. That was the last message he sent.

It was an hour ago that the text came through. And fifty minutes since I responded *thanks*.

It's the first time I've talked to him in years. This is all that's between us now. Business. The small clock on the mantel ticks and I pick up my beer, setting down one of the folders on the coffee table, taking a large swig before sending Derrick another message.

How are things?

My eyes burn from reading the handwritten print for hours. It's all I've been doing: putting together the puzzle pieces written in the journals. The problem is Delilah contradicts herself. The locations are something we can work with, but the other things she's written… I don't know that I trust them. She's not a reliable source and it's frustrating and time consuming. If it leads to Marcus though, it'll all be worth it.

I try to remember the last real conversation I had with Derrick. It was about Laura, I know that. He wanted me to come back, he said he wanted me *whole*. All he ever talked about was Laura. He hung Cami's death over my head, reminding me that he'd never be all right again, but I could still chase after what I lost. Laura was still out there.

Damn, that has to be three years ago.

Are you with her? Derrick asks me in the text and my eyes narrow, my head tilts. There's no reason he should know that I am. I looked through her messages, searching for someone who could have sent her flowers; they haven't spoken in years. She told the truth when she said she hadn't spoken to him a long damn time.

Why do you ask? I write him back.

Fuck off with that. I'm still your right-hand man.

I huff a humorless laugh and it comes with a slight smirk. Leaning back on the sofa, I read the message, settling the beer bottle to rest on my thigh. Those were good times. When he was my right hand and Laura was my girl.

She'll be here in an hour when she gets off work, I text and then add, *She's a nurse now.* It's not until I send it that I realize he already knows. She'd already finished school four years ago so when they were talking, I'm sure she told him.

I know, he confirms. *She still loves you too.*

It's not like that, I text him and feel a deep ache settle in my chest. It'll never be what it was.

I down the beer and get up to retrieve another, leaving the phone where it is. It pings the moment I get to the fridge.

Opening the beer, taking a sip, I make my way back and read the message only to feel that anxiousness I was drinking down, creeping back up.

There's something you should know. They found a body at the warehouse. Does Laura know about her dad?

No. Setting the beer down, I feel the cold prick along my skin. *No one needs to look into that.* Years have gone by without her father being a blip on my radar. I don't like him being brought up.

They don't need to, but the evidence is there. She may find out either way.

I mutter *fuck* and close my eyes. Dread is a bitter taste in my mouth. *She can't know*, I text him back.

You've got her now. Just don't let her go. No matter what comes out.

Derrick's texts come hurriedly, one after the other.

I remind him, *I asked how you were*, wanting to get off this subject. I can't handle this right now. Not when I don't know if there's even a reason to be concerned. My stomach churns, knowing Laura's father is on Marcus's radar though. Maybe the evidence is already out and he found it before putting the pieces together.

There's a lot of shit that's changed since you left, but overall, things are good.

I text him the obvious question to move things away from business: *You got a girl?*

A minute passes before he answers, *Not yet. I have to go, but I'll keep you updated with anything going on at the warehouse.*

Thanks.

With that, I'm left with just my beer, too many questions I don't have answers to, and the time ticking down.

Derrick used to ask me if I was punishing myself or Laura. The memory of the last conversation we had comes back full force. I can hear his voice in my head, asking me that question like he was some kind of fucking therapist.

Maybe it was a punishment to be so close to her, but not have her. Although, I couldn't have known she wouldn't come to me. For weeks, I thought she'd learn I was here, that I was close to her, and she'd come to me. When her name came up on the alert and I knew she was searching my name online, it put an end to that speculation.

The alarm beeps and a moment later the headlights from Laura's sedan shine through the front window. We spent last night at her place, tonight we stay here. I know she's had a long shift, but my place is closer to the center, so it was easy enough to get her to agree.

I don't know what we are. I don't know why my head's so fucked. But I know she's mine. She'll stay here until I tell her otherwise.

Laura comes into the house the same way I came into her place last night, saying my name as she pushes open the door with a key in her hand.

"You found it," I say as I smirk at her. Even after a twelve-hour shift in baggy scrubs, she's breathtaking.

"The key in my sandwich bag? Yes, yes I did."

"It was unlocked, you know?" I tease her.

"Maybe I wanted to make sure it was to your front door. Since, you know, it just happened to be in the bag with no note." She shrugs as she adds, "It could have been anyone's key."

"It's yours."

Closing and then locking the door behind her, she cradles an overnight bag in the crook of her arm along with her purse. It's not a large bag and I'm sure she only packed for one night. I'll have to fix that. She needs everything here and a place for what she needs in the cabinets and dressers. I'll correct that issue tomorrow. Dropping her keys next to mine on the kitchen counter, she leaves her bag there too and rubs her eyes, sagging into the seat next to me.

I hold up the beer, offering it to her but she shakes her head and then rests her forehead on my shoulder, sleep weighing her down. "You don't drink after work. Now that is different."

She smiles in the crook of my neck and her shoulders shake slightly with a small feminine snicker.

Glancing up at me, she gives me a smile and then rolls to the side, giving me space. She lets out an exhausted yawn and tells me she's just tired.

"Bethany said I should take up a red wine nightcap to help me sleep."

"I'll grab a couple of bottles."

"Mmm," she half responds with her eyes closed. Eyeing her plump lips with a loose tendril of hair in her face has me hard in a split second.

"You're not allowed to sleep just yet," I tell her and those long lashes sweep up so she can look at me.

"I should probably tell you something first," she says and the sweetness and playful demeanor fall from her expression until all I see is my tired girl.

Setting down the beer and leaning forward, I pray it's not about someone calling from California with news on her father. I'm aware of how I tell her to tell me, relaxed and easy. I'm aware of how I'm breathing calmly, like I'm not worried at all.

"Walsh came by the center." Relief hits first, then pride when Laura looks down at her hands, watching her fingers wring around one another as she tells me, "Today and yesterday."

She feels guilty for not telling me. I like the look of submission on her.

"Did he talk to you?" I ask her, expecting to hear that he didn't. Why would he? He doesn't know she's with me. He doesn't know shit about her. Or about the diaries.

"He did. About a murder and one of my patients." She readjusts and then looks at my beer where I left it. "Maybe I should have a drink," she comments.

"I'll get you one; you keep talking," I tell her and stand up, moving away from her field of vision to listen.

"The fire that happened down at the farm." She speaks louder so I can hear as I open cabinets, pretending to look for a stray bottle of wine. Crouched down and staring at rows of clear and amber liquor bottles, I listen. "He thinks she has motive and it has something to do with Marcus helping her get revenge."

"The fire at the farm?" I question her, as I stand up and move to the fridge. "No wine, Babygirl," I add with a smile, easing her as much as I can.

"A beer?" she asks and even pouts. She can't know how I want to kill Walsh for talking to her. She can't know half the shit that's going on. She wouldn't want to anyway. If she knew, she wouldn't stay.

"The thing is," she keeps talking as I twist the top off and toss it in the garbage. She only stops talking to thank me when I retake my seat next to her. "He keeps bringing up Marcus. He's talking to me as if he knows that I know."

My hackles rise, the tiny hairs on my arms standing on edge.

"Whether he knows about the diaries or he thinks I've heard things and whispers in the center… I don't know."

"What did you tell him?"

"I played dumb. I told him if he needs anything from me, to let me know."

Her nervousness and insecurity are something I've never liked. I'm here and as long as I'm here, she shouldn't feel like that. I'll fix it. I'll find out everything and fix it.

"A cop came in questioning a murder, that's… nerve wracking," I answer her, taking a long drag of my beer after handing Laura hers. She doesn't move to drink yet; even though I'm staring at the fireplace, I know she's staring at me. "To add on to it, you have secrets. You know about him and his motives. That's what's gotten to you," I say as I finally look at her and rest my hand on her thigh.

I have to give her a small smirk when my gentle touch, the back and forth of my thumb, gives her shivers. A deep chuckle vibrates up my chest. "So easy," I tease her.

She finally smiles, a cute little smile that she tries to catch between her teeth. The soft pink of a blush rises to her cheeks and she asks me, "You really think that's all this is?"

"You don't like secrets and you're shit at keeping them," I tell her. "You're doing good." Patting her thigh and then giving a gentle squeeze, I tell her, "Don't worry about Marcus or Walsh. They don't know anything and it's all in that pretty little head of yours."

"You sure?" Even though she questions me, her body language relaxes. Everything about her believes me. Which is shit, because I'm lying to her. Marcus knows something. Walsh doesn't though.

I give her a smile, followed by a peck of a kiss that leaves her with her eyes closed and a simper on her lips. "I'm sure, Babygirl. You're just stressed, but you handled it well."

"It's just a lot and it feels like—"

I cut her off to say, "Because it is a lot. You're carrying a heavy burden on your shoulders every day. When someone makes you question yourself, it feels a lot worse, knowing everything else that could fall." Cupping her chin in my hand, I kiss her again. I swear every time we kiss she melts a little more. She doesn't worry, she doesn't buy into the voices in her head telling her she's not enough and she's in too deep. I should kiss her every moment of every day.

"So… what should I do?" she asks me.

"You already handled it. Nothing else to do but let it go. I know you don't like to lie, and you did today, a lie of omission, but you have your reasons. You don't need to be in the middle of anything and Walsh shouldn't have put you there."

"Right, right. And he doesn't know that I read Delilah's diaries," she says and keeps nodding to herself, even after she's done thinking out loud.

"I know what'll help you," I say as I get on my knees on the sofa and face her, towering over her.

She's huddled beneath me, holding on to her beer with both hands and looking up at me wide eyed although there's a smile on her face. "What are you doing?" she asks playfully.

"Hands up," I demand and she obeys, not letting go of her beer bottle. Her bra's a simple white number; it makes her look innocent and sweet. Like an angel laid out before me. An angel to play with, to dirty and taint with all the sinful lust I have for her.

"You make me want to do bad things to you," I murmur. Peeking up through her thick lashes, her doe eyes go wide with lust, proving her to be the vixen she is. Even her cheeks heat nearly instantly.

"You like it, don't you?" I ask her and she doesn't even give me a chance to add, *how much you get to me.*

She answers, "I love it" before I can finish. "I love everything you do to me." With her hands behind her, her shoulders back and her head tilted up to look at me, she's vulnerable and waiting.

I want her to remember this night. I want every moment to be different, every touch to be more than what she can imagine on her own.

I glance to my left and the brown glass of the empty beer bottle glints. Turning back to her, I tell her, "I'm going to play with you, and take my time with you."

She doesn't protest, although I can hear my name and the way she says it likes it's a warning lingering on the tip of her tongue. She swallows it and any argument she has that she's tired. I know she is. She'll do what I want though, because she knows I'll make it good for her.

"Strip down." I give her the command and she obeys. She doesn't try to make a show of it although she teases me by biting down on her lower lip when she drops her bra to the floor.

I wasn't going to touch her, but the pale pink of her nipples begs me to caress them. Her head tips back, her hair cascading behind her. Correcting myself, and ignoring the desire that has all the blood in my body stiffening my cock, I pull away from her.

Without her clothes, goosebumps play along her body and after she lies down like I tell her to, I blow. That's all I do, teasing her, going from a warm breath along her neck that makes her shiver, to a steady stream down her belly and lower, to her sex.

She tries to reach for me, to grab my arm or my shoulder, but I catch her wrist. "No touching." My command sobers her, and I know in an instant she doesn't like it.

"No. Touching," I repeat firmly, licking my lower lip and loving how her gaze darts to the movement.

Nodding, but still holding doubt in her expression, she lowers her hands to the cushion, gripping it and closing her eyes with a soft moan as I blow against her clit again.

"You're going to make me cum from just breathing on me?" she questions, her eyes alight with mischief and the sexy grin proves she's thinking she'll need more than that.

"No," I answer her, reaching behind me for the beer bottle. I lick the top of it where the cap was twisted on and test out its ridges.

The sound of her nails scratching against the fabric, combined with her chest rising and falling quickly, let me know exactly how she's feeling. "You scared, Babygirl?"

"Will it feel good?"

"Does it ever not?" I question her and the doubt and fear vanish from her eyes. Her thighs part, her heels digging into the cushion as she bends her knees and bares herself to me.

Arousal makes her pussy glisten, and when I press the cold glass to her clit, I watch her cunt clench around nothing. Letting out a short chuckle, I position myself between her legs, careful not to touch her. My greedy girl lifts her heel, and I know she's going to move her leg around me, pulling me in and showing me just how much she loves it.

"No touching," I remind her, staring up her gorgeous body. She looks down at me, puzzled until I add, "Keep your legs still."

She only nods, her skin flushed and her breathing still not even. Just the idea of using a bottle to play with her has her so worked up. I drag the glass down her clit and through her lips, watching how her hips subtly rise and listening to the pleasure that lingers in her soft moan. It's barely audible, nearly a murmur of satisfaction.

The sweet smell of her, the sound of her moans, the heat of her flesh… fuck, it's torture not to touch her, not to lean forward and suck on her clit until she comes apart for me. I focus on getting the one thing I want… her desire to become so much that she disobeys.

I want her so wrapped up in pleasure from this touch that she forgets the rules. I'll let her cum and then I'll flip her ass over and ravage her. Letting my head fall, I close my eyes, groaning from the thought and feeling my hard cock twitch with need.

Soon.

The sooner the better. Laura's eyes are closed and she swallows thickly, waiting for me to touch her again. Instead I blow against her sex, noting how her stomach clenches and her body sways from the sensitivity. I want the pressure to build slowly, giving her a higher high than she'll recognize, and then I want to watch her come apart at the seams.

Starting at her clit, I press the bottle against her, slipping lower and parting her lips with the mouth of it. Pressing the bottle inside of her, her breath hitches and her eyes open. She's staring at the ceiling, her mouth in a perfect *O* when I pull the bottle forward, brushing it against the front wall of her pussy. I don't pull it out; instead I move it back inside of her slowly, all the while pressing against her front wall. The pink in her cheeks darkens and floods into her chest when the neck of the bottle is fully inside of her. Rocking it back and forth, I wait for the moment when her head thrashes and her breathing quickens.

"I can get you off with anything," I tell her and I'm cocky, arrogant… and I feel like a damn king. Her king, her ruler, her *everything*.

I don't stop until she cums. The first time, she doesn't break the rules. She holds on to the cushion like a good submissive when I fuck her to orgasm with the bottle. The second time, she screams out my name, her hands on her face, covering her mouth and she cums hard and fast. I'm relentless though. I never stop fucking her, slow and steady with the neck of the bottle, only picking up my pace when I know she's close to falling again. The third time, her back bows and tears fall from the corners of her eyes as her body rocks and her toes curl. She grabs my arm then, desperate to hold on to anything while she's falling.

Thank fuck she grabs me. Thank God she breaks the rules right then and there.

I barely have any control left and I need to touch her. I need to be inside of her, falling with her.

CHAPTER 14

Laura

THREE DAYS IN A ROW WITH TWELVE-HOUR SHIFTS ISN'T THAT difficult. It's not my first time and it sure as hell won't be my last. So that doesn't explain why I feel so utterly and completely drained. Bethany called out, something about her sister. I asked if everything was all right but she couldn't say.

The shift is harder today since I'm picking up some of her workload. The temporary hire to cover Bethany being out for so long, is a bitch who doesn't know how to do a damn thing. So I'm basically pulling the weight of two people today. Why? Because I care about Bethany's patients, unlike Cindy Lou Who-gives-a-fuck and who even knows where she is right now.

Looking to my left, toward the nurses' station where Cindy better be performing the checklist so we can leave on time, the hall is empty as I quietly shut E.J.'s door.

I rest my head against the wall and just breathe. Breathe in. Breathe out. That's all I have to do.

My grandma used to say, *"You don't have to do a damn thing. Just breathe. And pay taxes. Even if you're dead they'll get those taxes."*

The memory of her in the chair in the corner of the living room, pointing her finger at me while she said it makes me smile and it's the first time I've smiled all shift. Damn does it make me miss her though.

I never realized how alone I truly am until recently. No family at all. I only have one friend here, really. Bethany. I'm chummy with Mel and Aiden, but they don't know me like Bethany does. Now she's busy, off with Jase.

I have Seth now. *Only Seth.*

Fuck, I don't like that. I don't like having to rely on him. Especially since all we're doing is fucking. I'm not blind to the fact that when we do talk to one another, it's like walking on eggshells. I don't like it. I don't know how to change it though.

Maybe with time.

Breathing out, *just breathe*, I stare down at the tray in my hand and the last cup of pills. Three colorful ones for Melody.

Maybe some people are just loners. There's nothing wrong with that.

Besides, I have my patients and there aren't a lot of people who get that.

I shake out my shoulders, feeling stiff from not sleeping well and bending over the tray all day. It was my turn to do the pill sorting, well, Bethany's, but I didn't trust Cindy to take on that task.

Before I can take a step forward, across the hall to Melody, I hear a bang behind me. At least I think I do. The noise wraps itself around my gut, squeezing. Something's wrong.

I drop the tray like a fool, turning as fast as I can to get to E.J.

There's nothing wrong with her, though. Not a damn thing is out of place. I swear I heard a bang, like something heavy had dropped.

E.J.'s in the same position she always is, on her side, her knees bent, her hands under her head. I washed her hair today though, marveling at how soft and silky it was. She struggled to tell me months ago, before it happened—although she didn't say what "it" was—she'd gotten a treatment on her hair.

There's no doubt in my mind she's from money. Big money, given the strings they've pulled.

"Are you all right?" I ask E.J. when her heavy eyes open and she stares back at me. Her slow reactions are partly from the medication to help her sleep without dreams, and partly from her crippling depression.

She nods her head slowly and just like in the shower today, she places her slender fingers at her throat and I know that means she wants to talk.

"They told me not to give you my name. Didn't they?" Her voice is scratchy and I can tell it hurts her from the way she winces.

She must be out of it. There's no way I'd know what anyone told her. I don't even know who "they" are.

The end of my ponytail brushes against my shoulder as I shrug and say, "I don't know what they told you. I just know it's not in your files."

My answer brings tears to her eyes; tears I think were coming regardless. Her face doesn't crumple or contort though and when the tears fall from her chin, down the pillow, she pulls back and then reaches to her cheek before staring at the moisture on her fingertips. Like she didn't even know she was crying.

"I lost everything… I can't lose my name."

"There's always more, you didn't lose everything." I'm quick to console her and I slowly, cautiously, pull out the corner chair to sit in it.

"Do you know what it's like to lose everyone you love? To watch—" Her head falls back as her silent tears turn to wracking sobs. "I have court on the third. For my own custody. For them to take that too." She moves as quickly as she can to brush away the tears, accepting the tissue I offer her. It's a good sign. It's a good sign that she's talking, that she's aware of her pain.

"None of that is in our files."

"Please," she says. Her voice turns hoarse and she lies on her back, calming herself down, just breathing. "Call me Ella… please."

"I'll call you Ella. It's nice to meet you, formally." My quietly spoken joke comes with a warm smile and she gives me one in return before turning her back to me.

"Good night, Ella."

"Good night, Laura."

Just breathe. It's all I can think to keep from losing it when I leave her. Her pain is palpable and it wreaks havoc on my heart.

Some patients leave and they never return. Their trip here is only a blip in their life. The one time they hit so low that they needed help. That's all this will be for them. I'm grateful we're able to give them that and that their life goes on.

Then there are other people. Patients who are admitted against their will. Patients who are a harm to themselves. Whether they want to die, or just get off on the pain, sometimes they just want to hurt outside like they do inside.

Those are the patients I worry about when they leave. When the doctor or judge says they can go. Sometimes they come back here, worse off than before. Other times they leave here and within a week, their obituaries are in the paper.

The cup and pills are waiting for me on the floor just outside her door. It doesn't take long to dispose of them and gather the last cup for Melody. It takes me longer to mentally prepare more than anything.

Melody's waiting for me, rocking but not humming, when I enter her room. All of the rooms are standard. A bed, nightstand, and dresser. A TV in the upper right corner and an attached bathroom. White sheets, white furniture and soft gray walls. The only difference is the artwork in each of the rooms. And we provide plenty and offer to change them based on patient preference. It was an idea Bethany had years ago. I backed her and we had to pressure corporate to give us the funds to purchase additional artwork. It took nearly a year, but they agreed. I think it makes all the difference.

Neither Melody nor E.J.—Ella—cared about the artwork when they first arrived. Melody decided to change hers nearly a week ago though and I'm hopeful Ella will also come around, although the third of October is right around the corner. And if she's right about having a court date, she may be long gone sooner than I think.

"You changed your pictures again," I remark when I come in and Melody smiles.

"I asked the new girl to do it while I was in the library. She seemed like she had the time just sitting in the back, watching us."

Is that where she was? Hiding in the library? That little… I stuff my snide remark into the back of my head, jotting it down on the memo pad of complaints to give Aiden before my shift is up.

"I like it," I say, nodding one by one at the row of prints.

"They're all classics," she tells me with plenty of pep in her tone. "*The Starry Night* is Van Gogh and this one," Melody gestures as she rises off the bed, making the metal legs squeak as she does so, "*Blue Nude* is Picasso."

I know she's right, because I picked out the classics when Bethany wanted help choosing what art to order. They're only cheap prints, but they're still beautiful.

"I love them. Wonderful choices," I comment and hold out the little cup for her.

Her smile fades and she gathers the covers before climbing back into bed and finally accepting the cup.

"What do you think of Officer Walsh?" she asks me and then lets out a small chuckle. "The good officer, as I like to call him."

The small hairs on the back of my neck stand on end. "What do I think of him?" I repeat her question, giving myself time to think of how to reply while she accepts the cup of water and downs the medicine.

"If you want to talk to him, you should. If you don't, you shouldn't."

"That's not quite an answer to my question, is it?" she asks as she crumples the little cup.

"The thing is, I have to tell someone. I used to have Father John," she says and her tone turns remorseful and longing. The cold comes back, clinging to my skin. Walsh said she was the last to see him. I just can't imagine this girl killing anyone. Conspiring to do so or otherwise.

"The priest who… passed away." I don't say murder. I don't want her mind to move back to the crime and go quiet. Some piece of me has to know the truth.

Walsh's words echo in my mind but they're quickly silenced by Melody. "I didn't know he'd go."

"I don't understand," I say, pressing her for more as I pull the corner chair closer to her bed.

She readjusts under the sheets, lying down as I take my seat.

"I told him everything. He knew what that man did to me and my thoughts. I told him all about the others too. He knew and he never approached any of them. He never did anything but absolve me of my sins."

"Father John?" I ask to clarify.

"Yes." She turns to look me in the eyes as she adds, "It's a sin to think these things, you know? When you want others to hurt… it's a sin.

"So when I told him… I helped…" she trails off as her throat goes tight and Melody closes her eyes. My pulse races and I can barely hear her over the pounding of my heart. *Is she really confessing?*

"When I told Father John in church that they were going to die, I told him where, I told him how and he asked me when." Melody doesn't cry. She merely stares at the ceiling, as if watching, not remembering, not a part of it. Only watching the scene unfold.

"I told him I wanted to be in the church when it happened and that it was happening now." She turns her head to the side, her wide eyes piercing through me. "I didn't know he'd go. I didn't know once he left, he'd never come back. I stayed there in the confessional waiting for him. I stayed there all night."

A numbing prickle dances over my skin. To be involved in something like that… and she's only twenty. Watching the remorse, the confusion, the guilt, but also the anger play in her eyes is frightening. A part of me is terrified that she did go through with a plan to murder. Even if she wasn't there. Even if they deserved it.

She heaves in a breath and the emotional pull of it all drags her down to the hells of her own mind. Her bottom lip quivers and her voice shakes. "He left me to stop it from happening. He said he had to save them."

"It's okay," I console her, feeling her pain, but also my shock, my own horror.

"Why did he go?" she questions me as if I have answers. "Why would he go to them?" Her voice breaks and the tears fall fast and furiously. Unable to stop. Her elbow props her up as the small girl asks me again, "Why would he leave the church, leave me there, to go to *them*?"

The way she says them resonates with anger, with disgust. It's the hint of a side to the young woman that sends a chill down my spine.

"I can't say," I answer her, keeping my voice even. I'm silent, she's silent. No one speaks as the air is permeated with an influx of anger and betrayal, finally ending with sorrow when Melody's face crumples and she lies back down on her back.

"Do you want to tell Officer Walsh?" I ask her and she shakes her head violently, wiping at the tears.

"He already knows," she confesses. "I didn't have to say it for him to know," she adds in a whisper.

I wait a moment longer and it's then the meds begin to kick in, her eyelids turning heavy. When I stand though, my heart leaps from the quick grab of her hand onto mine.

"He didn't absolve me of my sins." She rushes the words out as if she's being strangled. Pain from her grip rips up my arm and I struggle not to show it, my back teeth clenching.

"Absolve me… please. Please, absolve me of my sins."

Fear strikes me, witnessing the dire need of this girl. Watching her reality slip to the point where she truly believes I could help her.

"What is my penance?" she asks as her wide eyes beseech me.

"I'm not-" I start to get out. I can barely breathe.

"Please," she begs me. "How many Hail Marys? He never did anything ever when I told him what that man had done to me. He always did nothing. He sat there. He never did anything but listen. I didn't know he'd go… I didn't know he'd die! Please! How many?"

"As many as you need," I answer her and she shakes her head, releasing my hand to wipe the new tears from under her eyes.

"I keep saying them, but I don't feel better. Please!" she screams, on the verge of a breakdown, arching her back as she does and I answer, gripping her hand in both of mine.

"Fifteen," I yell and then swallow, quietly repeating myself as Melody lies back down, calming herself until she's eerily still. I have no idea how many is a lot or a little or whether she'll even accept the answer. I'm not Catholic. I've never been to confession, although I have plenty to confess.

"Is that all?" she answers sweetly, in a tone not unlike the one she used when she told me the names of the art on the wall. "Fifteen," she marvels.

CHAPTER 15

Seth

THERE ARE AT LEAST TWO HUNDRED BODIES IN THE BAR. IT'S PACKED for a Monday night. The Red Room is never quiet though. Never a dull moment. Just like Allure. Long legs barely covered by short skirts, hard bodies clad in tight jeans sway and grind on the dance floor. The bar is dark, but the lights transition with every beat of the vibrant music.

The dark red paisley wallpaper that lines the walls and the black chandeliers hanging from the sixteen-foot-high black ceiling keep the atmosphere sinful and decadent.

Alcohol is a constant and tonight I stand behind the bar, waiting for one person in the hundreds to show. The liquor bottles behind me give plenty of light, even in the half beats of darkness. They're lit. This entire side is always lit which is why I stay behind the bar, always watching the moves made in the crowded place.

"Did he say when?" Jase asks me, fixing his jacket as he walks behind the bar to join me and the three bartenders.

"Around one." Walsh left a message on my voicemail. *One o'clock tonight in The Red Room.* The last time we met, he blackmailed us. Tonight should be a better experience than that.

"Good. An update in a public place. Maybe Walsh has what he

wants." Turning to Jase, I watch the background fade and focus on him. Freshly shaven with his tailored suit, he looks more like a CEO than he does the head of a crime organization. It's the air around him though and the way others look at him, with a hint of fear, or perhaps jealousy, that give it away. He stands apart from everyone in here. I've been doing my best for years to blend in, but right now, I wonder if I stand out the way he does. I wonder if the way he's perceived now is the way I was perceived years ago in my own club.

"You think he really found Marcus?" I ask Jase, barely breathing the name aloud. Marcus. His gaze meets mine and we share a look. If that list led him to Marcus, Marcus wanted it to happen. We've been following his men for months and we still haven't identified the man in question.

Movement from the corner of my eye catches my attention. Walsh doesn't blend in like the other men in this club. They all have smirks, smile easily, laughing and enjoying the atmosphere. A few watch the dance floor, taking notes on potential women to pursue. Even the ones who are less than fine, and come for a strong drink after a long day, look like they belong.

Walsh is all business. He's always all business. Even without his uniform, he looks like a cop. As he takes a seat on the leather-enveloped barstool, a man in the corner of the room stills, the pause at odds with the remainder of the club, grinding recklessly and swaying to the music. That man I know well and I'm damn sure he can tell Walsh is a cop just from the straight rod shoved up Walsh's ass that keeps him perfectly upright with that grimace on his face.

Jase catches the eye of the man in the corner and waves him off.

"Drink?" I offer Walsh, watching every detail of his expression. His eyes are narrowed as he does the same to me.

"I thought the list would be something you'd find agreeable," Jase comments after a moment of silence. "You don't think it's helpful?" he asks Walsh.

Something's off and wrong. He has resources and two days later Walsh should know by now that the list consists of six men on a rotating schedule doing Marcus's dirty work. At some point, they'd lead to him.

"You don't know, do you?" Walsh's expression changes as he drops his gaze to the slick bar top of black quartz. "Vodka, no ice." Hard, late nights and no sleep paint the face of the man sitting across from me.

"Straight," I answer, nodding toward Anthony, a bartender to my right who's listening in. Everyone who works in this bar works for Cross.

"You got it." He's a young guy, earning his way and learning how things are done. Not bad looking and knows how to take an order, so Jase stuck him here. I know he's itching for more. He's motivated and wants to move up. This right here, having him close enough to hear is more than a test to see how he does, what he does and what comes out of his mouth after the fact. It's everything for him to be on this side of the bar right now. Given the nerves that are evident as he nearly drops the shot glass, it's showing.

"Don't know what?" Jase asks calmly, although I can see just beneath the surface rage is brewing. I don't like to think that I have a temper. Jase though, he's got a hot one for both Walsh and Marcus.

Maybe when it comes to Laura. I have a bit of a temper if she's involved, I'll admit that, but when it comes to business, I like to think I can set my emotions to the side. I think that's why Jase and I make a good fit. I've enjoyed working under him even. Watching the way he does things and learning new methods. I didn't start at the bar though, I started in the parking lot, with a gun in my hand.

The music pounds, the bass thrumming through my veins and the lights dip low with the sound of a roar of excitement from the dance floor.

Walsh exhales, low and steady, flexing both of his hands on the bar. I'm conscious of where they go and every move he makes. Public place or not, Walsh is a desperate man fueled by revenge. I don't trust either of those aspects.

"You gave me six names," Walsh starts and then a chilled heavy glass of clear liquid is placed in front of him. I nod a thanks to Anthony, and wait as Walsh sips it first. It takes Anthony a moment to get the hint not to stay close, but he gets it as Walsh throws it back.

"I put them through the database and got six addresses," he says flatly, tilting his empty glass on the table. In my periphery, I watch as Jase crosses his arms. The way his jaw is clenched is an indication that he's holding back and he's on edge.

"Another?" I offer, and Walsh shakes his head, meeting my stare. It's then that I realize, all his attention is focused on me. None at all on Jase Cross. He's barely looked at Jase. I don't like the unease that climbs up my spine.

"When I got to the first address, I knew something was wrong. The lights didn't work. Electric had been cut. Next to the body on the floor was a note. Same with the next address and the next. All but the blonde woman on the list. She's missing, but her body wasn't dead at her place."

My blood runs cold. *Dead*. "They're all dead?" Jase questions.

"Every single one of them." Walsh's nostrils flare and the tension between the three of us is at an all-time high. This is fucked.

"If you think you can fuck with me," Walsh practically spits, the anger but also the frustration showing in his reddened eyes.

"No one's fucking with you," Jase says and slams both of his hands down on the bar, getting the attention of a number of patrons. I don't touch him or hint to anything at all with Jase.

"What did the note say?" I ask Walsh, needing information. Information is everything.

Walsh's hard gaze turns to me and he says, "Funny you should be the one to ask. It said: *Was it Fletcher who did it, or Laura's father?*"

The confusion weaves its way through my expression quickly enough and that's when the coldness hits, followed by the heat of rage. Marcus got to them first. He killed the men, knowing we knew about them.

My jaw twitches and I move for the first time since Walsh has been in here. *Fuck!* Adrenaline courses through me.

"I knew of Fletcher and you. I knew that one." Walsh keeps

talking. I can barely keep my focus on the words spewing from his mouth. I can't even fucking breathe.

Fletcher or Laura's father. Marcus's note comes back to me. He's playing with us. One step ahead. He's always one step ahead. Motherfucker!

"I didn't know who Laura's father was referring to. Not until last night." Walsh continues. "I figured if Fletcher was related to you, so was Laura." Jase says something but I can't hear him over the ringing and slew of curses in my ears.

With my hands in fists, I raise them to the top of my head, closing my eyes and praying for calm. He's bringing Laura into this.

Marcus brought Laura into it, and put her on Walsh's radar.

I finally speak. "Marcus… he knew about the list and got to them first."

"How did he know?" Jase's question is accusatory and I sneer at him, "How the hell should I know?"

"Calm down," Jase urges me, his dark eyes narrowing as he watches me. I want to pace; I want to throw something across this fucking room.

"He dragged Laura into this." I can barely speak her name. I feel like a caged animal, ready to attack anything that comes near me.

"He brought *you* front and center." Jase's response is quick and again I catch a tone that I don't care for.

"What does the note mean?" Walsh asks.

"I don't know," I answer Walsh harshly. With both of my hands on the bar, I inhale once, then look around us. The barstools have cleared, no one daring to come around us. When I look up, no one has the audacity to look at us, but I know they're watching. Some of them are. Others are leaving as quickly as they can.

I turn my gaze back to Walsh, noting how he looks at me like I'm hiding something. "Both of them are dead. Laura's father and Fletcher. They're both dead and buried ten feet under."

"Marcus must have known about the list and he got to them first," Jase presumes and places a hand on my shoulder, urging me to stand back up. With the blood still rushing in my ears and my head spinning, I stand up straighter. "He killed his own men because they weren't good enough to hide from us."

I can't fucking breathe in here. Loosening my tie, I hear Walsh tell Jase everything he did.

"Maybe surveillance on your computer?" Jase suggests after a series of back and forths.

"It doesn't matter. The information is useless."

"We gave you good intel. It's not our problem if you fucked it up."

"It actually is," Walsh replies condescendingly. "We don't have a deal until I say so. And this?" he says as he puts both of his hands up and then slowly shakes his head. "No deal."

"What do you want?" I ask him, glancing at Jase whose face easily tells me what he wants. He wants to take that glass or maybe the bottle, any fucking thing he can get his hands on and smash it into Walsh's skull. I bet that's what's playing through his mind right now. On repeat.

"I want Marcus." Defeat colors Walsh's tone and he drops his head into his hands, putting both his elbows on the bar.

"Get him another drink," I order and Anthony's quick to reply, "Yes, sir" at the same time Walsh says, "No."

"We have information at least," Jase says beneath his breath and then nods his head at Walsh. "His computer's being watched."

"Potential information," I correct him. "There's no way to know how and when Marcus got that list."

"What's that?" Walsh asks. The second he does, the glass of vodka hits the bar and Walsh shoves it to the side.

I take it. Still feeling the rage of adrenaline coursing through me, I throw back the shot and then tell Anthony, "Another."

I can't get the thoughts of Laura out of my head. Marcus is shoving her right in the middle. He gave her over to Walsh. He's going to know about her connection with Delilah. He will soon if he doesn't already. It's fucked. Everything is fucked.

"We'll look into what we can give you," I answer Walsh and before he can respond, the shot hits the bar and I down it, hissing from the heat that rolls down the back of my throat and spreads through my chest.

"What can you give me?" Walsh's anger gets the best of him. "Don't forget what I have on you," he warns.

"Don't forget we've both gotten away with worse," I grit back. "We're helping you find him, against our better judgment. Be grateful for that."

Jase only observes and then orders two more shots from Anthony. "Unless you want to take us up on that free drink," he offers Walsh.

The officer is silent as Jase takes a shot with me. And then orders two more. My head feels faint with the alcohol hitting me, but my mind still races and whatever I do, I can't tame the anger.

Walsh watches as another shot goes down. It burns and settles deep in the pit of my stomach. It only fuels the need to get to Marcus. To be the one to take him down.

"He shouldn't have brought Laura into this," I tell Jase, feeling the swell of anger rise to my shoulders.

"You know what they call serial killers like him?" Walsh asks and Anthony pushes another pair of shots in front of us. When I look at him, his gaze is fixated on the empty shot glass, turning it on the table.

I've had enough. Enough of everything. Jase is quick to throw his back, slamming the glass down just as Walsh answers his own question. "Angel of Death. They don't stop. I may be your enemy, but he's worse."

Neither Jase or I respond. I watch silently as Walsh's guard drops as his true intentions come closer to the surface.

"It's only a matter of time before you do something he deems punishable by death."

"Is that why you want him so bad? The serial killer who got away back when you were an agent?" I goad him, wondering if he'll even mention Delilah.

Jase takes the last shot on the bar when I don't touch it.

"No," Walsh answers honestly, but he doesn't give away any of the truth. The way his gaze seems to look through me, I think he already knows that I know. He's connected the dots. Which means he knows that Laura knows too. He makes his final plea and says, "Help me. Give me information."

The thoughts of Laura and Delilah remind me of the notebooks. We have them. We have the locations.

I don't trust Walsh though. I don't trust his ass and that realization brings me to the conclusion that maybe he killed them. Maybe he didn't find them dead. But that can't be. It doesn't explain the notes.

My head spins and a low exhale of agitation leaves me.

"We'll see what we can do," Jase answers Walsh even though his eyes are on me. "Now get out of my bar."

My gaze shifts between the back of Walsh's loose shirt as he weaves through the crowd and Anthony, who's standing with his hands clasped in front of him to my right. I know he can feel my eyes on him, but he doesn't look. He doesn't turn to watch. The kid doesn't know what to do, so I ask him, "What do you think?"

He hesitates to answer and when he does, he clears his throat first before saying, "I think the note has to mean something, but he's a fucking psychopath and I don't understand."

A large hand grasping my shoulder pulls my attention away from Anthony. Jase doesn't ask, he commands, "Have another drink with me."

"I have to go to Laura. She just got done with work." Fuck, I need to tell her Walsh knows. *There's so much I need to tell her.*

Jase walks around to the other side of the bar, pulling out stools for both of us. "It's one forty. She's already at your place by now."

"He brought her into this. Marcus doesn't play by any rules. He hits where it hurts."

"We may be a step ahead of him though. Now that we know he's watching Walsh's computer."

I nod in agreement, or at least my head does without my conscious consent. Marcus just graduated to the top of my hit list.

"Grab her a bottle of red wine like you said you would and have another drink before you lose your shit."

It hits me that Jase is saying the same words to me that I've said to him a dozen times before.

"When did that happen?" I ask him with a smile, a sad and fucked up one, playing on my lips.

"What?" Jase asks me, not waiting on Anthony now that he's busy with the patrons who have taken up the momentarily empty seats. He reaches around the other side, grabbing a half-empty bottle, choosing to stick to vodka, and two glasses.

"When did I become the angry one needing to be calmed down?" I joke with him.

"Ever since I've known you, you've been angry." He places the shot down in front of me before adding, "You just didn't show it." His response is dead serious.

I pour the shot into my mouth, noting how he squeezes my shoulders and then swallow the chilled clear liquid, feeling the burn flow down my throat and then lower through my abdomen.

Jase takes his and then taps the glass on the bar, looking at the stool where Walsh was sitting. "Now you need to tell me…" he says and his tone changes. Not to one of a boss, but to one of a friend who's desperate to help his buddy clean up his mess, "…everything about Fletcher and Laura's father so we can figure out this fucking note."

CHAPTER 16

Laura

My shift is over but I can't leave this place. I can't walk away knowing Melody's in there and she just confessed to murder. I can't call Walsh. I can't bring myself to do anything but sit in my car. It's on and the heat is blasting since I was freezing when I got in.

Seth hasn't called or texted. I thought he'd be waiting up for me, but when I messaged him, realizing how late I was, he didn't respond.

That alone and lost feeling I felt earlier today returns. When you're with someone, shouldn't you feel it? I remember, years ago, feeling that security and knowing he was there always when I had Seth. This is different.

I don't really have Seth right now though, do I? I have him in only two ways. He wants my body and my obedience.

I put my phone away. 9-1-1 was waiting for me to press send. All I had to do was push send and ask to speak to Walsh. I assume this late though, he's not working. I was ready to leave a message, but I don't want to do that. I don't owe anyone anything. I'll write Melody's confession down on the charts. I'll let Aiden deal with it. I already called him and left a voicemail. I already filled out all the necessary paperwork per protocol.

It's not relief I feel when I put the car into drive and pull off onto the main road. There's this gnawing hurt that eats away at me. It points out that I'm not enough. I've never been enough.

I'm too weak to handle any of it. I always have been. Does Seth really want me? How could he when he knows more than anyone how little I can handle?

The green light and white streetlights blur as I drive by them.

I turn on the radio and put the volume up then roll down my window and turn off the heat. A shaky breath leaves me and then another.

I miss my grandma. I miss my father too.

Memories of the two of them flicker through my head as I drive, desperately trying to think of anything but my present situation.

I remember one night my dad told me he had to make a stop before going home. I never liked it when he had to make stops at this "friend's" house. He wasn't a bad guy. My father really wasn't a bad guy at all. There wasn't a day that went by where I didn't know he loved me. There wasn't anything he wouldn't do for me. The thing is though… he did bad things and he got himself into bad situations.

I knew that he peddled pills. I wasn't that naïve. So when he stopped in front of an apartment complex I'd never been in, I was already on edge.

He leaned over and told me, "If you hear bullets, drive away as fast as you can." He made me say I would and then he went inside. I still remember his smile and that should have given it away. I was fifteen, I didn't even have a driver's permit, but I got in the driver seat and stared at the front glass door on high alert the second he was out of view.

My father laughed and laughed when he saw me after he'd been inside for only a couple of minutes. After all, he was just joking. He gave me a kiss on the cheek when I settled back into my seat, and the smile he'd left with was wider than before. He would never know how scared I was.

Not at the thought of hearing bullets or having to drive away. But at the thought that I'd have to drive away without him. My father wasn't a bad man at all and I love him still, but damn did he put bad things in my head.

I don't even realize I've driven to Seth's house until I put the car in park. I pull up next to his, noting that the headlights are still on. Did he just get in?

As I'm walking up to his door, the headlights go out. That's the first thing that startles me. It's always an uneasy feeling when lights go out and leave you in the dark.

The second thing that nearly gives me a heart attack is when Seth opens the door without any notice at all. I choke on my scream and my hand holding the keys flies up to my throat. It's such a jarring quick response, I almost jab myself with the key I'm so on edge.

"Fuck," I sputter, my heart pounding in my chest so hard, it makes me question if I remembered to take my medicine this morning. "You scared the shit out of me."

Seth's grip isn't gentle when he pulls me into his house. "Where were you?" he demands in a low, threatening tone. Ripping out of his grasp, I look at him like he's lost his mind.

Fear, not anger is etched into his handsome expression. Everything about him reminds me how damaged he is. Everything but the booze coming off of him.

"Are you drunk?" The accusation in my tone is evident.

He breathes out heavily. Slamming the front door and moving around me to go to the kitchen sink.

I can't believe the sight of him. Never taking my eyes off of him, I toss down my keys and purse. Seth's busy washing his face at the sink as I take a look around the room. He couldn't have been here long, but still, there's a hole punched into the drywall that leads to the hall.

"You hurt your hand?" I bite out, feeling angrier by the second. *What the hell is wrong with him?*

His shoulders are hunched over the sink still as he braces himself with his forearms after wiping off his face. "I thought someone took you," he admits to me. His breathing still hasn't calmed and guilt quickly replaces the anger.

I never know what to feel when it comes to Seth. Right now though, I feel sorry for him. He's still in his suit pants but his shirt is disheveled and I can see from here the bruise already covering his battered hand.

"I should have texted sooner; I just had a bad night." I apologize with every ounce of sincerity I can muster. I know the wars he fought, both physical and emotional, have left scars on Seth.

"You had a bad night," he huffs out humorlessly and then covers his face with both of his hands, leaning his head back.

It's so fucking insulting. Like I can't have a hard night because I don't do what he does. It's hard not to be angry. It's more difficult than anything not to engage and let him know punching holes into walls and yelling at me because I'm late—even though he was too—isn't acceptable.

"I'm sorry you thought something happened to me," I say, speaking up to make sure he can hear me as I grab my keys. The sound of them jingling finally brings his gaze back to me.

He looks like he's gone through hell and back. I get that. I do, but I didn't sign up for this shit.

"I'm going home and when you're sober—"

"The hell you are." Seth's tone is demanding and desperate all at once. "Get your ass over here."

My feet are cemented where they are, undecided on whether or not I should have a backbone and leave, or whether I should go to him. The fluttering in my chest and the way my throat goes tight when he looks at me like that, desperately from across the room, that's what makes me put my keys back down and make my way to him.

The second I put a foot in the kitchen, he pulls me in tight and hugs me to him. Yes, he smells like booze. He smells like *him* too. This deep masculine, heavy scent that I used to dream of. A scent I swore I could smell on one of my shirts once so I refused to wash it until I could no longer make out his fragrance.

"Please don't treat me like that," I breathe into his shirt, my eyes still open. His are closed though. Both arms wrapped around me, he rocks me right there in front of the sink.

"I'm sorry," he murmurs and then kisses my crown.

It's then that I remember a similar night. A night like this. One where I was ready to leave, but I didn't. Because I love him. I love the way he holds me; I love the way he smells. I love what he does to me and what I can do to him.

But as I stand here, too sober, too exhausted, too wrung the hell out, I remember very clearly something I told myself for years as I cried myself to sleep.

If I'd left that night, Cami would still be here.

That thought is why I push myself away from Seth, not wanting to cry anymore. His rough fingers brush my skin when I back away. The counter hits my lower back and with both of my palms pressed to my eyes I walk out of the kitchen. The silence behind me proves he doesn't follow me.

Fuck, I can't take any more today. *I swear I can't take any more.*

"What's wrong?" he asks me, clearly having no idea.

"I don't know where to start," I say and breathe out heavily. Wanting to sit on the sofa, but also looking toward the door. Therapy taught me a lot when I was in school. It taught me I should be by myself when I feel like this. When it gets to be too much, I don't communicate well. I know I don't. "I had a really bad day and I just… I can't do much of anything right now."

"Can't what?" Seth questions from behind me and I turn around to face him. With his tie loose around his neck, the top two buttons undone and the one closest to the top hanging on by a thread, Seth looks rough. Rough has always looked good on him, but not tonight. Not the way he looks at me with his lips parted, still breathing heavily. He looks wounded beyond repair.

"Are you okay?" I ask him, swallowing the wretched emotions that come with seeing him like this. He nods, not telling me anything and that's okay too. He doesn't have to, not right now. Not ever if he doesn't want to. We do need to talk about him reacting the way he did though. His anger; his fear.

"I think we should sleep," I suggest, not feeling well myself. "If

I look the way I feel, you know I need sleep right now," I tell him although I can't look him in the eye.

"Talk to me," he urges.

"What's gotten into you?" I question him, not liking the way he looks at me like he's about to lose me.

"You don't want to know," is all he says, again shaking his head. The hand he bloodied rises to his eyebrow and it's shaking. My strong man is trembling.

"I'm here, I'm here," I reassure him, holding him like he held me. This time I close my eyes and I let him rock me. I whisper against his chest, fighting sleep and refusing to be anything less than a rock for him now. "I do. I want to know."

"I have secrets," he tells me and I don't know if I should laugh, or maybe roll my eyes. It would be insulting if he wasn't wasted right now. I watch his throat tighten, the stubble on it even longer without him having shaved since I last saw him, as he swallows.

"You think I don't know that?" As I speak, my voice is soft and it's meant to be comforting, it's meant to make him feel better. I know he has secrets and he hides things. I accept it.

"You don't know the half of it. You don't know what I did," he says and his voice goes tight and again he covers his face, forcing him to let go of me. He scrubs his eyes like he wants the vision to go away.

"Seth, tell me what's wrong?" The unsettling, gut-wrenching feeling takes over. Something is not just wrong, it's gotten to him more than I've seen anything get to him. He's scared. I feel it rock through my bones, his fear and despair. "Seth, please," I beg him and he only shakes his head, his hands on the top of his head, his eyes closed tight.

"Tell me," I demand and pull at his arms, forcing him to look at me, not knowing what else to do. Not knowing how to help him and not knowing what I'm going to do. I'm so on edge.

"I killed your dad!" Seth screams and the rage and brokenness that was written on his face changes quickly.

What? His words sink in slowly, like a dark red sky late at night before it all turns black. Shock is a reality. It's numbing.

"Laura." He speaks my name and reaches out for me with both hands. I shake my head, not accepting his grasp.

"You're drunk; you didn't kill him. He—he died in a car accident. He was in a car accident." It was an accident, but my chest feels hollow hearing Seth say something like that. There's no skip, no beat of any sort. My heart has fled.

I rip my arm away from him and he stays like he is, hunched down with his arms out to me even though I step away. "You need to stop and go to bed," I warn him, feeling my throat go raw with horrible emotions.

"I did." His wretched words are spoken like they're true, but they're not.

"It was a car accident," I say as I take another step back until I'm fully in the living area and he's in the kitchen. "You need to stop," I warn him again, raising my arm. Of all the days to bring up my dad, it would have to be this one. When he's been on my mind the entire drive here.

Seth takes a cautious step forward and suddenly I feel like I'm choking. Just from the way he's looking at me, like he's about to break me.

"He was a rat. That's why." My bottom lip wobbles when his eyes turn glossy.

"Stop it," I say and try to cut him off, but he keeps talking. "No he wasn't. You're just tired and not—"

"That's why Vito was going to hurt you. To get to your father." I have to blink away the shining haze of tears in my eyes as I back away. He's lying. My father would never rat. Seth would never kill him. It doesn't make sense.

"Stop it!" I scream. "You don't know anything about my father," I say, barely getting the choked words out, tears flowing easily down my cheeks as I take another step back, hitting the coffee table and nearly falling backward.

Seth explains, his eyes turning red and a tortuous tone in his voice as he says, "My father… he couldn't let yours live. I wanted it to look like an accident. I didn't want to kill him. I didn't want to, but he made me. He said it was the only—"

"Stop it, please," I say as my legs go weak and tremble. My shoulders hunch in as I round the coffee table, backing away as Seth gets closer to me. I need to get to the door. I have to get the fuck out of here. "Stop it," I beg him.

It's not true. He's just drunk. It can't be true, but the hurt in my chest, oh my God, it can't be true. Denial is the first stage of grief.

"He said I had to do it if I wanted it to be an accident." Seth's eyes reflect mine. Glossy and wishing what he's saying wasn't true.

I don't know how or why, but I slam my fist into his jaw, only once before taking off. It's all a blur. I don't remember thinking of reacting, choosing to leave. My body's hot and numb and disbelief turns me blind to what's happening. I do it, though. I hit him square in his jaw. Leaving Seth behind me, holding his jaw in shock. I run faster than him, I get out of the house and into my car before I see him in the doorway. The burning pain in my knuckles is nothing.

It's nothing compared to the pain ripping through me as I speed away.

CHAPTER 17

Seth

Fuck. That wasn't the way it was supposed to happen. My head's spinning. I shouldn't be driving. Jase was right, I should have stayed at the bar or with him or anywhere else. I shouldn't have let him and Anthony drive me home.

I wish they'd been there when I walked in and saw she wasn't there. I stayed outside while they drove off, gathering whatever composure I could. It was a recipe for disaster. Everything about our story is meant for tragedy. It all could have been different, if only.

Fuck! I slam my hand onto the steering wheel, feeling the stinging pain from the already formed bruises. I do it again and again, just to feel it. I deserve it.

Reckless. I was reckless with her. I never should have said a damn thing. Selfish. I did it because I needed to know she'd still love me after. *Selfish*.

The lights turn red. I swear every light has turned red on my way to her house. Praying she's there, praying she'll forgive me, doesn't offer me any hope. *Why would she?* I already knew she wouldn't. She wouldn't love me if she knew. She never really loved me, because she didn't know. It's why I could never make the first move; it's why I could never tell her those words she needed to hear, *I love you*. It was such a lie.

I was never worthy of that love. It wasn't real.

Thunk! I slam my fist against my window, wanting to feel even more pain. The pain is so wretched in my chest that swallowing feels like suffocation.

I wish I could take it back. All of it. I wish I could rewrite our story.

My head falls back against the leather seat as I slow to stop at another red light. My face is hot and my breathing staggered, but my body is wired. My leg doesn't stop the constant tapping.

Thank fuck the streets are barren. There's not a soul out tonight.

Time moves too slowly; all the while anxiousness eats me up inside. My tires squeal when I pull into the parking lot outside Laura's place. Her car's already parked.

My body sags with relief of at least knowing where she is.

She's safe. That's all that matters tonight. She's safe.

If Jase hadn't wanted me to tell him… If I didn't have to tell him, I wouldn't have had to relive it.

With my fist at my jaw, I stare at Laura's window. The lights are on; she's inside. The sad truth is that it was going to happen eventually. I always knew it would. Her leaving me was a blessing. I should have let her go. I shouldn't have brought her into this hell again. *Selfish*.

"I'm sorry," I whisper, feeling the loss all over again and knowing it's my fault. My hands don't stop shaking.

I did it for her though. I remember telling Jase over and over. I did do it for her. She didn't have to know her father was a rat. Vito wanted to hurt him by hurting Laura, and that wasn't something that could happen.

It didn't change the fact her father had ratted. He was a rat and he had to die.

Fuck, my chest sinks, remembering the old man. Everything was a joke to him. It was never serious but the shit he talked about to whoever would listen… it wasn't something we could allow.

My father knew he had to go the second he took charge and everyone agreed. They were going to do it in the warehouse, then dump him in the back alley.

Then what would Laura have had? She would have known. Everyone would have known with his body being left there and she would have been the daughter of a rat.

I wanted to hide it from her. I wanted to protect her. Everything inside me needed to protect her.

Then you do it. My father's voice echoes in my head as I stare straight ahead at the bright lights in Laura's living room. Her curtains are parted and I can see her silhouette move from one side to the other.

My father put the gun in my hand and I shot her father in the back of the head while he begged for his life. I never wanted to do it. I didn't want to kill him. I just wanted to protect her. I had to do it alone while they watched. Getting his body to the car, driving it to the top of the cliff, disposing of the gun in the cement pit round the back.

They were going to kill him one way or the other, but I did it.

I didn't want her to know. It would have killed her. She was already so alone.

"I'm sorry," I say again in the darkness, all alone where I belong. "I'm so fucking sorry."

My throat's raw, my body humming, my emotions thrashed, which is why I hesitate to believe what I see. Two sets of lights are on.

My body's cold in an instant. *Fuck, no. No.* It can't get worse tonight.

She's visible in her bedroom.

So are three other figures, in her living room.

CHAPTER 18

Laura

I hear the front door open and I know it's Seth, but I don't say a damn thing. I don't even know if I can speak right now without screaming incoherently through the pain.

My father's been long gone. I have to cover my face with my hands as it crumples and the sadness rips through me… he wasn't a rat. He wasn't.

They didn't have to kill him; he never would have told anyone anything. He wasn't a rat! My knees are still weak and I sniffle, angrily brushing under my eyes. I can hear Seth in the living room, but I don't go to him. I want to, I want to scream at him, hit him. I want him to lie to me and tell me he made it up. I want it to be a cruel joke I can beat the shit out of him for and for him to hold me until this shaking and the sobs disappear.

He said we'd be together to make the hurt stop, but it doesn't. It never stops with us.

A shuddering breath pulls the energy from me and I hear something in the living room. He moved something around.

I want to tell him to get the fuck out. I want to scream at him and shove my fists into his chest. At the same time, I don't want to see him or be around him. I don't want his large hands on me, his warm body pulling me in. *Why*? Because I desperately need someone to hold me right now and I have no one.

It's hard to inhale; harder to calm my wild heart down. It trips like it's falling down an endless staircase and it hurts. God it hurts.

"Get out!" I scream and the sound is ragged. My fingers fly into my hair as I hunch my shoulders down and cover my face with my forearms. I grip on for my sanity.

Just breathe.

I've been doing it all day, thinking it all day, but at some point, breathing doesn't help.

The bang sounds again from behind me. He's still moving shit around in there.

I know that he's drunk, I know he's hurting, but right now, I can't have him here. I can't allow it to happen. I'm crumbling into nothingness and he doesn't get to watch that. He doesn't get to be around me when it happens. I don't care how badly I need him.

"Laura," a voice calls out just as I get to my bedroom door and chills flow down my spine, sinking into my blood as I stop with my hand on the knob.

Thud, thud.

That's not Seth.

"Come out, come out," the voice sounds, "wherever you are," dragging out the words like it's a game. And then I hear another voice. Two men.

My pulse races with a new kind of fear. Whiplash dizzies my mind.

I could hide, but there's nowhere to hide in here other than under the bed defenselessly. I have a window in my bedroom, but the fire escape stairs are in the living room. The ones made of steel that go all the way down and lead outside.

Sometimes you can't just breathe. Sometimes, you just have to face it.

When I push the door open, listening to the eerily soft creak, four men face me.

Three of them have black masks, dark blue jeans and black shirts. All nondescript. None of them recognizable from their voices or what little I can see of their eyes. They stand in a relative half circle, my coffee table pushed back.

Three men who have come to do something awful, although seeing masks covering their faces, calms a side of me. The logical side, the side that thinks, is telling me they hadn't planned on killing me. If they had, they wouldn't have worn masks to hide who they are.

They came for something bad, though. That much is known from the slow clap and chilled laughter from the one on the right, the one by the coffee table. As if the masks and breaking into my apartment wasn't enough to give it away.

I may be terrified, but a part of me is ready. That little piece that screams inside my head that I should have put a bat next to my bedroom door.

"There she is," he calls out, his voice harsh with brittle humor. I don't know how I stand so tall when they're so much bigger than me.

I try not to look at the fourth man. Swallowing harshly, my bottom lip quivering, I search my whirling mind for anything I can do to stall as Seth moves quietly to close the front door. I don't want my focus to go to him; I don't want them to see him sneaking up on them. In his oxfords and disheveled suit, a gun already in his hand and not on the doorknob.

My lips part to say something as the hot tears slip down my face, but I can't even speak. The barrel of a gun stares at me, the man on the left raising it. Fear is a crippling bitch. She can fuck right off, but right now, she's got her grip on my throat.

The barrel of the gun pointed at my face is a dark hole, like one I've imagined falling down so many times.

The bang isn't from it though, and the next bang and hollering isn't either.

"Behind you!" the not-so-funny man yells to man number two. Man number one, the one who dared raise a gun to me, is already lying face-first on the floor with a hole in the back of his head. Blood pools around his face.

Bang! I scream instinctively. Seth shoots but so do the other two. Bullets ricochet and fly, something breaks and I can't track it all at once. I don't know what is happening, just that I need to move.

Even shaking, I can see everything clearly, but only seconds of it. A second of logic and clarity and then a whirl of chaos. Grabbing the clock on the wall, the large sixteen-inch barn clock, I run and scream, slamming it into the back of the man's head who's closest to me. Cursing, he stumbles, but doesn't fall. I raise the clock again to strike him, wanting and needing to do anything at all, but I hear another shot and then another and the frightful burst of the bang forces me to huddle down.

My heart races. My body hot, I blink away the chaos. My breathing screams in my ears and it's all I can hear.

Seth's still standing. I'm standing. My gaze moves to each of the men accordingly. One, two, three. All still, all not moving. I watch them each again, listening to my ragged breathing. *Is it over already? Are we okay?*

We're alive. My chest pounds, my heart pumping hard and fast. I feel faint.

"We're okay," I whisper, rocking as I lean against the wall. The bullets weren't clean and simple. There's blood everywhere.

Is that blood? There's blood on Seth. His shirt. There's too much blood. Not like the bits that have spattered behind me. Not like what's on me. It's a circle and it's growing.

A mix between a grunt and a groan leaves Seth as he checks his gun and then it clicks loudly as he heads back to the front door, locking it.

"Are you okay?" I ask in what feels like a yell although it sounds like a murmur, hoping he can hear me. Inhaling sharply, my heart beats wildly and my lungs refuse to move right. He's walking, he's okay. He's okay. He has to be okay.

Everything is shaking and my hands don't stop shaking. I clasp them, trying to calm down, but that's when I see the blood on my hands. There's so much blood.

He still hasn't answered me; he's just walking to the windows.

"Seth!" I scream at Seth to look at me, my eyes burning and my throat sore from screaming. He doesn't answer me, but the blood circle is growing. He's shot. My lip quivers. "Seth!"

He ignores me, stepping over a body to get to the window.

"Fuck," Seth hisses as a loud ringing wails. "Why are they here so fast?" he questions out loud, moving to the window and cursing again. It takes me a moment to even understand. Everything is ringing, my blood, my ears. Shock and fear still have their grip on me.

Sirens wail outside. Loud and they're only getting louder.

"Check them," Seth grits out, his jaw clenched as he breathes in deep.

"You need a doctor," I beg him to let me help him, but he grabs my hand as I grab his shirt. "Check them first."

My eyes are wide with disbelief. "For what?" My head is spinning and my thoughts are scattered. I don't understand. "Make sure they're dead," he yells out and then leans against the wall.

I could argue with him and I almost do. My body leans forward subconsciously, wanting to go to him and give the gunshot the attention it needs.

"It's in and out, Babygirl. It's not a big deal, just annoying the fuck out of me," he talks calmly, although his breathing is still labored. Heavy and deep.

I take a step back to do what he tells me. Check them. Dead bodies. Three dead bodies all in masks.

The sirens get louder and Seth tells me to hurry, dropping to his knees by one man behind the sofa.

"Dead," he calls out loud enough for me to hear him.

I have to crawl on my knees across the thick carpet to go from one dead man to the next corpse. My shaky fingers dig into their necks, waiting for a pulse that doesn't come.

I stare into the eyes of the man closest to me through the ski mask. He's white, his eyes are hazel and they stare at nothing. Pulling his mask back, I note that I don't know him. He's just a man.

"Who are they?" I question in a hushed breath and Seth only replies asking if they're dead. My body trembles, not knowing what would have happened if Seth wasn't here. *What would they have done to me? What did they want?*

"They're dead. They're all dead," I reassure Seth as he grips his side. I don't know how I'm still standing, or how any of this happened. Three men lie on the floor of my living room, all shot. All dead. Bullet holes litter my walls, the coffee table is broken from one of them trying to use it for defense, I don't know. It all happened so fast.

"Let me look," I demand, not waiting for an answer. I run to him as quickly as I can and pull up his shirt. He doesn't protest, holding up his shirt and seething.

In the front and out the back of him. Two holes and too much blood.

CHAPTER 19

Laura

The blood is so dark. Dark blood is never good. "Seth," my weak voice utters his name as tears fall down my cheeks. "Put pressure on it at least. Gauze, let me..." My hands shake and I try to remember everything you should do for a gunshot. I don't have anything here to help him. I need supplies. "You need to go to the hospital!"

It's surreal.

Holding his gun, still facing the dead men on the floor.

"We've got to get out of here." Even as he turns away from me, I stare at the blood seeping into his shirt. It grows slowly, pooling out and then sticking to his side.

He doesn't mention the pain as he opens the window in the living room. The way his face scrunches though and the way he's breathing make it more than obvious to me.

"Seth," I whimper and cover my mouth with both hands. Through the gaze of tears, I see the wreckage. The bodies lying dead, men who came to kill me.

Men Seth killed to save me. We shouldn't be running, he should be getting help.

"Out here, Babygirl," he commands as the knock at the door gets louder.

"Laura Roth," a voice calls out. "It's the police! Open up!"

My feet are cemented where I stand.

"Someone called them?" I blurt out as my head spins. They're here too fast. It all happened so fast; why are they here already?

"Laura." The urgency is clear in Seth's voice as he closes the distance between us and grabs my arm. "We have to get out of here."

It all snaps into place when he looks at me like that. The same way he used to look at me back then. Like he was put on this earth to save me. The desperation swirls in his eyes and it breaks me down to the only piece of me I truly know.

The piece that's desperate to save my broken hero. So damaged by a life he chose not to run from.

"You first," I whisper, shaking my head. "And you see someone," I tell him, already deciding it won't be me. It can't be.

It's pitch black outside, and a gust of harsh wind throws the curtains to the side as the policeman roars, "We're coming in!"

"Go, quick," I say as I usher him to the window. My hand brushes against his side, against the blood. Seth doesn't react, but his jaw's clenched tight. "Let me help you," I beg him as he climbs out of the window and onto the metal fire escape stairs that lead down the side of the old brick building.

He's quick to climb out into the dark night.

The police are coming and I'll be damned if I let Seth take the fall. He still has both hands on the windowsill. The gun sitting on the sill cements my decision.

"Come on, Babygirl." His tone is gentle as he waits for me to climb out too and to run. "I've got you."

I can already hear my defense. They broke in here, they threatened me. I did it. I killed them but it was in self-defense. He can get help, he can take care of himself. They can't blame him for this.

If he did it, if he's the one to go down for their murders… There's intent, drug wars, previous offenses.

I love him, but I hate him.

He hurts me, but he saves me.

Maybe I'm confused, maybe it's the endorphins rushing through me, the fear, the unknown. I don't know what it is, but I rip the gun from the sill, whispering for him to go to the hospital and slam the window closed the second his hand raises in confusion and defense. The look of betrayal doesn't register in his eyes until I lock the window.

Bang! *Bang*! Two kicks sound at the door behind me and I suck in a harsh breath.

My fingers are clenched around the edge of the curtains, ripping them shut and hiding him from the police as the door slams open.

It's chaotic and my head spins with uncertainty.

"Laura Roth, put the gun down slowly."

It's hard to breathe, let alone register what I've done. My knees give in and I slowly drop to the ground. There was one rap on the window, one harsh pounding of a fist and I know it's Seth's. But only one and then he's gone.

Run, Seth. Please, run for me. Get help. I can't stop picturing the hole in his side. He'll get help faster this way. He'll be okay. I have to believe that he'll be okay.

He'll understand. When it's all over and I'm free. He'll understand.

My body's hot and still trembling as I drop to the floor, following the instructions of Officer Walsh. I recognize his voice. Walsh. Walsh is the one behind me and there are other cops as well, walking around and checking bodies. They call out that they're dead.

"All of them?" Walsh asks and someone answers yes.

I don't even know how many police officers are with him as he grabs one wrist and then the other. I stare blankly ahead at the curtain. At the spot where I last saw Seth's face.

"I know you didn't do this," Walsh whispers as another cop behind me calls out that *he's gone too*.

The police sirens ring out loud behind the windows. I wish it were an ambulance.

"It was self-defense." I clear my throat and tell Walsh as he pulls me up and onto my feet. He huffs out like he doesn't believe me.

"One of them was undercover, Laura. Your excuse isn't going to work."

Undercover… a cop. A chill travels along my skin.

No. Fuck. No.

My heart slams, skittering to a halt and refusing to go on. I can't breathe. "You're lying." My voice raises as I start to say, "You just want me to—" before I cut myself off. He's lying. The cold metal of the cuffs digs into my skin as he turns me around. Walsh's light blue eyes stare into mine with pity.

"I'm taking you in even though I know you didn't do this. You're going to tell me everything though. You have to. Someone has to go down for this."

He's wrong. Walsh has to be wrong.

I didn't just confess to killing an undercover cop.

CHAPTER 20

Seth

There's at least three of them. A gun to my temple. A hand keeping the gag in my mouth. The cloth is slipping back farther down my throat, strangling me as I breathe harshly through my nose. With only a single streetlight a block away, I can't see shit. I heard the cops practically knock down Laura's door and bucked back, screaming, fighting, but it was useless. I'd already been grabbed.

The rage is brutal, just like the heat that boils inside of me.

They don't say anything. Not a fucking word as I scream out. The heavy arm holding my arms down around my front grabbed me the second my feet hit the steel grid outside Laura's window.

Laura. The thought of her tightens my throat, a raw scratching feeling at the back of it. Trying to breathe, the gag slips back more.

"She's all right." I hear a voice behind me that makes me pause. Not the man holding me, not the man in front of me with the gun to my head.

It's taken a while, but my eyes adjust slowly. Too slowly. My vision spins for a moment, the dizziness caused from the lack of air.

Breathe. Just breathe.

My fists unclench and I do my best to be smart. To figure out who they are. Dark eyes and white skin peek out from the black mask of the guy to my left. The one with the .22 caliber. He's the only one I can see.

I can't speak behind the gag, but I desperately want to. All I can do is wait. To see what they've come for. My heart races and my body's nearly numb waiting, each muscle coiled and ready to strike.

I can hardly feel the pain of the bullet wound, but the blood is seeping into my clothes. It's wet too fast. Too much blood. I'm bleeding out.

Footsteps come closer behind me. Calmly. Three to four men at least. Masked and prepared to be here. It could be Fletcher's old crew but the chill in my spine, the lifelessness of the eyes I can see…

Marcus.

It was never Fletcher. It was always him.

Goosebumps dance down my flesh as bile rises up. "Laura's fine. I can't say the same for you." The eerily calm voice lacks menace. Lacks any emotion at all.

"We have orders," the man holding me finally speaks and I don't recognize his voice. But it's followed, too quickly, by another sound I recognize. One I've heard countless times.

Click.

Seth and Laura's story isn't over just yet.
Their story continues with *Tempted to Kiss*.

TEMPTED TO KISS

From *USA Today* best-selling author W Winters comes the third installment to her emotionally gripping romantic suspense series Hard to Love.

I fell for someone I shouldn't have.

I'm not the only one to ever do such a thing. I know that. And I'm not an awful person for desiring his touch, his kiss, his everything… but I knew I shouldn't have indulged.

There's something about knowing it's wrong that tempts me that much more. The seduction became a game with higher stakes than any before him. In fact, it was only ever him.

The thing is, I knew I shouldn't have. Now that the game is over and the pieces have fallen… I know I should have just walked away.

There's no way out of the wreckage now.

It doesn't change the fact that I wanted him more than anything. I still want him more than anything.

If only we could just have each other without destroying everything else.

Tempted to Kiss is book 3 in a series. *Hard to Love* (book 1) and *Desperate to Touch* (book 2) must be read first.

This book is dedicated to everyone who feels as if they're at their worst.

It's okay. There's always a way out. Tomorrow may not be better, but better is coming.

I promise you, you won't be down for long.

PROLOGUE

Seth
Eight years ago

WITH EVERY DAY THAT PASSES BY, I HATE MYSELF MORE AND MORE. Only when she's not around, though. When she closes the door and the crisp lonely air reminds me what a prick I am, that's when the resentment creeps in. I have that sound memorized now. The sound of her closing the front door of her house is unmistakable. It's not like other doors. It's heavier, I think, and it has to be older because of the ragged groan it gives. Then there's a pause and a click, followed by the shuffle of the metal chain brushing against the door as she locks it at the top. It's so high up, she has to get on her tiptoes.

Then there's nothing but silence and a hollowness in my chest that reminds me why she's on the other side of it while I'm out here in the cold, waiting for the dark to set in.

The only saving grace I have is that when the light of daybreak peeks over the city's skyline hours later, I know she's waking up with every intention of letting me back in, giving me the only chance I have to make my sins right.

She should hate me for what I've done. She should loathe my existence.

Instead she unknowingly takes my hand and offers me the only peace I have in this life. If she knew the truth though… none of this would exist. These moments with her would only ever be a dream. Then I'd wake in the dawn, hating myself a little less than I hate myself now.

There are two sides to my life: The first is the side that protects Laura and holds on to the threads of her trust. Power, greed, and killing comprise the other.

That's what drives me back to her every morning. I like to pretend I can keep the dark side of myself at bay, if only for her.

The look in Laura's eyes right now as I stand in her kitchen, waiting for her to tell me I should go—I've seen it a million times before. The carefully restrained lust echoes in my own gaze. I'm certain she sees it. Just as I see it from her. I know what keeps me from turning my fantasies into reality. I don't know what keeps her from acting on our mutual desire. Maybe she senses what I'm hiding. Maybe there's a deep-seated instinct that warns her away from me.

If only it were that easy to avoid the bad things in life. Simply sense them, these situations, and turn them away. How wonderful this world would be if it were so easy.

"Thank you, Seth," she says and her soft voice is gentle and sweet. There's a hint of shyness that stays with her when she lets me in. Her skin flushes a little brighter, although this time of year, it can be blamed on the wind from outside. We're in her home though, and her cheeks are a touch rosier than they were before we came in here. I have no right to let her innocence stir the flames of desire inside of me.

The microwave beeps, alerting Laura that her hot chocolate is done. "You sure you don't want one?" she offers over her shoulder. She's looking more at me than she is at the hot mug in her hand, as if she's asking me something else entirely. She quickly sets it down when I shake my head and leaves it there, running her hands down her thighs and biting just slightly into her bottom lip.

Leaning against the doorframe to her grandmother's kitchen, I note that no one's home. No one else is here to make sure she's all right. Her grandmother works herself to death and her father…

"Do you want to…" her voice trails off and a warm blush creeps up to her high cheekbones. Nearly up to her hairline. Her nervous laugh brings an infectious smile to her tempting lips. They're the color of sweet, perfectly ripe berries. Maybe whatever berry her lips were made from were truly the forbidden fruit that condemned mankind to hell.

"Do I want to… what?" I question teasingly, crossing my arms and taking her in. It's taken a long damn time for her to warm up to me. It took months for her to ask me to come inside. It's been a few more months now and every day is easier, lighter. Until she's gone and then I remember.

Laura picks at the hem of her large, cream-colored sweater. Her leggings make her look so relaxed and at ease. It's been forever since I've seen her like this. No more red-rimmed eyes, no more tearstained cheeks. Almost a year, and she's seemingly whole.

She closes the distance easily enough; her strides don't give anything away. I'm only aware of how quick she is to get to me from the rapid thuds made by the pads of her feet. Shock and surprise consume me as her dainty hand grips my forearm, her nails barely touching my skin, teasing me. *Thump*, my heart pauses. She rises up on her tiptoes, barefoot and all, and presses those sweet lips to mine. *Thump*, my heart races with need and hunger.

At first it's soft and gentle, a peck on the lips and nothing more. Maybe someone else would take it as a thank you, as testing a boundary, or flirtatious innocence. It's anything but that to me. The barest of affections from her elicit a storm of want and need that floods my blood with desire. Even the feel of her breath so close is like heaven, so close I can almost taste it. Adrenaline races through me and I deepen the kiss. My arms uncross and wrap around her small waist before I know what's happening.

The kiss is searing, branding my soul as she moans into my mouth. When she parts her lips, I take it as an invitation, giving in to the perverse thoughts I've had for as long as I've known her. The air turns hotter around us, everything blurring and turning into nothingness. That's all life's ever been for me, nothing without her.

I make a vow to myself as she parts from the kiss, her eyes half lidded, her fingernails digging into my skin to ensure I keep my grip on her. She breathes heavily as I promise myself, she'll never know.

I'll kill the man who tells her what I've done. I'll kill him for taking her away from me.

CHAPTER 1

Laura

I WISH I DIDN'T KNOW. I WISH SETH HAD NEVER TOLD ME. I WISH I'D never pressed him.

Once you tell someone a secret like the one he told me last night, you can't take it back. More than anything in the entire world, I want to go back to that moment and beg him not to tell me. That little secret changed everything.

My cheek rests heavily on my fist, my elbow propped up on the metal table. It's cold and I can't stop rocking my right leg, which is crossed over the left. My muscles are tight and sore from sitting like this for so long, but I can't get comfortable either way.

All I can think about is how I wish I hadn't pushed him. I wish he'd had the sense not to tell me.

All the wishes in the world don't mean shit as I bite away at my thumbnail in this far too cold empty room. Does that make me weak, or less of a woman? To wish I simply didn't know something so awful and life altering? If it does, so be it. I just want to go back. I don't want to know any of it.

The air conditioner keeps coming on and each time it does my heart leaps. It's accompanied with a loud click, that fills the quiet space. It scares the shit out of me every time it clicks on. I haven't slept in God knows how long now. I know that's not helping, but how could I possibly sleep in this room? It's not designed for comfort. I haven't taken my medicine either and the beating organ in my chest runs wild. It doesn't want to be in this interrogation room any more than I do.

My thumbnail is jagged and rough from biting it down to the nub as goosebumps spread across my flesh and my foot nervously taps against one of the metal legs of the table.

Four chairs, a table and a long-ass mirror at eye level on the wall to my left are all that are in this room. I'm no fool and I'm fully aware it's a one-way mirror and they're watching me.

Officer Cody Walsh is watching me.

Maybe he's waiting for me to break. The question is: how long will he wait?

The door opens suddenly, ripping me from the trance I'd been in as I stared at my own reflection. From the scrubs I put on yesterday morning, to my red-rimmed eyes, blotchy from smeared mascara, I look like hell. Or rather like I've been to hell and come back to tell the tale.

Again my heart reacts at a sudden unfamiliar noise as the door opens, thumping and loudly protesting this man's existence.

Cody Walsh will always look handsome, I'm sure of it. There's a charming air that surrounds him as he lets the door close behind him, a coffee in each of his hands. He's not dressed in his uniform, clad only in faded jeans and a crisp white collared shirt. Classically handsome fits him well. Wholesome, even. With neatly trimmed hair and never more than a five o'clock shadow on his face to pair with his gorgeous blue eyes and pearl-white smile, he's a good-looking man to say the least. A little older, but good-looking nonetheless.

"You didn't sleep," he comments with compassion in his tone. I wish he weren't compassionate. That's how he gets me and I'm so aware, yet so in need.

I fall for it. My dreary night lends itself to a need for sympathy. The ball of emotions clouds my vision and I let my hand fall over my eyes, scrubbing them and reminding myself that I can't say anything to anyone, no matter how long I'm meant to wait in this room. Anything I can think to say to Walsh in greeting jumbles itself at the back of my throat. I suppose some piece of me would rather choke on the words than give them to the man who arrested me.

"The guilty ones sleep." Walsh's voice remains casual, friendly even. It's unavoidable to look him in the eyes as he walks over to me, confidently and nonthreatening in the least. "You didn't and I knew you wouldn't," he says as he places a cup of coffee beside me. It smells like cinnamon and he must notice how I gaze down at the cup longingly the moment it hits the hard, unforgiving table. Which is the only thing that's been my company for hours. I shift in my spot and suddenly realize how sore my elbow is from resting in the same position for so long.

The white paper cup is innocuous, the black lid standard, but it looks and smells like heaven to me.

Wrapping both of my hands around it, the warmth is everything. "Do you intentionally keep the room cold?" I ask as my shoulders shake with another click of the air conditioner turning back on. I knew it was coming, but still wasn't ready for the sudden sound. It's less of a shock with Cody distracting me though.

Officer Walsh looks up at the vent only a foot from me before turning, leaving the room without a word and then coming right back. The constant breeze is no longer present and he gives me a weak smile although his eyes don't reach my own. "My apologies."

The concrete floor protests in a loud screech as he pulls out the metal chair across from me. I take a sip of the coffee, unable to refrain any longer. The least I can do for myself is consume some sort of energy. I haven't eaten in a long damn time since I didn't take my lunch break on my last shift. I don't know if the coffee is decaf or not, but the warmth alone is welcome. My eyes close and the lack of cool air against them grants me a small sense of peace. It's short-lived, but it was there for a moment.

Walsh gestures to the coffee and says, "Cinnamon crumb cake or something like that. It was the special of the day. I don't know how you take it."

"It's perfect," I find myself saying as I open my eyes and stare straight ahead at the blank wall. I add after the tick of the clock, "Thank you."

He nods in acknowledgment but then what he's holding steals his gaze from me. There's a folder in his grasp and he puts it on the table but doesn't open it. Splaying his hands, he places them on either side of the folder and looks down at it as he speaks, rather than at me.

I wonder what it contains. Maybe evidence they found. Statements they took. Maybe it's all blank papers and the man across from me simply wants to make me scared. At this point and from everything I've learned in my lifetime, any of those options are possible.

"There are three ways I see this playing out." With the first bit spoken and my heart pumping harder, Walsh looks me in the eyes. He clears his throat and says the first option: "You're tried and convicted for the murder of a cop."

I swallow, the remaining cinnamon-flavored coffee suddenly making my throat tight. My pulse seems weaker and my head feels lighter at the thought. I could spend the rest of my life in prison. How is that justice? My conscience plays flashes of my life for me, each moment I got away with something wrong, something I shouldn't have done. Justice and karma are quite different, aren't they? When I push the warm cup away and fold my arms over myself, the cop continues, his voice a bit stronger. "The second option: I let you walk away and you go back to the man who had you take the fall."

I bite the inside of my cheek to keep from speaking up to defend Seth and I know Cody Walsh sees it. The metallic taste of blood is awful, but uttering a word right now would be worse. I have to work hard to school my expression to neutral. I won't say a word. I haven't got a damn thing to say to him. If I so much as mention Seth, they could bring him in. He's shot, he's not okay.

Seth would have never meant for me take the fall. Never. I all but pushed him out that window. He may not be a good man, but he's a good man to me. My heart sputters as the vision of Seth confessing to me last night comes back. I hide it, burying it beneath the image of him taking a bullet for me. How am I supposed to think straight when my world is so tilted?

My eyes close with the silent prayer that Seth's all right. That he did what I told him to. My eyes open again while wondering: what are the odds that he already knows I'm in here? They have to be high. He must know. If he's able, he'll save me. I know he will.

"Or the third option," Walsh continues. "Charges are pressed against you, you go to jail, and Seth, with the help of the Cross brothers, pull their strings to get you out."

Hope flutters at the thought of the last scenario being the case. That will happen. That is the most likely outcome, right?

I've never known Seth to abandon me. He can be crude, an asshole. He's lied to me and done so many wrong things. Worse than just wrong. He does things that are horrible, things that some say would send him straight to hell. But never once has he abandoned me. He'll go through hell, commit all those sins ten times over, just to save me. It's one of the things I'll always love about him. He's a damaged man beyond repair, but he wouldn't let me suffer if he could stop it.

The rustling of Cody's jeans as he readjusts in his seat brings my gaze back to his. "None of those instances lead to justice." Justice sounds funny. Like it doesn't belong in that sentence, let alone this conversation. "I think the third is the most likely, if you're wondering."

I have to blink away my surprise at his admission.

"Given the experiences I've had so far in this city, the men you hang around have a way of protecting themselves and I," he pauses to suck in a breath, his brow rising before falling back into place. He lets out the breath and continues, "I hadn't realized how close you were to them until recently."

Tick, tick, my heart beats faster than the clock. I want to tell him that I'm not close to the Cross brothers, but I don't say a word. Remembering that not speaking is my best defense. If they charge me, I'll get a lawyer. Right now I'm in holding and having a lawyer won't change that. I'm aware of my rights.

"I don't know what will happen to you after you leave here, and that worries me."

The concern he displays nearly makes me respond that I'll be safe with Seth, but that's none of his business. Not only that, but I don't know how I could ever be with Seth again. My throat tightens at remembering what started this domino effect.

I have to clear my throat before I can tell Officer Walsh I don't have anything to say other than the initial statement I gave. It was self-defense and I hardly remember anything at all. I told them everything happened so fast and I was so scared that I think I blacked out. It was the best excuse I could come up with at the time and now I'm sticking to it.

"The thing is, one of the men was a cop. So even if they get you out of here, the investigation won't stop."

Out of a nervous habit, I grab the coffee and sip. I'd rather drink than speak.

"There are men who aren't in the back pocket of the Cross brothers. Men who also break the law and they'll go around it to see someone pay for Officer Darby's death."

"Are you threatening me?" I ask and the shock is unrestrained, new fear coming to life.

"No. Not at all." His response is quickly spoken, his eyes wide like he wasn't anticipating my reaction in the least. The next thing he says is spoken with strength and sincerity. "I'll do everything I can to protect you." My question obviously shook him and his answer was quick and sincere. "I don't want you to be involved. It can't end well for you if you are."

My nod is imperceptible as I absently scratch my nail against the paper coffee cup.

Words sit on the tip of my tongue. An explanation that the cop is obviously in the wrong, but now I question everything. Seth shot first. The masked man had the gun raised though. I've played it so many times in the back of my mind that the sequence of events is a blur and for a split second I'm not sure if I am remembering correctly. Inwardly

I shake my head. Seth shot first. I know that truth. But those men threatened me with deadly force, the cop included. If I could go back, I wouldn't want Seth to wait and see whether or not the trigger was pulled. If he had, I might be dead.

It has to mean something that I was threatened in my own home. That has to be important. The most important thing. All the words tangle at the back of my throat and I can't swallow.

They strangle me.

Cody Walsh looks down at me with such sympathy, I nearly crack and ask him to tell me if it matters. It has to matter, doesn't it?

My ass feels numb as I readjust in my seat, suddenly aware of how uncomfortable I am. My eyes are dry and burning. Of all the fatigues and pains, they hurt almost the most. Almost.

My fingers spread across my chest as I feel the faint pumping of my battered heart. Nothing could hurt worse than this.

I haven't forgotten what Seth confessed. The pain is proof of that.

"Let me help you," the good officer suggests as if he can. Nothing can help me. I won't betray Seth. I barely survived the first time. I wouldn't be able to look at myself in the mirror if I do it again. With weary eyes, I close them lightly, refusing to answer.

I have to sniff, breaking the silence and suddenly feeling stuffy. I haven't cried and I'm proud of that. In the face of everything crumbling around me, I don't feel the need. What's done is done and now I wait. It's all I can do.

"The death sentence is a possibility in this state, Laura. You don't want to risk this," he stresses.

"I don't have anything to say, Officer Walsh," I say and my voice is eerily calm. At my decision, the click of the air conditioner returns. I keep my eyes on Cody, but he moves his to the vent.

Although it genuinely tugs at my lips, I let out a small humorless laugh when he turns to look at the door, as if he'll see through it to whomever has turned the air back on.

It's a long moment before he says, "We can hold you for forty-eight hours without charging you."

I don't look at him. The metal table holds all my attention because it plays my life back for me like a movie. From the first time I laid eyes on Seth King to the sight he was last night. Forty-eight hours in here. I can make it that long. The *tick, tick, tick* of the ever-present clock calms any anxiousness I have. It's a balm to my torn soul, even if my hands do shake in my lap.

"Laura." The way the officer says my name grips my gaze, forcing me to look him in the eyes. They're the most tranquil of blues and riddled with concern. It would be touching if I didn't feel so much peace at the thought of simply being alone. "He killed one of us. They aren't going to let this go."

I don't respond. I don't have anything to say and I've already made that clear.

"Please, let me help you," he beseeches.

My hands are hot when I press them to my eyes, breathing in deep and feeling the weight of everything pulling me under what feels like the roughest of tides.

I've been beyond help for quite some time. Forty-eight more hours isn't going to change that.

CHAPTER 2

Seth

I NEVER THOUGHT I'D BE GRATEFUL FOR THE COLD. I'VE ALWAYS HATED how cold it gets on the East Coast; it numbs the pain, though. Most of it. So the cold is something I need, something I focus on to keep me moving.

At least four men are guiding me, shoving me forward and keeping my arms pinned behind me. Listening to everything, every breath, every step they make—that's the only information I have to go on to figure out how many there are, how big they are and what I'm up against.

Without the cold, I'd be burning hot with the need to react. The clang of the metal grates beneath my feet sparks recognition immediately. Thank fuck for that, because I can't see a damn thing with the bag over my head.

The grates on the edge of the parking lot let me know my location without a doubt. I'm away from Laura and her place. That is the only silver lining to this fucking ending. They're moving away from my Laura. At least she'll be all right. The thought is calming in the best and worst of ways.

The sound of crickets, along with leaves blowing indicates the woods behind Laura's apartment complex are to my left. The longer

I'm out here, the more information I have, and the more settled I become. The telltale whoosh of a van door opening sounds to my right. I don't react; I don't let them know I'm even halfway with it.

According to the men taking me in, I reek of whiskey, I'm bleeding out and there's no way I'll make it.

Let them think I'm drunk. Let them think I'm slowly losing consciousness.

I want the elements of shock and surprise to be on my side when I get my opening.

This is on Marcus. The men in her place, these men waiting outside making sure it went down like it was supposed to. I know in my gut Marcus set it up. He's a dead man. Every fucking person who's involved is a dead man.

I'll fucking kill him but odds are he's going to kill me first. Unless I get a single opportunity. I just need one.

"Get him back, get him to talk. That's all you need to worry about," a gruff tone says. He doesn't hide his voice and I almost give a start at realizing I recognize it. I recognize the way he coughs and I practically see him doing it. I've seen him close his fist and cover his mouth with it. He doesn't do well with the change of season. He said that once. I know it's him.

"I didn't sign up for this," one man protests, his voice hushed but I hear it.

The response is pushed through gritted teeth. "We have one job, get him there alive so he can talk." I can hear a shove, a scampering back. "Do your fucking job."

The hair stands up on the back of my neck. I followed this prick, I watched him for weeks. He's one of Marcus's men. Tall and gangly, but he's got strength hidden in his thin frame. He was by the bridge, lugging crates. No one would view him as a threat at first if they happened to come across this man. Average in everything with the exception of height. His dark eyes and towering stature are the only marked traits.

"What if he dies on the way?" another man asks lowly in a whisper, as if he's hiding it from my knowledge. Concern is evident and I don't know if there's credence to it or if all this pretending I've been doing, making my body heavy and groaning with the pain is a good enough act to convince them I may very well be dying.

He speaks again in single syllables, loud and distinct with anger clearly evident. "Get. Him. There."

I've been listening ever since a gun was shoved to my temple. I only know the tall man with the gruff voice. We identified him as Steven Davis. Barely on the grid, but identifiable from a previous criminal record.

A hard shove to my right shoulder forces me to stumble and I exaggerate it, falling to my knees on the asphalt. As the man who held my arms grabs my shoulder, I test whether or not the ropes are tight on my wrists. They're not. It's a sloppy job that was done quickly. Only meant to aid whoever it is behind me. They may buy him some time if I were to try to fight my way out, but the knots will loosen.

"Get up," the deepest voice says. It came from the one closest to me. The way he grips me and easily flings me up makes it obvious he's got weight to him. I dub him: the muscle.

"Keep him alive." The words are gritted in a hiss and I immediately feel a prick in my arm as my footing is finally getting settled. It's a shot of something. "That'll help."

The grimace on my face can't be seen, and I'm grateful for that. It's so fucking cold and my head feels light.

Footsteps move farther away even though the hard grip on my arms remains. Three pairs of them. A car door opens and then another.

The four men around me has decreased to maybe two. At most. Two men are within reach. If I had to guess, the others are walking around the vehicle.

If I don't try now, it may be the last time I ever see Laura.

Laura.

My body reacts before I can think. Throwing my head back, it slams directly into the big man, The Muscle, who had my arms restrained behind me. He yells a slew of curses and without missing a beat I turn and shove my full weight into him. The ropes burn as I work them, doing my damnedest to wrest them free. It works. The relief is slight, but it's there as the coarse rope falls beneath my hurried feet.

The screams of "Get him!" trail at my back. I don't wait; I run as fast as I can. My muscles scream and I barely get the black bag off my head before I hit the edge of the brick wall that surrounds the dumpsters. My right shoulder slams directly into it, knocking me off-balance and spinning me around. *Fuck!* The pain is fresh and brutal from the hit.

In a quick glimpse I see everything. The single light in Laura's parking lot, the all-white van with no windows, and the four men racing toward me with a look of dread in their eyes. One of them is most definitely Steven Davis. Our eyes lock and I know he knows that one of us will die soon.

"I'll shoot," one yells, stopping to point a gun and I take off. He's a heavier guy who's hard to see this late at night, but his build, his voice, they're etched into my mind. Every single one of them, I'll remember for as long as I live. Or, at least, as long as they live.

Revenge won't happen tonight. This is my only chance to run.

Agonizing pain courses through my limbs, every muscle coiled and screaming with the plea to stop. I sprint through it, past the dumpsters, past the complex and down to the woods. The smell of dirt is fresh, like an autumn rain mixed with crisp auburn leaves.

It's dark, too dark to see much of anything between the thick grouping of old oak trees. The fall leaves crunch beneath my feet as I whip around the dense forest. The bark scrapes my forearm. Fuck! The sting only adds a touch more pain to my already battered body. My breath forms clouds in front of my face, the only warmth I can feel at all.

Run. My heart pounds in my chest. Run as fast as I can.

My pulse hammers and my gut twists inside of me. I can't fail. I can't let them catch me.

Three. Two. One. I hurl myself down the left side of the woods where the drop-off is. I knew it was there. Letting myself fall down the steep hill, tumbling and crashing through sticks and gnarled roots, I prepare for the large overturned tree. It looks like it fell some time ago, but the roots took hold and it made its home in the side of the hill.

The second my body smacks into the trunk, I cling to it, gritting my teeth so I don't scream out from the sudden blunt force to my chest. It knocks the wind out of me but with shaking arms, I move my body around the tree and stay silent, hunched down in the darkness on the dirt floor and listen. My breathing is sporadic and heavy.

Quiet. Stay quiet. Stay still. The trembling aftermath is a constant. Aiming to control it, I close my eyes. I prepare. I listen.

They don't throw themselves down. Instead they run, stumble and try to keep from falling down the steep hill. I can't tell how many there are. They move past me, even though I swear my heart is hammering so loud they should have heard it.

Two men pass by with precision and haste, following the trail. I catch them out of the corner of my eye and if only they turned to look, they'd see me. The moon is brighter now. They keep moving, making their way as quickly as they can, but it's damn near impossible with how steep the cliff is.

There are two more. I can faintly hear one a moment later, the twigs snapping under his weight. He's quiet. He's got to be the heavier man. The one who aimed the gun. Far quieter than the other two, despite his weight. He goes slowly, tracking and being patient. I don't dare swallow or move an inch until he's far past me.

Even then, I know there's a fourth. There's another man looking for me and I refuse to move until I know where he is.

I take the moment to assess, my eyes fully adjusted to the darkness and look up between the scattering of leaves still clinging to their home, at the small bits of light the canopy provides.

As quietly as I can, I lower my hand to my side, my teeth grinding against one another when I feel the soaked shirt. My breath is stolen from me at the small movement. How did I run? How did I run through this shit?

More importantly, how much blood did I lose?

My head rests against the tree and I blink away the memory of getting shot. I can barely breathe, I can barely stay up straight, exhaustion pulls me down and whispers that I should give in. I should let go. I reach in my pocket, but my phone's gone.

Fuck. Fuck! I can't die like this.

I need to go. I need to tell Jase what happened. They have to save Laura. The cops were there. She needs help and protection. I need to know what's happening.

Crack. Snap.

Branches break behind me. Thin ones and my eyes focus straight ahead as my back stiffens. The rust-colored leaves are eerily beautiful as I overhear the horrid words from one end of a conversation.

"If we don't get him, we can get her."

Steven Davis.

Her. Laura. Each realization is like dominoes falling.

My instinct is to react and with the small movement up, my body revolts. The need to vomit is strong from the sharp gutting pain. I hate myself. I hate being weak. *He's threatening Laura.* He will suffer a slow and painful death. But first, he'll give me three other names. The slight satisfaction is immediately drowned out by fear at hearing more of his one-sided conversation. I strain to hear the voice on the other side of the phone, but it's impossible.

"Yeah, she's in custody," he says. "Make sure they don't let her out and plant someone in the cell with her." My blood runs cold, freezing every inch of me down to the marrow of my bones.

"Make it clean, she doesn't need to suffer."

No. No, they can't hurt her. She didn't do anything. My body begs me to plead with the man. I've never begged for anything but I can't fight him, I have nothing left.

Thump. My heart pounds and my gaze shifts to the ground.

There's a set of stones on the edge of the hill. A path of them. It's a foot long, maybe longer and the rocks are strategically placed. They follow along the side of the steep hill, as if it leads somewhere. Hopefully, somewhere with a phone.

I have to save Laura. It's the only thing that matters.

The man breathes heavily, gasping for air behind me and I stare at the closest stone, imagining grabbing it and slamming it into the back of the man's head. It'd be heavy enough. Could I do it fast enough, though? If I can't, there will be no one to tell Jase. No one will know she's there, no one will know they're going to kill her. She has to live. I have to save her.

My right side screams in pain and I nearly pass out from my first attempt to stand.

Fuck. Fuck!

I hold my breath, waiting for the prick to get out of earshot before I crawl and climb my way down the path.

I can't die until I know she's okay. Wherever this path leads will have a phone. I just need to get to Laura before they can. I breathe a silent vow to save her. I'll kill them all before they lay a finger on her.

The promises I make silently to her are the only thing that keeps me going.

CHAPTER 3

Laura

I keep finding my hand pressed against my shirt as if I can calm down my freaked-out heart. All the while, my body rocks steadily on the metal bench. It's fine.

I'm fine. My arrhythmia has never really been an issue. It's just a butterfly feeling in my chest.

The first time I remember this feeling, the sporadic fluttering in my chest, was when I stood in the doorway of my grandma's house, lying to Seth. I remember it so clearly. I even held my shirt the way I am now.

The memory makes me smile; it's a welcome distraction.

The door creaked open and I stood there in my thin pajamas as the wind shook through the house. I folded my arms over my chest because I wasn't wearing a bra, and although I knew that when I opened the door, I hadn't anticipated the cold. The wind blew by though, forcing the door to open wider and I struggled to keep myself covered while still keeping a handle on the door.

"Why aren't you dressed?" Seth's eyes roamed down my body leisurely. It may have been cold that day, but he made me feel hot from head to toe. Ever since we'd had sex, with one look he turned my knees weak.

I wasn't his girlfriend though and I couldn't keep going like that. He didn't want anything more from me and I was convinced I was only going to get my heart broken. At the thought, my heart did an odd thing. I opened my lips to lie to him, but my heart protested.

I gripped it, telling it to shut up and calm down. That was the first time I remember feeling my heart acting up.

"You all right?" he asked.

"I'm sick," I said and the lie came out tight. I just need to be away from him right now. I need a chance to think. Because when I'm around him, I can't think right.

He stood there in jeans and a leather jacket, a jacket he'd put around my shoulders a week ago. I don't know how I could have lied to him back then so easily, especially with the way he made me feel. "I'm not going to school today."

He nodded, a short nod, and asked if he could do anything for me. Even as I shook my head he kept asking, "No homework to turn in?"

It physically hurt to lie to him, but I didn't want him to keep walking me to and from school. I didn't want him to feel obligated to do anything at all with me. My heart was all sorts of tangled up in his touch and the way he cared for me… it wasn't right. He never made a single move; I did it all. I knew what that meant. That's not how love happens. I could easily see a new woman walking by, catching his eye, and then I'd be gone.

When I shut the door, I hated myself. I spent the next twenty minutes doing what I'd done all morning, figuring out how to get the hell out of Tremont. I didn't have much money and I didn't have any family outside of this town, but I knew Grandma would let me if I found a way.

That's what I was doing when the knock sounded at my door. My jaw dropped when I looked through the peephole.

There Seth stood, with a plastic bag from the corner store a few blocks down. I couldn't unlock and open the door fast enough.

"What are you doing here?" I questioned him as if he was crazy and it only made him smirk.

He lifted the bag and said, "I got you soup and a few other things." I didn't offer for him to come in, but he did anyway, like he belonged there. As if he was supposed to be there in that moment, taking care of me.

The little pitter-patter in my chest lifted, trying to stop any words of protest I had from coming out.

"Sorry you're sick, Babygirl, but I hope you like chicken noodle soup." As I stood there, my back falling against the door, I watched him make his way to my kitchen, fully prepared to take care of me. I knew in that moment, I was utterly and completely in love. I was certain there was no way I could ever run from him. I knew I should. I knew it with everything in me.

The butterfly feeling hits me again, only this time it's harder and much worse than it was before. I don't remember it ever feeling like this, so painful that I can't ignore it.

It's probably just from the lack of sleep and stress. There's nothing here to distract me either; I'm focusing too much on it. The squeezing sensation and irregular, weak beats are okay. I'm sure it's fine. Why didn't I take my medicine?

Panic attacks are not uncommon and I sure as hell have a reason to dissolve into one. Seth was shot and I don't know if he's dead or alive. That's my first thought. My first reason. As if being charged with the murder of a cop isn't reason enough.

I would give anything for Bethany to be here right now. I could tell her everything and she'd make sure that Seth was all right and he knew. My one phone call went to her voicemail though. It's ludicrous that every situation keeps getting worse and worse.

A whimper leaves me, a pathetic sound as I hunch over, pressing against my chest even harder when the next pain hits.

I tell myself it's fine again and open my eyes to see a stainless steel toilet with no lid across the small cell from me. That's the only other object in this room. A metal bench and a toilet. Simple enough I suppose. At least it's not cold in here. There's a man at the end of the hall, so at least one other person is around and the lights are dim, probably because it's early morning or very late at night. I don't know either way, because there's no clock and the man doesn't speak.

I thought he'd gone for the longest time until I heard that horribly loud beep that goes off before the heavy doors open. He came from nowhere, his boots shuffling across the cement to open the doors, tell someone something lowly, I couldn't hear a thing, and then they shut again. He walked back to his post and silently stayed there.

The dark blues of his uniform complement his brown skin and light blue eyes. He must be mixed race, with one parent white and one black maybe, to have features like that. Cleanly shaved, he's handsome because of the sharpness of his masculine jaw. Any other day, I'd smile at him, make small talk. But the attractive police officer is not my friend. Not in the least.

He's the only company I have. I could tell him about being on the verge of a panic attack but the idea of him ignoring me, or not doing anything at all hurts more, making my heart thump wildly in protest. I'm not a criminal, yet I'm here. In a fucking holding cell.

The jail cells are nicer. I've been back here more than a few times for patients. I've hated that oppressive beep of the locked doors since the first time they made me shudder. I hate the sound even more now.

The jail is not unfamiliar with psychiatric patients. Oftentimes, a mental illness goes unidentified until a patient has done something worthy of being locked up. Behind bars they can't hide their symptoms and it's so much easier to see and identify.

So I've been here before, accompanying a doctor to diagnose or treat someone. It was never a good feeling. The sound of the doors opening and closing gave me nightmares the first time I came here.

I thought it was because of my family history, my father being a drug dealer and all, that I had such an aversion to jails. That's ridiculous though, no one likes a jail. No one likes the reason a jail needs to exist and they certainly don't want to be inside of one.

Sure as hell not behind these bars. Not alone in this cell, apart from the silent guard who I can't even see because he stands at the far end, tucked away.

The last patient I saw here died in her cell. She wasn't in the holding area; she'd been in jail a while for assault, I think. The cells are past this hall and through two sets of doors. I remember it well. She didn't tell anyone she was seeing things. She didn't tell them about the voices. It took another inmate being scared shitless for the guards to be informed.

The voices in my patient's head told her to hurt herself, which they'd done before. She told me about them in therapy. She went from thinking the pills caused the voices, to knowing she needed the pills to shut them out.

Maybe she was lonely in that cell. Maybe that's why she didn't say anything.

Either way, when I got to her cell, we were all too late. I can still see her wide eyes, staring blankly ahead when the orderly rolled her over. Death has a certain look to it. It stains your memory and waits there, refusing to leave you be.

"I'm on medication," I say, finally giving in to the sudden fear and the nurse in me, calling out to the man I know is here even if he's silent and out of view. I have to shake away the memory of that woman. I don't remember her name and somehow that makes me feel even worse. "I think I need my medication," I call out. My words run ragged as the pain gets worse.

I can't die in here from a heart condition because of my pride or shame. I can't die in here at all. I need to know Seth's all right.

Just breathe. Everything's all right. *He'll be all right.*

The hall is quiet behind the bars and I haven't seen a soul in a few hours, I think. So when the guard doesn't respond right away, I start thinking he's actually left this time. I have no idea how much time has passed. I couldn't sleep, not even with the blanket they left in here. I can't do anything but blink away horrible visions, go over every regret, and notice how erratic my heart is right now.

"Please!" I cry out and I'm immediately met with the sound of a heavy door creaking open and even heavier boots smacking against the cement.

The guard. I finally catch sight of his badge and it says Walters. He's accompanied by another man who looks like he's in his fifties and is a little too round to work in the field. He stops behind the bars, so I can't see his name tag. Walters is quick to speak into a walkie-talkie on his sleeve while the other man stares at me. His wide eyes are the same shade of brown as his khaki pants. "Miss?" he questions. "Did you say medication?"

His brow is pinched and concern is etched there. It's only then that I realize I haven't stopped rocking and my hand is a fist around the fabric at the front of my shirt.

"What's going on?" I recognize Walsh's voice along with the door beeping and opening again. The pain is unforgiving as I catch sight of Walters's back as he speaks to Walsh. Again, the other man just stares at me, maybe bewildered, maybe wondering if I'm acting.

A cold sweat breaks out along my skin and my head feels faint.

"Walsh." His name comes out stronger than I thought I could say it. I force myself to let go of my shirt and stare down the long hall until the officer finally looks at me. The gaze from Walters burns into me. He never takes his eyes off me. Even when he gives a command to the unnamed guard who then departs, Walters's steely blues stay pinned on me.

"Are you going to let me go?" I manage to squeeze out the question the moment Walsh comes over to me. "I need to get out of here."

The pain in my chest spreads and it feels like it's in my throat, hollowing it out but also burrowing inside of it. I can't describe it. I've never felt this before. My hand drops as I sway forward slightly, closing my eyes and focusing.

"I need to get out of here," I say again, louder and with enough forlorn sincerity to make sure Walsh both heard me and knows something's wrong.

"That isn't going to happen," Walsh says and he sounds resigned to the fact. "The state is pressing charges."

My heart skids to a halt. No longer tumbling uncontrollably, it simply stops and I sit there, shocked and waiting. Waiting for it to start again.

"I wanted to release you." *Thud*, my heart's weak but it's working. "I told them to watch where you go if we released you."

"So nice of you," I whisper because that's all I can manage. It hurts to talk. My chest is so tight. I'm fighting to breathe but trying to look strong.

What did he say?

I can't even focus. Officer Walsh said something. He's fuzzy. The room is so hazy.

"Open it up!" he screams, his grip tight on the bars across from me. "Who did she talk to?" he questions the silent Walters.

"No one, I swear. No one saw her! This doesn't make sense." Whether he's my friend or my foe, Walters's eyes flash with fear. I see it. I'm sure of it. At least he doesn't want me to die. It's a minor consolation as needles dance on my skin.

Their voices blend and blur. I'm upright one moment, then in the next I'm falling. Walsh grabs me, his fingers in a bruising hold. I can't breathe, but I can't move either. I can't swallow.

I'm blinking though. I can blink for a moment.

"You aren't getting out of this, Laura." Walsh uses my first name but it's shaky. My lips twitch in an effort to respond. Nothing comes out though. Still, I can blink. Even as I get colder and fear wraps itself around me. "Not this way," he adds as he shakes his head.

"Medic!" Cody Walsh screams. His skin reddens, panic overriding every other expression. "Medic," he screams out again behind him, laying me down on the hard cement floor.

His hands push against my chest, and then his mouth is on mine. It takes me a long moment to realize it's CPR. I can't breathe. I'm not breathing.

"Is there a pulse?" a new voice says. I barely hear it as my vision turns black.

My hearing is the last sense to go. "I'm losing her!"

CHAPTER 4

Seth

A thick coat of dirt and blood covers my hands. That's why the knob slips at first. I tell myself that's why it slips and not because I'm on death's doorstep.

The rusted metal turns in my hand on the second try and even that small movement sends a bolt of pain through my right side. Still on my knees, I lean against the doorframe as the backdoor to the worn, wood-paneled lodge creaks open. Someone built a house back here. The three windows in front were the only light in the darkness on this side of the forest. I could barely see it in the woods but as I came closer, I knew there was someone here. The red paint is long worn off and the back porch is barely stable, but at the very least, the lights are on.

It has to be hours since I've been shot. Hours of losing blood. Hours of fighting to stay alive. All I can hear is the rush of my breath as I sneak into the backdoor of the house.

The last thing I need is to get caught, or to unknowingly walk into the enemy's territory. I don't know shit about who lives here or how far I've traveled. It feels like miles and miles.

I swallow thickly, forcing myself to stand up and lean against the wall. I'm quiet enough, but the dirt comes with me, serving as evidence of my arrival.

The creak of the door is muted in the kitchen. The old linoleum floors haven't been swept in a long damn time. It takes three steps for me to close the distance to the counter and reach for a neatly folded dishrag. The kitchen is darker than I was expecting, faintly lit by a single light from the room beside it, most likely the living room since a dining room can be seen to my left.

The blood is still damp on the gunshot wound, but some of the skin has dried to my shirt. I grimace as I pull it back, revealing that the bullet passed through me cleanly.

Sucking in a breath, I press the dish towel to the wound both on my front and back and then open every drawer searching for plastic wrap or duct tape—anything to keep the cloth pressed against the wound. I've already lost too much blood. The lightheadedness tells me that.

I only spare a few minutes to address the gunshot. I don't have any more time to give it. I need a phone. Bracing myself against the counter, I eye the place. It looks like it hasn't been updated since the '80s and I'm praying that means there's a landline somewhere. Every step I take elicits a short groan from the warped floorboards.

There are no photos to go by, nothing to tell me if this is a family home or an old man living alone in this house. It could be a hunting lodge this far out in the woods, but I don't see any guns or trophy mounts. I have no fucking idea. I search the walls of the kitchen then the outlets before coming up empty-handed and moving to the living room. A TV was left on, but no one's there. Someone is in this house; I don't know who and I don't know where, but I know there's someone here. I wish I had my gun on me. I wish I had anything to go by. Anything at all, but I have nothing. It only takes me half a second to see the house phone, complete with a curled-up cord, on what looks like a foldout dinner table next to the worn, brown reclining chair in the back right of the room.

If I had to guess, I'd say an old man lives here. It reminds me of my grandfather's place when I was younger. The foldout dinner tables, the bared shag rug and the faux wood panel walls. Even the off-white color of the ceiling and the scent that lingers. It's from years of smoke.

If I close my eyes a second too long, I can see my pops rocking in the corner chair, smoking a cigar and telling me to keep it down because he can't hear the TV.

For a moment, it's too real. Too lifelike in my mind.

The vision is quickly wiped away at the sound of a toilet being flushed behind me. From the back hall.

The realization is jarring and I hide behind the threshold of the door. My back is pressed against it as the sound of a door opening and closing echoes through the first floor. There's no light in this hall, although it looks like it leads to a garage or maybe a basement. The stairs to the second floor are to the left, back by the dining room.

I pray whoever it is takes their ass upstairs to bed.

I don't have a gun or a weapon; I don't have the energy or strength to defend myself. If my grandfather saw a strange man with a gunshot wound in his house late at night, I can guarantee he wouldn't have asked questions. Shoot first. Or else the other guy might.

I'm as still as can be, barely breathing as I listen to the heavy footsteps. They're slow, giving more evidence that whoever is here is older or at the very least tired.

I listen to him open the fridge, every sound he makes sounding fainter and fainter as I wait with bated breath, feeling the life slowly slip from me.

He grabs whatever he was looking for and goes back into the living room. I'm just behind the wall, so close to the phone, but blocked by his presence.

My mind immediately wanders to Laura and in a helpless moment, I contemplate begging the man to listen and not attack me. I picture myself walking out into the light, hands up in the air, pleading with him to let me use the phone. How would he react to a dying man who snuck into his house?

I don't trust him. I don't trust the situation. I trust no one and if I fail, Laura dies.

I remember every moment I had with her and recalling every second I took advantage of her destroys me, warping my mind and my emotions.

"Hey." The sudden strength in her voice gets my attention. She's been quiet all this week. She doesn't speak but sometimes she cries, like something's just reminded her that she's all alone. Regardless of the fact that I'm there, walking her both ways, holding her hand when she needs it.

I get it. It's the way we mourn. We're fine for moments and then we fall victim to the memories. It kills us to come back to the present.

Even though it's only early November, the bite of winter is in the air and it's turned Laura's neck pink. The tip of her nose is the same shade. With her hand on her front door, keeping it open, she looks out at me.

A gust of wind goes by and I slip my right hand into my jacket pocket, so very aware of how cold the left one is. My palm is warm from her skin and her touch, but the back of my hand is freezing. She let me hold her hand though, so there's no chance I'm letting her go.

"Yeah?" I ask her, raising my voice as I turn on the uneven stone steps of this old townhouse. I think she's going to say thank you; she says it every day even though she doesn't want me to be her babysitter. At least that's what she says, but I don't believe it. "You already told me thanks," I remind her before she can say anything.

She's busy chewing on her bottom lip, her baby blues wide while I wait.

There's a moment, a vulnerable one between us. A moment where she wants something—needs something from me—and I'll be damned if I don't need it too.

This is all up to her though. Every move is hers to make.

"What do you want, Babygirl?" I ask her, doing everything I can to hide what I want from creeping into my tone.

The moment is over, waning slowly when she shakes her head, her long hair falling down the front of her sweater and hiding half her face from me. "Never mind. It's nothing."

I shouldn't feel hollow inside when I force the smile to my lips. It matches the one she gives me too.

"Thanks again."

"No problem." I nearly walk away. I'm so close to letting her shut me out, but just the thought of it makes me feel empty. I don't like the way I feel without her.

"Hey," I call back before I can stop myself.

"Yeah?" The way she says the single word sounds faint and it almost gets lost in the wind. She perks up with hope though and whatever it is she's hoping for, I hope she gets it.

"Do you eat?"

It takes her a moment, but she laughs at the ridiculous question and the sweet sound makes me smile as I jog up the steps to get back to her. "I'm hungry and I was thinking, if you're hungry, you want to come with me?"

I can't be so out of shape that I'm breathless after making my way up her steps to be closer to her but I blame it on that, and not on the nerves. "Come with me to dinner," I say, making it a demand rather than a question.

She chews on that bottom lip for a moment longer, debating as the blush rises to her cheeks. "Yeah," she answers. "I could eat something."

All that tension melts, all the nerves go away. When she's next to me, it's all just fine. It's perfect.

The click of the television and the silence that follows brings me back to now, back to the chance to make things right. *Just a little longer*, I think. He's got to be going to bed.

The stairs creak and with the old floors, I can easily hear him upstairs when he finally leaves. Thank fuck.

I should wait to call Jase, wait until I'm sure that the man upstairs is asleep and won't come back, but my patience is thin. I've already wasted too much time. At that thought, I move as quickly as I can.

I know Jase's phone number by heart so I dial it, holding my breath. I'm fucked if he doesn't answer. And Laura…

Fuck.

The other end only rings twice. Both times, I stare down at my hands as they shake.

"Who's this?" Jase answers in a deadly tone. It's the best thing I've ever heard in my life.

Please God, don't let me be too late. She needs me. She's always needed me.

I need her more. More than anything.

CHAPTER 5

Laura

My hands are still trembling. I'm huddled up, tucked away in the corner of this bed, bracing myself against the painted white cement wall of the cell. Hours have passed, but I still struggle to fully wrap my head around it all.

I'm a nurse. I've read about it. I comprehend the words. I just can't believe it's true.

Arrhythmia is apparently the least of my worries. The walls of my heart are weak.

Too weak. Even if I'd had my medicine, it wouldn't have helped. It was only a matter of time before my heart gave out.

That's what the doctor said when I woke up in the medical center at the back of the jail. I was out for hours; the defibrillator brought my heart back to a steady beat. I know about the medical center here, but I'm not familiar with the doctor who monitored me. He showed me everything though. I saw my charts.

I have systolic heart failure.

The doctor's voice won't shut up in my head. He keeps looking at me with those pale green eyes from behind his spectacles. *You have systolic heart failure.* His voice was so calm, his hand resting lightly on mine. He was a kind doctor, but as I wiped away the tears from the corners of my eyes, I couldn't help but hate him for having to deliver that news to me.

"Your heart is weak," he told me. *"You'll be high on the donor list; you're in good health."* He touched my shoulder, barely gripping me but I could only look at where his hand met the orange fabric of my newly appointed attire.

The scene plays again and again. It can't be real.

More tests need to be done and an appointment has been scheduled for the first of said tests, but the chest X-ray is a smoking gun. The second I saw it, I knew. He didn't even have to tell me; I knew just from looking.

"The arrhythmia has developed into something more dangerous."

I read all about this in textbooks when I was still in school. I've never had a patient with heart failure though. They're always older in the educational videos and on TV shows.

I'm in my twenties, relatively healthy, but my heart is failing me. Really, I've failed my heart. I knew something was wrong, yet I never followed through. I let my health slip. They could have caught this sooner.

The next appointment, once my current situation is more concrete either way, will consist of an EKG to confirm, and then I wait. I wait for someone to die so I can have their heart. That's the best option I have. Of course, there's medication to take and lifestyle adjustments to relieve the symptoms in the meantime… like removing stressors from my environment. There is no doubt though from Dr. Conway. I won't survive more than a year with this heart. That's what he told me. No more than a year at best.

I hardly notice the hot tears anymore.

Sitting cross-legged on the thin mattress in my new cell, I try to focus on all the other noise around me. At least I have a mattress now, and not just a bench. I have a blanket too, and a toilet identical to the one from before is in the corner.

I don't know if this bed is mine or if the one across from me was supposed to be mine. I'm the only one in this cell, for now. I was told several things while I went through the booking process. But it was all a blur as they took my fingerprints and mug shot. All I kept hearing was: *a year, at most.*

Clank, clank, clank, clank. Someone runs something down the bars of their cell. It came from the right and a bit of a ways down the much wider hall than the one in the holding area. There have to be twenty cells on each side of this wing. A guard tells whoever's making noise to quit it. The voice comes from a man and it reminds me where I am, bringing me back to the present.

In two days, my life has changed to be unrecognizable.

A few inmates hooted and made a ruckus when I was blindly led back here. I didn't pay attention to a thing. Not to where we were going. I hardly remember the sound the bars made as they were closing shut. Even the horrid beep of the lock is less than memorable.

They put me in here and I find it hard to care, but a piece of me does. A piece of me wants out and still has hope; the rest of me can't believe this is real. *Maybe it's shock.* I nod at the thought.

I want to wake up from this nightmare. From the moment Seth told me he killed my father, to the attack and murders in my apartment, to the doctor telling me, *"It's not a death sentence to be on the donor list."*

There are other options but they're risky, and even worse, temporary. He worries the walls of my heart are just too thin for surgery, but that's what second opinions are for. I keep hoping he's wrong. I keep hoping I'm wrong. This can't be real.

My head feels heavy so I let it fall, pushing my hair up as I lean against the cinder block wall. It's suddenly bitterly cold and it takes everything in me to keep it together.

One breath at a time is all I need. *Breathe in*, my heart thumps, *breathe out*, it ticks too quickly this time.

The jarring sound of the bars to my cell dragging open with a heavy creak causes my eyes to widen.

I don't recognize the guard. He's got to be in his late thirties, at youngest. His jaw is covered with a five o'clock shadow and his cheeks are hollow from his age. They match the wrinkles around his eyes. There are too many guards working in this place for me to tell them apart.

"This is your stop," he speaks and oddly enough, it seems like he meant the words for me. He stands there, his back straight as a rod as a woman wearing orange clothes that match my own, walks into the cell. He never looks at me, even though I stare at him. His embroidered tag reads Brown, I think. It certainly starts with a B.

I don't like that he, just like Walters, doesn't look at me. Or when they do, it's with an air of righteousness. It's possible I've made it up in my mind, but I hate it. I shouldn't be here. The thought desperately tries to turn into spoken words.

Instead of speaking, I drop my gaze, picking at an oddly thick thread in the blanket and waiting for the bars to shut.

It doesn't matter what he or anyone else thinks of me; none of this matters. Still, I want him to know I didn't do it. There's an itch in the back of my throat and a cold tingle that dances along my skin, giving me goosebumps, at the mere suggestion that he thinks I'm guilty.

I didn't do anything wrong. The small piece of me that's focused on getting out screams in my head even though it sounds like a whimper caught at the back of my tongue.

The larger part of me knows it doesn't matter. Where I'm sitting doesn't matter. I have no intention of moving if I can help it.

All that matters is that I don't miss my next visit to the doctor and schedule with another to get a second opinion. To find out whether the bespectacled doctor's diagnosis is correct. And whether or not I qualify for the donor list, like he said I did. That's what matters.

A rough ball scratches its way down my throat as I swallow thickly, finally looking at my companion. She takes her time walking to the other bed, pushing up the orange sleeves as she does. Black ink scrolls its way down her arms. It's a scripture of some sort but it's no longer sharp, it's faded and fuzzy from years of being on her skin. She blows a stray strand of hair out of her face.

Years of being conditioned to be polite and uphold formalities wins out. "I'm Laura," I tell her even though her back is to me as she smooths the mattress sheet. Although I'm sitting, I know she's taller than me, broader than me. Big-boned is an expression my grandma would have used to describe her. She carries a lot of weight, but it looks like she works out just the same. Her black hair is lifted off her neck in a ponytail that's not smooth at all. It's like she haphazardly pulled it up. I suppose to her, what hairstyle she chooses doesn't matter. I get that.

The bed creaks and squeaks as she climbs onto it with a bit of a bounce that comes with aggression, mirroring my position and leaning against the wall.

She crosses her arms while she talks. "I know who you are."

Thud, my instincts recognize that tone. It's a warning cadence, a deathly low one that's meant to strike fear. I've heard it plenty in the old bar I used to work at, the Club, and plenty on the streets. Instead of eliciting fear as it's intended, irritation flashes through me. A match is lit and it gracefully falls to a line of fuel, igniting its way through me.

How fucking dare she? I deserve to at least revel in my pity party. *How fucking dare she?*

It's then I see just how much muscle she has. Although I keep my expression calm and I don't hint in the slightest at the terror I know she wants to evoke, I size her up. Every inch of her.

"Oh," I say sweetly, "the guard didn't tell me your name." I smile naively at the bitch, staring into her deep brown eyes. Shrugging, I do my best to look pathetic. I'm sure with my red-rimmed eyes and tearstained cheeks, it's not hard to appear otherwise.

I'm ice cold down to the marrow of my bones when she hisses in a breath, "Damn, you'll be a hard one." She shakes her head gently, that hair behind her head swaying as she does, as if she truly has remorse. The chill in my blood pricks harshly, sending a bite of frost to cover every inch of me. "You seem sweet."

I let my lips part and feign confusion. The dumbass eats it up, leaning forward with an expression that tells me she's oh so sad to inform me. "I'm waiting on a note," she says.

"A note?"

"Telling me whether or not to kill you," she says and I let my eyes widen, halting my breath. As if I didn't know she was here to hurt me. *Kill me?* That part is new. Why, I don't know. This could all be a joke, a ruse. I don't give a fuck.

She might know my name, but she doesn't know who I am. She doesn't know where I came from. My hackles rise inside and an angry girl I'm far too familiar with emerges.

I swallow and then quicken my breath, letting her feel what she wants. My fear, my turmoil. "I didn't do any—"

She cuts me off, not letting my plea go on; thank fuck for that.

"I know. It's unfortunate," she says and tosses her head back. "I'm a killer for hire in here," she confesses. I stare wide eyed and think about Seth, about my father, about my fucked-up heart, all in order to bring tears to swell in my eyes. Outwardly I'm fragile, stricken with her confession. Internally, I imagine this woman killing inmates and getting away with it. *Calling them sweet.*

I let my gaze fall to the ink on her arm. Tally marks and trophies. My eyes whip back up to hers when she speaks.

"I don't want to do it, sweetie," she tells me and I make a mental note that when I kill her, I'll make sure to call her *sweetie.* A side of me I barely know anymore emerges. The side that kept a baseball bat at my front door and a pocketknife in every drawer of my home. A side that hates more than it loves, a side that doesn't have hope, because it doesn't want it.

"I see," I say softly, sniffling and wiping under my eyes, even though enough tears haven't gathered to actually fall. "A note?" I question, prying for more information.

"They said it'll be quick if Marcus gives the word. Sorry this is happening."

The mention of Marcus causes true fear to trickle in, but it's tainted, stained by hate that anyone thinks they can kill me. I've never heard of Marcus killing a woman. Never. That fact alone makes me think she's lying. Not about what's to come, but about who's behind it. Or maybe I just have too much faith in the faceless man I've read all about in those notebooks.

"Give me a smoke, will ya?" the woman asks as my mind wanders and a deep crease settles in my forehead before I notice the fingers reaching into the bars. A guard hands her a smoke and she gingerly accepts it, climbing off the bed and telling the guard thanks. Pulling a lighter from her pocket, she leans against the wall, flicking the small lighter back and forth as the tip of the cigarette turns a bright orange and she breathes in then blows out a billow of smoke.

"I didn't think you could have lighters in here," I barely speak, looking over her tattoos again on her inner forearm. I know them, I've seen them on psych patients before. They're gang tats and the ones on her right forearm are credits for kills. I only got a glance but there are at least twenty.

"You can't have lighters in here," she answers as she plays with the lighter she has in her hand. Shrugging, she continues. "You can't ask for a smoke and just get it. You can't have this either," she says and pulls a blade from her pocket. It's a simple pocketknife, with a corkscrew at the end and she taps it against her temple. "The blade is cleaner but takes too long. The corkscrew is more efficient. Bloodier, but more efficient because of the size of the wound."

Another guard passes and all the while, she has the knife out and a smoke in her hand. She takes a puff and blows the smoke my way.

"Why do they let you?" I ask and try to play up the naivety.

"Because we're all on the same payroll, working for the same higher command. Well, some of them… others, I pay off. I get paid to kill and I pay them to help me." She shrugs, taking another long inhale. "This shift is full of people who'll look the other way for the right price. It's that easy."

My breathing is shallow, my vision black around the edges. She's not fucking with me, she's truly going to kill me and the people in here will let her.

The true fear is back, but so much anger comes with the knowledge.

"I really am sorry."

She talks to me like it's a given. As if I'm easy prey.

It's her. And me.

I nod, my lips still parted in feigned disbelief and then the woman lies back, not even looking at me.

I bring my knees into my chest so I can bury my head in them. I keep my eyes on her though. She can't see my expression. She can't see the unbridled hate.

Every footstep beyond the bars steals my attention.

She's waiting on a note. I need to get that note first.

CHAPTER 6

Seth

Their graves were right next to each other. Side by side. I knew mine would be the third. The plot was empty and I knew I'd be buried there. My grandfather, my father, and then me. My grandfather was a stubborn old man, set in his ways and vocal about them.

I never liked him much. You can't ever like someone if you fear them the way I feared him. He died when I was young and as I stood there tracing the etching on his stone, I wondered if I'd feel the same way had I gotten to know him when I was older. After all, I feared my father, but I loved him. I hated him sometimes, but I respected and loved him. I understood. Children can't understand this life and I stood there thinking, that must have been why I didn't like my grandfather.

"You all right?" A small feminine voice broke through the hiss of the wind. Laura clutched her coat around her and I opened my arms so she could take refuge there.

"Fine."

"Then why are you here?" she questioned. Her no-nonsense bluntness always made me smile, even that day. With the bite of the cold nipping my nose, I sniffed and then shrugged. "I can't just come visit my pops?" I asked her, although it was rhetorical.

She peeked up at me through her thick lashes and said, "Please, Seth. Tell me what's wrong."

So much was wrong. She couldn't do anything to change it and she shouldn't have had to deal with that shit just because she was with me. I'd never make her take on my burdens.

"I was just thinking of my grandfather, that's all. I promise." I offered her a small smile, which she reluctantly returned and when she did, I kissed the crown of her head.

She leaned in closer to me, taking her hand from her pocket, wrapping her arm around my waist and she slipped that hand into my coat pocket. I liked the move. Even more, I liked that she'd been making them more readily. She wasn't holding back anymore. I don't know what changed, but she wasn't trying to run anymore. I had her. She really wasn't going to leave me, at least that's what I thought.

"You know you can tell me anything, right?" she asked me in a whisper. Her cheek was pressed against my chest and when another sharp gust blew by, she didn't complain. She stood there by my side, quiet and ready to wait longer if I wanted.

"I know," I told her although it was a lie. I could never tell her everything. There were some things she would never know if I could help it.

"Can I tell you anything?" she asked, and a hint of insecurity revealed itself in her tone.

Resting my chin on the top of her head I told her easily, "Of course." Although nervousness crept in, not knowing what she would say.

"I love you, Seth, and I'm afraid you're going to break my heart."

I thought I came there to that grave to pray that when I died, I wouldn't be buried next to them. That I'd be buried somewhere else, somewhere with a different kind of family. Instead I stood there praying that I'd never break her heart. It was the only good thing I'd ever have. I couldn't break it. I'd never forgive myself.

"If I ever break your heart," I told her honestly, "I'll never forgive myself."

My eyes barely stay open as the memory from almost a decade ago leaves me. My lids are heavy, but I fight it. I know I'm lying down; I can see the ceiling and fan blades whipping around. The light is bright and right above my head.

I'm hot, so fucking hot. But more than that, I can't keep my eyes open. I fight it, willing my body to obey me.

It takes only a few seconds to see the IV stand, to feel the prick in my arm of a needle, to sense there are people around me.

"Stop drugging me," I say and pull at the tube in my arm chaotically. *Get it out. Get it out.* The need to run is strong but I don't remember why. The needle slips out but not fully, and the hot blood in the crook of my arm spurs me further, ripping pain through my forearm as I hiss, rolling over on the sofa although strong arms keep me down.

My hands wrap around forearms, trying to shove them away. My muscles coil and a new pain shoots up my right side. Before I can kick my feet up, someone yells, "Get him," and pins my lower half down.

"Fuck," a man curses under his breath. It's strained and it takes me a moment to recognize it's Jase. "You need the fluids," Jase grits out.

My back presses into the cushions beneath me as the hands holding me down shove harder even though I stopped struggling.

"Stay down," he orders and I don't have the strength to answer. My head spins. It's hot and bright.

"What happened?" I ask and my voice sounds far away. I'm trying to remember. Nothing is coming to me though.

"You were passed out when we got there. Scared the shit out of the old man."

"The old man?" What's the last thing I remember? My face is hot. *The fight*. She threw something at me. Laura… she punched me. Her eyes are filled with pain in my memory. I shake it away. No, no, that didn't happen.

"What happened?" I question again, sounding delirious even to my own ears.

"You lost a lot of blood from the shot," Jase says calmly and then he tells me to hold still. A random detail comes to me, the prick reminding me of another.

"They gave me something."

"Stay still," he warns again and more of what happened plays in my mind. It comes in flickers. Black and white slides of what happened as the needle pierces my forearm, finding a new vein. My jaw hardens, tightening and I refuse to react as everything comes flooding back.

"Laura," I finally speak, the room starting to settle. "They're going to kill her."

"We know. You told us. This isn't the first time you've woken up like this."

"They said they'd kill her!" The words rush from me, my breathing coming in ragged as I remember what he said. *Make it quick.*

Jase doesn't respond and dread spreads through me. "I don't need anything," I speak as I try to sit up but Jase is there to push me back down. The force of his shove knocks my breath from me. My head is still spinning.

"You need fluids." His voice is harsh and although somewhere deep down I wonder if he's right, I deny it, shaking my head and telling him to fuck off.

"Two hours," he tells me like that will keep me down. "Just two hours." The second time he speaks it's like he's asking me.

"She may not have two hours," I say and my voice breaks. The words splinter with the lack of hope. "They're going to kill her because of me." I remember something important suddenly and speak again before Jase can say anything.

"Steven Davis. Find him, kill him." I remember the name. I remember that dumb fuck. "He's the one who said it. He's one of Marcus's—"

"You told us last night. We already found him, found the lot of them."

The lot of them? I don't remember. I struggle to recall the details.

"You said there were four and there were. The van was at the docks, looks like they were waiting on someone. Don't think they expected us to show up, but we had the trace on Davis still."

"You got them?" I want them all dead. Every one of them needs to die.

"They took off and he had a gun." Jase talks to me absently and I look between him and the thin curtains over the windows. I recognize the bay windows, the coffee table, the art on the walls. It's his girlfriend Bethany's house. It was probably closer than the bar for him to transport me from wherever I was. More importantly, it's dark outside. Everything comes back, drip by drip.

Jase keeps talking as I remember the pieces of what happened. "We had to shoot. We got him, he gave us the other three before he bled out and Declan got the plates on their vehicle. We've got their names and Declan has possible locations."

"Let me, let me go." I struggle to sit up.

"Just two hours," he says and then I remember how he said *last night*.

"What time is it?" I ask, my blood pounding in my ears. How much time has passed? All three of them will pay but first, I need her safe. I need Laura back and by my side. "Is she okay?"

"Eight. We didn't get you until four this morning. And yes, we have eyes on her."

My hand travels down my side and my fingers brush over stitches. Everything moves slowly as I get colder and colder. Too much time has passed. "Where is she?" I question and again Jase doesn't answer.

"We need to get to her!" I rip out the IV again and this time I have more strength, more alertness so when Jase's arm comes down I'm prepared with my forearm already braced and shoving back. Whoever's at my feet got a good kick to his groin and I'm up and off the sofa, breathing heavily like a wild animal and staring at a pissed off Jase Cross and some poor guy who's doubled over.

The doc, maybe. I don't know. I don't recognize him or his voice.

"Don't be stupid," Jase says lowly, taking a step forward but not reaching for me.

"Fuck, shit," the man I kicked sputters. I got him hard and if I wasn't so concerned about Laura, maybe I'd care.

"We have guys on the inside." Jase barely acknowledges the man. His focus stays on me.

"Who?" I say and the word comes out deep, rougher and louder than I intended. The man I don't know slowly rises, his face both flushed and scrunched like he's trying to hide his pain. "Sorry," I bite out when he looks at me with contempt. He doesn't respond but I can hear him swallow from all the way over here. Judging by where his hands are and the fact they don't move even as he walks out of the living room and toward the half bath that's down the hall, I hit him where it hurts.

Remorse courses slowly through me as my vision becomes clearer and the pieces of what's happened line up, one after the other.

"A few guards are keeping an eye out. Walters, for one. Williams and Shultz. Chris Mowers."

"Who's getting her out?" I question, hating how tight my throat is at the thought of her in a cell. She's not meant to be there.

"She shouldn't even be in there," I add before Jase can say anything and both of my hands fly to the back of my head. My breathing is quick, too quick as I pace in front of him.

It's dark in this living room, but the floors sound the same as they did before. The soft groan of old hardwood. I look Jase in the eyes, pausing my steps and noting how tired he looks, how his five o'clock shadow is far too long. "It should've been me," I say, dragging out the confession from the back of my throat.

A different kind of pain washes through me and I close my eyes, remembering how she shut the window even knowing the cops were coming.

"She took the fall and it should have been me." Shit, everything would be different if she hadn't done that. She'd be safe. "She shouldn't be in there!"

"Listen to me," Jase says in a hushed tone and he sounds closer. I open my eyes slowly and he is, he's right next to me, reaching out his hand and gripping my shoulder. "She's going to be fine."

"You didn't hear him," I start to say, my head shaking chaotically as I remember the voice in the woods, the dead fucker who said, *make it quick*. I'll never get it out of my memory. I won't be able to sleep without hearing Davis again and again the moment my eyes close. Not until I know for certain Laura is safe.

"That prick is dead," he says and Jase's tone is firm, but it doesn't matter.

"The prick works for *Marcus*," I stress, hating that I have to justify my concern to him. He should know I can't sit back. He should fucking know.

"He's never done anything like this. He's never come after a woman." Jase's voice is calm with his head shaking just slightly. The small, rhythmic movements are at odds with my own. He repeats, "He's never come after a woman."

My heart thuds. It's not good enough. I can't sit back hoping Marcus doesn't give the word and that the men on the inside are able to prevent anything bad from happening to her.

She's mine to protect. She needs me.

"I can't sit back," I say and my voice cracks on the last word as I close my eyes, moving my fisted hands to the crown of my head. I'm barely steady, but I'm capable of seeing her there. Watching her pace around a cell she doesn't belong in. Watching her walk alone when I should be there for putting her through it all. "I have to see her."

"Visiting hours are over," Jase speaks as if that's the end of it. Hate is brutal, coursing its way through me. I've never resented the man, but what I feel for him at this moment borders on unforgivable.

When I open my eyes, doing my best to keep from uttering the spew of curses that choke me, I see a jacket draped over the sofa arm, probably Jase's, and on top of it are his keys.

He's not my boss anymore. And he sure as fuck isn't a friend. He'll have to kill me to keep me away from her.

"My car still at her place?" I ask him casually. My gaze doesn't move from the glint of silver metal until he says, "We got it. It's out front. Your wallet and phone were in the van at the docks."

"Where are my keys?" I question him.

He doesn't respond verbally. Instead he motions with his arm behind me and lets it fall to his side.

I don't waste a second putting my wallet in my back pocket, my phone in the front and then snatch my keys from the end table to the right of the sofa.

"You're just going to leave?" he says, raising his voice as I make my way to the door. With my back to him, I pause.

"Bethany stitched you up, by the way. We had to come here to get everything she needed. She risked her job to get the meds."

Glancing over my shoulder at him, I tell him, "Thanks. I'll tell her thanks when I see her again."

"You just kicked her boss in the nuts. You may want to apologize at some point." He's resigned in his tone, but there's a hint of friendliness. He huffs in humor and bends down to grab his own keys and then his jacket.

"You have to know I can't just sit here."

"I do," he admits and then he adds, "Don't do anything stupid, Seth."

He doesn't look at me and he doesn't wait for a response. Instead he pulls out his phone and dials someone. I don't wait to hear who.

The pain is a dull white noise running through me. The adrenaline outweighs any and everything that could keep me down.

I'm not conscious of what I'm doing when I get in the car. The headlights are the only bit of light in the neighborhood, but the streets have a few cars scattered through them. I'm careful as I drive, recounting everything that happened. Making sure I know all of it.

My memory stutters at the pain in her eyes when I told her the truth about how her father died. Everything else is red. Blood colors and stains every moment.

A section of road on the way to the jail is nearly black from the lack of streetlights on this side of town, and there are hardly any cars out here. It gets dark early this time of year.

The bank is lit up though. It's a beacon in the night. Every window is brightly lit. I know it's closed. It closes at six every day and it's closed all day on Sundays. Everything around here closes at six except for the bars and the church.

I'm not even thinking; my gaze doesn't stray from the front of the bank. It's mostly glass. I know I'm conscious of that. Glass is easy to drive through.

My foot feels heavy on the gas and the rev of the engine sends a thrum of anticipation to my veins. I'm hot as I turn the wheel just slightly. Just enough to put the bank in my path.

Visiting hours are over. Jase's words echo in my head. We can't get in to the jail without signing in. I'm sure he thinks she's safe and that she'll still be there tomorrow, but I can't risk it. I won't. He has the distance to be logical, to allow the risks. I don't have that luxury.

My heart races as I keep my hands steady on the wheel, bracing myself.

If they won't let me visit her or see her right now, then I'll join her.

They can arrest me for attempted robbery, for… I don't fucking know what and I don't care. Either way, I'll get to see her. I just need to get through those doors one way or the other.

My foot slams down to the floorboard of the car. The lights blur in front of me and my muscles tighten, ready for the impact.

The shatter of glass and jolt of the tires meeting stone don't mean anything to me.

None of it matters.

The airbag goes off and slams against my face. My neck whips back, unprepared.

It's barely anything. I've taken worse hits.

None of this shit matters, I think as I wait, letting the bag deflate, listening to the screeching of the alarms and then within minutes, sirens.

Arrest me, charge me, lock me up.

I pull my phone out of my pocket and text Jase: *Just get me close enough to protect Laura.*

The ringtone goes off within a few seconds. He's calling but I put my phone back in my pocket, ignoring him as the sirens get louder.

CHAPTER 7

Laura

"WHAT ABOUT ANY BROTHERS? OR SISTERS?" THE WOMAN ASKS conversationally. She finally told me her name is Jean. No last name, just Jean.

I have to swallow before I can answer, since my throat is dry from answering all her questions. Back-to-back she wants to know pointless details. Occasionally there's a bout of silence, but I hate that even more. I can't decide if she's sadistic and wants to know particulars of my life before she ends it, or if she's trying to befriend me as justification to her own conscience that she's not a bad person and is just following orders.

"None. You?" I ask back. I've done this a few times, asking the same question in return. It's mostly out of habit but Jean only shakes her head, either refusing to answer, or simply saying no. I'm not sure which. She could have a dozen brothers out there and still she shakes her head like she's done every other time I've turned the question back on her.

I don't know shit about her but now she knows all about where I grew up, what I do for a living, why I chose the East Coast. Mundane questions that amount to nothing more than small talk. I think it's a bit tedious considering I hate her fucking guts.

Everything I told her was true, except for what happened yesterday. She got half the truth and half the lie I gave Officer Walsh. Just in case she knows about Seth, I told her I'm involved with him. I told her he took off yesterday after we got into a fight and that made her laugh. A deep guttural laugh that brought a genuine smile to her face. She's missing two teeth, in the back upper right of her mouth. I've gotten a good view of her smile a few times now.

Again she shakes her head, refusing to answer and lies back down, stretching easily, as if she doesn't have a worry in the world.

I haven't moved in the hours we've been sitting in here. My muscles are tense, every single one and my back feels stiff. Jean, on the other hand, moves easily in our cell. I haven't taken my eyes off of her while she looks anywhere but at me for the most part. She has a habit of tapping the back of her knuckles against the bars of the locked cell when she's thinking. I assume she's thinking about something. She could simply be waiting for that note to float by.

I hate her. I hate everything about her. As time passes, the hate only seeps deeper and deeper into my psyche. I've imagined rolling up the bedsheet, slipping it around her throat and choking her. She's taller than me, so I wouldn't be able to do it when she's standing.

It's not quite practical, but the image of it happening has ingrained itself in me.

She's stronger than me, so slamming her head into the toilet wouldn't work. And the toilet itself is similar to one on an airplane—there's no standing water. So I can't drown the bitch.

I want to ask her how many people she's killed and how she's done it. Simply to justify the obsessive and hateful thoughts that suffocate me, but a girl who's frightened wouldn't do that. I've done everything I can to make sure she thinks I'm terrified. I've even begged her to spare my life. I've brought on tears.

I'll act for as long as I have to, until one of these plots in my head becomes feasible.

A contented sigh leaves Jean as she lays her head back, staring at the ceiling but then closing her eyes as if she'll nap. It has to be late now. Lights out was called a bit ago and this floor went dark in an instant, making my heart race for a moment until my sight had adjusted. It seems like lights out would be a good time for something like a hit to go down. Nothing happened though. Nothing has happened since she walked in here. Only question after pointless question.

The squeak of a cart rolling down the hall rips Jean's eyes wide open. She props her head up with her forearms crossed above her, still lying on her back but other than that movement, she remains still.

Thump, thump, my heart is steady, but fast until the cart comes into view. It's a simple silver, three-shelved cart. That's when my beating organ falls down to the pit of my stomach. I swear I can feel it beating there. The nurse rolling it by doesn't stop, doesn't say anything; she doesn't even look our way. I barely even get a look at her. It's dark and her straight hair is black. She doesn't turn to us and doesn't come close to the cell. Jean sure as hell was alert though. I suppose now I know how she'll be receiving her note. It makes me sick thinking about it and waiting around.

Even when the nurse is gone, the thumping still feels far lower than it should be.

"Don't worry," she says and her tone steals my attention and she smiles grimly. "When it comes, I'll make it so fast you won't have time to wonder if what I'm given is the note, or another smoke." She says it so easily. Like it's a kindness and not a threat to instill uncertainty and fear.

Jean cracks her neck and then rolls over, facing me even though her eyes are closed. Time ticks by and still, I don't move. I don't know how much longer I can go without sleeping. My eyes are heavy and dry. They've never been this raw in my life. How could I possibly sleep though?

I could close my eyes, and never wake up again.

I don't know if she's feigning sleep or if she's really capable of dozing off right now. More time passes. Sleep threatens to take me and when I try to adjust my right leg, the idea of lying down and giving in seems so… alluring. As if my body could rest even if I stay awake.

I can't go to sleep, but I have to. Maybe I could scream and beg for them to let me out of here. I could tell the guards she's trying to kill me. Although she said if I did, she'd kill me regardless of whether or not she was given a note. If she's sleeping though, maybe she wouldn't hear.

With my hand over my eyes, I focus on breathing. I don't know what else I can do. I can't sleep, so I can only think about begging to be let out of here and risk calling her bluff. I hate feeling like a victim, but I've been backed into a corner with no way out.

Movement from the right, behind the bars, steals every ounce of focus I have left.

I recognize the guard, the one who was watching me when I was in holding. Walters. My gaze darts between him and Jean as he makes his way toward the cell. He's walking toward me silently, not yet in view for Jean. I could ask him for help. I could beg him even, but there's something about him, something that keeps me silent.

His eyes reach mine when I look back at him after noting that Jean really does look like she's asleep, and he holds them for only a moment before dropping to his knee right in front of our cell. From here I can see him clearly; Jean wouldn't be able to even if her eyes were open and she was waiting for him. He's opposite me and not her.

I question if he's the one who would give her the note and an animal inside of me screams in agony. He could have just killed me then. If he knew, why make me wait? There's a piece that doesn't fit, though. Walters lets me see him. He waited for Jean to be sleeping.

Again Walters looks up at me and I stare back, watching him place something just under the bars. He scoots it back, giving it a small quiet toss so it's closer to the toilet in the corner of the cell.

With a small nod, he rises and stalks off, back the way he came. Jean never would have seen him. Whatever he left there, it's meant for me.

My eyes turn back to Jean's closed ones. She didn't hear him, didn't see him either.

The tension that's been building in my stomach rises. It takes over my entire body until I feel like I'm trembling although I'm eerily still.

I watch her for too long, knowing I need to get to it first. I need to see what it is.

There's a feeling inside sometimes that urges you. It knows this moment will change everything.

The visceral reaction that takes hold when I slowly stand, giving Jean a tight smile as she peers at me through narrowed slits, is overwhelming.

The knots in my stomach nearly make me throw up. A cold sweat lines my skin and I pray the bitch can't see it.

"Just have to pee," I mutter and swallow thickly. *Please don't see. Please don't watch me.*

"Don't be nervous, sweetie," she says, giving me that pet name again but the spike of anger is nothing compared to the fear. This moment is decisive. I know it. Every part of me knows it. From the sweat on my skin to the very soul that'll leave me if Jean gets that package first.

My lips quiver as I huff and I try to play it off like I'm nervous about her watching me pee and nothing else. She watches me though, following me as I walk in the small space that separates our beds and stalk to the only toilet just feet from where she's lying.

My heart sputters. *Don't look down,* I pray. *Don't let her look to the floor.*

I'm still wearing my sneakers and in the few seconds it takes to get to where I'm headed, I debate on stepping on whatever it is in order to hide it. I don't know what's inside. I don't know if it'll make a noise that will clue her in. So I don't do it. I stand there, knowing it's by my feet and meet her gaze as my thumbs slip into the elastic waistband of the pants they gave me.

The beats are so fast in my chest, I feel faint.

"A little…" I barely get out the words, taking a long, unwanted blink. Now is not the time, but I can barely focus.

"Privacy?" Jean says and huffs a laugh and actually smiles. I can see the glimmer of her grin as she rolls back onto her side. "Make it fast," she orders.

I drop my pants quickly, just in case she looks and sit there, forcing a dribble of pee to leave me. It's only when I reach down, feeling my entire body turn to ice and grab the package with both hands that I'm able to release myself. I unwrap the package while I do and there's no note, not a damn thing but a sliver of metal. It's thin, very thin.

It looks almost like an arrowhead, with a very small handle that doesn't hurt to hold, but the edges of it are sharp. After wiping myself, I test its strength. Whatever metal it is, it's strong as hell.

A shiv. The package I was given, is a shiv.

They want me to kill her first. Seth? The Cross brothers? Someone aimed to help me. Or rather, to help me save myself.

Heat replaces the cold as I stand up, securing the piece in my palm from her sight. The wrapping is easily disposed of with the toilet paper and I stand on shaky legs, staring at her still form.

I was meant to kill her. I knew that the first moment she spoke. It's one thing to know. One thing to think about it. To daydream about bashing her head into the wall.

It's another entirely to do it.

It's like having an out-of-body experience; as though I'm only watching as I take the four strides. *One.* Tick. *Two.* My shoes are heavy. *Three.* That lightness is no longer there. *Four.* My body screams to do it. Adrenaline surges through my body. It's a kill or be killed situation.

I think it's the shadow of my body over her eyes that cues her to look at me. And that's exactly what she's doing when I bring the shiv to her throat with a single slash. The blood sprays down her body and I nearly do it again, but it's not necessary. I would have done it over and over to ensure she didn't get up from that bed ever again. But I don't have to. Once was enough.

Whatever word she was going to say doesn't escape.

The hate in her eyes vanishes and it's replaced with absolute shock, then terror.

She doesn't reach out for me. Instead she grabs her throat with both hands as if she could stop it. She tries to keep the blood in as it gushes out.

The puncture was deep. I'm a nurse. It was more than deep enough to do its job.

She's able to back away from the edge of the small bunk, her legs kicking out to push her into the corner. Her eyes are wide, her pupils dilated as she stares at me all the while.

I don't realize I'm crying until she goes still.

Relief is not something I feel. It's another feeling, although not guilt. Hopelessness maybe. It weighs me down as I reach forward to wipe off the handle of the shiv on her sheets, not disturbing the blood. Her hands have blood on them, but I feel like if she'd sliced her own throat, she would have dropped it before reaching for her throat out of instinct. Having no prints is better for forensics than having a bloody print that doesn't make sense. She wouldn't have tried to stop the bleeding and then reached for the shiv again.

It disturbs me on some level, I note as heat pricks down my skin, that I'm able to think clearly enough.

Until I realize I'm breathing again, my heart is rhythmic.

Fear of dying at her hands is gone. She made the first move. I made the last.

I wait until I rumple my own sheets, making sure I don't have any evidence of blood on me, before I scream, shrill and horrific. I hate myself and what I've become. This version of me who murders so easily. Anyone could do it, though. It didn't take strength or imagination. It only took being pushed. First by her, then a gentle push from Walters.

"Help!" I yell so loud it feels as if my throat is on fire. Sucking in air, I scream again. The lights shine brightly in the entire place. The groans and murmurs from other residents in the neighboring cells are barely heard. Someone tells me to shut up. Another inmate calls me a little bitch.

They don't know. It's only then that I realize I may really have gotten away with it. So long as no one saw.

"What happened here?" a gruff man asks and rips open the cell door, staring wide eyed between the dead girl and then me. At a version of how I truly feel, scared and huddled up in the corner of the bed, covering myself with the thin blanket as if it will save me. It's Guard B. The one who brought her in here.

"She killed herself," I say, letting my voice quiver and try to cry again. When I see her there and the pool of dark red blood that's soaked into the sheets, crying is easy. I don't like that I did it. There's not a damn thing about this that makes me feel anything but agony.

"Oh hell," Guard B mutters. I notice Walters standing just behind the opening to the cell just as Guard B speaks into a walkie-talkie attached to his shirt. He calls for a medic, as if a medic could help her now.

The guard who gave the gift of salvation, Walters, doesn't look at me. He doesn't say a word when the other man says into his speaker to check the security feeds after pronouncing Jean dead. My anxiety would be heightened if Walters had reacted in the least. He simply stands there, unfazed and waiting.

I'm stuck where I am, barely holding on to my sanity as everyone else moves around me. Everyone seems to shift about but no one tells me to move so I stay right where I am and just how I was before Jean was brought in here. It doesn't take long before they decide her death is obviously from a cut to the throat and that she can be moved.

Walters never leaves, but neither does Guard B, whose name is actually Bernard. I finally got a good look at his name tag. It was in between glances at Jean. She's dead. I really killed her.

I can't imagine what you're supposed to feel when you murder another person, but this doesn't feel adequate. I felt more remorse and more guilt when Cami was lying dead at my feet than I do now.

The squeaky metal of a gurney is what I focus on. Tears are too easy to come if I think about Cami. My knuckles are white as I grip the sheets.

"Get her out of here," Walters orders. He gestures for me to get up as the men leave the cell. "I'm taking her in for questioning," he says, addressing the first guard, the one who eyes me suspiciously, Mr. Bernard. The man doesn't protest. He doesn't say anything at all.

He knows. I can feel it in the way he looks at me. I think he knows a lot that goes on around here. He doesn't spend long looking at me, letting his gaze roam up and down my body, in a way I think will give me hives, before turning and leaving.

All of this, all of the moving chess pieces and the lives at stake—I don't want anything to do with it. If I could tell Bernard that, I would. I didn't want to do this. I *had* to.

I'm in far too deep and I didn't ask to be. I've only felt this way one other time. The night death lay on my hands as I cried on the floor. I feel like I'm back there on the other side of the country. I can't stop the visions of Cami and they bring fresh hot tears to my eyes as I stand there, waiting for Walters to stop patting me down.

I'm busy wiping them away, too busy to realize the cell is quiet and only the single guard is in there with me. The feeling of death slipping around me and gripping my ankles is one I haven't felt in so long. It's cold. Death is so cold. He may have given me my way out, but I still don't trust Walters. I don't trust anyone in here.

I stare up at Walters, wondering what would have happened if I'd stayed in California all those years ago. If I'd never run away. Would this have been inevitable? Another life dying in order to save mine… would it have only happened sooner if I'd never run?

"Don't worry about the tapes," the guard whispers although his hands are on his hips and the way he's towering over me is not at all comforting. I have to wipe my nose with my sleeve before I can breathe.

"What?" I say and blink, the constellation of tears in my eyelashes obscuring my view.

"You did good," he tells me and I do everything I can not to noticeably allow what I'm feeling to show on the outside. "I don't think anyone thought you'd kill her. It was just supposed to make you feel protected. But damn, you did good."

CHAPTER 8

Seth

Seven abrasions are scattered on my right hand and truth be told, I don't know where they're from. There's a large bruise on my wrist with a tinge to it that makes me aware it's not fresh. Not compared to the one I see on my jaw. That bruise came from the crash. I know that much.

I graze the freshest of the cuts with the rough callus on my thumb, letting the pain keep me awake. With all the shit that's gone down in the last forty-eight hours, I don't know what left which of the marks that cover my body. My tongue slips along the crack on the right side of my bottom lip. *Crash.* That one's from the crash too. I can identify some of them at least.

The door opens slowly with an ominous creak, and I wish it were anyone other than this prick. Walsh's back is to me as he silently closes the door. The soft click is the only indication that it's shut. I don't watch him, but I know from the noise that echoes in the small room that he's sitting across the metal table from me. I'm afraid of what I'll do to him if I look at him.

He's in the way. He's choosing to stand in the way of me seeing her. I know how this works; I've played these politics. He could have let me see her, could have put the two of us in a room together with no issues. He's choosing not to. That puts him on my list of people to fuck over the first chance I get.

"I need to see Laura," I say and my voice is hoarse as it fills the tense space between us.

The slap of paperwork that hits the table is greeted with the grinding of my back teeth. It's been hours since I've been arrested. Hours of her being alone and in harm's way. I haven't had a chance to talk to anyone I have on the inside. Not with this fucker hovering.

He needs to get off my dick.

"She was sitting there about..." Walsh pauses and takes in a deep breath, letting time slip by. "About twenty-four hours ago. No," he's quick to correct himself, sounding surer with the "no" than anything else I've heard from him so far. The chair legs beneath him grate on the concrete floor as he leans forward, resting his clasped hands in front of him. That's the only bit of him I dare to look at. "No, it's been almost two days actually since Laura's been brought in."

Forty-eight hours. Two days. A wave of pain hits me from behind my eyes, residual from God knows what and I pinch the bridge of my nose, my eyes closed.

"I'd like to see her," I say, trying to be polite and courteous. It's only a matter of getting out of this fucking room. The second I'm past this stage of questioning, my men will take me to her. They'll find a way. It doesn't matter how.

"A lot's happened." Cody's voice is tight. "She's had a rough few days, hasn't she?"

Sharp pangs of hate stab through me. Lifting my gaze to his, I bite out, "All the more reason I should see her." My throat tightens and anxiousness claws at the back of it. I don't like not knowing. It's the worst feeling in the world, not knowing what's happened.

It's silent for far too long and all I can do is think about her alone in here. In a fucking cell! *Why?* Because of me.

My chest pains are deep and brutal, like my rib cage is closing in on itself. Bracing my hand over my chest, I do my best to keep it all down. "I'll make it right," I say but my voice cracks and I hate myself. The sound of my words betrays me. I didn't mean to say them out loud. They weren't for Walsh. They're for Laura.

Everything was always for her.

How did it get so fucked? How did we get here?

One breath in, and my back straightens. All the heat suffocating me slowly subsides to the cold darkness that keeps me in control. "I'd like to see Laura."

"And I'd like an answer to any of my questions."

My lips part, then close again. He can't play both sides. I thought he'd decided, but maybe this is for show. Maybe there's someone else on the other side of that mirror and he has to be a fucking prick right now.

"You haven't told us anything. You've been mute since you were cuffed." Anger slices through his words. "I don't think you were trying to rob a bank. No one in here does. You deliberately crashed into the front entrance though, the footage shows that."

The rough skin on the pad of my thumb glides over a fresh cut on my other hand. I don't speak. I don't look at him.

"I think you just wanted to see her. Couldn't wait for visiting hours?" Walsh asks and his tone is so damn condescending.

My head lifts slowly until I meet him in the eyes. Dark circles lay under his tired icy gaze. Whatever fight he's forced into his words doesn't show in his expression in the least. I take him in slowly, calculating what's going on with him. His intentions, his motives.

"I want to see Laura and I want to get both of us out of here," I say, making my demand.

"I wanted you in here for something other than attempted bank robbery. For the murder of the men who broke into Laura's place." He's casual as he talks, slowly leaning back in his seat.

"Is that why you're keeping me in here? To get me to confess?" I practically hiss the words, low and full of venom.

"You won't. No man who'd let a woman take the fall—"

"I didn't let her do anything!" My fists land on the table, halting him in his place. The pressure of my jaw slamming shut to keep the thoughts at bay is too much. I swear I hear my teeth crack.

She never should have left me that night. If she'd stayed with me and never gone back to her apartment, none of this would have happened.

I never should have told her.

That's where we went wrong. I told her the ugly truth and she left. She always wanted to leave. Laura's not the kind of girl who stays, but damn I need her to. I need her back.

Everything slips back into place; my mask, my self-control. All I have to do is get her back. There's no more bad shit she doesn't know about. We'll be fine. I'll help her. I'll be her prince who saves her from this hell and she'll love me again. She can forgive me. She has to. Either that, or I'll lie. I say I don't know what she's talking about. I'll tell her I must've been drunk off my ass to come up with a lie like that. I'll do whatever I have to in order to get her back. What's done is done, but now we move forward. There's no other choice. It's a slow ease that overcomes my body. I flex my hand before looking back into Walsh's gaze. It's going to be all right. I can keep this from happening again. This is the worst of it. I know it is. It can't get worse than this.

"I'd like her out of here," I add, staring him in the eyes, "since we both know she didn't do anything wrong."

"She's being charged with murder."

"Is that what you told them?" I can't keep the anger down. "You're really going to hurt her to get to me?"

His eyes are piercing, his expression merciless. "I don't want either of you in here," he barely speaks. It's nearly impossible for me to hear and his lips don't move. I almost think I imagined it.

The next time he speaks, it's clear and spoken with intention. "You want to see her?"

The lack of trust separates us. It'll never be there. Ever.

"You should really see her," Cody adds when I don't answer. The air in the room changes. It's colder, deadlier.

"Then take me to her," I demand, but my power is limited on this side of the interrogation room.

"I have people to talk to," he says and rises from his seat as I curse under my breath, hating him and hating all of this. The scratch of metal is searing. A beep precedes the door opening and with his back to me once again he tells me, "This isn't how I thought things were going to happen."

CHAPTER 9

Laura

WALTERS SHUT UP REAL QUICK THE SECOND BERNARD CAME BACK to the cell. I don't know anything more than I wasn't supposed to kill Jean. He didn't give me that shiv to kill her and that knowledge makes me sick. But what other option did I have?

With no one here and my imagination running away with itself, I feel like I'm drowning.

If Marcus put out a hit on me, I'm dead. Maybe I got Jean first, but she gave me the upper hand by telling me. Sitting here all alone and not knowing a damn thing… I'm nothing but haunted and scared.

This room is larger. Bigger and without a mirror. It still seems like an interrogation room though even if I don't see any cameras at all. Wrapping my arms around myself, I sit back down in the lone chair, glancing at the small bed on the other side. It's not like a holding cell, because there's a solid door with a small window at eye height.

I don't know what this room is, but the bed, the lack of cameras, the unknown… it's fucking terrifying. All I can do is glance from the bed, back to the door, praying whoever comes through it will tell me something, *anything*, about what's going on.

I just want to get out of here. I can't take it. I don't like who I've become in here.

How long did it take for me to lose it? To lose the morality Nurse Roth has every day at work.

I search the walls for an answer to my rhetorical question and then belatedly remember there's not even a clock in here. Nothing at all to indicate the time. A humorless huff leaves me, and I close my eyes with it. Sleep is so tempting, and the bed is so close.

I can't sleep without knowing. There's a vent on the other side of the room that clicks on and off, keeping the room temperate. It's gone off six times now. That's the only way I've managed to keep track of time.

With my arms wrapped around my shoulders, I rock gently, trying to calm myself down. I haven't gotten my medicine yet. The set of four pills I have to take daily. I have faith, albeit a small bit of faith, that they'll provide them once another twenty-four hours have gone by. I can track time that way. I haven't slept, so I don't know how close I am to that time frame. Four pills once in the morning. I should be getting them soon, shouldn't I?

A shudder runs through my body, followed by a wave of nervous heat. With my eyes closed but my head leaning back, I keep rocking and pray that this will end. *Please let this be the worst of it.*

My eyes are too itchy, too worn out to cry anymore. I'm at the lowest low I could possibly be. *Please make it stop.* When I lick my dry lips, tasting the residue of salt from former tears, a loud beep warns me that God may have heard my prayers.

Does he find me worthy though? I don't dare to truly consider the question, because I'm certain the answer is quite firmly no.

A deep inhale doesn't settle my racing pulse as the heavy door, this one metal and most likely once a shiny silver, but now worn to a dull gray, opens with a heave and a groan.

"I'll tell you when," a voice says softly. The door stays open and a mumbled conversation is blocked by it, as is my view of the person belonging to that voice.

Seth. *Please, God,* I think and my lip quivers with a raw mix of hope and fear. I know it's his voice.

I'm not in control of my body when the door finally shuts with a resounding click and he becomes my sole focus. My heart cracks and splinters at the sight of him. The space between us vanishes and it's all my doing. He's frozen where he is, not moving, not reacting, simply watching me.

"Oh my God," I say and I can't help how both my expression and voice crumple. With a shaky hand over my mouth and the other on his jaw, I ask, "What happened?"

My gaze roams over his face. His stubble is so long it's scratchy and I've never seen such dark circles resting beneath his eyes before. "Have you even slept?" I ask before he can answer. My thumb brushes along a bruise as I murmur, "What did you do?" I can't stop touching him or asking him questions without even granting him a moment to answer.

There's a cut on his lip and I touch that too, gently, but I imagine it still stings. I have to hold my own hand, snatching it in my other and taking a step back. He looks like he's been thrown over the edge of a rocky cliff and managed to survive but hasn't slept in weeks.

I don't bother asking about the gunshot. Gripping the edge of his shirt, I pull it up, taking in the stitches and feeling a slight sense of respite at the sight.

He's alive. He's been taken care of, but… "What happened?"

I'm stricken, taking in every inch of him and not knowing a damn thing.

His warmth envelops me first. It's everywhere at once. Every inch of my skin is affected by his embrace. I don't move, afraid he'll move in response. It feels so good to be held. It feels like heaven to be safe in his arms. I bury my head in his chest when he shushes me. Shushes me! But still, his voice is the most comforting thing I've had in what feels like years.

My mind rewinds the days, stopping at the moment I saw him drunk and disgraced in his house. I have to close my eyes tight, ignoring the reminder of where that led. I can't. I can't not be held by him right now.

I know somewhere inside of me I hate him. I hate what he's done. The fact that he helped me mourn… At the thought I have to wipe my eyes and as I raise my arm, Seth creeps backward, but I'm quick to fist his shirt in my hand and shove my body against his. It's not a conscious move, it's like everything else that I've done since I've set foot in this place: it's an act to survive.

I know I hate him or at least what he did, but I need him. I selfishly need him right now. Is it possible to love someone, or at least crave to be loved by them while also hating them?

Simultaneously? I don't know that it is because it's only one way for me. Like the teeter-totter of a child's seesaw, I go from one to the other. Back and forth. But never both at once.

As my breath shakes and my shoulders press into his hard chest, I only love him right now. It kills me to see him hurt, and the idea of leaving this room without him destroys me.

At the thought, my eyes widen and I pull my head back so I can look him in the eyes. My hot face feels the instant chill of the air as I search his blue gaze for some sign of what's happening.

He still doesn't speak.

"Please, say something."

"The guard just told me something," he says and his voice is raw and pained.

Shattered is what I feel. There is zero doubt that any other word could describe it better. Broken and in disarray, all I can do is wait. His throat tightens when he swallows, his eyes holding nothing but regret in them. I'm fucked. That's all I can think. They have good evidence on the murder in my apartment or hell, the murder in my cell. Fuck! Fuck! How did this happen? I just want to scream.

My gaze falls as he tells me, "They told me…" he trails off and doesn't finish.

My hand is still wrapped around his shirt.

Something awful, something dreadful. If I could will myself to release him and back away, I would. But I can't. I physically can't. I'd rather be stuck here, a shattered girl unable to hate a man who's hurt me more than he'll ever know because I desperately need him to love me right now… yet all he bears for me is more bad news. Something to drag me farther into this hell.

"They told me you that you killed someone. I'm so fucking sorry, Laura. I don't know how you could ever forgive me." My eyes rise slowly to meet his.

Thump, my heart skitters as Seth attempts to keep his expression schooled, not letting the sorrow take over although it's so close to doing just that already.

It takes me a long moment to realize he's apologizing and that this is about Walters and Jean.

"It's about Jean?" I question him, finding a bit of hope. It loosens my grip on him and I'm damn quick to tighten it the moment I'm aware of it. "That look in your eyes and what the guards told you? They know? Who knows? What did they say?" The series of breakneck questions is nothing at all like the initial ones. I rise up, not letting go of him and pulling myself closer to him as his expression morphs to something else entirely.

"Only the men who need to know, know. Everyone else is convinced its suicide. Or they better be, for their own good. Are you okay?"

He searches my expression, probably finding a hint of relief.

"I'm fine. And what about you?" I say and swallow, trying to calm myself. His hand covers my fisted one and I watch as his thumb grazes my skin. "What happened to you?" I whisper.

"Not here," he answers in a single breath then looks behind him at the window of the heavy metal door. "Soon though," he tells me and pulls my hand from his shirt, lifting my knuckles to his lips and kissing them.

The revolving door of emotions is endless.

"What else did they tell you?" I find myself crossing my arms over my chest, closer to my heart. If he has eyes and ears in this place, does he know… I try to swallow but it hurts. With everything that's happened, I forgot for a small moment. I forgot about my heart giving up on me.

I watch every detail of Seth's face. I see the confusion in the twitch of his brow. "Are you okay? What else happened?" he bites out, coming closer to me and glancing at the window. "Did anyone do anything at all to you?" The way he asks the question, with the pain so evident, I'll never be able to look at him and hate him.

This man would do anything for me. I know he would. I've always known that though.

"No," I say and ease his worry. "No one did anything."

"I never should have…" Seth trails off and shakes his head, then wraps his arms around my waist. He pulls me in closer and I let him. I need it more than anything.

"You forgive me?" he questions, and his gaze pierces through me. Intense, raw, needy.

"Yes," I answer and I don't even know what for.

"Good," he says then breathes in deeply, still holding my hand to his lips and the warm breath sends a shudder to run down my arm and over my shoulder. He kisses each knuckle again and although I have question after question, I'm quietly waiting for more.

I get nothing, but at the same time, it's everything. He holds me for the longest time and it's the safest I've felt in God knows how long. Until he speaks.

"None of this should have happened," he tells me and I hear him swallow, my cheek pressed against his chest. "You and I will work. We will be okay, but I need to punish you for running."

My arm yanks back in an attempt to rip my hand away, but Seth's grip is unyielding. So firm it nearly hurts. Seething, I aim to bite back some response that involves the phrase *fuck you* or maybe *you're out of your damn mind*, but the heat and intensity coming off of Seth in waves silences me.

He means it. He's dead set on whatever it is he's concocted in his head. My heart flips and pauses like it does when he's around. As if the medicine has run its course and I need another dose.

The whirlwind of what my life is pauses when I look back into Seth's gaze.

Did they tell him about my heart? I find myself staring at the small tinted window as if it has answers for me. *Did they tell him everything? Or just about Jean?*

He would have said something. He would have. I know he would have brought it up if he knew.

He goes on about how I run. I can barely focus on his words, because all I can think about is my heart and how Seth will react when he finds out.

I can only stare into his beautiful eyes, listening to his voice, knowing he's here in front of me, here to keep me safe. I don't think they told him. I don't think he knows. I don't want him to. I'd rather he not have that to weigh him down like it does me. I hate this, the uncertainty. The pressure. Everything is falling to pieces but I need to be strong for the time I have left.

"Babygirl, you're mine. You know that, don't you?"

I'm nodding my head before I'm even aware of it.

"We're going to be fine, but you need to have your ass blistered red for running."

How can he bring it up so easily? I ran because of what he confessed and here he is, talking about it in this way. As if all of this is my fault. My heart ticks erratically again and I find it hard to care about it. I need him. I need Seth to hold me right now.

"Don't cry." Seth's voice is gentle but firm. He takes a half step closer to me so there's no space between us. "I can't let this happen again," he tells me.

I didn't even know I was crying. I hate how easily I cry now. Am I broken entirely? This is what it's like to be ruined.

"It won't happen again," I tell him in a whisper.

Finally releasing my hand, he wraps both of his arms around me and I let myself fall forward. *None of it matters.* He rocks me and I pretend not to feel the weight of my reality.

"I won't let anything happen to you," Seth promises me, kissing my hair. "You'll be out of here soon and then you'll stay with me. You're not allowed to leave me again."

His voice is what brings back tears to my eyes. These fucking tears. All I've done is cry. I should be through with them by now. But he's so sure, so certain of himself that I'll never leave him again. I can hear it in his tone and how much determination and hope are present there. If only he keeps me by his side, everything will be fine. As if he's capable of that. He doesn't know my heart is withered and frail. He doesn't know it can't last.

I wish I'd never loved him, so he'd never know the loss.

My hot tears soak into his shirt and I ignore them. He hushes me and rocks me, and finally he bends down to kiss me.

His kiss is everything I need; comforting but demanding, strong and yet loving. I pour everything I have into it, deepening it, parting my lips and feeling my body mold to his.

A deep, rough groan rumbles his chest and that only makes me crave more. More of him while I can have it. More of this while I'm able.

But Seth denies me, grabbing my small hands in his and lifting his head to breathe with his eyes closed.

"I have to punish you. Whether you hate me or not." I can't answer and the silence forces him to look at me. "You can hate me while I punish you, but you're not leaving me. Ever."

Ever.

A younger version of me, an unknowing one, would fall in love with that word. We don't get to decide how long our forever lasts, though. It's naïve to think we can.

"Seth, I'm not okay," I whisper and wish I could take it back. He can't know. I don't know why I said it.

A small bit of relief overcomes me when he answers, "I know."

"I'm losing myself," I say and grant him a small truth and rewind again. Rewind to a moment I felt the distance between who I thought I was and who I really am.

"I know," he repeats with nothing but sympathy.

"I… killed someone." I whisper the rugged confession as if he's not already aware.

"But you're here, with me. I won't let them take you away." I'm torn and twisted.

"They're going to come for me and they're going—"

"To either put you back in a cell with me, or to release us both. I made sure of it."

CHAPTER 10

Seth

SHE'S ALWAYS LOOKED THIS BEAUTIFUL BUT THE THOUGHT OF LOSING HER makes her skin look softer, more delicate. She's fragile beneath me.

Breathing in deep, the smell of her hair lingers in my lungs. She's okay. She's here in my arms. She's letting me hold her. I have to remind myself of the three bits of my reality. They're the only things that matter right now. Her skin touching mine, her trusting me, relying on me.

Thank fuck. I can fix this. I can make it all better.

I can't believe she killed that woman, though. Shock doesn't describe my reaction at all when I was informed.

I fucking hate myself for not being there. Walters said they didn't want to let on that they knew about the hit on Laura and they knew that Jean was in there to kill her. Whoever hired Jean Cinders would have known if they'd switched Laura's cell. So instead Jase and Carter waited for the note that was supposed to be coming. The men I trusted most gave that order. To wait and watch.

She isn't bait, though. My girl isn't bait and he should've known better than to let her sit there with that hitman. I might hate myself but I hate Jase and Carter too. They risked her life by allowing her to stay in that cell. They knew she was there and in danger, and they just let her sit there. How could they do that? If it'd been Bethany or Aria, that woman never would have been in that cell. Not for a second.

Walters said they were told to wait, to sit on it and wait for the next move.

In the meantime, Jase wanted to show Laura that she was protected and safe. But by giving her a fucking weapon? None of these people know Laura. She doesn't trust easily and when she's scared, she'll do anything to survive. He's a fucking idiot and I'll never trust him again with her. Never.

Kissing her temple, I smooth down her hair. She's sweet and loving, but my God if you try to hurt her, she'll hurt you first swift and severe. I should be grateful though, because she hasn't turned that venom on me yet. Even though I deserve it.

"Everything will be fine," I promise her and I mean every bit of it. "I'll make damn sure of it."

"I love you," she tells me and presses her forehead into my chest when she starts to cry again, turning her head down as if I won't be able to see. God, to hear her tell me that again. I'm not worthy. I kiss her hair again and again, wanting to say it back but refusing to give her those words for the first time in this room.

She has to know I love her more than anything. And I'll tell her just that, the moment we're back home where we belong.

Clinging to me, she rocks her body and I can feel how heavy she becomes as sleep attempts to pull her under.

I glance at the room for the first time. It's meant for conjugal visits. She shouldn't have to be in this position at all, let alone here. Looking at the bed, I hate myself for fucking up so badly that she's in this room at all.

"I hate these clothes on you." The subconscious thought leaves me before I realize I've spoken the words aloud.

"Orange isn't my color." She whispers the small joke back to me. Sleep drenches it but the hint of the girl I knew long ago is still there.

I can't close my eyes without seeing her alone in a cell, ready to kill in order to survive. Even as I stare at the back wall, the cinder blocks play the scene for me as I imagine how it went down. I know hate and I know love.

I hate myself but I love her.

It's as simple as that.

"You should lie down and sleep," I say, deciding not to tell her we may be here, in this room, until tomorrow. I don't know how long it'll take for my men to do my bidding and push the issue of keeping Laura in here when she has a solid self-defense argument. No judge should have allowed it and the lawyers are working on having it overruled. My one call went to Jase and he filled me in. It could be hours to have the initial ruling overturned. Or it could be days, depending on how easily the judge can be convinced. He isn't one we have in our back pocket.

"Come with me." With her lips grazing my shirt, Laura peers up at me, begging me, "Please."

It doesn't escape my notice that she hasn't let go of me since I've walked in here. She tried once at the thought of being punished for running away.

I should tell her what it does to me to have her want me like she does. Just as I should carry out the punishment. If I'm harder with her, more stern, she'll be safe. She'll see; it'll be for the good of us both. It's what we need.

"We just need to get out of here," I speak without thinking, a tired sigh escaping with it. With my hand tangled in her hair, I kiss her forehead at the same time that she kisses the dip in my throat.

A spike of want runs rampant inside of me. I don't know what I anticipated from her, probably another punch to the face, but I sure as hell didn't expect her affection.

"Please come lie down with me," she begs again in a whisper and with her doe eyes looking up at me, I can't say no.

"All right." Giving in, I walk her hand in hand to the small bed. The bed creaks and shifts as I lie down, keeping my upper half propped up and my eyes on the door. She crawls in just how she used to, and lays her head on my chest, searching for a comfortable position. Years of this and she always settles on my bicep, but starts on my chest.

"This takes me back," I comment.

"What?" she questions sleepily and looks at me through her thick lashes. I have to smile down at her, even if it is a sad one because comparing what we had before to what we have now only makes me feel regret.

"Nothing, just this bed is so small… like the one at your grandmother's house."

Her wide eyes go soft blue for a moment, and she gives me the same smile in return before she sinks back down. The kind of smile that doesn't reach your eyes. I take my time pulling the blanket around her, tucking her in and then settle back against the wall.

"Sleep." I give her the command when her small fingers trace every little cut on my hand rather than being still.

"Did they tell you what happened in the holding cell?"

"Your panic attack?"

She stares up at me, her lips parted slightly like a word is caught there. "Were you faking it?" I tease her, downplaying it so she doesn't freak out. I can't blame her. Out of all the things to be, she shouldn't be embarrassed about it, and that's a bit how she looks. I nudge my shoulder, forcing her to roll toward me and her small hand splays against my chest to catch herself. "I was going to tell the guys there's no way you were faking it, you've never been good at faking it."

My crude joke gets the smallest hint of a laugh from her. It's short but it brings a genuine smile to her lips. "You'll be all right," I promise her. "We'll get out of here and I'll keep you safe."

She doesn't protest what I say and I pray that it means she's let go of what I told her about her father. At least for the moment. I'll tell her everything if she wants. If she wants to ignore it, forget it, deny it, I'll let that happen too. Whatever I have to do to keep her.

It takes me a long moment as I'm staring at the knob of the door, trying not to replay that scene from all those years ago, to realize she's crying.

"So many tears," I tease her gently, but lean down to wipe the tears from her left eye. The tears from her right are stolen by my shirt.

"I just want to be safe with you," she whispers and then sniffs. She always looks pissed off rather than hurt when she cries. She doesn't now, though.

"You are safe with me," I say and I can't hide the despair in my tone at the thought that she doesn't feel safe with me. "You want to go when we get out of here?" I search for anything, grasping for a thread to hold on to and all I can think is that she never wanted this life. If I'd left eight years ago, given it all up, none of this would have happened. "We can go wherever you want. We can leave. As long as we're together."

Her sobs turn harder and she crawls onto my lap, no longer satisfied with only having her cheek on my chest. Her small form curls up as she rests her head in the crook of my neck. Wrapping both of my arms around her, I hold her tighter, not remembering a time she's been like this. She's so broken. My poor girl.

"I'm sorry," I whisper into her hair, stroking her back, doing everything I can to love her. "We're going to be fine." My throat is tight with emotion when I promise her, "If you want to get out of here and leave, I promise I'll leave. I'll do it for you."

She doesn't respond, other than to cry harder. I shush her, I kiss her, I don't know what else to do. I wish I'd just left with her eight years ago. I wish we had a different life together.

"Let it out, Babygirl." Still rocking her, I watch the door and let her fall apart. I'll be here for her always. She'll see. I mean it and when she sees that, she'll stay with me. I just can't lose her again.

She doesn't respond to the idea of us leaving and part of me thinks it's because she doubts I'll do it. "I'll do anything to keep you," I whisper when her sobs quiet.

She doesn't respond to that either. She sits up all on her own, her ass still in my lap and avoids eye contact. It's not uncommon for her to do that after a cry. With her nose red and her cheeks only slightly less so, she picks up the sheet and wipes her eyes.

"I'm sorry." That's the first thing she says.

"Nothing to be sorry about," I say, pressing my hand to her cheek and she leans into my touch. It's the first bit of hope I have when she closes her eyes and puts both her hands over mine. Her bottom lip trembles again and she asks, "Can I ask you, please, to hold me until the end?"

"To the very end," I promise her and she tries her damnedest not to cry again. Her eyes stay closed and I have to pull her in close because she sits there, not moving, not saying anything. "I promise you, it's going to be all right. Better than. I promise, I'll fix it all."

Time passes, a lot of it, before she tells me, "I know you will." It's only a gentle whisper until sleep takes her away from me.

I can't breathe. I know I'm able to, but I can't breathe. Clinging to Seth, I can't do anything but hold him closer and try to get rid of the vision in front of my eyes. It was a nightmare but then I woke up here. It really happened.

I killed her.

My eyes burn and I heave in a breath.

"Laura, it's okay. It's okay." Seth's trying to soothe me. He's doing everything he can, but the nightmare felt so real. I woke up only to remember it happened. It happened.

Slowly, I can move, although I'm trembling. "I need it to go away," I speak into his chest. Seth smells like home. He doesn't smell like here. If only I'd been sleeping closer…

I inch myself onto his lap. I don't want to touch any of the bed, only him.

Make it go away. Erase all of it. I want it all gone.

"Hey, hey, you okay?" he says. His voice is a balm, but his touch is salvation.

"Just hold me," I beg him, finally coming down from the terror. With his arms wrapped around me as I'm cradled in his lap, I lift up my head and tell him, "No, no, just kiss me."

Crashing my lips to him, I refuse to feel anything but him. He'll take me away from here. He'll save me. I know he will. His lips are hot, my kiss hungry.

At first he tries to pull back, although his lips have already softened and molded to mine, teasing me.

"Laura—" he starts, in almost a warning tone.

"Please," I say, cutting him off. "Please, Seth. Please kiss me." I am as desperate and pathetic as I sound. I'm so very aware of it.

The room isn't dark or small but either way, it feels like it's closing in on me. "I need you," I breathe with my eyes closed. He can take me away from here. He can make me feel like it's all going to be all right. He's done it so many times before.

All of my darkest moments are only blips, only small dips in a timeline because he was there showing me where to go, leading me away. He can do it all with a kiss.

"Kiss me," I tell him, although it comes out as if I'm begging. "I'll do anything for you to kiss me right now." I'm slow to open my eyes, my heart steady as my hands move up to his neck. His muscles ripple under my touch as he leans in with me, nipping my bottom lip then sucking it before finally kissing me.

Gratitude swarms with desire, the two swirling deep in my belly. His smell, his touch, his kiss. I want it all surrounding me, protecting me and making it all go away.

Neither of us breathe as we kiss and in the moment of passion, we break away, gasping for air as his hands roam down my body. "Please," I beg him.

My legs part for him, straddling him already although we're both clothed. "Laura." My name is both a warning and the only word Seth speaks.

I say please, with longing.

He says Laura, with a torturous tone.

As he lays me on my back, I keep his lips to mine, parting my own and licking along the seam of his until he parts them, deepening the kiss and melding our mouths together.

The feel of his length pressing against my leg is all I need to moan.

He doesn't make a move to undress either of us, so I do it. Ignoring his protests and stroking him before he can tell me not to.

I open my eyes to see his head arched back, his deep groan of pleasure filling the space. He towers over me with all this power, and with a single touch, I know he wants me. I know he'll do everything he can to make sure I feel the same way I make him feel.

A faint beat flickers in my chest and I love it. I love that he makes me feel all of this. "I want you," I beg him as my hand moves to his velvety head.

I already know I'm ready for him when his heated gaze drops to meet mine. Both of our lips are parted, our breathing heavy. Both of us in need.

I shimmy out of my pants, dropping them to the side of the small bed, all the while keeping my eyes on Seth. He doesn't move, his hands fisted and digging into the mattress on either side of my head. His shirt still on, but his pants are pushed down to his knees.

If someone were to walk in on us in this moment, they'd get a sight of his fine ass. And the very thought of it makes me smile. It's a small smile, but it shows.

I think that's what does it, that and the last *please* I have to give him, for Seth to lower his body down to mine.

He props up one of my legs with the crook of his arm, spreading and angling me. His lips drop to mine at the same time that he enters me. The motion is swift and harsh. The act tears a scream from my throat, but he catches it. Staying deep inside of me, Seth whispers, "You will be quiet."

It's a statement that makes my heart pound with desire.

"I will." The whisper is lost in his kiss as he moves at a slower pace, each stroke deep before pulling out nearly all the way. Every time he moves backward, I pray for him to come back. Each thrust forward is nearly too much though, stinging my eyes with tears as my nails dig into his back and my head thrashes.

It's torturously sweet and slow. My pleasure builds, taking its time and feeling like the highest of highs before crashing down. I can't kiss him when I do. Tears leak from my eyes while the convulsion of the strongest orgasm I've ever had paralyzes my body and I bite down on his shoulder to keep from screaming out.

Seth

The knock at the door is followed by it opening, only a couple of inches. Laura is sound asleep on my shoulder and even though my arm is fucking numb, I haven't moved.

Carefully, I maneuver my way out from under her, hating that I have to leave her at all. I'm afraid if I leave, she'll remember why she left. Not that she can go anywhere in here, but she could realize she doesn't want me. I can't let that happen. All of this is too good to be true and I'm waiting for the other shoe to drop.

Staring down at her, I make sure she's asleep. Her readjusting and inhaling deeply is followed by the smallest of hums and not a stir afterward.

On the short walk to the door I shake out my arm, trying to bring it back to life. I'm tired as all hell. My eyes feel it, my body feels it, and all I want is to fall asleep with Laura in my own bed.

When I pull open the door wider, I catch sight of Walters first and I'm concerned by the expression he gives me until he nods his head behind him, at fucking Cody Walsh.

My gaze moves back to Walters. Walsh isn't on our payroll and whatever truce that was between us is long gone as far I'm concerned. My jaw hardens, and I play out every way this can go in my mind.

Before I can say a word, Walsh speaks up. "We're letting you both go."

His eyes don't look past me but even still, I shut the door to hide the sight of Laura sleeping from him and speak quietly. "Is that right?"

"The DA came to the decision. We don't have enough to charge either of you."

"And the cases?" I ask Walsh but look back at Walters, nodding and dismissing him.

"Yours is closed. Hers is still open."

I don't respond, pissed off and knowing that I need the Cross brothers to cover my ass in that case. I hate them for leaving her in that cell. It needs to go away in an instant, though, and they have far more pull than I do. I haven't forgotten that I promised her I'd leave, and I will. The second she says the word, we'll go wherever she wants. I don't know what that means for me and Jase. I know I'll lose her again if I don't, though. I'm willing to do anything. Anything and everything.

Walsh speaks when I don't say anything. "Passing out at the wheel is your defense, in case you didn't know." The humor isn't lost on me, but I don't show a hint of it to him.

I can't stand the sight of Walsh after he kept me in that room for as long as he did. I could have been with Laura sooner; I could have stopped the bullshit that was going on behind the scenes in her cell if he hadn't kept me in that damn interrogation room.

As far as I'm concerned, Walsh can go fuck himself.

"And self-defense against a dirty cop is hers."

I know the lawyer will tell me what he's talking about, but lawyers only know so much. "Care to elaborate?" I ask, needing to know the intel on the cop involved in her case.

"He had no reason to be there, or to be with the other men. He was undercover, but not on a case that involved them."

I nod, peeking back at Laura for only a moment and ensuring she's still passed out.

"Thank you." He earns a single point of gratitude for giving me that information. He can still go fuck himself, though.

"I wasn't going to let her go down for your mistake." Walsh's voice is harsh and my grip on the doorframe turns white knuckled. "I didn't know how close you two were until last week. I looked up everything between you two, and I think I have a good idea of what went down."

The guilt is there and I know he's right, but I don't like him. I'll never like him.

He must know exactly what I'm thinking from my glare because he tells me, "We don't have to be on the same side, but you don't know the shit I had to pull to get you both out of here."

Jase said it could take days to get to the judge and this is faster than I thought it'd be, but I doubt Walsh's honesty.

"That judge would have never turned. Judge Lainson wants the Cross brothers and he knows you and her are a way to get in."

"So you convinced him that the cases were too weak to hold up in court?" I ask, still not believing what he's telling me. He could simply be taking the credit.

"No, I didn't. I had the DA get involved and told him about an incident with Lainson. All of his cases have been handed over."

"An incident?"

"It doesn't involve you. What matters is that your case was given to a different judge because of it. A judge who happens to be on your payroll."

I'm silent, searching his gaze for honesty and that's exactly what I find.

Walsh looks over his shoulder, down the deserted hall and a look of shame is barely registered on his face. "I did what I had to do. You don't have to like me; I don't have to like you either. But I'm very aware that you and the brothers are the fastest way for me to get what I want." He looks past me, not able to see much at all in the room and then meets my gaze. "Get her, and get out. I'll get Walters for you since you seem to have a preference."

He doesn't fail to remind me, "Remember this, King. You owe me."

I only nod in agreement. That I do. For the first time since I met this asshole, I'm grateful for him.

"As a show of good faith," he says and looks as if he's debating something but decides to say it, "the evidence I have on you and Jase, it's in the mail."

"You have backups." It's not a question. Any smart man would.

"Had," he corrects. "I don't think you realize what he did to me.

All I want is Marcus. None of this matters and I'm willing to risk a lot to ensure Marcus and I meet sooner, rather than later."

"Why do you want Marcus so much?" I have to ask. He's gone out of his way to help me… all for Marcus?

His lips set in a straight line and he stares at me for a moment. "A while ago, he let things happen to a woman I cared about. He knew she was at risk, and he allowed them anyway." The last bit morphs into a harshly spoken whisper. He nods, staring at the crack in the door rather than at me. "She forgave him because he saved her from the end. But he was never held accountable. He believes every action has a consequence. He needs to have his. She forgave him, but I didn't."

CHAPTER 11

Laura

"YOU'RE ON THE DA'S WATCH LIST. STAY HERE. STAY LOW. THAT'S my professional advice." The lawyer is a no-nonsense man. In a sharp suit and with even sharper deep brown eyes, he's laid out everything for Seth and me.

"I understand." Seth's response is professional even though he's dressed in plaid flannel pants and a white t-shirt, both of which he slept in, and his lower right jaw is still bruised. The two of them are at complete odds in appearance, but one hundred percent in agreement on what happened.

I was meant to be leverage to get an in for the judge to take down the Cross brothers. They didn't care about the cop. This wasn't the first time the cop cut through red tape and was caught doing things he shouldn't have been. They knew. They withheld information in order to charge me.

My mind has wandered most of the meeting. It's late and I'm still tired. I don't think I slept for very long in that room with Seth. I've never been one to be happily woken up from sleep but hearing Seth tell me softly that we could leave? My eyes jolted open at that and I got my ass moving, still half asleep, just to get out of there.

"Always a pleasure," Seth says and the two men stand, the lawyer giving a polite laugh to the joke. They're shaking hands by the time I stand up and I reach out my own. Mr. Grayson's hair is swept back on the top and short on the sides. He has a look to him that's nothing but clean cut. He even apologized to me when he used profanity.

I don't know how he got involved with the Cross brothers and Seth, but I'm grateful for him and his insight. There's no way the case will stay open. He's sure of it.

Seth's arm wraps around my lower back as he walks the lawyer to the door, smiling while the lawyer insists that I'll be fine now that the investigation regarding the cop truly has no legs to stand on. It seems easy enough, case closed, but from the look in Seth's eye, the way the smile on his face is only polite like the lawyer's laugh, he's hiding something. And the second the door closes, I turn in his embrace, take a step back and question him.

"Why is he saying it's over and done, yet you're acting like it's not?"

Seth's jaw is lined with a rough coat of stubble. It's dark and combined with the bruise, his charming look is gone. He's rough and deadly but even still, the smirk he gives me and the gentle peck he places on my lips make him nothing but the man I remember him to be.

I'm a hair's breadth away from laying into him for not answering me, but he does. Honestly, and it makes a part of me wish he had lied. "Because it's not over."

"Legally—"

"Legally, we have nothing to worry about," he agrees with me, cutting me off and using his other arm to pull me into him. As if this one will be more effective than the last. And truthfully, I don't want to fight him. I don't want to leave his hold so long as he's giving me what I need. Right now, that's information.

"The guy I killed wasn't only a crooked cop. I think he–and the rest of them—worked for Marcus and I think whatever they started, isn't over."

"The mention of that name…" I trail off as chills flow from the base of my skull down my spine. The name elicits fear because it comes from years of whispers and authority.

"He's only a man."

"Why though? Why would Marcus want anything to do with me?" It doesn't take more than a second of staring up at Seth to know that he's the reason why. I am only a pawn. "What did you do?"

"I'm not sure it's him. When I know, I'll tell you."

It's silent as we move out of the foyer but then I remember something.

"Delilah wrote a lot of things in her books; some were about cops. She was a lawyer, you know. She knew things." I wish I were rested and had a better memory. I can't for the life of me recall a single name or anything specific about the men Marcus 'worked with.' "Maybe something useful is in her notebooks."

"Declan's looking," is all Seth responds but it's enough to ease my worry… some.

"You really think it was Marcus?" I question him. There was never a time in my life where I thought, *I'm going to be on the end of that man's wrath.* I never even wanted to see him. I wanted to pretend he was only a myth. Seth is right though; Marcus is only a man.

He's one I'm terrified of, though. And now he has men working for him. Which is the first I've ever heard of this.

"I don't know," Seth answers me grimly, taking his time to sit on the couch and instead of retaking my seat on the chair where I was during the briefing, I settle down next to him. I can't explain it, but right now I have to be touching Seth.

It feels too lonely, too cold when he's not right there. Not only that, but I'm still scared. I know I don't have to be. I'm safe here, but it's easier to not be scared when someone's holding your hand.

Just as Seth is holding mine now. He lifts my hand in his and stares at it when he talks. "I'm going to lay low but do some digging. I want you to stay here."

"I have work."

"I know, and you'll be safe there. Jase is sending some guys to watch the place."

I peek up past the living room windows and note the lights from a quarter mile outside on the edge of Seth's property. "Like he has guys watching out there."

"Yeah, they're on watch right now. Everything is safe and protected as long as you're here, at the Cross estate or at work." His steely blues hit me hard when he tells me, "If you go anywhere else, tell me. They'll follow you and keep you safe. That way I can work, knowing you're all right." He's looking at me with his brow raised as if I wouldn't tell him.

"I don't have a death wish," I try to joke but the mention of death forces me to subconsciously raise my hand to my chest. It splays over my heart and I consider for only a half second telling Seth about my condition and then I do what I've been doing. I drop it and my hand, using my other to squeeze his hand tighter.

The plan right now regarding my systolic heart failure diagnosis: I'm going to call and make an appointment with the specialist and until that appointment, I'm going to take my medicine and pretend like pills will fix it. I would rather hide it until I know what my options are.

"Hey." Seth's firm voice brings me back to problem A, away from problem… where does my heart even fall on the list? "Promise me you'll let me know where you are at every step and you'll listen."

A small submissive smile graces my lips, meant to appease him. "I promise, I'll listen."

With his hand still wrapped around mine, he taps my knuckles against his thigh rhythmically as he looks at me, searching for something. He doesn't like whatever he sees, judging by his expression, which is raw and open. He's undecided.

"What's wrong?" I question.

"It's just that I can see you taking off again, even though you're sitting there telling me that you won't. I know I want to prevent that and I know how, but you don't like the idea of being punished," he answers without hesitation. "See that?" He stops the rhythmic tapping and holds up our hands, still embraced but barely. "You tried to pull away at just the thought of it. And you did that yesterday too, when we were—"

"In jail," I finish the statement bitterly. I'm pissed that he has the nerve to bring it up again, but I don't want to fight. Swallowing, I press my fingers back between his and scoot closer to Seth. "I don't like the way you say it."

"Is that all? Because I don't think that's it. I don't think you want me to be..."

My gaze moves from his to the hole that's still in the wall. I was able to clean up the pieces of drywall before the lawyer came in, but the remaining evidence of the other night is still there. I don't want it here. I don't want anything to do with it.

When I move to stand, I have to rip my hand away from Seth's. How dare he bring it up.

"You don't get to punish me for leaving because you told me you killed my father." I don't even know how I'm able to say the words. The truth kills me, it chokes me, it smothers me. I don't want it.

"That's not—"

"It is!" I scream at him, shaking my head wildly. I can't take it, and my heart races. I can't go through with this conversation. I simply can't control what it's doing to me. "Please don't do this. Don't hurt me like that."

"Is that what you think I want to do?" As he speaks, he raises his voice like I do. "I don't want to hurt you!" He says it like I've spoken something offensive. As if I'm in the wrong. A moment passes with silence and the next time he speaks, his voice is calmer, lower. His hands are in the air like he's approaching a wild animal. "It's not about hurting you."

"It's not about the act of punishing me," I say and it takes everything to get the words out. "It's why!" *Thump, thump, thump*, the beating races through me, and I struggle to breathe.

Calming myself, I try. I try to appease him while protecting myself. "My father wasn't a rat. You didn't kill him. I don't want to believe it."

"Laura, it's about you leaving—"

"Stop it. Both times. Both times I left..." My strength weakens and my pulse is hard in my veins. I'm hot all over. "Can't you understand? I don't want to remember why I left."

I cut him off the moment he tries to speak. "You can't bring it up. It brings it all back and I can't go back, Seth. I can't live in the past, not when my present—" My throat tightens, silencing the rest of my thought.

"I'm not trying to hurt you," he says. His tone is calming and I know he's telling the truth. I know he is, but I can't allow the mention of it. Everything tumbles downward after it. I can't stop the falling of memories.

"I'll make a truce," I offer him, desperate to end this. "I never bring it up, and you don't hold my sin over my head."

"What's that?" His question is softly spoken.

"I never left. I never left you. I had no choice. If you get to live with a lie, so do I."

Only feet apart, we couldn't be further away from one another. Both of us struggling, but we can live this way. I know we can. We can pretend and be happy. That's all I want right now, for a little while. All I have is a little while anyway.

"Can't we just pretend? Please," I beg him. "I don't want to remember why I left. You say you're going to punish me for it, but saying that only brings it all back up. I don't want that. I don't want to remember. Can't we just pretend?"

"We can't pretend that you don't leave when things get bad."

My voice raises and I slam my hand against his chest, trying to shove him away as my cadence cracks. "And you can't pretend that things aren't fucking horrific."

I can pretend all I want but we are so badly broken, and the realization weakens my knees. I'd fall if Seth wasn't still holding me.

"Please don't do this," I beg him again as he pulls me into his chest. "Please, I don't want to cry anymore."

Seth's hand on my shoulder, his forearm against my back, steadies me. He rocks me softly and it's completely at odds with everything else. We are so broken, but this is all I have and all I want. I've lived my life without Seth in it. I can't do that anymore despite everything I now know.

It's a whirlwind of emotions and betrayal, yet a constant in the storm is how he makes me feel when we're like this. Me, broken and not knowing how to fix myself and him, steadily holding me.

"I need you," I whisper. Pulling away from the warmth of his chest, I tell him, "I don't need you to punish me."

"I need to know you won't run." His answer is simple.

My gaze is beseeching. In an attempt to crack this armor he's put up, I say, "I'm telling you I won't."

His lips part and I can almost hear his unspoken words declaring that I told him that before. My heart stumbles and falls so quickly. "Seth, I can't leave you," I say and swallow thickly, needing to tell him that what little time I have left, I need to be with him. The truth doesn't come, though. What if he decides he can't be with me when I have a faulty heart? He can't love someone who's only going to leave him. After all, that's what I do. I leave him.

"I'm afraid," I admit, opting for a new truth. Barely breathing as my eyes turn glossy. Haphazardly wiping them, I hold on to the anger. I pull away from him to bitch, "I hate fucking crying. When did I—"

"You can cry." Seth's voice is calm when he takes my forearm, pulling me back into him.

I don't have enough time to cry.

"I'm afraid of this horrible side of me. It bothers me… how I always fall into this world. I'm drawn to it, Seth," I confess and look him in the eyes. "There's no point in leaving you when I know this bad piece of me is just who I am and it leads me into this… this…"

"Nothing about you is horri—"

I cut him off before he can console me and feed me some bullshit about how I don't have that in me. I know I do. It's there waiting and ready, almost greedily wanting to come out and prove itself. "There's plenty of bad in me! I killed a woman. I killed her. I—I—I—" Words fail me.

"You had to."

"A part of me *wanted* to," I confess.

"Calm down." With both of his hands on my shoulders, he tells me sincerely, "There's nothing wrong with you."

"There is—" he doesn't let me finish.

"No there isn't."

He doesn't get it. He doesn't see the point.

"I can't leave you, Seth, because I accept it. I accept that I'll always be led back here. I promise you I won't leave. Because I know I need you." It's not all the truth, but it's jagged pieces of it. Reckless and scattered, but it's all true. "I won't ever leave you because I'm afraid of that side of me. But I know you understand it. I know you'll protect me from it all." That tiny last bit is so raw and honest that it shakes me to my core.

"Can I tell you something?" Seth asks and waits for me. I peek up at him, nodding.

A sad smile I know so well greets me. It's the kind he gives me when he tells me something he doesn't want to. "You're my good side."

My brow pinches with confusion until he leans in, kissing it, kissing that crease and then he says it again. "If there's a good side and a bad side to every person. You're my only good side. You can't leave me again. I'm nothing that I want to be without you. Imagine that feeling when that dark side threatens to take over. Imagine that, and only that."

Seth has been so steady, so strong, I haven't viewed him as broken, not like I view myself. Never. Not once.

All I can do, as quickly as my body is able, is to lean forward and hold on to him. No matter how hard I hug him, he hugs me closer, his warm breath in the crook of my neck. I wish I could just go back. There are times in life when I wished that, but never so much as now. Thinking back to that first time I saw him, I would change it all. I'd save us. We could have had a different life. I know in my heart he's the one I'm meant to be with, but why does this life have to end like this? Maybe in the next we'll remember. Maybe we'll remember this love and be drawn to one another again.

"I promise I won't ever leave your side. Just please, pretend with me. Please."

He doesn't say he'll pretend but when he kisses me, he promises not to bring it up again, and I'll take that.

"Can we just agree on one thing?" I dare to ask, to put it to bed and let it rest where it is. "I don't want you to bring up me leaving again. You don't want me to bring up," I have to pause and breathe in deep, pretending I'm not saying these words right now, "my father again."

Seth is still and quiet.

"Right?" I ask him, prodding him to agree with me.

"You have to know I'm sorry."

"Don't, Seth," I beg him, swallowing down the pain. "I need you to drop it, this talk about me leaving and needing to be punished for it. Drop it and never bring it up again and I'll do the same."

Seth doesn't say anything. He doesn't agree and he doesn't disagree. He holds me though, close and with a grip that isn't going to let up. That's all I want right now. With everything going on, this is all I need.

"Hey," I tell him, "I love you."

"That's all that matters," he answers and then kisses me. He's right. Right now, all that matters is this. I can be okay with this. I make sure I tell him, "I'll never stop loving you."

There's a moment when he's holding me, where I'm warm and so safe, that nothing else feels real. It simply can't be true because when we touch, everything is right. So all of the wrong that is happening around us, all of this awful shit, it's not real.

I let my lips slip up Seth's throat. There's always a little rough stubble there. The tip of my nose drags along it and when I inhale deeply, calming and settling, all I smell is him. I plant a small kiss right there, right on his throat and I'm awarded with a groan, deep and rough, vibrating against my entire front.

He readjusts and I know he must be hard for me. It's so easy to get him worked up, to get him wanting me. Truth be told, it's the same back. There isn't a moment where he kisses me and I don't want and need him instantly.

"You really love me still?" he questions with his piercing blue eyes focused solely on me. I'm so hurt inside. For him. For us.

"I could never not love you, Seth," I tell him honestly and kiss him before the swell of emotion takes over. All I want is him. To be held by him. To be loved by him. Everything else, in this moment, I choose to ignore.

Crashing my lips against his, I slip my hands up his shirt. One slides up while the other moves down, slipping past his waistband. I love the feel of him in my hand. How hard he is, yet soft and smooth. All of him was made to be a sex god. Every inch of his body. I grip him once and beg him, "Please," in a heated whisper.

Seth inhales and lets his head fall back. With his eyes still closed, he commands me, "Get your ass undressed now."

I can't help that I smile, that I feel a rush of warmth from my cheeks, down my chest, all the way down at the thought of him taking me right now. With my teeth digging into my bottom lip, I'm quick to remove every article of clothing. Seth is slower, lazily stripping as he watches me.

"I love it when you smile like that," he comments before pulling his shirt over his head.

"I love it when you make me smile like this," I tell him back, feeling a dull ache in my chest, a pull to him that I need to hold on to forever. Until my last breath. Because it's the best thing I have in this world. He's the only thing that feels good. This. This moment and what's between us, it's worth living for even if nothing else is.

Both of us bared, he stalks toward me and I wait, standing with anticipation, goosebumps traveling over my skin, but I'm so hot, the shiver doesn't come with an ounce of cold, only want.

He keeps his gaze pinned to mine until he has to break it to plant a single open-mouthed kiss in the crook of my neck. It's then that I reach out to him, both of my hands on his chest until I move them up to his shoulders. His hands roam my body and I squeal when he lifts me into his arms. His cock is nestled between my sex.

He braces my back against the wall and it doesn't escape my knowledge that the hole from the other night is still there, just to the right of me. That's where he fucks me, hard and ruthlessly.

He doesn't try to silence my strangled cries of pleasure. He tears them from me with each forceful thrust. His eyes never leave mine, even when he kisses my jaw.

"Seth," is the only word I can say as he takes me, pounding into me relentlessly. He hits the back of my wall every time and I swear it's too much, but the moment he's gone, I want it again. Always.

CHAPTER 12

Seth

"SHE'S GOOD?" DECLAN ASKS AS HE PULLS AWAY, LEANING BACK IN HIS seat and taking control of the polished steering wheel with one hand. Resting my head against the passenger side, I check the side-view mirror as the lights in my front room windows fade into nothing. The car jostles as Declan turns and hits the edge of a pothole.

"She's all right," I say, giving him a vague answer. I have to move, setting my elbow on the rest and letting my thumb tap against my bottom lip. She's not all right, but she's better. I know her and this isn't her. She's not addressing what I did, she's backing down from the fight. My babygirl doesn't pretend, and she doesn't hold things in. She's not all right. Something is wrong with her. Something's wrong with us and I don't know what.

"Are you good?"

"Tired and pissed." I answer him before looking at him. He knows I'm pissed. I haven't told him that I don't like that they left her in the cell with the hitman, but he doesn't need me to say it. I can read it on him and I'm sure he can tell I'm pissed just the same. Laura should have never been left in there. It was a calculated risk. And I hate them for it.

Declan is the spitting image of Carter, but with lighter hair, lighter eyes, and a more approachable personality. Every hard edge Carter has worked at having, Declan's cultivated the opposite. He wants people to come to him. He wants them to feel that they can trust him. It works.

"She's not bait." Apparently, I can't let it go. It's what irks me as I sit in this expensive sedan while Declan drives me away. They know I'm pissed. They know it was fucked. And yet, here I am, at war with an unknown man and pissed at the only allies I had.

"I know." Declan's tone is easy. He's always easy, but I've seen the way he handles situations. There's a grace about it, a calming air and then a brutal ending his opponent didn't see coming. It's all about the way he handles it, with both control and ease. "I told them that girl should have been taken out of Laura's cell the second she was placed in there."

The sun's only just peeking over the horizon, the pale pinks and oranges kissing at the edge of the skyline. Laura slept soundly for a little while, then woke up screaming again. He wants to know if she's all right? She's not. Part of the reason is because they let that situation occur. They could have stopped it. They didn't. And now she's not all right.

"She's not all right," Declan surmises. I only look at him in response, mute. "You can't hide it."

"How do you know that what I'm thinking is about her?"

"How could it not be about her?" he questions back. A deep ache settles in my chest and I have to look away.

"I can't stand this. She just had a hard time sleeping and now I'm leaving her. She woke up screaming, grabbing me. She has nightmares about it, Declan. She's not all right." He should know. They let that shit happen.

"She'll be all right," he answers. After a moment he adds, "She's strong… maybe it's better to be alone if she's doing that."

"Better to be alone?" I don't hide how I truly feel about his comment. How could he think that's better? Anger swims inside of me. He's the only friend I have out here. Him and his brothers. Yet here I am, wanting to beat their faces in.

He glances at me quickly, with confusion at first before explaining himself. "Well if she's grabbing you when you're sleeping… I was just thinking… you know, you react to that. Being grabbed in your sleep."

My head falls back and I stare at the visor and then up to the sunroof that still displays the fading night sky. "She's screaming, Declan. My first instinct is to find her." I explain it as calmly as I can remember something Declan told me that makes me feel like shit.

His first instinct isn't the same. I forgot about what he told me a year or more ago. That must be why he said what he did. Why he assumed her grabbing me wouldn't end well. And now I feel like shit. This edge I have needs to go. I need to get out this aggression before it gets me killed. Declan is not my enemy, even if I am pissed.

"Sorry," he says and adjusts his grip on the wheel, then looks out of his window, away from me. "I didn't mean for it to be taken like it was. It wasn't meant to be… cold."

"It's not," I say. "I get it." The streets are vacant as we drive. I'm quick to change subjects and put this to bed for now. "Everyone's going to be there?"

"The four of us. Daniel's staying back."

"Carter, Jase, you and me?" I question to clarify and Declan looks away to nod. I don't like it. I don't fucking like this one bit. Not when I'm pissed at them and they know it. "I'm not all right with the way things went down."

"We know," he answers and that's what causes the cold prick to travel down my back. I'm not comfortable against the leather. It's hot and this seat feels too small.

"If you knew I'd be pissed, then why?" I can't help but bite it out. "Why use her as bait?" They left her in there, hoping to get more information about who put the hit on her. I don't know how I could ever forgive them. Worse, I don't know how they'll react to knowing that.

"Carter got the note. It was never going to get to Jean." This is the first I'm hearing about it. I've been out for half a day now, and Declan's just now telling me?

"When?" I question and quickly spit out more. "What'd Marcus say in it? Where is it?"

"It's not Marcus. It's not his writing. Check the glove box," he says, reaching over. As the click of the lock fills the small cabin, he tells me, "We got it just after Walters gave Laura the package. If it had been delivered a moment before, things would've been different. I swear to you, if we'd already had the note, she'd have been in her own cell. She'd have been alone."

The small note is familiar; the type of paper, the handwriting. Marcus has a tell and these notes are it. It's his primary mode of communication. Thick handmade paper with deckle edges, his writing style, even how it's ripped. There's always a way to know it came from him and this looks like it did. My head spins reading it. Shock and fear come back with full force.

The note reads: *Make it quick. It's not her sin to pay.*

My veins freeze with the ice that courses through me. The need to rip it up, to crumble it, to smash my fisted hand against the window rides me hard. "He gave the order," I say and the tragic truth is ripped from me as my throat tightens and I read every word again. "She was going to die in there."

"Again, it's not Marcus. Someone wants it to look like him."

I stare at Declan for a moment, who gives nothing away, then back at the note. Bright lights from the streetlamps come and go, casting more illumination for me to see clearly.

"How the hell is this not Marcus?" I don't see it. It's everything we know that comes from him.

"Look at the tail ends of the letters, they're not like Marcus's handwriting. I put it through the system." Declan turns left, driving down a dirt road and past rural farms with bales of hay on either side of us. He explains, "It compares writing samples. This isn't from Marcus."

"What about the ones last week?" I can't help but to think back to the notes. The ones that convince me Marcus knows about my past.

"They're his." Declan's condolences are evident in his tone. "You ever decide on what you think it means?" he questions, taking a turn in the topic of conversation.

Which will it be? Fletcher's right-hand man? Or Laura's father?

"Did he want to kill them or did he have to…" I tell him the only conclusion I've come to. "I didn't want to kill Laura's father, but I had to. Fletcher was different. One was surviving this life, the other barely surviving life at all. I killed Fletcher for business. I killed Laura's father because I had to. Otherwise, I was dead and he'd have ended up dead too. There was no choice."

"Well, those were left by Marcus and obviously for you. He's been following you, talking to you, but this last note wasn't from him. He didn't order a hit on Laura."

Thank fuck.

It's silent for a moment before I tell Declan, "It's a power play either way. He wanted me to know that he knew about me and Laura and what I'd done. He called my hand and I showed it."

"Anyone would have," Declan tells me like it's all right, but it's not.

"Everything's fucked because of it."

"I think you did something to piss Marcus off. He's creating problems for you."

"I haven't done anything worth him even noticing."

"It's the same shit that happened with Carter. Everything was an easy truce until he took Aria. We think it fucked with Marcus's plans, so he came for us."

"I didn't do anything though."

"If not you, then Laura," he tells me, meeting my gaze as we turn down a long dirt drive.

Anger consumes me at the mention of her name. "She's innocent in all of this and you know it." The threat is barely hidden in my tone.

"Delilah is still a factor. She has connections to Marcus and Laura knows her. We don't know what Marcus knows about the two of them or what he thinks Laura knows."

Rage pulses through me and I have to close my eyes. "He didn't write the note though. He wants me to know he knows, but maybe he didn't send those guys to Laura's place."

"That's what I was thinking," Declan agrees. "Marcus is digging into your past. But someone else is going after you too. Someone who wants to pin it on Marcus."

"Walsh?" I question.

"No. No, not Walsh." The way he answers me, it's like he already knows.

"Who?"

As Declan puts the car into park, the dome lights giving off a soft glow inside the car, he smirks. "I think I know. I got a print."

"On the note?"

He only nods and continues. "And that print isn't in the system but it matches another print I took from Laura's place."

"One of the three pricks who broke in?"

"You are correct." Nodding, I crack my knuckles one at a time, peering outside. There's an old barn, the painted blue walls fresh compared to the wood on the doors, but still, it's worn down. Bright lights shine from inside the barn, and I make a note that there's nothing around here for miles and miles. Woods, and on the edge of the bay.

Another smirk shows first, followed by a grin. "I know you're pissed at me. But I have a gift for you."

Before I can respond, he turns off the car and slips out of the driver's door, leaving me there with apprehension. It only takes me a moment to get out, following him as he walks to the large sliding wooden doors to the barn.

Using both of his hands, he parts the opening and more light spreads across the field.

It's quiet, except for Jase's voice. "Took you long enough." I can barely hear him, walking a few paces behind Declan, but I know I heard him right.

I'm still rounding the front when I finally get a good look inside. The barn is at minimum twenty feet high and twenty feet across, but at least double that in length.

Carter and Jase stand side by side. Both cleanly shaven and each wearing slacks, black and gray respectively, and dress shirts. Carter's is rolled up to just above his elbows whereas Jase opted to keep his crisp white shirt sleeves down, complete with cuff links.

The two of them in this barn doesn't make sense. With the crowbars, hammer, and nail gun on a short wooden bench to their right, anyone could easily connect the dots.

They aren't the only ones waiting for us.

All three men are bound, on their knees, with burlap bags over their heads.

"Mine wasn't burlap," I comment, knowing in my gut these are the three fuckers who waited for me outside Laura's place. Their body types match up. My fingers itch with the need to rip the bags off their heads and make sure it's them.

Jase rolls his eyes and extends his hand to me as I follow Declan to them. "You good?" he asks me, my hand firmly in his.

His prying gaze sinks deep into mine, searching for what I'm thinking.

"You know I'm pissed," I answer honestly, finally letting his hand go. His nod is nearly imperceptible, but then he tells me, "I would be too."

"You want to hit something," Carter speaks up and tilts his head to the man closest to him. "You can take it out on them."

Although it's not said in humor and it's not said casually, I know it's his attempt to ease the tension between us.

One of the men, the middle one, tries to say something, but he must be gagged because every loudly spoken word is muffled and the dumb fuck nearly falls forward on his face. He barely braces himself, still struggling to be heard.

"They say anything?" Declan asks, tossing his keys down next to the hammer and rolling up his sleeves. He takes them up inch by inch.

"That one is spilling everything," Jase answers him and gestures to the middle man. Of the men that night, I barely remember his figure. He's not the muscle, he's not the heavier one. He's the other guy. Inconsequential, but there. "The other two haven't given up shit."

"One may be a little hard to get to talk," Carter speaks up, flexing his hand and then crossing his arms. The knuckles on his right hand are split. "His jaw might be broken."

"Why'd you do that?" Declan says almost jokingly, making his way to the line of silver tools on the bench. He's weighing a hammer in his right hand when Carter tells him the prick spit on him. "Anyone ever tell you that you have anger issues?" Declan says and then offers a smile as he holds up the hammer for me to see. Jase chuckles, Carter's still quiet and I shake my head in response to Declan's offer.

I haven't moved from my spot, unsure on what the plan is. Truth be told, I want them to myself. All three of them. They got to take out Davis. They shot him down, easily taking his life. I didn't get that justice. I haven't gotten anything. I wanted to hunt them down and take care of this myself. I don't want anyone else around when I take my anger out on each one of them, one at a time.

Although having them together, all at once does offer up a unique opportunity.

I want them to hear the sound of what happens when I'm crossed. I want the other two waiting and listening to their friend being beaten to death. It's fucked up and sick, but all I can wonder is what they were going to do to Laura. And every answer that comes into my head justifies beating them to death. And taking my time doing it.

"How's the gunshot?" Jase asks.

"All but forgotten about."

He nods and I catch Carter taking me in. "I've had worse and the bruise on my jaw is already letting up. I'll be fine," I answer them and I mean it. With everything going on, I haven't even thought about the gunshot. I take a pill in the morning for the pain, plus a pill in the evening. "Vicodin does wonders." My answer gets a laugh from Jase and Declan, not from Carter though.

Walking to the bench, I ask, "How'd you find them?"

With the doors still open, a breeze makes its way in and the faint smell of fresh water from the lake behind the barn comes with it.

The man in the middle leans forward, his shoulders shaking as he lets out a sob. A look of disgust plays on Carter's face.

"Middle man was the easy one. We had his license number from when we got Davis. It was linked to a credit card and that was linked to other bills, including an address."

Carter leans forward, ripping the bag off the man's head. His hair is matted on the right side, his face red and blotchy and a dingy rag spills from his mouth. He screams behind it, but the words are morphed into nothing that's identifiable.

His face, though, I recognize his face. "Yeah, that's one of them."

"He told us where the others were. It was easy enough to collect them."

Carter continues pulling off the bags and revealing the other two men. I didn't imagine I'd feel this much relief when I laid eyes on this crew again. It matches the animosity though.

I wanted an outlet for my aggression… here it is. Wrapped up in a pretty bow.

"He say anything interesting?" Declan asks and nods to the one in the middle. He shrieks behind the gag and that time I heard him. *Please.* He cried out please. It's muffled behind the rag, but I heard. I'm not going to give any mercy. He can scream whatever he wants to scream. He's as good as dead. The only consolation I have is knowing he'll regret ever stepping foot into Laura's apartment until the moment he dies.

"Yeah," Jase answers, leaning against the barn wall, propped up with his leg bent and one foot against the wall. "He said we're working with Walsh, and therefore we're free game."

"Free game?" Declan questions at the same time Carter huffs darkly, with true humor at the mention that the Cross brothers are *game*.

"Remove his gag, I'm sure he'll tell you we're as good as dead like he told us." Jase doesn't take his eyes off of him. His expression is empty of mercy and the man continues to beg. The other two men don't speak, they don't try to do a damn thing. One stares straight ahead while the other watches the four of us, focusing on whoever's speaking. He's the one with the broken jaw.

"Did you ask them why they went rogue?" I ask. That note is everything to me. The one made to look like Marcus's handwriting. I want to know why they did it. Why they decided to threaten Laura, to take her life, and why pin it on Marcus by writing the note the way they did.

"With the note?" Jase asks to clarify.

"Yeah," I say as my voice hardens and I have to shove my hands in my jean pockets just to keep from reaching out to them. "One of them wrote it, right?"

Carter kicks the back of the man seated directly in front of him, the one staring straight ahead.

"We didn't ask. You should though," he informs me. "His print is on it."

Every step is careful as I move toward the man. He's in blue slacks and a collared shirt, almost like a uniform. He's the tallest of the three. I crouch down in front of him, but an arm's length away and rip the gag from his mouth, tossing it into the dirt. No matter how hard of a man he wants to appear, he still retches from the cloth being removed. He spits on the ground at my feet and I wait, letting the anger pass. I need to know: was it just them, or was Marcus involved in any way at all? I have to know who all of my enemies are.

"Why'd you want to pin murdering my girl on Marcus? Did he send you to her house?" I ask and when the prick doesn't answer, I add, "He's pissed about Walsh, so he goes after a woman? That doesn't seem like Marcus."

Silence.

"Seems like something a dickless coward would do. There's no way a man like Marcus would go after someone's girl. You want to be Marcus, but you aren't." My last line triggers something.

The man's eyes flash for a moment and he clenches and unclenches his jaw, still not saying anything. I don't mean to do it, at least I'm not conscious of it, when I strike out and slam my fist into his nose.

"Fuck!" the man screams and leans backward, which only makes him fall. The blood from his broken nose leaks into the dirt, and Jase lets him lie there for only a moment before forcing him back to his knees. All the while he fights it. I shake out my hand, reeling inside. I need to know. I have to know who wanted her dead. Every name. Every single name involved. They all have to die.

"Look guys, he's not mute," I say, deadpan. "For a moment, I thought I was having a one-sided conversation." Everything on the outside of me, is at odds with what's going on internally. Even the control. I need them to talk, to tell me what happened, or else I have nothing. They're on their knees, at my mercy, but I still have nothing.

The middle man speaks up again, his eyes wide and his words muffled. Both men on his left and right glare at him.

I rip the cloth out of his mouth. "You have something you want to share?" *Please. Please,* I pray, *give me something. Tell me what happened that led to this.*

"Please, I'll tell you everything, just let me go."

"No." My answer is immediate and the man's eyes dilate as they go wide. He's hit with shock at first. He'll still tell me. I know he will. I have to believe that; I need him honest in his final hours. *I'll be honest too, just tell me.*

"We told them it was up to you," Carter informs me. "Guess he was hopeful that you would have mercy."

"Please!" he begs, his single word yelled in such a high pitch it breaks from his throat being dry. "I'll tell you everything. Anything you want to know."

"You think you could do that? And then you could leave here and Marcus wouldn't kill you?" Tears leak from the man's eyes. "If you could do that, then whatever you have to say isn't worth enough to even hear it."

"It is! Marcus is leaving. He's not going to be here. Please! I can tell you everything."

My gaze shifts to Carter, who's looking at Jase. A chill creeps into the silent room as the man heaves in air. "It was a mistake. I just want out! I want out of it all!"

The man who wrote the note, the one with the print on the letter, he curses in what I think is Russian before heaving his body at the middle man, his teeth sinking into the man's cheeks and blood gushes from it. It's not too deep, merely a gash, but blood leaks freely and the middle man screams out in agony, toppling over. I don't make an attempt at all to stop it. I want chaos, I want them to attack each other. In violence there's truth.

Carter grabs the first man by the back of his shirt, forcefully righting him and the man spits once again at the dirt under the middle man's feet. A tinge of his blood remains.

Standing up, I walk backward, assessing the scene in front of me. One man on his knees, glaring at the rat he used to work with, blood staining his mouth. The middle one wriggling on the dirt, his cheek slashed. The third still only watches, the one with the broken jaw, hanging lower than it should on the right side. All I need to know, is which of these three will tell me the truth.

"Marcus is leaving?" Declan asks Jase before I can. Carter stays where he is behind the three men, glaring at them and waiting. He's a brooding man and silent. Jase tilts his head for Declan and me.

"He said earlier, Marcus is picking a successor." He's not whispering, but he's not speaking loud enough for the men on their knees to hear us. A successor? He choosing someone to take his role?

"He's condoning going after women?" The disgust in my voice is evident.

"He gave a list of ways to prove themselves. It's up to his nominations to execute them."

"Free rein to do whatever they want to prove themselves," Carter says and Jase nods, agreeing with him. "That's what it looks like." Marcus told them he's leaving, and that whoever proves himself worthy, can take his place.

"Free rein?" I question, needing answers and not knowing who will have them. "My name was on a list, and they decided to involve Laura? Or was she included in the free-for-all?"

"Just you," the middle man whimpers out the answer that gives me my first bit of peace.

Although anxious heat sweeps across my shoulders and chest, the knowledge that Marcus isn't going after us, after Laura and me together, is a relief I didn't dream of having. Maybe he is still coming after me and he's digging into my past, but Laura isn't in his sights. She's safe. She *should* be safe. These fuckers will pay the price for dragging her into this hell.

"Which one of them decided that Laura would pay? Which one?" I speak up loud enough for everyone to hear, my last question coming out harder. "Marcus sent his men out to prove themselves, and one of you decided to hurt her." The men are silent, and I look past them at Carter. "I want him. I want the man who decided she needed to die." He gets that price on his head for his print being on the note. I don't even know if he made the call, but he's the one I'll take care of last.

"You can have them all," Carter answers, bringing all three of us to stare back at him. The middle man is back on his feet, his head hung low.

I eat up the space that separates us from them, leaving Declan and Jase behind me. Gripping the man who tells every secret, I drag him up to me by the collar until we're face to face.

"I'm going to ask you a simple question." He's already nodding his head, eager to tell me whatever I want to hear as I ask, "Did Marcus tell you to go after Laura?"

"No. He didn't. It was Jared's idea. He said it would send you on a spiral downward."

"Is that one Jared?" I nod to my left and even though Carter's nodding behind the man in my grasp, he answers quickly. "Yes, and that's his brother," he adds, motioning with his head which is the only thing he can move.

I drop the man, letting him fall to the ground.

"They just needed me to drive… I shouldn't have been there. I shouldn't have done it. I knew I shouldn't have," the man bawls.

"Jared goes last," I announce, feeling strangely calm considering the amount of hate that's fueling my decisions.

"Whatever you want. This is our apology," Carter announces and as fucked up as it is, I answer, "Apology accepted."

I take the gun out of its holster and weigh it in one hand and then the other.

"I've been trying to decide… if I should shoot you first, since you gave up everything so easily." The man in the middle looks hopeful for a moment, although he still shakes his head. My tone when I speak again clues him in to what I'm thinking before I crouch down in front of him, both hands on the gun between my legs. "The thing is, I don't trust you. So I can't give you that mercy."

"No! No! I told you all everything!" He's still pleading when I nod at Jase and he picks up the gag, shoving it back into the man's mouth. Chaos swarms him, but it dies down easily, settling into hopelessness.

"Him first, I think." I speak out loud and the three brothers nod in unison. He can't speak so it makes sense to get rid of him first.

"I have another question," I mention as the thought hits me. "Who sent her flowers?"

The look Jase gives me is unexpected, but Declan knows what I'm referring to. "Who was it?" I harden my voice, and the man in the middle mentions a single name.

Marcus. He told me that Marcus said she deserved a warning, another beginning to an end.

I do exactly what I pictured when I first saw them here. I don't use a single item from the line of silver metal. I opt for my fists. It's brutal and taxing on my body. It takes a lot to beat a man to death. After the first one, I have to take off my shirt; it's covered in sweat and blood and I'm so damn hot.

Middle man must've been speaking the truth because he was still pleading for his life, giving the same information over and over again until his windpipe collapsed under my knuckles.

The man who wrote the note, the one responsible for all the pain my babygirl went through, he goes last and before the second man hit the dirt dead, the bitch was crying, begging me.

Every man will break. Some are easier than others.

All three of them stay, watching and helping me when I ask them to.

I can't go home when it's over, since I'm covered in blood and angry. I'm still raw and wound up and the cuts on my hand have worsened and split. Declan takes me back to the estate instead, leaving Carter and Jase to clean up the mess. She's got work in only an hour anyway. That's how long it took. I can't let her see this shit right before she leaves and has normalcy. I can't drop this burden on her.

Declan's quiet until we park. "What are you going to do with Laura?" Declan's question catches me off guard and I don't like it. He should know better than to even say her name right now.

"What do you mean?" I'm fucking exhausted and I don't have time to decipher what he's getting at.

"Last time I asked you, you said you didn't know."

What am I going to do with her? "I'll do right by her. Get her a ring when all this settles." Declan nods at my simple answer and I find myself doing the same. I'm going to love her. That's all I can do and it's what she deserves. I'll do anything and everything that she wants. It's an easy answer, but every one of my thoughts stays bottled up. He knows about the ring, he knows she's mine, and that should be good enough. Everything else is just for me and Laura. It's only for us.

"And she's good with that?" The car is still running and the headlights shine into the woods. I focus on the lights.

"I think so." Declan's quiet but he's watching me. I can feel his eyes on me. Swallowing, I tell him, "She leaves when things get rough and this life is rough." I think about telling him that if she wants to go, away from here, away from this life, I'm out. So I do. I lay it out for him, and he accepts it. As if he saw it coming.

He's silent, but nods in understanding. His jaw is hard though, his brow pinched.

"So you two are good?" he asks again. Prying and the more he asks, the more I find myself telling.

"I don't know how to set boundaries with her. Every time I try, it goes wrong, everything falls apart, things get worse." It's her running away from *me*. I don't know how to stop it. "She can't leave me. She needs to know that's not an option."

It takes a long moment of silence before Declan answers me, "She doesn't strike me as a woman who likes boundaries."

"She's mine. And she needs to understand that."

He throws his hands up and says, "I didn't say that she didn't. Some women… they aren't submissive." His grip on the wheel gets a little tighter, his voice a little harder before he leans back, forcing himself to relax.

There's an edge to him. Declan's never had a woman he loved, as far as I know. He has needs though and I know he goes to this place, a club of sorts. He has experience in that way. But he doesn't have experience with loving someone. He doesn't know Laura at all.

"I like submissive. I need that control, you know."

"Yeah."

"You love her, and she's not submissive—"

"You haven't seen her in that way," I cut him off. Laura likes it when I take control. I know she does.

"In the topping from the bottom in bed kind of way? I'm sure I don't need to see it to know it."

"I'm sure as fuck not the submissive if that's what you're getting at."

"It doesn't work like that. I'm just saying, maybe she needs control as much as you do. You two work. I've seen it. You love each other. That's enough, man. You don't need to force her to agree to boundaries that have hurt her before. It'll happen when it's supposed to. Let her have the control she needs, and you might be surprised."

"I'm just afraid she's going to leave me." I speak the honest truth. I've had this with her before. It's the only thing I want. The only thing worth living for. "If I lose her again…" my voice trails off and I have to look away.

"You won't," Declan tells me confidently. It's only then I can meet his gaze. He nods, and adds, "You aren't going to lose her. You two are meant for each other. Nothing's going to come between that."

He sounds so sure, so confident, that I believe him because that's what I want to do. I want to believe I'll have her forever.

CHAPTER 13

Laura

"YOU AREN'T SUPPOSED TO BE HERE," AIDEN SAYS. THE AMOUNT of irritation he grits out in his comment is enough to make me roll my eyes, which I do since my back is both to him and the door to the back office. "I'm serious, Laura, you shouldn't be back until you're given the okay."

I hear him, but I'm not listening as I shelve the thick binder of medical records.

"It's a mandatory leave." His voice hardens when I ignore him, opting to continue exactly what I'm doing instead.

I am needed here and I'll be damned if I'm going to let him send me away. Melody's been transferred while she awaits trial. She's not here anymore, which I'm silently grateful for, but I have paperwork to transfer. Early yesterday morning, I left jail. This morning, I'm back at work. I don't see the problem, just a striking difference in scenery.

"Laura, are you going to make me call security?" he asks with exasperation and my answer is just the same.

"No. I'm sticking to my schedule." I guess the saving grace in all of this is that I didn't miss a shift. I want normalcy and this is the easiest way to get that.

His relief is palpable as he sighs and says, "Please just stay home for the week."

I turn to him, my ponytail swinging and the tips of my hair tickle my shoulder as I look him in the eyes and tell him, "No. You aren't calling security and I'm staying."

"We're doing an internal investigation, for fuck's sake," he practically hisses beneath his breath. The door's still open and Bethany takes the opportunity to walk in.

Thank the Lord for her. I thought her shift would never start.

"You're back," she says brightly, oblivious to Aiden's irritation and I return her smile, but mine's thin-lipped and cut off by Aiden.

"No, she's not."

"Yes, I am."

"We need her." If Aiden sounded exasperated, then Bethany sounds desperate. Grabbing both sides of the threshold to the small room, she leans in and whispers harshly to Aiden, whose hand is currently running down his face. "Cindy isn't good for a damn thing."

"I know," I stress to Bethany, giving Aiden the cold shoulder. "How did she even get through her boards?"

He may be my boss, but I'll be damned if he's going to keep me away. Especially given the activity he's been involved with around here.

"There's an investiga—"

"Over the woman with only initials?" I question him. "Over her being in here with limited information and files? Or over what happened when she had to have emergency surgery?"

He pales and when he speaks his voice is so dry, he has to swallow and then try again. "This is about you."

"If you push this, I'll push too." It hurts me, truly and deeply to look my boss in the eyes, a man I respect and make that threat. I don't know what he's up against, but he doesn't know what I'm dealing with either. Bethany's silent and I see her shrink back, but she doesn't leave. Maybe due to curiosity, maybe she wants to serve as moral support.

"Laura, this isn't about—"

"I don't care what it's about, I'm not leaving." My throat squeezes and I feel hot all over as I hug the binder to my chest. They can't make me go. Work is my life and the only thing that makes me feel good right now. "I need to be helping someone," I plead with him.

"We have to. It's procedure."

"Then she doesn't have to check in," Bethany pipes up. She looks nervously at me before meeting Aiden's gaze. "She can be here unofficially. You know we need the help, so as long as it's not documented..." She leaves the sentence unfinished and the two of us stare at Aiden.

He's cornered. Figuratively and literally. His answer is a very quickly spoken *fine* before he leaves. He's pissed and I get it. Everything around here is falling to hell.

"I'm so glad you're back," Bethany says and takes a step in as I stack another binder on top of the one I've already placed on the desk. Bethany sits on the edge of it before asking, "Seth all right?"

I nod, my voice suddenly lost. It's easy to stand up to Aiden, since he doesn't know everything. Bethany knows it all though. When you call someone early in the morning or late at night, and you lose your shit over the phone, it can be hard to look them in the eye the next morning. That's what it feels like right now.

"I still haven't seen him, though." My voice nearly cracks and I pause my motions, holding a binder that isn't the right one and slowly but surely, resting my head against the shelf. "He hadn't come home before I left." I called her when I woke up alone. I spilled every detail.

Except the part about my heart. And the part about Jean.

I told her enough that she knows I'm not okay. And that Seth and I were fighting. It's enough for her to understand. There's so much going on and everything feels like it's coming to a head.

I want to tell her about my heart, but not yet.

I'm not telling anyone until after the appointment confirms it. I just... I just have to make sure I don't skip the appointment. Which means Seth's men will follow me, but at least they're only following. They won't know why.

"Did you call him, though?" she asks and I only shake my head, feeling the swoosh of my hair before getting back to the binders.

I don't answer her question. Instead I confess the conclusion I arrived at after I spilled my guts on the phone to her and sat there alone in a quiet room with nothing to do but think. That's really what drove me to work. I couldn't be alone with my thoughts.

"Even if I called him, I don't know what I would say."

"Every couple has that moment," Bethany says with slight dejection. When she shifts on the desk she opens the binder. The telltale creak is the only reason I know she did. "I think getting to that moment is the start of something better. That's what I think."

"When did you become an optimist?" I question, pursing my lips when I find the last binder and turn to finally look her in the eyes.

With her hair up in a messy bun, she shrugs. "I like your scrubs though," she comments and I have to utter a small laugh. We're wearing matching *I love my patients a latte* scrubs with little coffee cups all over them.

"You have good taste," I tell her, closing the binder she was absently fiddling with and placing the third on top.

"I'm glad you're back. You're never allowed to leave me again," Bethany says and pouts. Literally sticking out her bottom lip, which makes me laugh a bit louder than the last time.

"Love you more than coffee," I tell her, placing a quick kiss on her cheek and slipping out of the room as she moves to find whatever it was that she needed. She calls out to my back, "Me too, but don't make me prove it."

It's nice to smile. It occurs to me that this is the first time I've smiled in days when I'm back at the nurses' station, pulling out the file numbers and testing a pen on a sticky note before opening up the binder to fill out the first bit of information.

"Do you have a pen for the sign-in sheet please?" a feminine voice asks and I peek up. Plastering on a smile, I answer her, "Right here," and pass her my pen that I know works, opting to grab another.

"Thank you." With the thinning of her gray hair, the woman's much older and I think I recognize her as the mother of one of our residents who's in and out. She's the mom who smiles to everyone's face but cries behind closed doors and at the back of empty halls. Even when you find her there, she'll smile and say she's all right, when in reality she's breaking inside.

I know her type and I feel for her.

"Have a good day," she tells me kindly, setting the pen down and taking in a deep breath as she prepares to go down one of the far halls. They aren't my residents down that hall. We're sectioned off but I watch her go, wishing there was a different way. It hurts to feel helpless, even more so when someone you love is in pain or a situation that's hurting them and they don't know how to get out.

She wore a dress and rouge for the occasion. Some call that lipstick courage.

I retrieve my pen, since the next one I try doesn't work and it goes straight to the trash bin under the counter.

The second I drop my gaze to the paperwork, a splash of blond hair catches my eye. The elevators are closing and the woman is off to one side of it, but a familiar chill spreads through me. Recognition mixed with fear and regret flows through my veins.

My lips part as a breath leaves me and I drop the pen, moving to the side of the desk in an attempt to get a better look.

Cami.

I swear it's Cami.

The doors close before I can fully see her and my deranged self decides to take the stairs, nearly running down the hall to get to the stairwell and therefore her, before she can leave. *It's Cami.* That's my only thought the entire way to the stairs even though I know she's dead. It can't be her. It's not possible, but I *feel* like it is. I can feel *her.* As I wrap my hand around the railing, taking each step as quickly as possible, I argue with my sound mind that it's Cami. There is no logical explanation, but there's a feeling when someone you know and love deeply comes close to you. You can feel them and it's her. I know it's her.

"Excuse me." I'm breathless as I give the apology, nearly bumping into an orderly as I round the last set and swing myself into the door. I pry it open in just enough time to see her leaving. A gust of wind blows her hair to the side as she slips out of the front doors across the room.

Her name is trapped in the back of my throat as my heart races. Just as the doors close, I call out, "Cami!"

The receptionist stares at me. She's the only one here and she stands awkwardly as I run past her.

Hustling to get across the reception area, I make my way while avoiding the prying eyes of the receptionist and whatever she's saying and slam my hands into the door, forcing it open. It's cold and unforgiving; the leaves have all changed color seemingly overnight. The sky is gray and the parking lot is empty. Wrapping my arms around myself, I walk down the front stairs, searching for her.

I even call out her name again. As I stand there all alone in the cold, I realize it's the first time I've said her name out loud in years. Years.

There are no people, no cars, no lights or sign that anyone is out here.

It's like she disappeared.

"Are you all right?" the receptionist asks me from behind.

"Of course," I answer her with my head lowered and look up one last time down the empty sidewalk and then to the parking lot.

"Do you need me to call security or help?" she offers and I only shake my head. Asking her if she recognized the woman proves she doesn't. She hadn't seen her come in and didn't get a good look at her when she left.

When I get back to the nurses' station, still feeling the cold blistering my cheeks, I check the log for visitors, and I recognize most of them. There are no new names on the sign-in sheet and no one named Cami.

She was here though; I know she was.

CHAPTER 14

Seth

THE FRONT DOOR OPENS WITH A SOFT CREAK. IT COULD HAVE BEEN silent and Laura still would've heard. She's waiting for me.

"Where were you?" The accusation is out of her mouth before she can even lift her head from the back of the sofa to glare at me.

Guilt-ridden, I close the door behind me and toss the keys onto the entryway table.

"With Jase and Declan."

She grabs the remote from next to her and taps it against her thigh, an agitated sigh leaving as she does.

"I didn't mean to be gone so long." I tell her before she can yell at me, "I felt like shit leaving you here." I felt like shit there, which is why I took so long. The meds work for pain, but I fell apart the moment I sat down at the estate. Sleep and an IV proved useful for getting me back on my feet. I could have done that here, though. Next time, I will.

She doesn't respond, but her gaze softens at least.

"How are you doing?" I ask as I take each step to her with careful intention.

"Okay… Work was fine," she answers, flicking off the television in the middle of a scene. If I had to guess, she wasn't invested in it.

Licking her lower lip, she stares at her socks as she pulls her legs into her chest. “How long have you been home?”

“Two hours. I couldn’t sleep.”

“You want me home when you sleep?” I ask her, needing to come up with a solution before she can even finish the complaint. She nods, her chin nestled against her knees. “If I’m not allowed to leave, you should at least be here.”

“I know,” I agree and fall onto the sofa, wrapping my arm around her and pulling her in. “I know. I’m sorry.” The second she settles her head onto my chest, I kiss the crown of her head. She’s still got her arms hugging herself and is in a huddled ball, but at least she doesn’t seem to be angry. Pulling her in closer, I tell her, “I had a difficult time this morning and it lasted a few hours. I had to decompress for a moment and when I did, I realized I lost track of time.”

“Where?” Her question isn’t spoken lightly. “You couldn’t decompress here?”

“I was pretty worked up,” I answer her although I’m hiding a lot of it. I’m still angry. More than angry. The three of those men could die a thousand deaths and they’d still deserve more. The anger I can push down, but damn was I worn out. I felt like death. The doc told me I shouldn’t be pushing it like that, but I have to do what I have to do.

“You can be worked up and still come home,” she says and her tone is less pissed off and more pleading as she peeks up at me. “There’s beer in the fridge.”

Before she can look away, back to the blank television screen, I grab her chin between my thumb and forefinger and plant a quick kiss against her lips. “Thank you.”

Her eyes stay closed for a long moment and she asks before she opens them, “For what?”

“For not being too mad.”

A sad smile graces her lips. “I don’t want to fight. I’m finding it hard to be mad these days.”

I don’t care for how she says it. It shifts something inside me although I don't know why. "I got you a gift." I wasn't going to tell her but seeing her like this, I had to say something to make the smile turn genuine.

"What is it?"

"It comes in the mail, so you have to wait." The answer makes me feel like an ass and when she rolls her eyes, that makes it worse. "It's flowers. Every two weeks, flowers will come in the mail."

"Really?" The interest in her voice and the sweet blush on her cheeks make it worth it.

"Really." I add, "They had options for the kinds you like and I picked the wildflower type and roses too. I know you like a mix, but you always smile at the roses too."

With sleep in her eyes, her hair still damp from a shower and wearing nothing but my t-shirt and a pair of short shorts for bed, Laura looks up at me and instead of saying a word, she steals a kiss.

It's quick and in return I give her a smile; the kind you feel in your chest. That's all I want. That warmth in my chest, that love from her. It's fucking everything.

"Better?" I ask, feeling the weight of the world leave my shoulders.

"A little." She bristles and adds, "I still don't like being alone here."

Rubbing my neck with my free hand, the one not wrapped around her waist, I answer her, "I know. It won't happen often. And you'll like it here more when you move your things in."

I anticipate her arguing based on her initial reaction, judging from the small gasp of protest that leaves her and the way her lips part, but she hesitates and then closes her mouth, opting for a small nod. "Yeah," she says, stretching forward and then standing. "You're right. I need to move my things in." Her tone drops, as does her gaze.

I don't know what to make of her reaction. Something's wrong and off and I don't know what. She isn't right. "You sure you're okay?"

"Fine," she says as gets up.

As she makes her way to the kitchen, I see she's spackled the wall over the hole I punched in it. She cleaned up and that spackle is the only evidence left of anything that started our recent downfall. I hate the numbing prick that climbs over me at the memory of it. I'll paint it in the morning, getting rid of any evidence at all. Maybe that's it. Maybe that's what made her react like that.

"You want a beer?" Laura asks me and when I move my gaze to her, I get a full-on view of her sweet curves as she bends down, opening the fridge and taking out a bottle of ginger ale in one hand and a beer in the other, holding it up in offering.

"Yeah," I answer, readjusting on the sofa. She could do anything, anything at all and it would be sexy as fuck. But offering me a beer in short shorts has to be at the top of my fantasy list now. "No wine?" I question her as she closes the door with her hip.

"My stomach is messed up. But I've got it when I'm ready for a glass." Her tone is flat and sleep weighs down her eyes. With the ice tinkling against her glass, she sits back down, sipping her drink and passing me my beer.

It's quiet as we both have a drink in silence. I fucking hate the odd tension between us. "Are we okay?"

"What?" She's confused at first and I simply wait for her to answer. "Yeah, we are."

"I just want to feel like we're okay and something... I want to see you happy."

"You're sweet." She smiles up at me, squeezing my hand. "When did that happen?"

"Guess you're rubbing off on me."

"I don't feel sweet."

I lean down to kiss her, just once, a small peck, but keep my nose touching hers. "Still taste sweet," I whisper against her lips. All I'm rewarded with is a small smile that doesn't last long. "I know things are off right now, but give it time. Everything will be better. I promise."

"You're making a lot of promises," she says and her voice is soft, low, and full of doubt. Doubt that wouldn't be there if we were as good as she keeps saying we are.

"And I aim to keep every one of them, Babygirl." That nickname does it every time. Her eyes light up, her lips turn up, everything goes up and everything is better when I call her *Babygirl.*

It's only a flicker though and then she falls back into this state she's in… It drives me crazy.

"Tell me what's wrong. Tell me now," I demand.

"I just really want to go back to what we were. What we had, you know?" she asks me and the sincerity, the desperation is too much. Her voice cracks and she closes her eyes as she adds, "Can we just pretend to go back and never go through all of this?" She opens her eyes when I don't answer and says, "I just want to go back to the very beginning. Back to you being on my porch steps."

"I never left." I answer her with all that I have. If that's what she wants, she can have it and more. There's an emptiness that she used to fill. Even when I didn't have her, I could still feel her there. She's slipping again. I can feel it but I don't know why.

Her response is somber as she sets down the glass in her hand. "Right, I'm the one who fucked that up."

"Hey, don't do that. I'm just saying, I never stopped…" I trail off although the words *loving you* are there. Right there, but I still can't say it. Not when I feel like there's something between us and I don't know what it is. "I was always *yours,*" I stress. "Whatever else I am in this life won't ever hold a candle to that flame. I'm nothing if you're not there, so I pretend you're waiting for me at that door. It's how I got through it and I never left. In my head I was always there, so close to seeing you again."

I don't anticipate her crying. She's not one to be so emotional but the last few days have been heavy and I wish I could find a way to make it right. Fuck, I'm trying. I'm trying to hold us together and failing. As quickly as I can, I wrap my arm around her but she pulls back, resisting me.

Her words are muffled angrily. "You can't say things like that."

"Like what?" *What the fuck did I do?*

"Like your only good side is me, and that you being with me is…"

"What's wrong with that?" The beer bottle clanks on the coffee table as I set it down. It's exasperating; I don't even know why we're fighting right now. We should be good. She keeps saying we are but we aren't.

"You aren't leaving me, right? Because it sure as hell feels like you are." Panic stricken. As I sit here, I am panic stricken and helpless. When did I become so helpless?

"I asked you to hold me until the end, right?" she asks and her voice gets tight. "That's all I want. It's my only wish right now. I just want you to hold me."

"Then why are you so sad? I've never seen you like this. I can feel that things aren't right."

She falls forward, her head in her hands and this time when I try to hold her, she lets me. Something is off. Something's so wrong and I can feel it. I know there's something she's hiding.

"Tell me what's wrong," I whisper and then add, "I'll fix it. I promise."

"I just want you to hold me, Seth."

"I'm so fucking sorry," I tell her with a ragged voice. I can't control the emotion inside of me. It's screaming that I'm losing her even though she's telling me the opposite. "What can I do? Just tell me; I'll do it."

Seeing her like this wrecks me. She's not supposed to be sad like this and broken. "I hate myself for putting you through this."

"It's not your fault," she says and shakes her head, even as the tears fall.

"It is my fault. It's all my fault and I'm so damn sorry."

She does the opposite of what I expect. She climbs into my lap and holds me. Her arms are around my neck and her head rests in the crook of it. "I love you, Seth King. I love you."

Hearing her whisper that calms me, but only slightly. So long as she's hurting, I won't be all right and it only forces the aggression to build.

"With nothing to fix, what can I do?"

"Just hold me."

My phone goes off at fucking 4:00 a.m. Laura's asleep in the crook of my arm and the insistent buzzing won't stop. My eyes are burning from the lack of sleep, but I scrub them with one hand as I slip Laura onto her pillow. She wouldn't let go of me. She won't tell me anything else either.

I've never felt so helpless with her.

I'm groggy as fuck and I can barely see as I make my way out of the bedroom and answer the phone although I don't actually listen to whoever's on the other end yet.

It's pitch black in my hallway but the second I get to the living room, the lights from the porch make getting to the kitchen counter easy enough. I lean on it and hear the muted "You there?" from the other end of the line.

"I'm here," I breathe into the phone, finally lifting it to my ear.

"Are you listening?"

"I am now," I answer Declan and take in a deep inhale, my eyes still half lidded as I lean against the counter. "What's going on?"

"You said Walsh told you he looked into you and Laura?" he questions.

"Yeah." I perk up slightly at Declan's tone, but I need strong black coffee if I'm going to make it through this. "What's going on?" It's hard to shut off the thoughts about Laura and just focus. I can't get over this nagging feeling that everything is wrong.

"There's no alert, Seth." My eyes open at what Declan just told me, staring at the coffee maker with the mug in my hand.

"Walsh said he didn't know about Laura and me until recently." I repeat the conflict out loud, "But you don't have an alert that he searched my name?"

"Right." He adds before I can ask, "Or Laura's."

"So go farther back with the dates on the system."

"I did that already. I searched for a month. Bethany was curious about you, by the way."

That part doesn't strike me as odd. I bet she hates me for putting Laura through all of this too. So long as she doesn't tear her away from me, she can hate me all she wants. That makes two of us.

"Check his work computers. The computers that aren't registered. Maybe it looks like someone else."

"No. No one looked up Laura other than Bethany until Laura was arrested. Not a soul. I wanted to do the search to see if we got any hits. There's no search for her or any information regarding you that included her." I'm silent, still trying to process what all this means and Declan keeps talking.

"It hit me a bit ago that Walsh told you he did. He said he looked you up. I never got an alert. He's lying."

"Could have been a paper trail?" I ask although that's unlikely. A chill runs down my arms as I hit the button to brew a pot of coffee. Why would he lie about something like that? It doesn't make sense.

"No. I looked into the police transcripts in your hometown. Nothing has been moved or requested."

"Either he already knew or he figured it out without searching online, and if that's the case, who did he talk to?"

"We have eyes on all our men. We've had eyes on Walsh. He hasn't seen anyone."

"I know. No one who knows would have told him shit." I don't know what to make of it all.

He tells me firmly from the other end of the phone, "My instinct is that he's lying. I think he knew about you and Laura all along. He went to her work, he befriended her."

"So he's playing us?" I can practically see Declan nodding the way that he does before he says, "Yes."

"And to think I'd just started to come around to him."

"You're a liar. You don't like that prick." I huff a short chuckle at Declan's response. Bringing the coffee to my lips, I take a long sip before asking, "So what do we do about it?"

"That's why I'm calling you. I thought you'd want to take the lead on this. Get ahead of it."

"Another gift?" I question and make my way to the sofa, taking a seat. Before he can answer, I tell him, "I told you, apology accepted, it's all behind me."

It's quiet for a moment before he asks, "You sure?" Thinking back to the barn, I flex my hand and then crack my knuckles.

"I'm sure."

"Still," he says on the other end of the line, "what do you want to do about Walsh?"

"He knows more than he's letting on. We all do. We keep our cards close. I don't trust him and I want him gone as quickly as we can get him out of here." I think out loud, "Marcus is supposedly leaving, maybe Walsh goes with him. I don't want anything to do with either of them."

"They both have their sights set on you. The question is, why?"

CHAPTER 15

Laura

Life is an oddity when you're waiting to see a doctor who is, more than likely, going to inform you that your death is coming shortly. The days blur together because every so often time pauses while you remember, and then it goes on, but in the back of your mind you're caught in that thought.

It's a constant. I can't shake it and it's wearing away at me. To the point where I made the damn appointment, even though I'd rather just hide. I'd rather pretend I don't know that I have heart failure. Apparently I'm shit at pretending.

"Hey, it's just a checkup," Bethany says sweetly beside me and I smile as she pats my shoulder. She does a little circle with her hand and then pats me once more in finality.

"Haven't you ever heard, doctors make the worst patients… and nurses aren't much better," I joke back at her, forcing myself to be the person she knows me to be. That's the way I've been with Seth too. I think they both see through it. I wish I was a better liar for their sake.

The waiting room is virtually empty. It's just us in the back row of these rather uncomfortable seats, closest to the magazines. There's a pregnant woman a row up. She's been on her phone the entire time; her hand is rubbing circles over her belly. It's calming to watch.

A single laugh is belted out by Bethany in response and then she flips the page to her magazine. "Speaking of that, I need to schedule a checkup too."

"Ooh, hypocritical much?" I taunt her.

The magazine makes a slapping sound as she tosses it down on her lap. "You look like you're going to an executioner, not a doctor."

My smile falls and it happens so fast and honestly that I don't have time to correct it.

"Hey," she says and her voice falls gently as she leans in, her hand on my thigh. "You okay?"

"I'm fine," I lie and at that moment my heart sputters, like it's scolding me for doing so. I have to clear my throat and pick up my coffee, which is the cue for her to remove her hand. "Just a lot on my mind." It's a lame excuse, but Bethany buys it.

"It's Seth, isn't it?"

"What?" The word is only a single breath. I can't even take a sip of the coffee. Why would she think it's Seth?

"You used to tell me everything. Literally five months ago, you described the worst date with at least decent consolation sex. You've been with Seth for like... weeks? And you haven't told me anything."

"It's been almost a month," I say, correcting her. "He's not like the other guys. This isn't a one-off to have drinks over and laugh at. He's not a date... he's... he's more."

"But you aren't happy," she emphasizes.

I'm happy with him. I don't know how to tell her how wrong she is. "I've changed and I know that, but it's not because of Seth. I promise you."

"If you don't want to be with him, don't. He can't force you—"

"I love him," I say, cutting her off. I'm not angry at her; I'm shocked, though. "I've always loved him and even though..." I trail off because I don't even know where to start. Our love story isn't a straight line, it's chaotic scribbles on a page. It's fucked up. "I need him right now. Why would you question that?"

"You haven't seemed right. Something's going on," she presses and I don't know what to tell her. I can't tell her the truth. I can't tell anyone. Not yet. I can't make it real for them like it is for me.

"Will you give me some time?" I ask her. "I just need time to figure it all out."

Her smile is small but genuine, and I get another pat too. "Of course." As she's telling me, "All the time you need," a nurse calls out my name.

"All righty," she says then stands with me and tells me she'll see me at work. I hate that I'm lying to her and to Seth, or at least lying by omission to hide the truth. I make a promise to myself as I watch her go before handing the papers to the nurse, that I'll tell them. I'll tell both of them everything the moment this appointment is done.

I can't keep lying and pretending.

"Miss Roth?" The doctor is short like me, although her shoes add at least two inches. *Cheater.* "Right this way." She's professional but walks quickly, as if she's in a hurry. It only makes me more anxious. She doesn't speak the entire way to the room, which is in the farthest corner of this place, adding yet again to my anxiousness.

"I'm Doctor Tabor."

"Hi, it's nice to meet you." Formalities take precedence although internally all I can think is that it is not, at all, nice to meet her.

"I see you've already had your blood taken?" she questions and I nod, my fingers drifting on the small bandage in the crook of my arm.

"I don't know why it was necessary." I didn't ask the nurse when she told me. I was too busy talking to Bethany who looked like she wanted to pry, but didn't.

"So, I had a look at your charts," she begins as she's closing the door and before I've even had a moment to sit.

"Yes, I know we're getting more tests done today concerning my heart condition and I" I try to speak confidently, remembering that I am a nurse and a grown woman. I can handle this. Before my ass even hits the exam table, she cuts me off.

"I can tell you right now that I can make a firm diagnosis with what we have. More tests will only tell me if your condition has gotten worse in the last week, and quite frankly, I don't see how it can get much worse."

All the blood in my body seems to go to my toes. It makes them heavy and numb while my body turns cold. As I swallow, my fingers grip the edge of the exam table and the white paper crinkles under me.

"I see." It's all I can say. I suppose sometimes when you get a second opinion, the doctor can be blunt if it's the same as the first. Even as I try to embrace it and somewhere deep down I already knew, I still want to deny the truth. "So, I'll need surgery then?"

"A transplant would be best. The walls of your heart are far too thin for a repair. I'm afraid it would tear."

"Is there another doctor—"

"I am the best heart surgeon there is on the East Coast. I'm confident I can perform a transplant. I'm also confident that there is no other doctor who would agree to attempt to repair your heart knowing very well the damage to the walls of your heart." She takes a moment and I can hear her swallow before she rests the chart on her lap and adds, "I'm sorry to lay this all on you. I realize it can be a shock, but I assure you, the donor list is your best option."

"If someone dies and I happen to be a match." The reality is brutal and it picks at me, bit by bit. The chill spreads, the pain sinks in deeper. I'm really dying.

With her lips pressed in a thin line, the doctor informs me, "Organ transplants happen every day. You are not the first and you won't be the last. It's scary and not a guarantee, but we can work on other ways to keep you healthy in the meantime."

I don't want to die. It's all I can think as I sit there. It's what I've been thinking since the first doctor told me. I'm not ready to die. I just got Seth back. And now all of this?

"One thing we need to discuss…" She pauses to clear her throat then continues, "You are high on the list due to the severity of your condition, and how likely you are to accept a donor heart given the rest of your health. However, if a viable heart is selected in the next few months, you have to know there's a risk to your pregnancy."

Pregnancy? My head spins at the word.

The doctor continues speaking even though I'm stuck on one word. She's talking about term and risks and I don't understand.

"I would know. I would know if I were pregnant." I can't remember my last period but I'm on the shot. I'm not at all pregnant. She has it wrong. My head is dizzy trying to process what she's saying.

"I'm not pregnant." My statement comes out weaker than it sounded in my head.

Pursing her lips, the doctor picks the chart back up from her lap, flipping over a page, and then she looks back up at me. "Blood was taken at your most recent visit. The hormone levels were indicative of pregnancy. You are in fact pregnant, Miss Roth."

I can't breathe. "No, I'm on birth control. I'm not..." My head spins. "When did I last... My gynecologist administers them. I'm on the shot." I don't have words.

"Looking at your history, you missed your last appointment for the shot with Dr. Gaffner. You never rescheduled." Closing the chart, the doctor looks up at me with nothing but an expectant, professional look.

I imagine I look like I'm going to pass out to her. Because that's exactly how I feel.

I'm pregnant? My hand slips to my stomach, smoothing over my belly. I have a little extra weight on me, but I thought that was only because of stress. I haven't been working out in weeks and...

Oh my God, I'm pregnant. My eyes widen and all I see is a doctor who'd rather be anywhere else staring back at me.

"You didn't know."

"I didn't," I tell her with my bottom lip quivering. "I'm having a baby," I say out loud and somehow that makes it all the more real.

"There are risks," she informs me, as if breaking the little bit of a happy bubble I'm in. "I'd like to discuss your options for the pregnancy."

I never imagined I'd be a mother. How could I know how to be one when my own left me the first chance she got?

As the doctor rattles off statistics and possibilities, I ignore everything she has to say. I only have a year but that's enough time for a baby. Before I left I'd make sure that baby would know it's because I had no choice.

I cut off the doctor, unable to focus on anything she's saying. "I can't decide anything right now, I'm sorry. Would you give me some time?" I'm polite and the doctor although hesitant, complies, leaving me for a moment to simply wrap my head around the fact that I'm pregnant.

Seth is going to be a father. That's even more shocking than me being a mother.

What would he say? What will he do?

I lied. That promise I made when I walked in here is bullshit. I can't tell Seth. I can't tell Seth any of this.

It's been so long since I've been inside a church. I sure as hell won't be going today either. It's not too cold in my car as I sit here with the heat on, staring at the stained glass windows. The moment that doctor left the room, so did I.

I got the hell out of there to think. All the white sterile walls and carts… I just couldn't process it in there. Let alone have a conversation about whether or not to accept a heart when it's available and risk endangering this baby. At the thought, my hand lifts from my lap to my belly.

"You sure do know how to fuck with someone," I whisper as I watch a woman enter the church. I'm all the way on the far right side of the parking lot and it may only be six at night, but service is long over and the early evenings of autumn have made the sky turn dark.

My grandmother used to pray. She didn't do it often, but if she lost something, she'd pray to Saint Anthony, I think it was. I'm pretty sure. She said Saint Anthony helped you find what you'd lost. I don't even know if that's a Catholic thing or Baptist. I simply wasn't raised to be religious.

Yet, when times get hard, I always find myself at a church. Maybe it's because the graves are in their backyards, or that a church can always be found near a hospital. I don't know why but I drove here eight years ago when I first arrived on the East Coast and I couldn't stop thinking about Cami and Seth. The two came together, different kinds of pain. If one left, the other appeared. So I came here, to this church.

Always at night, when it's most empty.

Once, when I was little and had no idea just how hard life could be, I asked my grandma, *"If you lose your way, do you pray to Saint Anthony too?"*

She looked at me with a sad smile and crouched down in front of me. She always smelled like peppermints and at the memory, I swear I smell them again.

"When you lose your way, you pray to God."

A mix between a deep breath and a sigh fill my lungs. I have prayed so many times, and yet here I am, with a faulty heart and now a baby I don't know if I'll even be able to carry to term.

Maybe it's because I only pray at my weakest moments. I've only prayed when things were horrible and I had no way out. Maybe that's why it just gets harder. God is forcing me to keep praying.

It's a ridiculous thought and I huff a sad laugh as I sniff away the tears that prick my eyes. No more crying.

My phone buzzes again and I pick it up, thinking it's another call from the doctor's office but it's only a text from Bethany asking what my schedule is at work next week. I need time to absorb all of this, so the impatient doctor will have to wait.

It takes me a moment to search through my email and copy and paste my schedule to Bethany as my thoughts travel to all of the details I looked up about pregnant women with heart failure.

Maybe those scenarios are what led me here.

I nearly call Bethany. So many times as I've sat here for hours I've thought of calling her, telling her everything and then begging her to tell me how I can tell all of this to Seth.

How do I tell him I'm pregnant, but this baby might not make it? Oh, and I may not make it either. How do I tell him I've known for over a week now about my heart and that I lied to him?

A light in the car a few spots over goes off and then back on catching my eye. It's the security detail and I when I see the phone in his hand I wonder if he's telling Seth. The clock tells me I've been here for three hours. I don't know how. I've only been thinking. Apparently I'm slow today.

"Have you been taking all my mental energy?" I ask in a soft voice, that motherly voice every adult female seems to have around a sweet little infant. "Is that why I can't think straight anymore?" I ask this little bump.

My security detail lowers his phone and the flash of light distracts me again.

The woman is already leaving church, the same one who entered a moment ago. I wonder what she came here for and then I wonder if she has a baby.

I want a baby. That is the only conclusion I have come to repeatedly since I've been here. I would love to hold my baby.

CHAPTER 16

Seth

I'M A BASTARD. LAURA CAN'T EVEN LOOK ME IN THE EYES ANYMORE. SHE doesn't want to touch me. She avoids me all the time now. It's been a week of her doing this and I know it's my fault.

She's drifting away from me even though she's right here. She's always here but she's not. It's fucking killing me. All I can do is check the messages from the security detail on her. It's gotten to the point where Jase won't even have a conversation with me if my phone is out.

He can be pissed all he wants. I cannot lose her.

When I get home, her flowers are in a vase on the coffee table. It's the first sign of life I've seen from her.

For a week now. Ever since she went to the doctor. She said she's feeling sick and that's all it is, but she's lying. She goes out, she comes home, she goes to bed.

That's been her schedule. I've fucking had it. Screw Declan and his advice to give her space. It's obviously not working.

I'm not a fucking fan of *space*, apparently.

With a bottle of wine in my right hand and Chinese takeout in the other, I shut the door and listen for her.

No sign of her in the house, but I know she's here.

I call out for her as I lay everything out on the counter. I got her favorites, even the crab rangoon I think is… less than appealing. Crab and cream cheese just don't work together in my book. The wine was damn expensive and the man at the register said she'd love it. As if he knows her. Still, I got it.

"Chinese?" she says and her small voice comes from over my shoulder. She holds me from behind, hugging me first, which is new, and rests her head on my arm as she takes a look at the options. "Sesame chicken, I call that one." The smile is genuine and I'm floored. I don't understand, but she's acting normal. I'm afraid to breathe or she may go back to the sullen shell she's been wrapped up in.

"All yours, Babygirl." I stare down at her as I speak and her response is to lift up onto her tiptoes and kiss me.

It's a small peck, sweet and short although she lingers a moment longer when I lean down to go in for another. I'm granted a hum of satisfaction and then she's moving behind me to get the plates from the cabinet.

I don't miss that when she sees the wine, that bit of happiness falls. Like it was just an act. It's already gone; the smile, the blush in her cheeks.

A worried look replaces it all and I can see the wheels spinning as she takes her time getting out two plates. One and then the other.

She's killing time until she has to go back to putting on a show for me. It's so damn clear and I can't stand it. It's eating me up inside, gnawing away at whatever makes me a semblance of a good person.

"What's wrong?"

"What?" she says as she turns around, her lips parting in shock. Both of her hands grip the counter behind her as she shakes her head. "I'm fine."

"The hell you are," I say and I don't hide the raw pain in my voice. "You think I don't see you? I know you, Laura Evelyn Roth and I know you're not happy. You're not even close to being okay."

Her sad eyes stare back at me, but the frown on her face keeps her mouth shut.

"I'm trying everything here," I tell her as I open my arms, the empty plastic bags in one hand and then I ball them up, holding on to them as if they'll ground me.

She starts to say something but then she looks past me and worries her bottom lip before catching it in her teeth.

"It's killing me, you know that? I lost you before, but this?" I throw the bags away, which makes me turn my back to her, but only for a moment. "This is hell," I tell her, the words scratching their way out of me. "It hurts to see you hurting and you pretending you're not for me."

"Would you rather I go?" The question is riddled with such loss that even her whisper mourns.

"No! No!" How can she even think that? I can't breathe. I have to loosen the fucking tie on my neck because it's choking me. "Don't leave me. Please. I want to be here for you," I say, and I am begging her. "Whatever it is that makes you cry at night; you need to tell me. I promise I won't think less of you or… shit, I don't know what you're thinking will happen if you tell me because you don't tell me anything."

Her expression crumples but still she doesn't say anything.

"I know I hurt you—"

"No, stop," she says and Laura's hand flies out in front her. Her palm faces me as if to silence me.

"I know I did." I rush out the words, hating myself. "If I could take it back, I swear to God that I would. I don't deserve you but it doesn't mean I'll ever stop wanting you. I don't want anyone else to have you and I can't walk away."

Her shoulders shake with each shuddering breath. "Stop! It's not that. Stop. Stop!"

I feel crazy and lost and reckless. Dropping down to my knees, I stare up at her. "Tell me! Please! I'm begging you," I practically yell but I don't mean to. Just like I don't mean for my eyes to turn glossy. "I can't lose you but I am. I am losing you and I hate it. You aren't here with me and I can't be without you. I will do anything, whatever it is. Please, just tell me."

Breathless and in a hell that is limbo, I watch her. She's right there, only feet away from me, but she feels so far from my grasp.

Hope stirs when she slowly drops to her knees, never taking her eyes off mine. She crawls to me and lets me hold her. That is my only salvation. It's the only way I've survived this last week; she lets me hold her.

I kiss her hair as I rock her, "Please tell me what's wrong. I love you. I love you so damn much and I can't lose you."

She has to know I love her. I know she already knew, but I can't let her walk away from me without telling her. "I love you, Laura. Please, let me love you. All I want in this world is to love you."

CHAPTER 17

Laura

I will never forget the way he said it. He brought it to life by speaking the words. Seth King loves me. I'll never let him take it back. He's not allowed to take those words back. Ever. They belong to me now. I knew he did, I've always known, but hearing him say it is something else. Something bigger, something I couldn't have prepared for.

"I love you more." It's all I can do to whisper the words. I cling to him, literally, holding him as close to me as I possibly can.

"Impossible," he breathes against my neck as I hold him. "I love you so much it hurts."

Till the day I die, I'll remember this moment. The moment Seth King first told me he loved me. It pains me, literally, a slamming pain in my chest, that it's because he thinks he's lost me.

"I'm just upset." My ragged excuse leaves me and he doesn't let me bury my face and hide it. He doesn't let me get away with it. I can't figure out how to tell him that if I have this baby, I will most likely die. If I take the heart, our baby will die. If I even get a chance at a heart. I choose our child. And I don't know how to look this man in the eye and lay all of that out for him. I've tried all this week to figure it out but I can't. I can't hurt him like that. All he wants me to do is promise I won't leave him and here I am, choosing to go but in my place, we'll have a child. He'll have a baby to love and I… I don't know what he's going to say. It will kill me to tell him. I know it will.

"Tell me why, tell me," he begs me, holding my arms and forcing me away enough that he can look at me.

"There's a patient and I lost her." I bite out the quickest excuse I can think.

"She died?"

"No, no. It was because of a court hearing and I'm sad she's gone," I say and wipe haphazardly at my face but my face burns with shame and embarrassment.

I can't look at him. Not in his eyes. I should be better than this. I struggle with everything now. I don't know what's right or wrong and all I know is that my happily ever after is so much different than I'd planned.

"There's nothing else? Nothing else going on?" His blue eyes beseech me and pain is there, the type of pain when you know you've lost someone.

I have to tell him. I haven't had the courage to call the doctor back. I haven't been able to fully accept it all and what will happen at the end, but I can't keep it from him any longer.

I feel like a liar. Not even speaking the falsehood *nothing else*, the lies consume me. I can't let him live like this. How could I spend this time, this short time left, allowing him to feel like I'm already gone? He'll know soon. He'll have to find out. It's not like I can hide a baby.

So will Bethany. I've almost told her so many times, but only to have someone to lean on. It's been a week and a half and instead of facing it, I've hidden. I'm not ready to tell the world and lose this little peace I have. They'll judge. No matter what I do, it'll be wrong. I just want to stay here, in this moment, for a little while. Knowing that I have a little life inside of me to love. But Seth should have that too. He should know.

"Seth, I'm pregnant and—" I want to get it all out. All at once. It's my intention, my plan. It's the only way I see it getting through to him, the gravity of it all.

He cuts me off before I can say anything else. "You're pregnant?" Shock lights in his red-rimmed eyes. His light blues shine back at me as they change to reflect nothing but happiness. I'm lost in those eyes. A gaze I have dreamed about for so, so long. It's my fault. I shouldn't be so selfish, but I don't press on when he interrupts me. I let him have that happiness. One of us should truly be happy.

His smile presses against my belly as he leans down, capturing all of me in his response. "You're pregnant," he says, no longer a question. The words resonate with gratitude. With his eyes closed, his lips pressed to my stomach, I lose it. I cry like I have never cried in my entire life.

"That's why?" he asks me even through the smile on his face. "Babygirl, I'd say don't cry, but that's why? That's why you're so emotional?" he questions although the way he says it, it sounds like he's convinced himself.

He's so happy and lost in it, that I nod my head and breathe, "Yes."

One lie. One lie. I can live with one lie to keep him here with me, holding me, happy and at peace. One of us should have it. His expression is filled with relief more than anything, but his smile never leaves. His handsome and perfect smile.

"I hope it's a boy," he tells me, wiping the corners of his eyes with the palm of his hand. "I don't know what to do with a girl, so…" he trails off and sucks in a calming breath. I don't know that I've ever seen him like this. So overwhelmed with happiness. "I'll be a good dad," he says quickly when his smile vanishes. "I swear it to you."

His pale eyes lose their shine for a moment and he asks, "Is that why you didn't tell me?"

"No, no. I just…" I would say anything to make him smile again. "It was just so early. I—"

I don't have time to finish because he cuts me off with a searing kiss. Stealing all my fear and giving me a moment with him that I thought days ago, would only be a dream. He only breaks the kiss to tell me he loves me and our baby and that we're going to be fine. Better than fine.

"We have to get so much stuff," Seth says as if he's just realizing everything that comes along with a baby.

My heart is wretched as he looks down the hall, already planning. "We can use the guest room. It's big enough for all his furniture and toys. All that… the diapers."

"His?" I joke because it makes me smile and that keeps me from crying. "It's far too early to know." Although the look on my face must be torn between the two.

"I thought I lost you," Seth breathes out. "I'm so happy right now. I don't know how I could be happier." There's only sincerity from him. No fear, no anger, no worries in the least. "Oh my God, I love you so much and now we're having a baby."

"I love you too," I tell him back and both love and hurt radiate through me.

"I promise I'll be good for you two. I swear to it," he whispers against my lips and I kiss him as hard as I can, holding him close to me before telling him I know he will.

As he lifts me into his lap, one thigh in each of his strong hands, I squeal in genuine giddiness. In this moment, I pretend. I pretend that I'm not sick. I don't do it for him; I do it for me.

Because I want this so badly. That other version of us I saw in this room the first time he brought me here, they would be doing this. Right here, exactly as we are. I want that. I want that other life where we can have our happily ever after. A real one with all the bells and whistles.

"I love you so much," I whisper in the dip of his throat and he's quick to capture my lips in a kiss before telling me, "I love you more."

Impossible.

CHAPTER 18

Seth

I leave Laura where she is in the bed, feeling on top of the world. She's sound asleep after hours of me worshipping her body.

Of all the scenarios I'd imagined, her being pregnant never occurred to me. Not once did I think that she was keeping that from me.

She said she wanted to be sure before telling me. She wanted the baby to be healthy and live past those first twelve weeks. She shouldn't have had to carry that burden alone.

Never. She never has to carry the weight of anything alone.

The only reason I'm leaving her now is because Declan said his news couldn't wait.

Whatever it is, whatever he found, it couldn't wait.

The entire drive to the estate, I think about how I've never even held a baby. Not a little thing.

I hope it's a boy. Although a little girl with Laura's eyes would make the world stop. Shit, my heart feels like it's exploding. I went from one extreme to the other, feeling like I was trapped in hell to being lost in heaven.

I can't stop smiling. Even when I reach the estate, I can't stop it. That's why I sit there for longer than I should, and the only reason I get out of my car is because Declan comes out and walks toward me.

"Hey, sorry it took so long," I start to tell him. Laura wants to keep it a secret, but how could I not tell everyone?

The look on Declan's face is what finally rights me, what grounds me to the paved drive of this place and the merciless world I live in. He's deathly pale and there's not a hint of humor on his face.

"It's the PO Boxes." Declan starts talking before I can say another word. He's got papers in his hands and he looks down to read one before getting frustrated. "Get in," he says as he gestures to the car and pulls the handle of the passenger side before I can even unlock it.

The car beeps softly, the headlights flashing and by the time I'm sitting in the driver seat, he's turned on the interior light above our heads.

"It's been too long, do you blame me for what happened?" He reads the first line of the paper in his hand. It's not folded but there are creases that show on the sheet.

"What is this?" I question him before he can read the next.

"Letters," he says and shakes them in his hand. "Walsh didn't lie to you. He's been talking to Marcus. Marcus is the one who knew and told him."

Blood drains from my face and I snatch the photocopies as Declan tells me, "Two weeks ago Walsh went to the PO Box." He finally sits back in his seat but he stares blankly ahead as I read the lines of letters. Some in Marcus's handwriting, others in a different style.

One starts *Old Friend*, the other *No Longer Friend*. Marcus refers to Walsh as *No Longer Friend*.

There are dozens in my hand but before I can ask, Declan tells me, "There are hundreds. He stores them there, but none postmarked from two weeks ago. He must have taken it with him to reply."

"This is how he knew about Laura and me? It's how he found out about us?"

Declan nods somberly and says, "It has to be. He photocopies the one he sends to Marcus and keeps them together. He's been doing it for years. It looks like Marcus used to give him information."

"What? Marcus is an informant?" No fucking way. My head spins with scenarios, including one where the FBI allowed him to get away with murder in order to keep tabs on other men in this world. Men like us.

"No, it's in riddles. Like he was toying with Walsh and they developed a rapport. Marcus handed over men he wanted to get caught."

It's all in riddles and ciphers and we need more time for the rest, but we've already deciphered one code. Birds are protected, dogs are men to be killed.

He grabs the papers and flicks through them before picking one and reading.

"It's heard I'll lose you soon. Are you traveling far from the woods? The dogs are barking in a way that tells me you'll leave them alone to roam. Tell me that can't be true."

He flicks to another page, the light casting down on his face and illuminating the letters.

"No, no, I've only given them the idea, I'm moving the luggage. You know sometimes you must let mutts play in order to determine the breed."

He only reads small passages of long letters. "He's not going anywhere," Declan tells me, his head still shaking as he swallows. "He's letting the men beneath him think he is in order to see what they'll do."

"How do you know?" I question although the puzzle pieces of what he read line up, one after the other.

"It doesn't make sense otherwise. You know Marcus. You know his riddles and the way he fucks with people. He must've sent Walsh a letter years ago and Walsh found a way to write back."

"We've only been through a dozen from the last month, but they talk about us, Seth. They call us birds until months ago. This one," he says and points to a page, tapping it and making it crinkle in the silent cabin, "this one has to be Carter."

He reads the first halfway down the page. I know it's Walsh's writing. It's a line that's highlighted and I can already see the page beneath it has a highlighted line as well.

"I thought you said that bird was a friend? What did the thing do to warrant such hostility?"

"The Beast of a bird went after another, taking a small female. It flies so low; it must think it is truly a dog. I cannot have it in my woods. I told you, only birds must stay." Moving to the page after, he reads, "I see the list of numbered dogs has changed, what did the one do to have vanished?"

"Numbered dogs?" I question, stopping him from continuing.

"There are numbers at the bottom of every letter, they have to be how Marcus identifies names to Walsh. We haven't figured them out yet, but between the two letters Marcus sent to Walsh, one set of numbers disappeared."

"Carter's numbers?" I surmise. He nods and then continues, switching out the page and it's another from Marcus. "The female belonged to him; you know birds have good memories. It appears they have mated." He pauses, looking up at me to say, "He took her, Carter took Aria and it put him on Marcus's list. But he took it back."

The wealth of information in those letters is dangerous.

"How many have you gone through?" I ask him and then add, "How did you get these?"

"We broke in after closing, picked the lock, and took copies. It took hours and I don't think Walsh knows, but Marcus does."

"How do you know he knows?"

"He left a letter on Carter's car at The Red Room. He was there. He addressed it, Beast." Declan swallows before telling me, "He said to tell you to bring Walsh to him." He glances at the house then back to me before closing his eyes. "It's inside. You can read it... he calls you King," he says and brings his palms to his eyes. "He said you would be the one to show Walsh to him. That it's time the two of them met."

Declan's expression is devoid of anything but concern. I'm intimately familiar with his expression. It's the look you give someone when they've been sentenced to die.

"Is that all he said?" He nods once. "Walsh wants to meet Marcus.

Marcus wants us to bring Walsh to him. I need to read the note, but I am fine doing it."

"Seth," Declan warns, "I don't trust it. We have information on him, we have intel no one else has ever known. I don't think he's going to let you walk away. He could have told Walsh to meet him." He raises his voice when I shake my head. "He could do this on his own!"

"He likes to see if we'll listen. You know that. He likes to give a demand and have it met." This is the last piece of the puzzle for me. I bring Walsh to Marcus, I follow through on my word, and then I leave. I let it all go. For Laura and my baby. This is my way out.

"I have to do this," I say, cutting him off as he rambles on about not trusting Marcus.

"Marcus has been focused on you. I don't like it. I don't like a damn—"

"He has, and now he can have me."

"You could be walking to your death," he tells me evenly although his voice cracks. He swallows so harshly I know he believes every bit of what he told me.

"I could be ending this," I answer him in the same tone. "I need all this shit with them to end. When does he want to meet?"

"Tonight."

CHAPTER 19

Laura

"WHERE ARE YOU GOING?" I WOKE UP TO AN EMPTY BED. JUST as my hand reached out to test if the sheets were still warm, I heard him in the room over.

I don't tell him I saw the guns. Seth usually leaves with one on his waistband, but he grabbed two more today. He doesn't think I pay attention but I do. His bruises and scrapes have all but healed, and I get the feeling he's on his way to get fresh ones.

"Nowhere important, Babygirl. I'll be back soon. Within hours."

"How many times have you told me that?" I question him, crossing my arms and leaning against the threshold where the hall meets the living room.

With his boots tied up, he leans back on the sofa. Blue jeans, boots, and a button-down white shirt that's rolled up to his elbows. The tats on his right arm show and it gets me all worked up.

"Come here," he says then spreads his legs and pats them. It's easy enough to go to him; it's what I want more than anything. "It's late." I murmur the protest against his chest as I breathe him in.

Whatever he smells like, I'll never grow tired of it.

"I know and I'm sorry, I have to do this tonight but then I'm staying in with you. We can be lazy together at night. Shit, we can be lazy together in the morning too." A charming smile meets me when I look up at him. "I want to be lazy with you," he tells me and I have to laugh. My shoulders jostle against his chest and I scoot in closer to him, one hand on my belly.

"I'm sorry it has to be tonight. Of all freaking nights," he says, sounding as exasperated as I feel. "Don't be mad at me." He brushes my hair back behind my ear. "I just have something to wrap up," he answers so casually, but there's this gut feeling I can't shake.

Something inside of me is screaming to tell him not to go tonight. I close my eyes and when I open them, the lick of the flames in the fireplace stares back at me. It's got to be the fear of loss. That and the guilt that I still haven't told him about my heart. The surgery isn't guaranteed. I just want to have the baby first.

The first doctor gave me a year. I can have this baby before then. Is it so wrong to keep this secret? Judging by the swell of emotion in my throat and the dreadful feeling that stirs inside the pit of my stomach, yes. Yes, it is wrong.

"Seth," I say and I almost ask him not to go tonight. I'm so close to blurting out that I need him to stay because I have to tell him something that's been killing me.

"Babygirl," he says and his voice is so calming as he repositions me on the sofa so I'm no longer on his lap. The weight of his body rests on his knee that's beside me and it makes the cushion tilt, bringing me into his body. "You don't have to be worried. One more night and after that I'm telling Jase I want to ease out of it all."

"What?" My eyes widen with shock. "I didn't ask you to do that." I know who this man is and what his life is. You can't leave the life. I'd never ask him to. "You can't just—"

"You didn't have to," he stresses and settles down next to me. "I can't leave, you're right… but I can back off. Sebastian is Carter's right-hand man. They get it and with everything going on, it's better anyway for me to lay low."

"What's going on?" I ask him breathlessly, adrenaline picking up. I don't like any of this. Nothing feels right.

"Nothing you have to worry about," he tells me as he leans his forehead against mine. "I promise."

"You make lots of promises," I whisper with my eyes closed and my hands on his at my shoulders.

"And I'm keeping every one of them. All you have to do is promise you'll be here when I get back."

"I promise," I answer wholeheartedly. It seems hollow in my chest though. Something's wrong. I can feel it. As if I may not be here. My heart ticks and then thuds. "Seth," I say and close my eyes, ready to tell him.

"I mean it, Laura. I want to have stability. I can run the bar; I can be here more. I'll be a good dad."

There's so much hope in his voice and it's more than soothing, it's addictive. Just the idea of him holding our baby… I want to hear him say it again and again. My breath stills and I lean forward, capturing his lips with mine and surprising myself as much as him.

He smiles when he whispers, "That's my girl."

After telling me to go to bed, he says he loves me again. I love hearing it. For years I pretended he'd say it, and now I have it. I make sure the last thing he hears before he leaves is, "I love you too."

I can't bring myself to get off the sofa, but the room has a chill. So I search for a throw, but Seth doesn't have one. I decide I should hire movers tomorrow as I stare at the flowers on the coffee table that obstruct my view of the fire. The first batch I received are beautiful. The size of the bouquet is ridiculous. But damn are they beautiful. There's a mix of white and pink flowers but what really makes it are the pale blue velvet leaves. I keep wanting to touch them. They're soft and feminine and smell divine. They're the only feminine touch in this place.

I'm busy tallying a list in my head of everything to do tomorrow so I can square it away and make a new list for the baby when I drift off, my hand on my stomach.

Sleep doesn't last long though, because of my phone ringing. I leave it out in the kitchen so I can sleep easy and of course I'd fall asleep here, early in the morning to be woken up at 7:00 a.m. I hustle to the phone charging on the counter and nearly trip from my sleep-induced gracelessness.

"Hello?" I answer it after taking a deep breath. It's the hospital. No more waiting. It's time to move forward.

As she speaks, I keep my eyes closed. "Miss Roth, it's Doctor Tabor?"

"Yes, I remember," I say and my voice is even and calm. "I apologize for leaving so abruptly. I—" Before I can spit out an excuse, she stops me.

"This is not my first time, Miss Roth. I understand it can be a lot to take on. I do have to stress though, that decisions need to be made. You are very high on the list and without the transplant, I'm not sure you'd be able to successfully deliver."

"So I need a C-section?"

"Yes, we can schedule one for eighteen weeks from now, but if a heart becomes available before then—"

"Eighteen weeks? I'm sorry, but no." I'm suddenly very awake. My hand on my belly, I start pacing and ask, "How could we deliver him so early?" I only catch that I say him after I've said it. The baby could be a her, but those semantics aren't important right now. Eighteen weeks? My baby would die. "I can't be more than a month along," I stress, swallowing harshly and waiting for an answer in the silence.

"You are far more than a month along, Miss Roth." The doctor is so sure of herself and I find myself shaking my head, my eyes closed as I brace myself against the counter.

"Due to the high levels of hormones, we estimate that you're roughly twenty weeks pregnant given the results from your initial blood taken. We could have confirmed it with an ultrasound, but since you left, we were able to confirm with the additional blood drawn at your last visit. The hormones confirm it. Roughly twenty weeks pregnant. I do need that ultrasound though, Miss Roth."

"Twenty weeks," I barely speak.

"I assure you, at thirty-eight weeks pregnant, your baby will be healthy. What I need to know is what the protocol will be if a heart is available before then, and Miss Roth, I need to give you my professional opinion. You should accept the heart."

The memories come back in a rush, starting with the missed appointment. The phone call from Bethany about her sister. "I was on my way in, but a friend needed me." That was months ago. Five months ago. I missed my birth control appointment five months ago. Next month I would have gotten the alert for the six-month shot. How could I have been so reckless?

I feel faint. I've only been with Seth for a handful of weeks. Almost a month.

"Twenty weeks?" I speak louder and again the doctor keeps talking. She doesn't understand apparently that I can't listen, I can't even think straight, let alone comprehend what she's saying. Twenty weeks is five months pregnant.

Conception happened before Seth.

Oh my God.

The baby isn't Seth's.

"I can't breathe."

EASY TO FALL

From *USA Today* best-selling author Willow Winters comes the epic conclusion to the heart-wrenching, romantic suspense series, Hard to Love.

With her I was always on the highest high. That's why it was so easy to fall.

I never stood a chance without her. The two of us were made for one another. It's as simple as that. The world could try to rip us apart, but it would fail.

Until this.

She told me once that love isn't enough. I never would have believed it…

I won't stop fighting. Not until the very end.

Two words will help you cope when you run low on hope:
accept and trust.

—Charles R. Swindoll

PROLOGUE

Laura

THEY SAY DEATH FEELS LIKE FALLING. YOU PLUMMET DOWN TO THE center of a large black hole, blind with nothing to touch. Only a sinking feeling in the pit of your stomach and the rush of air around you makes you aware that the descent is happening. At first there's a dip in your tummy. The same kind of dip that happens on the road when you drive as quickly as you can down a hill. Like you're on a roller coaster. That same concoction of adrenaline and dread that forces you to either scream or smile in the face of what's instinctively fearful. And then it's gone and you're simply falling. That's what death feels like.

It's funny how similar that description is to falling in love, isn't it? There's no controlling it. You can keep your eyes open or you can close them. You can scream on your way down, or you can lift your chin and wait silently for what's about to greet you on the other side. Your death or a kiss.

Sometimes, it's both.

One or the other just takes a bit longer to happen, but you were falling all the while.

I didn't realize I was falling at the time, but now as I lay here, waiting for the end, I can pinpoint the exact moment when it happened years ago. I know the very moment I slipped and tumbled down.

Hindsight is twenty-twenty and all that.

I didn't even get a kiss when I started falling. One look at Seth King and I was done for. I've fallen many times since then, all those little dips that made me both smile and scream. Always for Seth. I guess you could say I died for him many times. But this time… this time will be my last. I know it will.

The difference between the two, love and death, is that you can come back from love. Death isn't as forgiving.

CHAPTER 1

Laura

Ten years earlier

"You know you can sit with them if you want," Cami tells me in between bites of her apple. It's just us on this side of the cafeteria table although at the other end on the opposite side, two freshmen girls are currently having a heated but hushed conversation. I guess they wanted privacy for their gossip and they've planted themselves on the very end of our table to get it. "You don't have to sit with me when you're dating Seth."

I shake my head in disagreement, my gaze moving from the brunette ponytail swishing behind one of the intruders at our table to Seth's table. Of course it's his. He owns it.

He smiles when he sees me. It's slow and charming, genuine too. The kind of smile where wrinkles form around his eyes when he does it. He's so damn handsome, it's not fair. How could I ever not want him? There's simply no denying it. My whole heart wants to beat with his.

That doesn't mean we have to put a label on it. I know damn well that it will be the kiss of death if we do.

And it sure as hell doesn't mean I can't sit with Cami anymore.

"We aren't dating," I say, denying what Cami suggests, even as my heart goes pitter-patter in protest. It's too warm in my chest, with too much commotion going on in there at the mere sight of Seth's smile. My eyes are caught by his steely gaze. There's a sense of tension and electricity between us. There's no use fighting it anymore.

"You're one of them now," she whispers, leaning closer to me for comedic effect with no trace of malice, only humor. And it works. I laugh, this ridiculously high-pitched laugh as my cheeks burn and I turn to her.

My lips part to object as I reach forward and unscrew the cap on my iced tea, but Cami doesn't give me a moment to form a rebuttal. "You hang out at the bar. You play pool with them. They walk with you on your way home."

"Not the whole way and not always," I protest.

She tilts her head and makes an expression like I'm being unreasonable denying it and maybe I am. In the last two months, I've spent every waking moment with Seth and his crew. And it feels like I belong there, like I was always supposed to be on that side of the room. It's like they're my new family. Not by blood but by choice. Cami is my family too, though. Nothing will change that. Ever. We will always be inseparable.

"Semantics," Cami argues and takes another bite of her apple. She doesn't bother swallowing before telling me with a nudge of her shoulder, "You should sit with your boy toy."

"Boy toy freaked me out a little yesterday," I say. I'm going off script, changing the subject and hiding behind huge news. I'm not sitting with Seth whether Cami's here or not. It would make what we have more real. And if it's real, it can be taken away from me. So my ass is staying put.

"What?" Cami's happy-go-lucky façade vanishes and she quickly glances behind me. "What happened?" she asks lowly, barely moving her lips as she keeps her eyes pinned to mine. I have to laugh, my shoulders shaking gently.

"Nothing bad," I start to tell her and my stomach does this weird flip that coincides with my heartbeat as I remember last night.

"So I was doing our biology homework last night, you know how there's that genetics question about kids? Like about what color eyes they'd have if both parents had blue eyes?"

Cami's in the middle of nodding and taking a sip of water when her eyes go wide, and she whips them to me. "Kids?" she questions, getting right to the point.

Again, my stomach does something strange, almost like it's cringing. Which is exactly what I feel like doing too.

"He said we'd make cute babies," I say and blush.

"Oh. My. God. Seriously, go sit with him," she says, brushing me off jokingly and then laughs. It takes her a half minute to completely change her tone. "You are not allowed to get pregnant in high school," she reprimands me although there's nothing but humor there. She knows how driven I am. Still… the thought, even if it was a quick one, of having a baby with Seth feels like the world shifting under my feet.

"As if," I half-heartedly joke and remember the next bit of the conversation. How Seth laughed, but it was a sad laugh, and then he told me he'd make an awful father.

I bet whatever it is that makes him feel that way is because of his own father. I never knew the man, not really. I only knew of him. Instead of replying to Seth's offhand remark, I simply kissed him. He told me, "You're too good for me, you know that?" Which earned him a quiet laugh and another kiss from me.

He's wrong about that. He's wrong about a lot of things, but one thing he's right about is that we would make cute babies.

Flip, tumble, I willingly fall all the way down…

CHAPTER 2

Laura

Present day

THERE'S THIS SICK FEELING I GET IN MY GUT SOMETIMES. IT HAPPENS when I know I've messed up or when I'm highly aware that someone's going to be mad at me. My grandma told me once it's something that *people-pleasers* get. It's like this churning that's too deep and low to be due to my stomach but still wants me to throw up. Ever since I got off the call with Doctor Tabor, I've had that nauseated feeling.

I still have to go in for the ultrasound for more precise specifics, but the hormone levels in my blood are conclusive proof that this baby is farther along than a few weeks. She's sure of it. Months. Months and months. Not weeks along like I originally thought.

Suddenly, I'm even colder than I was just a moment ago and the blanket isn't helping. I don't cry. I won't cry even if my breath skips and hitches.

That revolting feeling churns again and I have to close my eyes. I haven't cried yet but I want to. *This baby isn't Seth's.* Just the thought makes my throat constrict and bitter tears prick the back of my eyes. I'm physically not all right. Not in the least.

Instead of giving in to the harsh need to let it all out in useless tears,

I lean forward, picking up my cup of hot tea and take a sip. It's caffeinated and part of me thinks I shouldn't drink it because it means I'll just be staying up that much later. The other part of me thinks I shouldn't drink it because caffeine isn't good for the baby. But it's the only thing in this damn house that I can pretend will soothe me right now.

And that's all I'm doing. Pretending. Because nothing is all right. Not a damn thing. Rocking back and forth, my mind races and I try to work it all out in my head, but I can't.

I have an urgent need to get up and go to work. Not because I bury myself there when I want to run away… well, maybe partly that. But also because the answers I've been avoiding await me at work. I can reference the dates I went on by checking my old work schedules and I can make use of the equipment for pregnant patients.

I need to know exactly how far along I am. Hate and resentment burn inside of me, knowing I've been running all this while. I've known for weeks that I was pregnant. *Weeks!* At the very least, I could have gone in at any point to make sure this baby was healthy. Instead, I was running from the truth and burying my head in the sand.

Seth's right, I do always run. I fucking hate myself right now.

My hand splays across my stomach as I stare out the window, watching a late-night thunderstorm crack open the sky with an occasional bolt of lightning. I pretend this doesn't hurt and that I'm not scared. And more than that, ashamed. Ashamed of being a horrible mother to this tiny life that hasn't even been born yet.

If it wasn't so cold, I'd slip outside onto the porch and listen to the sounds of the rain beating down on the roof. It's so soothing to hear. From in here, I can't hear the rain, and I can barely see it at all once the lightning ceases.

I haven't felt a single kick. I've barely gained any weight at all. In fact, my jawline is tighter than in recent months and my stomach only looks a little bloated. *If I'm really months along, I should be bigger.* Even as the thought hits me, I strike it down. Women carry differently. Every pregnancy shows differently. I need answers. I need to take care of myself and this baby.

Months. My chest pulses with pain as another burst of lightning rips the sky open. Thunder comes many seconds later. All the while my eyes are closed.

Months of drinking.

Months of stress at work and late nights.

Months of sex with various men. Only seven months ago I spent the night with one man and the very next night with another. Was I already pregnant then? *Impossible.* I can't be seven months along. No, no, I can't be that far along.

I need to know how far along I am and I need to know right now. Because the one thought that's been screaming in my head feels accurate. It feels right. *The baby isn't healthy.* No kicks, no weight gain. Maybe my heart is failing my child.

The tears prick again and this time one escapes and rolls down my cheek. I brush it away, pretending like it didn't happen and stare out of the window into the dark sky, speckled with blurs of the pouring rain.

I have work this week. Work will have answers. And I'll schedule every appointment my doctor wants first thing tomorrow. I just need to make it through tonight. *I'll be a good mom,* I silently promise my baby. I may fail everywhere else, but I promise I'll be a good mom.

More tears escape as I hold my stomach and I can no longer stop them.

I don't know how I'll make it that long. I can't take any more. From my heart, to Seth, to this pregnancy and jail. Jesus Christ! I can't take any more! My heart spasms in my chest and I grip at my shirt, stifling the useless sobs of self-pity. I've taken all my medication; I'm doing everything I can, but I can feel myself breaking.

So I do what I've done for years now. I pick up the phone and call Bethany.

It rings and rings. All the while I stare out of the window, watching the wind whip across the darkened tree line of pines. Something, anything, please take away this pain because my mind is going to the darkest of thoughts. How could it go to anything else? All my life has ever been is tragic.

"Hey, you okay?" Bethany answers, sounding slightly out of breath, which makes me lean forward, my comfortable blanket falling from my chest to puddle in my lap.

"Are *you* okay?" I stress, roughly wiping my face and getting a grip on my emotions.

"Yeah, just," she pauses and breathes out heavily before continuing, "yeah, I was just on the other side of the hall when my phone rang. I didn't put it on silent like an idiot."

"Oh," I say and settle back in the sofa, readjusting my blanket. "You have a minute?"

"It's bedtime over here, so I've got all the minutes in the world for you, love."

A smile lifts up my lips as I pick at lint on the blanket.

"I just… I have so much to tell you." A sadness washes over me at the realization that I haven't told her a damn thing. Secrets kill people. They bury themselves deep down where they hurt you but you can't feel it until the damage is already done. I should know.

My head falls back against the sofa as I stare aimlessly at the ceiling, feeling a hollowness of regret run through every inch of my insides. I'm always telling her to confide in me, yet I haven't let a soul in.

No one but Seth. And I can't tell him this.

"Yeah, I bet you do. You haven't told me anything," she answers and sounds of papers shuffling and slapping down on—probably the reception desk—come in through the background. It goes silent for a moment, then she sighs and says, "I feel like we've barely talked lately."

"I just…" I say and trail off, acutely aware I keep repeating this nonsense. *I just… I just…* I hate it.

"Where's Seth?" Bethany questions.

"He went out for a bit," I answer as if it's a normal night in the King household. Just like any other home. He went out for milk. He went out to pick up dinner. He went out to cache guns everywhere he could hide them and he might not come home. You know, *the usual.* The dread comes back and I squash it all the way down. There's too much else for me to worry about.

"Why does everything get worse and worse?" I ask her the rhetorical question, knowing I'm simply procrastinating and being a downer all the while. A thread comes loose on my chenille throw from my picking and I scrunch up my nose then put my hands under the blanket, resting them in my lap instead. Dammit. I love this blanket.

"What's going on? You're scaring me," Bethany replies in a single exhale.

My right hand travels to my stomach as another bolt of lightning illuminates the night.

With my lips parted and my eyes closed, I think of how I should tell her. It's so much to reveal. My heart. The pregnancy. How far along the pregnancy is.

An inhale, long and deep is what I give her, unable to tell her on the phone.

Why did I call, then? And when did I become such a chickenshit?

"Do you need me to come to you? I can call Cindy in." Her tone drops, becoming humorous as she adds, "I want to pay that bitch back anyway." A snicker leaves me.

"I... no. It's okay. I only needed to hear your voice. Guess I'm feeling a little bit lonely is all." *Chickenshit, chickenshit, chickenshit.* Although there is some truth to my statement. I feel very much alone right now.

"I can come right now, no questions asked." She would too. I know she would. It wouldn't be the first time one of us has dropped everything to help the other. Although in the past it's been because of her sister, or my unfortunate choice in men or alcohol, or both.

That's when the realization occurs. I have Bethany at the very least.

I always knew I could never really have Seth and if this is the last of it, of us, at least I have Bethany and so does this little one.

I should probably tell her about said little one before something bad happens.

"It can wait until tomorrow."

She heaves in a breath that sounds more like a sigh and says, "All right then. You should know I'm planning on passing the hell out when I leave here at five."

"Par for the course." I smile as I respond then take a sip of now lukewarm tea that doesn't do anything to soothe the ache in my soul.

"Love you," she tells me and I tell her I love her back.

I'll go to sleep and ignore these feelings. Tomorrow, when the sun is up and I'm able, I'll go to the doctor's and I'll take it from there. That's all I can do right now anyway.

Seth

My father always told me to trust my gut. He said there's something about humanity that tries to make us hide our baser instincts, but it's those instincts that keep us alive. Right now, I feel sick. I feel like something awful has happened. It's a hollowness in my chest. Not when I think about Marcus though, and not while Declan talks to me on the way to the corner store to meet with Walsh.

I may be headed to my death right now, but that doesn't affect me in the least.

It's when I look down at my phone and see Laura hasn't texted me back. That's when I feel like something's wrong. I don't know what it is, but I know something's wrong.

I try to convince myself that she's sleeping, but my gut tells me I'm a liar. There's something very wrong. The seatbelt across my chest feels tighter now and I can't get comfortable in this seat. She was fine when I left. I know she was fine, better than fine, even. Maybe worried but she always worries and this is the end to that.

The bright light from my phone pierces the darkness in the cab of Declan's car, getting his attention.

Love you, Babygirl. That was sent two hours ago.

"You all right?" Declan questions, turning down the radio station that was already barely on to begin with.

"Fine, just give me a minute." *Thump, thump*, something's wrong. I can feel it.

A quick call to the security team confirms she's inside the house, safe and sound.

"You sure?" I question Dominic and his confident voice reassures me she's inside, with no signs of distress. "Do you want me to go inside and check?" he asks and I tell him no. "Thank you," I say then hang up the phone. She was awake when I sent the text. They confirmed it.

The concerned exhale that leaves me gets an unsure look from Declan. With a fresh shave and a now empty orange energy drink that I can smell from here even though it's sitting in the console, he's wide awake and alert. "What's going on?"

I don't have an answer to his question.

Maybe it's just that I'm not ready to be a father. Maybe that's why I get this feeling every time I've thought about her tonight. Maybe I'm not used to telling her I love her and not hearing it back. There's some fucking karma for me.

"She's okay, right?" he questions as he readjusts his grip on the wheel. The motion is what I focus on as I shove the unwanted feelings aside.

"Yeah, Dominic said she's inside still and from what they can tell she's sleeping." *She probably didn't see it,* I lie to myself. She always checks her phone and plugs it in right before bed. Always. Laura is a creature of habit.

"Are you having second thoughts about this meet with Marcus?" he asks me as we roll by the Rockford Center, the large building and parking lot lit up while everything else has closed down this late at night.

The black leather under my ass groans as I readjust in my seat, staring out the window and listening to the rain beating against the car. The windshield wipers slide back and forth, clearing the way for more battering.

"No, no second thoughts. We need to end this and see what the hell he wants."

"It pisses me off. For months we've been trying to get in touch with him and no response. Then this?" It's quiet in the car as I stare at him, his anger attempting to disguise his concern. "If we had more time, we could go through the transcripts of their letters and have the upper hand."

The feeling vanishes at the mention of the letters. And just like that, my phone vibrates in my hand. *I love you too. Come home as soon as you can.*

She adds a moment later: *And in one piece.*

I may make her heart skip, but she does something to mine too. There's a sense of warmth and calm that hits me every time she says she loves me. I think it's because my heart knows she's telling the truth. She really does love me.

It's a fucking miracle that she does. An unjust one at that, but I'll greedily take it.

That stir of anxiousness leaves me instantly. She's all right. We're all right. *Damn, when did I become so insecure and self-conscious?* Oh yeah, the second she told me I'm going to be a father.

"Guessing your fight is over?" Declan asks, the cocky smirk on his face revealed easily via the light of my phone in the dark night.

"We weren't fighting."

"Whatever you say, King." Declan uses my last name when he replies, which is something he doesn't usually do. I notice it, but I don't know what to make of it.

He hasn't called me King in years.

I note how easy it is to shift my focus back to the point of this drive and tonight. Knowing Laura's all right, I can put everything into this meet with Marcus.

Declan's at ease, well as much as he can be. Letting the anger dissipate, he drives with one hand now as we pass the police station. Like the Rockford Center, it's brightly lit, a beacon in the barren streets.

Declan gives me yet another reason we should push off the meet. "We still haven't decoded all the letters."

"I bet that's why he wants to meet tonight, so we don't have time to figure out what they've been talking about," I comment, bringing the conversation back to Marcus, to the point of tonight's venture. It's far too calm now as we drive straight into the eye of the storm that is Marcus.

"That would make sense, which means technically, we do have the upper hand."

"Possibly," I say, correcting him. Absently, I tap my knuckles against the window, thinking back to every piece of information I was able to gather in the letters Walsh and Marcus wrote to each other.

"I wish they hadn't written the notes in fucking code," I mutter, pissed that it couldn't be as easy as simply reading them. Although there are literally hundreds of them, dating back for over a decade.

Declan's huff of a laugh lacks all sense of humor. "Tell me about it," he comments offhandedly, lowering his head slightly as he makes a left at the light.

"We know Marcus taunted Walsh at first but then they shared an interest in something."

"In what?" I question, wanting every piece of information. Declan had more time than I did to scour the letters. I only got a briefing and not a damn bit of it makes me feel prepared for what's to come.

"Killing a man who deserved it."

I swallow thickly, nodding. Marcus has always played a part in who lives and who dies in this town. Even Carter acknowledges that. The Cross brothers were never on Marcus's radar; the two men never had a problem that stirred between them.

That changed when Carter took Aria. That much is clear in the letters as well.

"Walsh said Marcus could have him." Declan's comment brings my attention back to him rather than what Marcus wrote about Carter.

"Who?"

"The man they agreed needed to die. It was a case, Walsh's case and he gave Marcus the green light to murder. That's when their friendship began and the letters came in more frequently."

"Right." I wonder if that's why Marcus wants Walsh there. "Maybe they're closer than we previously thought."

"Walsh said Marcus was an angel of death, a serial killer deciding who would live and die based on what they deserved."

"Do we trust what Walsh says?" I question Declan, who pauses. The windshield wipers are the only sound I can hear as we wait at the last red light.

"He's not wrong. He hasn't lied to us yet either."

"That we know of. But he's sure as shit held back."

"All I know is if Marcus is our moral compass, we're fucked," Declan comments.

"We take the train to the warehouse together. We take two trains back separately when we leave."

"At least your train is first," Declan says.

Nervousness pricks along my skin as I tap my thumb on my knee. This is it. An end to all this bullshit between Marcus and us. It fucking better be.

I have a child coming. A life I want to live. All this bullshit has to stop or else I know it will end the same as last time. I can already picture her leaving me. I will chase her to the ends of this world, but I won't let the danger accompany me. I won't let her be involved.

Marcus was wrong about Carter. He was wrong and he knows he was… it's in the letters. So he can go back to playing God and leaving us to our own devices. Or else… as Carter said last night, there will be a war.

That can't happen. Not again. I can't let that happen again. If it does, I will lose her forever.

"You all good?" Declan asks me and it's then that I realize we're here at the train station. "Ready?"

He parks the car on the left side, the tracks in front of us and empty spaces all around us. The night train leaves in half an hour.

A half hour, a twenty-minute ride, and then… it's the end of all this.

"Yeah," I answer him, "I'm ready."

CHAPTER 3

Laura

It's cold. I can't get over how cold it is. It's all-consuming, the freezing chill. My thoughts stay focused on it even as my surroundings come back to me. The stark white brick walls. The paint is so thick, like it's been coated a hundred times. The light is dim, because it's "lights out." That's right, I can't sleep. Not with Jean in here with me.

Shivers run down my spine. It's odd how I can't even focus on her lying across from me in her orange uniform. The one that matches mine.

All I can think about is how cold it is; the thin blanket in the jail cell simply isn't enough. Anxiety threads itself slowly through the thin fabric, followed by fear. So much fear. I can't sleep because if I do… she'll kill me. She's going to kill me. I know she is but still, my eyes close. I can't sleep, but terror grips me. Exhaustion keeps me still, fighting against the need to sit up so she knows I'm awake. So she won't kill me. I can't die. I want to live.

My eyes fly open, my heart galloping away at the sight of her. Taller, stronger, and more experienced in killing. Who was I to ever think I'd be a match? The terror is so encompassing that when she stands up, the blood dried around her neck and hands, I can't move.

Run! *I can't. I can't move.*

All I can feel is the pounding in my chest and the frigid cold along my skin.

Scream! Fight! Do something! *I can't do anything, though. I could never outrun this. I was supposed to die a long time ago. I'm living on borrowed time.*

My body's practically paralyzed, everything is so still and I'm about to be a victim as she makes her way to me.

Even when she pulls out her pocketknife, smiling at me, I'm trapped in a body that refuses to move. Her little nickname for me nearly forces me to close my eyes. Sickness coils in my stomach. I hate her and everything she stands for.

I stay still, as still as can be. All the while she waves the knife at me, giddy and proud. I can't move. I can't scream. I'm only watching.

Seth. Seth, help me. *I cry for him, even when I know he can't hear me. He can't save me here. Could he ever really save me? Wasn't I supposed to be the one to save him… and I didn't. I failed and now I'm going to die.*

I'm alone. So alone. All I'll ever be is alone.

Miraculously, my hand moves to my lower stomach.

Baby.

The soothing thought is only a word. I won't be alone. Tears fall down my face and that's when Jean smiles at me. You can't keep him, *she tells me, taunting me.* You don't deserve him.

Thump, thump. No! *Adrenaline scorches my blood as it races through me, challenging the pounding of my heart.*

Screaming. There's so much screaming.

It's all I can hear. My own voice screaming "no" as she closes the distance. But I still can't move.

And then both of us scream as she plunges the knife into my belly with one swift motion.

I jolt awake from the horrible nightmare and nearly vomit instantly. Somehow, I manage to keep it down, although my body shudders. A cold sweat bathes every inch of my skin as I sit straight up, my gaze darting around the empty room. My trembling hand covers my mouth and goosebumps line my skin.

Breathe.

I do just that.

Lift your shirt. See? It's okay. I go through the motions to prove it's a nightmare. Even with the fear lingering in my every thought.

It's only a nightmare.

It takes a long while for my heart to knock it off, and the fear to subside. Even longer to breathe normally.

Jean is dead. She's long gone. She will never hurt me or my child. Never.

One hand is still clutching the sheet with a white-knuckled grip and the other is protectively laid over my stomach. The light that filters in beneath the door from the hallway is the only light I've got besides the clock on Seth's nightstand. The digital numbers read 3:15.

One breath in and then another. It takes a moment to steady myself, but I do.

Blinking away the little bit of sleep I got, I finally notice that Seth isn't home. He's been gone too long. My first instinct is to check my phone and I'm glad I do. He texted me an hour ago saying that there was a delay. A few minutes later, he messaged that he hoped I was sleeping.

"I wish I were sleeping too," I mumble, rubbing my tired eyes. My shoulders shake with a shiver that won't quit. Sighing out the frustration, I rip off the covers and go to the bathroom to take my pills. Four of them, every morning, for my heart. And then a prenatal vitamin.

I've never taken so many pills in my life. It's a bit early to take them, but there's no way I'm going back to sleep. Not after… that.

I wash my face and when I do, the vision of Jean comes back, only this time I'm saddened by it. By the memory of what happened and what I did. I suppose I'm not over the fact that I killed her. With the water still running, I lean my weight forward and rock slightly, gripping the porcelain sides of the sink.

I did what I had to do. And I can live with the nightmares if they're my consequence. I accept it.

It isn't the worst nightmare I've ever had. It isn't even the worst thing that's happened to me, murdering someone in cold blood—it's not even the most frightening thing. If I just ignore it, the nightmares will go away. I nod at that conclusion. It's true. I've been here before with worse terrors. This isn't the most horrific thing that's happened to me and it won't be the last event of my life that gives me night terrors. Well… so long as I live long enough. A sarcastic chuckle comes paired with an eye roll.

I'm not giving up on my heart just yet.

I'm just not myself. Right now, I am not myself at all. But I'm okay. The baby's okay.

My thoughts eventually give way to a whispered mantra. "The baby's okay. The baby's okay." It's the only thing I can repeat that calms me down. The adrenaline, the chills, the fear—it all means nothing because my baby is okay.

My gaze rises to the mirror, where dark circles under my eyes greet me.

I can't stand to look at them or the redness gathering in the whites of my eyes. I can't get back into bed either. Not with the nightmare still fresh over the sheets.

One look at the rumpled covers and I have to turn away before her voice hisses in my ear again.

I tell myself I'm just getting tea and then I'll climb back in bed, but that doesn't explain why I grab a thick sweatshirt and throw it on over my pajamas. I know my boots are at the door.

I was always a bad liar, even to myself.

I told Seth I'd be here when he got back, but I can't stay. I need to get out of here. I still have time to catch Bethany before she leaves at five, the start of the morning shift. Work will be slow and I have to tell her.

I'll bring her a cup of coffee so she can power through this next hour—that last hour is a bitch, after all. It's always the most boring, just doing rounds on patients as they sleep.

The rain from earlier has stopped, but I still manage to walk right into a deep puddle the second I make it down the porch steps.

"Fuck," I mutter as the freezing cold water splashes up the right leg of my pants and I curse my way to my car in the cold night. My breath fogs in front of my face and all the while my keys jingle happily beside me.

The radio's on when I get in my car and I'm quick to turn it down. The car starts with a rumble and I sit back in my seat, digging my phone out from my purse.

I'm smart enough to at least let Seth know where I'm going. He doesn't get a say in whether or not I go though, given his ass isn't even here.

I whisper the text as I write it out in my phone, "Getting Cami coffee and going to the center. I'll be back before six to go back to sleep." I nearly send him the message when I realize my mistake.

Cami.

I wrote Cami.

Fuck, that pain is sudden and fresh. It's a familiar pain of loss I haven't felt in a long time. *Fuck.* My head slams back against the headrest.

I could tell myself I'm just tired, but that's not all this is. I miss her. I miss her so damn much with everything happening. Cami would know what to do and how to tell Seth the truth. Damn it hurts and forces more tears to well up in my eyes. I wish Cami were here. "No more fucking crying," I mutter to myself.

A sharp pain that feels like a knife twisting in my chest makes me struggle to take in a steady breath. My eyes close tight and my neck arches back so my face is toward the hood of the car. I cover my face with my left hand and drop my phone into my lap. "No more crying," I whisper into my clasped hands. "My baby is okay and I can't cry because it'll upset the baby," I say. Making the bold statement helps me. It truly calms me through and through.

With a shuddering breath, I admit I'm all sorts of fucked up this witching hour, but I change *Cami* to *Bethany* and hit send, gathering my composure and continuing with this plan I've barely put together in my head.

I pull out of the drive before Seth can text back and tell the men at the gate where I'm going.

There are two men on security duty in the brick shack at the end of the drive. At least that's what I call it; although I'm sure it's armored and reinforced to high heaven, I still call it the security shack in my head every time I look at it. With a single look at each other, they decide which one will follow me and tell me to wait until he's behind me.

Security detail is still a thing, I guess. This time it's a man named Garett with dirty blond hair that looks charming like it is even though it's all messed up. He also looks far too awake for 3:00 a.m., but I don't question it. I only nod and sit there in silence, waiting for him to get the car. I don't care if Seth wants them to follow me for the rest of my life, to be honest. They can follow me through the coffee shop drive-through that's open twenty-four hours all they want.

Which Garett does.

Follow me wherever. Just don't tell me where to go.

The entire ride is silent. My stomach bothers me and it grumbles. Right before the turn to the center, I swear I feel a bump or a kick, but I can't tell for sure. I hold my breath as I turn in and all the while that I'm idling, my keys still in the ignition, my car still running and the smell of a large mocha coffee and a large hot chocolate still permeating the small space, I wait for another kick.

But the kick, if it was that, doesn't happen again. I swear I felt it though. A little hope stirs in my chest.

I rack my brain trying to remember when kicks start as I put the car into park, absently noting that there are three other cars parked here. Two of them I recognize as Aiden's and Bethany's. Kicks start up earlier for some women, like within two months. Others around four or five months, I think. So that doesn't do me a damn bit of good.

I fight the urge to rub soothing circles on my tummy as I make my way into the Rockford Center. Mostly because each hand is grasping a foam cup of hot liquid.

Gesturing to the handsome babysitter, also known as my security detail, I motion that I'm going in as he parks his car and I hit the handicap door button on the exterior of the building for the front entrance to open for me.

My memory is shit this early in the morning but I still wish I'd paid more attention to the maternity chapters of all the textbooks I've had to read and all the classes I've had to take. One thing though that always stood out is that every woman is different, so therefore every pregnancy is different. Which doesn't offer me any comfort as I take the elevator up. Not a damn bit.

Nerves build in my belly as the elevator rises one floor at a time.

Ding.

The elevator arriving is the only noise on the entire floor. It can be unsettling this late at night, with the hallways empty and the lights on overnight mode, so they're off until motion is detected. It's creepy as fuck, to be honest.

Luckily, the main light is always on since someone is always here.

The view of Aiden leaning out from his office is a welcome sight, even if the look on his face isn't.

With his brow furrowed he asserts, "You aren't on the schedule for today." *Well, that's a nice hello.*

"I know," I answer him, shrugging off my coat at the reception desk and laying it on a cleared-off spot free of fall décor and paperwork. The cold still clings to me, so I pick the hot cup back up the second I can. "I just brought Bethany coffee."

"She should be done with her rounds in a few minutes." His answer is simple, welcoming even, but his face is still pinched with concern.

"Are you all right?" he finally questions and I give him an honest answer, saying, "I couldn't sleep and something's been bugging me that I thought Bethany could help me with."

I half expect him to tell me that now is not the time, don't bring personal life into work, blah, blah, blah, but he only nods once and tells me, still leaning just outside his office door, "If you ever need anything, I'm here." It's sincere and his tired eyes reflect nothing but genuine warmth.

"Thanks." The word leaves me a little too quietly and I have to clear my throat before I can say it louder.

With a pat on his door, he vanishes back into his office, the door being left open just an inch. *Nosy fucker...* The snide thought does nothing but lessen the tension in my shoulders and put a smirk on my lips. I do like that nosy fucker, even if he's been weird lately. I've been weird too, after all.

The moment I pull up an extra chair beside the one behind the reception desk, Bethany's there.

"What the hell are you doing here?" It's nearly an accusation, probably the exact words Aiden wanted to say. With her wide eyes riddled with concern, she smiles back when I smile up at her, holding out the hot cup of coffee.

"Brought you coffee and a dilemma that won't let me sleep." Inwardly I grimace, remembering the real reason I woke up. I imagine Jean will haunt me for the rest of my life and I sure as hell will never breathe a word of what happened to anyone. *No Jean. No nightmare.* But this early morning, before the sun has a chance to slip out, I'm telling Bethany everything else.

All the tension leaves her squared shoulders and she eagerly accepts. The clipboard she held in her hand claps down on the desk as she sinks into the chair beside me and takes the coffee with a grateful simper.

With her pink scrubs bunched up her arms, she blows across the top of the coffee and takes a sip. With the steam pouring out of the small opening at the top, it must still be too hot because her sip is short and Bethany's a girl who gulps down a drink, rather than savoring it.

I fidget in my seat, twisting the chair back and forth and waiting for the right words to come, but they don't.

An easy hum of satisfaction from Bethany is followed by the easy demand as she says, "Spill it."

Thump. My heart slams in protest, but I ignore it. It wants to fight everything nowadays.

"I have a heart condition and it's worse than I ever could have imagined."

Bethany's demeanor changes in a blink. Setting her coffee on the desk, she leans forward, the blood draining from her face.

"Okay," she says, in the tone we use when talking to patients, although fear drowns the neutral word. She looks like she's about to break down and she expects me to tell her I'm going to die. Which… I would, if I were to be completely honest.

I pick at my nails, feeling this wave of heat roll up my body.

"I'm on the donor list for a transplant because surgery is too risky."

"Oh my God," Bethany blurts out and covers her face, her body crumpling in on itself but only for a moment. She's quick to correct her posture and reach out a hand to me, which I accept. Her hand holding mine, just a little human touch, is everything that I needed.

"I'm not concerned about that as much as something else."

"What the hell?" Her answer comes out in a single breath. "You need to be," she adds and she's harsh with her rebuttal, tears gathering in her eyes and falling just as quickly.

"What can I do?" I say and shake my head gently. "I have medicine, I take it. And now I wait. Why concern myself when there's something more important?"

Her bottom lip wobbles for a fraction of a second before she rakes her hand through her hair, pulling her hand from mine, and starts listing everything else I can do. "Diet, stress levels, there's so much you can do."

"Is there really though? I'm doing the best I can with it, but we both know sometimes it's not …" I trail off and swallow thickly before continuing. "I promise you, I'm doing everything the doctor told me and praying for a donor match to become available so I can have the surgery." As Bethany nods in understanding, although I'm not sure she believes me, I watch her swallow and promise myself I won't tell her the doctor only gave me a year. I'll lie if she asks. She doesn't need to know that. I accept whatever comes to me on this front. I'll do everything I can, but I've prepared myself for death before and I can't run any longer.

"I'm also pregnant," I blurt out before the sadness overtakes this entire conversation.

"What?" she exclaims and I practically chuckle at the whiplash Bethany just went through.

Her eyes are wide and her expression simply shocked until I tell her what she needs to know.

"I'm pregnant and I'm so happy," I say although my voice cracks during the last part and I hate it. "Why do I keep crying?" There aren't tears yet but I swear if they come I'll be pissed.

"Because you're pregnant," Bethany answers as she gets off her chair to hug me. Her embrace is steadying, just like I knew it would be. A safe place full of shared happiness and love.

"All these tears," I say, wiping at my eyes to keep them from coming and then wiping my hand on my pajama pants. She takes that as her cue to sit back down, although she doesn't take her eyes off of my stomach.

"It's because you're pregnant," she says again, sniffling and plucking tissues out of the box on the reception desk. She hands one to me and keeps another for herself.

"Oh yeah? Then what's your excuse?" I jokingly push back.

"Because *you're* pregnant," she says comically, quietly laughing and I join in with her.

After the laughter dies down, the realization slowly hits her. "How is your heart going to hold up with…"

"The doctor wants to do a planned cesarean to avoid the stress of labor."

It's a sobering thought once again, but I keep a thin smile plastered where it is. I won't let this light be dimmed. My baby will be okay. My baby *is* okay. That's what matters right now.

"I …" I pause and take a deep breath, hating the next part. "I don't know how to tell Seth—"

"He'll be so happy," she says, cutting me off, so certain that I'll get to have that part of a happily ever after. She reaches for my hand and I pull away, shocking both her and myself.

"Sorry, it just hurts." I swallow thickly before continuing. "Because he *was* happy, when I told him." Confusion mars her tired eyes until I add, "But I just found out that this baby isn't his."

Bethany can't tear her eyes from mine, not even as she reaches for her coffee as if it will protect her from the uneasiness of this conversation. Tears cloud my vision and prevent me from clearly seeing the shock on her face.

"Do you know who?" she asks and I shake my head.

"I literally have no idea. I always used protection. I may have been a little ... promiscuous... but I wasn't reckless." The defensiveness in my tone isn't needed. Bethany's never judged me. She never would.

"I know you did. I know."

"I have my schedule from the past few months in the office and I can look through it to see the dates." She nods along with my explanation.

"I want to tell him but I have to go to an appointment first to make sure everything is okay. To make sure the baby is healthy and find out exactly how far along I am."

"You haven't gone to a doctor?" Her question doesn't hide her shock and how ludicrous she must think this situation is. "You just went. I went with you! You were right there." I squirm in my seat. There's that shame again.

"I didn't realize I was pregnant. Definitely not this far along—"

"How far?"

"I don't know... That's partially why I'm here." I glance down the hall, past Aiden's office, where I know there's an ultrasound machine.

I don't even have to tell Bethany what I'm thinking before she grabs my hand, her ass already out of the seat as she says, "Let's go see your baby."

CHAPTER 4

Seth

"He set the meet, he shouldn't be late," Walsh mutters without breaking his steady pace. He hasn't been still since we got on the train.

Nervousness keeps him pacing in slow but steady circles around a staircase in the center of the nearly empty warehouse. It's driving me fucking crazy. Maybe this is what Marcus wanted… for me to kill Walsh before he gets here.

Letting out a controlled exhale, I slip my hands in my pockets and glance past the iron rails of the staircase to the large, sleek silver doors of the elevator behind it.

"It's always a warehouse," I murmur so low, Walsh doesn't hear.

He stops in his tracks. "What?" The fact that we're both in suits doesn't mean shit right now. Exhaustion is evident on his face and I can feel it weighing down my own expression. I don't have to see myself in the reflection of the elevator doors to know I look like hell.

Pinching the bridge of my nose, I tell him, "Nothing."

"He's never made me wait before," Walsh tells me then takes a few steps, walking closer to the edge of the room where boxes are stacked. "He's always waiting. I bet he's here. Just waiting."

This place must still be in use, which makes me think there are cameras, although I haven't seen one yet.

I've gone over how to phrase everything we need to discuss so that if there are security cameras here, I won't be implicated if footage turns up later.

I don't trust Walsh. I don't trust Marcus.

At this point, an hour past the time agreed upon for the meet, I don't trust my gut either. It told me to come, and now it's screaming for me to leave.

"Seth King." A deep voice booms from somewhere to my right through the barren warehouse. The familiar chill that comes with it travels up the back of my neck.

Marcus.

Just his name irks me, so the sound of his voice feels like someone digging even deeper into a fresh wound. "Finally we meet," Marcus states, but the voice comes from the left this time. Nervousness travels down my spine, starting at the base of my neck.

"Is that what this is?" I question, keeping my voice even and letting my gaze roam from the left side of the room to the right, slowly going over every shadow and stack of boxes. There are three levels, with the main floor open all the way up to the third floor with a railing along the hallways that line each floor. The building itself is at least thirty feet high. In this tin can of a warehouse, Marcus could be anywhere. "Usually when I meet someone, I see them," I add, raising my voice and feeling my spine straighten, my shoulders squaring.

The voice, in response, comes from behind me. "Did you really think I'd allow that?"

Walsh turns to face the sound, irritation clear on his expression, not the fear I imagine Marcus intended. I don't follow suit. My feet stay planted right where they are and I force myself to remain in control. Despite everything he's done, Marcus is only a man. "Yes." My voice is strong and every emotion except for irritation flees. "I did think you'd meet me face-to-face."

Everything Marcus does is deliberate, and I'm sure not showing his face is part of his plan, but also this theatricality with scattering his voice was done for a reason.

"I'm not entertained," I add.

"Then you're more foolish than I thought and perhaps I've made a mistake."

"Was it meant to frighten me, Marcus?" I question him, walking toward a pallet of stacked boxes in the corner. There are wooden toys inside of them. Little knickknacks that toddlers would play with. Over here, the light is scarce, making it more difficult for him to see me… I presume. "Or did you want me to be aware that you don't trust me?" I ask a bit lower, not bothering to raise my voice this time.

As I open a lone box lying behind the stack, I peer at Walsh from my periphery. He stays where he is, leaning against the rail and waiting patiently. Both his hands grasp the rail behind him while he watches the elevator doors.

"Have you done this before?" I direct my question at Walsh, who stares down at me since I'm now crouched. "Come to meetings with Marcus that are more of a show than anything?"

"It's always a show." Walsh's response is easy, although his expression is anything but. I respect the man at least for that.

"I can see you're frustrated," Marcus answers, his voice coming from a level above and to my right. The light doesn't reach that corner. "I never had any intention of showing myself to either of you. You should know that. You are a smart man, Seth."

"What are your intentions?" I ask. Walsh's footsteps clack on the concrete floor as he walks closer to me, where he could get a view as well. There's nothing to be seen from the corner on the second floor, but the next time Marcus speaks, there is no sign of a speaker or any device. It's him.

His voice bellows down from the second floor as he says, "I have a proposition for each of you, and I'm scarce on time." He must signal someone, because a thick shadow shifts in the distance. It's the only sign of movement.

There he is. Still hidden, but there nonetheless.

"You know how to reach me," Walsh says carefully.

"Our form of communication has been compromised," Marcus admits from upstairs and Walsh's brow furrows.

"Isn't that right, Seth?" Marcus's voice is accusatory.

"We found your letters, if that's what you're referring to." Heat dances along the back of my neck and my palms itch as Walsh's gaze moves to my form. I don't take my eyes from Marcus though. Or rather, where I know Marcus is.

"Where at?" Walsh questions and I answer, still not averting my gaze although I can feel Walsh's piercing mine.

"The post office."

"You could have told me on the way over so I didn't feel like a dumb prick," he mutters beneath his breath for only me to hear. The anger is temporary.

"We have other ways," Walsh speaks to Marcus.

"I don't trust them any longer," comes the reply. Marcus's harsh and darkened voice seems… tired, resigned even as he talks to Walsh. He corrects it as he raises his voice to say, "I thought you'd like to hear this as well. It's quite interesting, if nothing else."

My pulse quickens as my palms sweat. Waiting for whatever it is to come, still, I can't hold back a line I've been rehearsing in my head the entire silent train ride here.

"You made a mistake targeting the Cross brothers. We know you know that. You admitted it in the letters."

Walsh peers at me, his head dropping and I note that he stares at the floor as I speak. As if considering what I'm saying, debating whether it's true or false.

Marcus's silence urges to me to continue. "They don't need to be on your list. All we want is to go back to our former relationship."

"That's not going to happen," he says and Marcus's response only makes my hackles rise. Anger stirs in my blood.

"Then what is it you want?" I question, my voice coming from deep in my gut. "War?" I hate him in this moment. A bloody battle is the last thing I want.

His answer hits me hard in the chest, not just surprising me, but instilling a new fear. "To save Laura."

"Don't you fucking dare mention her name," I say and the sneer leaves me before I can think twice. Fists turn my knuckles white and I step closer to the edge, hating that he's not on this floor.

"You can't play God," Walsh bites out.

"I'm not," Marcus answers. "God has mercy."

"Don't you touch her," I say and I don't bother to hide the threat in my snarl.

"I don't plan on it. Let me explain."

"Explain," Walsh pipes up, reaching out for me. Not holding me back, but simply putting out his arm as if to stop me. There's nowhere for me to go, no way to get to him from here.

A new terror binds me in place at knowing she's anywhere near this man's radar.

It takes everything to be silent as my vision turns red.

"You had what I had. On the West Coast, you had control and power. The streets whispered your name like they do mine here. So naturally I had to keep an eye on you."

He pauses, although I don't know why or what he expects from me. All I keep thinking is that the moment he mentions her name again, I'll kill him. I will find a way to kill him.

"It became very clear that you followed her to the East Coast. Laura Roth. Love is so unpredictable. While everything else is… easily controlled."

"I'm warning you." My voice is barely contained. A deep-seated fear of losing her takes over. It claws at my stomach, tearing up everything inside of me. I don't let it show. Not an ounce of it. But I can't react either. I can't speak or else he'll hear it. He can't know.

"I want to save her." Marcus repeats what he said before and my head drops.

A sick, twisted smile lingers around the threat that leaves me, keeping the words steady as I say, "If you kill her…"

"I won't."

"Is she a target? Who's going after her?" My voice holds nothing but a menacing tone. All I need is a name.

"You should talk to her," he says and Marcus's easy response angers me even more. "Seth, she isn't well."

Questions race in my mind while emotions run through me. Is it a threat? Is that what this is? Does he know she's pregnant? Does he think there's something else going on with her? What the fuck does he mean by, "she isn't well?" My mind races and I can't stop it from going to the darkest of places.

As if reading my mind, he speaks, "It's more than her pregnancy. You'll see."

"You're lying." I hiss the response and oh so subtly, Walsh nods in agreement with me. His gaze is fixed on the spot where Marcus remains hidden.

"She'll tell you. I have faith that she will."

"Fuck you!" I can't control the chaotic response and Walsh grabbing my wrist is the only indication I have that I've stepped forward once again. "Stay away from Laura," I warn Marcus while shaking off Walsh's grasp.

"I have a way to save her." Marcus's voice is calm and at his admission, Walsh's expression turns quizzical. He stares into the darkness as I glance between the two of them. "And I promise you," he says, his voice becoming easy, like it was earlier with Walsh, "I have no intention of going anywhere near her or hurting her."

The pounding of the blood in my ears calms me. *Save her.* I would beg on my knees for him to save her if I truly thought he could. Or that he would. Or if she truly needed saving.

"I see you're skeptical," Marcus says, "but I've made the gathering of valuable information my life's work. I see everything, even things I don't care to see." He practically whispers the last line.

"What do you want from me?" I question him, my eyes narrowed.

I can practically hear the smile in his voice as he says, "I want you to owe me something."

"Tell me what you want," I say, pushing for him to get on with it.

"Walsh," Marcus says in a way that causes chills to roll down my arms, "this is where it gets interesting."

CHAPTER 5

Laura

"SO… IF THE BABY ISN'T SETH'S?" THE SMALL ROOM IS FAR TOO STERILE for this conversation. "How do you think he'll react?" she says and I take in a deep steadying breath.

Bethany gives me a moment to think up an answer, glancing between me and the tall machine in the room with the monitor that I can't take my eyes from.

The ultrasound gel is being warmed up, the machine is on and a textbook is open next to the keyboard on the desk for Bethany to reference.

I answer honestly, "I don't know." I genuinely have no idea how he'll react. But I know it'll crush the happiness he had. I'm all too aware of it.

Laying my head back on the small and thin disposable pillow, I listen to the rustling of the paper under my ass. I opted to take off my pants and I still have my shirt on, just lifted. Aiden better not come in here or he'll get an eyeful, that's for sure.

"I'll have to go through the dating apps I had and the schedule I kept to even narrow down who the father is." My throat is tight at the confession and shame forces my eyes closed. "I should at least know that before I tell him, I think." I nod with my eyes closed, as if agreeing with myself. "I should know everything before I tell him."

Bethany doesn't agree with me and neither does the pang in my chest.

It's quiet for a long moment and in that time I envision the conversation. I can barely stand the imagined sight of his sadness and disappointment. He wanted this. He was elated when I told him. My throat gets tight and I have to open my eyes to stare at something else, anything else. I can't take this baby away from him. It's going to hurt him. No matter the details, I know it's going to destroy him… and us.

"Okay, hold on." The sound of Bethany flipping a page in the textbook makes me turn to her. "You know we could wait for Sheila to come in tomorrow?" she says, but she doesn't take her eyes from the book.

"I don't want anyone to know until I know."

Insecurity runs rampant on Bethany's expression. "It's been so long since I've done this and I don't want to fuck this up," she practically mumbles.

"Just do it. We have to hurry anyway before Aiden realizes I stole you away."

"Cindy can cover for me. She should be here any minute now." She stares at the textbook, reading something rather than looking at me and my pleading expression for her to hurry the hell up.

"Cindy can't cover her own ass." I keep my tone light and so does Bethany with her response: "You're not wrong."

My chuckle is silenced by the squeeze of a bottle and gel plopping onto my exposed stomach.

"I think there's a bump," she says and Bethany's voice holds a hint of awe as she stares down at my tummy, now covered in goo.

"You're going to regret that if all of this is a mistake and I'm not really pregnant."

Neither of us laugh because she puts the transducer right beneath my belly button. Neither of us do anything at all other than stare at the monitor as the black screen turns to white streaks that resemble the waves of an ocean as they crash on the shore. The wand moves to the right and still nothing. There's no little blip. No sign of life and fear cripples me.

There's no little sac, there's nothing.

Not until the wand is moved to the left and at what I see, my hand reflexively covers my mouth.

"There's the baby." Bethany's sweet voice is all singsong and happy and I can't say anything at all. I'm too choked up.

My eyes burn with happy tears at the sight on the screen. I can't think of a single time, in my entire life, that I've ever cried happy tears. Not until today.

There's a flicker on the screen. A little tiny one right where the heart would be and it's in tune with a steady rhythm that comes through the speakers.

"It sounds like a little train," I whisper, listening to the *chugga, chugga, chugga, chugga* that is so steady and perfect. So perfect. *Please don't have a heart like me, little one.*

With my bottom lip unsteady, I get hold of my bearings enough to ask Bethany, "Is that you moving the wand or the baby moving?"

"That's just me. It looks like the fetus is sleeping." Bethany's eyes are glossy, but she keeps it professional. Still she whispers, "You're having a baby."

It's okay that there's no movement yet. Everything's okay because of the *chugga chugga*. Even so, I want to see him or her move. Some other sign. I want all the signs, if I'm being honest. Every sign in the world that this baby is okay and I didn't unknowingly hurt him or her.

Just like that, the little baby moves. He—or she—moves. I see it!

"Maybe that was a kick?" Bethany questions, obviously as thrilled to see the leg jolt like that as I am.

"I can't feel it." I shake my head.

"It's different for every pregnancy and mother. There's nothing wrong with that," she says, ever reassuring.

"I know, I know." I can't look at her. I watch my baby all the while. I barely even register the word until she starts moving the wand again.

Mother. She referred to me as a mother.

A tingle spreads down my skin and I can't move my eyes away. That's what I am, a mother. My head lays back, easier this time, waiting to see if the baby will kick again. I can see the legs, the arms, the big ole head and forehead. There's a little baby, a little life, inside of me.

Bethany never stops moving the wand and I wish she would hold still over his or her precious face. I want to see my baby. My first thought is that I want to see if the baby looks like me or Seth.

That sudden pain is a fast blow to my gut. I force it down and away though.

"That is the skull, we have a skull forming." I'm grateful for the distraction in Bethany's observation. I don't want anything to steal this moment from me. *I'm having a baby.* This is a happy time. I want my baby to know I'm so happy to see him or her. All I want this baby to feel is loved. Regardless of how fucked up I am.

"There are each of the sections of the skull..." Bethany's professional tone catches me off guard until I realize why she said it.

"Okay, so how far? How far along when the skull forms?"

"I don't... wait, let me..." Bethany doesn't refer to the textbook but instead continues to scrutinize the screen. "There's no yolk sac so you're more than ten weeks along." She's just rattling off facts.

But that's a fact that hits home.

Ten weeks. There's a dull thud in my chest. That confirms it. Seth hasn't been back in my life that long. Plain and simple. I was pregnant when I got in that car with Laura and saw him for the first time in years. I was already pregnant.

Even though it kills a piece of me, the piece that let him hold me in the living room, pretending we were a happy, perfect couple, I stare at the monitor and force myself not to feel the pain from knowing this isn't Seth's baby. *My baby is okay.*

"Do you want to know if it's a boy or a girl?" Bethany asks, quickly moving the wand from wherever it was positioned so I can't see for myself. As if I could tell what's going on down there. The rotation I did for maternity went by in a blur and the only thing I learned is that I didn't want to work in maternity.

With a quick sniffle to shake any bad or negative energy away, I nod and say, "Yes. Yes, I want to know."

She moves the wand just slightly to the right and the picture on the screen changes. At first I see a little foot, the tiniest little foot and all five toes. Then a leg, followed by both legs and a lean tummy.

"See that?" she asks and I shake my head but don't respond verbally. I'm still in awe that there's a baby in me.

"Boy," she says softly and gently.

"Are you sure?" I question her and then the pain hits again. *Seth wanted a boy.*

"I'm positive," Bethany answers and I smile. Genuinely.

"I'm having a baby boy."

I'm overwhelmed with so many emotions. There's a calmness in seeing my baby boy and knowing he's there and from what I can tell, healthy. But I don't know how Seth will react and that discomfort, that anxiousness, that fear of losing him—it all lingers over the small bit of happiness, tainting it.

"There's hardly any fat."

"What?" I question Bethany's comment.

"That's in the book. It's in here." The excitement from Bethany isn't contagious. Maybe we'll be able to tell how far along we are. There I go again, my mind picturing Seth with me through all of this… "Hold this."

I obey Bethany and hold the wand as still as can be over my belly.

The second I take it, my little boy touches his face. I saw it and I can see each little finger as he does it. My heart swells with the kind of happiness that also makes it ache.

"Did you see?" I whisper the question but Bethany didn't see. That little movement was just for me.

Bethany talks to herself, turning over a page then turning it back again instead of answering. I don't blame her. I hope she's close to knowing.

"He's a little shy of a foot long." Her exhale is loud before she tells me, "I think you're around twenty-two or twenty-three weeks. Definitely not twenty-five weeks because he's not tall enough." She sounds so certain.

"What if he's just short?" I ask her, remembering how my grandma used to tell me how small I was as a baby. I was a teeny tiny preemie.

"Umm, I don't… there's also… I don't know for sure but there's not a lot of fat on him like in these pictures and that's around twenty-five weeks."

"So more than twenty-two but less than twenty-five." So somewhere around June. I have to take my phone out to double-check. But it would have been a date in June. I can't even begin to think back that far, but I didn't go on many dates at all this summer and the double-dipping I did was in April or May. That's what Bethany called my two nights back-to-back with two different men: double-dipping. Technically I was the one dipped, but either way it doesn't matter. I imagine it won't be hard to figure out what fling led to this little blessing.

Then there's the matter of telling the man… and telling Seth.

"Is that something you can live with?" Bethany asks me and it takes a moment for me to understand what she's referring to. Weeks along: twenty-two to twenty-five.

"Yeah." I don't skip a beat before asking her, "When is it safe to deliver?"

"Thirty-seven weeks… some say thirty-eight."

"What if I get that heart in?" The questions tumble out of me.

"You need to see your doctor." Her tone practically scolds me as she takes the wand from me, taking another long look at the baby. My little prince.

"I will tomorrow." I will do everything right starting tomorrow. Every appointment, every pill. Whatever I have to do.

"It's almost five a.m. love, so you will *today*, but probably after a nap."

"Right, I will after a nap. I will *today*."

"How far along did your doctor say you were? Based on the hormones?"

"She said twenty weeks."

"Okay so maybe I'm wrong… but I mean… he's way longer than ten inches."

"Maybe he's just tall then?" I make a joke but it sounds sad.

"Well make up your mind, is this little one going to be short or tall?" Bethany brightens the joke a bit while she cleans the gel off my stomach. "Just go to see your doctor."

"I can do that," I offer, those emotions still coming in waves but now exhaustion weighs them all down.

"I've got it." She balls up the tissues and then flicks off the machine. "I'd print you pictures but I don't know how, so… go see your doctor later today. Promise me."

"I will. I just…"

Bethany grabs my hand, squeezing it until I look her in the eyes. "I'm here for you and for this little blip."

"I know."

"But you have to tell him."

"I know." This time when I tell her that, I practically whisper because I don't want to tell him.

"Do you think he'll be mad?" she asks nervously, although she tries to hide it.

"I think it will devastate him." I swear to God I'll scream if I cry, but that's exactly what I feel like doing.

"What if… no. No, you can't lie to him. I'm a fucking awful person for even thinking that," she says then shakes her head and I let out a small sad laugh.

"I was thinking if it was anywhere near the date, I'd lie. I'm awful too."

"The truth always comes out anyway." She offers me a hand to sit up and I take it.

"Just tell him the truth already, get it out so it stops stressing you out." She emphasizes, "You don't need that stress. Neither does the baby."

"I know. You're right." My head feels light when I sit up and I have to take a moment to steady myself, crinkling the paper under me.

"You hid from him for how long? You can't hide this."

I would say "I know" again, but… well, she gets it.

Bethany questions me, "You think he'll leave you?"

"I don't. I think it's going to hurt him, though. And make him worry about…" I can't even voice it. *Me running.* Because it's what I always do and why would I stay if I'm pregnant with another man's baby?

Bethany guesses my fear. "He'll think you'll leave him?" I can only nod. "Will you?"

"No." My answer is so firm it's nearly ripped from me. "I'll find out who the father is and then he can be a part of his life or not."

"Seth isn't going to like that."

"I know, but that's what's right, isn't it?"

"I think so."

A moment of silence passes, with nothing but the clock ticking in the background. We have to get going, but I can't move yet.

"I don't know how I can look him in the eyes without telling him but I also don't know how I can tell him this."

"Well, you have to tell him and if you think it will be less stressful for you, you could write it out now and give it to him. You could call him and let him know. So there's distance."

I still can't answer her.

"There are options and you know the less stress right now for you, the better." She puts her hand on my stomach and I smile faintly. "This baby has to cook a bit longer."

"I can't believe I'm pregnant, much less this far along." It's crazy. Life is one crazy journey.

"Well that's probably a blessing. Looks like you got to skip out on the morning sickness and went straight to the honeymoon phase in the second trimester."

"Right, the horny phase. And to think I thought that was all Seth's doing." I have enough humor to roll my eyes. "Although I really haven't been eating. I just thought my stomach was messed up."

"Why don't you just call him? Let me check out, make sure Cindy is here and I'll stay with you," she practically begs me. "I'm here for you. You call him, and I'll be right here by your side. That way this is done."

I manage to get off the table, imagining calling him to tell him. I won't have to see the devastation on his face and it's selfish, but it's also a relief. A slight one, at just the thought of ripping off the Band-Aid, so to speak.

"Is that okay? Do you want to try calling him?"

I can only nod a response.

"Good. We can hide in here," she tells me over the sound of her balling up the paper that was on the exam table. "Just give me a minute to check out and I'll be back."

All the while she's gone, I think about how I'll tell him.

I'm going to start it the way I want to finish it. *I love you more than anything.* My hand instinctively moves to my belly, wondering if that will hold true. I speak out loud, imagining his reaction to every word. "I'm not leaving you, unless you want me to." The third statement comes out stronger than I thought possible, due to the way it fucking kills me.

"I couldn't sleep tonight, because the doctor called after you left and told me something."

I stand there, alone in the room, and I say everything from the news about my heart to how far along I am. When Bethany comes back, I say it all again, crying through most of it. And leave it all on voicemail because Seth doesn't answer.

I'm all right with that. I'll be home soon. At least I said it all.

I might be with him when he listens to it, but at least he'll hear it all.

It doesn't make me feel any better, though. It doesn't help shield me in the least from thinking my world is crumbling apart.

CHAPTER 6

Seth

The early morning sun peeks out over the horizon as Declan's car drives away, the image of the train station reflected in the rearview getting smaller by the second.

"You going to say anything?" Declan asks with a hint of humor, but the concern drowning in his gaze and the way he keeps glancing at me even though he's driving and the light ahead is green, says otherwise.

My throat is tight and I clear it, but the unsettling feeling is still there. I can't even look him in the eyes.

"I can't." My eyes feel heavy and the strain of it all is weighing me down even more. "He made me an offer, and it involves silence." *That's a lie.*

"An offer for what?" Declan questions and I let my eyes close as my head falls back.

It can't be true. It hurts too much to even think about it. Laura is all right. I want the videos from the projector filling the high walls of the warehouse and everything he showed me, to be made up. Just a cruel trick. It can't be true.

Rubbing at my eyes with my fist to rid them of both the need to sleep and the sight of what Marcus showed me, I try to answer Declan.

"It involves Laura."

I can feel it happening again, just like it did when I was a teen. The feeling of my world slowly falling apart until there's nothing left but pain and anger. It's happening again.

I lie to Declan, staring straight ahead as the light moves more quickly over the skyline and say, "I can't tell you." I give him a bit of the truth though and add, "I don't even know if he's telling the truth."

Marcus never said a damn thing about keeping secrets. But what he wants from me… I can't tell Declan. I can't tell anyone.

"He threatened Laura?" Declan's tone is a mix of pissed and troubled. His grip slips on the wheel and he stares at me instead of the road.

I shake my head, unable to voice anything as the images come back. I don't want it to be true. Swallowing, I prepare to give Declan any bread crumb I can, but that involves speaking about Laura… and I can't. Not until I talk to her.

The vibrating of my phone in my lap spares me the sorry excuse I was going to give Declan.

It's her. It's my Babygirl. The image of her face fills up the screen as the phone rings and I know I can't answer it. Not here. Not with Declan listening.

I imagine she's upset with me. She woke up and I wasn't there. I told her I would be and I wasn't.

"You going to answer that?" Declan asks, his voice sounding concerned.

Again, I only shake my head. Still holding the phone, unable to let go, but unable to answer just the same.

"What can I do?" he offers and that simple kindness nearly breaks me.

"I don't know yet," I say, finally answering Declan honestly. I've never felt so lost and helpless. "I have to ask Laura something."

I don't know how I'll even get it out of me. The questions and the accusations are caged deep in my chest.

I feel hopeless, but worse than that, like a traitor. Like I don't deserve to live.

It's silent all the while in the car, up until we park and I notice Laura's car is missing.

It only takes a second to go into my texts and read them. Shit, my heart couldn't beat for the second spent thinking she's already gone.

"I can't leave you like this," Declan says, giving me the side of him I know too well. The true friend I have in him.

"I'll be all right," I say, lying to him again and I know it's a lie as I pull the handle of the door, letting the wind whip at me as I climb out of his car.

It's not until I'm inside that I listen to the voicemail and completely break down.

The sick feeling in my stomach that I had before meeting with Marcus is back full force as I stare at the cup of coffee on the end table. The smell of black coffee invades every inch of space as I rest my elbows on my knees and wait. I can't move off the chair in the living room. I can't drink the coffee even to stay awake from this brutal night.

All I can do is sit here and wait for Laura to walk through the door.

I believe everything Marcus said after listening to her message.

Her heart. The baby.

She didn't tell me the timeline though. She kept so much from me.

My head falls into my hands as I do what I've done for the last half hour. I wait for her.

Everything is wrong. It's all wrong. It's not supposed to happen like this.

I shouldn't have to make a deal with the devil to keep her alive. I shouldn't be this helpless and at his mercy. Not over this. Not like this.

I'm supposed to be able to protect her and keep her safe. I have so many regrets. Too many to count.

The churning in my gut intensifies when I hear a car door shut out front.

My heart breaks slowly, but it still beats. I don't know how it's possible to still function when I know damn well that it's shattered.

There are two things that keep me upright. Two things that prevent me from falling to the ground and giving in to the pain like I did eight years ago when I thought I'd lost Laura forever.

1. She still loves me. She told me she did.
2. Marcus's deal.

I might hate myself for it, but if Laura gets to live, I'll do it. I will do anything to save her.

My phone moves from my left hand to my right when the doorknob on the front door turns. Anxiousness creeps up my throat and suffocates me.

The small creak of the door opening fills the room and then she's there, my gorgeous girl. It takes everything in me to stay where I am.

She freezes in the doorway, her gaze caught with mine, but the howl of the wind behind her releases us from the moment. The clicking of her boots is all I can hear until she shuts the door, keeping her hand on it and her back to me to speak.

"You got my message?" she asks even though she already knows.

I flip my phone in my hand and do everything I can just to breathe. "Yeah," I answer her. "Come sit here." I give her the command although my voice isn't as strong as I'd like it to be.

The hollowness in my chest seems to grow, the vacant spot filled with agonizing pain.

Laura sniffles at the door, the tip of her nose bright pink but I'm not sure if it's from the cold or from crying. My poor girl.

Her keys fall onto the foyer table and she kicks off her shoes, leaving them there. Taking her time before coming around to the living room, glancing at the black coffee that's probably cold by now and not a sip has been taken.

Her blue eyes are glossy as her bottom lip quivers. "Are you..." she starts to say before pausing as she slowly takes the seat on the sofa catty-corner to me. The crack in her voice keeps her from getting it out.

"Are you..." she tries again to question me about something and fails as I sit up straighter, still on the edge of the chair and waiting for her to get it out.

Her long lashes flutter as a silent sob seems to make her breath stutter. "I love you," she whispers as her expression crumples.

I can't stand her like this. I can't take it. In a quick single motion, I take all of her. One arm slipping under her ass and the other around her back. I'm on the sofa with her in my lap before I can think twice.

She's warm and soft in my arms, so fragile as I hold her.

With her head laying in the crook of my neck I whisper the only thing I'm sure of against the shell of her ear, "I love you too." Holding on to her as tight as I can, I rock her as she tries to stop crying.

I know the feeling. I understand her when she says she hates crying. I wish I hadn't cried either, but I can hold it together for her. When she needs me, I'm so much stronger than I am without her.

"Shhh," I murmur, rocking her back and forth, grateful that I'm able to just hold her finally.

Time passes, and I wish we could fall asleep right here, and wake up to find last night was just a nightmare. A fucking horrible nightmare.

I know better than to pretend though. Bad things happen when we pretend we're all right.

"I want you to tell me everything," I say, speaking calmly and softly.

"Did you listen to it all?" she asks me, her lips brushing against the rough stubble on my neck with her question.

"I did." Three times and nearly a fourth, but I don't tell her that extra information.

She's still in my arms, her chaotic breathing steadying with each deep inhale and exhale.

The sound of her licking her lips steadies me, preparing to do as I ask. Her not running from me… that steadies me even more.

"I need a transplant for my heart and this baby is further along than we've been together."

"Five months," I cut in, very much aware.

"I think so. I'm going to make an appointment tomorrow."

"Good, schedule everything. I want to go with you." I don't give her the option to say no; it's not a question. And thankfully, she doesn't object. I'm on edge wanting to take control but knowing full well that I lack it in the ways that matter most.

"I should have told you everything. I just couldn't. I couldn't look you in the eyes and tell you. And I'm so sorry."

"And the baby?" I don't even know what my question is.

"I didn't know that until you left last night." Her knees dig into the sofa as she leans back, the words spilling from her lips quickly and she finally looks me in the eyes. "I didn't know how far along I was… I'm sorry… I just…"

I kiss her before her voice can hitch again and before fresh tears fall from her wide eyes. Her lips mold to mine, her hands slip around my neck and she holds on to me as tightly as I hold on to her.

The kiss deepens and that's her doing. Her desire and her need make a deadly concoction as they stir to mingle with her sadness. I'd get drunk on that taste every night if I could.

When she breaks our kiss to breathe, her chest brushing against mine, I whisper, "I love you." I'm drowning in the heat between us.

"I love you too."

I have to ask her before I lose the nerve, before the moment is over. I need to know. "And the father? Are you going to tell him?"

She didn't mention him at all in the message. I imagine she's unsure who he is, but I'll damn well know before the sun sets tonight.

"I'm going to tell him when the baby's here."

She holds my gaze, and hers is mixed with uncertainty as she confesses, "I think he deserves to know."

I nod in agreement although that's not at all what I think. I lie to her like I did to Declan and say, "As long as you want me there at your side, then the world can throw whatever it wants at us, because I know it'll be all right." I don't know if anything is going to be all right. All I know is that I made a deal with the devil and I pray he keeps his word. All I can do is pray and I hate it.

I can hold her all the while though. Every moment I can love her, I will. Her message was very clear about the condition of her heart although she neglected to mention that she'll likely die within the year and that if she doesn't get a donor transplant, she most certainly will.

"Go the bedroom and get undressed," I command her, again not giving her a choice. And again, she's agreeable, kissing me hurriedly as if afraid I'll change my mind and then she slips off my lap.

I miss her warmth instantly, but she has to go without me. I need a moment. Just one to forward the message to Declan and then text him to listen to it.

And then I listen to her again.

I'll need his help to find out who the father is. I add in a message, that Marcus knew. That this is what Marcus told me, which isn't a lie, but Marcus told me much more.

The floor creaks and that's when I see Laura's come back.

"Are you okay?" Laura whispers, drawing my gaze to hers as she stands in front of me, her legs between my knees. I nod into the palm of her hand when she cups my chin.

"I just need a minute, Babygirl." She rewards my whispered response with a kiss and I tell her to go. That I'll just be a minute.

Hate is so much easier to hold on to than any other emotion. And that's all I can think as she leaves me.

She's mine, not his.

This baby is mine, not his.

I text Declan as I listen to Laura's feet pad softly down the hallway: *Find out who Laura dated five months ago. Go through her texts, her emails, the dating apps on her phone. I want to know everything about him.*

CHAPTER 7

Laura

I LOVE HIM WITH ALL MY HEART.

Every piece of it beats for him.

My hands tremble as I undress, taking more time than it should and I know that, but I can't stop picturing him there, his shirt unbuttoned at the collar, his broad shoulders hunched over with a dejected look on his face.

I'll never unsee that look in his eyes, like he was questioning if he still had me, if I was still his, and desperately needed to know.

Because he wants me still. He loves me still.

And I've never needed to feel that more than I need it now.

The door behind me creaks open just as I unhook my bra. It hits the floor just as I spin to face him and before I can move or speak, he's almost on me, closing the distance between us in three broad steps.

His strong arms wrap around me as he gathers me up, capturing my squeal of surprise with his lips in a kiss. I can't hold him close enough as my arms wrap around his broad shoulders. They only stay there for a fraction of a second before I tear at his shirt, needing it off and desperately needing his skin against mine.

I've never felt so close to him, yet so far apart at the same time.

I need more of him and all of him. I want him to surround me and consume me until I am nothing but his. Protected and loved and cherished.

My kisses devour his, but somehow he does just the same to me.

Although it all feels reckless and desperate, he lowers me to the bed as if he has full control. Of course he does; he is so much stronger than I am.

The thought reminds me to tear at his clothes, a button popping off as I do and neither of us care.

In a single motion, Seth parts from my embrace, removing his shirt with one hand over his head and tossing it somewhere behind me.

"On your back," he groans, the depth of his dark gaze stirring with a fire that burns me, singeing my core.

I watch the cords of his muscles tense as he removes his clothes, and then he crawls up the bed to where I'm lying. He slowly inches up my naked body, kissing and nibbling which sends both a chill and a thrilling wave of heat to descend over my body. He takes his time, teasing me while my nails dig into the sheets, desperately holding on to patience. I want him now. To say I'm in need would be a profound understatement.

I suck in a breath before his lips press against mine and in that same moment, he enters me. A swift motion that brings about a stinging pain just as much as it brings an all-consuming pleasure.

His pace is set before I can breathe. His grip on my hips, pinning me in place.

He only stops kissing me to moan in the crook of my neck, "I need to get lost in you." And with his deep voice and rough cadence, raw with need, I feel myself clench around him. Already the heat of the act dances along my skin, from the tips of my toes all the way up my body.

My blunt nails dig into his back, not piercing his skin, but holding on to him for dear life as he rocks himself in me all the way to the hilt.

It's all too much, but that's the only way Seth ever is. Too much, all-consuming. It's the only way he's ever been and I've never been so grateful.

As the pleasure builds inside of me, I stare in the reflection of the dresser mirror, watching his powerful frame as he moves in deep, controlled strokes.

He's a sex god, a man I was never supposed to have. And he takes me with a force and a need that's undeniable. He may be getting lost in me, but I've forever been lost in him. And that's all I want. I would happily roam the earth for all eternity not knowing a damn thing other than what it feels like to be loved by him.

As his pace quickens and my climax gets closer and closer, I pull my eyes away from our reflection, my neck arching with a need to pull away from the intense feelings.

"Don't," Seth scolds me, forcing me to keep my eyes open and stare into his gaze. "Don't stop watching now," he says in a single breath that sounds too easy compared to the cold sweat growing along every inch of my skin. He groans, the sound deep and sexy as he props up my left leg so he can enter me even deeper. "This is my favorite part."

With that confession, he pounds into me. His hips piston and a scream tears through me. The pleasure blazes up my body as I cum, but he doesn't stop. He fucks me harder and more ruthlessly, our reflection only adding to the intensity of the scene before us.

I scream out every time I cum on his cock and he rewards me with nips and sucking along my neck.

He fucks me like he owns me. He makes love to me like I've always been his.

And I love both ways I get to have him, because I love all of him.

When we're both breathless and spent, my body weak from his touch and my heart soothed from him whispering he loves me as he leaves kisses on my neck, he lays beside me, his arm protectively draped over my body.

With my back to his chest, I stare at us in the mirror, loving how we fit together so perfectly, but feeling the pain of uncertainty sneak in between us.

There's so much I don't know about how we'll get through this.

"Everything's going to be okay, right?" I whisper even though I know there's no way for him to know. Somehow, I convince myself that he could know. He could make it all right if he wanted to. Because he's Seth King and he has always ruled my world, my thoughts. He is my fate.

"Of course it is, Babygirl," he answers me and kisses my neck before telling me to sleep. His voice doesn't have the confidence I hoped for. I snuggle closer to him and tell him, "I love you," thinking that I need to make sure I tell him every day, just in case it's our last day together.

"I love you too," he says and his answer soothes me, threatening to lure me to sleep with a wonderful dream. But a truth I've known for far too long keeps my tired eyes open, staring at his in the mirror.

If only love was enough to make all this all right...

CHAPTER 8

Seth

I FEEL FUCKING SICK. LIKE THAT KIND OF ICE-COLD TINGLE THAT TRAVELS along your skin, but your face is burning up type of sick. I hope I vomit on his cheap knockoff shoes.

That's what this prick is. A knockoff. He's no one.

He's no one echoes in my head as I stare back at him, watching the sweat bead on his neck.

"So you own this place?" Declan asks Jim. Jim Howard. This spineless prick sitting in front of me knocked up Laura.

Squirming in his seat, he puts a false smile on his face. He knows who Declan is, he recognizes our names. He's a pussy, a limp dick. God I hate this bastard. I hate him with everything in me.

I hate the color palette of this rinky-dink shop. Home Brew Coffee looks like every other coffee shop that exists. Except there are rows of bagged ground coffee lined up on shelves to buy. There's a bell above the door. Generic paintings of coffeepots on off-white walls. And red metal chairs around six small tables. Like the one we're sitting at right now.

He clears his throat and starts to say, "Actually," but the one word cracks. He's nervous, jittery, and Declan leans forward, calmly telling him to relax. His crisp suit, fresh shave and charming features make this douche look even more like a pile of shit.

How did she even find him all the way out here? It's hours away. Oh, right, that was his doing. To keep her at a distance and every other hookup he has.

I wish I could reach across the table and smash his face in.

His smile turns more firm and he nods as he says, "Actually, I own it with my wife."

That right there. That hot prick of nausea comes back to me. That's why I hate him like I do.

"Your wife?" I question him, keeping my voice as even as I can although my grip on the glass of ice water tightens to the point that it's strained. Everything is so fucking hot as I sit across from this sorry excuse for a man.

He only nods. It's all he can do.

He can lie on his dating profiles. Give a half-real name with a barren social media profile he made up. And cheat around on his wife while texting his friends about it so they'll cover for him.

"That's right," Declan says and nods, speaking before the man can do anything but glance at me and then back to Declan. "I did see that on the lease."

A full background check and hacking into his phone took less than two hours.

"She's pregnant, right?" I question him, my throat so tight I'm getting light-headed.

Every document Declan handed me this morning I wanted to tear up and shred. I haven't felt pure rage like this in a long damn time.

How could she have been with him? My Babygirl with *him*?

All loathing aside, he's decent looking, though there's nothing remarkable about him. Physically he's more built than average, with a nice-enough smile and charming way about him. It's the charm that hides the asshole side. I know the type.

He told her he had a business, which he does, but the online coffee sales barely break even every year. Even this small-time coffee shop, where he really makes his money, is failing. What the hell did he say to her that led to the two of them in bed together?

I imagine he lied. Because that's what pricks like him do. They lie.

The mental image of Jim and my girl is what I see when the bastard responds, "He was just born. Nine pounds and healthy."

"Congratulations," Declan tells him, his smile nice and even. It relaxes the man, and I watch as the tension in his shoulders visible lessens. Like he's genuinely happy he had a son.

I don't expect the other emotions to creep in. The jealousy, the pain and agony. It makes everything in me tense and tight.

He had a wife, he had a baby coming. And he risked losing it all for a "fuck night," as he referred to it in a group message to his friends.

Fuck him.

I swallow down the unwanted emotions with a gulp of water.

"See, I was just wondering," Declan says and his tone changes, lowering as he hunches forward. It takes everything in me to just sit here. Simple as that. Just to stay seated, I am at the edge of my sanity.

His cock was inside her. Did she even get off?

I can't stop fucking wondering. Pissed off and brokenhearted is a strange combination. Jealousy disgusts me. And yet here I am, jealous of this piece of shit.

"Your profile, the one you've been using to see some of the women around here, it says you're single."

I can hear the prick swallow, the sound giving me slight relief. I want to see him choke on his fear.

If Laura knew, she'd hate herself. She'd blame herself for sleeping with a married man. I know she would.

"If I..." Jim pauses and throws his hands up in a defensive gesture as if he's being robbed and I turn to my left, just enough to see the young woman at the register pausing as she cleans the glass coffee mugs.

"Maybe you should go to the back, sweetheart," I tell her and give her the hint of a smile that narrows my eyes. When she glances between me and Jim, I add, "Nothing to worry about. Just asking questions."

I surprise myself by how easy it all comes out. I don't feel a hint of that ease inside of me.

The conversation pauses as the woman leaves the main room, hesitating at the doorway to the storage room.

"We'll only be a minute, promise," Declan reassures her although she doesn't take her eyes off of her employer, whose eyes are pleading.

"Look man, if I slept with someone I shouldn't have, I swear I didn't know." His plea tumbles out followed by heavier breathing.

"Relax." Declan keeps talking, giving him a false sense of reassurance. "We're just confused. We want to know what kind of guy you are because we're moving a little closer and wanted to get the lay of the land is all. You're not in any trouble with us," Declan says and motions with his thumb for emphasis.

The fuck he isn't. I keep my thoughts to myself, though. I'm still not able to speak.

"So you're a married man with a baby."

"Three kids now. Two are in school and we decided to do it all again."

Three of them. I can't stand this man, so how could I be jealous of him? I hate him. I hate everything about him.

The clock on the far wall ticks steadily with every second that passes and I have to stare at it instead of him.

"But you get some side action," Declan questions easily.

My thumb moves in a steady motion across the beads of water on the outside of the glass.

"Yeah," Jim says and leans back, breathing out. "It's just a release."

Crack. The glass in my hand breaks out of nowhere. I only gripped it for a fraction of a second. The glass lays in pieces on the table, the water splashing.

Adrenaline races through me.

Just a release. Laura was "just a release."

"Sorry about that," Declan says and I can barely hear it over the ringing in my ears.

Just a release.

"My friend has a strong grip."

My gaze falls to the prick who just referred to my Babygirl as "a release" when he speaks. "I can see that." The nervousness is back, the jitteriness is evident.

Declan places a hand on my forearm that's under the table, keeping it down. With my free hand I make a fist and lay it on the table, not bothering to clean up the small bit of blood that's there.

If I move, I know exactly what I'll do.

I'll lay into him. I envision it as Declan and he make small talk. I picture slamming my fist against his mouth. The mouth that got to kiss her. He was able to be with her and that's what he refers to it as? *A release.*

Every time he looks at me, I hope he can see what I want to do to him. Judging by the way he averts his eyes the moment our gazes meet and how he turns paler and paler, I think he knows.

"Give us a minute, will you?" Declan asks him kindly. He sounds so friendly, but even with all that ease he gives to the man across from us, Declan grips my forearm harder, silently letting me know what I'm feeling.

It fucking hurts. It feels like my chest is cracked wide open and this bastard did it.

The second the man is behind the counter, I storm out of there, shoving the door open. The harsh wind and bitter cold greet me, chilling me to the bone and I'm thankful for it.

Thankful for anything to dull this pain and this heat that's suffocating me.

"A release," I finally speak as we get to the car. My muscles are bunched, my nostrils flaring when I get in the car, barely taking anything in as my vision goes red.

My voice trembles when Declan takes his seat, the driver's seat. "A release. That's what she was to him!"

I can't control my temper or the way my chest heaves.

"First, don't fuck up my car," Declan says and I whip around to face him. A humorous smirk is waiting there for me.

It dulls the edge of it all, but only just slightly.

When I fall back into the seat, a hand over my eyes, my palm pressing slightly to try to calm myself down, he adds, "He's a prick. He's a liar. But you have to think, what did he mean to her?"

"She was 'a release' to him," I say dully, swallowing the bitter pill before looking at Declan.

"And what was *he* to *her*?" Declan repeats, carefully with emphasis, and his hand lands on my shoulder in a way that's meant to calm me, to get through to me.

But all I can see is that bastard fucking my girl.

"She's going to have his baby." The words choke me as I say them.

"You know how it is. Laura's a smart girl; she never messaged him again. He was just a release for her too."

My voice raises, the anger showing with a spiteful tone, "Well all that's changed now, hasn't it?"

It's silent, apart from the sound of the wind howling so loud and commanding outside that it rocks the car. I rub my hand down my face, trying to rid myself of the need to do something about what he did to her. How he lied to her and used her.

"I want to go back in there and beat him to death," I confess to Declan although I stare down at my shoes, the black leather impeccably polished and shined. They're expensive as fuck, but they feel like nothing. I feel like I'm not worth a damn thing compared to that prick.

Just the sight of him makes me feel like I'm nothing. Because it's his baby. He has what I so desperately want. If he wanted, he could have a family with her.

"I hate him too," Declan finally answers me, his hand patting my back as I stay hunched over in the car. "You want to kill him… fuck him up? Whatever you want, I'm here for you."

I nod. Yes, that's exactly what I want.

"But think for a moment about what he was to her," he implores me. "He doesn't mean anything to her."

"He gets to be the father of her baby." The second I speak the words, I hate them. I want to take them back and do everything I can to keep that reality from happening.

He got his release, so as far as I'm concerned, he doesn't get to have anything else. Anger is blinding me to reason.

"Block him everywhere and erase it all." I give the command to Declan and add, "She won't be able to find him. Their only contact was through that dating app. He's the only one she slept with that month, so she'll know it was him when she looks at her schedule. Block him everywhere. Erase him from her life."

As Declan takes in a slow breath, his expression falls. He doesn't agree with my decision. I can see it written on his face.

"He can't be in her life or I'll kill him," I say and wait for Declan to look back at me before I hold his stare. "I will kill him. I know I will."

Pulling his hand back, he scratches the side of his jaw like he's thinking, right before telling me, "Don't take her control away."

My head shakes as I release a huff of a breath. "I'll do it myself then," I say and the words sound spiteful as they come out.

"Seth. Listen to me," he says and his tone begs me. "She wants to do the right thing. She always wants to do the right thing."

"I know." I can't stress it enough. "I know who she is. I know what kind of person she is." I'm pissed and I can't not be pissed because all that's left for me otherwise is the hurt.

Declan keeps his voice low and calm as he says, "I'll make it so she can message him and it'll show as seen but he won't ever see it."

With the ringing in my head it takes me a moment to absorb what he's saying. She can message him, but he won't see it. He'll never know. He won't be able to respond. It's what he fucking deserves. "Can you do that?"

Declan nods as a car drives by us and that's when reality sneaks back in. It's fucking cold and we're having a therapy session on the side of the road in a parked car.

"I can," he tells me and I sit up straighter, clearing my throat and focusing on getting my shit together.

"He'll be out of the picture then," I comment, feeling lighter and more relieved than I imagined I would. There's still her heart to worry about, but one problem solved makes all of this feel like it could work. I can keep her and my baby.

She'll still love me. She won't leave me.

But then that leaves me with Marcus's deal.

"I'm getting my guys on it now," Declan says although it's a question more than anything.

"Yeah," I answer him and then clear my throat. "Yeah, thanks man."

I picture her staring at the screen and not getting a response and it fucking kills me because I know it will hurt her. "She's going to be wrecked by it."

"She just wants to do the right thing," Declan says, disagreeing with me. He doesn't know how emotional she is, though. She's strong and smart, but emotions rule her every thought and action. "She can do that. She can message him still." Even though he's talking to me, he's texting. Sending out demands for all this bullshit.

I'm barely hanging on, the anger's got nowhere to go and all I am is fucking wrecked.

My voice is tight and my words crack when I tell Declan, "I waited too long."

The truth hurts. It's brutal and unforgiving. More than that though, it's deserved.

"What?" he says then looks up and at me. His eyes on me beg me to look at him, but I don't. I can't. There's a prick in the back of my eyes and I feel like a little bitch. Licking my lips, I take in a deep breath, expecting that to make it better, but it's worse.

"He's what she had. A release is all she had." I barely get the words out and I ignore Declan when he reaches out to comfort me.

"I could have been there with her. I was so close for so long and I could have been with her."

"Hey, man, don't—"

"She's dying and that's what she had," I say, cutting him off as tears cloud my vision. She's dying.

I can fix this problem named Jim Howard, though. I can get rid of the man who didn't love her but has a rightful place in her life. I won't allow that. I can't.

This baby is mine and so is she.

But I can't fix her heart. I can't fix that; I'm so damn helpless.

"I waited too long."

Marcus's promise, his deal, whispers darkly in the back of my mind. He swears he can save her. He promised. He's willing to make that deal.

Declan's still trying to console me when I say, "I have to tell you something."

Fate's a bitch though, choosing this exact second to make his phone ring in his hand.

Pulling me from the moment.

"Get it," I tell him and then stare at the window, pretending like everything isn't still crumbling around me. "This can wait."

It can't.

None of it can wait.

Marcus will want his answer soon. And time isn't on Laura's side.

CHAPTER 9

Laura

"So good news and bad news," I start to tell Bethany. The hot chocolate on the table smells divine and with how tired I am, I'm going to need another one in no more than thirty minutes after I suck this one down just to stay awake for this shift.

In the last ten days, I've had every test done and every checkup imaginable. The days have blurred to the point where all I can see is Doctor Tabor's face during the day and Seth's at night.

"Spill it." With her coffee in hand she stares at me, waiting expectantly. She'd look very commanding and badass if it wasn't for the puppy dogs on her pale blue scrubs.

"So the good news," I say and pull out the slippery paper with the black-and-white image on it. The one with my baby boy's perfect little face as he sucks his little thumb.

My insides turn to warm goo every time I look at him. "He's perfect," I tell her and the smile on my face is infectious.

"And beautiful," Bethany adds, taking the paper and staring at it.

It's quiet for a moment as we both pretend we're not emotional wrecks still. We don't talk about my heart and when I feel it racing, I just keep it a secret. I don't want them to worry, but both Bethany and Seth tiptoe around me whenever I go quiet. It is what it is. A baby will really throw a wrench into being a hard-ass like I used to see myself. So instead of telling them that my heart feels like it wants out of my chest, I tell them I thought the baby was kicking. That always makes them smile. I would so much rather them smile and celebrate with me, than be scared … like I am. I'm so damn scared I can barely function.

I have to tell someone though and Bethany is the someone who can handle this.

"What's the bad news?" Bethany asks, handing me back the photograph and opting to hold her coffee with both hands.

"That copy's yours," I tell her and force a smile but it wavers. Clearing my throat and staring at the large clock to the right of the elevators, I tell her, "Because I won't accept a donor organ or surgery until it's safe for the baby, my placement has dropped on this list." The air leaves my lungs and said heart does a quick race, pounding against my rib cage. It does it every time I think about it, but I'm quick to look down at the picture. "I accept it," I tell both of them. Both Bethany and my little one. "I accept waiting to make sure this little one makes it out healthy."

There's no response but I can feel her gaze on me. It's too damn quiet this late at night. The ticking from the clock is all I get so I pick up the cup of cocoa to have a drink, only to find it already empty. I must've sucked it down without realizing. It makes a hollow sound when I set it down on the front desk.

"I've thought a lot about it, Bethany. I choose the baby. Please don't ask me not to." I have to whisper the last statement. I know that's what Seth would do. Seth would want the heart as soon as possible. He wouldn't risk another day. But this baby isn't ready and I don't want to live if it's at the expense of my child. I want to give this baby everything and I choose to start right now with these days, however many of them I can give him.

"What did the doctor say?" she asks.

"She said it's not wise." As I speak, I mimic the way the doctor said it. As if I was supposed to answer with absolutely no emotion and only logic. "My heart does more work as the pregnancy progresses. She said that's probably why my symptoms have been worse recently."

"That worries me," she says and Bethany's response is quiet, smothered with concern and I wish I could allay her fears, but she's right. It's a risk and a very real one at that.

"We're going to plan for a C-section roughly sixteen weeks from now, and the baby is already getting steroid shots for his lungs and other organs to develop. With the C-section there will be far less stress on my heart, so there's that positive."

I try to keep my response upbeat, but Bethany doesn't buy it.

She's silent and it takes me a long moment to bring myself to look at her, but she's staring down at the slip of thermal recording paper from the ultrasound in my hand. She wipes away the tears in her eyes when she sees me looking at her.

"Right. And then when he's born, what happens as far as the surgery for your heart?"

"Top of the list."

"Okay…" She seems hesitant although my answer was quick and confident. "And what happens in the meantime?"

"Vitamins, medication and appointments … baby yoga and a less stressful schedule. Which means …" I pause to suck in a breath and then reluctantly let it out. "I'm trying to decide if I should take leave. I don't have to be on bed rest, I specifically asked… but my doctor did recommend taking a leave of absence so I could eliminate as much stress as possible."

"You should," she says and Bethany's response is immediate and adamant. "Go home. Stay home."

"Part of me wants to … but the bigger part of me doesn't. I want to be here where I'm needed … It's not like Seth can just up and quit. You know how it is. So I'd just be home alone. Worrying constantly … I'd rather worry about everyone else in this place than think about myself for even a minute."

"Do you really want to be on your deathbed wishing you worked more?"

I shrug, even though I know the answer to that. I've thought so much about it these past few days.

If I'm on my deathbed, I know exactly what I'll regret.

Every milestone I didn't have with Seth.

I have this horrible feeling that we won't make it to any more of them. It's okay. I just want him to love me and he does. That is enough. It's more than enough for now.

With only that shrug from me, Bethany lets out an exasperated sigh.

"Don't you think Seth would want to be with you right now?" I pick at the sleeve of my scrubs where the fabric is worn as the heat kicks on and a visitor gives us a small wave as she signs in. If only they knew what we were talking about. I glance at the clipboard on the table, knowing I need to sort meds soon, rather than answer Bethany. "What did he say about all of this?"

I rub my tired eyes with the sleeve of my old white scrubs. Mascara mars the pretty fabric. *Sweetie*, which is written all over the scrubs and mixed in with the pattern of peaches, is unrecognizable on my sleeve now.

With my lack of a response, Bethany questions me again, her tone more confrontational. "What did Seth say?"

Looking her dead in the eyes, I answer, "I'm not telling him."

Fuck, it hurts. My throat goes tight at the thought of keeping this from him. He told me he wants to know everything, but I can't tell him this. I can't do it.

Her wide eyes swirl with disappointment.

"He doesn't need that stress. I want him to think everything is as good as it can be. And it is. I'm doing the best I can and I just want him to be happy with me." I swallow my conviction. "I want him to be by my side but not running my life right now."

I'm prepared for Bethany to be the other half of the argument that I've had in the back of my mind every night as I lie down with him in bed.

He holds me tight, his hand splayed across my belly.

"He keeps calling him 'our little prince.'" My eyes tear up and I have to close them, the watery vision of the silver doors to the elevator turning black and instead I see him. I see the love of my life holding me, talking about my son as if he's his and everything is going to be okay. "I love that he is being the father figure and..." I have to pause when emotions tackle the words as they climb up my throat.

"If I choose this baby over me and he knows... I'm afraid he won't feel the same way. The baby won't be his little prince anymore if something happens to me."

The warm tears come and go now. I'm so used to them I don't fight them.

"Laura." Bethany's pained voice forces me to open my eyes and all I can see is her leaning closer to me, holding me as she shushes me and tells me it's going to be all right.

It's what we do. We say it'll be all right even when we don't know it will.

I love Seth and he loves me. But if I die and this baby lives, I want him to love the baby like he does now. To hold this baby the way he holds me at night.

I don't want to risk him blaming the baby.

"You know my mom left... she blamed me. My mom and dad split because of me. It's what people said anyway."

"Your mom was a bitch and you are not. She was selfish." Bethany knows all about it. We've shared our stories with each other on drunken Wine Down Wednesdays. My mother and her father... what a pair they would have made.

"I might never get a heart but if this baby has Seth, all of him with how hard and fiercely he loves... it'll be okay. And you, of course. His godmother." I deliberately pull away and change the topic as quickly as I can.

"His godmother?" Bethany plays along, ignoring the worry, sticking with the "it's going to be okay" strategy. I want to pretend too. We can all pretend together.

"Yes, if you would be his godmother, I would be so happy."

"Of course." Her nod is furious and her voice sounds ecstatic although the worry still dances in her gaze that's glued to mine.

"Well that's settled then," I say and nod, trying to forget the last bit of our conversation, one of the many worries that keeps me up at night.

With a hand on my belly, on top of a very clear but small bump, I rub my thumb in soothing circles.

My baby will be all right.

I'll get a heart.

Seth will love both of us forever.

We're going to be a family.

Even as I list the positives to counter every doubt I have, I know it's too good to be true.

"Hey," Bethany says and whispers my name, "I know life hasn't been the best to you, but you do deserve your happily ever after."

My hand trembles a bit as I reach for the cup of cocoa, only to find it empty—again. A huff of sarcasm leaves me as I smack it down on the tabletop.

I struggle to respond, not knowing how to tell her one of the greatest truths in life: *not everyone gets a happily ever after.* It's not about what people deserve. Sometimes fate just takes what she wants and there's no rhyme or reason to it.

CHAPTER 10

Seth

"YOUR STOMACH BOTHERING YOU?" I QUESTION LAURA AT THE sound of her fork scraping against the porcelain. "You've barely eaten."

The dining room is something I've barely ever used since moving in here. Tonight's the first night we've used it together. That'll change when the baby comes. A lot of things are going to change.

She leans forward, an elbow resting on the walnut table and glances down at the Chinese food on her plate. It's her favorite, and she still hasn't eaten. She barely eats; she barely sleeps.

With bags under her eyes, she gives me the smallest of smiles. "I think if I eat it, I may in fact throw up."

"What about the lemons?" I offer, changing the subject and shoving the last wonton into my mouth. She has supplements to help her retain whatever nutrients and fats she can eat because she hasn't gained enough weight. I don't think it's the pregnancy at all. It's the stress. I'm guilty as fuck when it comes to that.

"Oh my God, if I smell another lemon." She breathes out the statement in one long line. "Maybe it works for some women but not me. I'm just not hungry. It's not like I'm nauseated. I'm just not hungry and if I try to eat, that's when my stomach gets upset. There's no morning sickness… I just can't eat."

"What about something else? Anything else?" I offer.

"Let's just lie down on the sofa and relax?" she questions and I'm already standing, the feet of the chair scraping against the hardwood floor making the only noise in the room. "Maybe I'll grab a bowl of ice cream after. A bowl late at night has been wonderful."

"I'll get the dishes," I offer. "Go lie down and put something on the TV."

The light from the black iron chandelier above the table reflects off her hair as she stands up. It gives her the look of an angel.

"I can get it. I'm not useless, you know?" she answers with a simper and the glint in her eye turns soft and tempting.

The gray walls and sleek slate-colored chairs with expensive fabric look cheap compared to the way Laura looks right now, standing there in a simple silk chemise.

"Get your ass on that sofa." To say it's a demand would be comical, but she obeys, giving me a view and when she turns, I get a good look at her little bump.

The click and light of the TV turning on are followed by dull sounds of channels flicking and by the time I've cleaned up and made my way to her, she's nestled under the chenille throw, a pillow propping up her head as she lies on the end of the sofa, leaving me room behind her to spoon.

Just how she likes it. Which happens to be how I love it.

Just the sight of her like that, knowing she's all mine right now, makes me eager to feel her body pressed against mine.

I'll never not want her. There isn't a day in this life that I wouldn't be drawn to this woman.

She peeks up at me as I slip behind her on the sofa. All of her soft curves molding to mine and warming every inch of me.

As she snuggles against me, she holds up the remote to the TV, flicking through the channels without actually waiting to see what's on the screen.

"What are we watching?" I ask her, sneaking a small kiss on the crook of her neck. Her eyes close and the corners of her lips slip up. I love it. I love the way she reacts to something so small.

The moment she opens them, she shrugs and sets the remote down, leaving the TV to play an old cartoon although the volume is so low, I can barely hear it.

"You're going to be a good dad, you know that?"

She picks nervously at the end of the throw and I don't answer her until she looks back at me. "You will be."

If only.

"You'll tell me if I do something wrong, won't you?" I play it up, wanting her to be happy, needing her not to have a worry in the world other than what flavor of ice cream she wants tonight.

"I would say that you won't do anything wrong… but you totally will." Her brutal honesty does nothing but make me smile, which in turn puts a grin on her face and I swear it's the first time everything has seemed right all day. That sick feeling inside that haunts me, warning me that nothing is all right is silenced by the way she looks at me.

Pulling her body close to mine, my forearm against her front and her back against my chest, I live in this very small moment for as long as I can.

When I kiss the crown of her head, she hums a sweet sound, my favorite sound.

"I wanted to talk to you about a few things," Laura says just beneath her breath and then gently turns in my arms. I have to loosen my grip some for her to get settled right.

"What about?" I ask her, knowing damn well whatever she's going to bring up, she's been thinking about for days.

"I think I may quit… or go part-time." She stares at the dip in my throat as she talks. As I answer her, she rests her pointer against it before dragging it up my neck and back down. I stare at her all the while, from the curve of her neck to the tip of her nose. How every feature of her is utterly gorgeous.

"You never have to work if you don't want to."

"I don't know what's best to do."

"Whatever you want to do, I will be here. I will support you. And I will love you regardless of your choice." That's what I tell myself every night. To love her, to stay with her. Because it's all I want back from her. If that happens, we'll be okay.

When all of this is over, we have to be okay. That's the bottom line. I won't survive if we aren't together.

Or if she doesn't love me anymore. So I'm careful. Careful not to do anything that will push her away.

"I mean it," I tell her adamantly, waiting for her gaze to meet mine. "Whatever you want to do."

"Thank you," she whispers and then her breath hitches. The next question is muffled as it comes out, like it didn't want to be asked. "Can I ask you something?" She's quick to follow it up with, "I don't want to upset you."

As she clears her throat, looking down at my chest again rather than into my eyes, I nod and say, "Of course, ask me anything."

All of the innocuous questions she could have possibly asked are nothing like the one she utters.

"Did my dad die quick?"

I'm gutted by her question. I can't speak for a second, I can't do anything but stare down at her as she tries not to cry.

Her inhales are deliberate and even as she says, "I just wanted to know. I've been thinking about him a lot, you know?"

The memory of him on his knees in front of me is a flash in my eyes and I'm grateful she doesn't look at them for fear the reflection in them would give it away.

"It was fast," I answer her as evenly as I can. "I'm sorry."

"Just a shot to his head?" she questions further and it fucking kills me. "Did he know?"

"He knew. When he got there, he knew." I don't know how she can lie here with me during this conversation. It makes me feel like that much more of a bastard.

"Right and then it was fast." She keeps picking at the blanket, staring at my chest as her shoulders move gently up and down with her even breathing.

"It was. He wasn't greedy. He was..."

"He was stupid," she answers for me, with no resentment or emotion. Just simply matter-of-fact. "He never should have been a part of that life."

I want to agree with her, but I'm afraid to speak at all on it. It's not my place.

"He used to tell me all sorts of things he shouldn't."

I'm grateful she hasn't pulled away. I'm thankful she doesn't break down either. But damn does it hurt. "If I could go back and..."

She peers up at me, her eyes darker, wider, swirling with a knowing truth as she says, "It wouldn't have changed it, would it?"

With my throat tight, I shake my head and hold on to her tighter.

"He just didn't think it through. His mouth would move before his brain. Grandma said it too. She worried for him because he couldn't keep his mouth shut."

"I'm sorry." It's all I can say."That's who my dad was." She keeps talking, although it's as if she's talking to herself rather than me. Her gaze firmly set on my shoulder this time, her finger trailing along the seam of my t-shirt. "A know-it-all who didn't know a damn thing and a man who ran his mouth faster than he himself could run."

"There were good parts to him," I offer her, remembering her father. "I wasn't around him often, but when I was, he loved to make jokes. He liked for other people to smile."

Her hand pauses and worried, I gaze down at her, only to see a small smile gracing her lips. "That's true. He did like to make other people happy."

"He did." Picking up her hand, I kiss her knuckles.

A long moment passes, the comfortable atmosphere dampened and the irony of childhood cartoons playing in the background only adds to the somber effect.

"Thank you for still loving me." I don't know how I'm able to speak with the way every part of me dies inside. What I did was unforgivable. I stole from her in a way no one had a right to. And yet here she is, letting me hold her and soothe the pain I caused.

"He wasn't the best father, but he loved me."

"He did."

"Promise me, Seth, that you'll love this little boy."

"Our little boy," I correct her and then kiss away the tears on her cheek.

"Yes," she says and smiles through the pain. "Promise me you'll love him always."

I hate the way she's talking right now. Maybe she thinks I don't see through her words. To the very idea that she's planning a life for me and for our little prince without her. I won't let it happen. I can't.

I can't live without her.

"Always. I will love you and our son, and all of the other little ones to come, forever."

"I love you forever," she whispers, tilting up her chin and brushing her lips against mine. It's the way she used to do it. She'd say she loved me, then kiss me, so when I didn't say it back, it was okay. Like she'd silenced me and not as if I was deliberately holding back.

I pull away from her, breaking the tender kiss and stare into her baby blues as I say, "I love you forever and ever, Babygirl."

CHAPTER 11

Laura

I CAN'T HAVE WINE. WHICH IS MY NORMAL GO-TO FOR STRESS.

And just the thought of carbs makes me want to puke. So my junk food choices are a no go. My mind races whenever I try to nap, even though I'm exhausted as all hell.

So what's a girl to do? Shop.

"We are buying all the things. Every single thing," I state comically as I toss another blue binky into the cart. "I didn't realize they were called pacifiers," I comment as I read the back of another package. This one contains a binky with a little blue airplane on the front and even comes with a strap to hook it onto a onesie so it doesn't get lost. *How smart.*

"What? What did you think they were called?" Bethany questions and I shrug. "I've only ever heard it called a 'binky.'"

She's still busy reading the side of a bottle warmer. It's the third one she's picked up. None of them seem to be good enough and I'm not sure what deems them unacceptable.

"You know you can't get everything on your own. You need to have a shower so we can get you stuff too."

"And who exactly am I going to invite?" I almost say Melody, just to jokingly name a patient, but then the last time I saw her comes back to me, along with a chill that silences me.

"I think..." Bethany starts to answer me but she's distracted by another box, which she picks up to examine then puts down. She pushes the cart down the aisle further and I walk with her, resisting the urge to grab every bath toy on the display wall as we go.

For noon on a Wednesday, the Buy Buy Baby store is practically empty and it's just us two. "You know, I think it would be good if you met the other girls," she says and finally looks at me, standing still with both hands on the handle of the cart.

"Other girls?" I question and she pulls her gray shimmery sweater up her forearms and bunches it just before her elbows. It is a little hot in here, after all.

"You know, Aria, Chloe, Addison."

The wives of the Cross brothers.

"Oh," is all I can answer. I'm shocked, to be honest. And then a little petrified. I got out of the life. I know Seth comes with it. But this is different. Things are different now. Aren't they? Loneliness and longing are two emotions I didn't expect to feel at that thought. "Is that because you and Jase are... you know, a real thing now. Like for real, for real?"

"For real, for real." Her cheeks get fuller when she smiles. Every time I mention his name, she smiles like that.

"I think you'd really like them and Aria... last night she did a reading for me. And I picked a card for you. She said you're not supposed to and it doesn't work like that. But I think it fit you well."

It takes me a moment to realize by reading she means tarot cards.

"What card?" I ask her even though I turn my attention to a pile of baby blankets. I run my hand along them, but I don't really feel them. Just the thought of the Cross brothers and those women gives me pause. But if they're a part of Seth's world...

"The three of cups. She said it's the card of sisterhood."

I turn to her with a smirk and say, "Sisterhood?" She only nods.

"Look, they would love you and you would love them, and," she stops and sighs like whatever she has to say next is a given before continuing, "if I have to be around them, so do you."

A single laugh comes from deep in my chest and makes me smile.

"Well then—" I start to answer her, but that's when I feel it. "Oh my gosh," I say as both of my hands fly to my lower belly. Very low, close to my hips. And he does it again.

"What? What is it?" Bethany's voice is riddled with unease until I smile the widest grin I've had in weeks.

"He kicked." I take her wrist as she gapes and gently put her hand right where mine was. I'm careful as I do it, worried he'll stop. The anxiousness keeps me on my toes, holding my breath until Bethany squeals, "He kicked!"

He kicked. My grin stretches all the way across my face. My baby kicked for the first time in a baby supply shop, right at the start of aisle ten. I never want to forget this moment. The smile genuine, the happiness and relief so very real. This is what it's supposed to feel like. It's what normal women must imagine when thinking about being pregnant.

No matter what happens, I got to have this moment. With my best friend hugging me, and my baby safe and healthy. I'll be forever grateful that I at least got to have this moment.

"One cup of coffee, two cups of water." The waitress looks at me like I'm crazy for about half a second before she corrects her maybe-seventeen-year-old face.

I'm tired as all hell and if I need a cup of coffee… well then I need a cup of coffee. My doctor said a cup is fine as long as I drink water constantly and it might help me with other issues I'm having too. The headaches, the lack of being able to go to the bathroom.

The second the waitress, I think she said her name was Angel, turns away from us and moves to the next table, Bethany tells me, "I am taking off for the next one."

"It's on Thursday." Because I'm high risk, I have to go in for stress tests constantly.

"I'm going to miss you at work, so I want to come along."

"I'd love that." With both of my arms folded in front of me and resting on the table, I try to pick an item on the menu that calls out to me. The menu is printed on paper with a checkerboard pattern and the tabletop is red lacquered. It fits the '50s feel of the place.

The linoleum floors and pleather bench seats do too.

There are a lot of yummy smells in the Bells Diner but one thing in particular smells divine. "I'm actually craving something," I mumble and when Bethany asks me what, I can only shrug. "I'm not sure what. But something..."

That gets a laugh from her and although I hate to interrupt the happy day with one little thing, I have to do it. Better now than later.

"I have something to ask you," I say and tap my finger on the menu, no longer searching for my Goldilocks dish, fidgeting with a ring on my middle finger. It's a rose gold ring with a white quartz stone and flowers on the edges of the band... little daisies. Cami gave it to me a long time ago and I rediscovered it last night when I went looking through things as I packed them up to take to Seth's place. He hates it when I call it that. It's *our* place now. I could roll my eyes at that all day long. I'll make it ours, but right now it's his place with a bunch of my boxes and things in it. Like this ring. An old friendship ring she told me once that was supposed to guard us from bad things. I didn't wear it for the longest time, thinking it had done just the opposite.

"If I die, will you take care of him?"

The thud in my chest is nothing compared to what I feel every night. I won't feel better until he's in my arms. That's simply the way it is. The unknown isn't just uncomfortable, it's scary as fuck. And it's weird between Seth and me without knowing for certain that there's a backup plan. A "just in case" plan. I can't talk about it with him though.

The shock on Bethany's face is temporary. It morphs into something more mortified but then solemn.

The cords in her neck tighten as she averts her gaze but starts to say something.

"Here you go." Angel, our waitress, interrupts us. The cups hit the table one by one, the waters, coffee, and a latte for Bethany, and then she asks us if we need another minute to look over the menu.

"We do, please," I answer her quickly and pray that when she scuttles off that the only thing Bethany will say is, *of course.*

"What about Seth?"

That's the last thing I wanted her to ask.

"I don't know how he'll react if I… he's been very emotional lately. I worry about him." My hand travels to my lower belly, and I wish my little prince would kick again. "I just need to know that our baby will be all right. I can't imagine… I just can't see him dealing with me not being there and also having a baby dropped in his lap.

"It will be hard for him to keep it together," I explain calmly, rationally. There are no tears when I say it out loud. Because I know it's a true fear of mine. If I die and Seth is left with a helpless baby… If he breaks down, our little boy is going to need someone there.

"I'm just coming to terms with the fact that a heart may never come and I don't know that Seth will be able to take care of him on his own, at least in the beginning." I don't know that I'm describing this right. I've been too busy picking at my nails to realize Bethany is silently crying.

"You aren't allowed to cry. We're in public and we aren't drunk," I mock scold her emotional reaction comically. I hate to see her like this. It hurts a piece of me that's always wounded. The part that knows I can't help that one day, I won't be there for her. For my baby boy. For Seth. One day, I won't have them and they won't have me.

"They're going to need you. I need you there for them. Both of them." This feels like the last piece of the puzzle. Seth doesn't know it, but at least I'll feel more at ease.

"I know that you're just planning." She toys with the fork on the table as she talks. Breathing in deep, she finally looks back at me and says, "I promise if you… if something happens to you," I don't miss how she doesn't say, *if you die*, "then yes, I will make sure your baby boy is safe and happy and lives the best life a little boy could."

"Thank you, Bethany." She nods.

"I'm not ready to die and this life wasn't what I planned, but I want to make sure he'll be all right. Seth too."

"You're going to be okay, though." She sounds far too confident, but at least she's stopped tearing up.

"Sure I will," I answer her with a smirk and have a taste of my far too bitter coffee before reaching for the sugar. That's when I see the long blond hair out of the corner of my eye.

Chills sweep over me and I turn sharply to my left, to the booth where a blonde woman was seated with her back to me.

I only blinked and now she's gone.

She was there, though. She was right there. Fear whips around me, nearly making me knock over the sugar.

"You okay?" Bethany questions. "Hey, love, you all right?"

"Yeah, yeah," I struggle to answer her while also trying to find the blonde woman I know I've seen a handful of times now. I know I saw her.

"Did you take your medication?" she asks softly, her hand over mine.

"What? Yes, yes, of course I did." Even though she's not there, I'm still uneasy and it's hard to shake it off.

No one's there.

"I have a question then. What if Seth doesn't want me involved? That's the only thing I worry about. What if he wants to leave with your son and go back to the West Coast? What if he takes him… what are we calling him? Have you thought of any names?"

I answer, "Little prince."

I can barely focus on her question, still struck with the image of the blonde who reminds me so much of Cami.

Fuck, I really am going crazy.

"Well, what then? What if he leaves?"

"Seth isn't a loner. He doesn't do well alone, so that won't happen." I surprise myself with my quick answer and confidence, but it's true. It's simply not in his nature. Neither of us likes to be alone.

"And you'd be fine… if Seth is fine, him being on his own with the baby?"

"Yes. I just know Seth will need help, is all…"

I imagine Seth holding a little baby boy. He's always been so protective and he's nothing like the reckless youth he used to be. "He'll make a good dad. He wants to be a dad."

"So you just want me to be the cool aunt?" she jokes and the dark clouds around her slowly fade. "That was the plan anyway."

"I guess…" I can't help but smile just a hint of a grin. "Seth sometimes doesn't respond well. Like the last time I left. And I just want to make sure everything will be all right."

A sarcastic laugh leaves her in a huff as she lifts up the menu, her eyes wide with humor. "Is that what you call it?"

She has to keep talking before I fully grasp what she's getting at.

"Jase told me about what he did when you left him last time. Not that it was… not that it's the same."

"Right," I answer the single word, any bit of hunger vanishing as the conversation progresses.

"Marcus called him the black widower in the letters," she comments, her gaze on the menu.

"They're still going through them?" I question her. Truth be told, I'm curious to read them. I'm more anxious for Delilah to show up. Any day now. And I'm reluctant to quit for that one reason. Delilah has to know who Marcus is. Or at least what he looks like. I know Seth told me not to concern myself with it, but she could help them if only she told them—or me—who Marcus is or anything about how to find him.

"Yeah, there are a lot of them, years' worth, and a lot of decoding."

It's quiet as we both stare down at the menus. The ding of the front door opening, the din of chatter and clink of silverware on dishes is our backdrop.

"I'll put it in the paperwork," I tell her, taking in a deep breath and feeling more at peace. More ready for whatever may happen. "That you'll have secondary custody."

"Paperwork?"

"I want my affairs in order." Everything from a will to life insurance is updated. Absolutely every *I* dotted and *T* crossed. "We'll sign them on Thursday."

Dropping the menu, I stare back at Bethany, only to see that look back on her face, the solemn one.

"Thursday it is then."

I nod in agreement and say, "Thursday."

It's easy to talk about some things with Bethany and some things with Seth. Other things are best to keep to myself.

Tossing the keys onto the foyer table, I take in the crowded living room. Boxes and more cardboard boxes filled with things from my old apartment are taking up so much space, and here I am, adding more bags to the mess.

"Seth?" I call out and the plastic crinkles as I set the last bag down with the rest of them.

My feet ache and my back feels a bit like shit, to put it eloquently, but there's so much work to do.

"Babe?" I call out louder and peer down the hallway, which is lined by boxes too.

There's a single light on down the hall, coming from the room that we decided would be the nursery.

He always calls out when I'm home. It's odd. I know his mind is elsewhere with everything going on but still.

My steps are careful as I walk quietly down the hall. Thoughts of the blonde, of Marcus, of every bad thought that keeps me up at night make me second-guess going down the hall at all.

The faint thuds in my chest get harsher and I call out, my voice a bit shaky, "Seth."

The sight of him, poking his head out of the room, his brow furrowed and a headphone dangling from one ear while the other's still firmly in place eases the fear that was running through me.

"You all right?" he questions me, concern changing to protectiveness as he strides confidently down the hall, taking the earbuds out completely.

"Yeah, I just… I'm home." I stumble over my words, feeling foolish, but when I say I'm home and Seth's eyes light up, his hard features soften and he leans down, both hands finding their place on my lower back, his lips brushing against mine… well there's nothing foolish about that.

With my hands against his hard muscles, everything inside of me melts. A small hum escapes me when he breaks the short-lived kiss but then bends down to nip my neck. My head falls back and I could stay there just with him, in a crowded hallway full of boxes, forever.

"Let me show you what I've been doing." He's too eager to move me, even though my feet are planted firmly where they are in protest.

I let him lead me away, taking my hand. His is so strong, so large it wraps wholly around mine.

"It's paint that's safe for babies. That's what the clerk said. And for you," Seth informs me before the room comes fully into view.

"It's mostly dried," he says and lets go of my hand as I walk into the brightly lit bedroom that smells faintly of fresh paint. The former modern fan has been replaced with one that has alternating blue- and white-colored blades. A dark navy blue compared to the pale blue on the far wall, the one with the bay window.

I can't speak as I take it all in. The pile of cardboard in the one corner, the newly built whitewashed crib and matching dresser. I almost step on a screwdriver; Seth grabs my waist to pull me back. Pulling me into his embrace, warm and strong and everything I could ever want.

"I know it's a mess, but I'll clean it up tonight after I finish putting the rest together."

"It's so beautiful. I love it. You did all this?" I say and turn in his embrace, still stunned and so overwhelmed.

"Yeah, I needed something to do." His answer comes with a handsome smile, a charming one, but it doesn't reach his pale blue eyes.

"You all right?"

He starts to say yes, I can hear it without the word even being spoken, but shifting his gaze to an empty box that needs to be broken down, he leaves me where I am and gets to work, doing just that, breaking down the cardboard with a box cutter so it lays flat.

"I'm good with us. Good with this. Just," he pauses and takes in a deep breath, stretching out his shoulders with his back to me. The white shirt stretches tight over his shoulders and it's then that I see a bit of paint he got on it. Seth looks handsome in suits, but he was made to be blue collar. In those jeans, with those muscles. No suit, expensive fabric and tailored perfectly or not, is justified to hide all that.

"Just what?" I ask him and make myself busy too, grabbing the stack of white wicker baskets laying on the corner of the floor by other bags of baby items and lining them up on the dresser. There are a few empty plastic bags scattered around the room, so I pick them each up, balling them up and putting the smaller ones inside of the largest.

"I'm messed up right now," he admits, his voice lower than usual.

I pause what I'm doing, watching him as he keeps working, not looking back at me.

"Can I do anything?" I offer, silently praying, no—begging, God please let there be something I can do. I hate seeing him like this.

"No," he answers, sitting back on his heels, wiping his forehead with the back of his hand. I watch as he takes a moment to look at the crib, a genuine smile slipping onto his face, but it's gone in a moment. With his head hung low, he grabs another box and continues what he was doing.

"What's wrong?" I dare to ask, not bothering to do anything now. Instead I find a clear spot in the corner of the room, sitting on the floor and trying to get comfortable.

The second my ass hits the ground, Seth looks up. "I ordered that rocker that matches the crib. The one you wanted," he tells me and my heart does a little flip. "It's delayed but it'll be here next weekend."

I love him like this. For some reason, it gets me all choked up and my eyes glaze over a bit when I smile and whisper my thanks. "That can't be what's wrong, though? A rocking chair getting you like this?" I try to keep it light. My arms wrap around my knees and I curve my back, stretching out my sore muscles.

"Marcus told me to do something I don't want to do."

His answer both surprises me and sends alarm shooting through me. That cautious feeling that came over me when I first came home, comes back with full force.

"What is it?"

"I can't tell you and I don't want you to stress. I just need you to know that I'm off right now, and I'm doing my best to be here for you how you need me. If I seem out of it, it's because of that, not because of us. I love us. I want to be here for you."

"Well why you?" The second question comes out even faster. Why is Marcus involved? Why is he telling Seth to do anything? I hate him in this moment. He doesn't scare me. That's what happens when anger takes over. Nothing scares you when you're angry.

"Delilah will come back to the center—" I can't finish because Seth cuts me off.

"Babygirl," he says and pauses, crawling over to where I am to put his hands on my shoulders, staring into my eyes. "I promise you, I'll figure it out. I just don't like what I have to do."

My inhale is unsteady until he leans down and kisses my cheek. My eyes close and when they do, he kisses me tenderly, surprising me when his lips mold to mine.

He breaks the kiss, and my eyes stay closed as he whispers into the warm air between us, "That's what I needed. That's all I need."

The cool air surrounds me the moment he leaves me, going back to piling the last of the cardboard before grabbing a box that holds some other sort of crib that we're supposed to have. One that's portable and rocks.

"I have more too," I tell him and force myself to get up and get the bags so I can organize all the little things in drawers and baskets.

Seth is quiet as I leave, but he looks over his shoulder to give me a look that warms me from head to toe. It's the kind of look where you know the other person wants you, that they love you, and that if they could, they'd lay with you forever.

My fingers brush against my lips when I get to the hall; I can still feel his kiss there. And I know I'm blushing because my cheeks are warm.

We work in silence for a little while, me taking things out of the bags and plopping them into the newly designated baskets for such items. Binkies, rattles, bath toys. I did end up buying nearly half of the ones on that display.

"Oh." The sight of the bath toys makes my eyes go wide when I remember.

"What? Are you okay?" Seth answers quick and I'd laugh at the look on his face if it wasn't so heartwarming.

"He kicked today," I answer him and all those emotions come back.

His gaze moves to my lower belly. "If he does it again, I'll tell you," I offer and a handsome grin stretches across his face.

He crawls over to me, such an odd thing for a powerful man like him to do. Lowering his lips to my belly and slipping his hands up my shirt, he whispers for little prince to wake up and give him a kick.

He jokes that it's not fair that "Mom" got to feel it without him. He called me Mom.

I wish he was the biological father. I wish there was no backup plan needed and I knew for certain everything was going to be just fine.

But even if those wishes don't come true, I still feel so damn lucky. At that thought, Seth pulls back, his hands still on my belly, just a split second after a small kick lands near my ribs.

Seth's stubbled jaw drops in awe. "He did it. That was him?" he asks me.

Nodding my head, I whisper, yeah, and watch him watch my belly, telling our son to do it again.

He doesn't, but that only prods Seth to kiss my belly. Right where the kick was.

"Thought he might take the chance to get me." He mumbles the joke and it makes me laugh.

"Thank you for doing this."

"Of course."

I can't stop myself from asking as he rubs soothing circles on my bump, "Why can't we smile like this all the time? Just have this forever?" It was meant to be rhetorical, but Seth answers me.

"Because I am terrified to lose you. And I have a lot of reasons to believe I might."

"If it's up to me, you won't. You know I'm a fighter." I barely whisper my promise.

He only smiles at me before kissing my belly and then the tip of my nose.

"I love you."

He responds with a hand splayed across my lower stomach, "I love us."

"God is so unfair," I groan.

"Why?"

"Because you're fucking perfect."

He's on me in an instant. His lips hot against mine, his hands traveling down the curve of my waist and then lower.

"Seth," I say and his name is a gasp on my lips, stolen between a heated kiss. Emotions swirl with an ever-present desire and all my sadness drowns in it.

Every nerve ending between my legs sparks with recognition and need.

My breath is his, his mouth never leaving mine, even as his forearm braces my back. Lowering me to the ground.

Desperation would have me ripping his clothes off, needing to be one with him in this very instant. Every second is torturous as Seth does just the opposite.

His fingers barely graze my skin as he undresses me slowly, one piece at a time. And he does the same for himself, not letting me move an inch beneath him. With his body above mine, I'm never cold, always warmed and protected.

If his lips ever leave mine, they travel down my jaw, my neck, my collarbone, leaving a tender trail that's ravenous just the same.

"I need you," I whimper and Seth pulls back, staring down at me with complete devotion. There's a sadness that swirls deep in the depths of his gaze, but it's gone as quickly as it came. His voice is filled with wretched emotion when he says, "I wish I could go back and tell you every day that I loved you. Every day."

"Seth," I say, trying to comfort him, but when my hands cup his strong jaw, he takes them by the wrist. He kisses my palms and then plants them above my head. Lowering his lips to mine, he whispers, "Know that if I have one regret in this life, it's that I didn't tell you I loved you every single day I could have."

My fingers spear in his hair, but before I can give him a response, he devours me as only Seth can.

He enters me in one swift motion. My neck arches as the sweet pain of being stretched stirs with the hungered need for more.

I wish I could meet his pace, but he alternates between deep, slow thrusts and a pistoning every time I come close to the edge. He doesn't hold back like I expect him to when I get there. He forces me over, screaming out his name as my orgasm tears through me. And then he slows, pushing himself deeper until he's pressed against my back wall, groaning his need for release in the crook of my neck.

Over and over he takes me, until my throat is sore from crying out his name and my body trembles with overwhelming pleasure.

CHAPTER 12

Seth

"I WANT TO ASK YOU SOMETHING," I SAY AND MY VOICE COMES OUT stronger than I'd like, breaking up the peaceful silence. Her eyes open and she peers up at me through her thick lashes. I knew she wasn't sleeping. Neither of us have been able to sleep, and for good reason. We have these moments that are pure happiness, but then reality dampens them.

She rolls on her side, the bed groaning as she does and the dim light kissing along her bare skin emphasizes every curve as she turns to give me her full attention.

"Yes?" Her barely spoken question fills up the master bedroom.

I've never been anxious to ask her anything. Never in my life. But the truth she has for me could cut me deeper than any knife would.

"You've been asking me lots of things. A lot of hard questions." I'm fully aware that I'm stalling. I fucking hate what this situation has done to me.

"I know. I promise I've asked all of them. No more hard questions." She promises me as if she's done something wrong by asking them.

Licking my lower lip, I settle my hand on her lower back over the thin sheet and kiss the tip of her nose.

With my forehead resting against hers I whisper, "You can ask me anything you want, whenever you want. Hard or not."

She nods ever so slightly and then lifts up her lips, kissing the tip of my nose just as I've done to her.

"What is it?" she asks.

"The father… do you know who he is?" Although we're both so still, and the room itself is eerily quiet, my pulse races and my blood rushes in my ears.

"I have an idea. I just haven't reached out." She reaches for the sheet, bringing it up higher like I knew she would. Putting anything she can between herself and that question. "I don't plan on it until after the baby's here."

"Do you have to?" I ask her and there's not an ounce of anger or authority there. It's a simple question, one that aches inside my chest. I don't let her hear it in my voice, or see it on my expression, but I know she knows. She always knows.

"I haven't decided," she whispers quietly. The vulnerability that I keep hidden away, she wears openly. I know if she does, she'll never hear back. But still, I don't want him to be on her mind. I just want it to be us. Only us for her.

Readjusting on the bed, I pull her closer to me and kiss her gently. Keeping my eyes closed, I ask her, "Did you enjoy it? What you had with him? Or any of the men you were with while we weren't together?"

The second the question is spoken, I know I've officially gone mad. I'm fucked up and nowhere near the man I once was.

But if that's what she had while I wasn't there, I want to know she was happy. I need to know that much.

"That feels like a loaded question," she says. This time she's the one stalling, staring back at me as if she's not sure if she should tell me the truth.

"He didn't hurt you, right?" I ask, rolling onto my back, pulling away and pinching the bridge of my nose. I'm so fucking weak and helpless. I've never hated myself more.

The sheets rustle as she props herself up, placing a palm against my chest. She stares down at me.

"No. No, none of them hurt me in any way. It was… it was just a hookup mostly. I don't know what you want me to say." Her last statement is spoken nervously.

"Did they break your heart?" I ask her, finally pulling my hand away to look back at her.

"They never had it to break." She'll never know what her answer does to me. How much it means but how much it hurts just the same.

I give her a weak smile that I'm not sure she can see in the darkness. "I guess I'll let them live then."

She utters the smallest of laughs and says, "Is that why you asked?"

"I don't know," I answer her honestly. "I don't know a lot anymore when I used to know everything."

"My broken king," Laura whispers, kissing the dip in my throat.

"My broken queen," I say in reply, not knowing how true a title that is for her until the words have escaped into the air.

A beep from my phone interrupts the moment. Leaving my scattered thoughts where they are, I kiss her knuckles before removing her hand from where it lays on my chest and reaching over to my phone.

"I have to go, Babygirl." It's the notification for the meeting tonight. For what must be done. I plant a kiss on her lips before reminding both myself and her, "Security's outside."

"I know," she answers with a small smile that doesn't reach her eyes. The blues of them carry so much depth of emotion as she stares back at me.

"I'll be back as soon as I can."

"I know."

I cup her face, feeling her warmth and running my thumb over her kissable lips. "I love you," I tell her.

"I know. And I love you too."

I know she does. That's why I have to do this. Whatever it takes, I'll do it for her.

It's almost three a.m. and the bar is just winding down. The music's off since it's closing time and the only patrons left are ones who have business outside of liquor consumption.

Anthony is behind the bar. He's the first one I see, drying glasses with a bright white dishrag as I walk through the front door. The man I want to see has his back to me, seated on a stool just to the right of Anthony. Just like last time. I don't want this setup to become anything more than what it is. A one-time exchange of information.

With a nod, I give the order for him to move to the other side of the bar. Five men are in the main room right now, with maybe two more in the back. All of them are men who work in this bar, and therefore for the Cross brothers, and then there's Officer Walsh and myself.

"I was just getting ready to order another," Walsh comments as I approach. No doubt the sound of my footsteps alerted him. "Do you need a drink too?" he questions, his voice dull. Which is appropriate for the occasion.

He knows exactly what I'm doing. Giving Marcus a firm yes or no. Setting everything into motion, as he likes to say.

The legs of the stool scrape on the ground as I pull it out, taking the one to the left of Walsh. He doesn't move his pale blue gaze from the back of the bar. The reflection in them shows the rows of colored glasses in front of us.

"I'll have one with you. Just one, though."

He nods, swallowing thickly and then motions toward Anthony. His gaze darts between Walsh and me until I nod. He's a damn good kid, learning quick, but I feel for him. One day, he'll be in the same place I am. It always comes down to this. Making deals to save the ones you love.

"What are we having?" I ask Walsh even though I see Anthony pull out an amber bottle of what I know is expensive whiskey.

Walsh waves me off and says, "Doesn't matter. I'm buying."

The two shots thud on the bar as Anthony sets them down in

front of us. Walsh lifts his in salute and I toast mine against his before throwing back the neat whiskey.

"He wasn't always like this; you know?" Walsh starts, his gaze still focused in front of us. He hasn't even looked at me yet.

I square my shoulders toward him and that does the trick. His eyes are red, with dark bags underneath. With his dark jeans, a t-shirt with some sort of logo on it, and a black leather jacket, he has the look of a man on the edge. On the edge of losing it all.

"There was a time when we saw eye to eye. When it was only the criminals and men who killed for sport who were on his radar. And then… one case… one case changed everything."

He holds up two fingers, indicating two shots and I tell him just one. His response is that both are for him.

"It was then that he decided even the smallest of crimes could lead to something horrific that needed to be prevented."

"What was the case?"

He looks like he's going to answer me, but instead he puts a shot to his lips, throwing it back and fiddling with the glass.

"It was five years ago. In all fairness, it changed me too." His gaze turns distant and he tosses back the second shot.

I nearly ask him what Marcus wanted from him at the warehouse. But he slams the shot glass down and then faces me to ask, "Do you have it?"

I can only nod, the temperature of my blood getting hotter and hotter as he holds his hand out, waiting. If I do this, I know there's no going back. If I don't, I don't know that Laura will live and she has to live. She has to make it through this.

"Yeah," I finally answer him, desperation making me sick to my stomach.

Walsh's gaze falls slightly, looking something like disappointment when I grab the envelope from my back pocket, folded and creased in half, and hand it to him, although I don't let go of it.

"Are you sure you want to do this?" he questions in a breath just above a whisper, still not looking at me.

"Like he said," I say as I remember what Marcus told us in that warehouse, "I'm aware of everything I have to lose, and I won't risk her." I may hate myself, but if I don't, I know with everything in me that I'll lose her. By the hand of the devil named Marcus, or by the hand of God.

So this has to happen.

"You made your choice then?" he asks and attempts to take the thin envelope, so thin it nearly looks empty, but I still can't let go of it.

"Yeah," I answer him and finally let go, releasing it and taking the consequences in return.

"Then this is for you," Walsh says simply, reaching inside of his jacket. I watch the men reach for their guns, but Walsh doesn't pay attention. He retrieves an envelope, just as thin. "For what it's worth, I believe him. If he says he can save her, he can and he will."

I nod at his statement. "I do too," I confess, my voice turning tight. "It's the only reason I agreed to this."

CHAPTER 13

Laura

I'VE NEVER GIVEN NOTICE OF LEAVE BEFORE. I'VE NEVER QUIT. I HADN'T realized that until just now as I get in my car to go to the Rockford Center and do just that.

It's all I can think about on the drive there. How much I busted my ass for this job. How it's my first real job. How much I love it and what I do and my patients.

The roads are icy and even though I'm fully aware of that, I nearly fall on my ass when I open the car door to go in and tell Aiden I have to quit. *Shit*. My grip on the edge of the door is so tight, I'm able to hoist myself up and grateful the door itself didn't snap off.

Thump, *thump*, *thump*, my heart races along with the wind whipping at my face and destroying the limited effort I put into making my hair look semi-decent.

Just breathe.

In and out, I focus on breathing. The morning air is nippy, but it feels worse than that. Everything just feels wrong. Everything feels off.

"I'm not quitting," I whisper into the frosty air, the words turning into fog in front of my face.

"This isn't running and this isn't giving up." I finally find my footing and stand up straighter, more relaxed and calm. More sure of myself as I stare at the building I've practically lived in for years now.

It's only a temporary leave, I promise myself.

The damn wind isn't quite as bad when I finally close the door. The resounding bang of it closing seems too final. It all feels too final as I stand there, so I slip my hands into my pockets and wait. Just for a moment. Nothing in this life is final. I know that, but why does it feel like it is?

Cars drive by the busy road to the right of the center. A few here and a few there, but the parking lot at the Rockford Center is mostly empty.

It's a Wednesday morning, so no deliveries are scheduled. And with the holidays coming, everyone seems to have already taken a bit of vacation themselves.

It's slower, colder, and the bitterness of it all is getting to me. Winter isn't my season. I may have been born in winter, but it doesn't like me much. And I don't like it either.

It's as if everything is smothered, everything depressed in some way during this season. I'm not a fan and neither is my shaky mentality.

Even with my hands in my pockets of my black wool coat, the heaviest coat I have, they're freezing. So I force myself to move, one step and then another. Tomorrow I'll find my gloves, wherever I've put them.

The thud in my chest doesn't quit. My boots click on the sidewalk and my heart beats with it. That is until I hear my name, called from my right.

The chill bites down all the way to the bone as I stand there, staring at her vision through the clouded fog of my breath.

"Delilah." I call out her name but it's ragged and cut short. I have to clear my throat and this time I walk faster, to the edge of the roundabout at the front of the building where she's standing.

A mix of emotions overwhelm me but the first is relief that she's checking in. I will always love my patients. Then quickly the reality comes back, falling like a building that's collapsed. One floor buckles, then it's slow for a moment, disbelief kicks in, then the whole damn thing crashes down.

Delilah, Marcus, the threats, the letters. I don't know what to do but she can't leave. I can't let her leave.

"Delilah," I call out her name louder, her on one side of the street while I'm on the other.

"Miss Roth," she calls to me and her voice is confident and comes with a recollection of nostalgia. As if we're old friends.

Her thick red coat falls to her calves, hiding the tops of her leather boots. She always looks like New York. Not just like any New Yorker, but this woman gives off an energy that represents NYC itself. I told her that the first time I met her. That she looked like New York. Even though that night she wasn't nearly as put together as she is now.

"I was hoping to see you," she tells me as she gets closer, checking both her right and left side as she crosses the street. One would think she's a powerful woman, capable and confident. But depression doesn't know a social status and I can't tell just from a simple conversation how she's faring either.

"I'm so glad you're here." The words rush out of me as the wind whips by again, blowing strands of my hair into my face. Hers stays where she put it, high in a perfectly arranged bun on the top of her head. All I can think is that she's seen Marcus. If I could convince her to tell me his full name, or to talk to a sketch artist if she doesn't know it… if only I could do that, I'm sure it could help. I've never been surer of anything.

Her red lips complement her dark skin and her auburn eyes stare back with the hint of the smile she wears on her feminine face.

"Are you leaving?" I ask her, finding the cold wrap itself around me tighter and tighter as the tip of my nose seems to freeze.

"I was just making an appointment. I didn't check myself in this time but I thought it'd be wise to come in for a consultation."

I nod subconsciously, knowing she needs to do that for her prescription as well.

"I—I agree," I say, forgetting my predicament for a moment. But then I think twice. My place is beside Seth. My place is with him and what he needs. I owe it to him to at least try. "I need your help with something."

"Can I ask if it's for professional or personal reasons?" Her question catches me off guard, but only for a moment.

"So you know that personally—"

"That our respective personal worlds are no longer..." she trails off as her smile falters and a flash of a woman I used to know, a woman I used to hold as she cried, flickers in the swirls of amber.

"A dear friend told me how you're involved now. You know what I know. I don't have to say it. And I respect him and his wishes. He's only ever tried to help me. You know that, don't you? I'm sorry, but I can't help you if it's about that."

"Please, I just need you to tell me who Marcus is or what he looks like. Please, he's—"

The smile she gives me doesn't reach her glossy eyes when she says, "I've been told not to speak to you any longer." Her voice is choked when she cuts me off. "But I am so happy to see you." She pulls a tissue from her pocket, dabbing at the corner of her eyes and looking to her left and right rather than at me, before telling me she should go.

I'm speechless. I've stayed up with her for hours on countless nights by her side while she needed me. I only need this one thing. Just this one and then the man I love won't keep himself busy, his mind focused on a task this Marcus wants him to do. "Wait," I call out and grab her wrist, the pain and agony mixing like a potent cocktail with the anguish.

"Marcus. Just tell me who he is. Please, please?" I'm not above begging. "He's hurting my family." It's the truth and she must know it is.

She doesn't show any reaction, she doesn't acknowledge what I've said, but she does look down slowly at where I'm holding her. As if to warn me that I better let go.

"You know me as a person who wants to see you whole and healthy. Someone who's kept your secrets." I let go of her, but her gaze is steady as I continue, the wind turning icy. "But there's a side of me that comes out when it has to. A side that I hate and a side that I don't want to come out. I need your help and if I'd had it, so much would have been prevented."

"Oh, dear girl, none of it would have been prevented. Not a damn bit of it."

"I killed someone." I whisper the confession, and I know it's not lost in the wind because of the sadness that echoes in her eyes. No shock, no fear, only sadness.

"I can't help you." That's all she gives me.

"I can't let you leave. I need your help," I say and desperation flutters in my tone.

"You don't need me..." she says, lowering her voice before she continues knowingly, "a man does."

"A man I love," I correct her, raising my voice, and then feel foolish and like a petulant child.

My hand covers my mouth and the fear that I'm going to fail comes over me. She's really not going to help me. She's not going to help us.

Before I can explain anything to her, before I can beg her to let me take her out for coffee and could we just talk, she stares into my eyes with a piercing gaze that only comes from a woman who's been to hell and back.

"Yes, a man you love, a man you'd do anything for and he'd do the same for you... Even things you both know are so very wrong. I know that story. I know it well." Her eyes are riddled with a mix of emotions as she whispers, "Do you want me to tell you how it ends?"

Her bottom lip trembles and mine does the same as I stare at her, so clearly in agony.

"Please," I beg her once more.

"He told me not to speak to you," she says softly, with remorse.

Shaking my head, I turn from her, my head spinning and not knowing what to do. What's right and wrong. But knowing I have to tell Seth she's here, I hurt for her the most. It all runs through my mind, every scenario, every fear... until I hear the squeal of tires.

"Laura!" Delilah's voice is heard so clearly. Everything slows. I don't realize it's a car at first. It's just a blur of red. I didn't even realize I was in the street.

The roads are icy.

The brakes aren't working.

Thud. Thud.

My heart stops working… the third thud never coming as the car crashes into me and I tumble over it. My thigh hits first, my body's limp, maybe from shock, I'm not sure. It's all so cold, so sharply violent.

I know that I tumble over the hood and land on the asphalt, unforgivingly hard. The pain is immediate, but it doesn't feel real. None of it feels real until I see Delilah standing over me, but looking at something else, someone else, screaming to call an ambulance.

CHAPTER 14

Seth

I used to revel in these moments. The talk of the business, the exchange of money. I wanted to know all the ins and outs of every deal. I craved the power of it all.

But as I sit in this room, Carter's office in the Cross brothers' estate, I can't stand to be here.

My thumb keeps tapping on the hardwood armrest of the walnut chair. My mind keeps racing. I imagine this is what men look like when they have something to hide. Exactly what I look like now. And ever since that warehouse meeting, it's been getting worse and worse. Every day, I break down more as I come to terms with it. If only I could tell them, but Marcus needs to go through with his promise. I won't say shit to anyone until she's healthy and safe.

I'll do it for her. I'd do anything for her.

"And what about Nikolai? We just let him leave?"

Jase questions Carter about men in the upper west area of our territory. Each section is essentially cut into fourths and the income that comes and goes is analyzed, problems sorted, men, police and drugs alike. I can't focus on a damn thing.

There isn't one topic I've spoken up about. Not even the bar.

"What happened at the warehouse?" Carter's deep voice breaks through my racing thoughts. It's at that moment when my phone rings. I silence it without looking, unable to look away from Carter's dark gaze as he broods in his chair behind the large desk. Placing it on vibrate, I answer him, "Nothing that concerns you. It was about Laura."

The sky is white and angry behind him in the large paned windows. It only makes him look that much more foreboding. I don't fear him; there isn't anything I fear right now more than losing Laura.

I feel remorse for all of them. But they'll understand. When it's done and over with, they'll understand. I trust that they'll follow through accordingly.

"Bullshit," he bites out.

"We know something happened." Jase's voice is calmer, less threatening as he leans back in the seat across from me, both of us on the other side of Carter's desk. Declan's across the room. He likes to sit there, in the back corner near the books.

"Walsh is leaving. He retired. So Marcus told him something," Jase prods, and I can feel all three of them staring at me. Wanting answers.

I don't look at the roaring fireplace with intricately carved marble; I don't glance down at the expensive rug beneath my feet. My gaze moves easily from Carter to Jase as I tell them I'm not privy to what was said when I left.

"All I know is that Marcus wants a meet and that he traded information about Laura's health for me to make it happen."

It's not all a lie, but it's not all the truth either.

"Right," Jase says then drops his head and his gaze. "I know I've said it before," he says as his foot taps on the rug, creating a dull thump each time that mirrors the sound in my chest. "But if there's anything we can do…"

"There's nothing," I answer them and carefully breathe in and out. Marcus said he could.

He said he'd come through first. And then, I come through for him.

I'll save her first. Gentleman's honor. That's his promise. Once she's saved, the events are put in motion. Then I'll tell them. One way or another.

The letter is already written.

My phone rings again, vibrating in my hand.

I clear my throat, wanting to give them something. I feel like a rat, sitting here with them, with men I respect, men who have been there for me and I've been there for them.

"I get the idea that you're hiding something," Carter prods and a sick smile kicks up my lips when I look back at him.

The air between us all is different now. It feels thicker, heated, suffocating.

"I am," I admit to him, but I don't elaborate.

"If Marcus made you a deal—" Jase starts to say but then his phone vibrates loud on the desk and he has to silence it.

"I want to tell you, but I can't… it doesn't concern you anyway." I add the last part more for reassurance than anything. Even though it's not true.

I know what happens to men who keep secrets. Men who admit them are signing a death wish. I won't lie more than I have to, but I can't tell them.

"You're really going to keep something from me?" Carter questions and for a moment, a small moment in the silence of this room, surrounded by three men who would kill me, three men who are positioned all the way around me, all carrying guns, I fear they will.

It's gone quickly and it's the first time I've felt it, not because it's the first time Carter has thrown his weight around, but because for the first time, I can't die. I have to follow through on my deal with Marcus. If I die, there's no way in hell he'll save her.

"I ask that you trust me. That's all I ask. I'll tell you everything when I can."

"Tell us what?" Declan questions, then his phone goes off and so does mine again. They're both only on vibrate, but all of us notice in the tense room.

Irritation mars Carter's face, creating hard lines in his features. "It's about Marcus and Walsh and I'll be damned if that doesn't involve us."

Jase and him share a look before he says, "You can tell us anything."

"I will. When it's time."

Carter's fist slams down but as it does, his own phone rings, the shrill sound of the tone filling up the room.

"What the fuck is it?" Carter roars, clearly pissed from my insolence. I'm only doing what must be done and I know damn well he'd do it too.

His expression falls as silence overcomes him. When his gaze lands on me, I know it's bad. Not in the way he elicits fear, but in the way that's often followed with "I'm so sorry about your loss." I know it's Laura. I know it is from the look on his face.

"Take this." Carter's tone is full of remorse and a sick gut-wrenching feeling comes over me. I don't know how I even stand and take the call.

"Hello," I answer and swallow thickly, prepared for whatever happens, silently praying I'm wrong. That she's just fine. But I wasn't prepared for the sound of Bethany's choked voice or her sobs.

"It's Laura."

CHAPTER 15

Laura

It's all in and out. A white haze floods my vision and my eyes are so heavy. There's a pounding in my head but it flows through every inch of me and it hurts. Well, for a moment, and then…

I know it hurts, but more than anything I'm tired and my body feels light, not in pain. There is no agonizing feeling. All it is, is falling.

The stark white walls of the hospital fade and so does the chaos of yelling and the man barking out orders above me, his white coat open, his baby blue scrubs taking up all the space as he leans over me… it all blurs and I don't mind. His stubble comes into focus and then out, his hazel eyes seem to hover over me and then it's all gone and I fade into them.

Because I'm falling and it's so light, it's so easy. It's comforting to let everything fade and blur and then there's silence in a rush of peace.

But then I'm back again. Bright white lights, screaming and the pain.

In and out.

"Keep up compressions," one voice says, or rather demands.

"It's thready but it's there." A woman's comment is rushed, panicked.

I suck in a breath, my eyes going wide. *No, make it stop!* Fuck, the pain is all-consuming. I can't move, even as I feel like I'm choking and the instinct to grab my throat takes over, I can't move. Something holds me down and it digs into my skin.

Help me, it hurts so fucking much.

"Miss Roth, Miss Roth." Someone's calling for me, talking over the storm of worry that thunders with every sound in the elevator. "We're taking you up to surgery."

"What happened?" I swear I speak the question aloud but he talks over me. My throat hurts. Why does my throat hurt? What happened? Why does everything hurt? A deep crease runs down my forehead and I try to move, to turn over, but I can't.

"You're in good hands," he says and his statement comes with a ding of the elevator. "Let's move!" his voice booms.

In an effort to get a grip on reality, I lift my head only to be met with the dizzying need to lie back down. Be still. In this moment, I want to fall again. I don't want this.

A striking pulse of pain, as if in anger at my thoughts, races from my heart up my chest. A strangled cry leaves me as I writhe in agony.

The car. The accident. It floods back in a hurried tumble.

"My baby," I whimper, my expression crumpled. It's only a whisper forced into a plea for something. To stop this. *Make it stop*, I pray as my throat tightens and tears leak from the corners of my eyes. *Please, I only want to fall.*

The hot tear rolls down my cheek and the salt meets my lips as I cry out again in pain. I can't move and that makes it worse. Everything hurts. Every moment, every thought. Every breath steals strength from me.

Make it stop. Please, please.

My memory whirls with thoughts of how I got here, but with the pounding I can't remember it all. I don't know what happened. It's in and out and I can't hold on to it.

Where's Seth? I want to cry out for him. He's still with me, isn't he? Seth would never leave me. Seth is here. He has to be. I cry out his name, Seth, but he doesn't answer.

"We're losing her," a voice says. She sounds young and scared. My head falls to the left as I sob through another bolt of aching pain.

It's my heart. My heart. *Did I go to the doctor's?* I can't remember. *Did I tell him about my heart?* The way it pitter-patters.

Slowly I remember the doctor. And then leaving. Leaving the woman who was dressed for a date, so distracted. I remember her. I remember coming home. *Cami. Cami. "No, no,"* I scream a hollow sound that I don't recognize, tearing at the restraints holding me down.

"You have to stay calm, Miss Roth, calm down!" they yell. Both at me and at each other.

Cami. Other memories rush back to me.

It takes me a moment, watching the fluorescent lights blur above me as we're rushed down the hall. One deep breath. The white and silver blend into a pattern as a prick hits my arm. I barely notice it. Another deep breath. It's the chill of whatever they've shot me with that brings the action to my attention.

My eyes burn, but my body relaxes. On the third breath I can't even feel the rise of my chest anymore.

My blood chills and with a deep inhale, I remember. That was years ago. It's been years.

Fuck, why does that make it hurt even deeper? A heaviness weighs down on me, and with it, a numbness in my toes and fingers.

I ran. The memory forces the tears to flow easier, harder, although I'm silent. Watching the years of my life come and go in waves.

I left him.

No. No! He's here. I know he's here. "Seth!" I scream out, knowing I can't live without him. I could never be without him. My head shakes and strong hands object to the movement. There are yells and demands but I don't hear any of them because they aren't Seth's voice. He's not here. Seth, I murmur pathetically. Pathetic, painful, lonely. My voice echoes all the mournful emotions. I don't want to be alone. I could never bear it if the last person I ever said I love you to wasn't Seth King.

Memories flash. His hands on my wrists, his lips on my neck. Seth, I whisper to no one. He's not for them.

I remember now, the last weeks coming slower, more detailed. I can feel him, his hard body and the heat of his embrace.

Seth. I don't bother saying his name. It's not for them. It's for me.

The car is the last thing I see. Delilah and the shock, the fear that rolled through me and with the impact, my body jolts and another wave of pain.

My head is heavy, and so are my eyes. It's cold, freezing cold as goosebumps dance along my skin. The loud ringing in my ears is unbearable and then suddenly the noise is faint, soothing. It's not so cold anymore.

It's only as cold as the breeze when I fall.

I recognize her voice. The doctor. My doctor. Doctor Tabor.

Fuck, the pain. With the recognition of a voice, the pain comes back. I feel it first, then the ringing. It's so loud. The pounding, the ringing, the screaming pain.

Blinking rapidly, the lights come back. Everything whirls and falls back into place. No, no, let it be over.

"Miss Roth," she says and the force in her voice grips me. I know her voice. Her hair is pulled back tight, making her look even thinner, even frailer, although I know her to be an imposing force with the strong will she has.

The light in my eye is blinding and I fall again.

"Laura, can you look at me?"

I know her voice. The doctor. My doctor.

I nod my head ever so slightly without moving my neck. I can't now, I can't move it. The brace is tight, but not constricting. I can breathe better. I can breathe.

It takes me a moment.

"Miss Roth, do you know where you are?"

Hospital. I don't know that I've spoken the answer until Dr. Tabor tells me that's correct.

"Do you know what happened?"

With the inhale, I wince from the pain and in an instant I'm moved from the gurney to a table, bright lights shining down in my eyes.

The headlights. The impact.

I can't breathe.

Car, the screech of tires. Delilah.

"Miss Roth, you were in a car accident and your injuries are severe."

Baby. My little prince.

I try to move my hands to my belly. He's not kicking. *Please kick.* Fear cripples me and they tell me to stop, but I can't see. Did the car hit my belly?

"My baby," I say and barely get the words out as my doctor hovers over my face. All I can see is her and her stern look although her eyes hold compassion.

"We're doing everything we can," she tells me, but her expression slips.

It lacks confidence because it lacks hope.

"Save my baby," I beg her but she doesn't listen. Someone else is talking. "My baby!" They don't listen.

"She needs a transplant right now." She answers someone else. She doesn't listen to me.

"Stay on the line with medical."

"They don't—"

"Keep calling," my doctor screams in response.

"We're going to do everything we can, Laura."

"My baby," I cry and I wish Seth were here. He'd fight for what I want. He'd tell them to save our son. He'd hold my hand. He would have hope.

"I'm going to do everything I can."

Did I tell him that I loved him? I can't remember. Did I at least tell him I loved him before I left?

CHAPTER 16

Seth

I'M SUPPOSED TO SIT HERE.

Tapping my phone against my suit pants in rapid succession, I stare down at the movement thinking, *How am I supposed to just sit here and do nothing?*

Gritting my teeth, I lean back in the simple chair and then stand up without conscious thought. I can't sit still.

I can't leave though.

There are fourteen wooden chairs in this room, all with squared backs and fabric with a navy pattern. It's like small petals scattered on them, I don't know. I've been staring at them for hours and I can't even say what they are.

Two rows of seven chairs, two long coffee tables between them and a large single-pane window on the far right. It's dark now that the sun's gone down. So it's just two black rectangular squares that I can see and the only light is from the fluorescent tubes above my head.

It's not supposed to happen like this.

Marcus promised he'd save her.

He swore he would.

Yet here I am, on death row with the Cross brothers, while Laura lies open on an operating table. And I can do nothing. This is my penance and I'll take it all and more, as long as they get to live.

When my hand starts trembling again, I shove the phone back into my pocket and pace.

My head is light from not breathing right. I can't do anything right. All I can hear is Bethany's voice when she called.

There was an accident.

Her cadence was full of dread and it ricochets in my mind, hitting every vulnerable place and with every impact, I see Laura, smiling, laughing, biting down on her lip as she peers up at me.

I just want her back like that. *Please, God.*

I've made a deal with the devil. I'll make one with God too.

I'll make every deal I can with every man in power on the face of this fucking earth if it means she gets to live.

"Hey, you want one?" Bethany asks, her voice small and quiet in the large room even though it's just the two of us.

"No thanks," I answer her as evenly as I can, even though dread seeps in regardless.

Her eyes are red and the mascara's no longer there where it was hours ago. She's barely moved from her seat. I don't know how she does it; I can't sit still at all. A few people have come into the room and saw her in scrubs so they approached her. Other than that, she's only gotten up to get coffee from a machine down the hall that takes two dollars to spew out an inferior form of caffeine.

"What about something else?" she asks me and when I look up at her splotchy face, I can see she's begging me to give her something to do, something to make it better. I can't tell her how much I relate. If only it was as easy as putting two wrinkled dollars into a machine.

"I could use a water maybe," I get out and the back of my eyes sting. I imagine they're red like hers.

"You might need some caffeine," she offers, a little more hopeful although the horrid look on her face doesn't change.

"I won't be able to sleep without knowing." Somehow I answer her without suffocating on that truth. On the possibility that it was all for nothing.

If she dies, I have no reason to live anyway.

"They should be able to tell us something. They should be here any minute to tell us she's all right." Jase's voice is unexpected. I didn't even hear him come up behind me. He's still in his stone-gray suit, jacket and everything. Mine's rumpled in comparison.

When Bethany falls into his arms, his kisses the top of her head before resting his chin on her crown and then looking at me.

"She's going to be all right. That's the only thing they'll say; that she made it. I know it, they have to," Bethany speaks into Jase's chest and I hear it.

"You okay?" Jase asks me and I only shake my head. I can't speak.

I want to thank him for just showing up. For being here for me in this dark time, but I don't deserve it. He knows it and so do I. After today? Things are going to be different between me and the Cross brothers. I know they are. And it was for nothing.

"She and our baby boy are going to be okay. They'll be all right." Bethany speaks as she wipes her eyes, breaking from her embrace with Jase. It's the first time she's broken down out here, although a few times, she's gone to the restroom and come out with her face much redder than before. "Your little prince, right?"

"Our little prince," I barely breathe, my hands trembling again.

"Still no word? Nothing?" Jase questions, and I can feel him looking at me but Bethany answers no, her hair swishing as she shakes her head.

She asks Jase if he wants a drink from the vending machine before leaving us alone.

"I just talked to Carter, he's coming with the guys." A chill flows over my shoulders.

I nod and think a moment before saying, "You know I would never do anything to risk you or any of you."

"I don't know what deal you made, but if he tried to kill her—"

I cut him off, realizing that he doesn't know. "It was Aiden's mother, the manager's mother." The words rush out but my inhale is slower, attempting to steady myself.

"Just an accident?" he questions with disbelief.

"The ice…" I can't finish. I saw the older woman, banged up and looking scared while she sobbed uncontrollably. "She was bringing him something for lunch."

Fuck, the pain. I hate it. I hate this.

But it's what I deserve, isn't it? They don't deserve it though. They don't deserve any of it.

"I've never been able to protect her." I speak without looking at Jase even though he sits down next to me. With my shoulders hunched over, I explain. "That's why I did it, why I planned it the way I did. Because I knew I couldn't protect her. I couldn't save her."

I see him lower himself, hunching like me, trying to look at me, but I don't let him. A hand covers my face.

"I would do anything for her, but I can't protect her."

"Say it." Jase's voice is firm.

"Say what?" I ask him, ready to say whatever he needs to hear. I don't have it in me to fight anymore. Whatever he wants to know, I'll tell him.

"Say she's going to be okay. Say she'll be fine." His words come out harsh but I can hear him swallow the pain down. "She's going to be okay and you need to say it."

I nod, even though I don't know that I believe it.

"She's going to make it," he says and he's firm.

"She has to." My eyes burn. "Both of them are going to be fine."

CHAPTER 17

Seth

IT WAS AN EIGHTEEN-HOUR SURGERY IN ALL. I SAT THERE, IN THAT WORN-OUT chair, staring at the pile of dog-eared magazines with torn pages and counting every second.

Jase is silent, apart from comforting Bethany.

There's a heavy weight on my chest that still won't let up. Even when the doctors came out, all three of them, the weight only got heavier.

They did all they could.

Beep, beep, beep.

The room is simple; there should be flowers in here. She loves flowers.

"Seth, is there anything…" Jase starts to ask as Bethany's silent cries break into hysteria. She has both of her hands on Laura's. Her body collapses with the next sob and her knees hit the floor. Her colorful scrubs are the only bit of life in this room. Everything else is bland, stark white, and dated.

She wouldn't like this room at all. There's nothing with any personality in it.

"Flowers. I want her to be surrounded by flowers when she wakes up." I give him the answer, but all I'm met with are sad eyes from the doctor.

"Mr. Roth," Doctor Tabor begins, pausing and breathing in deeply, but her dark brown eyes never leave mine.

I almost correct her, I almost tell her it's King, but I don't. Instead, I prepare for my rebuttal to whatever is going to come out of her mouth. The doctor is short, plain with no makeup at all, but she's determined and logical more than anything. A powerhouse in her field. Next to her is the neurologist, the one who can't look me in the eyes as the cardiologist tells me we have to prepare for the likelihood that Laura is never going to wake up.

"I understand what you said, and I know you understand what I said. I want extraordinary measures to be taken. She just needs time," I say although I lose the upper hand I have on the last line because my stern voice cracks and my eyes glaze over.

Beep, beep, beep, the steady sound of her heart beating is what keeps me going. It's steady. Her heart is a good heart. She's going to be okay now.

She finally got a good heart, so she should be able to use it. I'll be better with this one. I won't break it. I'll make sure it never breaks if she'll just wake up.

Wake up, Babygirl, please. Wake up.

"The surgery went well," I say, giving her the words she gave me. "You said the surgery went well. All of them."

The surgeon, the one who fixed her heart, nods, and as she does, she swallows. She's frail and skinny, but something tells me it's simply the way she's built. Clasping her hands professionally in front of her buttoned-up white coat, she answers, "That's correct, the transplant went perfectly and now we monitor her to make sure her body accepts it."

"And so far?" I question.

"So far everything looks well but we need twenty-four hours to be sure.

"All of her injuries are stable and at this point we're just waiting for her to wake up, but she sustained various trauma. We lost her in surgery and she was gone for a number of minutes... and sometimes patients don't recover."

"She should have woken up by now, Mr. Roth." The neurologist speaks again, not giving me a chance to thank the other doctor who just spoke.

"She hasn't slept in days. She's just tired," I answer them and part of me really believes it. Like she's just in a deep sleep because she's exhausted from all this bullshit. God knows she needs it.

Laura's hair is pulled back with a bandage that wraps around her head. The rest of it is a messy halo on the stark white pillow. There's another bandage on her wrist that travels up to her elbow, where her arm was placed in a splint and they set the bone. But other than the bandages and the bruises, she looks like she's just sleeping. She's only resting.

"She'll wake up." My confidence forces Bethany to look at me, and I can see in her eyes that she wants to believe me but she doesn't.

No one says anything. They just stare at me.

"And what about our son?" I ask the nurse closest to me and my throat gets tight. "We will wait for her to wake up and I want to see my son."

Bethany's been quiet, her grip never loosening on Laura's hand, but her focus moves to the doctors now. She wants to know too.

"We had to intubate him as he wasn't breathing on his own. Other than that, he appears to be stable. It's a good thing that we started the steroids early, but he's still not in a good condition. The pediatrician is with him now. Statistically, every day is a better outcome, but he will be here for weeks so long as he remains stable. We have to monitor him closely and the likelihood of permanent damage is very high. His quality of life, if he does make it, is unknown at the moment."

"Can he be brought up here? So he can be with his mother?"

"Unfortunately not. Given his condition, he needs to stay where he is in the neonatal intensive care unit right now.... You should prepare yourself."

Bethany's cries are accompanied by Jase shushing her, calmly trying to soothe her. As if words and a tender touch can heal this kind of brokenness.

"Is there anything at all I can do to help either of them?" I ask, somehow still standing on both of my feet although I know for a fact I'm shattered and everything that makes me human is on my knees, crying and begging. Yet here I stand, asking questions.

"At this point, we wait." The neurologist is the one who answers, and I hope he can feel how much I loathe him.

I hate all of them.

"You can pray, Mr. Roth." The cardiologist, a woman I didn't at all suspect to be religious, with her cold manner of speaking, offers me. She nods once, looking only at Laura before leaving us and saying one more time, "Praying is all we can do."

It's quiet for a moment, and they mumble something about leaving us alone and letting me know when I can see our son.

"Of all the ways it could happen… a fucking accident. A car crash," Bethany says and barely breathes as a suffocating sob leaves her. She buries her head in the white sheets. Her head brushes against Laura's arm and Jase is there all the while, stroking her back.

"I need to get her flowers and a different blanket," I say then clear my throat, noting how tight it is before continuing. Jase's gaze reaches mine and he doesn't have the same wounded look as all the others. "When she wakes up, I want her to smell flowers and be as comfortable as she can be."

Dropping my eyes to Laura's closed ones, I take in the bruising on her face that travels from her jaw to her neck.

When Jase makes Bethany leave, that's when I finally go to her, letting my fingers gently trail along where she's not bruised.

I kiss her head and remind myself how she hasn't been sleeping. She's only tired. That has to be it.

She's the strongest woman I know. She's only tired. There's fire in her blood and we finally have a family. "Wake up, Babygirl, we have to see our little prince. Wake up."

Beep, beep, beep.

The pediatric floor is one level below and it's silent on the walk, silent in the elevator. I pass rooms and halls, desks and plenty of other people, but all I see whenever a bed comes into view is the image of Laura, lying in that bed, her skin pale and her body motionless. The only indication that she's alive is the steady beeping of the monitors.

She can't leave me this way.

She can't do it.

She promised she wouldn't leave me. She said if it was up to her, she wouldn't. All she has to do is wake up.

It's been twelve hours and I drifted in and out for four of them. At least now I can finally see my son.

I do something I haven't done in a long damn time; I pray on the walk to pediatrics. I pray for both Laura and our son to make it. Really pray. I pray for them, and I pray for myself. If they don't live, I don't want to live either.

When we get to the glass wall with all the little carriages and babies sleeping soundly, or otherwise, I anticipate walking through those doors, but we don't.

"He's back here," a nurse tells me, her expression sympathetic. Of course my son wouldn't be in there; he's not healthy, he's not well. He isn't with the others because those babies are going to make it out of here just fine.

Tears would come easily if I wasn't so beat down already, as reality grips me. I don't stop moving, even when my throat squeezes so tight that my breath is absent. I walk steadily, listening to my footsteps and following the older woman with kind eyes and pink scrubs to the far corner of the floor, to a room without large glass panes. A room they don't want bystanders to see because it's so tragic.

There are only two other babies in this room and all of them have plastic walls covering their tiny plastic cribs. There are two with pink blankets and one with blue. So I know which one is mine.

All of them have tubes, the smallest ones imaginable. I can't stand to look at the other two children. Even when one of them moves, her little fist making a sudden motion, I see it but I can't look at her. It's crippling. They're so small and alone. It's the saddest thing there is in life.

"Here's your son," the nurse tells me, as brightly as she can although the sadness lingers there.

I take one more step forward and then another, until my hand lays against the plastic. He's so small. So tiny I could hold him with one hand.

"Did you two have a name?"

"Not yet," I answer her and take in an unsteady breath. "We weren't expecting him so—" The words refuse to come out to finish the sentence. They stay back, choking me instead.

"If you want to sit, you can hold his hand, here." She points to a small opening in the plastic enclosure. A slot is all I have.

This is my fault. The truth is a landslide of accountability.

They're suffering for my sins and it's not fair.

None of this is fair.

He hasn't even had a full day to live. And Laura is all that is good with the world but the two of them are here in critical condition, helpless and their lives uncertain. While I get to breathe freely. Please God, don't do it to them.

It's not fair and it's all my fault.

"When we remove the tubes from his mouth, you can hold him, so long as everything is steady." I can't speak for a long time and the nurse doesn't pressure me to. Instead, I slip my pointer finger onto my son's tiny palm. And he squeezes. It's not very strong but I'll teach him. He'll get better. He'll hold on.

I have to believe that. If there's any mercy in this world...

"What is the likelihood of..." I catch myself using the word "likelihood" because that's what the doctors upstairs kept saying.

Likelihood she won't wake up.

Likelihood he won't make it past tonight.

"We're monitoring him closely and doing everything we can. If we make it through tonight, it's likely we'll be able to remove the breathing tubes. He has other issues and he won't be able to leave, but you could hold him then."

I can only nod, not trusting myself to speak.

Four days pass and it only gets harder because my confidence and hope wane. Nothing is getting better. Laura is stable but unmoving, unchanging and there's nothing we can do.

I thought, if I lay next to her, if I talked to her, if I reminded her of everything we have to look forward to, she'd wake up. If she knew her son was just downstairs, I could've sworn her eyes would open and she'd demand that I take her down there right now. And I would, God I want that more than anything.

But she doesn't respond to a damn thing. She doesn't give me any signs at all. No one knows why she doesn't wake up. *Sometimes, it just happens.* That's what they tell me and I hate them more and more with each passing day. Especially the cardiothoracic surgeon who only peers through the door. She never comes in here, but she watches and waits. I hate her the most. She was supposed to fix her, but what good is a heart if Laura can't use it?

I'm helpless with my Laura, but even more so with our baby boy.

Staring at him through the plastic box is the second-worst thing in the world.

Even yesterday, I couldn't hold him. He wasn't stable. He's a fighter, though. So is his mother but I don't know why she won't wake up.

Tonight Doctor Peters, the pediatric surgeon, said I could hold him. She said it would be good for his body to be against mine. Tummy to tummy, although really it's chest to chest. She said it's so his heart can learn to beat and I wish his mother were here. I wish Laura were here because her heart is good now, and she could do this if she were here. I know she'd love that.

"Right there is fine," she says and I take the nurse's orders of sitting down and unbuttoning my shirt. Yesterday was the first day I showered since the accident. I had to leave when the nurses all rushed in to save my son from dying and I couldn't remain. They forced me out as I screamed and demanded they save him. I had to leave the hospital for a bit; I couldn't stand to be so helpless. So I showered and packed clothes to wear. And I went back to the hospital to tell Laura she needed to wake up.

I held one of her hands in both of mine and prayed when she didn't grip my hand back. I just needed a sign, any sign. I've never cried this much. Never in my life. I've never felt this low.

The worst part is that I know this is my fault. I couldn't protect them and all I've given Laura is the consequence of my sins. I'd take it all back. All of it. I'd take it all back for them not to suffer.

What came from me praying for her to hold my hand back was a nurse three hours later telling me our son made it.

Our son.

But not Laura.

That was yesterday and today I can hold him. Doctor Peters promised me I could.

"Okay now, there are some wires here to monitor him so just be careful, all right?" She sounds more hopeful today, happy even, and I take it as a good sign as Nurse Morison sets my little prince down against me.

My hands are on him in an instant, both of them even though my fingers overlap. With the way I'm leaning back to look down at him, I'm sure he'd stay put, this tiny little baby without being held at all, but I have to hold him just to be sure he's okay.

"There we go," Nurse Morison says and quickly grabs a little blue blanket to cover him and I move one hand to hold the blanket to him, but the other is still firm against his back.

I can't move it, I can't let go, because I can feel him breathing.

From his chest to mine, I can feel his heart beating so fast. So much faster than mine.

Even when I lean down to kiss his little head, covered with a small smatter of fine dark hair, I keep my eyes on him. I can't let go and I can't look away. Today is his best day yet.

"I'll leave you be." Her voice is so quiet, I barely hear her but I hum a response and rock side to side ever so gently, watching as my little prince yawns. It's the smallest movement in the world, but it's everything.

"You've got to make it for Mommy," I whisper as I rock. How could he not make it? He's perfectly fine, this little bundle. Look at him, he's got to make it.

He's going to be okay. I know he will. He can't leave me too.

"Mommy is going to be so happy to see you when you wake up," I tell him and he wriggles against me. See, he's fine. He's healthy and fine. He's going to make it. He has to.

"I love you, little prince. When Mommy wakes up, we'll give you a name," I promise him. With my thumb stroking against the side of his little head, I tell him about Laura, about his beautiful mother and how perfect she is. I tell him how much she loves him because she can't tell him right now, but I can. "Let me tell you a story about your mother. She's a fighter like you. Even more than me, I think. She's going to be so proud of you. Probably even more proud than I am and that's… that's…" That's when I have to wipe my eyes. I don't stop rocking and I don't stop holding him though.

Not for the whole night. They let me hold him for hours and hours.

I kiss his head in between stories about Laura. And when the nurse comes back, she lets me stay, holding him to me, as she checks on him throughout the night.

The only reason I leave him at all is because sleep comes hard just before morning and they say I can't hold him if I fall asleep.

I spend the nights with Laura, holding her hand and sleeping in the small hospital bed next to her, and the days are split between our little prince and her. I tell her everything about him, from the way he makes little noises to how tight he's holding my hand now.

"He's going to make it for you, Laura, so wake up, Babygirl. Please, I love you. Wake up."

CHAPTER 18

Laura

I WOULD KNOW HER ANYWHERE FROM SEEING JUST THE BACK OF HER HEAD, but the hoodie is what gives it away. It's bright pink but faded at her wrists, the fabric worn out so much that she poked her thumbs through the ends of her sleeves.

"Cami!" I call out to her as she's sitting on the hood of her car that she parked in the middle of the field behind the school. "You're going to get in trouble for parking out here," I yell out to her although there's a smile on my face that won't go away. It's at odds with the gloomy weather. The overcast sky threatening to rain although nothing's come down yet. I can see the storm ready to break right above us, but we're dry. So, so cold, but dry.

"Why did you park out here?" I question her like she's lost it although she must've had a good reason to park her car in the field.

I feel light but so cold and my heart is heavy although I don't know why. Or why I'm wearing these scrubs. They're scrubs, aren't they? I do want to be a nurse one day… confusion overwhelms me, putting a deep crease on my forehead. Why the hell did I wear this to school?

"We have to get to class," I tell her, picking up my pace to get to her because I don't think she can hear me and I'm so lost right now. The tall grass tickles my legs as it slips up the loose pants. I don't remember how I got here or why we're out here. I must've hit my head hard on something. Thank God I found her.

She doesn't answer me, even when I bang my fist on the car. The metal is hard but it doesn't hurt like I expect it to. That's when I realize how quiet it is.

Is there even class? There's no one else here, no one on the roads. A shiver runs down my arms, making me cross them as I look up to Cami.

"Cami!" This time when I call her name, she looks at me, peering down from where she is on the roof of the hood of the car.

"Hey," she says, but her voice sounds so far away. There's something wrong with my hearing. There must be. I really did hit my head.

"What are you doing out here?" I question her and the wind whips away my words. I can hear each one being moved in the air, further away from Cami. I stare down the empty field, watching the overgrown grass blow as if I can see what I've just spoken hiding among the dried-out crops.

The cold slips down my spine. "We have to go inside," I tell Cami with all seriousness. There's something wrong. I can feel it. And it's far too cold to kick it out here. "Hey, let's go inside," I suggest to her again and this time my hearing is fine. It's fine. Everything is fine.

"This is where I like to stay. Sometimes Derek comes back here and if he's not here, I can still remember our first kiss right over there." She points off into the field.

"You and Derek?" I ask her, shocked and when I blink, I remember. Like a forgotten dream. "That's right!" I say and the smile grows larger on my face. "You two," I say as hope blooms but then fades and I don't know why.

I feel like I've lost days or maybe weeks. Why don't I remember?

"Come sit with me for a minute? We have some time," Cami says in an eerily calm manner but it eases something in me. I just want to talk to her, to be beside her, so I agree. Climbing on top of the car, I sit next to her but when we brush shoulders, she's so cold.

"Are you okay?"

"Oh, yeah, I'm fine, just reminiscing. It's so good to see you. You have no idea."

Something is definitely wrong. It all feels so wrong. "We should go," I warn her again. "It's going to rain and it's so cold."

"It won't rain," she tells me and smiles. Her lips are a beautiful shade of red. The color is from matching lipsticks we got together when we got our friendship rings. "I promise it won't rain."

"Hey, I got you coffee, but I think it's cold." In an instant, the surrounding environment changes to a house I don't recognize but it seems familiar. My stomach sinks and lightheadedness nearly makes me topple over. What the hell just happened? Fear chokes me and I feel sick.

We were just at the school. We were at the school.

"Cami, there's something wrong. I'm not okay." Gripping the hood of the car, I clench my teeth and try to calm the terror that rides through me. "I'm hallucinating or something."

Slowly, my eyes open and just like I thought, we're suddenly in front of a house. There's a red door. And I know I know this house. It scares me. The memories of it evade me still, but I'm terrified.

"I want to go," I say and my voice is firm this time but Cami grips my wrist with her ice-cold grasp.

The shudder that runs through me stops my heart. Or was it already stopped? I can't feel it anymore. I can't feel anything.

"I'm scared," I plead with her. I'm never scared. So little is able to scare me but I'm not okay right now, I'm not at all okay. "Something's wrong."

"I'm sorry," she says and she's quick to pull back. "I'm sorry," she repeats with less shock and more finality. "I forget sometimes."

Sitting on the edge of the car, I debate running, but my head spins and I think I'm going to be sick.

"Don't think about it right now. Don't think about that night or why you feel the way you do. Just... just talk to me please. Please. I miss you so much. Even when I see you, I miss you still."

Her light blue eyes gloss over and I get back to where I was, crawling closer to her and huddling together, my knees in my chest.

"You don't have to miss me. I'm right here," I say to comfort her even though something's wrong. I'm vigilant, looking out for whatever is coming. Something's coming, I know it.

"What's wrong?" I ask her.

"Sorry, I didn't mean to freak out. It's just that sometimes I'm so sorry."

"I don't understand." It's even colder here than it was in the field.

"Don't be scared."

"I'm terrified," I confess to her, beseeching her to get off this car and go back. Back home, back… back… I don't remember where we were.

"I don't like it here. I don't… Cami, I want to get the hell out of here," I practically yell at her but I don't mean to. "I'm just so scared."

"There's no reason to be."

"Cami, stop. This isn't funny." Trying to reason with her is… it can't be done.

"I think you should remember. Sometimes we go back to a happy place and I couldn't know what yours was. I'm so sorry."

"Remember what?" At my question, she places her hand in mine and there's warmth, the only warmth that surrounds us, but it's followed by a flood of memories.

Slowly, each one taking its time.

Bringing me back to yesterday. To the sight of my body lying in a bed.

I have to rip my hand away to hold my stomach.

"He's okay," Cami whispers. "Please," she begs me, wrapping her arm around my shoulders and I lean into her, the tears streaming down my face. "Don't leave me. It's okay. You're okay. I've just missed you so much."

Wiping my eyes haphazardly, I come to the conclusion that it's only a nightmare. Or maybe a twisted dream. I don't know what's real and what's not.

"I miss you," I manage to say, as if… if this is real, I could at least tell her that.

This is all a torturous nightmare. It has to be.

"I miss you too." She brushes her shoulder against mine again and this time it's not so cold. "At least I get to see you sometimes."

I wonder if it's her I've been seeing, the girl in the diner but as I'm thinking it, she shakes her head.

"You have to stop being so sad, you know?" Cami gives me a half smile and swings her legs down the front of the car.

"I'm not sad."

"You're a horrible liar," she tells me and I don't know why I lied to her.

"I feel so guilty," I admit. Thinking back on that day, the day here in this house. The last time I ever saw her or it. "It was supposed to be me."

"We don't get to know fate," she tells me as if it doesn't matter. As if her dying wasn't a horrible tragedy. It was horrible and the worst thing in the world. She wasn't supposed to die. It was supposed to be me. She should have had a full life. She was sunshine in a world that desperately needs it.

I can only shake my head, everything coming back so much clearer. I want to wake up. I need to wake up from this nightmare. "I miss you so much. You'll never know how much I wish it had been me."

"You know what I was thinking all the while when I was in your house and they were hurting me?"

When she squeezes my hand, it's warm, so warm, as if she's really here with me. I hold hers with both of mine. I wish this weren't a dream. I wish this were real.

"I was hoping that you wouldn't come back home until they were gone. I'd made that decision, Laura. They thought I was you and I let them believe that. That was my choice."

It kills me to hear her say that and I search my mind for any part of me that would think she'd want that.

"It's not okay. It was supposed to be me."

"All the while I kept thinking of what excuse I would give if you walked in. How I could convince them that you were only a friend and to beg them to let me send you away. That's how I made it through it all. There were so many lies I could tell if you did come home. It was quick you know, in the scope of things."

"I'm so sorry," I whisper.

"You shouldn't be. It wasn't in your control."

Her skin looks so youthful. She hasn't aged a day, but her eyes are full of a wisdom that she didn't have before.

"Even as I was lying there dying, I prayed for you to not come home until they were really gone. Then I heard them leave and all I could think then was that I hoped Seth found me and not you or Derek. He wouldn't have let you see."

She rocks me as I hold her tight, wishing I could go back.

"You know what, though? What I'm really looking forward to?"

Wiping my eyes, I take in a shaky inhale to ask her, "What?"

"Babies and sometimes young kids can see us. Sometimes they know and I think it's because they don't know better to be scared or maybe it's because of something else I don't know. But I'm hoping he'll be able to see me."

The second she says "he," I see my son. I see a flash of him. In a little plastic box with wires attached to his chest and I gasp as I pull back from her.

I hate this nightmare. I want to wake up. Please let me wake up.

"My baby," I say and put both hands against my flat stomach and silently pray for him to kick. To tell me he's all right.

"He's all right. I've made it my mission to watch over him." Cami smiles so bright and so wide as she adds, "He looks so much like you."

"You saw him?" I question her and a panic sets in. "I haven't held him. I need to make sure he's all right." I close my eyes tight, trying to see him again. I need to get back to him. My little prince.

"You should probably wake up; they need you."

"Come with me," I beg her and I don't know why. I know this is only a dream. One I both love and hate. One that scares me and one that I cling to. "I miss you too much."

"Hey, I'm already there. Every time you remember me, a part of me is there. It's why I like to stay in the field. Derek has the friendship ring… he knows I picked out these rings specifically because the pattern on the bands looks like the little daisy flowers on the edge of the cornfield where we first kissed, you know. It makes me laugh really. I got them for us, but anything that had to do with us always had to do with them… didn't it? It was supposed to be the four of us together forever. Did you tell him that when you gave it to him? Because he says that a lot."

"How did you know?" I question out loud how she would know that I gave the ring to Derek at the bar that night, but of course, she's only a figment of my own imagination.

She smiles knowingly and shakes her head, as if she read my mind. But of course she did.

"He started dating girls who looked nothing like me, intentionally… as if blondes aren't his type. Isn't that…" she trails off and simply huffs then shakes her head. "He doesn't want to love again but that only makes me cry harder here. I can feel his pain." She admits that to me with tears in her eyes. "One day he'll be happy again. One day he'll love a girl and just to spite him, I hope she looks just like me," she jokes and wipes under her eyes. "He needs to love again. That's what I'm waiting for in that field. For him to tell me how he found someone. I love him too much to ever want him to be lonely. Would you tell him that? Please, tell him that."

"I'll tell him. I promise."

"I love you, babe," she whispers and then she tells me to go. I don't even get a chance to tell her I love her back before she's vanished and my world turns black.

CHAPTER 19

Seth

THERE WAS ONE RULE LAURA MADE THAT I ALWAYS FOLLOWED. ALL the others I broke. I kept the lights on constantly, which she hated. I came home late and made too much noise. I did all sorts of shit that broke her rules.

But I never woke her up in the morning. No fucking way. I did once and I learned my lesson.

The memory makes me a huff a bit of laughter as I sit in the uncomfortable blue chair in the corner of her room. It's too small for my frame and too hard to sink into. The bags under my eyes feel heavy and exhaustion, both physical and emotional, have beat me down into a man I don't recognize.

The memory of her when she woke up before she was ready, years ago when we were first dating, will always make me smile though. I can't help it. She's an angel, heaven sent just for me, but a demon if woken up before her alarm goes off. It's what caused her to shove me away for the first time. True bitterness from being woken up when she had twenty more minutes.

My Babygirl needed her beauty sleep. Or else she turned into a gremlin spewing curses.

So I never woke her up and if I had to, I'd sneak out of the room before she could see me. I'd never make it obvious that I was the reason she was up so I could hide from her wrath.

Another short laugh makes my shoulders shake and that warmth from the countless memories of her shuffling her bare feet while she made her way into the kitchen, desperate for coffee, mixes with profound sadness.

She looks so beautiful when I think that she's just sleeping in. She's just having a wonderful dream and she doesn't want me to wake her up.

When reality comes back though, the smile falls and there's not an ounce of warmth. It's hard to feel anything other than cold and dreadful. It kills me to see her like that. She needs to wake up. I'm dying without her.

"You have to wake up, Babygirl," I plead with her for the thousandth time. "Little prince has another surgery today." My voice tightens as I speak and I'm barely holding it together. "He did really well with the first one, you'd be proud."

They're pressuring me to give him a name. There's so much paperwork and they said I need to do it soon, but I can't name him without her. "You have to wake up. I can't do this alone."

I sit back in the chair, wiping my eyes harshly, pretending like I'm not the shell of the man I was. "I told him you were proud and then I told him about that time you helped Derek after the surgery on his arm. You remember that?"

I keep asking her questions like one of them will do the trick. One of them will wake her up. She's going to answer one of them. She's stubborn like that. She can't let me get the last word in. That's the girl I fell in love with. She's going to answer me one of these days and I'll be so grateful for her to wake up and put me in my place.

My heel taps on the floor as I grow restless in the stiff chair. I thought the smell of flowers would do it, so I lined this room with them. Two dozen vases and then some. The windowsill is lined with them. All sorts of colorful petals from wildflowers, sunflowers, and orchids. But none of them got a reaction at all from her. I thought a kiss, a squeeze of her hand, something, anything would let her know I'm here and she should wake up.

But she only lies there, not responding to anything.

So now I talk and pretend she can hear. Sometimes I hear her answers. Maybe I'm just crazy at this point. I hope somewhere inside of her, she's listening and that she knows I keep the vases full of water and the second the flowers wilt, I get her fresh ones. I hope she can feel that I kiss her temple, then her jaw, and then her lips every morning and every night. I desperately hope she knows I'm doing the best I can with our baby boy but he's not doing so well.

He's a fighter, but he's far too young to have to fight this hard. It's not fair. It's not supposed to be this way.

"The doctors said the likelihood of survival is lower for this surgery than the first but if he makes it, then he'll have a very good shot," I say then have to pause, closing my eyes and resting my forehead in my hand, my elbow on my knee. My throat is so tight and dry. I've been through hell and still I know it's nothing compared to what he's been through. "He's a fighter like you and it was either choose not to do the surgery and say goodbye, or do the surgery and fight."

I pretend I don't hear the tears drip onto my pants and I don't feel them rolling down my overgrown stubble. "He's a fighter," I repeat, swallowing harshly and squaring my shoulders. "He's got fire in his blood like you do. You should feel the way he holds my hand." I'm here to protect her and him, because I'm supposed to be the strong one. I will be steady for them through this storm. No matter what happens in the end.

"He's going to make it," I tell her although my voice is tighter than I want. Wiping my eyes, I add, "He has you for a mom, how could he not make it through?"

My question is only answered with the click of the heater turning on. I get up to brush the back of my fingers along her cheek, making sure she's not too hot, not too cold. The salty taste on my lips is from my tears and when I selfishly kiss her, I hope she can taste it. I hate myself for thinking it, but she never did like to make anyone upset.

I hope she knows I'm crying without her. I hope she knows I'm breaking. What good is a broken king if he doesn't have his queen? I've always been nothing without her.

"You should wake up," I whisper. "He wants to hear your voice."

"Hey." Declan's voice behind me snaps me back to reality. Brushing her hair from her face, I stand up straighter and pinch the bridge of my nose to get myself under control before turning to look at Declan. He has to know I've lost it, but he doesn't let on; he's quiet as I gather composure.

"What's going on?" I question Declan, finally turning around to see him slipping his hands into the pockets of his jeans. I should wear jeans and a black shirt like he is. They wrinkle less. Not that it would matter with the way I look. Disheveled and wrecked just the same, regardless of what clothes I wear.

"Just checking in." It's been weeks of the Cross brothers doing rotations. Jase is here a lot with Bethany and I'm grateful for it although Bethany's been breaking down more and more. It's killing her too. Three weeks is a long time for someone to not wake up from surgery. But she's going to. Our baby will make it out of surgery with flying colors and then Laura will make it out of this. I have no other choice than to believe that's the truth.

Declan stays in the doorway until I pull the chair around the dresser and closer to the one I'm sitting in. "Have a seat," I tell him, leaning back and sucking in a steadying breath.

The constant *beep, beep, beep* never lets up as we talk.

"I found a letter in your room," Declan tells me, then reaches in his back pocket. All the while my pulse stalls and my blood turns colder, knowing he'll pull out the letter I wrote. "Care to explain it?"

He must've been snooping for something to find it. That's my first thought, but then I forget where I left it and when was the last time I even looked at it. It could have been on the fucking coffee table for all I know.

"How did you get that?" I ask as a chill lays itself across my shoulders.

"I went to your house because you need more clothes and shit."

I stare at the letter.

The deal with Marcus; the only way out. My explanation to Declan once I did what I had to do. I had to explain to make sure they understood. I knew they'd get it. They'd understand why I had to do it. They would protect her when I was gone.

I decided the day I bought the fan for little prince's room. I knew I didn't have a lot of time, so I started getting his room together. I was so sure I'd get everything done. I would have everything planned for Laura. She'd never worry again in her entire life.

"What's this about?" Declan asks.

We haven't talked business since the day of the accident. I've been waiting for them to confront me. None of them have.

Until now.

"It's the deal I made," I confess to him, feeling a prick dance down my spine, making it harder, straighter. When his gaze meets mine, I clarify, "With Marcus."

Declan's gaze falls to the linoleum floor and I swear the heat turns off just because I said the name *Marcus*.

"He made a promise to me. He would save Laura if I killed one of the Cross brothers."

There was never a choice as to which one and Marcus knew it. Daniel, Jase and Carter have their significant others. Carter just had a baby himself. When their pictures showed, all three of them lined up, I couldn't even look at the other two. I didn't have to choose; Marcus knew because I could only look at Declan.

I tell the Cross brothers Declan is meeting at one place.

I tell Declan another.

I remember Marcus's exact words: *Pick a Cross brother to die. You do the deed.*

One of the brothers. All alone. That's the deal.

A life for a life.

"It took me a long time to find a loophole. But I did."

"And this is it?" he questions, waving the letter before tossing it down on Laura's bed. I don't like it there. Something so impure shouldn't touch her. It shouldn't be anywhere near her, so I pick it up.

"He told me to kill one of you and he'd save her. He promised he'd save her first, so… so as far as the deal goes, it's nonexistent. None of it matters anymore."

"But this letter?" Declan questions.

"As far as I could tell, the only reason he'd have me do it, was so that the remaining brothers would kill me. I'm sure it was a test in one way or another. I couldn't see clearly; all I could think about was Laura." Just saying her name makes me close my eyes and grip the armrests. I would do anything for her. "I could have told you but then he said he would stop the motions that had started that would save Laura. I couldn't tell anyone. I was trapped. So I agreed."

"But this letter?" he repeats, more anger and impatience showing.

"I could never kill you. I could kill myself, but then he'd go after Laura. He said he'd be there to make sure it was me so it had to take place. I lied to him and said I'd do it." My gaze shifts from Laura to Declan as I confide in him. "But I wanted you to kill me instead."

"So… once Laura was well and Marcus had done his part, I planned to give you the address like he told me to. I'd go, I'd lift my gun and when I fired the blanks, you'd kill me. I would honor my deal with Marcus and by that point, Laura would be safe and healthy. And I wrote the letter with the intent of sending it the day of the meet. That way you'd all know the truth, so you'd protect Laura in case Marcus didn't feel that I held up my end as best as I could. You couldn't know. If you knew, he'd know. I didn't see another way."

"You thought I'd kill you?" he asks me with a dull tone, not even looking at me.

"If I raised a gun to you? If I fired?" I pause, feeling all the agony of my decision again. "I knew you would. I had to leave you the letter so you knew it was only to save Laura. She had a life here before I came back into it. She was happy. She loved it. She would find that again. I didn't want you to carry the weight that you'd shot me. It was my decision and I needed you all to still love her. To still protect her—"

"You were ready to die."

"To protect her? To end all of the bad shit in her life that follows her because of me?" As I speak, my voice raises and I hate myself even more. Whenever we're together, bad shit rains down on her. It was the only choice. She was happy once without me; she'd be happy again. One day. And I would have everything prepared for her. All the money I've made, plus the house would be set up for her and our little boy. The Cross brothers would protect her because they'd owe me. She would be safe forever. It would have been worth it.

"All of this is because of me. I'd leave her the money and everything she'd ever need. You'd protect her. There are more of you than there are of me and I've already failed her so many times. She would finally be safe." Maybe he doesn't understand because he doesn't love someone like I love her.

"If I'm not there… it was the solution to everything. And then this happened."

"You could have just killed me," he offers, looking dejected as he stares at Laura's motionless body hidden under the chenille throw from the living room.

"I could never kill you." My throat's tight just thinking about that. "You and Jase … you're family… you guys are the only friends I have. The only semblance of a family I've known for years."

I try to lighten it up and my next comment gets a huff of a laugh from Declan. "Besides, if I did that, your brothers would kill me…" The half-smile on my face that matches his falters when I add, "And then she wouldn't be protected. There are more of you than there are of me. And a family. A real family." The last part hurts the most. She deserves that. She's never had one, not since her grandmother died, but she has one now. I couldn't take that away from her. "Our son deserves that too."

"You're talking like you aren't a part of our family. Like you're not one of us. When did that change? When did you decide to leave?"

"When the idea of killing you was something I actually considered." Looking him in the eyes, it's hard to admit it. "It was only a moment, but I considered it. I don't deserve to be your family and—"

"Bullshit." He's quick to cut me off with a venom I don't anticipate. "You don't get to just leave. You're still like a brother to me."

"I'm sorry," is all I can say, truly feeling like less of a man.

"So, that? That's what you were going to do?" he asks me in a tone that makes me sick as he points to the folded letter.

"A life for a life. That was the deal. Mine for hers is what I decided." I lean closer to him, making sure he looks me in the eye as I add, "I'd make that deal any day."

He shakes his head, staring at me like he doesn't even know me. "And here I thought you were coming to terms with killing me," he says as his expression changes to one of sympathy and sorrow, "not that you were coming to terms with your own death."

Beep, beep, beep.

The monitor is steady as I process what he's saying.

"We wired the warehouse before you went in. We couldn't let you go alone, and we had arranged for backup. We were ready to protect you if anything happened."

"You knew?" Disbelief shows in my tone. Betrayal creeps in.

"Yes, of course we did. And Marcus knows we wired it because once you left, he told Walsh he had to stop the eavesdroppers and everything went out."

"You knew this whole time." I can't fucking believe it. My hand scrubs down my face. "You fucking knew?" I snap at him, hating them for putting me through this shit when I was already suffering. I fucking died more and more every day keeping it all to myself.

"Carter wanted to know what you'd do. I told him you wouldn't go through with it." His tone holds condolences. "I knew you wouldn't."

"I can't breathe."

"Did you think we didn't know?"

"How would I ever think you'd know?" I practically sneer, betrayal but also relief running through me.

"He played you."

"And he didn't save her." The words are torn from me. "That was all that mattered. And he didn't save her." My anger doesn't mean shit. The reality is that it didn't happen. In another life, in an alternate story, I died to save her. But this is what's real. I'm alive and she's… *Please, Babygirl, wake up.*

"I'm sorry." Declan's words are the sincerest he's been since he stepped into the room. His hand lands on my shoulder. "She's going to make it."

It's quiet for a moment and I take the time to lean forward and hold her hand. As my thumb brushes against her knuckles, I keep praying she'll squeeze my hand.

Any sign. I just need any sign.

"I came here to tell you I got a note from Marcus."

Hate mixes with absolute contempt in my blood. I let her hand go, unwilling to hold her while I feel like this. He was supposed to make her better. Instead, now she's here. I would have given him more for him to do it faster. Why didn't he help her? He said he could help her.

"He wants to meet with me. Doesn't say why. Just lists an address and a time."

"I guess this is his backup plan," I snidely comment.

On the edge of my vision, Declan shrugs. "If he wanted me dead, he could easily do it."

My gaze doesn't move from Laura's lips, down to the curve of her neck.

"I never should have made a deal with him." I finally look at Declan. "I never should have said I'd help him with shit."

"You did what you had to do."

"Hey." The sound of Jase's voice comes in along with a knock.

"You're supposed to knock first," Declan reprimands him although it lacks strength.

Jase glances at Laura but not for long. He never looks at her for long. I know what he's thinking: She's already gone.

Pulling up the final chair in the room, he drags it over to where we are and sits with us.

But first he puts a vase on the windowsill. A single rose in a simple vase. I take that time to calm down as best I can.

I watch him and I know he can see the question in my eyes. "She didn't have any red roses in here. I thought a red rose… you should get her roses."

He clears his throat as he sits down.

"You talk to him?" he asks Declan and he nods in response.

"Good," is all Jase gives him in response.

Looking past Declan I question him, "You aren't going to ask him what I said? What I was going to do?"

He shakes his head and says, "I don't need to. I know you'd never do it."

Struggling to feel deserving of his trust, I press my back to the chair and sit there, my elbows on my knees, my hands clasped in front of me.

"You might think we don't know you, Seth King. But we know you. All of us do. And you'd never betray us."

"I feel like I betrayed her." I can't help but give the statement just under my breath. She was supposed to be safe with me, and I couldn't protect her.

"Bethany's with little prince," Jase comments, thankfully changing the conversation. "Did you think of a name for him?"

Emotions make my answer tight as I say, "I'm waiting for her to wake up."

I can't look at them when I say that, because then they'd see the doubt that breaks my chest in half as I look at her.

"Don't get mad."

I lift my gaze to Declan's, ready to tell him if he feels the need to lead with that, then he knows I'm going to be pissed.

"I just want to make sure we're on the same page," he emphasizes, his hands in the air in a defensive gesture.

"If… if Laura doesn't wake up and little man downstairs is released… He's with us, right? He's not going anywhere even if… Laura…." He has the decency not to finish.

"He's my son," I answer him adamantly with an edge of a threat.

"Of course." Jase is quick to agree with me and Declan follows suit.

"I know, I know. I was just making sure we're on the same page is all. Same plan. We stick to the same plan as before."

"Regardless of what happens, I'll take care of him. I'll be the father Laura would have wanted me to be."

I don't like talking about her like she's not here anymore, when she's right in front of us.

I have to cover my face with my right hand to keep from fucking crying. It's all I can do to hold myself together.

"Hey." Jase keeps talking, like I'm not entirely breaking down. "You know adopted kids, they say they look like their adopted parents. It's because of the facial expressions. When you're around someone so much, you start to mimic the way they say things, do things, it's what makes a person a person. So even though… biologically speaking, he's… you know. He could still look like you and no one would ever know."

It takes a long time for me to even breathe, let alone think about what Jase just told me. I know his intent was to make me feel better or distract me, but all I can think of is that in that picture, Laura's not there.

After a long moment, I tell them, but I plead with Laura, holding her hand in both of mine. "He can't be left with just me."

CHAPTER 20

Laura

I'M IN AND OUT. IT'S THE FIRST TIME I'M AWARE OF IT. AWARE OF THE FACT that I'm in a hospital bed. Although it smells like I'm in a field of wildflowers. It's wonderful, but I want to see Seth; I want to hold my son. I keep hearing bits of his voice in the distance and they're talking about little prince. I just want to open my eyes so badly.

Trying to wake up has never been so difficult.

I struggle to listen and sometimes it's easy, sometimes it's all black. I'm not falling though, not anymore. There's no dip in my stomach, no wind rushing around me. I'm simply still. Motionless. Waiting and unable to do anything but struggle to listen.

Sometimes it's Bethany's voice, sometimes it's Seth. Sometimes it's the nurses like it is today.

What are they saying? I swear my eyebrows pinch; I can feel it happening. *Just wake up!* Frustration is overwhelming until I hear their conversation.

"I'm telling you." A hissed voice is hushed as she speaks. "It's the sweets."

My fingers move, I know they do. It's only a centimeter at most. But they moved. *Wait, what did they say?*

"For the love of God, it was just a vial in her pocket, there was none of it in her system."

Are they talking about me? I didn't have a vial in my pocket.

"That was a good heart," the second voice says. I got a heart. I have a heart. A wave of warmth flows through me from head to toe. Disbelief and elation swarm through me. The steady beeping corresponds to the pounding in my chest. I wish I could feel true relief, but I'm so scared that I can't move, and I can't speak. I'm terrified every time this happens... unless Seth is here. *Where's Seth?*

"She killed herself on the table." The comment is made harshly. All I can do is try to move my fingers again. *Please, move, some part of me move.*

"I still can't believe she did that. I can't believe that poor woman killed herself."

What? No I didn't. I try to swallow so I can scream at the woman making accusations that aren't true but it's so dry it hurts. Fuck, it all hurts. Writhing is futile, there's no escape from my still state.

"She tried to kill herself before even being on that table..."

"I don't understand why. I liked her. She was so sweet, always bringing in the hats for the babies and the random flowers."

I stop trying to do anything but listen to them.

"I was shocked too but then I got to thinking, why was she always here? For months that blonde was hanging out on the benches at the park constantly. She'd be in the lobby all the time..." The one nurse's voice trails off.

"You know she was troubled and she was mourning." The second nurse's tone is riddled with remorse.

The first female voice, the skeptic who first brought up the sweets, says, "I think she'd decided she was going to kill herself here and she was just waiting for the guts to do it."

"Then why do it at a hospital where we could save her if she really meant it? It doesn't make sense."

"I'd like to believe she didn't want to die, but when she did it on the table...."

"Well either way, it's a bloody miracle she did it when she did."

"And how she did it... if she had bled out, that heart wouldn't have been any good."

"I don't want to talk about this. It's too much."

"That's too much? Of everything you've seen."

"Just stop… what's her pulse?"

"It's high."

"Give her more meds."

"You know they say she's one of them."

"What?"

"The blonde girl… the one whose heart this one got. The one with the sweets in her pocket. Maybe God didn't want anyone else to have that heart. And that's why she's not waking up."

"One of them? Like one of… Marcus's?" I barely hear her when she whispers, but still the goosebumps run down my arms. Do they see it? Can they tell that I can hear them? *I can hear you!*

"Yes. You know she is. One of the troubled ones."

"No, we don't know that. As far as I know, that man, Marcus, doesn't even exist. She was a sad woman who lived a horrible life and went through hell. She didn't want to go through it anymore. That's all. And luckily, she happened to end her life the moment that this woman needed her heart. Like I said, it's a bloody miracle."

"What the hell are you two doing?" A third voice interrupts the morbid conversation.

A woman killed herself… she killed herself and I got her heart as a result? If I was capable, I'd be sick. I'd be physically sick. Everything processes slowly. A blonde who hung out. A blonde who was waiting to kill herself.

As it stands, I'm merely lightheaded and feeling the edge of my world turn cold and dark.

Their conversation is barely audible and only pieces are heard.

The blonde girl.

The sweets.

Why isn't she waking up?

I hear them, but I can't answer. I can't question them. A blonde girl. For the longest time, all I can see, all I can think about is Cami. But when sleep pulls me under, I remember the girl in the coffee shop. The girl who looked so much like her. The girl who gave me chills.

I hope I remember when I wake up. But the conversations blur and the next time I'm in and out, I don't remember anything, but I can move my fingers that much more.

Beep, beep. My head hurts. My body's stiff.

When I open my eyes, all I want to do is rub the tired ache from them but I can barely move my arm. It feels as if I've run a marathon and I can't even stand power walking. Everything is so damn sore.

Rolling my head to the side, I feel the groan before I hear it leave me.

Fuck, it all hurts.

"Miss Roth, Miss Roth," I hear someone say. The voice is peppy and comes from my right. "I'm Nurse Hale."

My blurry vision comes into focus to show me a young brunette woman, her hair pulled back in a simple ponytail. Her blue scrubs are loose on her. She's a tiny little thing and her feminine tone matches her aesthetic.

"Water." Before the word is even fully out of my mouth, I hear her pour a cup of it but then she's frantic, looking for a straw.

"A straw, a straw… she's up! Page neurology." I don't know who she tells the last part to, but she's in my face with a plastic straw and I greedily suck it down.

It smells like flowers. Like heaven. As I pull my knees up, stretching my aching muscles, I feel my chenille throw, my favorite throw from the sofa and I pull it close to me, smelling it. It usually smells like Seth. Like his cologne or his body wash. Right now it doesn't and my chest feels hollow.

"Seth," I say, whispering his name, feeling the loss and suddenly very scared to be in a hospital.

"He's here, he's just waiting downstairs. Let me get him for you," she says and the nurse rushes her words out, obviously excited but I reach up, gripping her arm.

"Wait," I say and my heart races, but it's different. It's a steady gallop. "What happened?"

The smile slips from the nurse's pretty face.

"Do you know who you are?" she asks me.

"Laura Roth." She nods at my answer, holding my hand and taking a seat on the edge of my bed.

"And do you know where you are?"

"Hospital. I know… I know I was waiting on a transplant… I…" The memories come back slowly. Delilah… the accident. "I was hit by a car."

"Yes, and you suffered a number of injuries, most of them minor and healed now. In the process you also got a heart transplant."

"And my baby?" I ask and my voice is strained. My hands pressed to my stomach that's obviously flat. My eyes are watery.

"He's downstairs, survived the delivery, had an immediate surgery and then two more. He's a trooper and a sweet, happy, healthy baby boy."

"He's healthy?" Overwhelming emotions force me to cover my mouth. As she nods, all I can think is that we made it. We're okay. We're all okay.

"It was a rough road, a bit touch and go for him at first, but he's much better now." She continues, "Your… significant other, Seth, is downstairs with him in pediatrics as we speak. I'll go tell them you're awake."

Before she can stand, I tell her to wait. "I just… I need a minute."

"I understand. You've been in here for quite some time. It's been almost a month."

A month. That knowledge is crushing. I've been in here for a month? My hands shake and I cover my face again, lifting my legs up and holding my knees to my chest.

"The doctors will be in shortly to make sure everything's all right."

I can only nod, my forehead resting against the blanket. The sweet nurse rubs my back the entire time.

"The important thing is that you got a new heart, the surgery went well, and now you're all right. We were worried you weren't going to wake up."

As I sit there, gathering my composure and swallowing down the fact that a month of my life is gone, my baby boy is here, and I have a steady heartbeat, little memories start to come back. Overheard conversations.

"You were very lucky that a heart happened to become available when you were brought in. If someone had planned it, it couldn't have been more perfect timing."

A distant memory comes back. A conversation.

"From the blonde who killed herself."

"What?" The shock in her voice makes me raise my gaze to the wide-eyed woman.

"I heard you talking. Or your friend. I don't remember." My head hurts and I need more water. She holds it for me, apologizing profusely for her lack of professionalism.

"You couldn't have known that I could hear."

"I'm so sorry, Miss Roth." She looks mortified.

"I won't tell anyone," I offer her with a smile and then take another large gulp. "Who is she? The woman?"

"I didn't know her personally."

"But you knew of her? A few of you did."

"She was a troubled woman, about your age. She'd been in before for overdose; it was an attempted suicide. And then she hung around outside and donated baby blankets she'd crocheted. She was here a lot… and then when you came in, it wasn't even ten minutes later that she arrived and tried to cut herself out front. We brought her in and before we could do anything…"

She doesn't finish, but I remember what the one nurse said. "She cut her throat open."

"Yes. There was no way to save her. It wasn't a cry for help." Her somber voice drops even lower. "She was just ready to go. And she happened to be a match for you, so…"

"I'm freezing," I comment to change the subject and pull the throw around my shoulders. I feel awful for the poor girl. Benefiting from her sadness feels so wrong.

"Hey… she may have died, but she was able to save you. And that's a beautiful silver lining if ever there was one."

All I can do is force a tight smile. "I am happy to be alive."

"You're not the only one… do you want to see your baby?"

CHAPTER 21

Seth

"ONE TIME, WE'D ONLY BEEN DATING FOR…" I RACK MY memory, trying to place the moment as I rock in the chair. Our little boy likes to hear stories about us. In the last few weeks I've learned the more I talk to him, the longer he sleeps. So I tell him stories and our little prince naps in between bottles. Three more days of him doing this well, and we'll be able to leave. It's both the best news and the worst, because Laura still hasn't woken up.

I only tell him the good parts to make sure he has the sweetest dreams and it helps me too, to remember all the moments in my life with Laura. They are the best memories I have.

I let my nose fall to his little head, where his soft baby hair tickles my nose as I kiss his noggin. Turning my cheek to his head so my breath doesn't disturb him, I tell him, "We'd been dating for a few months. Back then, your mommy didn't want to believe I loved her. And I know I didn't love her as much as I do now, but I swear I did. She was strong and beautiful and even though I knew I wasn't good enough for her, I still wanted to kiss her because I thought it would make her happy and I wanted so badly to make her happy."

My voice breaks for a moment and I close my eyes, rocking him.

It happens sometimes, when the reality creeps in and the overwhelming sadness keeps me from being able to tell him the good parts.

"She loved me though. I could feel it. There's this little piece inside of you," I whisper as I rock him in the nursery. It's only the two of us in this room. "There's something inside of you and it tells you where to go. It always led me to your mommy, little prince. And I could feel it, I could see it in your mother's eyes. She felt it too. So I knew if I waited long enough, she'd always come back to me."

I open my eyes so they stay dry. They're sore and bloodshot from not being able to sleep. How can I? When any moment she's going to wake up for us. I know she will. She has to.

Swallowing thickly, I get back to my story, to the good part that our son needs to hear.

"This one time, she nearly said it. She almost said 'I love you' even though she wouldn't even call me her boyfriend. Your mother… she's a stubborn girl with a wild spirit but she's so good to the ones she loves. She's the best of any person I ever met and she loves so hard. She loves you. If she could tell you that now she would. She's the kind of person who says it every day even when she's angry. Even when she doesn't know if it'll last or if she'll hear it back.

"She said it first and she told me all the time but I never said it back to her. I waited too long. Little prince, when you fall in love, you should tell the girl. Even if you don't know if she'll say it back. Or else you'll end up like me, remembering all the times she said it and that moment she almost did where I wish I had said it instead of just kissing her."

I almost ask him to promise me, but then I realize how ridiculous I am. This little life can't promise me anything; I'm the one who should be making every promise to him.

"I'll tell you every night just like she would have… like she will, I mean." My throat gets tight and I take a moment to calm myself before promising him, "You'll get all the good I have, little man. I'll give you everything in the world and I'll tell you every night too. I love you. Your mom loves you. And there's so much love there from her, it'll protect you always. We'll make it, you and me, because she loves us so much we don't have a choice but to do otherwise. That's what love does. That how strong it is. So when you feel it, say it, let them know. Something as strong as that shouldn't be kept secret. I promise you I'll show you that. I'll prove it to you."

I'm too busy talking to my son to see Nurse Morison in the doorway. But the moment I see her, I know something's changed. My heart doesn't beat until I grasp it fully.

"Mr. King, she's awake."

CHAPTER 22

Laura

I'll never forget the look on Seth's face. Even as I'm torn between the two, my small little prince wrapped up tight in a blue and white blanket, and the man I've loved my whole life.

I'll never forget the relief and gratitude in his piercing blue eyes or the way his throat tightened and his strong jaw trembled just slightly as he whispered my name.

"Seth." I wanted to say his name with strength but the single syllable is lost in a sob. My hands tremble as I reach up to him, the moment he closes the distance in only seconds.

His collared shirt, normally ironed and smooth, is a rumpled mess. The top buttons are undone, revealing his skin underneath. His pants look like he's slept in them. The sight of him like this, a complete mess, my Prince Charming who's been through hell and back, somehow living to tell the tale… that's the sight before me. My hero. Forever my hero even in a life where the villains go unseen and there is no happily ever after in sight.

The gasp that comes from me is unexpected, but so is the sight of my baby boy's face. His eyes are closed but he yawns and it's the sweetest thing I've ever seen in my life.

Seth is gentle, ever so gentle when he lays my baby boy in my arms.

My body rocks, my eyes close but only for a moment, only so much so that I can feel the overwhelming reprieve and devotion that envelops me. I have never felt like this. Safe and at peace. Seth's stubble brushes my jaw when he kisses my cheek. It's rough and comes with a wave of warm air that smells like him. That masculine smell that waits for me in the early morning on his pillow. The scent that comes with memories and sentiments of affection. It's either that smell or the tender touch of his lips on my skin that brings mine to his in a heated embrace.

His lips mold to mine, brushing against them and then deepening. I can barely breathe; I can barely do anything but try to convince myself that this is real.

I get to live. I get to have the love of my life. And we get to keep our child.

The small sound of our baby boy interrupts the kiss and I hold my son closer to me. He's so tiny, engulfed in the blanket and nestled against my chest. His little hands gripping the cloth between the two of us so tight. All I want in this world is to protect him, to make sure he lives the most blessed of lives. I will do everything I can so that he doesn't live like we did. His life will be so much more than a series of tragic mistakes and running from the past.

"He looks like you." That's the first thing Seth says to me. With a broad smile on his face as his head falls in the crook of my neck and his hand slips around my waist. I hold on to our son and he holds on to me. Leaning my head against his, his hot tears leave a wet trail in the crook of my neck.

"We'll give you two a minute," Nurse Hale offers us, polite and only speaking loud enough to be heard as the two of us lose ourselves in the moment.

We made it out alive. All of us. It's a miracle and I'll never take a second for granted. I'll never run again because this is all I want. Seth King and our little prince.

"We're okay?" I question Seth the moment the door to the hospital room shuts. Brushing the tear from under my eye and glancing down at our baby and then back to me, Seth nods, his expression adamant for the first time since he walked in here. "We're better than okay," he answers me, never breaking our gaze.

My inhale is shaky at best, not knowing how it's possible, but grateful that I got my happily ever after.

"I love you," I say, getting out the words just before Seth takes my head in his hands, giving me a searing kiss and then resting his forehead against mine.

"I love you too," he whispers and kisses the tip of my nose.

He wipes under his own glossy eyes, staring at our baby boy while he reaches behind him to drag a chair closer to the hospital bed.

"When can we leave?" A gruff laugh leaves him at my question. "I just want to go home with you and him."

"Well, we should probably name our son first," he says as his large hand takes my free one and then with his other hand, he strokes the side of our baby's face.

My son's closed eyes scrunch, as if he doesn't want to wake up and my baby wriggles in my arms.

"He's so much bigger now," Seth says with reverence and the admission tightens a vise around my heart. I remember what the nurse said. A month. I missed the first month of my son's life.

"Is he…?" I trail off as my bottom lip wobbles ever so slightly.

Seth's answer is everything that I need. "He's perfect."

He never stops stroking the side of our baby's head as I gently rock him, not wanting to disturb him.

"He had to have a few surgeries and he was a champ through all of them." As Seth talks, my inhales come in shaky and it takes everything not to cry even harder. I could drown in the sadness of what we've been through, or I can rock my perfect baby to sleep while the man I love tells me he loves me too.

I choose the latter.

"He loves to hear stories and I swear he knows your name," Seth says and I look into his blue eyes, shining with devotion as he looks at the sweet bundle in my arms. I never stop rocking as he tells me our little man stops crying when Seth says, "Laura." He pauses, like he's waiting for the rest and Seth swears if he tells him some mushy story from when we first got together, he stops crying. He wants to hear the good stuff, that's what Seth says.

Most importantly, he says so many times how much he loves us, the three of us.

I love us too. I love all of us and although it hurts how we got here; I'm so grateful that we did get here. This is all I ever wanted. To love and be loved and share that love with our little prince.

"Can we name him Cameron?" I ask Seth. Judging by the way he peers at me, with long-ago memories in his eyes, I think he knows why. "I just feel like…" My throat's tight and I want to cry just thinking about Cami.

I don't remember much, barely anything at all really. A month went by and all I did was sleep. There's some part of me though that feels like she was holding my hand. Like I wouldn't have gotten through any of this without her. Maybe I just miss her that much. Maybe there's more to it, I don't know. "I just want to remember her always and honor her in a way… is that… I don't know. It's—"

"I love it," Seth says, cutting me off, kissing my cheek and preventing me from crying even more. "Yes. Yes, let's name him Cameron."

CHAPTER 23

Seth

"YOU'RE GROWING SO FAST," I SAY AND MY WORDS ARE LOST SINCE they're whispered to a sleeping baby boy. Even though he's dreaming, he holds my thumb with all his might. His wrists are chubby, his cheeks full. He's gaining weight and the pediatrician is happy with his progress.

We're in the clear. It took three more days after Laura's release, but we're finally able to breathe now that we're in the clear.

I never knew how much relief those words would bring me, doctors telling us we can all go home. Bring *us*.

"I love it when he holds my fingers like that." Laura's comment is gentle and comes from the open door to the nursery.

In only her silk robe that clings to her curves, she tempts me like she never has. Seeing her with our baby boy, little Cameron, makes me ache for her.

I'm already hard by the time her eyes move from Cameron to my gaze. She must know because even with only the faint light from the hallway behind her, I can see her blush rise up from her cheeks to her temple.

"You're impossible," she huffs humorlessly, wrapping her arms around her front. Her bare feet pad on the floor as she comes to me, although I know it's only to scoop up Cameron into her arms.

We have another week before sex is an option. I am counting down every fucking hour.

She teases me even more, taking Cameron from me, but settling down into my lap. With my arms wrapped around her, I keep her close to me, smelling her fragrant hair as I sigh easily.

I never knew how badly I wanted this. Her with me and a child too. A family.

It's more important than anything else, which is why I'm continuing to lay low, only running the bar for the Cross brothers… indefinitely. I don't ever want Laura or our son mixed up in anything else. So I took a step back and everyone was on board with that.

"I want a million more," I comment and with my admission, our little prince stirs in Laura's arms.

She only laughs, soft and easy. Her shoulders shake against my chest with it and then she rocks Cameron. I expect her to joke about another being too much or that I'm just ridiculous. She doesn't though. "I do too," she whispers.

"Could you not sleep?" I ask her.

"I got six hours straight," she answers with a smile and then looks deep into my eyes, still rocking our baby as she adds, "I dreamed I was missing you two."

A soft hum leaves me, vibrating down my chest and she snuggles in closer to me.

As much as I love this, as much as I want to live in this moment forever, I know what day it is.

The reminder makes me hold Laura closer to me. I kiss her temple, her hair tickling my nose when I do, trying not to think about what's going on outside these walls.

I want to stay here forever with her. In love with her and loved by her.

Declan told me it was all right. He said the note told him he had to go alone and there was nothing I could do. Still, I want to know what happens. I need to know this shit with Marcus is over. Forever.

I got my happily ever after, but I don't know at what cost.

"You all right?" Laura's question brings me back to this moment and it's then that I realize my heart is racing with fear for Declan.

"Fine," I lie to her and kiss the tip of her nose. She shouldn't worry, not when I don't know what to tell her.

"I love you, Laura," I tell her rather than confess my fear. "I would do anything for you."

She has no idea how much I mean it. I'd sacrifice everything for her.

"I know," she answers with a soft smile on her lips as Cameron coos in her arms. "I love you too."

"You need to sleep," I comment, noting how our little prince is falling asleep in her arms. "Let him sleep and you get into bed."

"I'm not tired," she protests and I'd smack her ass if it wasn't firmly in my lap right now.

"You will be when I'm done with you," I whisper at the shell of her ear. Her eyes close and her breath hitches.

"But we can't—"

"I know what we can and can't do," I say, cutting her off. "I'm far too aware."

As quiet as can be, she sets our son down in his crib, giving him one last look before peering back at me. She catches me standing up and her gaze goes straight to my cock. I'm so fucking hard for her. I take my time closing the distance, watching that rosy color in her cheeks grow.

Cupping her cheek in my hand, I press my lips to hers and then give her one last warning. "Get your ass on that bed, Babygirl."

I don't have to swat her ass, because she immediately turns around, making her way to our bedroom. I do anyway though, a slap that makes her gasp that sweet sound. The smile's wide on her beautiful face and there's a happiness and a lightness in her step that I haven't seen in so long.

She's mine forever like this. And I'll make damn sure it stays that way.

Marcus

He came alone like I knew he would.

The youngest of the Cross brothers has always been the most trusting. He doesn't remember the events of his past like the others do. He didn't have to go through it like they did. That's the only explanation I have for his trust in me.

He shouldn't trust me. No one should. Just like I don't trust a damn one of them.

Seth didn't trust me either, but he sure as hell was willing to make a deal.

He may think I didn't follow up on our arrangement, oh, but I did.

Little Audrey, with her long blonde hair, would have killed herself so many times before. She begged for death and her tragic story pleaded for me to let her let go in the years I've known her. In an effort to convince her otherwise, an effort for her to see the greater good, I told her she couldn't do it, unless her death became someone else's miracle.

It worked for a while… until she happened upon Laura. She found a picture online of two girls. One that looked like her and the other was Laura Roth.

She was too wise for her age. Finding Laura and knowing she could save her was the way out she'd been hunting for years. *She said it was a sign.*

It certainly gave me leverage, but if I could have saved Audrey, I would have. I tried. Some souls are just too far gone.

Audrey's death, her suicide, hurt me more than anyone would ever know, even if she did save a life.

Seth got what I promised him and it killed me to allow it, to tell Audrey the moment I knew about the accident. But I won't hold him to our deal. It wasn't for him anyway. It was a test of his dear friend.

Declan steps closer to a stone carved with his own last name on it. His brother's first. The dried leaves beneath his feet crack and crumble.

Declan came to me for this. He came months ago wanting something I didn't know if he deserved… So I tested him.

No man would allow the woman he loves to die. Seth could never say no. He would have done anything for her. I allowed Declan to know. I let them plant the wires, I let them listen in as I offered the deal.

He knew his best friend was made an offer he couldn't resist. Declan knew Seth had to kill him in order to save the woman he loved.

After seeing what happened…

Declan deserves what he asked for and I'll give it to him.

I do have regrets, for the pain it put Seth through, but that's on Declan. Not on me. All of these men, they want, want, want, but I have never gotten what I wanted. Not until now.

Snow gathers in the sky, making it a cloudy gray to blanket the darkening evening. The chill is biting and it reminds me of the night everything changed for me.

The night I met her.

A stream of light descends between us and it casts his shadow long against the stone and grass that litter the graveyard. More importantly, the light gleams from the metal in his hand.

I'm certain his gun is loaded. Maybe he has less trust than I thought he did.

No matter. If he thought I'd let it end like this, he thought wrong.

"Declan." I call out his name before he can leave. His back is to me, his shoulders tight and tense. So at odds compared to my easy posture.

He doesn't turn around, which only brings the corners of my lips up into a smirk.

"I have one last deal to offer." One more. Because I have to. "I know something you don't. Something you really, desperately want to know."

"What is it?"

"Turn around, Declan."

"Are you going to kill me?"

"No," I answer him and a nervousness rolls up my spine, coupled with a sickness in my stomach. It's been so long since someone's learned who I am.

It's a risk, but one I have to take. I need to for her.

She begged me for this.

Declan's slow to turn and face me. The recognition lights in his eyes, his expression turning from stone to one of confusion and then quickly, betrayal.

I give him a moment and he speaks a single word. "You?"

Marcus's story is up next.

For an extended epilogue of Laura and Seth's story, sign up for my newsletter. Spoiler alert, she got a baby shower, even if it was a little late. xoxo

ABOUT THE AUTHOR

Thank you so much for reading my romances. I'm just a stay at home mom and avid reader turned author and I couldn't be happier.

I hope you love my books as much as I do!

More by Willow Winters
www.willowwinterswrites.com/books

Printed in the USA
CPSIA information can be obtained
at www.ICGtesting.com
LVHW040733051023
760204LV00004B/56